RAVEN'S WYRD

A NOVEL OF GERMANIA AND ROME

HRABAN CHRONICLES: BOOK II

Alaric Longward

TABLE OF CONTENTS

RAVEN'S WYRD   **1**
TABLE OF CONTENTS   *3*
A WORD FROM THE AUTHOR   *7*
OTHER BOOKS BY THE AUTHOR: *8*
MAP OF NORTHERN EUROPE B.C. 12   *10*
NAMES AND PLACES   *11*
CAMULODUNUM, ALBION (A.D. 42)   *19*
PART I: RAVEN'S FLIGHT   *25*
CHAPTER I   *27*
CHAPTER II   *38*
CHAPTER III   *50*
CHAPTER IV   *62*
PART II: CLAWS AND SPEARS   *71*
CHAPTER V   *73*
CHAPTER VI   *89*
CHAPTER VII   *114*
CHAPTER VIII   *123*
Then I remembered nothing.   *157*
CHAPTER IX   *158*
PART III: SPRING TIDES   *164*
CHAPTER X   *166*
CHAPTER XI   *177*
CHAPTER XII   *182*
CHAPTER XIII   *189*
CHAPTER XIV   *201*
CHAPTER XV   *210*
CHAPTER XVI   *217*
CHAPTER XVII   *235*
CHAPTER XVIII   *251*
CHAPTER XIX   *276*
PART IV: THE EAGLE AND THE FOX   *302*
CHAPTER XX   *304*
CHAPTER XXI   *314*
CHAPTER XXII   *325*
CHAPTER XXIII   *341*
CHAPTER XXIV   *354*
CHAPTER XXV   *379*
PART V: THE GATHERING STORM   *391*
CHAPTER XXVI   *393*
CHAPTER XXVII   *405*
CHAPTER XXVIII   *412*
CHAPTER XXIX   *425*
CHAPTER XXX   *440*
CHAPTER XXXI   *449*

PART VI: EAGLES AND WOLVES	470
CHAPTER XXXII	472
CHAPTER XXXIII	482
CHAPTER XXXIV	498
CHAPTER XXXV	522
CHAPTER XXXVI	529
CAMULODUNUM, ALBION (A.D. 42)	545
AUTHOR'S NOTES	548

Copyright (C) 2015 Alaric Longward

ISBN 978-952-7114-89-6 (mobi) 9781517767037 (paperback)

Cover art by Markus Lovadina (http://artofmalo.carbonmade.com)

Cover design by (http://www.thecovercollection.com/)

Dedicated to Woden, who suffered and sampled death so men could gain the gift of poetry.
And for my mother, who gave me the gift of life.
And, as ever to my wife Marjo and my children, Lumia and Arn, the lights of my life.

A WORD FROM THE AUTHOR

Greetings, and thank you for getting this book. I hope you enjoy it and possibly also The Oath Breaker and the Winter Sword, books one and three in the series. I humbly ask you rate and review the story in Amazon.com and/or on Goodreads. This will be incredibly valuable for me going forward and I want you to know I greatly appreciate your opinion and time.

Please visit

www.alariclongward.com

and sign up for my mailing list for a monthly dose of information on the upcoming stories and info on our competitions and winners.

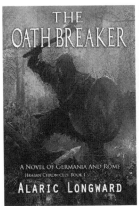 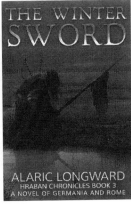

OTHER BOOKS BY THE AUTHOR:

THE HRABAN CHRONICLES – NOVELS OF ROME AND GERMANIA

THE OATH BREAKER – BOOK 1
RAVEN'S WYRD – BOOK 2
THE WINTER SWORD – BOOK 3
THE SNAKE CATCHER – BOOK 4 (COMING 2016)

GOTH CHRONICLES - NOVELS OF THE NORTH

MAROBOODUS - BOOK 1

GERMANI TALES

ADALWULF

THE CANTINIÉRE TALES – STORIES OF FRENCH REVOLUTION AND NAPOLEONIC WARS

JEANETTE'S SWORD – BOOK 1
JEANETTE'S LOVE – BOOK 2
JEANETTE'S CHOICE – BOOK 3 (COMING LATE 2016)

TEN TEARS CHRONICLES – STORIES OF THE NINE WORLDS

THE DARK LEVY – BOOK 1
EYE OF HEL – BOOK 2
THRONE OF SCARS – BOOK 3

THIEF OF MIDGARD – STORIES OF THE NINE WORLDS

THE BEAST OF THE NORTH – BOOK 1
QUEEN OF THE DRAUGR – BOOK 2 (COMING AUGUST 2016)

'The Bear will roar, beware you gods,
for time is come to break the bars, sunder the rules, break
the words.

The road from the shadow will begin, the Raven to bleed on
the evil, rocky skin.
A sister, a brother, wrongful act share, a deed so vile, two
children will she bear.

The Raven will find the sister, the gods to look on as blood
spills onto the Woden's Ringlet.
A raven will show the way, a bear is slain, cocks will crow,
men feel pain.

Youngest sister's blood is needed, her heart rent, onto the
plate of Woden, her life is ended.
Released is the herald, the gods will bow.

After doom, life begins anew.
A selfless act may yet the doom postpone.'

MAP OF NORTHERN EUROPE B.C. 12

NAMES AND PLACES

Adalfuns the Crafter – mysterious old man trying to help Hraban fight Tear. Will help Hraban three times if Hraban proves himself worthy.

Adalwulf – champion of Hulderic.

Adgandestrius – a Chatti adeling, son of Ebbe, brother to Gunda.

Adminus – Catuvellauni noble in Britain, brother of Togodumnus and Caratacus. A schemer and former exile in Rome.

Agetan – son of Tudrus the Elder, brother of Tudrus the younger, twin to Bohscyld.

Albine – daughter of Ebbe the Chatti.

Albis River – Elbe River.

Ansbor – Hraban's rotund friend, sarcastic yet staunch.

Ansigar – Hraban's scheming friend.

Antius – also Gaius Antius. A trader and negotiator, a servant of Rome who is plotting the downfall of both Germania and certain Roman nobles.

Aristovistus – in the past, a famed leader of a confederacy of Suebi. Tried to conquer Gaul 58 B.C. Defeated by Gaius Julius Caesar. Grandfather of Balderich, the old leader of Marcomanni.

Armin – Arminius, a Cherusci noble, son of Sigimer, husband to Thusnelda, foe of Rome, of Maroboodus and of Segestes.

Arrius Vibius Bricius – a Mediomactri Gaul noble living near Rheine, father of Cassia.

Aska – first man created by Woden, Lok, and Hoenur.

Balderich – grandson of the famous Aristovistus, grandfather of Hraban, leader of the Marcomanni.

Bark – brother of Wulf, priest of Freyr, foe of Maroboodus.

Bero – brother of Hulderic. Followed Hulderic from Gothonia to regain his ring and vengeance. Foe to Maroboodus.

Bohscyld – son of Tudrus the Elder, brother to Tudrus the Younger, twin to Agetan.

Burbetomagus – shared capital of the Mediomactri Celts and the Vangiones.

Burlein – youngest brother of Isfried and Melheim, noble of the southern Marcomanni.

Camulodunum – city of Camulos, former capital of Trinovantes, now lorded over by the Catuvellauni.

Caratacus – Catuvellauni in Britain, brother to Togodumnus and Adminus.

Cassia – daughter to Arrius Vibius Bricius, a Gaul, and a healer.

Castrum Flamma – a Roman fort in the lands of the Luppia River.

Castrum Luppia – a Roman fort in the lands of the Matticati.

Catualda – son of Bero, cousin to Maroboodus.

Catuvellauni – a tribe in Britain, foes to Catuvellauni and Atrebates. Lords of Camulodunum, where Hraban is hiding Thumelicus.

Chatti - a fearsome Germanic tribe living north of the Maine river, south of the Cherusci.

Chauci – mighty Germanic tribe of the north.

Cherusci – a mighty Germanic tribe living at Weser and Elbe Rivers.

Chariovalda – lord of the Batavi, allies of Rome, client to Drusus and Hraban's captor.

Cornix – optio of the nineteenth legion, servant to Gaius Antius.

Danubius River – Danube River.

Draupnir – ring of Woden. Every ninth day, this wondrous, dwarven-crafted ring would spill eight others.

Draupnir's Spawn – spawn of Draupnir, Woden's ring, and the influential ancient ring of Hraban's family.

Ebbe – Chatti noble, father of Gunda and Adgandestrius, ever ready to oppose Rome.

Embla – first woman created by Woden, Lok, and Hoenur.

Ermendrud – daughter of Fulch the Red, lover to Hraban, then Wandal's wife to be.

Euric – father of Wandal, a blacksmith.

Felix – a Celt slave to Maroboodus and Hraban. Hraban's friend.

Fulch the Red – warlord of Bero, father of Ermendrud.

Fulcher – Hraban's conscience and friend.

Gaius Julius Caesar Augustus – the first man of Rome, seemingly keeping Rome a republic, but in reality, creating an empire where he would hold the power over the military and much of the legislative power. Strove to ensure the continuation of his line in charge of Rome.

Gaius Julius Caesar Augustus Germanicus – Caligula, the Roman Emperor whom Hraban sacrificed to elevate Claudius.

Gaius Sentius Saturninus – a Roman consul, supporter of Augustus. In the book, he is helping Drusus with the wars of 12 B.C. to 9 B.C. A fair ruler, a wise general. In reality, he would not arrive in Germania until 4 A.D. and would he replaced by Varus in A.D. 6.

Galdr – magic, spells, rhythmic spell singing.

Gau – a Germanic county, administrative area.

Gernot – Hraban's weak-willed brother.

Gnaeus Calpurnius Piso – son of famous Gnaeus Calpurnius Piso, a praefectus of auxilia.

Gothoni – old Germanic tribe from the Baltic Sea.

Grinrock – capital of the southern Marcomanni, home of Isfried.

Gulldrum – ancient abode and shrine of Tear's clan and god by Elbe River.

Gunda – a Chatti noble, daughter of Ebbe

Gunhild – sister to Sigilind, Hraban's aunt. Daughter of Balderich.

Gunnvör – Burlein's archer, slayer of Guthbert.

Guthbert – Batavi rider of Maroboodus, brother of Leuthard.

Hadewig – Thumelicus's real name.

Hagano – Hraban's friend, youngest of the Bear Heads.

Hands – a Chatti bounty hunter.

Hard Hill – capital of the Marcomanni, oppidum hill next to Rheine.

Harmod the Old – champion of Hulderic.

Hengsti – the war king of the Matticati, allies of Rome, famed riders.

Hermanduri – vast Suebi nation covering much of the Weser River. Roman allies.

Hraban – the Raven, the Oath Breaker, the main character of the story. Son of Maroboodus, he is telling his story to Thumelicus, so he might one day have his fame redeemed and his daughter Lif know him.

Hulderic – Hulderic the Gothoni, noble of ancient house, father of Maroboodus, grandfather to Hraban, brother of Bero.

Hunfrid – a Vangione noble, son of Vago, brother of Shayla, Koun, and Vannius.

Inguiomerus – a Cherusci noble, brother to Sigimer and Segestes, foe of Rome, but envious of Armin's growing power and of Armin's ability.

Isfried – lord of the southern Marcomanni, head of his own large family. Ally to Bero, Balderich's lord. Brother of Melheim and Burlein.

Ishild – daughter to Tear, sister to Odo, she is a girl entwined in her mother's and brother's attempt to destroy the world. Torn between her family and her love for Hraban, she makes Hraban's life full of hard choices.

Koun – a Vangione noble, foe to free Germani. Brother of Shayla, Vannius, and Hunfrid, son of Vago.

Leuthard – a Batavi warrior who served Bero, then Maroboodus. Brother to Guthbert, Maroboodus's bodyguard.

Lif – Hraban's and Ishild's daughter.

Lifþrasir – son of Odo.

Lok – a trickster, half deity, half giant. Bound by the entrails of his own son for causing the death of Baldur, son of Woden, and for his chaotic nature.

Lucius – a man of Maroboodus, who deserted.

Luppia River – Lippe River in middle Germany. Where much of the Germanic wars took place.

Maelo – famous opponent of Rome, Sigambri Germani noble.

Marcomanni – the bordermen, Suebi Germanic tribe divided into two gaus, counties. Led by Balderich and Maroboodus.

Maroboodus – son of Hulderic, father to Hraban and Gernot, husband to Sigilind. A man returning home after a long period, bringing with him war and threat of destruction of the whole world.

Marcus Romanus – a Roman exile living with Hulderic, teacher to Hraban. Servant of Maroboodus.

Mare Suebicum – the Baltic Sea.

Mare Germanicum – the North Sea.

Mattium – famed capital of the Chatti, home of Ebbe. Oppidum.

Mediomactri – Gauls living west of Rheine River, opposite to the Marcomanni. Share their land with the Germanic Vangiones, foes of Maroboodus.

Melheim – brother of Isfried, brutal and treacherous. Noble of the southern

Marcomanni.

Moenus River – Maine River, where Hraban lives as a youth.

Moganticum – a major Roman military base started by Agrippa, it kept growing into a naval base and a trade city. Mainz of today, located where Maine River combines with Rheine.

Nero Claudius Drusus – Stepson of Augustus, son of Livia, brother of Tiberius. The leader of the early wars against the Germani east of Rheine, and the greatest, best liked leader of his time.

Nihta – a Germani warrior of the Rugii tribe, a harii, night fighter, and champion of Maroboodus. Deadly with a sword.

Odo – son of Tear, brother of Ishild. The driving force behind the god who wants to destroy the worlds. Hraban's nemesis.

Oldaric – the other Chatti lord, father of Albine. Stubborn and slow to oppose Rome.

Pipin – a Batavi guard of Hraban.

Quadi – a Suebi tribe, allies of the Marcomanni north of Maine River.

Radulf – a Batavi guard of Hraban.

Ralla – a völva at Hard Hill.

Rochus – a Cherusci noble, brother of Armin, son of Sigimer.

Ragnarök – the final battle of Germanic mythology, the end of most of the living things, the gods included.

Segestes – also Segestes the Fat, a Cherusci noble, brother to Inguiomerus and Sigimer, uncle of Armin and father of Thusnelda. Roman sympathizer. Ruler of the Cherusci lands west of Weser River.

Seidr – magical power of Freya, the war goddess, mistress of seduction. Völvas use it.

Shayla – a half Celt, half Germani druid, opponent of Tear, trying to steer away the prophecy of the end of the world. Sister to Vannius, Koun, and Hunfrid.

Sibratus – Quadi noble, brother of Tudrus the Older and Tallo.

Sigambri – old Germanic tribe living around Lippe River. Always at war with Rome along with the Bructeri, Usipetes, Marsi and Tencteri.

Sigilind – daughter of Balderich, wife of Maroboodus, mother of Hraban and Gernot.

Sigimer – a Cherusci noble, father of Armin, brother of Segestes, ruler of lands east of Weser River.

Suebi – a vast confederacy of Germanic tribes stretching from Sweden to Danube River.

Tallo – Quadi noble, brother of Tudrus the Older and Sibratus.

Tear – also called Zahar, the mother to Odo and Ishild. Reluctant servant of her old god bent on destruction of the world.

Tencteri – Germanic tribe from the Lippe River.

Thumelicus – the man Hraban is spinning his story for. Son of Armin and Thusnelda, rescued by Hraban. He is recovering in Albion, Camulodunum.

Thusnelda – a noble Cherusci woman, wife of Armin, daughter of Segestes and mother of Thumelicus.

The Three Spinners – norns, the Germanic deities, or spirits, sitting at the foot of the world tree, by the Well of Fate, weaving the past, the present, and the future of each living creature. Also called Urðr, Verðandi, and Skuld.

Togodumnus – king of the Catuvellauni, lord of Camulodunum where Hraban is hiding Thumelicus. Brother to Adminus and Caratacus.

Trinovantes – a tribe in Britain, foes to the Catuvellauni.

Tudrus the Older – brother of Tallo, nephew of Sibratus, a Quadi noble, and leader of the westernmost of the Quadi.

Tudrus the Younger – eldest son of Tudrus the Elder, the brains of the three Quadi brothers.

Vaettir – Germanic nature spirits.

Vago - king of the Vangiones, foe to Marcomanni and the Quadi. Leader of I Vangiorum, a Roman Auxilia unit. Father of Shayla, Koun, Vannius, and Hunfrid.

Vangiones – a Germani tribe serving Rome.

Vannius – a Vangione noble, son of Vago, brother to Shayla, Koun, and Hunfrid.

Varnis – Sigambri Germani noble.

Varus - Publius Quinctilius Varus, supporter of Augustus, took over Germania from Saturninus. Did not understand how to treat the Germani, and Armin took ample advantage of Varus's shortcomings, causing the destruction of three legions.

Veleda – the girl Hraban must find for Tear and Odo.

Visurgis River – Weser River.

Wandal – Hraban's ham-fisted, slow-witted friend. Son of Euric.

Woden – also known as Odin, the leader of the Aesir gods, one of the creators of men and the world.

Woden's Gift – spawn of Draupnir, Woden's ring, the influential ancient ring of Hraban's family.

Wulf – a vitka from village of Hraban. One of the few who are trying to stop the prophecy that will end the world. Hraban's former tutor, foe to Maroboodus.

Wyrd – fate in Germanic mythology.

Yggdrasill – the world tree, where the nine worlds hang from. Source of all life.

Zahar – see Tear.

CAMULODUNUM, ALBION (A.D. 42)

It appears you might survive your wounds after all, Thumelicus. At least you have hope.

It is in the hands of the wyrd, but your improved condition is partly due to my tireless efforts, Thumelicus, or Hadewig, whichever name you will prefer, should you recover. The former one is your Roman slave name, which you have obeyed since your birth, and the latter your true name, given to you by Armin the Cherusci, your mighty father, and the man who never met you. That was something that changed him into a wreck of a man, and one who rarely smiled. Oh, he was calculating, harsh, and fierce and had many plans to topple Rome and my filth of a father, Maroboodus, but if you shared ale and mead with Armin, spoke of heartbreakingly beautiful women and fine victories, he would be merry as a newborn lamb on a meadow.

Not so after losing your pregnant mother, though.

Losing a wife and a precious, unborn son to an enemy is a thing to change any man. He no longer cared for pretty girls or past victories, as he spent the rest of his life hunting for heads.

To be honest, the Romans have a flair for names, and Hadewig sounds, at least to me, something a man choking on a sharp fish bone might utter in his final moments. 'Hadewig, hadewig!' I mutter aloud, sputtering gutturally, and laugh generously at my own joke as you groan in your feverish nightmares. Forgive me, lord. I am lonely and old.

You may call yourself what you will, my lord, if you pull through the scorching fever. You paid the price when we sprung you from the Roman ludus, and the swift trek to Albion did not improve your condition. Swords and spears nicked you, and I am sorry for you.

These Herculean efforts of mine to keep you alive are my penance for a life wasted. Surely I have outlived any plan the gods had for me. I am still strong as an ox, but I am old, and few live to see my age. Saving you from the Roman captivity is the only oath to your famous father I have truly kept, and even that I kept over a decade late. I have failed, my lord, so many times to grasp the right clues from the whirling chaos of choices. Others have a knack for the right ones, but I never did. That is the way of the wyrd, our fate, the tapestry of all life, which the three spinners effortlessly and tirelessly weave. While you never met your grieving father, thanks to the malicious choices of others, my orlog, my choices led me to a confrontation with my own father, when I was but a youth. Your age, in fact. You remember this, if you read my last letters.

Maroboodus. He was my father.

He was the great Marcomanni, and the clueless Roman historians write of him as the hope of all the Germanic people. To them, he was the man who rivaled your father, Armin, as a deadly threat to Rome. Maroboodus did rival Armin in famous stories written on scrolls and pages, but in truth, my father was a shrewd politician as much as a warrior, and his heart was divided equally between Roman promises and Germani glory. He was a man who betrayed his people, and saved them when it suited him and his many selfish needs.

And yet, despite this, he falsely named me the Oath Breaker. He did this before all our people.

He came home from Rome, a stranger to us. He was exiled from the Marcomanni before we were born, and when he came back, he was exiled also from Rome, a reputed murderer of Agrippa. He came home an enemy of Rome, and he saved Gernot and myself from the Vangiones, even if my mother, Sigilind, and grandfather, Hulderic, his father, died in that horrible attack.

He was a hero, wronged and sad. Many admired him, and yet, he hated me, as I had a dark hair and he did not, and he had been away for a long time. He knew his wife had been lonely, and he was plagued by questions. While he thought I was illegitimate, he gave me a chance. He used me to oust Balderich, our grandfather from my mother's side, leader of all the Marcomanni, and also Bero, his uncle. He grasped for the power, and I helped him. He made me trust Catualda, Bero's traitor son. He gave me hope, pretended to love me, and when he had slain the brothers, Isfried and Melheim of the southern Marcomanni, who were rebelling against his rule, and had used me in deeds that were foul and unworthy, he gave me away.

Without a blink.

He gave me to the vitka, Odo, son of the völva, Tear, leader of a sect of maniacs who had for thousands of years sought the end of the world. They wanted me, as our family hailed from far Gothonia, where all-father Woden created men in Midgard. Our family descended from the first men. Odo's god, jealous, had cursed Woden's men, and then spawned his own people, Odo's equally old family. Our families would always be entwined in a deadly game where a man, the Raven, would one day lead Odo's family to a quest that would unravel all of Woden's work. Our world would fall. Their god would mold a new world. Men would die. Gods would as well. The curse and the prophecy were penned down on a parchment, and the hazy, twisted lines promised many things. I was the Raven. Doom-ridden. This was a heavy duty, Thumelicus, for any man to carry.

And Father gave me to them, naming me the Oath Breaker, blaming me for crimes he had committed. He betrayed me. Even Gernot abandoned him. He smeared my fame with shit, sullied my honor in piss, and men hated me. I was helpless, as I had trusted his promises. I was a fool.

But, he was happy. Gods, he was strong, and he had plans.

I suffered.

We admire men who suffer. Even our heroes who are usually already in Woden's golden Valholl, or with Freya in her fine hall of Sessrúmnir, and I was to join them. I was to serve Odo's needs and then die, eventually at Odo's hands. But, I did not. I escaped Odo, lord. I fought like a wolf, crawled out of the thick, strangling web of lies and blades, and I made myself a man by deeds of blood. I killed Vago, King of the Vangiones and a man Maroboodus had used to slay my loved ones. I was far from home, across the Rhenus River, covered in Vago's lifeblood, and surrounded by hostile tribes, but I, as you know, vowed to go back home to the Marcomanni. Oh, despite the ominous prophecies for the end of Midgard, the many waiting foes, I would go and right the many wrongs. I was determined to pluck the eagle of Maroboodus, hoping to skin the bastard Bear. I knew what he was. In my imprisonment, I found the truth about my father.

The truth was, Thumelicus, that he was Roman. So was his nephew Catualda, Bero's son. Together, they had schemed against the simple, true Germani tribes, and all of our glory was to go to Hel.

He was a Roman masquerading as a Germani, a man who served Roman interests. He sought many things when he came back home, as a fugitive from Rome, but reuniting with his family was not one of them. He had a mission. He was to become a leader of the Marcomanni, and as a leader of my tribe, he would combine the mighty Cherusci and the powerful Chatti tribes under common cause, and oppose Rome that was then attacking our lands. His skills would make sure there were to be victories, and that some high Roman men would die. Those Roman men were a risk for the new Rome Augustus had built. They were men who yearned for the Republic, and would see it reborn after the old man died. Father's masters could not murder these men in Rome, no. They could not risk discontent by poisoning these men. Had not Rome been wrecked by civil wars for decades? No, they needed a foreign threat.

Father was to be that threat. He was to be the mighty Germani who would slay the honorable Romans, foes of Augustus.

Then, when the time was right and the Republic had no defenders, Father would lose the war, and the Germani would fall with him. Our lands would be pillaged, but he would be rewarded. And it was not Augustus, Thumelicus, who planned on slaying these Republicans. It was a third party who hoped to reap the fruits of new Rome, and thrust both the

Republicans and the old man into oblivion. There were many agendas in Rome, Thumelicus. Augustus had his, Republicans had theirs, and those who wanted neither Augustus nor the Republic, many more.

My father, the infiltrator scum, was important for these bastards. And Maroboodus thought he would lead the Germani. There were none to challenge him.

Except for your father, Armin the Cherusci, his foe, it might have been so. Maroboodus never anticipated he would find true competition within the rude chiefs as a strategist, as a supreme warrior.

As for me? I only wanted my reputation restored. I didn't care for Republic. Fame. That mattered.

Instead, I discovered my honor.

Learn the difference between the two, Thumelicus. Being famous without honor was a thing of no worth. I was a child still, despite my war-like, Woden-given battle-rage and the abilities as a warrior as I went home. I learnt one's happiness was a greater miracle than the fragile fame men would salute in the feast hall.

I had plenty of scars from this time, especially one on my face, and another on my chest. I chuckled as I ran my finger over them. A blade made one. A scarred, evil hand-made one.

Now, let me renew my pledge to you, my lord.

As I explained earlier, an old man was always in a hurry.

Elders were not sure what they should accomplish with the time that is left, but I knew I wished to write this story. I also knew the story needs a willing agent to spread it after I was gone. So I beg: should you recover, go to the deeps of Germania, find my old daughter, and tell her of me. Tell her of Hraban of the Marcomanni, of the vile Oath Breaker and dreaded Lord of Bones. Do so, and I shall serve you in the afterlife, as I promised. Few listen willingly to heroic poems of Hraban in their halls over there; even now, few would believe I am anything but a piece of shit soaked rat skin. I accept this now as an old man, but lord, be fair to this lost, old man and help me. At least my daughter should know why and how her fool of a father lost his fame but regained his honor, and why I could not meet her again, ever, after I parted with her.

I promised to fight, and to win you a seat near your father in Valholl, should you do this for me. I will serve you like a lowly servant, and sit and sleep at your feet in the mud and dust. I promise this still, even if on the hindsight serving you in the halls of the dead, shivering at your feet might be very uncomfortable. Yet, I care not, as long as she knows of me.

Now, as for your survival. You might ... you should live if I keep an eye on the wyrd and help it along and that it will be due to my efforts if you keep your life. Today, I found you a healer, a fine druid, and killed a man of the chameleon Claudius; a mercenary recently arrived here by a ship, trying to find our whereabouts. One day, should we survive, I will tell you what I have done in Camulodunum for us, and I will be surprised if you do not appreciate the deeds this old man has performed.

Now, I shall tell you what happened after I escaped Vago's lands, and crossed the river to enter our Black Forest, bent on revenge, hoping to regain my fame, and I shall tell you how I became a Roman with an intact honor, but no fame with our people.

PART I: RAVEN'S FLIGHT

'Happy crows hopping on rotten corpses. That is the only certainty in this world of ours, Fulcher.'
Hraban to Fulcher

CHAPTER I

Sitting all those years ago at the gates of Burbetomagus, the seat of the Vangiones and the Mediomactri Gauls, I watched my former slave Felix ride for the west, his home, and felt terribly, utterly alone. I had sawed off Vago's head in his own bedchamber, my enemies had been humbled, and I had made a man of myself, happy with my success, sad over the loss of Shayla, the druidess I had learnt to love, and then I was alone, afraid again.

Felix was my friend, a runt but a friend.

Yet, over the river, he was a slave.

He deserved better, despite helping Catualda and Maroboodus scheme with the Romans, which resulted in the deaths of my mother and grandfather. Yet, I had forgiven him, and even rewarded him with Vago's helmet and my farewells. Woden knew I feared the trip home without him. I would miss his company, and I would especially miss his wit.

I looked east, for a dark road waited for me, one that required a keen, cool mind, and I had to rely on mine. I would go home, reviled by all, my fame utterly smeared by my father's outright lies. 'My fame, my vengeance,' I repeated to myself, bent on recovering the first by regaining the latter. I had done many unworthy deeds, I knew that, but I had done them for my oath to Father, for the love he had pretended he felt for me.

Father had to fall.

How? That was a mystery to me, for I only possessed a sword called Nightbright, my ancient Greek bronze helmet, and a chainmail, while he led a vast nation, a dozen savage champions, and fifteen thousand willing spears. He would not expect me, but others might. Odo was looking for me; enemy to me, enemy to Father, the vitka who wanted to capture me, the madman who wished to control me and to find his youngest sister, Veleda. The girl was to die; a girl whose blood had to mix with the ring of our family on some silly ensorcelled stone somewhere far away, and then the world would end.

I snickered at the curse that had plagued our family since the beginning, and damned Odo. I thumbed Draupnir's Spawn, the gift of Woden to the first men, the precious golden treasure that was part of the prophecy. I fingered the flower-engraved thing I had just recovered from Catualda, relative and former ally of Father, a fat-lipped piece of shit who wanted it for the power it gave in the north, where Woden's blood ran strong in the veins of the Suebi nations. Many men would follow its holder. Father coveted it. Odo wished it for the prophecy. Catualda wanted it for the Cherusci, for Armin, your father, Thumelicus, the man who hated my father for the betrothal of your mother to my father and the alliance. The ring had power, mysterious and also real.

Now, it was mine.

I would take it and go home, and there everything would be risked.

But, gods, I missed Felix. I was afraid and felt witless.

I glanced at the yawning gate with the two alert, if young, guards, knowing I should make haste out of it. I was wondering if the guards would react to the dark-haired Germani who did not look fresh out of bed but instead battle. I sniffed in disgust at the smell of blood wafting from my clothes and the stench of arid smoke. The terrible fire, spewing thick smoke and cinder to the ochre sky, was my doing. I was tall, wide, and easy to remember, a berserker born with the gift of battle, but I had no choice. I hoped they had not seen me when I was brought in months ago, wounded and senseless. I hesitated just one moment longer and kicked the flanks of my stolen horse, which reared, drawing unwanted attention. I needed not worry. All animals in sight had grown skittish as the inferno of Vago's hall apparently spread outside the compound, threatening to ignite the surrounding hay roofs of the manors.

I spat as I glanced up the hill.

Let it go, let it burn to cinders for all I cared. I had lost Shayla, Vago's druid daughter, a woman whom I had grown to love during the time we were waiting for Vago to sacrifice me. I had slain Vago, and while I had spared his eldest son, Hunfrid, I felt no love for the town. I nodded to myself, took a deep breath, and guided the horse towards the guards at the gate, the dog I had previously kicked growling at me from the shadows, perhaps smelling there was a fresh meal of meat in a pillowcase I had strapped on the horse. I intended to take Vago's head home and show it to Maroboodus, my father. I would flaunt the great deed at his face, for had he not used Vago's threat to gain power with the Marcomanni? Had he not let Vago slay my grandfather, Hulderic, his own father, and my mother, waiting until it was too late to save them? It was symbolic, at least.

Yes, I had business in the Hard Hill.

Not only vengeance and my fame, other issues worried me. I wanted to rescue Ansbor, my wounded, rotund friend. I wished to see if my best friend, Wandal, ever made it home from the battle I lost him in, at the Roman Castrum Luppia where I had gone to chase after Catualda, my hated relative, the man I then thought solely responsible for the deaths of my mother and grandfather, until I found out later that Catualda was in league with my father. Catualda had his own agendas as well, oh yes.

I also wanted to rescue Ishild, my childhood friend, Tear's daughter, and mad Odo's unhappy sister, whom I did not love. She was strange and had secrets, but she carried my child. It was a child Odo desired for the prophecy as well. Odo had many needs. None I approved of.

They were fine goals, but vengeance was the one that burned me the most, my fame second. I was shamed, my soul on fire for the ignominy of father's public accusations. I wanted to show my people I was Vago's slayer. A warrior, not a worm.

Negotiatore Antius told me everything, thinking I would die. Maroboodus was Roman, a traitor, and I would carve the truth out of Father and regain my fame, my place, and finally gain a hall for myself. I would be what I was meant to be. A lord and a ring giver. A Germani. Not a fugitive with the clothes on his back and nothing more. I was also of Balderich's blood, and my vanity made me dream of an even loftier position. The one Father had stolen. The noblest noble of our tribe.

I spat in disgust as I reached the gate. The guards aimed their heavy spears my way, their concentration broken by the huge fire as they tried to do their duty. I hailed them. 'I would be leaving, back to Moganticum. Which way is the best?' I asked, as if there was nothing unusual happening in the town. Screams could be heard as Vago's hall collapsed, and I smiled, flashing a look up the hill. I had a cropped, dark beard, jet-black hair, unusual in Germania, but usual with men of Woden's own blood, Tear had once told me. My green eyes twinkled with mirth, I was sure, as the flames roared up there on the hill, consuming Vago's headless corpse.

And then I cursed, for Catualda had escaped that night.

One guard shook his head, his long beard swinging. 'Don't know the road? You came with a ship? Yes? Just take that road north, and it leads back there. Do you know what is happening up there?' He thumbed to the direction of the mayhem. 'Is that the mansion of our lord?'

I guided the horse past them and nodded my head. 'Oh, aye. I know. The Oath Breaker cheated Lord Vago, pissed on his corpse, and burnt down his home. Hraban the Marcomanni, that is,' I said as I rode on to the road, heading north through shops and shanty houses. The guard looked after me in confusion, alerted by my knowing words. He noticed the blood in my clothes as wind ruffled my cloak.

'Hraban? And who are you?' he yelled after me, a note of panic in his voice.

'I am Hraban, the one whom he wanted dead!' I laughed unwisely, with spite dripping from my voice, and spurred my horse wildly. I rode hard, only to slow down when a patrol of Vangiones passed by, little heeding anyone in their haste to reach the burning town. At some point, a tired Roman squad was crossing the road, and I hailed them happily, feeling mad and foolish. Soon, I left the lands of Burbetomagus behind me, and I wondered if Augustus himself was in the castrum of Burbetomagus, wondering about the fire. The old man had toured the lands not too long ago.

'Come, my friend,' I told the head of Vago, bumping against my thigh, 'hopefully they think we are riding for Moganticum. Let us cut for the river, and try to find a boat,' I drawled, and checked my short sword Nightbright was loose on the sheath.

I did not enjoy the silence and chuckled. 'But, we just stole horses!' I mimicked Vago's drunken, gruff voice.

'Hopefully, they think like you,' I chided the head. 'Like cheap bastards with no guile.' I guided the horse for the banks of the mighty Rhenus River, having spotted a small fishing village nestled on a small bay. It was a bit too near Burbetomagus, I thought, but I wanted to be across the river as soon as possible. I was looking at the filthy people in their chores, wondering why so many were still up, but apparently, they were having some sort of a celebration. I was gazing at the houses, guiding the horse carefully around, trying to find a suitable boat, and spoke to Vago with concerned voice. I would have unpleasant company very soon; I was sure of that. 'On the other side live wild Germani and tribeless Gauls, none of the Marcomanni. Burlein's lands start some thirty Roman miles to the north, I think. We have to get there, and past that land,' I told the dead Vangione carefully while squinting at the village, and at the same time, I started to understand why Felix had not come along.

I was likely committing suicide.

In the lands of the Marcomanni, I had no friends. To revenge myself on Maroboodus, I would need an army. I would have to cross the hostile southern Marcomanni lands first, and I shuddered at the thought of Burlein, whose family was dead, thanks to the favors I did Maroboodus. They had opposed him; we had lured them to a trap, and I had lied to Burlein's brothers, Isfried and Melheim, though to be fair, they had tried to trick me as well. He would not love me, should he capture me. I mimicked triumphant Vago. 'Burlein is sure to welcome you after you broke your oaths to his brothers. Oh, yes, he will roast you slowly, savoring your whimpering and cries, and he shall serve his pigs a filthy fare.'

'I will try to avoid meeting him and his pigs,' I answer myself ruefully, kicked the head with my knee, and rode carefully by the village, gazing across the fluttering torches in the darkness, trying to see past a thick, neglected barley field and few trees. Surely there would be boats?

'Where, exactly, are you going then?' the head inquired, a small panic in his voice. I was growing cautious and no longer bothered changing my voice to Vago's.

'Hard Hill. I will go there, and murder my father,' I told him, 'one way or the other, but first, I need to see to my friends.' He began to argue, but I thought better of it and went silent. I was close to the village now. I finally spotted the boats. Some simple rowing rafts were moored on the bank some thirty yards away, near the village's larger houses. I got down from the horse and looked around. I began to smile, thinking I might make it across after all. There were no guards with the boats, but then horses neighed, and I stiffened.

A group of Vangiones rode to the town from the west, holding flaring torches. Their leader was a man in shimmering armor, with axes tattooed on his bruised and slashed face. Hunfrid, Vago's furious boy. There were some twenty of them, armed to the teeth with Germani spears, the thin-tipped framea, axes, and heavy clubs.

'It seems they know their land, Hraban,' said Vago's head with a sneer, and I cursed. 'My boy Hunfrid will take a shit in your skull, scum.'

'Indeed,' I said, depressed. 'It matters not, for we have to cross here. They must have men watching all the woods from here to Moganticum by now, so this will have to do.'

I should have gone west first, then cut to the south, but I had been arrogant, and Hunfrid, Vago's eldest son, the man I had bested before butchering his father, was after blood. The Vangiones dismounted, and were asking brusque questions from the scared and roused men and women living in the cruddy huts and halls. They had seen nothing, by their wild gestures, but then they shivered helplessly as Hunfrid raged at them, his horse turning in many directions under the heels of the enraged lord. His hair was disheveled, singed from fire, yet he looked a formidable lord, his trimmed beard shivering with rage. He was, I realized, now the King of the Vangiones.

'Your boy is the King now, Vago,' I told the head maliciously. 'A king of shit walkers, he is. Perhaps he will squander all your fortune while you weep unseen in his hall.'

'He can squander all my money and hump all my women as long as he walks on your shit first,' Vago insisted with a whisper, and I reluctantly thought it might be possible.

I decided I would take a rowing boat, despite the men searching the village. I told myself Woden would aid me, which of course was a lie, for the gods expect us to help ourselves. I tethered the horse on a branch. I hoped someone would find the beast before it died of hunger and infection, as it had done no ill to anyone that night. I began to walk slowly for the boats, leaving the bloody pillowcase with the head by the horse.

'All the village is there, bowing to Hunfrid, they have no eyes to spare this way,' I whispered to myself, hoping to be right. And I was, as I managed the dark obstacles of the harbor area and sneaked down to the waterline, pushed the first boat to water, and cut the rope, hoping the blade would not flicker brightly as the torches waved in the village. No one saw me.

I waded to the water and started to pull the boat to the side. I glanced back towards the village. Hunfrid was stroking his horse as his men were searching the last of the houses. The simple peasants and smelly anglers living in the village watched in helpless rage as their belongings were ransacked and thrown into the mud. With Hunfrid, there sat a group of men. They looked like a practical sort, mercenaries in greasy leather and chain mail, some wearing caps and hoods, all rich with silver rings. They had a curious red mark on their foreheads, and I realized it was a burnt scar, the result of some sort of a ritual they performed. I decided and wanted no more to do with them. Their leader, a tall beardless man with dark, lank hair, was maliciously riding around the peasants, kicking them on the backside, while a bright torc glittered in the torchlight. His scar on the forehead was thick and old.

I struggled through the weeds and sticky, sucking mud, trying to decide how far I should go. I was nearly on level with the tethered horse now, and I decided that would be enough as I dragged myself back to the land, crouched as I went to fetch my gear.

There was an arrogant yell from the village. I turned, and saw the fuming lord thinking hard, his hand in the air, contemplating on leaving. Something stopped him, and I cursed the fickle gods. 'Go away, and bury your filth of a father,' I willed him, but he did not heed my wishes. Hunfrid snapped his fingers, stopped his men from searching the village, and sent some men up and down the dark river to search the banks. 'Ass,' I told him softly, rushed to my gear, grabbed the sack, and waded to the river, keeping an eye on the encroaching riders. I hoisted the head, and gingerly placed it on the boat, thinking hard. There was no choice, I decided, and so I climbed to the boat, cursing the oars rattling hollowly on the bottom. I would row towards the north, perhaps escaping notice, and then to the east across the river. I'd hide the boat, and find a swift horse.

It was a good plan, the only plan, but as you remember, lord, I kicked a dog at the gate that night, and dogs have unsettlingly long memories. The very same dog was sniffing at the place where the sack had just been laying. I gazed at it while its fat, wet snout was on the turf, slowly puffing at telltale hints of blood from the sack, some having trickled to the moss below. I tried to remain quiet, glancing towards the men riding closer. It was a large hound, mottled and ugly as a hairy ass, likely ever hungry and malicious.

I moved my foot. The oar banged. The dog looked up, its beady eyes gleaming dangerously.

'Please be quiet,' I said pleadingly. I could swear it smiled, and in my head, I heard Vago's lips smack foully in happiness, though, of course, that was just my imagination. The dog sat down, raised its snout to the heavens, and barked. It barked hard and long, the sort of a sound that grinds into man's ears and nerves. It started to howl. I wanted to go back to murder it, but I glanced at the village where Hunfrid pointed a quivering finger in our direction, the torches coming closer all over the area.

So I rowed, and cursed softly. At least Felix would not be hunted, for they would all go for me.

The night air in the middle of the river was surprisingly cold, and I shivered as I rowed, but soon forgot about such mundane problems. Some arrows splashed into the water nearby, and I noticed frantic activity around the still baying mutt. More arrows flew, some men yelled with excitement. A clatter of oars. They were out there; soon coming after me with whatever they could lay their hands on, anything that floated. The boat was picking up speed in the middle of the river, and I would soon be out of their bow's reach, but they were sure to find me again. I thought about just letting the river take me home, the wide lane running freely towards the far sea, passing Marcomanni lands, Hard Hill even, but the Roman navis onageria patrolled the waters. I would be caught, I might run into rocks, even go through deadly, sucking rapids. I did not know the river.

Horns blared ominously on the Roman bank. Up ahead in the river, torches fluttered as well. They already had ships blocking the waters out there. That simplified things.

I rowed forcefully across Rhenus, jumped off the boat with a splash, stumbling on wet rocks as I dragged the pillowcase after me, glancing up a wet, muddy climb to a thick wood of alder and beech. Torches were now flickering all across the other side, as if there was an army out there preparing for a hunt. Then I froze, for some of the torches were in the middle of the river. I swore, and wished I had risked exposure in the village and cut the ropes of the other boats.

I ran up the hill to the woods, to the unknown, wild lands, and hoped to find friendly faces. I plunged to the darkness of the Black Forest, wondering how to navigate my way in the dark for the north. It would be slow going. The men across would know the woods. Some would, at least. I dodged under some fir boughs, and ran wildly in the dark, begging not to break my leg, sliding over a moss-covered trunk, cursing my luck. My triumphant night had turned into an inglorious hunt, and I was the prey. I begged for gods and spirits to guide me to the right path, but it was equally possible the night spirits and the evil vaettir would guide me to my pursuers, then enjoy the show from their shadow lands. The Vangiones, happily, took their time. I glanced at the bank through the trees every now and then. Most of them were still on the other side. Some few torches were at the place I had left the rowboat. They were not numerous on my side of the river, but they would soon be on the trail.

Later, I abandoned the bank and ran to higher ground. From a craggy hill, I saw a horde of rowboats descend on our side, and a larger ship rowed down the river, a navis lusoria, going to fetch the horses and perhaps even Hunfrid. There was frenzied barking in the night. I was sure the village I had stolen the boat from had sent local men to look for me as well, for there was more than one hound out there. One was, surely, the beast I hated.

I pulled the helmet Tudrus the Older had once given me out of the bag, and stared at its empty eyeholes. It was an old helmet, and I remembered Marcus Romanus, my tutor, speaking of the warriors of old Athens and Sparta. It was bronzed and beautiful, with symbols of our gods carved on its surface. There was the mark for Tiw, the Even-Handed, for Donor, the Smiter, and even Woden, my god of tricks. I prayed to them, and pulled the thing on my head, sure I would need its protection before the hunt was over. I begged for help and happy faces. I contemplated on abandoning the heavy chain mail, but decided to keep it. It was precious, rare in Germania.

I abandoned the hill and navigated for the north. Stars were bright and far away, the burning of Burbetomagus looking like an ethereal, strange spirit. I ran through that night with a rotting head inside a sack, not bothering discussing our plight with it. It would only enjoy my sorrow and worry.

Morning came, the mists of the night parting for the rays of light.

To my alarm, I now heard the dogs barking, not too far. I took to a shallow stream, and ran towards the east for some long hours. I did not run into any people, but only saw untouched, wild lands. Some startled stags ran away from me, eyes huge in terror at likely the first human they had seen. This was the Black Forest, dim and dark, full of vaettir, sprits both formerly human and non-human. It was a place few men braved alone, and some did not return.

At midday, I heard horses pass not far, riding hard for the north through the thickets. I withered in indecision and decided to take after them, as I heard no barks of the damned dogs near, and hoped the stream had diverted them for a time. I had to stop several times, spying men sitting on horses far in front of me. They would go on through the thickets, then stopping again, cautiously listening. Some had the red mark on their foreheads, and I spat in anger for these were men looking for me, not casual hunters. The mercenaries and the Vangiones were careful, skillful warriors, now spread out. It was touch and go, and I was nearly caught many times as some of the mercenaries stayed behind, often on purpose, having hunted for wily prey before.

Eventually I heard a horn blare mournfully, and they all looped back to search the area they had passed, as there was no sight of me ahead. I slid to the mud and hid under a bank of moss. Soon, a horse was whinnying two feet away from me. I grabbed Nightbright tightly, sweating as some ants were crawling on my back, finding their way to my pants. Eventually the horses went away, the riders patiently making hand signals. Woden helped me that day, and I thanked him profusely as I slowly crawled out from under the moss. I took off towards the north, and did not see a soul. The dogs barked to the west, near the Rhenus, and I began to run now I could see where I was going.

I had begged Woden for help and friendly faces, and so I found Fulcher.

37

CHAPTER II

By afternoon, I thought I had run some twenty miles in the deeps of the Black Forest, having made my way across pristine mossy valleys and clear streams. A pack of lazy wolves had stared inquisitively at me while panting in the sun, but they left me alone. Perhaps they were waiting for the night, or had eaten some other fugitive running before me. I laughed, offering the sloth-like beasts a mock bow. The woods were still thick, but there were some signs of life now. Germania was not all deep, brooding forests, like the Roman authors liked to think, but amidst these woods there were many clear valleys, fertile and breathtaking, and the closer I got to Marcomanni dominions, the more I started to see some small villages and houses amidst the trees, with fields having been cut and burnt to the woods.

I ran on, starting to feel tired and hungry, and wondered what kind of a hunger it would take for me to roast and eat the damned head.

Cows ogled at me amidst the trees, stopping mid-chew as I jogged past, sweaty and worried, for surely the Vangiones had not given up. I dared not approach the houses. They were perhaps Marcomanni, or men close to them, but I could not be sure, and would not risk it. No matter the tribe, the men living there in the deeper woods had their own loyalties and agendas, and they might very well sell me to my enemies, especially if they wanted no quarrel with armed men used to violence. Of course they would. They had families in those houses.

I felt paranoid, not sure where to go, unless forward, hoping for Goddess Frigg in her mercy to guide me, as apparently the gods I had already prayed to intervene were asleep. I had the sun, it told me where the north was, but no matter that small mercy, I was starting to feel very anxious. The nasty head bumping on my thigh with each step was a reminder of what might soon befall me. I grunted in anger, driving such thoughts away, swearing my father's head would join Vago's inside my pillowcase, lip to lip, and went on, chuckling. I missed Felix, who would laugh with me. Or even my dull Wandal and surly Ansbor. I briefly wondered what had happened to my bastard of a brother, Gernot, who had sided with Odo. I had cut his hand off, and gods knew how he fared. I had left him there, without help or care. Perhaps he died with Ansigar, my former friend, another traitor, whom I had whipped bloody to the bone while Gernot watched.

I navigated down a small incline, hanging on to boughs and cursing as I slid and bounced down painfully. On my right, the land rose, and far off in the mists, there was a fine-looking mountain range where Burlein and the southern Marcomanni gau traded iron ore. There was bound to be a road to transport it north, I realized, and I started to navigate towards northeast. I ran on, cursing the torn moss hanging crazily on many a boulder from my passing. They would have an easy time tracking me, should they find the trail.

Soon, I smelled smoke. I heard horses neighing, and also upset yells, and I knew Hunfrid was close and they had not given up. I crashed through some thickets of thick ferns, and abruptly stopped with a curse, hoping none had heard my clumsy landing.

Below me, men had died.

A small, sturdy hall was burning.

One end of it was smoking, and some small flames were licking through the wet thatch roof. On the trampled field surrounding it, there were twisted bodies. Men, old mostly. Some horses were tethered at the side of the house, snorting uneasily, and a few men sat on other tall horses, questioning a tall, sturdy man with a long red beard and matching hair, his face angular with brooding eyebrows. He was on his knees, staring wildly at the hall as the riders prodded him with spears, asking questions, his hands tied in front of him.

I recognized some Vangiones who had escorted me to Burbetomagus. A large, thick brute in a fur vest and a drooping hat was seated on one rich horse, looking around, bored, his shield a yellow sunburst as he guarded the man. And there were men of the red-scarred band as well. Their leader was the lank-haired lout with a beautiful, chestnut horse and the thick golden torc, and he sat on a Roman four-horned saddle with silver studs, his face as long as a fox's. He was arrogant and dangerous, the thick scar on his forehead angry red.

A woman screeched inside the house.

The tall red-headed man tried to get up, swearing vile oaths, but the fur-vested man kicked him on the back, and smiled at him brutally as the redhead fell on his face, helpless as an overturned beetle with his tied hands under him. I spat in anger, my hand tingling with rage, and I felt Woden's Dance, the call of a berserker, the vision of the shadowy figure stomping the ground in a ferocious dance hovering somewhere at the edges of my consciousness. I pushed the urge back, trying to calm myself, wiping clammy, sweaty palms on my pants. There were five of them on sight, apparently more inside. I stared at the scene, and contemplated on going past them. Then the woman screamed again, and I cursed softly, hesitating.

A child cried, and I moved.

I pulled Nightbright out, and snuck carefully near the horses, which moved unsteadily, their eyes large as they stared at me with suspicion, but happily, they did not make a noise. They were all nervous because of the fire, wise animals as they were.

Fur Vest spat. 'Forget them, man. Where is your hidden cellar and your paltry treasures?' the Vangione demanded. 'What you had there was a sad joke. Give us the rest, and perhaps I shall call the men here, and spare what is left of her.' The man was not asking about me, and I wondered if they had given up, and were just looting now. Likely, they were doing both.

The tall man shook his head as he rolled back to his knees, his shoulders strained with anger and helpless despair. 'The man you are looking for is not here, and you have everything of value! We have no use for trinkets in these woods! Let them go!' The leader nodded at the fur vest, who got down, ready to question the man even more vigorously.

So, they had already asked about me.

The leader leaned down, his fox face a tad bored. He gestured at the men around him indolently. 'I am Bricius of the Red Finger.' He sneered, as if his name or the name of his band should mean something. He noted no awe or respect in the kneeling man's face, and pointed a quivering finger towards the hall. 'I have no patience for gutless, cheese-smelling mongrels like yourself. No more than for these former slaves of yours.' He spat on a bleeding corpse of a young man. 'Since you have no wealth, we shall let her know some of the best cocks west of the river.' They laughed like a group of fiends, drunk on mead and power. 'But, I am not sure you have not seen our man.'

'Hunfrid will wish to see us soon,' a young man in their group said nervously, apparently nauseated by the butchery and torture. 'He will not approve if we make war with the Marcomanni. There are bound to be many warriors scattered around these woods, and we might get surprised,' he tried to reason, but the rest jeered him.

They were well armed. Shields, framea, and heavier spears, some held nasty cudgels and stubby knives. I stretched my neck in the tall grass and noticed the cow shed was on the other side of the house, as was the norm, and some animals were running free from that end. I crouched, sneaking there as quietly as I could. I slithered by the wall, glancing inside, but it was terribly smoky in the hay-ridden stalls. Jumping over a fence, I entered the hall from that side, stumbling blindly.

Hay and thatch were smoldering nastily in the damp, but the blaze began picking up. Part of the roof threw up sparks in the air. A woman sobbed inside the house. I went forward, and saw a small door that was ajar at the end of the space where the animals lived. A light was shining through the crack, and I snuck and peeked inside. A large, sturdy pine table dominated the center of the room, a stone laden fire pit light with logs and shingles, and a spilled dinner of lentils strewn on the floor.

On the table, a large Vangione was raping a semiconscious woman.

He was happily grunting over the pretty face streaked with grief and pain, and I felt and heard Woden laugh at the soon-to-be corpses, for the man was not alone. In the corner, another was leering at the sight while holding a spear point on two children, a silent, white-faced boy and a small girl, crying silently, her face buried on the boy's shoulder. The boy had blood on his face, and was not moving.

Rarely had such rage filled me.

Woden's anger entered me as I stopped thinking about stealth and surprise, opened the creaky door, and walked swiftly for the man holding the spear on the children. He turned his head in surprise, the red, burnt gash in his forehead scabbed and new. 'Your turn will be next, after Morg has finished. He is taking a second turn ... ' he said with a wicked smile, and his face screwed up weirdly as he looked at my strange helmet. 'Hey, who—'

I rammed Nightbright to his crotch and tore it up, spilling his whole belly on the hay, and he fell over it, silent and shuddering. I forgot him and walked for the other one.

He saw me coming, but did not move nor scream. He was staring at his partner, his rot-toothed mouth open, and his manhood was there for all to see as he pulled out of the sobbing woman, raising his hand protectively in front of him. He was a big bastard, bigger than I was, but like all rapists, a foul coward. I rammed the sword through his mouth, tore it out sideways, and slashed him across the throat, and he fell wheezing, terrified, and gurgling. I kicked him until he was silent.

The woman tried to get up, her face streaked with tears and a bruise on her cheek, and I put a finger over her mouth.

'Your man is outside held by these Hel born turds, and if you scream, he might die. Tend to your son, woman,' I told her, and she, summoning all her bravery, went to her children while I searched the hall. I heard her sob silently, holding her son, holding back a scream of loss. The boy was dead. He had been a brave boy, having tried to save her. I hoped he would be well received in Woden's or Freya's halls. Woden whispered to me of more death that was needed. I would deliver it. I picked up two spears and

42

peeked outside. They had beaten the man now, who was lying on his side, spitting blood desperately, and trying not to suffocate. Only Bricius was on the horse, looking even more bored than he had.

'Where … have you … buried your wealth?' he was asking again, articulating slowly, as if the prisoner was stupid. 'And what trails are there near here? How is it that a man with so many slaves has not seen a soul running past here this morning?'

I nodded to myself, took a deep breath, and yelled, 'Here, there is something bulky buried under the table!' I tried my best and faked enthusiasm. The man on the horse snapped his head toward the hall. 'It is heavy, I cannot lift it,' I said with a groan and prepared the spears. Bricius nodded with a greedy look on his long face, and three of the men came swiftly towards the doorway, running with fleetness born of greed, Fur Vest amongst them. I picked up one spear. I saw the first one was the careful youngster, hoping to escape the torture. He seemed a good sort. It did not matter.

The young man entered the hall, his eyes slanted as he surveyed the dark corners. I threw the spear with a grunt. It went lower than I intended, piercing the boy on his thigh, and he fell inside the house, hollering incoherently. The second spear flew in the air at the next man, Fur Vest, piercing his chest just above his fancy shield, sinking in as if his skin was made of water, spilling him forcefully on his back. He was shivering as death claimed him. The last man blanched, and went back, crablike, holding his shield up. They all stared at the hall with their mouths open.

'Did you search it? There is someone else there!' Bricius shrieked. 'My cousin?' He was eyeing the doorway, and I gazed down at the terrified youngster. I grinned and pulled Nightbright, and crouched before him.

'Name?' I asked him.

'Tarn, of the Red Fingers,' he said painfully, gritting his teeth as he bled. 'I am the cousin!'

'Die bravely, Tarn, and you will be loved,' I told him and stabbed under his armpit, and his shocked face turned into a grimace of death, his lips

43

foully curled as he shuddered to the next world. I grabbed him, heaved him up, and threw him out of the door. There he lay, in a heap.

'Your cousin, Bricius!' I yelled, and the fox face clawed at his face, in shock.

'There was no-one there, master!' a man said nervously.

Bricius cursed, tearing his eyes off Tarn and rode cautiously closer. 'Here. Come out. I do not care if you are God Leucetios himself. I don't care that you killed King Hunfrid's men, but what you did to Tarn earned you such pain as to make you sorry for your birth. I'll flay you. I'll feed your cock to you, and laugh as you choke on it! You will come out, or we will burn you in there. Come out and fight! Stay there and roast! Choose, you filth.'

I glanced at the unhappy family and cursed the Vangiones. I would fight for them to the end, but to go out there would mean I would be surrounded. I turned my attention to the red-haired, tall man who was struggling to his knees, eyeing the doorway with hope. I nodded to myself, hating what I was about to do. 'What kind of a hero rapes helpless women and kills small boys?' I asked scornfully. They just laughed, but with a nervous edge on their voice.

The effect of my words on the prisoner was remarkable.

His son was dead, and so he forgot his pains and fears. He got up swiftly behind the men, his face a mask of unfathomable madness. He walked to the back of the nearest, unsuspecting man and turned him around, took a hold of his jaw with tied hands. Then he snapped his neck so hard the man was nearly looking squarely back at his own ass.

I ran out, and Bricius grimaced, as he understood I was the man they had been searching for. Few wore a helmet like mine; ancient, beautiful and hauntingly dangerous-looking. A thing of the old, battle-mad Greeks. The father of the dead child hollered and attacked the last man, swatting his spear aside without heed for his safety, grabbing for the now retreating, confused Red Finger mercenary, and wrestling him to the ground, smashing the Vangione's head to a stone time and again, where it eventually broke like an egg.

44

I advanced on Fox Face, sword out, my helmet spattered with gore. I danced in front of him as he guided his horse away, keeping a careful eye on my movements.

'Hraban? You do not butcher men of Red Finger and mock us. You will be caught, and I will have my turn to defile your body after the King is done! And as for my cousin? You will know I loved him,' he spat, and turned his horse with a yell and rode off so swiftly the beast whinnied in surprise. I contemplated on riding after him, but decided against it. I would ride to face too many foes, stumbling around like a fool. The hall burned fiercer now, spitting flames and embers to the morning air.

I looked carefully at the man who had been beaten as he stared at the burning house. He gazed at me, and I nodded as I walked over him and crouched before him. I slid Nightbright between his hands and cut him free. The man was perhaps ten years older than me, below thirty, but weather-beaten, and his hands were calloused from hard work. His eyebrows were thick and red, so was his hair, running all the way to the ground as he kneeled there. He was strong and tall, and he would have to face his loss now.

'Your boy is likely dead; a brave boy he was. Woden will take him, surely. Your wife is alive, but hurt, you know what they did. You have a sweet daughter there, alive. Go and get them. You cannot stay … '

He nodded gratefully, his dark brown eyes gauging me, and went inside with a heavy heart, his steps faltering.

I fidgeted as I waited, taking hold of the sturdy horse Fur Vest had been riding. Then, the man came out, carrying his son's corpse. His wife came out next, unsteadily leading the weeping daughter, her clothes torn. All had a stricken look on their face. He laid the poor boy on the grass and mourned over him, his beard mixing in dirt with bright tears.

I looked at the horses, miserable with the whole scene. They were fine beasts. I hunched next to the corpses. The men had some silver and bronze coins, a few proper bracelets, the sturdy sunburst shield, and a number of serviceable spears. I took a spear and Fur Vest's yellow sun shield and grunted, as I noted the family had not moved an inch, entirely sunk in their sorrow. The heat from the burning house was nearly scorching now, the sweat under my helmet started to pour on to my chin, and I moved the horses away.

'Man, your family needs you,' I yelled after some time, feeling the urge to ride away. He did not budge, but rocked on in his pain. 'He is gone. Mourn him, but leave this place. Those men will be back. You must take your family to safety. And I cannot stay,' I tried again more forcefully, and he looked up. He looked hard at me as he laid his hand on the son.

'Are you this Hraban they were looking for?' he asked calmly, and I tensed, wondering if he was not done with his vengeance yet. He walked over to a corpse and took up a spear with a grunt, and Woden whispered a warning to me.

I nodded brazenly, the horse snorting while I rode around the man. 'I am Hraban. They are looking for me, indeed. I am son of Maroboodus, and they have hunted me for two days now.' I glared at him from under my helmet. 'I am sorry for your losses.'

He nodded softly, his face unreadable. 'I have heard of Hraban.'

'They say,' I leaned towards him, 'that I am the Oath Breaker. A liar. A traitor.'

'A murderous cur?' he asked.

'Yes,' I told him, stopping the horse. 'That as well, certainly. Though I call them liars.'

'Yes,' he said carefully, 'a man with those titles would have moved on, and we would all be gone now. But, I think you are a murderous cur, and I thank the gods for it.'

I wondered if he was trying to put me at my ease, but then I shrugged. It did not matter, for I would not relax. 'Yes.'

He nodded and glanced at his son and wife. 'So, what does the man called the Oath Breaker, a supposedly vile murderer and an exile, hope to find in these lands?'

I laughed at him dryly. 'Justice for those very lies, justice for my slaughtered family, and other things I will not share with you now. I wish my fame returned.' The woman looked at me with distrust, despite what I

46

had done for her. 'You see, I am in a hurry now. You also must be away. Do you have anyone you can stay with?' I asked him wryly, still wary of the spear in his hand.

He shrugged. 'There were signs, but I did not heed them.' He nodded towards the daughter who was now listless, staring at the corpses around her, her sweet face ashen. 'She begged me to take us to the woods when the hunters told us of the strange men in area. The fault is mine. My name is Fulcher.' His face was briefly a grieving mask of self-loathing, but he quickly adopted a stone-faced demeanor, apparently struggling to keep his calm. 'I will not use this to skewer you, though perhaps I wanted to, for a moment.'

I smiled sadly at him. 'Happy crows hopping on rotten corpses is the only certain thing in this world of ours, Fulcher. Wyrd. He will be missed. Will you burn him here? Thus was my family buried.' I gestured for the hall, nearly all the way in fire, from one end to another. An animal screamed in a brief agony.

'I will do so,' he said and turned to his boy, lifting him. His wife cried as he carried the boy to the flames. He went inside the inferno, and I thought he had killed himself in his guilt, but he soon ran out, coughing raspingly, and they watched as the hall was consumed, with a goodly part of their happier life. I lingered, nervously glancing at the way the mercenary had ridden, but I felt I could not go and leave. They were strange, oddly stricken, and in a peculiar mood, uncaring of their fate. If the Vangiones came back, there would be a brief butchery, if they were lucky. Finally, they turned towards me, and I decided they would have to make their own way now.

I looked at the man's eyes. 'Now, I must go. Take the horses, they are worth something,' I said, and nodded at the gathered beasts as I turned my horse for north.

'Let me see your face, lord?' Fulcher said, and I turned in surprise.

'Why? Do you wish to see the eyes of a man you will try to kill, after all?' I asked with a grin.

'No, lord. Just your eyes.'

I hesitated, and flipped my helmet forward, revealing my sweat-soaked hair and face, my bloodshot, green eyes, and strong features, and so we stared at each other.

'You are a perilous man, Hraban. You are on more than one quest, is this not so?' He shook his head. 'Gods are gazing at you, no? Fearing you? I hear them whispering.'

I nodded at him, perplexed by anyone claiming to speak for the gods, and I waved my hand dismissively, replacing the helmet. I had had enough of vitka and völva with their sight and spells. 'So they say,' I grunted. 'Gods will die, the world will change. But, I only wish to get what is mine. My guiltless friends, my unborn child, my vengeance, and above all, my fame. I will be a man of the Marcomanni once more, respected.'

He hesitated, whispered to his wife who nodded, and glanced at me with utter distrust. She took some of the horses, choosing them with a practiced eye, and raised her daughter on one. Then, without turning back, she walked towards the east, painfully holding her belly, eyes towards the high mountains. Fulcher watched her go, indecisive, mumbling something, and I was about to ask him what was going on, but he nodded at me. 'I am coming with you. I owe you a debt, one that is hard to repay. I will help you, until you need me no more.' He went to fetch a shield, grabbed a horse, and hopped up to it. 'And I have that man to kill as well.' He grinned savagely. 'I am sure you will run into him. I will be there.'

'I am … ' I began to deny him, but he shook his head.

'You will need friends. And advice,' he added humbly. 'And I need to see Bricius dead.'

I did not move, not entirely sure I enjoyed the situation. 'Your family?'

'They go to her father. He will understand,' Fulcher said calmly, and checked some of the sloshing water gourds on his horse.

I shook my head, trying to dissuade him. 'Understand? You are her husband. How will he understand that you take off with a man called the Oath Breaker? It is hardly something to make them sing praises about you as they struggle to feed more mouths.'

He flicked his gaze over me. 'I said, I have payback to do, as well. That they understand, at least.'

I nodded. 'Ah, they would, perhaps.' I fidgeted uncomfortably, and then pointed for the north. 'You see, I am not entirely sure where I am going. Hard Hill? Under cover of the night, like a thief? I cannot promise you vengeance, not even the safety of your skin. So I think it is best you went with them.'

He nodded towards north. 'That way. Quickly.'

'Why that way?' I said, as I sipped some sour ale out of a water skin strapped on my horse. 'Did you have a sight? Gods whisper to you?' I sneered.

He spurred his horse. 'I need no sight for this, just my damned ears. There are filthy dogs coming. Two- and four-legged,' he said, and rode off, leaving his hall and burning son behind.

He was right. The dogs were barking, howling like denizens of Hel. I cursed, and spurred the horse after him, my doubts forgotten in a common plight.

CHAPTER III

The dogs were herding us mercilessly for some hours. There were few things as scary as a pack of fleet, slavering beasts loping after you under the boughs of the forest. Should they catch you, you would suffer, bleed, be torn and ripped, until you could not move. You would be waiting for their masters to show up. We could see fleeting shadows of the beasts far in the woods behind us, but Fulcher knew the hidden, useful trails, and we kept riding hard. At one point, we briefly saw some horses and men far in the thick woods to our left, but they disappeared into the forest.

Another hour went past, and we heard no more hounds, saw no men or horses.

I let myself dream we had lost them. Fulcher, as if reading my thoughts, turned his head around as he guided the horse forward, avoiding a tangle of slippery roots. 'They might have men with them, people who know these lands. Some people were missing from a household near us the other day. Prisoners likely, forced to help them, so let us not smile yet,' Fulcher said and grunted as he stopped for a while, and I joined him, both sitting on lathered horses.

I nodded, tired to the bone. 'No, they will not stop. At anything short of an army.'

He nodded at the bag, suspiciously. 'What's that then?'

I opened it up to him and he nodded, squinting the head of Vago. 'Rations?' he asked calmly, face slightly green.

I shook my head. 'Not that desperate. This is Vago, formerly a king to the lot. He lost his head, and I picked it up.' I nodded backwards. 'His son is a bit upset, though. Should have killed him as well, but there are always brothers and relatives to take up the vengeful sword. I bested him last time we met, but this time? Gods know.'

Fulcher nodded and looked ahead. 'That man who led them to us. I will want his head when I ride home. But, now, Hard Hill, eh?' he asked curiously.

I shrugged. 'I have a friend in Hard Hill. I hope he is alive. Another might be there as well.' I thought of Wandal, and prayed it was so. My mountainous friend had fallen from the palisade in the battle for Castrum Luppia, and I had not seen him since. 'I will sneak in there, take them out, their women as well, and figure out a plan on how to gut my father and regain my fame.' I shuddered as I thought of the women. Cassia, the Celt I had promised freedom, was a dark-haired beauty of a biting tongue, but she had promised to heal wounded Ansbor when Maroboodus had sent me away. Then there was Ermendrud, the girl who had thought she would marry me, but whom I hitched to Wandal. Neither loved me, I was sure.

And Ishild.

Tear's daughter, held by my father, as was Tear. Odo was at large, still serving the prophecy, certain Ishild will one day be with him again, as would be my unborn child. The bastard hoped to whelp two children with her, his own sister, as the prophecy demanded. I often wondered if this was the reason Ishild slept with me that one night, hoping to curb his plans.

Yet, the plans were there. Odo would sire two children, or take mine, and they would survive the end of the world. Gods only knew if one of them was to be my child, or if he had to kill it and make his own. There will be a boy and a girl, the prophecy claims, but I spat at the ancient words, determined to take Ishild to safety with my daughter. Wherever that was.

Fulcher was observing my inner turmoil calmly, nodding softly every now and then, as if reading my mind. I gave him the evil eye, and he pointed at the fine bronze helmet Tudrus the Older had once gave me. I loved the Quadi like a father, and wondered where he was and how he was doing. Father had ousted him from the Quadi tribes with the help of renegade Quadi, men who served Maroboodus now. 'You might want to take off the helmet; they have heard of the Oath Breaker here. The day you betrayed Isfried and Melheim, Burlein's brothers, is not a day they love. Gunther, their second cousin, ruled us. A good man,' he said glumly. 'Now buried.'

I did not remove the helmet. 'I did what my father asked me to do. And to be fair, I only escaped by hair's breath. They did not mean to keep their oaths to me any more than I to them. Wandal saved me that day, my friend. I'll keep the helmet, thank you,' I said, tired and irascible.

He did not give up. 'It is no excuse, Hraban, that they meant to betray you as well. And your father's men spin a different kind of a story. That he wanted a peaceful solution to the problems.'

I spat. 'Peaceful? No, he wanted the southerners all dead and buried in pig shit. I knew it, Fulcher, and I went along with it. It was something I had to do, and I nearly died doing it. A lord is a lord first, and lords, they told me, have no qualms.'

He nodded as he gazed at me. 'That might be the prerogative of a lord, my lord, having no honor. Such a man might have fame across the land, but is rotten inside. Are you such a man? A broken soul?'

'Am I a broken man?' I asked him dangerously.

'Are you proud of the deeds you performed for your father?' he sneered.

'No, of course not!' I told him with a scalding voice. 'Who would be?'

'Then how is it that you could ever regain your fame?' he asked simply.

'With vengeance?' I sneered.

He laughed, and his eyes glinted. 'Vengeance is a fine thing, Hraban, but it won't change the things you did. They will never forget. No, you can only try to find your honor. Forget the fame.'

'I have honor, and I have also had enough of your advice. Is this why you came with me?' I ground out, trying to quell my anger.

'Perhaps,' he agreed. He looked away, as if searching for the right words. He waved his hand. 'Go and avenge yourself, Hraban. I will help you. I will help you until you are happy again, until Bricius's head is rotting in my bag, and then I shall return to my family, if you have no need of me. Just remember. By being an honorable man, Hraban, you need no fame. Men will see you as a good person, the few who matter.'

He said nothing for a while, and eventually spoke softly. 'You will like yourself better. Watch the lords in the halls, the famed ones. Some are honorable ones, who truly deserve the praise poets pour on them. Others look embarrassed as children, for they are like you. The lords who have both deserved fame and honor suffered and fought to remain pure. The ones who betrayed and murdered their way there cheated the gods. You are not innocent. Never will be. You can only be the sort of a lord who is ashamed of the songs in his halls. Perhaps it would be best you had no hall with false poets but only your horse and people who know you as honest and just?'

'I am done speaking about this, Fulcher,' I told him with finality.

'Fine,' he growled. 'I have said my peace. Now, as for your vengeance. You have to settle things with Burlein. I know you had a part in his family's death and that of our lord's, and so you will have to speak with him. Grinrock is over that hill.' He nodded behind my shoulder.

'You have led me to the man who has a hard time deciding if he hates my father or me more? After I saved your wife and daughter?' I asked. 'He will never let me go. None shall speak for me.'

'I shall, and others will,' he said resolutely. 'You will sleep better.'

'Sleep?' I sneered. 'I made myself a man by slaying a king, and decided I would not let anything stop me from slaying my father and gaining my goals,' I told him. 'Dying in Burlein's spear point would give me eternal sleep, but no vengeance.'

'Meet with Burlein,' he told me frankly. 'There are a lot of people you need to compensate, and start with him. What you did with our lords, Hraban, might have been just in your father's eyes, but it was still dishonest, a murderous treachery.'

'It is my guilt, Fulcher, not yours,' I growled. 'And I feel much more guilt for the pains and losses of my friends who have suffered, than for these nobles of yours.'

'Yes,' he said stubbornly, 'but with Burlein, you can start rebuilding the things you lost. Your honor.'

'And honor again,' I sneered.

He ignored my contempt. 'It will be hard, but it will also be well. It is a man's duty to set wrongs right, yours as well.' He leveled his spear at me calmly, his grip steely on the shaft. 'I will help you with your vengeance, will gain mine, but only when Burlein believes in you. That is my duty, to take you to the lord of the land, and hope you both find ways to trust each other.'

I cursed him and shook my head tiredly. 'You think I came back from Hel itself to fall into his vengeful hands? He might kill me, easily. Even torture me, certainly. He might hand me over to my father. No!'

He looked at me steadily. 'The first two, yes, certainly and easily. The last one? We have few men who returned from your father's war with the Matticati. They say he let the southern men die in his war, betrayed, and punished Burlein, even after we lost Isfried and Melheim, and most of the nobles. It is a dark land, Hraban, with much sorrow and sad contemplation. When you arrived, I saw the chance of a bright future again. Go to Burlein. Trust me. Hard? It will be hard, but I did not see aught but possibilities.'

I wondered at him, his calmness, and the spear in his hand. He was resolutely demanding I do something that might doom me before I reach my rightful home. He spoke of honor and separated it from fame, and I saw both equally important. I wanted to feel like a good man, yes. Yet a peasant had honor, and I wanted poets to sing my praises, for that was a warrior's true measure. Honor without fame felt like a kiss from a favored dog. Loving and wet, but still a kiss from a dog. Fulcher seemed utterly courageous, and righteous to his core. I felt ashamed of my fears, but I would not risk avenging my family. Burlein hated me deeply, very deeply, and I did not really know the third brother of the southern lords, except for a brief feast in their hall, and for his spite later.

'Very well,' I said, and rode up to him, holding my hand out, eyeing his spear, planning on hamstringing his unsuspecting horse. He smiled and nodded, as he raised his hand to grasp at my wrist.

I tightened my grip on Nightbright.

A line of brooding, tense men on large Roman horses followed some muzzled dogs out of a thicket. Bricius was there, his lank hair covered by a cowl, and Hunfrid as well, his face a mask of surprise, then of hate. They stopped, the dogs baying softly under their muzzles, and we stared at each other. My hand was still stretched to Fulcher. Hunfrid broke the idyllic scene. 'There! Finally! Bring him to me! If you cannot capture him, slaughter him. Rip him apart. I want the heads, at least. Both heads.'

He meant Vago's and mine, likely, but Fulcher did blanch.

Men vaulted down from their saddle, un-muzzled the dogs, and all of them flashed a feral smile full of sharp fangs. One of them was the damnable dog I had kicked and suffered for. Some ten men kicked their horses' flanks.

'Tyr's lathered balls! Come on!' I turned the horse so quickly I nearly fell and then I rode off, towards Grinrock. There was no need to think about my options anymore. Hanging there later would be vastly preferable to getting disemboweled and skinned at Hunfrid's cruel hands. Bricius would make me squeal, I was sure of that as well.

It was a madly wild, very dangerous ride as we kept guiding and whipping our horses through the perilous wooded hill. One wrong turn could cost one of us our lives, and the nimble dogs kept gaining on us, the constant baying reaching a near unbearable level, disturbing our efforts.

I dodged an old alder tree just to see a jutting boulder behind it. The horse nearly fell over it, just managing to keep its footing on the slippery grass and moss. Glancing back, I saw a dog streaking very close, a brown hound, mouth full of teeth and eyes glittering with determination. It was the bastard again. Thus, we rode for ten long, suffering minutes, and the enemy was gaining steadily. The dog was running next to my horse, its tongue lolling as it enjoyed the chase and the eventual joy of sinking its fangs into my calf. I could see its eyes measuring the thickness of my muscles, its mouth salivating with the anticipation of blood, skin, and meat filling its maw.

Suddenly, before us there was a former field with some uncut trees, and we ploughed amongst the old abandoned stalks of barley growing wild, aiming for a village that was very near now. I saw Hunfrid curse at his men, and the dog snapped at my horse's legs, but my beast had had enough and stepped on the ugly thing, leaving it yelping and barking with but three legs in the mud. I laughed like a lunatic and grinned at Hunfrid, who leered back, knowing he would reach me unless something stopped him from doing so.

He did not know Grinrock was near.

Some twenty Marcomanni rode up from the village now in sight, men ready for war, armed, and some even armored in leather. Hunfrid spat in distressed anger, and yelled at his men to attack.

'Hraban, be brave!' Fulcher yelled nearby, and he did not mean the mercenaries, the Vangiones, or even Hunfrid. Burlein, the young, blond man with an unreadable look on his wide, formerly happy face, rode a bit further than his men, gazing at us. He saw me, I was sure, racing for him, but not a muscle moved on his face, his long moustaches and plaited beard prominent on his chest. Behind that callous look, I was sure he was contemplating ways of impaling me, disregarding one after another as too kind.

Hunfrid's men stopped as some of the Marcomanni lifted their arms and launched swift arrows at the first dogs, hitting one. The beast yelped and flew on its side, breaking the arrow with a nasty, meaty crunch. The others stopped and put their mottled tails between their legs, taking off as more arrows hit the muddy ground around them. The enemy stopped their horses, and blithely ignored Hunfrid's frantic commands to charge.

I prayed to the gods, plunged to the group of Marcomanni, and stopped the horse amidst the glowering men, none of whom liked me. I looked at Hunfrid who was in the forefront of his own men, cursing, hissing, and agitated, riding back and forth. He did look like Koun, having the same eyes, the Vangione Maroboodus had captured the night my grandfather and mother died. Koun was the man who had killed Hulderic, my grandfather, in battle. He had something of Vannius as well, the youngest of brothers, the one who had been given to the Quadi after the battle, and the one who had betrayed Tudrus for Father.

Hunfrid was the eldest, and now impotent in his rage. 'You possess something of mine!' he yelled at Burlein, pointing his spear at the Marcomanni lord. And then he spat at my direction. 'I want him. And he has something that belongs to my father!'

I nodded, catching my breath. 'That I do, Hunfrid. Your father did not let go of it willingly, but as you know, he thought killing me would make him a god. I wonder if it would have been so, but now, we shall never know,' I mocked him and then cursed softly, not knowing if Burlein might entertain similar aspirations. The Marcomanni lord had not moved, not one bit. 'Yes, I have his head. Come and take it? I will meet you halfway?'

He guided his massive horse back and forth, a beautiful beast, contemplating on taking my challenge. I pulled my sword; he had an axe and a spear, but he did not come forth. 'Ah yes! Ride forth, and fall victim to another treachery! No thank you, but I shall meet you on another field, if you evade me this day,' he hissed, and pointed a finger at me. 'You shall never humiliate me again.'

Silence reigned as we stared at each other.

I grew bored and looked down to Rhenus River. I noticed Grinrock could be seen from there. The familiar jagged harbor was intact, and fires burned in houses sprouting hazy smoke. Winter was quickly arriving, and deep cellars were being packed with precious food and drink. I realized it was the end of the Haligmonath, the month when warding spells were cast before the cold arrived. A thanksgiving celebration was to take place, one that lasted much of the month.

In Grinrock, there was not much to give thanks for.

Burlein's blond hair and beard was whipping with wind as he rode forward easily, swaying in his saddle as if weary and uninterested in anything that was happening on the field. He spat at the direction of the

Vangiones, and stopped the horse in front of us, facing Hunfrid. 'I do not recall inviting you beggars. Did I?'

Fulcher grunted and rode to him. 'Lord. This is Hraban—'

Burlein's voice was as cold as the north wind at Yuletide. 'I know who he is. He always appears from the woods, riding with ill will as a companion, death as a mate, and is often followed by men with readied weapons. He is an evil omen, like a crippled raven. That the case now? You have a thing they want?'

Fulcher nodded and answered for me, adjusting his seat nervously. 'He is running from the Vangiones and carries King Vago's head. They chased after him and started to loot our lands in the meantime. They killed my boy, raped my wife.' The dog my horse had stomped on howled pitifully, suffering, and the wind blew. 'He killed most of them, save for that one rat bastard.' Fulcher pointed at Bricius amongst the Vangiones, and scowled, hefting his spear.

'Sounds like Hraban,' Burlein said dejectedly, 'except for the saving part. Why did you bring him here? But, King Vago's head? He does know how to make an entrance.'

'Lord,' Fulcher said dutifully, 'he needs help. He has wronged your family, and given you false oaths for his father, but he is out here to avenge himself on his father.'

'A petty vengeance, eh, Hraban? He ousted your womanizing, traitorous ass, and you—'

I grunted rudely, and the Marcomanni tensed. I flipped the heavy helmet off my head and wiped my lathered hair aside. 'He orchestrated the attack on my village, the one that killed my family. He used me like a whore.'

'Did you like being his whore?' Burlein rumbled. 'You helped him with my—'

'I did. I loved him, for a while, before I knew the truth of him,' I told him. 'Now, I only wish to go and—'

Burlein shook his head, interrupting me. He yelled at our enemies. 'What shall we do, Vangione? I have sent men to find your friends, rest of your marauding men, but here we are. Will you not fight him? Perhaps you two will skewer each other, and spare me the trouble?'

Hunfrid cursed Burlein softly, thinking hard. 'Turd spattered Marcomanni rat! Poor and thieving dogs. For every man you kill out there, we will enslave ten. We are no friends, it is true. But, today, we meant no evil towards you, we just want him. He … ' Hunfrid choked in anger, 'killed my father.'

'So, you are the King now,' Burlein rumbled. 'Should I bow?' A horn sounded somewhere far. Marcomanni had indeed begun the slaughter of the scattered Vangiones looking for me. Hunfrid did not enjoy the subtle mockery as he growled at his men to stay still, some who became skittish at the sound of the horn.

Hunfrid shook his head. 'Give him to me.'

'It is for you to choose, Burlein, with what to do with me,' I told the lord resolutely, seeing Fulcher nod at me encouragingly. I cursed the man and his faith. 'I have no love for my father, and I saw what he did to your men at the battle of the Matticati lands. I fought bravely there, you saw it.'

'It is true you fought well, Hraban, and it is not your prowess I have reservations about; it is your heart,' Burlein said calmly. 'You are not a good man.'

Hunfrid shook his axe at Burlein. 'Give him to us, give us the Oath Breaker. We know of him, and we know you have suffered much for him and his father. Give him to us, and you may dream of the things I shall do to him, for it will not be quick. Give him to me, and we shall leave and war another day!' Hunfrid screamed, mad as a bull, frustrated.

Burlein shook his head. 'If I wish him dead, I will do the deed myself, and I dare say, my imagination is at least as keen as yours. And shut your mouth. You sound like a lesser son of a greater man. Vangiones will be less wily and brave while you rule, so I shall let you go, fool.'

'If you do not give him to me,' Hunfrid continued, more composed by the reproof, 'I will lead an army of Vangiones on to your lands. It will burn, even if we are driven out eventually. You shall starve, and we will entertain ourselves with your women. It will all be gone anyway, soon, for

I hear this one's father does not love you. Give yourself some time, least of the three brothers, and buy us off this day.'

Burlein's face reddened as he watched his ragged band of men around him. Something was missing from them. Spirit, confidence? They had suffered terrible losses, despair, and my father had made them a sorrowful people. They doubted their prowess and their future. Once, Burlein's vast family had ruled the southern Marcomanni with ancient rights of blood. Now, few survived.

'What say you?' Hunfrid asked, grinning at his enemy, sensing their silent weakness and despair.

I ignored him, and stared at Hunfrid's horse, puzzled. It looked familiar. It could not be. Surely it could not. I choked, sputtered and then I laughed. Of course. It was! I turned to the blond man as I guided my horse forward. 'If I give you Hunfrid, they will find it hard to attack you. Keep him alive, a hostage. Take time, and rest your people, never fearing the dogs. Until you have recovered,' I said, smiling like the sun.

Burlein looked at me in wonder. 'He can just ride off. He will not fight. He threatens now when he does not have enough men here, but he will soon, and then they will come back, perhaps before the winter. Your father will help, but only after we have bled more.'

I laughed wildly and rode forward. 'Here, let me give him to you. Hunfrid, come here!' I made summoning gestures, like he was a hound, slapping my thighs. The dogs looked at me suspiciously.

'Is this the way you let him treat an enemy king?' Hunfrid sneered, utterly enraged. 'Very well, I—'

I yelled, 'Minas, here boy!' I whistled a certain, flippant tune. Minas, my grandfather's prime warhorse, one of the beasts they stole that night my family died, pricked up his ears to the familiar call and galloped forward, and the terrified, surprised Hunfrid was clinging in the saddle. His men tensed and stared in stupefied astonishment. Some rode forward instinctively, but none came close to us. Instead, the great black horse picked up speed, resisting all the enemy king's attempts at turning it, and Hunfrid did not have the sense of mind to jump down. Unsteadily, he just held on as the beast plunged for me. In an eye blink, the horse stood in front of me. My sword was on Hunfrid's throat. He was pale and shivering, surrounded by the Marcomanni, his bravado forgotten.

'Lord Burlein, I give to you Hunfrid, the King of the Vangiones. His father is in the sack.'

Fulcher grinned darkly at the shocked enemy king, and Burlein, for the first time after the death of his family, smiled and laughed merrily. Then he punched me out of the saddle, and his men gleefully bound both the King and me.

CHAPTER IV

Vangiones rode off reluctantly, and we were escorted to Grinrock. Burlein was as silent as a stone as we rode forward calmly. When we dismounted, he had men take hold of me, and they escorted me to a simple, wattle- and mud-walled house near the middle of the town. A few burly guards were posted. Fulcher spoke briefly with Burlein, and then pushed me inside the sparsely furnished main hall and untied my hands deftly, looking down.

'So, what will he do?' I asked Fulcher.

He shrugged. 'He says he does not know. But, you got a better house than Hunfrid! He is a king, after all.'

'I don't feel like this plan of regaining my honor is going well, Fulcher, house or not,' I spat and cursed him, but slept in peace that day and night. I was tired to the bone, deciding I would not benefit from trying to escape in such a condition. Fulcher stayed with me, and infuriatingly, before I did fall asleep, he sang softly and sat by the gentle flames of the fire pit. The song was a mournful lament, and I dreamt of many faceless dead by a green meadow.

Next morning, Burlein rode up to the house. Fulcher got up, went out stiffly, and came back. He pointed a quivering finger at me, giving me a cold smile. I nodded, got out where Burlein stared at me, his face unreadable. He nodded at the stable of the house, and I understood. Soon I was taking Minas out of the stall, and then saddling him with Hunfrid's fabulous Roman saddle while stroking his fine coat of hair, and nodded gratefully to Burlein, who could have easily claimed the horse. In fact, he still could. At least the Vangiones had taken good care of the old beast, I thought, and I missed my grandfather Hulderic, the true owner of Minas, and not even his death could change that. Burlein sat on his horse, patiently and silently, and let me take my time. When ready, I mounted my horse, and he guided his next to mine and looked at the Rhenus flowing by, swirls of blue and green, reeds swaying as birds skimmed the surface.

'I never liked my brothers, you know this. You don't like yours,' he said.

I nodded. 'I cut off Gernot's hand, you know.'

He looked surprised. 'Really? He has not been seen in the Hard Hill. Perhaps he died of blood loss. What did you do to Odo? I heard your father tried to give you to him. Then something happened, and everyone involved disappeared.'

'He got away. You know about the prophecy, of course. Bark, the vitka told you, no?' I asked him.

'Yes, he told me. He told us. He said you have to die for the world to survive. I nearly believed him.' He laughed in derision. 'Had the fool not wanted a personal revenge, you would be buried here now.'

'Yes, lord,' I told him. Bark had indeed wanted to slaughter me personally, reluctant for anyone to rob him of the satisfaction of seeing me die at his feet. I had killed his wife, the act that forever sullied my soul, though the priests and priestesses were hardly innocent babies, having sacrificed men and women, young and old. And no god had punished me for the deed.

Yet, I suffered nightmares of the night. Even if Maroboodus and Odo had manipulated me that night, the act was mine. I waved my hand vaguely around the countryside. 'A druid explained many things to me, Shayla did. Worlds end, it is their nature, and in our Midgard, our world, men decide this fate, men of my family, of the old blood. If Odo is right, I will risk everything one day, and it is my wyrd to decide such things. I do not believe in it, but many do. Vago did. The world will have to trust me to do the right thing,' I said. 'Unless you wish to hang me.'

Burlein grinned. 'Ah, yes. What should I do with you?'

I sighed. 'I am not begging, Burlein. I am not interested in explaining myself. I will go and kill him, my father, or not. You decide.' I looked at Minas and remembered the good years with my grandfather. Burlein smirked at me and guided his horse away from Minas who lightly bit his steed in the ass. The horse nearly threw him, and we laughed briefly as he calmed his beast. Then he nodded to the north. I swallowed my suspicions as we rode on.

'Maroboodus? What is he, really?' he asked languidly, adjusting a light cloak around him, for wind was blowing with biting, sudden cold. Some crows were croaking loudly.

I spat in anger. 'A traitor.'

'Traitor, Oath Breaker?' he laughed.

I did not enjoy his mockery. 'He is that, and more. Catualda, Bero's son, helped him, but he is trying to become a leader of the Germani, while working for his masters in Rome.'

'Catualda, eh? I always distrusted that sweaty rat's skin,' Burlein said. 'Scheming and ugly. Those lips would have made excellent fish bait.'

I showed him the fine ring, golden and brilliant, sparkling and precious, carved with leaves and old symbols. 'Catualda wanted this. He wanted to rule men under Armin's banner. He left Father as well, you see.'

'Why would Armin the Cherusci,' Burlein drawled as his eyes flickered to the ring, 'care for the worm?'

'They are relatives; his mother was a Cherusci,' I said. 'One day, he will suffer.'

'Relatives, eh? We will all suffer one day, but let us speak of the more urgent matters now, Hraban,' Burlein told me, 'though you seem to know much I am interested in.' He was not much older than I was, but being the lord of the southern Marcomanni had grown him from a merry young drunkard into a serious, overly careful ruler. 'Over there,' Burlein nodded, and we rode to a light woods full of young oaks, hung with ornaments and bizarre symbols.

'There a vitka with a sharp dagger and a sturdy rope waiting there, Burlein?' I asked, half amused, half scared. He did not answer, so I continued. 'What are we doing here?'

Burlein grunted noncommittally, and we came to a pristine, silent clearing. It was almost a shame to disturb the peace of it, and I said nothing. Even Minas seemed subdued, for it was a place for the dead. There, a multitude of sad mounds, one after another, lay in a haphazard order, like a thousand anthills had suddenly sprung up. Some were pale green with grass, others dark and dirty, fresh. All held bones and ashes, and the few possessions the dead should take with them. Few were larger than the others, likely holding remains of a horse and some finer treasure.

Burlein's voice sounded hollow. 'Here lies my whole family. Most of the people I knew and grew up with. Merry uncles, drunkard cousins, great warriors, men, and fathers. We were happy, free as the wind and prosperous enough. Yes, Isfried and Melheim were ever worried about our fame, and our place under Balderich. They had ambition, but a man should have some, at least. When your father ousted Bero with Isfried's help, he failed. He trusted the wrong man. He should have helped Bero and trusted Gunhild; Balderich's last daughter would be married to us after all. There was no reason to believe Maroboodus would keep his promises.'

I nodded, and wondered how I had forgotten Balderich, the great former ruler of the Marcomanni, blood of Aristovistus, and my other grandfather. I had loved him, especially after I found out Father had framed him for the deaths of Mother and Hulderic. Balderich had disappeared when Isfried had been lured to the trap. Perhaps I would find him as well, if I managed to free myself. Then again, I suddenly thought, Woden whispering to my ear, perhaps he was not far, as Father had claimed. Perhaps he was with Maroboodus. Perhaps dead, perhaps alive. I would find out. 'None,' I said.

Burlein continued, 'And the lesser nobles. They trusted us. They were our men, believing in us to make the right choices. We made none.' I nodded but said nothing. 'There is the suspicious Isfried, and rapist Melheim, buried after they gave the corpses back. I wanted them dead, quite often, but they were family. So, I buried them with honor. We used to play together as children, wildly, and we had many good times, before they grew up into beasts. There is my favorite uncle; there, my cousin. The whole line of my family.' He clapped his large hands, and the echoing sound bounced eerily off the trees. The crows went quiet. 'Everything we were, lies here. Except for me. Hunfrid called me the least of the brothers. He is right. What am I to do? I hear your words, and see what you do. You were sent away in shame to die, and come back with Vago's head, never heeding danger. Where do you find the will to crawl through Hel to get what is yours?' he said, miserably. 'I am no Isfried, Hraban. I am the death of my people. I only know how to sever weak necks. Your father's is strong and thick.'

I turned Minas towards him, not sure what to tell him. 'As you said, Isfried made mistakes as well. I suppose ruling people is harder than severing necks.'

'I feel stuck, constricted…,' he said with a ragged breath. 'I long to be the man who drinks himself senseless, and lets someone else carry the burden.'

I grinned at his distraught face. 'Did not Isfried ever drink himself senseless?'

'He did, but—'

I laughed. 'I think, Lord Burlein, that you need to do what I have done. Let go of the fears, and make decisions. And bury your sorrows in sour ale, trusting men like … well, Fulcher. Build your lands anew, my lord, and grow your family. One day, your sons and grandsons will walk this place, pointing out your mound in awe. Perhaps they will say that there is the man who saved your family.' I stopped. 'Or, they might come and piss on the mound, cursing you for their thralldom to Maroboodus, laughing at the fool who failed. Just try, or don't. If you don't, let someone else build something with the dregs of the southern Marcomanni.'

He stared at me incredulously and then laughed raucously, the horses neighing with surprise. He got down and walked to a large mound, and pissed on it, a long, pleasurable piss that ran down the hill in rivulets. He finished and tucked his manhood away and cursed the piss that soaked his foot as he stood there wondering. He nodded at me happily. 'So, you tell me to brave it all or wither away, but one must decide, and play it to the end. As if I didn't know this already?'

'As long as you try, it matters not what you knew or didn't,' I laughed with him. 'I have nothing to risk but my life, so who am I to advise you? But, I think you worry about the fight so much you do not think of what you might accomplish. Though I am not sure what you will try? Will you obey Father, and slowly grow stronger? Ride away with your people?'

He sighed. 'No, we will fight him. We will not go away, like beaten dogs, nor will we bow to him. Very well. If I die, we are gone, our people left with very few men of my old family, and we will be lesser slaves to Maroboodus. Your father would not mind this. Do you know that the remaining Quadi lords are mostly dead, the ones that did not join your father? Poison and blade, they say. Your friend, Nihta, is slowly making Maroboodus a king. The Quadi Sibratus is now forcing even Tudrus's brother, Tallo, out. That Vannius helps him. No, I shall not wait, nor flee. I would rule happy, proud people, not beaten ones.'

'I know very well what you mean,' I said as I patted Minas, who was struggling with my reins so he could eat grass. 'It is never too late for the living to try to change things. The dead can but weep. I told Fulcher just now I would regain my fame one day.'

'Your fame as Hulderic's grandson?' he smiled. 'You are so young; you had little fame.'

'I have slain men. I have Vago's head. I fought in Castrum Luppia. I have fame. I want men to praise me for it,' I told him with a growl.

'You sound like Isfried,' he chuckled, and silenced me with his hand.

He looked to the sky that was cast over. 'Winter is coming. They will celebrate all over our lands, at least some four days. Hard Hill is very prosperous now. They looted so many cows from the Matticati, took so many of the greatest of horses and mightiest of weapons, a veritable hoard of Roman ones, that restless men flock to your father. The people of the mountains trade iron there now, not with us. I wish to change this. So, to answer your question, I will have revenge in order to secure happiness for my family.'

I held my breath. 'I will help you change it. If I can.'

He nodded. 'Gods know if I should fillet you now, but I won't, and, yes, you can. I give my oath in front of high Woden, before my dead people, that I shall not rest until the land we have lived on is made new again. I will find a wife, be happy, our people prosperous. He will pay for what he did to us in the Matticati lands, and what he did to Isfried.'

'I give my oath to help you, but I doubt you would trust that,' I said bitterly. He shrugged and climbed back on his horse, and we sat in silence for a while, mulling it over.

He then glanced at me and gave me a small smile. 'A man came to see me, few days past. He was looking for you. His name was Ansbor.'

My heart raced with unfathomable joy, and I nearly grabbed him to hug him, but he raised his finger in an unsubtle warning. 'He came here? Was he a fat man? Grumpy?'

He laughed at my happiness. 'Well, it is cheerful, this graveyard today. I have come here daily, and always left the place with tears, but not so today. No, this man was not fat, but he looked like he had suffered a lot lately. Perhaps he had once been corpulent, gods know. As I said, he was looking for you, had been looking for you in all the directions of the sun. He said he had been to see the Quadi already. I gave him no hope, but I respected him for daring to come to me. Your enemy. This is possibly why I did not slit open your throat yesterday, for filth to have such loyal friends with such high praises of his qualities, means the man might not be as evil as it is said. After all, they still call me a drunkard, and I have not drunk in a while.'

'What did he say?' I asked desperately.

He waved his hand north, towards Hard Hill. 'He confided in me. He worried that you had been betrayed, and he said he knows where Tear and Balderich are held by the orders of your father, in Odo's former hold. I was shocked to learn Balderich is alive. The true leader of the Marcomanni, but what can we do? He told me he came to me, for it seemed to him we would be natural allies, seeing how the southern men came back with no loot but empty horses, and the northern men with fewer dead but all the wealth. He was right, of course.'

Ansbor was always the keenest of us. My head spun. So Ansbor already found Balderich. I would free him. 'And Ishild?'

He nodded as he eyed me. 'The girl you made pregnant? The deed that nearly condemned you to losing your hands? He did not need to tell me this. Ishild is with Gunhild, your aunt, your father's wife. Ishild is still pregnant, and your father does not trust Odo. He watches her closely. Moreover, Tear and Balderich are being watched by that bald shit Leuthard, they say.'

'Leuthard,' I said grimly, for the warrior was terrible news. Catualda's father, Bero, had many champions, but Leuthard had been the greatest of them, a spear terror, breaker of walls, brother to Maroboodus's lieutenant, Guthbert. Burlein snapped his fingers. 'No, it's not going to be easy to conquer him.'

'You knew much about my matters already, Burlein,' I said, gritting my teeth at the thought of Ishild being held a prisoner, despite our differences. Once, we had been friends, nearly more.

'Yes. And I think your friend is right,' he laughed. 'I will do what you have done. I will try to reverse my fortunes. And we will do so together.'

'To do this, my father has to die,' I said calmly.

'We will kill him, and restore the rights of free men,' Burlein nodded and turned the horse. 'We will calm our ghosts, and make them happy.'

I smiled inwardly. 'Did you know Gunhild is not happy with my father?' He glanced at me, and could not help but smile. I continued. 'The whole issue started with my father withholding Gunhild's royal blood from your family, reneging on the promise he gave. But, she is still there. Perhaps she might be without a man one day, and you are looking for a field to plough.'

'She has not been a fertile field, Hraban, childless,' he said, intrigued, for Gunhild was of the high, ancient royal blood. Who married her, ruled all the Marcomanni, not only the South or the North.

69

'Father wanted to marry another for the children, and keep her for the blood and pleasure,' I snickered, and he actually blushed.

'Shut the hell up, Hraban, and let us go and plan,' he told me and turned to look at me. 'I am glad the Raven flew this way. I hate the bloody, ill-omened crows, for we have had few too many here lately. Let us entice them to move to the Hard Hill, and soon we will piss on your father's grave.'

'I'll not have him buried, lord,' I told him.

'I'm fine with that,' he agreed.

I smiled at him, thinking Fulcher was wise after all. But, he was wrong about my fame.

It could be regained.

PART II: CLAWS AND SPEARS

·

'I do hate you, boy. Not sure why, but there you have it. Sometimes the dogs just hate each other, for what would the world be like if we all loved each other, eh? We would be bored to tears. I will see you in Valholl.'
Leuthard to Hraban

CHAPTER V

I rode off with Fulcher the next morning. I was riding Minas, and we led a string of sturdy, old workhorses loaded with mottled, ugly bags full of hides and rubble. We followed the same routes we had ridden with Wandal and Felix earlier that year, and I was deep in my thoughts. I had cast my die.

The sky looked like it was about to rain, and one could not be sure if it would be wet snow or ice-cold water. The leaves were turning yellow and red, and it was freezing cold in the night. I wore a bearskin tunic with matching pants; a hood was covering my face. My helmet was hidden in a sack, and I had a bag of silver, some gold mixed in, and Vago's head was packed in yet another heavy leather sack. We rested when the sun went down, and Fulcher was quiet as he guarded the woods. He noticed I did not sleep. Instead, I stared at him, and so he stared back. Finally, he shrugged. 'I was right, was I not? About Burlein?'

I grunted, not willing to admit anything.

'And that you feel hope now, less guilt?'

'Maybe?' I said reluctantly.

'Definitely,' he said happily.

'Had you heard my friend had visited the town?' I asked and frowned. He did not answer, but dug around the grass with the butt of his spear. 'You had? You knew Burlein had spoken with him about me?' I mused. 'You bastard.'

'I am not privy to my lord's councils,' he told me with a hurt voice. 'My sight told me Burlein was not entirely hateful to you, and I had heard some gossip when I visited Grinrock. But, my sight is true.' He got up to take a piss in the dark. 'I told you that you should meet Burlein,' he said from the darkness. 'And now, you have real plans.'

'Do you have sight on what is going to happen in Hard Hill?' I growled back at him. 'What do we need to succeed?'

He laughed. 'Wyrd, lord. Fate. Luck. I do not see that far. Call it what you will, but luck we shall need!'

'I call you an idiot, a charlatan, and a liar, but I like you,' I said grudgingly.

He was quiet for a while. 'My lord is dead. He was never replaced. I asked Burlein for a leave to serve you. I will give you my oath, but of course, you must give me wealth and protection, as a lord should. And help me with my vengeance.'

I laughed, surprised. 'You ask me for protection? If it is not a Vangione with slavering dogs, then it is a powerful Marcomanni, an army of the Matticati, or a mad, world-hating vitka trying to slay me. I would need an army to keep you safe.'

He laughed in the dark but said, 'No, lord. I mean protection in small ways. That you shall not betray me. I just need a lord, and a lord who saved my family is a fine choice, no matter if he is considered excrement by all the rest.'

'Give your oaths then, Fulcher, and I will do the same. I suppose I will need you, even if you think I am an evil man,' I said, and he did, his long face betraying a brief smile, the first real one since the death of his son.

'What is the plan?' he asked, sitting down.

'Well, we will take Father's hall with Burlein,' I spat and glowered at him.

'Burlein is taking a chance, then,' he said, and nodded with approval.

'But, I am changing the plan a bit,' I told him.

'How?'

'We will see, but I have a hunch where Balderich is, and gods know I will want him there when we face Father.'

'Where is he?' Fulcher asked carefully.

'If Father is holding Tear a prisoner in her former home, then there are most likely other prisoners there.'

He nodded, his eyes worried. 'That means you would have to kill the guards. Leuthard. Without Burlein.'

'Yes,' I told him. 'We will see. I need an idea how to deal with that beast.'

'You need sense. If you will not sleep, then you can guard,' he crumbled and fell to his side. 'Lord.'

We rode out the next morning, and soon, emerging from the thickets, Marcomanni riders from Hard Hill could be seen, patrolling the land languidly, for there was little evidence of a war. The weather was chilly, there was a bank of clouds racing across the northern sky. I was afraid, yet determined, as I gazed the horizon for the hill I knew. At midday, I saw it; the long, flat hill our tribe had so long ago made their capital. It was strangely different from the past spring, when I spied it for the first time. Yes, the Matticati had burned part of it down, and those halls and huts were still being repaired, but it was mostly still lightly wooded, save for the very top, where Balderich's old hall stood, the Red Hall, now apparently the home of Maroboodus. The colorful clusters of halls were strangling the slopes. The gardens and stables were still there, and the sturdy planked harbor attracted some long-hulled traders, but it was different, nonetheless. It was Maroboodus's town, and no longer lovely to me. It had been so when I first spied it with Nihta, Maroboodus's deadly lieutenant.

Hate changes so many things.

A troop of mounted Marcomanni rode up from a nearby village. One of the war parties charged with the safety around the town, the hulking warriors held better shields, long beards, and wild hairs braided with their elaborate suebian knots, spears and axes glittering in the pale sunlight. They stopped in front of us, and we halted the horses with difficulty, cursing the packhorses that seemed reluctant to yield to each other.

A man laughed gruffly at our struggles, good-natured, but still annoying. He waved his hand around. 'Welcome, and who are you?' he said with a slightly bored voice. Clearly there were many people visiting the hill those days, and they had little time to enjoy the last of the dwindling sunlight and sour ale.

Fulcher rode forward and bowed. 'I am Fulcher, from the mountains to the south. I bear ore for your smiths and some hides. Will they buy, you think?'

The man nodded. 'They will buy. The month ends tomorrow; winter is upon us. The long months of being starved of ore and coal makes this a perfect time to be selling. They will need it, surely, like a drunk needs dice. Who is he?' he pointed at me.

Fulcher rolled his eyes, tearing softly at his red beard. 'Ah him! That is my son, he is an idiot, a hulking thing good for carrying and fetching, and perhaps breeding,' Fulcher said, and hit me lightly with the end of his spear. I growled softly but held my peace. 'One has to guide him like a mule.'

They laughed with Fulcher like a pack of bastards and rode off, their shields banging on their backs, beards flying behind them. I glowered at Fulcher, who pretended not to notice. He might seem a taciturn, sad man for his recent losses, but he certainly enjoyed himself, when the time was ripe. We rode to the bottom of the hill, dodging some halls and a cellar surrounded by a lush garden. The area looked prosperous. Some new houses were being built, and the fields were still full of fat, though small, cows. Many people streamed around in the wooded ways of the place, more men rode in patrols, and harried traders and craftsmen came and went.

We found a busy market set up downhill from Bero's old hall, near the harbor, where my friends might still live in Wandal's father's smithy. Sweet wine and expensive mead, unusually sizable cows, and even rare sheep, many handsome items were being sold. Some weapons by skilled smiths, as well, were on display. A grizzly man in a bear cape was selling a live, fairly tame wolf and also a savage, rare beast on another cage, the size of a dog, growling with hate at a pack of children poking it with sticks. I stopped to stare at it.

'Maroboodus is doing well,' I noted, and Fulcher nodded.

'It is opulence he has brought, and men do love opulence. Even men seem to enjoy the jewelry,' he said, noting a warrior rifling through a hoard of fine bronze arm-rings. 'South is different.'

'Men should love war,' I spat as I groped for the silver I had been given by Burlein. 'But, jewelry makes them look war-like.'

'Women love fineries, and that I understand,' Fulcher said sourly. 'My wife was always unhappy about our secluded hall, hating the trip to the town. She would not be kind to me, some days and nights after she visited Grinrock.'

'She denied you your happiness,' I drawled lecherously, 'and you got back to her bed by buying such trinkets?' He hummed, not getting pulled into such a discussion. I turned towards him. 'You mock me in front of the enemy, enjoying it, and I cannot make mockery of you?'

'She was raped,' he told me morosely, and I started to argue, but decided not to. He was certainly right, but his wife lived, and that meant something as well. He was an enigmatic man, brusque and efficient, but also moody. I wondered how he would enjoy Wandal and Ansbor's company, for we were young men with young men's amusements. I huffed and decided it was his problem. I went to banter with the man in a bear cloak and parted with much silver. I gave him instructions, and he nodded.

'Why?' Fulcher asked, as he eyed what I had bought.

'I got an idea for Leuthard,' I snickered. 'A mad, crazy idea, but better than a dozen of Burlein's spears.'

'You are mad,' he said softly, and he was right. It was mad.

We rode on, cumbersomely taking the horses past crates and jugs being carried up the Hill from the harbor. There were celebrations ongoing up there, I decided, my eyes scouring the Red Hall and Father's home. Fulcher nodded at my scrutiny. 'He has a guard of men, fifty strong, with the looted Roman armor. That includes the surviving riders he brought home. You know some of them, no?'

'Yes,' I said with a small voice. Nihta was a deadly man, worth a dozen warriors. Guthbert, the huge bastard I liked, Leuthard's brother, a Batavi originally, but Father's champion nonetheless. Another man who was worth a dozen men. We would run out of men if they should fight us fairly. 'He was training men in the east, the Roman way. They are not here, no?'

Fulcher continued, while guiding the horse past some women scolding their irate children. 'They are not. And he is still training more. He brought some of the looted Roman armor here, and gave it to young and hungry men, but most went east. The old families, he seems to despise, even if he has to bear with them. I hear the Quadi, whom Sibratus and Vannius led to the Matticati war, have some Roman armor and weapons as well. Few Germani have such a force,' he said neutrally, as he guided his horse around some Marcomanni maidens, who were not yet made old by the joys of parenthood, and smiled happily up at him, for he had wonderfully long hair and a fiercely handsome face.

'Your wife would not like the looks they gave you,' I teased him. 'Would need to buy her a crown to get back under the sheets.'

'Those women used to live in Grinrock,' he said with mild reproof. 'Hope they keep their mouth shut.'

'They follow the men after riches and glory. We will see whom they follow soon. Force of men, all armed in mail, eh? Likely all in the Hall up there.' He nodded. We had already spoken about this with Burlein. That night, we would deal with them, armor or not. Before that, I would go and do a deed. And before that, I would have to see if Wandal was home. And Ansbor.

I rode to Euric's well-ordered yard. It seemed ages since we were there, since Nihta had fetched me to be judged by Father. The hall seemed strange indeed, the yard unfamiliar. We dismounted, and I gave the reins to Fulcher and stepped to the door, opening it softly with my foot for I heard the dull clangs of a smithy.

Euric was hammering on a spear point, his eyes red, back hunched.

I stepped in and he looked up, eyeing me hopefully. Then he slumped and just nodded slowly, trying to see past the hood covering my face. Gods, Wandal had not returned. Surely that was it. He put his hammer down heavily. 'Selling or buying?' he asked dully. Ansbor came to the room from the side, his brown beard long and unruly, dark rings around his eyes. It was true he was no longer entirely fat, though not thin either. The wound Cassia had been healing had made him a suffering husk of the boy I had known. He seemed older, in many ways like me.

I stood there, in my hood. Cassia followed Ansbor to the room, her pretty face curious, wiping her hands to her tunic and her long, lustrous black hair was disheveled. I was half surprised she was still there. I had promised the Celt woman freedom after Ansbor was healed. I scrutinized my friend, and wondered if there was something that was not hale yet. Cassia had an inquisitive face, one with thin, sharp eyebrows that moved animatedly, adorably, and I knew her father had been a famous Celt noble across the water. Yet, there she was, still.

'What is it,' I heard Ermendrud call out from the side room. 'Trouble or amusement?'

'Gods,' I whimpered softly. I had been Ermendrud's lover; she had thought she would marry me, but I had been briefly promised to Gunda, a Chatti princess, and so I had taken an opportunity to force her on Wandal. Now she had not objected too loudly, but neither did she love me for it. Yet, at her insistence, Wandal had joined me in my exile. I grinned briefly at the thought. Perhaps she had wanted to be rid of both. She appeared, her slightly flat face unchanged, the blonde hair sweaty, and cheeks smeared with a web of flours. She stopped to stare at me, and dropped a rag she had been using to wipe her hands and put a hand before her face, surprised.

'What is it, girl?' Euric asked.

'Hraban is back!' she gasped and rushed forward but then checked herself suddenly.

I thought she wanted news of Wandal. I sighed, and pushed my hood back. 'Hello, Ansbor. Euric.' I nodded at Cassia gratefully, her face scowling now, and then I bowed slightly to Ermendrud.

Euric's eyebrows shot up, Ansbor rushed forward, and we embraced. 'Thank Woden, thank you, high god,' Ansbor breathed, his eyes wet, his beard tickling my chest.

I pushed him further and looked at Euric, Ermendrud, and Cassia. 'I do not know where Wandal is, not even if he is alive or dead,' I told them, and they looked away, disappointed mixture of relief and disappointment on their collective faces.

Euric grunted. 'They say he fell in battle, and songs of his heroism are being sung in the feasts. They give me little happiness, though.'

I nodded and sat down and told them everything. How we had survived Odo and Gernot, and chased after Catualda for the ring and revenge, and how in Castrum Luppia, we had done great deeds worthy of a dozen men, fighting for a ballista that Nihta's men finally used to kill many Roman soldiers. Wandal had fought like a berserker, like I had, but had fallen from the wall. I had followed him down, falling to my doom due to Catualda, and the retreating Roman cohort had captured me. Fulcher entered slowly, and Euric served him a mug of good mead as I spoke, and they nodded. Cassia looked pale at my words, and Ermendrud was pulling at her dress, agitated. She cared for Wandal, after all.

'I do not know he is dead, at least he was not struck by a weapon,' I told them. 'Likely, he is a prisoner, somewhere.'

Euric nodded sadly. 'I did not blame you for his death, Hraban. He followed you, and you served him well. That he might be alive is good news, but where would we start looking?'

I felt shame for having let him fight alone in the rampart while I went for Catualda, and Ermendrud noticed this, slamming her fist forcefully on the table, startling everyone. 'I blame you, though. I am sure you let him down. You grasp at bright stars, and when you fail, you climb over bodies of friends and their women alike. He was a good man. Is!' I noticed Ansbor looked uncomfortable, but stole glances at Cassia, full of star-eyed wonder. Ansbor had grown attached to Cassia. I snorted at Ermendrud's anger, but waved my hands to mollify her. She fumed and stayed her tongue, with difficulty.

I faced Euric, pointedly ignoring the fuming woman. 'We should start with the Matticati, and then Rome,' I said, then looking down. That would be a hard promise to keep, should I fail that very night with my terrible father. It was a ludicrous attempt we were involved in, but one we would try, nonetheless.

Euric nodded, but the Celt woman spoke, her voice as thick as ice. 'After, of course, you topple your father from his seat, save Ishild, find this Catualda, and achieve many other things?' Cassia said, tartly.

'Yes, because we shall have no peace to search for Wandal unless we have a home and fewer enemies. And I am not sure why you care. Are you not free to go home?' I slammed my fist on the bench, and she turned red from anger. 'I told you that you would be free to do so, after Ansbor was saved. You saved him, no?'

'I am their friend, Hraban, and no slave to you,' she told me imperiously. She was highborn, a woman used to riches and respect in the lazy Gaul, but wanted to stay?

'You don't have friends at home? You said you had a man you were to marry and lands to govern?' I insisted, but she turned her face away from me imperiously and not willing to answer, and so, I cursed.

'She is a friend, Hraban, so behave,' Euric rumbled.

I felt a moment of suspicion the old man had fallen in love with the spoiled brat, but then I felt remorse and waved my hand. 'I give you my word I shall try to find him. But, today, I need to find out where Balderich and Tear are.'

Ermendrud spat. 'Here we go.'

Ansbor nodded, uncomfortable with the tension. 'I followed some of Odo's men soon after you left for Isfried. I sent a slave to warn Tudrus the Quadi as well. '

I clasped his forearm. 'They possibly saved his life, Ansbor.'

He looked embarrassed by my words, and both women glowered at him. He looked sheepish and red-faced as he continued. Gods, the women were terrible, and I rubbed my forehead. I swore I saw Fulcher grin briefly. Ansbor spoke, his voice neutral. 'Odo's men, yes. They were buying some supplies from the market, simple foods, jugs with herbs, and strange leafs. Of course, jugs full of ale, for they were men, despite following Odo. They packed it all up and rode north.' His face went deathly white as he recalled his fateful day, and then he went on, painfully reciting his story. 'There is a rock there, some few miles away from a hidden road. A huge, flat rock. This is miles and miles east of the place Bero was captured, far from the river, far from it. There are heavy woods around this tower, and water flows on its base, swampland really. The rock is many heights of man, and as wide as a hall.' Cassia took his hand in support as he faltered, and I cursed the woman. Ansbor was likely entirely mixed up in his head for the hussies in that hall. *I had to give him his freedom,* I decided. He smiled at Cassia gratefully. 'Atop that rock is a tall building, made of wood. Men lived there, and I followed the fur-clad men, Odo's spawn, as they walked a path through the swamp, a path that held their weight. I saw Tear on top of the building, chanting and praying; Odo was with her. They tortured a man, I think. Held his head, and the man cried. I do not know what spells they were casting,' Ansbor said, squeezing Cassia's hand.

I placed mine on top of theirs, and Cassia recoiled. I smiled at her, and Euric snickered.

'Go on,' I mocked him, and he grunted uncomfortably, flushing. Cassia was now rubbing her hand energetically, as if I had soiled it.

Ansbor looked away from me to the dark, reminiscing. 'Anyway, I have never been so scared in my life. The men went forward, crossing a copse of rotten, smelly woods, and so I tried to see where the route went, stumbling along as quietly as I could, but I suppose not quietly enough. I saw a mad man's face appear from behind the tree. I knew I had been caught. I yelled, and I remember stumbling.' He was visibly reliving that the terrible day.

'Balderich or Bero?' I asked, and he shook his head quizzically. 'The man Tear and Odo were using for their spells,' I elaborated.

'The man was likely Bero,' Ansbor said. 'I never saw him, remember? But, he was older, and had your hair. He was likely this man. What was left of him. He looked… drained, not sane.'

I grunted. I had liked Bero until Maroboodus had duped me into thinking he was to blame for my family's deaths. *Would he be there still?* 'Bero? But, Balderich was there?'

82

Ansbor shrugged. 'Perhaps. Someone yelled something, challenging the two, Odo and Tear. Not a happy voice. Never met Balderich, not properly, so I cannot be sure of his voice, but I think they told a lord to be quiet. Next thing I remember I was running and stepping on a bird that was hurt, trying to take flight, only to fall injured to the water, a terrible omen. For some reason, I remember that. Some men in furs ran after me. There was a horn blare. An arrow flew by. But, I ran.' He licked his lips, and gave me a brief grin. 'I remember cursing you for asking me to do the deed. Oh, I wept and cursed you.'

'We all have wept and keep cursing him,' Ermendrud said sourly, and I wondered how I had ever enjoyed her company.

Wandal shook his head to stop any further argument. 'I have never been so scared. Ever. Odo was cursing me, I think, from afar. I heard him screaming. I did not want to be captured by him, by Hel.'

'Did you hear what they were doing with Bero?' I asked.

Ansbor licked his lips. 'No, not really. Of course they were summoning evil spirits, a god, calling for creatures not meant for this world, and Bero stood there, looking more dead than alive. Likely they were asking about that prophecy, and Bero was left a broken man after, I am sure of it.'

'So how fares the prophecy?' Ermendrud said sweetly. 'It's a surprise we are still alive.'

'I pissed on the prophecy, woman, now shut up,' I told her. 'Go on,' I beaconed Ansbor as Euric put a finger over Ermendrud's pouting lips, just briefly, for likely the smith feared for his precious digit.

'Not much more to say,' Ansbor said. 'I managed to climb away from the swamp, nearly losing the pursuers, but one man was coming towards the tower from the town, and seeing me, he pulled a knife. He was fast. I killed him, but not before he stabbed me.' He was rubbing his belly. I remember his terrible wound, and I flashed a grateful smile at Cassia. She blithely ignored it, her face turned away from me. She had a flushed look on her cheeks, and I noticed it was not so hot in the hall. *Was she in love with Ansbor as well?*

I shrugged. 'Anything else, Ansbor?'

'Odo called out for a name,' he added. 'I am loath to say it.'

'A man, a filthy beast?' Euric asked. 'You never told us this.'

'The name of a god?' I asked breathlessly. 'The one that tricked Woden? Their ancestor?'

Ansbor was nodding and shaking his head, confused. 'It was a goddess.'

We sat there quietly for a while, waiting, until Euric pushed him. 'Which goddess?' Euric asked angrily.

'Sigyn? Goddess Sigyn,' Ansbor said softly.

I nodded. It was a name we knew, and all of us blanched, save for Cassia, who looked around confused. She was a Celt, and they had their own gods, and those of the Romans, even if some of them worshipped the better known gods of the Germani as well, like all-father Woden, the boar god Freyr, and Tiw the Even-Handed.

'Tell her,' I growled, and felt pangs of malice reach across the lands, as Odo's words about their ancestry echoed in my mind. Somewhere, there was an abode called Gulldrum, where their tribe was born off the loins of the god who put a curse on Woden's first men. It was possible, I felt suddenly, but then refused to believe in it. A sane man would run far away, but I would stay, for what else could I do?

Fulcher stirred as no one spoke. 'Sigyn is not well-known, it is true. She is rumored a gentle goddess, certainly that. If this vitka and völva are raising her, then they are trying to reach her husband, really, one that is bound by the gods after Balder the Golden was killed by that god's malice. He is lounging in immobile thralldom, suffering. Yet, one day, this god will be freed, it is said, and it is also said that this god will lead the terrible Jotuns against the ill-pressed gods when the world ends.'

I nodded at Fulcher's direction. 'He has sights. Usually he knows the sort of information everyone already knows, but he is right in this. Odo's god finally has a name. It is no minor spirit, then.'

'The harbinger would be free, I know,' Euric said. 'Perhaps you should take Odo's prophecy seriously, after all.'

'They have been trying to either capture me or slay me for the past year for it, that is serious enough.'

Euric grinned humorlessly. 'So, let us name him. His name is Lok, the Shadow of Niflheim, Father of Night, of Woden's blood, god, and no god and so Odo is onto something, eh? If they free Lok, the end is nigh indeed. Woden's own blood, traitor Lok,' Euric spat and eyed me. 'Poor bastard.' I was not sure whom he meant with that, Woden or me.

Lok, the trickster.

Shayla had not mentioned him. It was terrible luck to do so, for the bound one might hear. I knew I saw Woden dancing by my side when I had to fight, most of the times, at least, and knew our family was related to the god. However, Lok's children were many, and Odo was amongst them. The powerful god felt suddenly very real; the vitka I had mocked a serious threat to be sure. I thought of the dark one, thinking about the many deeds he was rumored to have committed, foul trickery and cruel jokes, murder and adultery, his nature utterly chaotic. It was an evil being, they said, malicious beyond understanding, but for some reason, I felt sympathy for the creature, for was not my life chaotic and full of trickery?

I was unsure of what to think, but I saw them staring at me. 'Do you know the full lines of this prophecy now?' Ansbor asked with curiosity. 'None knew before, but have you found out the truth?'

I nodded carefully. They did not know much about the prophecy. 'Listen,' I said, 'this is what Shayla read to me.' I clapped my bag where the scroll rested.

'The Bear will roar, beware you gods,for time is come to break the bars, sunder the rules, break the words.
The road from the shadow will begin,the Raven to bleed on the evil, rocky skin.
A sister, a brother, wrongful act share,a deed so vile, two children will she bear.
The Raven will find the sister,the gods to look on as blood spills onto the Woden's Ringlet.
A raven will show the way, a bear is slain,cocks will crow, men feel pain.
Youngest sister's blood is needed, her heart rent,onto the plate of Woden, her life is ended.
Released is the herald, the gods will bow.After doom, life begins anew.

A selfless act may yet the doom postpone.'

They sat there, listening, and when I was done, they stared at each other. 'That is cryptic,' Cassia said. 'Only some of the lines make immediate sense.'

'That is true,' I said. 'But, I am to find Veleda for Odo, and he seeks the ring as well, for it is needed.' I showed the ring to them. 'And there was much more, of course. If all these things take place, Lok will build the new world with Ishild's children. Odo plans to whelp one on her, perhaps another, if mine is not ... right for Lok's purposes. Woden's world will go to the abyss. I am the Raven, my father is the Bear, and the ring is Woden's Ringlet, and is to be drenched in the blood of Veleda. The two bloods of gods will mix, and that will spell doom for Woden's creation. Odo wishes me on a short leash, but not hale while he holds it. He wishes me eyeless and armless, a suffering husk for what Ishild did with me, and he still expects me to lead him to his small sister.'

By the end, they all shook their heads, Fulcher included. Cassia was fidgeting. 'You must not find this Veleda. Can't you see this is powerful and dangerous? Wulf, Bark, and Shayla all failed at killing you. Vago failed to take your head. Surely, it is not such a sturdy head to beat the malice of all these powerful men and women? Lok protects you. Even Woden would like to see you finally fall.'

I spat. 'Yes. But, Woden has helped me so far, so he has more faith in me than you lot.' They all looked down, even Fulcher, and so I groaned, biting down an angry comment. I needed no more warnings. 'If I do find her, I will protect her or die trying, but I shall not let them gain hold of Ishild. She carries my baby. Odo might kill her, the baby as well,' I stammered and continued, 'or he might keep her. So I do not give a shit about these warnings, and the way few think me worthy of such a burden. I will meet my fate head on,' I growled and looked away.

Cassia did not buy it. 'You said men in your family have faced this same curse previously. That they either died or fled? And you seek to save your baby? Is it not so you want revenge and satisfaction? You would not be content at snatching Ishild and fleeing?'

Fulcher smiled at me wistfully. I cursed him. 'No, I wish to regain my fame.'

'Yes, fame,' Ermendrud growled. 'He is selfish to the bone.'

'I have made mistakes, but I will not run away, hunted to the end of the worlds. Odo does not give up, ever, until his head is a rotten skull, buried in my shithole. It is better to be selfish here and face them, than live as a noble, hunted hermit in the mountains. Besides, what if some other man of our family is a suitable second choice? What if there are people in the north, far in the depths of snow-covered Gothonia, who carry my blood, and they will find such a man? No. I will remain, for my vengeance, for Wandal, for Ishild, and for you lot, even for Balderich, for Bero, and for my father, who deserves to be gutted. And yes, my fame, for that was robbed from me.' Ansbor slammed his hand on the table, shutting Ermendrud up before she could retort. She sat there, simmering like sodden firewood. I nodded thanks at Ansbor. 'That is all. Lok it is, our enemy, mine at least. I have a plan. One that might change everything and make us powerful.'

'Gods,' Cassia said in despair, but shut up as I fumed.

Euric grunted. 'She is a friend, Hraban. She healed Ansbor, and she healed Guthbert. Respect her, I told you already. Your father's Batavi was sick this month; fever and some strange disease wracked him. She has helped the villagers as well; they love her.' He looked strange, as he fidgeted. 'There has been strange happenings in the area. She healed a woman who had been attacked, bitten savagely. Something tried to kill her, then eat her.'

'Wolves grow bold, I guess,' I said, nodding apologetically at Cassia, who just stared at me woodenly. She was uncannily beautiful in the light of the fire, and I knew I had stared at her for too long, for Ermendrud scoffed.

'No, no wolf,' Euric said strangely. 'They say it was a human. The victim claimed it was so. Something akin to a man. Shadow, fangs, walking with two legs.'

'Human tried to eat this woman?' I wondered. 'Has there been famine here?'

'No,' Cassia said, blanching. 'There is something about at nighttime. Something that is not sane, someone. She had been gnawed on. I had to remove her leg. She says it was a huge man, singing. She kept saying it. Repeatedly. Human, not human. Singing. Evil. People fear.'

I shrugged. 'Singing cannibal. Might make a good poem. This night, we are the beast, and will feast on our enemies' unsuspecting flesh.'

'You assume they are our enemies, as well,' Ermendrud said coldly.

Ansbor grunted, and so did Euric. 'They are.'

'Listen,' I told them, and something growled outside. They all froze, thinking about the man that was no man. A door opened, revealing a shapeless mass, and another growl echoed from under a wooden crate that was covered with a thick, dirty woolen blanket. The men carrying it came in to receive payment, and I grinned at them. A beast was needed, indeed, to topple the beast of Maroboodus.

For I needed Balderich.

And Leuthard guarded him.

CHAPTER VI

Maroboodus had taken over Balderich's hall. I noticed the guards were inside drinking, so I took the chance to put my head inside the doorway. The hall was much changed from the time my old, famous grandfather had lived there. It was now a luxurious place, with the vast Matticati loot adorning the walls and tables, and it looked like some kind of a barbaric treasure hoard, with the victorious warlord uncertain what to do with all of it. Shiny gold, brilliant silver, dull gems, and glassware from Rome adorned the tables. Forgotten was Maroboodus's claim of hating anything, and everything, Roman, and I snickered. His opulence now topped that of Bero's, whom he had condemned as a traitor and given to Tear.

On the walls, broken enemy shields and trampled banners hung, including Hengsti's standard of white horse hairs on a cross pole, the famous Matticati lord's loss displayed publicly. Even the lord's bloody helmet was nailed on top of the crossbeam, where all could see it. Hundred high men were feasting, celebrating the coming of the winter and the end of Autumn. The Yule feast would be held in a bit over a month. The Germani found reason to celebrate many things, for life took so many of us away, so suddenly, and we had many gods to thank for the time we still had.

All this I noticed, as I gazed inside from the doorway, cowl hiding my face. There was also the man I hated. At the table, sat my father, merrily talking with the former Vangione Vannius, Hunfrid's third brother, the boy who had betrayed Tudrus and torn the Quadi apart. There was the lithe, nearly sober, Nihta as well. He was armored, and sat uneasily with a gladius on his hip. All knew that a gladius was snake fast, and the man wielding it as merciless as a blizzard. There was also Guthbert, now apparently healthy, who was sitting at the end of the hall, sulking and silent, and scattered around were some ten of the famous men who had come with Maroboodus, apparently exiled from Roman service.

Liars, the lot of them.

I had once admired them, crashing through leaf and wood to save us, but they followed a lord whose mind was rotten. The dreaded Leuthard was not there, and that was fine. We knew he was in the woods, guarding Bero and Balderich. And Tear. I was unsure what I would do with her, should I see her. Slit her belly, likely.

My mother's sister, Gunhild, was walking at the end of the hall, with a severe look on her face. She was tall and thin, like Mother had been, yet with nervous energy in her, where Mother had been calm. She had been the pawn of the alliance between the Southern and Northern Marcomanni, the one available woman with Balderich's, and thus Aristovistus's, ancient blood, and Father had had no intention of giving her to Isfried. He had married her himself, taking the place of Bero, and, as Balderich was missing, at his orders he now enjoyed true legitimacy.

I would try to change that.

I pitied Gunhild, the poor woman I loved. She liked me just fine, but she was also a virtual prisoner with Maroboodus. My father had not been the loving, heroic lord she had imagined. Once, she had envied her sister for Maroboodus; now, she tried to survive. I spat in disgust as my father was kissing a slave girl. Many Germani frowned at this, the old families who respected modesty and family, but he was now at the pinnacle of his power, and out to change the tight ways and minds of the Germani. I wondered when a Thing was last held, and if the men attending truly had a choice to voice their opinions. Father hated our ways, like Gernot had.

He wanted to become a king, something most Germani abhorred, being stubborn and intractably proud, wary of any loss of their ancestral freedoms.

I asked an older man to fetch Gunhild to me. He complained, and I growled, as I gave him silver. He nodded and went, though he was still complaining. Gunhild came out, putting on a cloak of fox fur. 'Yes? Who are you?' She was worried.

I bowed to her deeply, my hood swiping the dust on the doorsill. 'Tell me, lady, are you happy with your hero, Maroboodus?'

Her mouth opened in astonishment at my audacity. 'Who are you to ask such things? Answer me, man.'

'My father's business does interest me,' I said calmly. Her eyes narrowed, and then she looked utterly shocked.

'Hraban?' she whispered softly, shaking in terror. I nodded slowly, my eyes on Father, who was now laughing happily. Oh, I would make him cry, I would. Men were passing by, and glancing at us curiously. 'Why are you here?' she asked with a show of calmness, and pulled me outside, and then to the side, beside some Roman jars.

'You do not know?' I said scornfully. 'Come, Aunt. I am here to avenge my mother, your sister, and my grandfather. My father set the whole thing up, and Catualda was his follower. It is a long story, one that will disgust you, I am sure. Have you seen Gernot?' I glanced around, sensing trouble, and noticed the youthful face of blond, handsome Vannius coming outside, where he threw up near the corner of the doorway, drunk and sick. I had liked him once, but he was a schemer my father had lured with golden promises. I wondered if Father had kept them.

Gunhild glanced nervously at Vannius. 'No, but they say he is alive. He is with Odo. Your father holds Tear and Ishild. He wishes Gernot back, though I hear your brother has a life with your enemy now. It is possible Tear is not alive, even. I know not. He is wondering about the fate of his ring, the Draupnir's Spawn, for he needs it for the Cherusci. He is holding Ishild … safe for the ring, I think. Odo was supposed to have the ring. And then, there is Koun,' she said softly, shaking. 'None have seen him since the Matticati attacked us.'

91

I nodded. Koun, Hunfrid's and Vannius's brother, had been my friend, and Gunhild had fallen in love with him. 'Odo had it only briefly. Catualda took it from Koun after a battle.'

'Took it from Koun?' she said with a small, shivering voice. 'Is he—'

'Catualda murdered him. I know it is of little condolence, but Koun tried to come here, and trade the ring for you. He was a good man.'

She was sobbing briefly, her face torn with unfathomable sorrow, but her survival instincts took over and she calmed herself with such a struggle, I had to admire the survivor inside the daughter of Balderich. 'Why did Catualda want the ring?'

I sighed. 'It was Bero's ring originally, remember? His father's ring. He wanted it, and as he is also related to the Cherusci, the latter tried to get the ring without burdening themselves with Maroboodus. But, I have the ring now, here.' I showed it to her.

'Is Catualda dead then?' she asked hopefully, eyeing the beautiful thing.

'I know not, lady,' I told her, truthfully. 'One day, he will be. Let it be while he is still young.'

'Let it be so,' she sobbed. 'Why are you here? You have no hope ... ' She put her head down and looked at her hands. 'I am alone, Hraban. Very alone. He has not even bothered to lie to me. He only holds me as a relic to Aristovistus. He plans a wedding with the Cherusci Thusnelda, and I know he is not alone at nights.'

'You helped him, you poisoned me, made me look like Bero's victim for him,' I told her sad face, shifting my gaze to Vannius, who was retching again, seemingly insensible, or close to it. He might die that night as well, and I was not sure I enjoyed the thought.

She wiped tears off her eyes, and pushed me, forgetting caution. 'Oh? Yes, I did. It was not deadly, you know. And what have you done for him? Killed, Hraban, betrayed men and women both.'

I calmed her with my hand. 'It is true, Aunt. And so, we have a common cause, and a ton of filth to wash off our shoulders. His foul plans will crumble, if you but help me. You are not alone.' I put my hand on her shoulder, and saw Vannius grin at Gunhild, with some vomit still on his short, blond beard, his eyes twinkling.

The bastard apparently thought she had a secret tryst with a strange, fur-clad man. He raised his hands, and went inside, not appalled by the thought. Perhaps he did not love Maroboodus, if he didn't care whether Gunhild was unfaithful, or not. In our lands, an unfaithful wife was to meet the rigid, cold waters of a swamp, weighted down by trunks of wood. Often, the other party to the crime would already be down there to welcome her. I stared after Vannius, a former Vangione, a third boy forever far from the helm of power in his homeland, now likely at the peak of his with Maroboodus. He had ambition, and yet, he had had some honor, at least, enough to help me once with Gernot.

Life would be easier for Burlein and us, should the Quadi be gone that night. And now, unknown to him, he was actually not far from the helm of power with the Vangiones.

'Vannius is my friend,' Gunhild explained. 'He knows I love Koun, his brother. He does not know his fate.'

I nodded, an idea formulating in my head, one that might make a world of difference that night. I glanced inside the hall. At least a third were Sibratus's Quadi, high warriors, with able men accompanying them. Apparently, Vannius was their lord now.

She grasped my hand, and pulled me from my devious thoughts. 'What are you planning, then?' She was sweating with fear, her voice trembling, and I wondered if she was up to what I was about to ask her.

'Is Ishild here?'

She looked around, as if uttering her words carried some ill omen. 'She is. They attacked Tear's abode in the woods, and plucked her out of there. She is with me now, but not allowed to leave the room. The baby is fine, growing and kicking like a small piglet. She is sick still, even now, vomiting like Vannius. Pregnancy does not become her, but otherwise, she is doing well. She is scared. Of being returned to Odo? Of Maroboodus? Of something else? She is distraught over something she will not share. She tried to escape once. Where she would have gone, I know not.'

'Has anyone touched her?'

She shook her head. 'Guthbert stopped Leuthard from doing that, they say. Made him swear an oath.'

I was suddenly grateful to Cassia for healing the dangerous warrior after all, and I glanced through the doorway at the huge, grizzly Batavi, with gray in his temples, his nose broken. He was a boulder-like man. He reminded me of an older version of Agetan and Bohscyld, brothers to Tudrus the Younger, my former childhood Quadi foes. 'I will want her safe. I will need you to lead her out this night, and then hide her for me. Do it after I return later. From the side door. I will let you know when. Prepare her, if you can. Also, when I return, I will speak with Vannius first. Do not alert him, though.'

She nodded at me, looking dubious, opening her mouth, but apparently decided she would risk it. And, if I failed, she would need to do nothing. 'I will do it.'

'I have a thing to do first,' I told her. 'Do you miss your great father?'

She hesitated, but nodded. 'Terribly. You know he only wanted to retire in Roman Gaul? He had nothing to do with Rome, treachery, and such. Nor did Bero. Maroboodus promised me he would be safe, even if he was powerless, a relic more than anything, but lacking nothing.'

'Did he lack nothing after Maroboodus ousted Bero?' I asked her with a smile.

She shuddered, as she took a deep breath. 'His honor was intact, but not so his fame. He even went hungry, and they robbed him. Maroboodus promised to restore him, and I know not what would have happened, had not the Matticati taken him. Maroboodus says he did not find him, or evidence of him, in the north during the war. He says he keeps searching for him. I think he is dead.'

'He might be,' I told her carefully. 'But, if so, he died in the same place Ishild was held at.'

'What?' she breathed. 'Why?'

'Maroboodus is a Roman more than Germani, aunt. He has great plans that serve Rome, and his own interests. Balderich had to disappear at some point, and the Matticati had to fall. He simply made it look like they took him, that day I saved you right here. He put him in that tower, where they held, or hold, I know not, Bero. And Tear. He might be alive.'

'He is a Roman?' she said, her mind whirling, but there was steely hate in her now, and I knew she would not falter.

'He led the Vangiones to our village, Gunhild. His hand struck down the Vangiones, only after Hulderic had fallen and Sigilind taken. Your sister. So, this evening is yours, as well.' She nodded, swallowing her bile, shuddering still, though only with anger this time. 'Let us see, Gunhild, if, by Woden, we might restore your father. He might be, by tomorrow perhaps, the leader of the vast Marcomanni tribe, again. With Burlein helping him, of course,' I added and grinned under my hood. She went inside, and her step was lighter, her hands in clutched fists. She was a very willing ally now, even if Balderich would not truly rule anything ever again. That much I had agreed with Burlein. He wanted new rules, and new blood, to govern the Marcomanni, and I did not blame him.

I rode downhill calmly. There was some snow billowing in the chilling evening air, as I joined Ansbor and Fulcher.

'She said yes, so let us do our hard part,' I mumbled, and rode after Ansbor.

'There will be many hard parts this night. In fact, I see no easy parts,' Fulcher said sullenly. 'Perhaps we should just wait for Burlein.'

'No, I want Balderich here when we oust Father,' I said.

'Why? What difference does it make?' he asked, exasperated.

'I don't want Leuthard to kill him, if he learns Maroboodus is dead. I owe Balderich,' I said and spat. Besides that, I did not trust Burlein to let him live, should he find the old man a prisoner where none knew of him.

'Life is short, so best enjoy some challenges, no?' Ansbor answered him. 'Suicide to serve you, my friend, always knew it.'

'Ansbor, what is it with Cassia and you?' I teased him, pulling the hood deeper.

'The boy,' Fulcher chortled, 'is as helpless as a doe with a broken leg, when that enchanting creature so much as moves.'

'Yes,' I chuckled to Ansbor's back. 'I think he would sigh with admiration should she fart,' I added mischievously.

'She is not the sort to fart! She is a fine woman, wealthy ... ' Ansbor turned, fuming, and we mocked him with laughter. I was happy, even if Fulcher's laughter was brief, apparently not happy with himself for being happy.

'She is wealthy, yes,' I said laconically. 'But, a bit severe.'

'She is severe at you,' Ansbor spat out, and then pouted for a moment, continuing with a subdued voice. 'She smiles like the sun to the rest of us. With us, she is as happy as a bird hopping on a fresh turd.'

'My, what a splendid way of describing the girl,' I teased him still, but also wondered at his words. Why did the woman hate me so? Had I not saved her from slavery by the Sigambri Varnis who held her?

We rode under the canopy of trees finally, and I noticed Ansbor stiffen as he stared at a space nearby. Likely, that was where he had been found. How easily he could have died there that day, I thought. *Wyrd.* Now, he was alive. I shook my head, as the dark woods closed around us, evening claiming the sky, and it was gloomy and bitterly cold. I had thrown my dice. There was no turning back. There never was, I realized. Nothing I could have done would have changed Father's opinion of me. I prayed to Woden to help us that night. I am sure my friends prayed as well. Lok flashed in my mind, and I pushed him away. His shrine was somewhere in front of us.

Ansbor was conscious of the ground turning into swamp. 'This should hold. It did when I was here.'

'I thank you, Ansbor, for coming here alone for Ishild,' I told him, as I navigated Minas through the morass. 'It was a very brave thing to do.'

He grunted, bothered by the praise. 'I heard later from Cassia—'

'I bet,' I snickered.

'From Cassia,' he said indignantly, 'that this wood is called Skuld's Wrath. Ermendrud told her. They gossip terribly much. I know not what this Lok god does here, but the legend tells how Skuld, the Valkyrie, spared a fallen lord's life around here.'

Fulcher nodded. 'Valkyries are fickle. They should haul the dead off to the sweet afterlife, but sometimes the women resurrect the dead. Sometimes, they fall in love. Though they say such love is short-lived and the recently resurrected find themselves dead again.'

Ansbor nodded at Fulcher. 'It was so in this legend as well. Skuld, a Valkyrie, had ridden to this lord, who was dead amidst the debris of battle, soiling her mare's hooves in congealed blood, fully intending to take him to Valholl for his bravery in war. But, having seen how the man was fair and tall, a better looking man than any of us, she had felt stirrings of fierce love for him. She guided her stallion to him, refusing Woden this man, his trip to Valholl canceled, even after he begged, his ethereal spirit bent over his corpse. She ignored such prayers, and, in her lust, offered to spare his life, return him to our world, and have him as her lover.

'A fine offer,' Fulcher said. 'Few men would refuse.'

'He refused,' I said. 'Is that not so?'

Ansbor grunted with amusement. 'He did. He had no wife, no. He had a lover, a man in his war band. Learning this, Skuld was determined she would never be mocked for her mistake. Her rage was earth shattering, and so she returned him to life, but not entirely. He was left to walk the lands, a broken creature of pain, but her tears of raging anger raised a swamp around here, for a woman spurned is a creature of no mercy.'

'I know that,' I said, thinking about the unforgiving Ermendrud and disdainful Cassia.

'Thank you for this story,' Fulcher said, and pulled a cloak around him. 'A cheerful story for the fools like us, walking the very woods.' An owl glided over us, and Ansbor nearly shrieked.

The trees around us were struggling to live in watery banks of mud. Snakes slithered in the water, and mosquitos buzzed around us, as Ansbor guided us forth. We rode for a short time, and suddenly, the horses were up to their knees in murky water, their eyes flashing concerned looks. The trees turned sparse, save for rotting trunks.

'Gods, Skuld must have cried for days,' I mumbled as I looked forward. 'Are you sure this is the right way?' Around us, in the dark, spread a stinking morass.

'Yes,' Ansbor said tediously, while jumping down from his horse. He sunk his chest to the water, cursing vilely, and groped around, dragging himself towards a copse of trees. Suddenly, he climbed up to an unseen bank of sturdy land. 'I walked amiss. It's here.'

Fulcher spat as he guided his horse forward, and I followed him cautiously. 'It is just that you got wet, for missing the road.'

'I was running away when I was here the last time,' he grumbled, as he shook with disgusted shivers. 'I hope I survive to get wet again. But, we will die out there, no doubt, so getting wet is nothing.' He pointed a stubby finger towards north.

There, far ahead, a huge rock formation rose from the rigid water. A pale light was lit on top of it.

'They are sure to have guards, Hraban,' Ansbor said, and tied his horse on the wooden remains of a trunk, his face ashen gray. 'I was discovered around here. Lucky they have none here now. Sorry. But, I forgot the distance, and it is dark.'

I placed my hand on his shoulder in consolation. 'By gods, Ansbor. You have done well.'

'Well enough,' Fulcher said, as he eyed the rocks. 'It is good it is night, indeed. Hard place to take in the light.'

'Hard place to take at all,' Ansbor said with worry. 'They could just hole up there forever. You have men coming to help us?'

'No, cannot alert Leuthard with a clamoring war-band. We must make sure Balderich survives,' I told them, as I stared at the rock. Ansbor gaped at me, as if I was mad.

'Alone? We go there alone?' he whispered, but I went ahead.

'You will see. It is cold, the last days of the celebration. They are bored out of their minds, and they are likely drinking mead and ale, for they are Germani,' I said softly. 'Our people have little discipline, and even less when mead is on the table. Romans would be impossible to drive out of

98

there.' I thought briefly about the Roman cohort in the Castrum Luppia, of the fabulous short men who had fought on, even when everything fell apart around them. They would have had a guard on the road. An alert one.

Fulcher said nothing, but Ansbor spat. 'If you admire the Romans so much, why did you come back? Never mind. Up there!' There was an audible voice of an opening door, revealing a sputtering light inside. There was also a chatter of gruff voices, and the light briefly shone strong enough to reveal part of the wooden tower build on top of the large rock. A man stalked the rock, dragging his framea behind him listlessly. He burped loudly, scratched his hair under a helmet of leather, as he scanned the surroundings briefly, and then went promptly inside.

'This Leuthard is keeping lax guard over the place, eh,' Fulcher said mischievously. 'How do they get up there?'

'I told you. They have a rope they throw down. Men climb or gear are hauled up,' Ansbor said irascibly. 'They do not keep horses here.'

I nodded, and we tethered the rest of ours. 'Let's go then.' Without any further discussion, I led them forward silently, wading carefully in the freezing water, clasping the spear, but I had no shield.

'How do you plan to take care of Leuthard?' Ansbor asked dubiously. 'He is the most famous warrior in these parts, even with your father's men shining like stars in battle. He has—'

'I ... ' I began to tell him to shut up, but then I slipped on to my knees in the water, and a flock of surprised birds took off right next to us. We froze. Three men, Leuthard's hulking form amongst them, came out. They had long hunting bows and wicked spears, and they squinted into the darkening night. An inhuman howl tore the night air, originating from some unfortunate creature inside the tower.

Ansbor paled and mouthed: 'Bero?' I shook my head stiffly, as the enemy was trying to adjust their eyes to the night.

They would see us.

I cursed, and thought about dying there, in the murk, a place of death. I noticed clumps in the water, moving slowly. At first, I had thought them to be ferns or rotten timber, but then to my horror, I realized my father had not bothered burying the servants of Odo, after he took possession of the tower along with Balderich and Bero, and captured Tear.

'Lie down,' I whispered, and slowly sunk to the filth of water, where a corpse of a fur-clad man was staring sightlessly to the sky, his face half skull, eyes missing. 'Pretend to be one of them, or you shall be,' I hissed, and we all lay down with the dead.

It was uncomfortable, freezing cold, horrifyingly agonizing as I gazed at the tower. Leuthard held the men there in the open for a long time. The bald man was stroking a long, braided beard, trying to sense where the sound had come from. His bony brow was jutting over his beady eyes, his many times broken nose sniffling at the nightly air, as he gazed around, the huge man sensing something was wrong. His eyes passed us, the clumps in the water, many times.

The corpse next to me turned around, the gasses inside it escaping through its rotten lips, and I nearly retched in disgust. The man's face turned underwater, exposing his neck. It was a mass of red, a terrible wound, as if something had ripped the meat off it.

Then, mercifully, the birds flew back to the tree they had taken off from, and Leuthard grinned and pushed the nearest man, nodding for the tower. 'The corpses fart, that is all,' he rumbled. They all turned to go, but Leuthard glanced back, some vestige of uncertainty still haunting his animal-like mind, and he stopped a lanky man from following. He grabbed something from inside, and threw a blanket at the man. The man cursed helplessly, and sat down near a wall, facing east, a miserable lump of disappointment, not really keeping watch.

'Come then,' I said softly, and we got up slowly, shivering nearly uncontrollably. 'Not a sound,' I added, and so we sneaked from tree to rotten tree in the deepening gloom, trying not to make too much noise, three pairs of eyes staring at the tower.

'We could use Felix now,' Ansbor grumbled. 'He would find a way. A sensible way. Why don't you tell us the plan?'

'We knew there would be guards here,' I told him with a hiss. 'We knew we would have to kill them. And so, we will. It is a long shot, it is, but it's our only shot. Balderich must not die so we cannot take it by force. We go with the long shot.'

'Tell us what it is!' he hissed, and put a hand before his mouth in fear of being heard. The guard did nothing, and we waded forth.

Eventually, we reached the rock, all of us holding our breaths while the guard was sitting on top, grumbling and cursing. A wind was picking up, the breath of the north promising snow and misery. Then the guard got up, and we froze in concentration, but he went inside, and came back out, evidently having fetched something to drink. Leuthard was calling him a grunting pig, and the man was returning the compliment as he shut the door. It was a soft retort, so Leuthard would not hear it.

'Right, lean on the rock,' I told Ansbor with a whisper.

'Lean on the rock?' he asked incredulously.

'No, in fact, to your knees. Come, come, do not be a woman,' I whispered, and he obeyed, cursing softly, grimacing at me with hostility.

'I am not well, not yet,' he added very softly, as it started to snow, as the wind had promised. It was eerie, but a huge, silvery gray bank of clouds covered the sky, as if summoned by a powerful vitka. Dull, white flakes came down in an ever-increasing amount. 'We'll freeze to death,' he said miserably, trying to keep his face from the water, where nearby, a rotting corpse of a woman floated.

I stepped up on Ansbor's back, and took a step up to his shoulder. If Fulcher were to climb on mine, we could reach the top. The wooden tower was reaching up above us, but around it was plenty of walking space on top of the huge rock formations. Just up, there was some sort of a wooden platform. I poked at it with my spear. It was durable, if moldy. The tower, on a closer look, was made of sturdy trunks. It had holes in the wall, great for firing arrows and some good for even throwing spears. I grunted softly.

'Fulcher, give it to me,' I whispered. 'We will do it here.'

He carefully took out a torch. 'What is that? Are we not going to climb?' Ansbor grunted in pain.

'You wish to fight Leuthard?' I asked him. 'I do not.'

The guard got up, yawning, and went to the door, opening it, braving Leuthard's ire. 'It is his turn! Is as cold as the shit frost of Niflheim out there! Did you drink my ale?' the man cursed, and I heard Leuthard curse him back. Something broke with a crash, and an old man cried in terror. I shuddered at the thought of what we would find up there, should we manage to kill Leuthard.

Fulcher took out a flint and a dagger, kneeled, and placed the torch precariously on his knee. 'Don't drop it!' I hissed.

'What is he doing? Is he afraid of the dark?' Ansbor hissed back. I wish I had told him the plan, but I was sure he would not have approved the next part. Fulcher struck the flint on the dagger, creating a host of sparks and a bit too much noise. It did not catch. He did it again. No light.

The man came out, escorted by threats. 'Shut your mouth, and do as you are told, you rot-tit woman,' Leuthard shouted, and the man who had received the guard duty walked directly above us. I looked up and cursed, holding my balance with one hand, calming Fulcher with the other.

Silence, shuffles, and I looked up. In horror, I looked down.

A stream of piss drizzled down, dripping on and streaming down the wet rock, falling on us. It took a long time. He had drunk a lot, mostly ale, by the smell. Then, he gave a pleasurable sigh, and I hoped he had no other needs to take care of. Luckily, he turned to go, and we waited, sitting miserably under the meager cover of the wooden tower.

'And, to think, I wanted you to return home,' Ansbor complained, miserably.

'Again,' I whispered, ignoring him. 'Carefully.' Fulcher scraped the blade softly across the flint, making a soft, jarring noise. A spark caught; the oiled torch lit. 'Here,' I stretched my hand, and Ansbor groaned as the weight shifted. I took the torch precariously, gazed towards South, and waved it in the air, many times. Nothing was showing in the gloom. I gave it some time, and did it again. Then, after a third time of waving the torch, I got down carefully, trying to avoid making splashes. The guard above was coughing and mumbling as the wind picked up.

102

'Who is coming?' Ansbor hissed at me. 'Burlein?'

'Wait, my friend,' I told him. 'Now we need luck.'

'Now we need luck?' Ansbor said skeptically. 'What—'

'Fulcher, the bows,' I told him softly. 'Gods be with us. We have to hurry.'

Fulcher grunted. 'Here,' he said, handing me a sturdy bow from under his cloak and two arrows, and he pulled another out, testing the string.

'You are terrible with the bow,' Ansbor whispered. 'What was the torch business?'

'Fulcher said he is excellent with the bow,' I told him under my breath. 'Right?'

Fulcher looked uncomfortable as he was scrutinizing an iron-tipped arrow. 'I'm fair, to be sure.'

'Fair?' I hissed, 'You said—'

'I bragged!' he said, a bit too loudly, and we froze. The guard was singing, some sort of a heroic tune, with a voice so bored, I nearly felt sorry for him.

'Come then, braggart.' We made our way so we could nearly see the guard and the door, positioning ourselves as sturdily as possible amidst reeds, shitty water, and another half-submerged corpse. Time passed, and Ansbor was staring at us. He was fingering his spear uncertainly, and contemplating if he should join us.

'Wait,' I told him softly and watched the dark tower intently.

Ansbor's eyes fixed to the gloom, his mouth opening in surprise. 'There are people coming this way, Hraban. Who is out there?' he hissed.

I glanced that way, not seeing anything. Soon, however, two stooped figures came from the dark, snow-filled gloom. They carried a pole cumbersomely. Between the pole, there was the large, square, wool-covered mass, swaying with the unsteady steps of the obviously suffering people carrying it. They stopped uncertainly, but then the shorter one pointed a finger our way, apparently having excellent eyesight, and their suffering trek continued across the sloshy, pollen-lathered water. The weight of the burden began to sink them. Some fog was gathering, as the snow whipped across the woods.

'Who the hell are they? Surely, they cannot be with us? I had to show the way, and … ' Ansbor began to whisper.

Fulcher snorted, but I shook my head. 'Ansbor, they followed us. I did not want to start to argue with you, and I wanted to keep them away, until we knew what was out here. Go and fetch them, quietly; leave your spear and be careful,' I whispered.

'The guard?'

'Will fall,' I said. 'And now we need the luck. Or this will end in tears. Ours. Go.' We moved briskly with him, the bows trained upwards for the guard. 'Make noise.'

Ansbor nodded suspiciously, and started to walk with splashes forward in the billowing snow and frozen swamp water. We were cursing the guard, who was still singing. 'How is it he does not hear anything?' Fulcher whispered. 'Surely even a deaf idiot would at least imagine having heard something?'

'He is as drunk as a fat, lazy lord, he is. Be ready,' I told him, and Ansbor was still walking for the pair of people carrying a burden.

'We kill him. We kill him, and hope he does not make too much noise in death. If we miss, it doesn't matter, and we will all suffer.' I flexed my cold fingers.

I glanced back. Ansbor was up the sunken road, talking animatedly with the figures, gesturing for us and waving his hands like a windmill. I was sure he did not like the fact Cassia was there. I had not invited her, but Euric had no helpers, and Burlein's men were not there, so there was no choice.

I took a shuddering breath, my neck aching with the strain of the bow. I was risking the whole night for Balderich. If I died, it would leave Burlein alone and suffering, as he faced Maroboodus.

Cassia. I wondered about her.

She was utterly brave, I gave her that, but she also complicated the plan, for I had not dared tell Ansbor. Apparently, Cassia would not be an easily controllable woman for him. I laughed softly at the thought, and Fulcher hummed. Seemingly, he thought the same. Ansbor was still fuming, but I saw Euric silence him, and they precariously started to feel their way forward after Ansbor took the pole from Cassia. He lifted the cloth just a bit, and I saw him blanch with understanding over what I had bought that day. They felt their way forward, but then Ansbor fell on his knee, making a loud, sloshing noise.

The guard above moved.

He got up with a scrape, and walked briskly to the edge of the stone, draped in a blanket, squinting as a small blizzard of snow blew across his face, hiding the road. When the wind had passed, his mouth fell open at the bizarre sight.

We both grunted, Fulcher and I, and the arrows flew.

The deadly shafts sped in the air. I did not see which one hit the man, or if indeed any missed, but at least one shaft pierced him in the chest, spinning him down on his back, his skull making a small cracking sound on the stone. One of his legs could be seen, twitching, as the man was dying, or at least terribly hurt. I waved at Ansbor to hurry, and in a minute, they arrived.

'Cassia should not be here!' he started to yell, but it withered into a hiss. I waved him down. 'No, she should not!' he continued. 'And this thing? The thing you bought from the market? Will it spare us? I want her gone, at least!'

'No,' she said.

'No?' Ansbor answered. 'What use are you here, where we might all die?'

'Sounds like I will be of much use, if things are so desperate,' she told him imperiously, her thin eyebrows high. 'Shut up, and hear what the lout is thinking.'

'She should not … ' he started, but I shook my head tiredly. Euric grabbed his jerkin.

Euric grunted. 'I told you, she volunteered, and I have none to spare with this chore. I could have used a slave, if I had one, but I don't. She is a sturdy girl; now shut up, and be a man.' Ansbor huffed and closed his mouth, though with difficulty.

'Now we have to get it up there?' Fulcher asked, shivering in the cold.

'We need the ladder. Euric?' I said. 'There, put it there.'

Euric uncovered a wooden ladder, half as tall as he was from a load he was carrying on his back. The man was so large it did not look strange at all.

'Nobody wondered as they walked laden like that?' Ansbor asked, his face screwed up in curiosity. 'And the cage goes up there?'

I nodded. 'I agree it is not safe, but we will be down here, at least. It is for Leuthard. We could all climb up there and rush the room, but we do not know what is in there. But, we know Leuthard is. I do not wish to fight him, fairly at least. So this will do,' I told them, without a shred of shame. 'Let us set up the ladder. There is a wooden platform, and we must get it up there, facing the tower.'

'Hell to boost it up there. It's not over heavy, but the load will be unhappy,' Euric grumbled as he carefully groped under the clothing of the box and pulled out a coil of rope, one end attached to it. 'Make sure this does not get caught while we try to lift it. That would be uncomfortable. And, I want to say, Hraban, this is an utterly mad plan.'

'Fits him perfectly,' Cassia snorted.

'Need I remind you, girl,' I told her, the woman slightly older than I, 'Felix and I concocted the plan to spring you from Varnis, and here you are. This will work, as well.'

'That you trusted Felix's plan to work was as mad as this is,' she told me regally, exasperatingly.

'She is right in that,' Ansbor supported her, and she rewarded him with a smile that would light the deepest night. I hated them both, and spat in disgust.

'Let's see how this one turns out, then,' I told them with hurt feelings.

We placed the ladder to lean on the rock. It was not tall enough, but I climbed it. Ansbor climbed next to me, shaking his head in desperation. He cupped his hands, and I boosted myself up, hauling myself on his shoulders, then up to the wooden platform, where I crouched for a moment, listening. The guard was moaning in pain, barely moving. Below, Euric and Fulcher lifted the covered box with grunts and vile oaths, Ansbor grabbed it and pulled at it, and they all pushed it up the slight rocky incline. Soon, it was above their heads, slamming against the rock. They panted and kept it there, Ansbor complaining as he felt it slipping on the stone surface.

'Quickly!' I told Ansbor, who wheezed and lifted the box from his end, the stone grating against wood. 'Don't put your fingers inside,' I told Fulcher as he panted with supreme effort, shaking with exertion as he pushed. I grabbed the top of the box, avoided the rope coiling down, and pulled, nearly slipping as I wrestled it further up. 'Hold on,' I hissed, and we got the edge of the box higher, and I was shaking with exertion. Something large moved inside the box, nearly unbalancing it.

'This plan seems most excellent, Hraban,' Ansbor said, as the thing inside the box again moved, and scraping sounds could be heard.

I swayed, grunted, and pulled, my neck and shoulders taut. I pulled, they pushed, and suddenly, the box was on the platform. I tugged at it, and it was secure. I adjusted the covering, checked the rope was free, and looked down. Below, Fulcher slipped and fell to the frigid water, his eyes huge with shock. I glanced over at the tower's door. Nobody had noticed anything. I climbed down, and jumped to land in the filth as Fulcher got up.

'Will the rope work?' I asked, grabbing it carefully, making sure it was attached.

'Proper pull will do it,' Euric assured with a sniff, certain in his craftsman's pride. I jumped down, hoping the plan would work.

'Let's prepare, and call out for them,' I said. Then we heard some scraping noise up there, and that did not come from the creature in the box, which had been suspiciously, broodingly quiet the whole time we fought to get it up there. I stretched my neck and noticed the leg of the guard was not to be seen, and a continuous scraping sound could be heard. The guard was crawling for the door. 'Looks like we don't have to beg them to come out. Ansbor and Fulcher, go and get our shields from the horses.' They nodded, and ran off cumbersomely. I waded briskly after them, dragging the rope behind, making sure it did not get caught on anything under the surface. The others followed me, and I stopped in full sight of the tower door.

'What about their bows?' Fulcher asked cautiously, as he looked at the dying guard crawl the last inches for the door, spitting blood, leaning painfully on his side.

'We make a small shield wall,' I said, my heart racing. 'Cassia, hide behind Euric's shield,' I told her, and added: 'Please.' She huffed, and I noticed she was wearing a short axe on her belt. 'You know how to ... never mind.' She glared at me, as if I was a thing made of horse turds.

Ansbor and Fulcher got back, handing me my shield, and Euric his. We stood in a row, linking the shields together, and I pulled on my helmet as well. They would know me when they saw me. Leuthard and I had no love lost between us. I thrust my shield forward, and so it was we waited.

The guard was finally scraping at the door.

Leuthard opened it, ready to give nasty reproof, then looking around in confusion, his bald head twitching left and right. Then he looked down and dropped his drinking horn as his guard bled to death at his feet. I nearly chuckled, for his look was comic, one of utter astonishment. Nearly, for I was scared shitless.

'Arms! Get your weapons, shields. Hurry up, louts!' he shouted like a mountain would. He disappeared inside the tower like a wraith. A man wailed inhumanly inside, and we all shuddered. I prayed to Woden, and I heard the thrumming sound inside my head, Woden's dance savage, and my blood was boiling. I would fight for his honor. If I fought Leuthard, I would die for his honor. But, I had no plans to do so.

I had a champion. I nodded at Euric, and he took a tight grip of the rope, running under the water.

We waited nervously, as they got ready. It took some moments, but then a man walked out, a red painted shield in the fore, then another with a bow. They had no armor, not even Leuthard, who was following them outside. It takes time to pull chain mail on, a cumbersome process at best, and I was happy Leuthard had left out the priceless lorica hamata he usually wore. I still had mine under my tunic, the one I had taken from the guard at Burbetomagus, but it was of bad quality, and such things did matter. The men cautiously checked on the man lying on the doorway, who was as still as a stone. They walked around the top, looking around for dangers, but Leuthard walked carelessly for the edge now, the sword my father gave him swinging angrily in his hand, and he was also grasping javelins. He came to look directly at us. He knew where we were, his instincts those of a predator. The snow was billowing around us, and he squinted, with his arm blocking the flakes, but all he could see was our shadows.

I walked forward, and noticed an archer stare at the box.

'Who are you? Come here so I can see you!' Leuthard snarled at me. I drew Nightbright and hefted the sunburst Vangione shield I had looted. 'A pig sticker you have? I will use it to scrub my ass!' He laughed, as two more men followed him outside, carefully, but gathering confidence. The archer was poking at the crate. I stopped some steps in front of my friends and held my sword down in the blizzard, not bothering with any insults. 'It is foolish to try to rob us, stranger. This is no simple guard tower,' Leuthard said, cocking his head, but his voice faltered, as he noticed my helmet. I was staring up at him. He recognized me. 'Hraban!' His voice sounded incredulous, then happy, for he would love to eviscerate me.

I nodded. 'Hraban it is. Back from the exile. The foe to my father, I am here for Balderich, Bero, and Tear. And, of course, I will scrub this sword inside your ass, as you are entertaining such thoughts anyway.' He was nodding madly, unstable and perhaps a bit drunk. The archer had removed the cloth covering the box, and was peering inside it through a small hole. It would be dark in there.

'You are a stupid boy, Hraban. Always was. That is why your father screwed you over. He cannot abide stupidity, no, he cannot. Who could? Why did you come here to die? You cannot get inside the tower, and I am not stupid enough to come down there. Who knows what evil you have brewed up in your little, filthy mind,' Leuthard laughed, hefted a javelin, and threw it at me in a blink of an eye.

I put up my shield, and it clanged off the leather, spinning wildly and broken to the swamp. The men laughed at me.

'Well done, cur,' Leuthard took up another, and started mocking throwing motions towards me. I did not budge.

'You are party to the deaths of my family. You helped the murderer, at least, and you betrayed your lord, Bero, and his wife. You are no man. Spineless as Catualda is,' I sneered at him. 'Such cowards, of course, would stay up there where I cannot open up your filth-filled bellies. Will you not come down?'

He shook his head. 'I, the traitor? You are the one they call the Oath Breaker, boy, and it is not all due to your father. I was there when you made oaths to my former lord, Bero,' he said maliciously, and thumbed inside the tower. So he was still alive, my relative. 'You are like we are, only weaker. As for raping your ass down there in filth, Hraban, I would love nothing more, but I am a warrior. Have been for a long time. Despite my appetite for yellow-blooded pretenders, I am not a fool. I will come, when it is clear I will not be ambushed. It might be this very night, it might be a year from now, but I will, one day, find you. Then, you will cry in fear. My word on that.' I felt cold, shivering fear at his words. He spat at my direction. 'You are not to be trusted.' He made a lewd face. 'On Ishild, when she is not pregnant, perhaps I will marry her? She is a fair woman, and I fear no magic.'

I spat. 'I am not her man, but I will be happy to fight for the mother of my child. Cowards threaten women, Leuthard, makes them look as weak as liver. I bet even Guthbert hates you.'

His eyes twinkled. 'Oh, he does. Wants me dead, like you do. Yet, I will not speak about that, not with you.' He threw another spear at me, wickedly, snake-fast, and with such strength that it shattered through my shield, bowling me over, missing my forearm by inches. I got up, holding the pierced shield up, dazed, and despite the yell of warning from Euric, another fell by my torso, inches away.

Fulcher was running for me, hoping to pull me back, but I held my hand up with a savage snarl. I yelled at Leuthard. 'Well thrown, for a mead sodden drunk. Now. Come down. Die. Or give me Balderich.' I spat filthy water from my mouth. He growled, and whispered something to his men. Here was a prize worth taking to Maroboodus, but to take it, he would risk much. I spat at his direction. 'There is a reason why you are the one guarding a swampy tower, while they feast up there. The Marcomanni? They know you. Mothers spit at your sight, youngsters are told not to be like you, and men dream of killing you, yet are loath to do so, for there is no honor in it.' I yelled as I pointed my sword at him. 'They say you are here with these men, because you have an affair with them.'

Perhaps he would have come down for that. Never was a man as insulted as he was, and so were the men with him. He said nothing, a sure sign of the man contemplating a violent, dramatic move, but still he gritted his teeth. The archer now had his dagger out, and was grunting as he pried at the box. It cracked, and Leuthard glanced that way.

'Your brother is the best man in your family; I heard Romans call you the fat, bald cow. They say you could not challenge an elderly matron to a single combat, and your foes die from behind!' I yelled up at him. 'And now, you will come down, because I will it. Or die there. Euric!'

Euric pulled at the rope, running between his fingers. It tightened, rushing up from the filthy water, and the archer crouching next to the box fell back in astonishment as something clicked, and the end of the box fell open. I heard Euric sniffle with pride at his construction.

Have you ever heard a mountain wolverine growl, my lord Thumelicus?

It is a deeply thunderous sound, as if a storm is raging somewhere near you, but you do not know where, exactly. In any case, it fills you with trepidation, with wild terror. The sound is as primal as if torn from a mad god, the beast as awe-inspiring as an earthquake, its claws as merciless as a stormy sea, despite its relatively small size. The sound that emerged from the deepness of the box was a reverberating song of death, rushing from deep inside a cavernous, muscle-knotted hairy chest, a noise of the purest form of hate, raw, unforgiving. It was the voice of vengeance.

The dog-sized creature was utterly furious of the bouncy ride it had endured, its captivity to begin with. It had been a mother, before it fell into a trap, and sharp teeth were the first thing we saw as the brown streak flashed out of the box. They sunk to the feeble throat of the terrified archer, a man who had no time to so much as scream. He died in an eye blink as the animal tore his throat out, the corpse flapping on the ground, and staying there. Then, it raised its beady eyes up towards the men staring at it with utter surprise. It was just warming up, and the unholy light playing in its eyes told the men on that rock that their boring life was about to change, drastically.

'It cost me a lot at Hard Hill, Leuthard! Now, show us your mettle, or come down!' I laughed as the men around Leuthard shook in terror.

Fulcher whispered to me, 'What if it kills the lot of the louts and then eats Balderich? And this Bero? Or us?'

I cursed softly, and prayed to Woden. A man cannot plan for every eventuality.

A wolverine can smell terror. It loved every moment up there on the rock. It was fast, the rock was small, and the men were weak. Its awkward gait brought it towards the nearest man; it jumped and clawed at his crotch, tearing a weirdly bloodless chunk off his forearm, the man uselessly trying to ward himself. I nodded at Fulcher, Euric, and Ansbor, and they ran up, following me as we sprinted forward, pale as they saw the rare beast rage at the enemy.

Two of the enemy dropped their weapons and jumped down, falling to the frigid water. I ran after one, a man who tried to wade away. I caught up with him with a huge bound, sinking my sword in his back, pushing him under the water, where he struggled weakly for but a moment. The other one limped north, towards the swamp. Fulcher grunted as he threw his spear, the weapon spinning in the air, splitting its way through the light snowfall. The man fell, crying, as he groped for the thin blade protruding from his belly, pierced through.

Up on the rock, another man screamed in fear, and we all heard how Leuthard's sword swished in the air. There was an animal-like yelp, and then a deep curse, a pained oath, and then a savaged hand flew in the air to bounce off Fulcher's chest. Another oath bellowed forth, as Leuthard attacked the beast again, and then he screamed like a child. We could not see what was going on.

Suddenly, we saw a ball of fur, arms, legs, and blood roll down from the top as Leuthard kept his savaged forearm in the mouth of the maniac creature, his sword buried in its belly. They fell hard, but the beast did not give up, its legs furrowing meat out of the bald man's chest, making small yelping noises as the sword was sawed back and forth. We moved to stand around them. Finally, Ansbor threw a spear, and the wolverine shuddered, going still. Leuthard was bleeding profusely under it, trying to keep his face on top of the water, his face in a pained daze. His right hand was raw and red, one finger nearly lost, all skin gone from the hand. I walked casually forward and stepped on the fingers holding the sword. They did so limply, he let go with a grimace, and Ansbor picked up the tall sword.

'What shall I tell your brother?' I asked, as I placed Nightbright on his throat. The man was full of wounds, his chest a mass of red. He was surely dying.

'Tell him to burn me, and send my ashes to our father. The old man, he would appreciate it,' he said with a raspy breath, and shivered. I saw a bloody foam break out of his savaged chest. I nodded.

'I will send both of you to your father, Leuthard,' I said, and prepared to kill him.

He shuddered as he laughed bitterly. 'I do hate you, boy. Not sure why, but there you have it. Sometimes, the dogs just hate each other, for what would the world be like if we all loved each other, eh? We would be bored to tears. I will see you in Valholl,' he said, and shook in brief terror as I pressed the blade to his chest. Before I could plunge it in, he jerked crazily, rolled on his side, his face going under, and so he died, his flayed hand on top of the water.

I nodded, taking a relieved breath. I had feared that man. But, I also feared what was to follow. 'Come. I have to see what is inside.'

CHAPTER VII

We cautiously climbed up, and dispatched the one man who was still alive, his guts flowing on the ground; so many ropy entrails it was incredible. The beast had gotten stuck on the mess, for much of it was cut savagely, torn around in a struggle. Ansbor retched at the sight. I pushed the door open with my blade. I saw a hefty table, a nicely warming, roaring fire, a half-eaten horse leg, some overturned benches, and a few hay-packed niches, where one could sleep. It was a filthy room, yet, in some ways, homely.

In the corner, a chain mail was draped over a bench, one that Leuthard had used. It was heavy and free of rust, a fine thing, with a serpent's face of carved bronze in the chest. 'I'll take that,' I said, as I ran my fingers over the precious thing.

Ansbor shook his head enviously. 'Another level up there.' He pointed to the end, where a sturdy ladder was leaning on the wall, and there was a yawning darkness up there. We walked to the ladder and I got up on it, climbing up with Nightbright at the ready. Gods knew there might be someone hiding there with an axe, and then my story would be at an end. I noticed the room above was not entirely devoid of light. Something was burning up there as well, giving some comfort in the darkness. Rats scurried around. I climbed up, cautiously turning around, trying to sense danger.

Nothing. Shadows.

I stood in the semi-darkness. There were rottenly constructed wooden cages around the small cramped space, and a horrible stench filled my nostrils. I turned over a jug of water with my foot, and realized it was rancid piss.

'Hey!' Ansbor yelled from downstairs as the rivulets found a way through the floorboards.

Looking up, the snow-filled sky was plain in sight, for there was no roof and I could see a small platform up there, a place where Tear and Odo had uttered their spells, and recited terrible curses in the name of Lok. I looked at the cages. I tried to fathom the jumble of things inside them. One was a skeleton, I was sure. Then, another. I squatted to look more closely at it, and noticed it still had its hair, a silvery thing around the bony face. I fell back in terror, drawing my shallow breath, and I understood it was not a skull after all, but the emaciated face of Tear. She was unconscious in a ragged heap of filth, her old face ashen gray, and she still breathed.

'Asses,' I said. 'Damned shit-eating animals.' Even if Tear was my enemy, she had shown some remorse for the events that had taken over our lives.

'Hraban?' Fulcher asked, his voice suspicious. 'Wait, stop!' he added, and someone was climbing the ladder. Cassia's face appeared, her axe in her hand. I waved her down cautiously.

'Euric? Can you get him? And the others. Have Ansbor stand guard,' I asked her, and she blanched but nodded, whispering down the ladder. While they were climbing over the loud protests of Ansbor, I poked at Tear with a piece of wood. She stirred ever so gently, and one bloodshot eye glared at me.

'By Mogon, they have kept them in their own shit,' Cassia said, as she squatted next to me. She pushed me away as she tore the door open, stepping inside, and gently began dragging Tear out of the cage. Euric helped her.

'Odo has a lot to answer for, acts of foul cruelty and many deaths on his head, but so does my father,' I said, as I kneeled outside a cage that held a dark mass of shadows.

'Balderich? Grandfather?' I poked the shadow; it slowly rolled over, and a man came forward, pressing his ravaged face to the wooden bars. I

115

recoiled at the dirty, old face, his one good eye rheumy, and his few teeth rotten.

It was Balderich indeed.

'Hraban? Can that be you? They told me you were dead, they told me Gunhild was dead, and they laughed,' he said weakly, as he was trembling and wearing but a torn tunic. 'So cold, Hraban. So cold.' He coughed. He was skin and bones. 'I did not betray your family. No! It was someone else.'

I wiped tears off my face. Father had duped me into betraying both Bero and Balderich, and I shuddered with hate. Cassia laid her hand on my shoulder briefly, and I nodded gratefully at her. 'I know, Grandfather. It was Catualda, and his master was my father.'

'Maroboodus,' he asked, suddenly seeming sane, for hate has a way of clearing one's mind.

'Yes. He has a lot to answer for. We are here to take you out. To safety. Burlein is out there, this night,' I told him.

'I always liked Burlein. Third son, but he had wits. No. Not wits, but he could at least laugh,' Balderich said. 'I only wanted to retire, you see. In Gaul, before we went to war with Rome. I was too old for war, and Bero, while loving peace, was no friend to the Roman Wolf.'

'Let us discuss later, Grandfather,' I said with a broken voice. 'Now, we have to get you out. Did Tear hurt you?'

He grunted in terrible anger. 'No. I was brought to them only days before Maroboodus raided this place, but what they did to Bero those nights? I believe in the gods now, Hraban. I have seen, and heard, terrible things, I have.'

'I have a battle ahead of me. Many battles, in fact, and so we shall spare her. She might talk, after all, despite being a fanatic.'

He nodded. 'You are in charge now, boy. I thank you. I do thank you. My spear and shield?'

I laughed, astonished. 'Old man, you need not worry about them. We go and get them. You will have them back. And, if not them, then you will have Maroboodus's head. They were Aristovistus's once, but what we are about to do, is more important than such relics.'

He looked at me in wonder, as Fulcher helped him up on very shaky legs.

I glanced up to the platform. Balderich noticed it and nodded, taking a shuddering breath. 'He might be alive. Best kill him, Hraban.' I swallowed, and went up a creaky staircase. Cassia followed me. 'Spells were cast on him, Hraban!' Balderich screamed. 'He might not be alive, but do not touch him in any case!' Cassia was nodding at his words. We got up the stairs, and glanced around. We were very high, and could see far, if the weather and time of day allowed it. Wind was bitterly cold up there, and Bero was chained to the floor. Cassia gasped, and I had to look away.

He had no eyes and only one ear. His fingers were broken, and his knees smashed. He was a creature, only barely living, lost in the mists of pain, and he howled an inhuman scream of hate and desperation curiously mixed together, as he sensed our presence. I kneeled next to him, and could not recognize this relative of mine, a lord of the Gothoni, then of the Marcomanni. He was a careful warlord, a guardian of the people, a man Hulderic, his brother, had wronged in his fear of the prophecy, a man my father had robbed of one son, and whose other son, Catualda, had turned traitor. He was a lord I had sworn fealty to, and whom I had betrayed. He was my great relative.

'What shall I do?' I asked him weakly.

He heard me. Cassia crouched, and put an old blanket over him. He shuddered in reaction to the sudden change, terrified of the touch, whimpering weakly. I sat next to him and drew my blade. His head was sniveling around, instinctively trying to see, but he had no eyes, which did not apparently stop the tears, for he wept bitterly. 'Who is there? Who is it?' His voice was croaking, sadly begging, bottomless with fear, and hopeless. Cassia looked at me with begging eyes, making a stabbing motion.

I sighed, holding my head with my other hand, but decided to speak to him. 'Lord, it is Hraban. I have set Balderich and Tear free, and—'

He shuddered. 'Hraban, the boy who lied to me.'

I shrugged, breathing deep. 'Yes, it is I.'

He shook his head. 'Tear! The witch, the whore. She gave herself to Adalfuns, rather than me, all those years ago.' He cried a bit, and I nodded. Once, Bero had tried to woo her then kill her. There were vitka who knew of her blood and her Lok spawned family, and their uncouth plans for the prophecy, and her family had been hunted.

Yet, Bero had cared for her looks enough to spare her.

After that, the old man, famed Adalfuns the Crafter, had saved her, and then married her, and they had sired their children. Ishild, and Veleda at least were his, but Odo, that creature, was spawned of evil itself. I briefly wondered where Adalfuns was, for had he not promised to help me three times in my hour of need? Yes. But, no, he was not there to help me deal with the broken Bero, whom I had betrayed.

He was sobbing. 'I let her go. I was weak. Bark wanted her dead, but I failed. And look at me now. Look what she did to me. All I wanted was to have Woden's Gift, my ring by right. I wanted to lead the people in peace, and win in war and rule well. I would have elevated you. But, you let them manipulate you,' he hissed, and I nodded and laughed bitterly.

'I am sorry, Bero. I am sorry for your losses and my failures, but then, having her raped by mercenaries was not very well done, was it?' I spat, and got ready to use the sword. 'You only failed to kill her.'

He spat and shuddered. 'I have paid,' he cried bitterly, writhing so hard the blanket fell off his tortured body. Cassia tried to relax him with soft words, but he had none of it. He hissed: 'Raven to find the sister, poor Veleda! They will sacrifice her; their own blood, and Odo shall use the children who are to survive to populate this world anew! After Veleda dies, the final wars begin! You will find young Veleda, then Draupnir will be set in blood, and the trickster is free of his shackles. This they found out from the goddess.'

'I know the prophecy,' I told him. 'I have bested it so far.'

'You think so? You have only slain their enemies, Odo's foes. Bested it? And, yet, you are here, risking it again,' he sobbed. 'I used to be like your father, and did not believe in it, but now? I do, oh, I do.'

I nodded. 'I learnt much from Shayla, a druidess. I'll brave it, my lord, and shall prove worthy enough to foil them all.'

He spat in anger and bellowed in pain. After it subsided, he said with a weak voice, 'Hulderic was weak. He chose not to fight our uncle, Hughnot, the Black Goth, when we were young. He wanted the ring kept safe. He was selfish and untrusting, costing us everything in the north. I would have been a better guardian for it. I would not have run. And, now, you say you are not going to run? Perhaps it is a sign. I hope you are right. The prophecy is real. They are of the blood of Lok. But, I guess you knew this as well.'

'I do, lord,' I said miserably. 'Let us see, then. I shall take you to safety. To … mend.'

He cried as he tried to laugh, for he was a thoroughly broken man in body, and then turned his head to me. 'No.'

'Great Uncle, Cassia is a talented healer; she might … ' She shook her head sadly.

'Lies, boy. Lies. I'll see your grandfather, my brother, Hulderic, soon. I will hail him, and then I shall flail him. We hated each other, but most of all, I hated your father. The man who gave the ring to them,' he said bitterly. 'Odo mocked me for it; he told me he would take my ring and extort Maroboodus, for he knew his secret. He told me he will bleed you, and set you on the road, eyeless and maimed, alive enough so that you will find her, in his leash.'

I put the ring on his chest. He jumped in surprise. 'That, Bero, is the Draupnir's Spawn. It is with me. He but briefly held it. I shall not give it to them.'

He looked towards his chest in wonder as if his unseeing holes could see it and cackled something unintelligible. 'Finally. Mine. Again.' Then, his back arched as if something otherworldly took hold of him, and I grabbed the ring off his chest. He whimpered, tore at his tight bonds, and cackled. His empty eyes jerked towards me.

'Woden's Ringlet is not golden,' a deep, vibrating female voice told us sweetly, and the hair in my neck was standing up crazily.

119

Cassia took my sword and punched it through his chest, while grimacing in fear. He took deep, gasping breathes and then went still, so suddenly it was hard to fathom. 'What did you do?' I shrieked, grabbing her painfully.

She whimpered as she stared at me. 'It was not Bero, Hraban.' She grimaced in my grip, but I held her and stared at my dead great uncle. She put her hand on my face, turning it towards her. 'It was not him. He is at peace now.'

'Who was that?' I asked, staring at her beautiful face.

'Sigyn?' she said with a small voice, and buried her face on my shoulder. I let go of her and stroked her back, letting her stay there. She continued, 'They used his life force and pain and suffering to talk to a goddess. She used him to come here, and say those words. He was but a vessel now, not entirely human.'

I nodded, and spoke in a small voice as I gazed at the dead man. 'Ansbor said they invoked Sigyn when they learned more of the prophecy. Why would she talk to us?'

She got up slowly, and looked at me carefully. 'She gave us a warning?'

I shrugged and smiled at her, wiping tears. 'Perhaps she wants to punish Lok and keep him under guard?'

She smiled. 'Or perhaps she loves him and keeps him near, and makes sure he is unable to flee far.' Her voice was husky, she blushed, and I understood I was in trouble, for I wished to kiss her.

Instead, I let go of her and pulled Nightbright out of Bero. 'Woden's Gift is not golden,' I said casually, trying to forget how close she had been.

'I do not understand it,' she said, and neither did I, then.

We went downstairs, and Euric and I carried Tear painfully out of the tower. I wanted to drop her to the bottom of the swamp, but I also wanted to speak with her. There was plenty of time to find other swamps later. She said nothing as she gazed at me, not entirely comprehending the activity around her. Yet, I did not trust her, and kept a close eye on her. 'Odo will die, by my hand. Veleda, your third child, will live,' I told her, and she nodded. 'And now, I shall fetch Ishild. Then, if we survive, we shall speak at length.'

A small spark in her eyes flashed, and perhaps she even nodded. I nodded back, hating her, but we left. We rode to the edge of the woods, and saw how Hard Hill was covered in a fine sheet of snow, which was still coming down gently. Dogs were barking nearby; some horsemen rode around the hill guarding the celebration. Up there, far up, I saw Balderich's Red Hall, and the fires sputtering merrily around it. My grandfather looked at it with an expressionless look on his face.

I clapped my hand on Euric's shoulder. 'Will you ride to Grinrock? Take Cassia with you, and Tear?'

He nodded. 'I will take them, and you will come there.' We clasped arms. 'Make sure you do not die. This was child's play in comparison with what you try now. We still have Wandal to find, you see.'

I shrugged. 'Wyrd.'

'Wyrd,' he said. 'I will meet Ermendrud at the edge of the town. And, Hraban, she does not hate you. She is mad as a hungry bear, true, but she lost a baby. She did. She has not been well.' His eyes flashed as he said that, and I knew he did not think Wandal was the father, for they had not married yet. I remember Wandal saying she had felt ill in the mornings, and I had ignored the problem then, but this would soon be something I had to deal with. She had lost it. I felt terribly cold at that, even if there was no future for Ermendrud and me. Finally, I turned to my grandfather. 'Will you go with them, or come see me become a Kin Slayer, as well as an Oath Breaker?'

Cassia hissed. 'I shall not go—'

I ignored her. 'Grandfather?'

He shrugged, his eye red. 'I have not eaten well for a while. I wish to see my hall, I think, and feast in blood and flesh. Let us share that meal.' We laughed nervously and rode up, hailing the guards on the way. Euric led fuming Cassia and unconscious Tear off towards the south, picking up a mule from a stable near the bottom of the hill. It held our wealth and his hammers, plus precious winter clothing.

Hard Hill would die that night, and we needed a new home.

CHAPTER VIII

We rode towards the top, Balderich disguised under a blanket, bravely holding himself erect, no matter his weakness. Fulcher wore my old chain mail, for I had taken Leuthard's. It was superbly heavy, uncommonly uncomfortable, and too large in the shoulders, but it did make me feel powerful. Ansbor carried a large hasta spear and wickedly carved javelins, and he was admiring Leuthard's sword, a weapon I had grudgingly given him. He had no idea how to use it, but I doubted he needed such instruction that night.

A man was lingering near the Red Hall. He noticed me, and I nodded at him. He ran off, grinning like an imp. He would set the plans moving with Burlein.

On top of the hill, I stopped Minas, observing the happy folk wondering at the snow that still blew in from the banks of clouds. Red Hall. This was the wondrous place where so much had happened that past year. Things of dreadful consequences, happy feasts, unhappy marriages, and the battle with the Matticati and Melheim, Burlein's rapist brother. I had taken his eye there, in rage, an arrow in my throat, and saved Gunhild. Tonight, there would be the final act, I decided. Minas was steaming in the cool air, looking about, distraught, demanding for something to eat. It was a magnificent animal, and there were appreciative murmurs from men who stood there near the Red Hall. I pulled the cowl of my furred cloak lower. 'Wait here, my friends,' I said softly and dismounted. I walked to the guards.

123

'Is Maroboodus in? I would pay my respects. I hail from the far east, and seek a good lord,' I clapped one of them on the shoulder, and he nodded in pride, admiring my sword and shield.

'The lord of this land is in. He is a generous lord, and the best warrior this side of Rhenus River. You find him in a hospitable mood,' the guard claimed. 'But, I am not sure he will hire a vagabond, such as yourself,' he said with an insolent laugh.

I laughed. 'We will see. I hear both his worthless sons are gone!' They snorted and nodded their heads.

'He'll make new ones,' said the other one, and we all laughed heartily. I would cull his balls, I would, and he would make no sons or daughters, if I had anything to say about it.

I entered the room where Balderich and I had met for the first time, and I shook my head, for to the left corridor was my former abode, my room for the month I had spent there. I stared at the crowds. There was a tumultuous party going on, and now there were perhaps twenty men of the old families of the Hill, fifty of Maroboodus's own picked men, and twenty Quadi getting drunk. Men roared drunkenly and cheered happily, and some men were wrestling with grunts.

Guthbert was not as sour as I had seen him. Mayhap he sensed Leuthard had gone to Hel or even Valholl, if Woden was in a merciful mood. He was gambling with a serving wench, throwing dice hopefully, and lost a silver coin and cursed deeply. Then, my eyes sought out the most dangerous man in the room, and found the lithe, sleek-haired man who arrested little admiration for his physical prowess, but no man who looked at his eyes would walk away without a flinch. Now, unlike earlier, Nihta was quite drunk, smiling happily while speaking with my father. He had been my friend. He had trained me dutifully, shared fey and funny stories of far-away lands. He had mercifully given me my weapons the day they had left me at Odo's mercy.

None of that mattered now.

Only few men had armor on, but all of Father's old band of men did. Most had access to weapons. There were many Roman chain mails scattered on the benches, things none of the lucky ones to own one would leave far from sight. Gunhild saw me standing there, and for a second, the look on her eyes reflected her terror. She calmed herself, and I nodded carefully, flashing her a smile from under my hood. She answered it, though it was forced. She remained still, tense, and ready.

Vannius.

I stared at the men in the hall. There were great many Quadi there, all Suebi as were the Marcomanni, sharing the same lineage, but different tribes. It would go ill with them, or us, that night. I had been thinking about Vannius, the man who had sided with Father to drive my friend, Tudrus the Older, out of the Quadi tribe. I wondered if he had loved Koun enough to help me. My eyes sought him, still wondering if I would approach him.

He took the choice out of my hands.

I found him sitting, strangely subdued, near the end of the table. I was surprised to see he was looking directly at me, looking very sober, and glancing at Gunhild. I realized she had spoken with him, for her face betrayed worry. He was her friend, she had claimed. Vannius could doom me easily, and as he did not have his happy smile adorning his face, I was sure he was thinking about it. He seemed like a lynx, sizing up a large boar, thinking keenly if he could down it. Cold sweat broke over my brow. He shuddered as he noticed Gunhild approaching him, to urge him to speak with me, but got up before she could reach him, took a mead horn from the table, and walked towards me. I relaxed my grip on Nightbright.

Vannius came to me, and grimaced wickedly. 'Let the sword be, and grab a horn. She wanted to spare me the surprise, Gunhild, for I am her friend, and Koun's brother. Little does she know I did not think of Koun too much when I helped your father and Sibratus with the Quadi. Such an amusing world, this shithole place of ours.' He was still not smiling, his eyebrows screwed with displeasure.

'Greetings,' I told him softly. 'So, how has life treated you? I remember you did not wish to return to the Vangiones, being the third son.' *My idea was doable*, I thought as his eyes flickered around the room.

He smiled wistfully, but then his mood changed, and his voice turned ice cold. 'Did you kill Koun?' he said, hand on dagger. 'I betrayed his hopes once, but Gunhild told me he is dead. It seems I have a conscience.'

That it mattered to him was important. 'Koun, your brother,' I smiled at him, and he bristled. 'The fool who worried for you, obeyed Maroboodus for you. He kept Father's secret. The secret it was not Bero, but Catualda who treated with Rome. The same Koun you left at Maroboodus's mercy, while you helped him subdue the Quadi for a personal gain?'

He looked away, swallowing, his long Suebian knot undone, and he tugged at it to make it unravel all the way. 'Yes, that Koun. And, I never wanted him to die. I hear he did, and I hear you told Gunhild it was Catualda. I just made oaths to kill him. But, then, I see you there, and you, Hraban, would say anything to hurt the men in this hall,' he told me, glancing at my aunt nervously wringing her hands.

I waved my hand gently around. 'Catualda did kill him. He reneged on Father, for he wanted the ring more than my father's promises,' I said, grimacing at my father, who was kissing another slave girl, and then saluting Freya for her generousness in women and war. Surely, the Red Goddess objected to him, but then, perhaps not. Gods were as fickle as men. Goddesses more so, no doubt. 'He gave Koun promises, but kept none. What is your game, Vannius? Gunhild's friend.'

He blushed. 'She is a fair woman.'

I snickered. 'She is also older than you by ten years, and the reason Isfried is dead and possibly Koun too, who loved her. Had he been less in love with her, Catualda could not have surprised him.'

His eyes scourged me strangely, and he hesitated and let go of the dagger. 'I will wish to hear the full story one day.'

'Aye,' I told him. 'So, I ask again. What are you doing now, dear Vannius?'

He was older than I was, but also youthful enough to be my smaller brother. He did not object to my tone. 'Your father did promise me vast lands and much honor. You likely know he plans on taking the Boii lands, far to the southeast, one day. These lands are still possible for me to gain, mind you, so tread carefully, Hraban.'

'Oh, I heard the story,' I chuckled. 'But?'

'Sibratus,' Vannius said cantankerously. 'The Quadi is above me in councils and trust. I have started—'

'To wonder if you are another tool he can, and will, discard, as easily as he squeezes out a turd, no?'

He looked like a man with a frozen turnip under his tongue. 'Perhaps. He is prone to treachery.'

'You betrayed my friend, Tudrus,' I said, emotionlessly. 'That we even talk, is a miracle.'

'Shut your mouth, Hraban; we are all soiled,' he sulked. 'I know not what I am to do now. Perhaps I shall skewer you? What can you offer, better than promises of Maroboodus? Your ass?'

I leaned forward with a smile. 'We hold Hunfrid.'

'Yes,' he said, uncomprehending. 'What?'

'We have your brother,' I repeated. 'The one you dislike. The one you both hated.' He frowned, though there was some disbelieving excitement in his eyes. 'And, holding your eldest brother, the brother you both detested, holds certain promise for ... you? Seeing how Koun is dead.'

'How is Hunfrid?' he asked as casually as he could, for he was suddenly closer to the kingship of the Vangiones than he had thought. Much closer than he knew, I snickered. He did not apparently know Vago was dead.

I did not answer his question. I picked up a mug of ale, apparently abandoned on the table, and shrugged. 'You know, when I was a ... guest in Burbetomagus—'

'You were in our home?' he asked, breathless. 'You saw our hall?'

'I did see your hall,' I told him with a snicker, not wishing to tell him I torched it over his father's corpse. 'I was going to tell you I admire the vast, rich lands there. All the wheat, fat cows, trade, and Roman wares. Mediomactri are veritable slaves to the Vangiones, I think. Your lands, my lord, are worth ruling. Rather than lands still held by enemies.'

He fidgeted. 'I asked, how is...'

127

'The axe-faced asshole? He is alive. Getting bored and fat, no doubt,' I told him. 'Burlein holds him.'

'And Burlein,' he said mischievously, his eyes calculating, 'the bastard who is a reluctant subject to our lord here,' his eyes flickered towards Maroboodus, who was discussing animatedly with Nihta, sharing some amusing story, for both chuckled deep and long, 'has not delivered this arch enemy of the Marcomanni here? Is there a reason for this, I wonder?'

'Ah, the prisoner is exhausted after giving me a chase and a horse. He is resting for now. Burlein will send men here to bear the great news,' I told him with a smile, and then we both tired of the game. 'Hunfrid might die, lord, of this exhaustion. Then you would be hovering near the throne of the Vangiones. Surely, with the vast experience in warfare you have lately received and the intricate lessons in betrayal and diplomacy, this situation might be something of an opportunity for you.'

He nodded stoutly. 'Lands in the future, as compared to lands now? After my father dies? It is tempting, Hraban.'

'Oh, yes,' I chuckled. 'Vago…'

Vannius was shaking his head. 'I loved Koun. Much more than I love my father and brothers. And sister, of course. Did you see her there? In Burbetomagus? You know they wanted you dead. For that prophecy thing.'

I took a deep breath. 'I liked her, very much indeed.'

His eyes took on a confused look as he examined my face. 'Liked?'

'She grew weary of life, Vannius. We cared for each other, as she cared for my wounds. She would have died had I died, and you know what your father did to her,' I told him grimly, begging Woden he would believe me. His hand was on the dagger, his knucklebones white.

'And you say you did not kill her either?' he hissed.

'This, I swear, Vannius,' I told him, opening my hands in front of me as a sign of honesty. 'We shared love, and I shall weep for her for years to come.' In that, I did not lie. She had been wise beyond time, as beautiful as the moon, and utterly miserable, and our time together in my imprisonment had been gentle, if doomed to end.

He looked away, bile in his throat. 'Vago. My father. He was unkind to her, all her life.'

'We need not discuss it anymore, Vannius,' I said calmly.

'I will see him one day, my father, and have words with him,' he said, with words devoid of love, and I smiled and nodded. *Sooner than he thought, if he did not leave the hall.* I was about to tell him Vago was dead, but felt brief anger as I gazed at him. He had caused many deaths amongst honorable men I loved.

'Evidently, you did not love Tudrus and his family? The man who treated you like a son,' I said with reproof, even if I should have just gotten rid of him by telling him he was an orphan. 'What happened to them? Did they lose anyone for your betrayal? You were trying to trap him, remember, and then slay him. Right here, even.'

He shrugged, taking a deep breath. 'Yes, and you fooled me to give you the means to help him. I liked him, curiously better than most men.'

'He is that, likable,' I snickered. 'His sons?'

'All survived the turmoil when Sibratus overran his dominion. Some of his warriors and villages fell, but he led most north, to the Luppia valley area, past the Matticati. He joined the Sigambri, I think, and likely fights Romans now, the poor bastard. I was sorry for it, Hraban. Tudrus was in the way, and man must make choices. You know this better than any. He wanted to stay independent; Maroboodus needed the Quadi to join the Marcomanni. Now, they are sad, divided people.' He skimmed his gaze over his men lounging in the room with uncertainty. 'Sibratus is the strongest lord there. Tallo is still independent from Maroboodus near the Chatti Hills. His half of the Quadi fight the savage Hermanduri and roving bands of Chatti, both, and they are doomed. I became famous when Hengsti died. There is a song about my deeds,' he purred.

'How much did it cost you?' I snickered. 'One silver per word?'

'Bastard,' he said, pushing me with a grin, and I liked him again, despite the past. 'So give me a way out of this, and a way to become even more powerful.'

'It is possible for Hunfrid to die in his captivity, it is indeed. There are diseases, food poisoning.'

'Murder?' he grinned.

'Such things do happen, Woden forbid,' I confirmed, peering over at Nihta, who was now staring at us. I did not have much time. Outside, I could hear many horses neighing far in the dark. Dogs were barking, nervous.

I nodded. 'As for you, I think the Quadi might benefit from not being present in Hard Hill this night.'

His eyes popped open. 'Truly? They are bringing news from Burlein this very night?' he asked sarcastically. 'And spears?'

'Truly. Also, I hear old Lord Balderich has been seen in the docks. Another rumor has it that he was seen riding east, for his old life. Not an hour ago.'

He glanced at me in surprise. 'I see. The old goat escaped from his cage, scampered behind the huge beast of Leuthard, strangled him with his old, gnarled hands, and slew all the men in the tower, eh? Apparently, he did not take Leuthard's armor, though?' He tugged at the cold metal peeking under my tunic. He ticked his fingernail on the bronze ornament at the chest beneath the tunic. 'So, which way should I take my Quadi? If I agree.'

I shrugged. 'I feel that riding for east would be prudent. You should not come back before tomorrow morning, or preferably, afternoon.' I looked deep into his eyes. 'You might be one of the most powerful men in the Suebi nations, able to choose your own way, perhaps topple Sibratus and Tallo and lead the Quadi? Young enough to do what you will. Or, go home, and take advantage of the chaos in the land.'

'That would pit us against each other, Hraban?' he said prudently. 'Perhaps both of those choices would do so.'

'They might. I know not yet what I shall do, if I succeed here this night,' I told him honestly. 'Why worry about it? All I want is my fame back. And, some other things, of course. Tell Maroboodus that Balderich has been seen, and volunteer to take after him.'

'Of course,' he said, and drank the mead and wiped the juices off his weak beard. 'Yes, I see that. I like you, Hraban. But, I still have a third choice. I can wait for what Maroboodus has promised, and also wait until Vago is dead. I doubt you will ever let Hunfrid go, anyway. I cannot go home and suffer my father, nor challenge him. Perhaps I should wait? Maroboodus!' he yelled, and I cursed.

My father's war-like face turned to stone as he gazed for the voice that hailed him. His beard was full and red, braided in gold and ale, his red hair unruly and long, golden torc shining on his armored chest. He was lean of waist, broad of shoulders, and powerful to behold, his face as merciless as the approaching winter. The man had claimed to love me. Now I saw he was incapable of loving, or if he was, it was not possible in the land so full of spears, and with his plans with Rome standing in the way. Here, he would never rest and lay down his guard.

I cursed Vannius softly and pulled him to me. He nearly pulled his dagger, but I grabbed the hand, saw Gunhild clasping a hand on her face, and I nodded at her quickly. She nodded back, as I hissed in his ear. 'Your father is dead. You are the king now.' Gunhild rushed out of the room, for Vannius had robbed us the time to prepare.

Vannius's face betrayed his surprise and bewilderment. Maroboodus got up and leaned over the table, banging on it and pointing a powerful, ring laden finger at me. 'Who is that man?' he growled, his voice a bit drunk. 'A man who is angry, while others revel? A man you do not trust, loyal Vannius?' Vannius looked at the ground, grabbed a vacant horn sloshing with ale, and seemed to mull over his choices. I cursed him. I had wanted Gunhild and Ishild out of the hall, before what was about to happen. 'Well?' demanded my father slowly, and I was afraid Nihta would recognize me too early.

Vannius clapped his hand on my shoulder. 'I know not this man, though his voice is familiar. This is but a rider, my lord. He tells wild tales, and, yes, I got riled at his claims!' Vannius was covering his tracks, in case things did not work out. But, at least he was trying to grasp the Vangione throne now. He continued. 'He spins a strange story. A ghost story, or one made up by a drunken imagination. He says Balderich was seen seeking a passage across the river just now in the docks, near Euric's smithy. Would you believe that?' He stopped and looked at me. 'Was it Euric? Yes? Smithy? He said he looked tired and dead. He claims others say he was seen riding east. Surely, the great Balderich is lost, still? In the deep Matticati hills? Perhaps dead?'

Oh, Vannius knew about Balderich, and Maroboodus knew he knew, and his and Vannius's eyes met as they were contemplating the meaning of my tidings. The Marcomanni did not know Maroboodus had hidden their highest noble away, a very subtle situation. Most lords of the various clans sat there, oldsters and some keener younger men, and not all loved my father.

Maroboodus looked momentarily frozen, and the party around him went silent. Nihta got up, Guthbert as well, though stiffly. The men of my father's band seemed to sober up quickly as they looked around to gather their weapons. They were old Roman guardsmen, and knew how to change from merry revelers into bloodthirsty slayers in but a moment. Maroboodus turned to Nihta, who nodded at some twenty men. They grabbed their chain mail, spears, and axes, and filed out. They were the Marcomanni warriors most dedicated to my father, the dangerous men. His closest men stayed put, though, clad in furs and Roman finery, tall, impossibly strong men who had changed so many battles. Their eyes gleamed.

'It is true then? He is alive?' Vannius queried. Men in the hall murmured, and some cheered merrily. Some looked at my father suspiciously.

Maroboodus shrugged, as he eyeballed Vannius murderously, warning the young fool to stay his tongue. 'If it is so Balderich has returned, it is a ghost, as why would our lord be running away? It is a dead spirit, and so, he has died. Nihta went to see if this ghost is stalking the harbor. You men … ' Maroboodus pointed at some of the drunken Marcomanni getting up unsteadily.

Vannius intercepted him. 'Lord, if there truly is a ghost stalking the land, let me take my Quadi to search the eastern roads. I have some twenty men, most hopelessly drunk, aye, but able to go anyway. Some will break legs and arms as they fall from the horse, but let us capture this ghost. I am happy to do you this favor.'

Maroboodus grunted and nodded. 'Noble Vannius, I accept.' His eyes flashed at the young man, and he motioned for one of his riders to accompany Vannius. I felt sorry for the man, should we win. Maroboodus stalked to the wall, and took down Balderich's ancient weapons, the blue-hued hasta, the huge cavalry spear with a chiseled, ornate blade, and the shield with a symbol of a black chain. He walked back to his seat, set the gear near him, adjusted his spatha, a long, sturdy butcher's blade, my grandfather's ancient blade called the Head Taker, and turned to the staring clan's heads. 'Please, keep drinking and eating. Make merry! If a ghost stalks the land, we will drive it away. If it is seen, we will mourn our lord. We will avenge his death, so we will.'

The men in the hall murmured, and raised their mugs in salute to Balderich. Everyone knew he had lost his power to Maroboodus, but he had led them for decades, and they respected him. Vannius left, grinning at me, and I followed him out. Nihta had jumped on a large, roan horse, and some twenty armored men were ready to stagger to the harbor. The lethal man guided them towards Bero's former hall, and I hoped to see him dead.

Vannius said nothing, as his Quadi followed him out of the hall, muttering to themselves, stroking their beards and suebian knots in the chaos. Many of them were soon rushing downhill, towards the houses where the Quadi were quartered. I thanked Vannius in my head for his duplicity, though I also cursed him. Gunhild and Ishild were still inside. I nodded at the young man, and thought Tudrus would slaughter him one day, but that day, he had served me fairly well.

He glanced my way. 'He is dead? Truly?' I grunted and patted a heavy sack at my side. A pungent smell rose from it. Vannius's eyes went to slits, and he nearly protested, but thought better of it. Shaking his head, he rode to gather his men. 'We shall be back. I'll bury you, should you fail. It is likely.'

'Enjoy your throne, wherever you find it, Vannius.' Gazing at the shadows of the surrounding halls, I knew we were ready.

I waited, fidgeting.

Ready, but for Gunhild. I waited still. Nothing. Wind blew mournfully.

I cursed, and went back in, furious at my aunt. The hall was half empty after my father's supporters had followed Nihta out and the Quadi had left, my father mumbling something to a few of his men. One left, evidently riding for the swamp. Then Maroboodus settled down to his seat, his hands thrumming the table. The jolly mood had evaporated as fog would in scorching sunlight. I waited for some time, leaning on the doorframe. I glanced out of the door, and saw torches carried by Nihta and his men disappear down towards the water line. It was time, Gunhild or not. I nodded at the darkness, and entered the hall fully, my eyes feverishly seeking her outside, but she was not there. She was still inside, or she had forgotten to signal me they were safe. Gods. She was failing me. Screw Vannius for making it so. I had to chance it. Woden, everything had been going miraculously well so far, so this was the price to pay for it.

Then, my father looked up, tearing himself from his contemplations. Here was the warlord of terrible deeds, I thought, gnashing my teeth together. A failed father, a failed husband, and an evil son himself, a treacherous dog for all the Marcomanni, nay, even the Germani. Fulcher and Ansbor came in casually, standing near me, and he glanced at them curiously, frowned at Ansbor, searching his memory for his face, which was partially hidden under a rough hood. Balderich walked in, swathed in rags and hoods, trembling in anger or sad memories of his own former hall, and scuttled to the side, his face hidden.

'Greetings,' I said loudly, and with little respect. People turned to look at me, many of the eldest Marcomanni lords wondering what was to happen next.

Maroboodus leaned back, truly resembling the Bear, as the prophecy named him. He waved his hand. 'It is warm here, my friends. Why not remove your extra clothing? Let us gaze at your faces. Perhaps we know them?' I ignored his request, and whispers began all around us. Guthbert roused himself, his mouth slightly open as he was trying to gaze at the sword strapped on Ansbor's back, Leuthard's blade. Then I witnessed Gunhild in a cape leading a stooped figure with blonde locks falling out of her covered hood, inching out of the side rooms, her face terrified. I cursed bitterly. She had not managed to get Ishild out of the side exits, and maybe it was not her fault. Suspicious Maroboodus most likely kept a close guard there, and I should have thought about that.

But, I had not.

Maroboodus waved for a seat after a lengthy silence, and I struggled to keep my face turned away from Gunhild, who was bravely trying to hold her end of our bargain. 'Sit down then, my ugly friend, and keep your face hidden. Tell me more of the ghost? Where did you hear about this creature, a vaettir? Or did you actually see it yourself?'

I walked to the middle of the room. 'I know nothing of ghosts, rather it seemed like a live man to me. Dead men do not seek passage across rivers. However, I might be wrong, and know little. Yet, now that I am here, my lord. Do tell me, oh mighty Maroboodus, do you truly have the head of Agrippa?' Maroboodus was a fugitive to Rome, and claimed to have slain the great, old Roman, a man who had been called the Sword of Augustus. It gave him great fame this side of the river, and made him a terrible enemy to all the Romans lurking on the other side of the Rhenus River. Yet, Antius the Negotiatore had told me, when he was sure I was to die, that it was but a ruse to invoke awe amongst our people, and the head came from a Syrian male whore.

He grinned, though a bit uncertainly, for I had changed the subject. 'I have it. Over there, in my chest of treasures. Do you wish to see it?' I nodded eagerly, and he gestured for one of his armored men to go get it. I saw Guthbert look at me now, his hard, cragged face twitching. I looked down at my feet under my hood, drawing quick breaths. This was what I had wanted. I could not turn back now.

'The head,' my father said, receiving it from his man, and then grinning at it before placing it with a bang in the middle of the table. It was nothing much more than a skull now, though skin and dark hair could be seen in patches around it. It stank, and I smiled at it.

'A fine trophy indeed, but— '

I shut up, for disaster struck.

Maroboodus turned his head casually, and saw Gunhild, and his brow furrowed. A suspicious look flickered on his face as he glanced at Ishild. 'Where are you going, my love?'

Gunhild took deep breaths and nodded outside. 'She needs air, husband. Air, for she is pregnant and very ill this evening.'

He hesitated, half getting up to inspect the woman, but then frowned. His animal-like instincts told him something was wrong. 'No.'

'Husband, I—'

'Will take her back to her room. You shall care for her, yes, but it is freezing outside, and I hear there are ghosts walking the land. No place for delicate flowers such as you two. You do not wish to stride the snow banks full of dead men, eh?'

Men chortled at him, but the mood was somehow dangerous. I sweated and shook, cursing the bastard. When Gunhild did not move, he indicated to Guthbert, who got up stiffly, and went to stand next to the women. Gunhild looked at me. They would not get out before the matter was solved. It meant great trouble, and I wished I could send word to Burlein, but it was too late. My mind whirled while seeking a solution. My father turned back towards me as Guthbert was whispering to Gunhild, who was still arguing, bravely. Balderich was sitting near the door, his hands clutched as he witnessed his daughter holding Ishild's hand, accosted by the terrible warrior, unable to do anything about it.

'What say you about the skull then? Why did you wish to see it?'

'It is a magnificent trophy, lord!' I told him with some sarcasm, as I tore my eyes from the women. 'What say you men?'

Men cheered happily, as I pulled up my sack. 'Yet, I hear this head belonged to a Syrian male prostitute. I heard it from a Roman, who knows

Maroboodus very well. He is a Roman who says Maroboodus works for him, and his mission, my Marcomanni lords, is to work the will of Rome, and thus ruin the Germani tribes.'

The silence was such, it nearly thrummed in our ears.

Those words were malicious, unproven, but like my fame had been torn from me, I knew there would always be tarnish over his. Men were always willing to believe in gossip. Men would doubt him, men enjoyed such doubts when high lords were concerned. I felt giddy happiness, as I saw the bastard squirm and steal glances at the shocked men around him. The fire pit crackled with burning wood, but even the mutts were silent, some slinking away with their fur standing up like a porcupine's, tails under and between their legs. The men and women all stared at me, a man about to become a corpse. Woden's Rage beat inside my skull, as I stared at the man I hated.

'I also have a head. Do you wish to see it? This one is a truly famous head. Not a former prostitute,' I said arrogantly.

'I think I know you,' he said with an ice-cold voice, his eyes darting around the room, taking in the leaders of the old families who were all thoughtfully staring at the skull and suspiciously at Maroboodus.

I spat and threw back my hood. 'Oh, you do. And I know you. I am the boy who killed for you. I helped you devise foul plans for the deaths of honorable men, and you, turd, manipulated us all so you would seem a hero in the eyes of our kin. You named me the Oath Breaker. I name you Father's Bane, or perhaps, Mother's Tears? You conspired with Rome so your very own family was murdered to make you look a sad hero, a valiant man who had been wronged. You are a Roman, who will betray us all to the legions. Oh, you know me. I am your son, the one you first denied, then used, and finally abandoned.'

They all stared at me.

Some mouthed my name, others cursed me, but I heard some curse Father as well. All father's warriors stared at me in utter stupefaction.

'You know this as well, perhaps?' I said, and I rolled the rotten, stinking head of Vago on the table. I turned it slowly by the hair to face him, and he furrowed his brow. Guthbert was grunting in agitation, as Gunhild was pleading with him. He half pulled his blade, a gladius of fine make.

'It is familiar, certainly,' Maroboodus said darkly, his eyes darting from the head to me.

'Let me remind you, Lord Maroboodus. It is the head of the man who killed your wife and father, another one you fooled, but one who did you a great favor.' I said venomously, but men around me surged up, and many suddenly knew the features of the head, the King of the Vangiones.

'Vago? King Vago! He lost his head then!' men shouted around us, and mighty cheers were echoing in the hall, and I grinned. Maroboodus got up unsteadily, but the noise did not abate. Mead was offered to me, despite the terrible promise of violence lingering between father and son, but I drank it down and threw away the horn. And Fulcher had said I could never get my fame back? Bah! I gazed at the elders, some of whom were now celebrating me, having forgotten the blood about to flow in the hall, as the great king's head was on the table. Many saluted me, but even they had a glint in their eye, reflecting hidden thoughts, and guarded approval. They did not trust me, I decided. But, Balderich would change that. I would get what was mine. If Father died.

After a long while, men went quiet, some still grinning. They were all on their feet now. My father lifted the head by the hair and looked at it. He spat in the eye, and placed it next to Agrippa's head. 'A man I hated, and a man who took a woman important to me. I thank you, Hraban. But, the rest of your speech is meaningless shit. You lie, my former son. A bad seed, rotten and bloody useless, you are. I doubt you killed him.'

'I bit his damned throat out, next to his own bed,' I hissed at him. 'And did you not tell everyone you would make their wish true, should they bring you this head?'

'What is it that you want for the head?' he asked sarcastically, his muscles rippling as he was readying for the inevitable.

I shrugged. 'I have something in mind, Lord Father of Lies. Perhaps something to be discussed in a Thing? Surly there is one tonight? It is not the custom to hold one at the end of the month? Or have you already turned into a king? As you always planned.'

He huffed, and looked around carefully, aware that men looked at him with hostility. His men glowered at the villagers. 'More lies, Hraban. There is no Thing. I am the war king, boy. The Thiuda. Things are places of discontent, and it is better that one man decides when war is afoot.'

'But, when war is no more, a Thing is to be held?' I sneered. 'One where one can settle scores, blood feuds declared? No? For I want to challenge you, Father, under the eyes of the gods. Woden—'

He slammed his fist on to the table with enough force to break a part of it. 'To Hel with the Thing! We need no simpering old men to decide on blood feuds, and we settle it now,' he shouted so hard the rafters shook. Some few of the elders, high men, got up, gnashing their teeth at him, and left the hall in a hurry. They were the leaders of the tribes, old men of much honor, and Maroboodus had been slowly choking the lot, especially the unyielding ones. Maroboodus glared at their backs with a vengeance, and then at me. 'You bring discontent to us, my boy. You sow evil, sad seeds to a merry field. What is it you want for the head?' he asked. 'And I don't care about the Thing.'

I nodded at my grandfather. 'I will let the ghost ask for it.'

Balderich stepped up, standing in the doorway. He pulled down the blanket, and all could see his haggard, tortured face, his lank hair drooping, and his one vacant eye and the rheumy one. The rest of the elders got up, their mouths open, their beards shaking with fear. 'Nay. I am no ghost. But, I was his prisoner, friends. For Vago's head, we want yours, Maroboodus, you winded bag of lies, and we shall piss in your skull. And Hraban does not lie when he says you had your wife and father killed, and he speaks the truth when he tells us you serve Rome. You traitorous scum, my torturer.'

People looked at him, astonished beyond words, save for Gunhild, who tried to run to him, her eyes running with bright tears, but could not, for Guthbert grabbed her. Many invoked the names of the gods in wonder, and there was not one man who did not look at Father, who, for once, had a brief moment of weakness. His face went blank and his mouth hung open. All his plans, his delicate schemes, his small games, and deceitful steps. Laid open like a gaping wound.

Balderich laughed hollowly. 'I am no ghost, no, honored men of my village, the best blood of the Marcomanni. I am your high lord. A fool lord, to be sure, a coward for not challenging him when he rode to this village, but I had a weakness. I wanted to retire, I did, and this slithering snake betrayed Lord Bero, who was nothing short of a great man. We shall honor him, we shall. So says a wronged lord, who was imprisoned by this Maroboodus, the liar,' said the old man with a quivering voice.

'So, Father, shall we get it over with, then? Your head, my worthless oath lord, I would have it for Vago's,' I spat as I pulled Nightbright out, my eyes seeking Gunhild who was being pushed by Guthbert to the side door. Ishild's eyes were strange, uncaring, but she followed Gunhild nonetheless. Her belly was round, and so I had a good reason to fight and win. I grabbed my helmet and pulled it on. Hate spilled out of the helmet's eyeholes, brimming over as I remembered the false tears of my father over the bodies of the ones I had loved. I got up to my full height, rivaling my father, and my knees shook, I thought at least, for if I died quickly, everything would be wasted. I would die a joke. I shook such gloomy thoughts far and grimaced. Fulcher stepped forward, and gave me my sunburst shield.

A violent energy was rippling in the air, something dangerous, coiling like a snake, building like a terrible storm, a primal creature you could almost touch. Soon, it would burst out into acts of murder, hacking and stabbing until flesh was dead. Balderich spat. 'Get out, my old Marcomanni, and leave the guilty to their judgment,' he said callously, meaning Father, his men, and his few truly loyal supporters in the village, his oaths men, and perhaps, me. Only the soft drawing of the weapons in the meeting hall broke the silence.

Fire crackled as the remaining lords of the finest families of Hard Hill, indeed, of the Marcomanni, took steps for the door. Men, who had cheered for my father, fought for him under his banner and believed in him, would do so no more, unless forced to. One-by-one, they disappeared out of the hall, pulling on coats and furs, mumbling in wonder, many touching Balderich's arm as they passed him. My father's face shook and looked like a man a vaettir possessed, his moods changing from rage to denial, his riders now a glittering wall of men, ready to kill as he gazed at the departing men he had duped. A dozen of his sturdiest followers stayed on his side of the hall, supporting their lord. More were in the side rooms.

'Nihta?' he gestured at the door, with a guttural voice.

I shook my head with a leer, for I was not feeling sorrow that moment. 'He is not likely to make it back here. Neither will your armored oaths men.'

As if to prove me honest, one could hear distant screams, for a battle had been joined. Then, outside the hall, horses neighed. The two guards ran in, snow billowing after them, barely dodged me, and went to my father. 'There are riders coming! The harbor is on fire! Men are fighting all across the town below. They slew some of the men who left here!' I glanced outside quickly. Burlein was supposed to spare the men leaving this hall voluntarily. Was he reneging on the deal, or just a fool?

My father pulled the guards aside. 'Who did you sell us to, Hraban? Vangiones? Matticati? Hermanduri, perhaps?' He pulled out the Head Taker, Grandfather's legendary sword, and the long blade glittered in the firelight, his eyes regarding it and then me. He grasped Balderich's ancient shield, the shield Aristovistus had once carried in his war against Caesar.

I shook my head. 'No, someone closer to home. Burlein has come to get vengeance for his people. Not to revenge himself against Hard Hill, but you, though both will suffer this night! We killed his family together, Father, but you fed his men as baits to Hengsti the Matticati!'

Maroboodus sneered at me. 'And worthy baits they were, for I fished a fat victory with their guts. They were worthless. It was just they died."

'Come now, you worthless father,' I laughed at him, and spat at his feet, over the table that separated us.

'Yes, we shall come,' he said, then kicked the heavy table into a heap of tinder, and they charged.

141

Balderich dodged out of the door, and Ansbor and Fulcher closed up on my back, a brown and red hair flanking my dark one, as we backed up towards the door. Men got in each other's way as we retreated, especially the men who had not been with Maroboodus in Rome, untrained and wild. Ansbor grunted as he threw a javelin, piercing a man's thigh. I carved a piece out of a man's face with a flick of my wrist, and Fulcher slammed his shield on a thin Marcomanni, who was struggling with too much mead in him. Father was pushing and pulling in the sudden press, to gain a foothold in front of the men, his fiery hair a halo of hate. We backed up, pushing at the enemy, getting minor scratches as our shields kept them at bay.

Outside, Burlein's best men stood in a spear-filled crescent on red, slushy snow, where lay many of the noblest Marcomanni who had left the hall. There were fierce fires all around the Hill, and Balderich was there, looking aghast at the carnage, talking to Burlein in agitation, but the young blond man had no interest in words.

I nearly fell as desperate men tried to pull me down, but managed to escape, and fell aside and out of the doorway.

Burlein pushed past Balderich, screaming a thin order, and a dozen of his demonically grinning men released their javelins at the fools trying to push out. Many of them died on the doorsteps, others screamed painfully inside. Some fools still tried to get out, another volley of projectiles impaled one in the mouth, and he shuddered in a pool of blood, dying in the snow.

I climbed up and ran to Burlein. 'Gunhild did not get them out! And why in Hel's name did you kill the men here?'

He snarled. 'To me, they are the enemy, just like he is. It is time to bleed this nation so it is more accommodating and easier to rule. And where did Balderich come from? That was not part of the plan! Only after your father is dead, were we to … wait. Didn't get them out?' Burlein said quickly, at a loss. 'That means we have to go in, after all.'

'Yes! Call off the men who were supposed to burn the hall; stop them! Post a guard at the side doors, but stop the burning! Call more men here, and we rush in and butcher them.'

He looked haunted, eyeing the burning town. There were sounds of fighting all over the Hill, hoarse screams mixing with alarmed cries. 'I do not think we have more than the fifty here. Nihta's men are facing a hundred, and we have another hundred riding outside the village, keeping reinforcements out, but it is impossible to pull the men here. Some will trickle in, but they are fighting. No, this is all we have.'

'You had five hundred! Are they looting the town wildly? Send a man to fetch those who killed Nihta!' I screamed at him.

'Nihta is still fighting!' he shouted back. 'Listen!'

I did, eyeing the harbor, where a mass of men was struggling. The best-armored Marcomanni had been surprised there by overwhelming odds, but would it be enough to push Nihta to Woden's arms? I knew not. 'Stop the fires, at least. They must not burn the hall!' A great number of other halls were to burn, nonetheless. A terrible number of fires were spreading across the Hill while the snow billowed in the air. Inside the Red Hall, Father gave terse orders amidst curses, and a huge table was moved to block the door, pushing out two wounded enemies into a sad heap before our eyes. I cursed and shook my head. 'We have to finish here. I'll go and stop the men from torching the place.'

He grabbed my arm. 'But, how will we conquer here, Hraban? He has to die.' I opened my mouth to curse him, but realized he was actually thinking about letting the enemy burn, and Gunhild and Ishild with him, rather than face Maroboodus with a sword in his hand. I shook my head tiredly.

'He has but some thirty men,' I told him as I gritted my teeth, trying to mold him into a confident leader with words alone. 'Nihta is likely dead. He will not be here. I saw Leuthard die at my feet. They are doomed.' At that point, some arrows shot out of the hall, hitting a horse that fell heavily on its side, its eyes large in pain and terror.

He was swallowing, holding his spear like he was a dead man already. 'Many inside. Some will be wearing Roman armor. We have to roast them. We—'

'Let go of me,' I told him, and he did. 'We have to get the women out, and keep the men in. We will need a miracle to do all that, but let me go and try.' I despaired as other fires were spreading downhill. Balderich was standing on the side, his face deathly pale as he regarded Burlein.

Burlein shook himself free of his terror. 'Go then, quickly, for they were supposed to block the doors and torch the rooms.' He turned to the blocked door. 'Come out, Maroboodus! Come, come alone and make a brave memory of your ending, one that is more befitting an honorable man than the memories of your past deeds! We have a score to settle with you!' Burlein shouted, but apparently, Maroboodus was not interested in such an arrangement, as a spear hit Burlein's shield.

'Let him rot inside,' Ansbor crumbled. 'Let us go!'

'Go, and stop them on the other side; we go this way!' I yelled at him, and pulled Fulcher after me. Ansbor hesitated, made some sort of an oath, and rushed off towards the cattle shed end of the hall.

I rushed, aiming to the left, to the side of the living quarters. Gunhild had been herded that way anyway, and so we ran in the slippery snow, begging fierce Woden and gentle Frigg to spare them. If they had torched the hall, then it would be desperate indeed. We heard warning shouts around us; riders were seen in the dark; confused scuffles were taking place. In the harbor, men were dying; it was evident by the high-pitched yells and screams. Women were sobbing or making oaths, children were horrified, dogs barked. It was utter chaos, a scene from some mad god's feast.

A hall was burning fiercely near us, one that once belonged to Fulch the Red, Ermendrud's dead father. Inside it, cattle cried with their pitiful squealing voices. Down in the harbor, a huge conflagration was suddenly spreading, and I wondered what in Donor's name was happening there. I rounded the corner, and noticed how a dozen of Burlein's men were throwing torches on the roof.

'Stop with the torches, the women are still inside,' I shouted to the men, but they ignored me, grinning like evil spirits as the flaring missiles arched over the roof. I stopped and grabbed a torch from a skinny man of Burlein's and eyed the doorway. It had been blocked well. A man of Maroboodus's was dead over it, having tried to get up and out.

'What are you doing, you rotting cadaver?' the man demanded, trying to grab the torch back, but I growled and punched him in the face so that he flew on his back crazily.

'The women are still inside!' I told him with a growl, as the other men were looking on in unreadable expressions. On the other side, I could hear Ansbor yell impotently.

The man nearest to me shook his head uncertainly. 'Lord, they are armored. We have to roast them inside their iron. This was the plan, no?'

'Plans change,' I spat. 'I will go in.'

'Lord! Do not! They will—' the man said, as Fulcher pulled me around.

He pointed up to the roof. The torches were sizzling in many places, but on some places, real fires had begun. 'We must hurry,' Fulcher urged. I nodded, and climbed the barricade so I could see inside. There, in a small room at the end of the house, two bearded Marcomanni with loose Suebi knots were surprised as my face appeared, but they swore quick oaths, and threw spears that missed me by a hair's breadth, spinning to the darkness.

'It is not possible, you turd humper, to get in anymore,' said the man I had struck as he got up, spitting blood and teeth fragments. I glanced back inside, and noticed many men milling in the corridor behind the two men. I grabbed Fulcher as some ten men rode up to the hall. One was apparently a man of Maroboodus's, nine others Burlein's. The man of Maroboodus sat there, looking terribly confused for a moment, until an arrow pierced him in the chest, and he fell from the horse.

There was now smoke coming from inside the doorway, as the thatch had begun to burn. 'Go and tell Burlein he must charge the door. Tell them they must do so on the other doors as well!' I yelled, with a hint of desperation ringing in my voice. 'They must try very hard to get inside, enough to convince Maroboodus to guard those doors well.' Gunhild was near, so close, yet I needed time.

Fulcher nodded carefully, clapped my shoulder, and ran off. The riders were about to follow him, but I stopped them. 'Wait. I have need of you.'

'You are not our lord, Oath … ' the bloody-nosed one began, but I gave him such a baleful glance he shut up and looked down. Fame. Gods, but my allies hated me as much as they hated my enemies.

I pointed my finger at the obstacle before the door. 'In a moment, I will break in from this side, and you lot will help me. We shall see what happens in there, but we are looking for two women. Two. Not one,' I growled, and grabbed a huge axe from a surprised man. 'Not a man will disobey, or I shall show you what I did to Vago.' They growled assent, some with wonder in their eyes, others suspiciously, most hefting their spears and shields, some cudgels and wicked axes. Germani are hard people to rule, unless you lead them shield first, spear bloodied.

I would do exactly that.

At the main door, men were yelling. 'We must charge them!' I heard Burlein scream manically, like a haunted, fearful man. I heard them charge, their yells mixing with the crackle of the burning thatch. He led them to the doorway, his former intrepidity forgotten, the men grunting and trying to push the great barricade down, hacking, ripping into wood and corpses.

Spears flew out; no doubt, vile curses and pained howls could be heard, as Burlein's men tried to bowl over the table. Maroboodus's men would not let it budge, but they would thrust spears at the faces of the attacking men, and death would take some. Then, on the far door, the same sounds could be heard.

I listened to Maroboodus bellow commands, slap of footsteps as men ran that way to help with the defense. I glanced again at the room, and I saw only one man there, fingering his sturdy spear unceremoniously, nervous to the bone marrow, as his friend was running for the main hall. Other men in the corridor were going that way as well. Angry men roared, as words of encouragement were ringing out on the hill. I noticed someone threw in torches from the main door, though men were quick to stomp them out or throw them to the fire pit.

Out front, Burlein's men tried to break in again, and a huge crash could be heard. I saw how a man of Maroboodus flew back on his side, his face opened by an axe, his mouth opening and closing in agony at the end of the corridor. I indicated to a wide man with a bow, and he slunk forward, his furred hood bouncing. I made a throat-cutting motion, pointed a finger to the barricade, and the man climbed next to me. Carefully, he eyed the man inside, who was now in the doorway to the corridor, gazing at the struggle in the main hall.

'Kill him,' I whispered, and the man nodded, took a bead of the enemy, and expertly let loose an arrow that tore its way through the man's back. He fell forward, shuddering in agony. He tried to claw his way forward, but apparently, the arrow had pierced him, and the tip was now wedged in the floor.

'Tear it down!' I told the men.

Together, with a strength born of desperation, we began to unravel what we had piled to keep the enemy in, and what they had built to keep us out. Loud cracks were heard as we ripped at a half-mangled door. We grunted and tore at an upturned bed, a trunk made of a whole, shit-thick log, some eight of us throwing bits of woods to the snow and mud. Then, I kicked at the bed frame, the remains of the door, which was very sturdy. I managed to rend some of the last planks aside, pushing and smiting at the obstacles mightily, cursing crudely, and some of Burlein's men came to help me.

I stepped inside, and came face-to-face with Guthbert and some of the Marcomanni, few in Roman armor, all bewildered.

They had not been fools to entirely ignore this door, yet, they were late to make sure the door was safe, for the obstacles were down. It was Guthbert, the meaty, strong Batavi, who had not always agreed with Maroboodus, and so I hesitated. Guthbert opened his mouth and cursed foully. 'Leuthard's sword and that mail,' he pointed at the iron glinting under my tunic.

I ripped it down to show it better, and he nodded as he saw the serpent's head. 'He is rotting in Hel. He sent his regards.'

One of Guthbert's men grew impatient and charged for me, while I was standing amidst a splintered door. He punched his spear forward, a fast man, but I dodged inside the room, and smote him on his back with the axe. He flew outside to the snow, and my men poured inside. We stared at each other, Guthbert and I, while our men charged forward, coming to stand behind me, filling the room. Some of Guthbert's men formed a small shield wall across the door, awaiting their leader incredulously. 'Guthbert. The women?' I growled at him. He spat, and pulled a bronze helmet on his head, wearily gazing at me and the men around me.

He nodded at me, his voice a bit strained, as if the tumultuous events around him were of little concern. 'Hraban. The toothless puppy that followed my master, has grown fangs, it seems. The women are alive. I do not know if you would enjoy Ishild's company. She wants her brother.' He growled like a bear would, and his grip on his sword was like iron. It was a gladius, and he had no shield. 'Did Leuthard die easily?'

I shook my head as I walked forward. 'No, he was mighty. I had him fight a wolverine. I suppose it was a tie, but he is gone, nonetheless. I promised his ashes would go with yours to your father. I am willing to renege on that, if you but run out of here and let me have the women. And why would Ishild want her brother? No creature enjoys Odo's presence!' I grimaced at him as thick smoke billowed out of the next room, and women coughed. 'Give them to me.'

He glanced behind him to the corridors and the rooms, concerned, but turned back towards me. 'No, Hraban, I will not betray my lord, never like this, despite his many flaws. The only way you will get them is if I will die in front of you, boy. Not an easy feat.'

I cursed him, the men around me tensed, and I nodded, my heart heavy, but not heavy enough for Woden to ignore the fight. I felt savagery conquer my soul. 'Let us find out then.'

He nodded. 'Wyrd.' His voice was steady. His bronze helm glittered as he settled into a fighting man's position, his legs wide and balanced, his sword low. His men stepped forward to cover him, grim Marcomanni of many battles, some armored and all ready. The warriors stood rooted to their place, men were begging to all-father Woden and old Tiw, smiter Donor and fierce Freya for favor. At the front door, Burlein's men tried to get in, still. A man shrieked for a long, long time, and that was our cue.

We charged.

There were nine men with me, and I thrust my sunburst shield at Guthbert savagely in the press, Burlein's men guarding my flanks. A mighty pushing-and-pulling match ensued, and we sweated, spat, and cursed foully over the shields. Guthbert stepped suddenly forward, punching out with his fist at my helmet, and my ears rang. He had been fast, so fast. His gladius flickered for a gut-opening strike, but I was fast as well that evening, and my shield rim pushed it down. He stumbled forward to my shield, I struck his neck and helmet with the pommel of Nightbright, and he grunted in pain. Near me, two of my men were skewered, panting their lives away on the floor, one dragging himself for the door. The archer in his furred cap was aiming a dark-feathered arrow at Guthbert, but a large man in iron ring armor was covering the Batavi as he danced back from me, hurting.

I threw my weight at that man guarding Guthbert, charged under his shoulder and punctured Nightbright up, so hard it went in through his armpit and came out from his neck, and we fell in a tangle. At that time, Guthbert spat in anger, about to stab at my back, but then howled in pain, and I saw an arrow pierce his armor. The large man fell on his back, and the Marcomanni fled around him. I got up, shrieking in anger, and pulled at the blade, which was stuck only for a moment. I ignored everything else, saw Guthbert was still on his back, charged to the corridor after the fleeing men, and saw Maroboodus turn to regard them, his face hard and sweaty as Burlein was making another costly brunt at the door.

I looked at the room that had once been mine.

Ishild and Gunhild were there, cowering on the bed, coughing. Their eyes enlarged as they regarded me. 'Hraban,' Gunhild said softly. 'Is—'

'I am fine, thank you. Guthbert is not, for which I am sorry. Come!' I told them, and pulled at them, Ishild's large blue eyes regarding me carefully. 'Ishild, I am not sure … ' I stammered.

She took a long breath, a shuddering one. 'Odo?'

I spat in anger. 'I do not know where the maggot is, Ishild. I know about the prophecy. He wants to whelp a child on you. Why worry about him?'

'You do not understand,' she told me. 'Mother?'

149

'Is safe,' I grunted as I glanced toward the end of the corridor. There, Maroboodus was pulling and pushing at men, pointing his sword one way, then the other. I pushed the women for the door. 'Quickly! Outside.'

I hesitated at the room where the battle had taken place. Men were there, the archer regarding Guthbert, who was on his back, his sword pointed at the men. The archer was aiming a bow at the champion. I slapped the arrow away, and pushed Gunhild and Ishild their way. I pointed at the women. 'That woman is Burlein's future wife.' Gunhild's eyes enlarged as he looked at me, and I had to remind myself she had once helped father poison me. Wyrd. I continued, waving her protests away, 'This other one is a völva's daughter. Guard them with your lives, and get them both to Burlein.'

The archer nodded dutifully, his full beard bobbling as I kicked at a broken table and then walked in front of Guthbert, angry. I had liked him, even if he was my father's man. His eyes were feverish as he regarded me, the sword still out. I ignored it, as I bent before him. Some of Burlein's men covered my back, stealing glances across to the hall, where Maroboodus was now screaming orders. We did not have much time.

'Go out and prepare to block the door again,' I told them. They did, and I faced the man again, who pulled his helmet off and sighed.

'Thank you,' he said. 'Was getting tired of showing a brave face there. Gods, archers are cowards. But, a good move that. Surprised me.'

'You were not fighting fully, my lord,' I told him. 'Halfhearted defenses. Normally, you would have slaughtered the lot with one hand, and no help.'

Guthbert smiled at me. 'True, Hraban,' he snorted. 'I am tired. It has been heavy serving your father. And I have been sick. Strangely weak for months. Losing weight. God Juppiter laughs, but your father is in a pickle.'

'He is a Roman,' I told him neutrally. 'Truly Roman. Not Germani.'

He smiled. 'Yes, he is that. So is our original band. He serves the many, many interests of some high noble, someone who intends to kill those who would upkeep the Republic. That's not old Augustus, though,' Guthbert said. 'Never saw the noble. Only the fat go-between. Antius.'

'I know Antius,' I told him sadly, as he was going to die.

He grabbed me. 'He will combine the mighty tribes, and fight Rome with Roman tactics. He will kill those suspected republicans, and be rewarded, as he lets the Germani die to Roman swords. I admire your father, Hraban, in many ways, but I also admire my father, and he would not approve of the many games we are playing. Filthy games. Now, I shall leave this place, and I hope he forgives me when he has my ashes.'

'Is it that bad?' I said carefully, as I tried to see to his wound.

He shook his head, humored. 'You are as brave a boy as your father is a man. You both know how to fight, but he has more experience. Do not face him, Hraban, for I do not want your company in the afterlife yet. I should fight you still, with my last breath, but you see … ' he parted a piece of a torn tunic. The arrow was embedded in his belly, having pulled some of the chain mail with it. 'It is too painful, yes. You will give us a proper burial, and send us to Father. I have a wife in Rome, and a daughter with her. Try to send them word, if you can. I miss them. Now, I suppose my mad brother Leuthard is waiting for me just beyond the shadows.' He groaned and let go of his sword, his heels thrumming the ground briefly in terrible pain. I did not know what to tell him as he fell on his side, groaning in agony, his sword tumbling across the floor.

'Tell Leuthard,' I told him, 'that I hate him.'

He was suddenly calm, his breath rasping, his arms groping for creatures I did not see. His voice was as calm as gentle rain. 'Mother? Father. But, I see no Leuthard. The beast is not there.'

His words made my skin crawl with skittering fear. I got up, and said my farewells to the mighty man, as he fell limp. I eyed the corridor briefly, gazed at ten Marcomanni coming forward cautiously, anticipating a trap, led by two of Maroboodus's riders, and I spat their way.

I stepped out, and Burlein's men blocked the doorway. I leaned on the wall and wept for Guthbert, for he had been a friend. I waved at the men of Burlein. 'Burn it,' I said heavily. They started to lob torches inside and to the roof again, and they would hold the door, the archer firing gleefully inside. A man screamed crazily.

'The women,' I asked him.

'As you commanded,' he told me, and kept at his fun, the slayer of Guthbert. A bow, my lord, was a terrible weapon where there was no shield wall to protect you. I ran around the huge hall for the pandemonium of the front doors. There were some fifty men of Burlein's there still, though some were skirmishing at the corners of the nearby halls with confused Marcomanni bravely trying to defend the town.

I nodded at Burlein, who threw his hand around in frustration.

'They throw the torches back out, and we cannot get in,' he cursed. 'I lost six men, and many wounded. But, you succeeded. I thank you. The women are in that hall, safe, for now.' He pointed at a sturdy hall, and I nodded, happy for the fact. Fulcher ran to me.

He pointed at Ansbor's end of the hall. 'That side is burning now. It will be terrible for them, soon.'

'Send more men around to the walled side,' I told Burlein, and he nodded, turning to look for the men he could spare. I gazed around, understanding my father was trapped. The Bear's coat would be signed soon, unless he charged out. Then, he would fall into mud and snow, and I would be at peace. I grabbed and turned Burlein, who had sent some men around to the other side of the hall, where there were no doors or windows. 'Charge the front doors again, and have your men lob in dozens from the sides. Keep at it and more to the roof, the torches. It is costly, but keep them defending at the front door. Find hay, and throw that in as well. Bleed and die, Burlein, my lord, your men will, but do not let them fight the fires. Have some more archers keep their men down in the side rooms.'

So, it was that Burlein led his men to the door again. They battered at the barricade, Maroboodus's men defended ferociously, men bled profusely and died sad deaths, but on the sides, the fires started to spread resolutely. Suddenly, thick smoke filled the hall, pouring out of the sides, and the front door and dozens of strained coughs could be heard. Burlein grinned at me, and I pulled my sword and grabbed my shield. The blond man snorted, and waved his sword at his men. 'Get ready. Some, at least, will try to get out. Make sure they do not. Perhaps they want to die in fire.

We will see. Thus ends the story of the Red Hall. But, you can always build new ones.'

Balderich appeared and grimaced, nodding. His face aged further, as he regarded the pouring smoke. 'It was always Aristovistus's seat,' he said glumly, and gestured at the door. 'His mighty weapons will be gone. His ancient standard, dust. Our family's artifacts, smoke in the air. Yet, perhaps it is fitting these mighty tokens will burn with the man trying to usurp his glory,' Balderich said, tiredly. I nodded. I did not care for the artifacts, save for the Head Taker. Hulderic had promised it to me, I still believed, though he had not been that specific. That night, I would lose the artifact, but would gain the death of my father.

'You still have Gunhild,' Burlein told him carefully, not sure where he stood with the Lord of the Marcomanni, even if it was evident Burlein would be the power behind him now. Yet, Burlein was not a strong man, and he eyed the great one with suspicion. Suspicious lords are dangerous.

Balderich flashed a rotten smile his way, though there was a careful glint in the old, wise man's eye, one that remembered the dead Marcomanni nobles at the door not moments before, victims of Burlein. Would he have died in the tower later, had Burlein come to rescue him? 'We will speak about Gunhild, but I think you have well-deserved her hand, Burlein.'

'I ... ' the blond man started, blushing. 'Let us see the bastard dead first.'

'A death deserved. I hope Hulderic and Sigilind are watching here with us,' I said, as I spat at the hall. 'And poor Bero.'

It seemed impossible for my father to survive the conflagration. Some commands could be heard, a man shrieking in horrible agony. 'Wait! They will come soon!' I yelled, and the men tensed, forming a hard shield wall. I bullied my way to the first rank, growling at men to cover me. Fulcher was there on my right, his shield banging into mine as we braced ourselves.

Then, desperate hands started to rip the splintered bench and tables out of the doorway.

Men rushed out.

Their beards were burnt, heavy tunics smoking, and they coughed. All had shed their armor. Man after man came, and Burlein's men butchered them on the muddy and snowy front yard. Some cried for mercy, others tried to give a fight, but they had no chance. One man, a rider of Maroboodus, charged out with an axe, and chopped down a surprised man in the shield wall, but Burlein speared him in the throat, and his mail-clad, smoking body fell to the mud, next to the bodies, twitching.

Then, they stopped coming.

'How many got out?' I asked bitterly.

'Ten? Another ten inside, at least?' Fulcher said.

'On the sides?' I yelled.

'Nothing happens there,' Burlein yelled, his men running back and forth. 'He is not going to give us the satisfaction,' he grumbled, flushed with the glory of the great victory. He likely thought about his family and the dead ones in the silent cemetery, and of their glory restored.

Yet, I felt something was wrong.

'Grandfather, is there any other way out of there?' I asked, and he just looked at me and shrugged tiredly.

'Not unless they made one,' he said with little emotion, and then we heard a wooden crash. We had not heard the axe strokes in the midst of the brief battles of the men rushing out of the front door, but his remaining men, most his former riders, had indeed used massive weapons to hack a hole on the back wall, and then the wall had fallen. It was a hard feat to achieve, but perhaps Maroboodus had deliberately weakened the wall for just such an eventuality. They would be going downhill now, escaping.

I cursed, and ran for my horse, abandoning the shield wall rippling with confusion. I grabbed Minas. 'They are getting away from behind! They made a hole in the wall! Leave some men here, follow!'

Burlein cursed in fear, and his men grabbed what horses they could find. Fulcher screamed at me to wait, but I mounted and whipped the horse hard. 'Haiyaah!' I pounded past the corner, past Ansbor's stupefied face, rounded the last corner, and rode past flames striking through the hall's sides.

There, I saw men struggle, coughing terribly, stumbling through a collapsed part of the wall. Maroboodus stood a few feet away from the hole, his face blackened, the Head Taker in his hand, the famous spear at the ready in the other, Aristovistus' spear. The shield was apparently gone. At his feet were some of Burlein's men, who had apparently been very surprised as the wall fell down. Maroboodus was armored in his fine Roman mail, but had little else with him. Inside, a bright jingle of glass rang out as the Roman wares exploded in the heat, and another scream could be heard, horrified, as someone caught fire. Father's face held no compassion for the loss of his men, as he gestured at his finest soldiers to get out of the jumble of blackened, soot-stained timbers. A fiend of war he was, a demon escaping some infernal plane of spirits. Some of his original band of men, one of whom was dragging his standard clear of the inferno, cursed as they stumbled out. Father nodded, pulled some men together, and they started to run downhill, some six of them.

I gave a terrible oath to Woden, offering the blood of a prisoner, if he let me conquer the terrible man escaping. I spurred my horse and drew Nightbright, as I bore down on the hapless man struggling with my father's standard, left behind. Minas bore down on him, teeth bared, and as he looked up, his eyes very surprised, he saw the tip of my blade coming, and then he saw no more. He fell like a sack, his armor jingling as he rolled on to his belly. Fulcher appeared in a blink, Ansbor following, running with more men, Burlein's men, chasing and bearing down on the fleeing warlord.

'Maroboodus!' I yelled, and my horse stood on his standard. Fulcher speared a hapless, blind man struggling out of the house, and Ansbor pushed another back to the flames, where he shrieked terribly, but then went quiet, his body roasting with a horrible smell.

'Father!' I screamed, and he turned, and Burlein's men hovered near.

Maroboodus saw Minas standing on his bear standard, the red, rampant animal soot-blackened and dirty, smoking. I saw the clump of hair that had been Bero's, and I noticed he had wound the chain of Aristovistus around the top, taking glory from the old hero. His men stopped, and squared off against me.

'Are you not going to defend it? Father? Come? Your fame and glory demands it, oh hero of Rome! Are you a cowardly eagle of Rome or the fierce Bear? Show your mettle!' I laughed at him, and gestured at the man whose eyes were glittering with terrible anger. He shuddered as he appraised Burlein's many men, now moving forward. His men spat, and a few had some heavy darts, which they threw, impaling a hapless horse and an arm of the leading man.

The rest reined in their horses.

'Come, take it!' I yelled, and got down from the horse to pick it up and carried it downhill toward him, dragging Minas after me. 'I am here! Come! Make a name for yourself!' I mocked him. 'So far, all your deeds? Shitty lies, no?' Not all, of course, for he had conquered the Matticati and conquered a Roman fort, no matter if Antius had helped with that. Burlein was collecting his men into a careful group as I walked forth, readying to kill the man. Many had horses. No matter what would happen, he would ride Maroboodus down. I stopped Fulcher and Ansbor with an abrupt gesture of my hand.

'Do not! Hraban!' Burlein yelled. 'We have him!'

'Do as your new master says,' Maroboodus sneered. 'Go away. Leave the standard. We will fight another day.'

I laughed at him, mocking him furiously. 'This is a fine night to do so. You will not go anywhere. I will shit on it, have cows sleep on it. I will burn it and throw the ashes on the graves of cowards and women, and you tell Woden I did this. He will wish to know how you let that happen, Father, how you let your exiled son to torture you so. They will look at you in the halls of the dead, and snicker at your stricken face as they show you their standards, knowing you have none!' I threw the pole to dust in front of me, the chain of Aristovistus clinking.

He smiled wickedly. 'I do not believe in the gods, Hraban, and I doubt we will sit in any hall after this life, but I will take the pole back nonetheless.' He told me, his heavy face emotionless as he prepared to fight, perhaps for the last time. He glanced back. Some Marcomanni could be seen downhill, walking their horses up cautiously. His reinforcements, but not many, not enough to save him.

Burlein gritted his teeth in fear of him, and ordered a charge. 'Take him!'

'No!' I yelled, and I jumped on Minas and charged like a bee-stung ox.

Many things took place in the next moments.

Maroboodus yelled, suddenly happy, and charged for me. 'Come then! Meet your grandfather's blade! You always coveted it!'

I grinned and kept going. I went fast, outpacing the others, the helmet diminishing what I could see; Nihta leading a dozen men on a mad charge, his men throwing Burlein's riders in to chaos, men falling from horses in stupefied surprise. Men were throwing more darts, and my father's few men were running for their saviors. I remember Minas shuddering as a dark dart was quivering on its neck. Strangely, it seemed to do so for a long time.

I remembered rolling, falling, hurting my face and side, and I got up, painfully climbing to my feet, my helmet gone. I remember Head Taker coming down for me, the tip glinting in the slight snowfall and fires, and the explosive pain in my face as the ancient blade tore down with a vengeance, my father's gleeful eyes bestial behind it. I remember falling, men yelling, horses whinnying, Fulcher and Ansbor grabbing me.

Then I remembered nothing.

CHAPTER IX

I came to on a strange horse, and Ansbor was leading it. He had a crude bandage on his side. Fulcher was walking next to me, his horse laden with gear, my helmet and sword strapped on it, many coats of mail as well. We were riding towards Bero's old hall downhill. I glanced behind painfully. There, behind, Balderich was riding heavily, his old spear in his hands. *Father,* I thought. *Did that mean Father was dead as well?*

As well. No, I lived, I thought. Or, were we all dead, marching for Valholl?

Burlein was waiting at the hall, his men riding around, his face sweat stricken.

'Is he awake?' he asked. I groaned, and he grinned. He walked next to me. 'Well, Hraban. The Hill is ours today, but we must leave. You do not look so good. Not as pretty as you were, but more like a warrior,' he laughed. 'I can see your skull, I think, just above your eye. Your horse is dead.'

I felt the side of my face, and cried for the pain. 'Shit. Poor Minas.'

'It can be fixed, boy,' Balderich said mournfully.

'By Woden!' I groaned and felt my face, which exploded in agony. 'By Frigg, how bad is it? I cannot see with my left eye,' I blurted in panic. 'Minas is dead? Truly?'

Fulcher grunted with sarcasm. 'The great horse died, I am sorry. Now, you have a nag. A fitting prize for failure, but such is often a fame hunter's fate. You will have quite a scar, but your eye is just crusted with blood.'

I nodded and looked at Burlein mournfully. 'He escaped?'

Burlein went silent, his face briefly scared and his good humor gone like a distant whiff of a baking bread. He looked at Rhenus River, the banks covered in a slight coat of snow. 'He has lost a lot of men and prestige, but, yes, he did. He was bleeding as well. I threw a javelin at him, and his armor saved him.'

'Nihta?' I pressed on, and he shook his head, uninterested in giving further explanations. 'The standard,' I asked him nonetheless. 'He lost the spear, but—'

'Nihta saved it. He broke out of the harbor just in time to save his bastard master,' Ansbor explained sourly. 'It was a mad scramble. Nihta killed many a man this night.'

Burlein grunted. 'We will see what comes out of this. He will come after us, if he can. Best leave for Grinrock. If that Vannius returns in the morning, we are dead. He will choose a side that is strong, and your father still commands the northern Marcomanni, no matter how many heroes he lost this night, and how much we hurt him. Perhaps it will be an equal fight, in the future.'

'We have Hunfrid, and Vannius will want him dead. We have tools,' Balderich told him, planning for war, the old, starved man. I grinned at him, and felt hideous, as the wound in my face was throbbing, flesh tearing with my facial movements, blood wetting my chest and side. I spied Ishild to the side. She made no move for me, her face blank, and I swallowed in anger. It was not the reunion I had hoped for, but then, we had bad blood between us.

Burlein glanced at her. 'Give it time, Hraban.'

I nodded and got down, swooning on my feet. 'Grandfather?' He looked at me, confused. 'Come to the shore with us. Burlein?' I asked, and the blond man nodded carefully.

'It is there, on the shore,' he said heavily. He pointed at a ship with rowers on board.

Balderich stammered. 'What do you mean?'

I turned to Grandfather painfully. 'Where is Bero's treasure?' I asked with a wince, and Balderich smiled knowingly.

'In a cellar under some gray mead barrels. Over there in the woods,' he said, and pointed to the general direction of the place. 'I think I own some of that,' Balderich said, a bit worried as Burlein snapped his fingers, and Ansbor rode with men to search the cellar.

'You will get half. Enough to buy you your retirement,' I told him, and curbed Burlein's protest before he could voice it.

He blinked his eyes. 'You wish me to go?'

'You are old and tired, like an overused spear. I know you will not live a long time, and so, you should get away from this all. I think the slave girls will be safe from you as well, surely,' I grinned, and had to grab the horse's mane as the pain overwhelmed me.

'Boy?' Balderich asked, and I waved him down.

'You should go to Moganticum, then find a ship rowing for the south, beyond Burbetomagus, far from here. Claim to be a noble from the far north. I am sure you will manage a suitable lie,' I said, while gasping for air.

'I should stay here, and fight your father,' he reproached me sternly, but his eyes flickered for the boat, where light shone invitingly. I actually envied him.

'You will be free, rich, and happy. Just avoid Antius the Negotiatore,' I told him. 'If you run into him, he will roast you for the pleasure of the sneering peasants. Hide your face, have some other man make your deals.'

He looked down at me, and we grabbed each other's arms. 'Perhaps we will meet again.'

'In the afterlife, Grandfather,' I told him happily. 'You will meet Hulderic and Sigilind first, unless the gods have a terrible sense of humor. When you do, tell them I miss them.'

'You are a better boy than you are given credit for. Come with me?' he pleaded softly, with tears flowing on to his scraggly beard.

'Maroboodus lives, but I will think about it, should that change. In the spring. We shall see.' I smiled at him, knowing I would fight until I regained my fame.

He took a deep, shuddering breath and handed the old blue bladed hasta my way. 'This is Wolf's Tear. I never told you the name of this weapon, for I wanted to give it to you with ceremony, our ancestors watching. I reckon they are watching now.'

There were so many fires around us, it was like daytime. He grinned at his former home's plight, and squinted Burlein with some hostility. I did as well. Burlein should have spared the lords of the town. Now, he made them enemies just as much as Maroboodus had.

Balderich grumbled and turned to me. 'Try to master him. He is the sort of a man who never thought he would command armies and men, and when he does, he is like an axe, instead of a chisel. But, the spear, Hraban. It was held by Aristovistus in the battle we rarely speak about, the one where Caesar destroyed our dreams. I carried it after my father, and it has taken lives, though never a wolf's, that I know of. It is sturdy and ancient, like your ring. Take it. It is yours. From me to you. Grandfather to a grandson. I once promised it to you for helping to beat your father. Had you obeyed then, we might all be happier today, but it is wyrd, is it not?'

Spear of Aristovistus.

I grabbed it gratefully. An old weapon of much honor, it was a great gift, and one I had not truly deserved. He smiled, and we waited. In an hour, Ansbor carried a large bag full of coins to us. He stammered, for even if the Germani disdained Roman coins, we had learnt their value in Hard Hill. 'There was silver, even gold! Bronze and strange, glittering rocks. Burlein was kind enough to take those, and let us have the silver,' he said, and Balderich laughed.

'Thank you, my boy, thank you. A word of advice: next time, take the rocks!' We laughed at Ansbor's shamed discomfort.

'Well, I am set. Burlein?' Balderich said, pointing a finger at the blond man, who was grinning like a thief as he emerged from the darkness. Which he, of course, was. 'Take good care of Gunhild, for she is dear to me. She loved Koun, but will learn to love a good man. Be one,' he said, with some doubt, and clapped the sack. 'A fitting gift for a father of the lady, even without the pretty rocks. I thank you for all you have done as well.'

Burlein scratched his sweaty head with a sheepish look on his wide face, and threw the old man a small pouch, no doubt holding some of the precious jewels. 'Indeed, lord. Fare you well.'

'I fare as well as I can,' the old man said as he rode down. We watched him stop next to Gunhild, and they wept and cried, speaking at length. Finally, the old man pushed his daughter away, kissed her, rode on silently, and finally mounted the boat, which slowly, silently started to row upriver on the slight snowfall. It was going towards Moganticum, and the old man was sitting on the prow, starting at the embers of the Red Hall.

'I hope they receive him well,' Fulcher grumbled.

'He is rich. They will. Or they will rob him. Wyrd. But, this is what Burlein insisted when we agreed on this work.'

Ansbor leaned forward, shivering as he stared at my ripped face. 'He wanted Balderich out?'

I nodded. I felt feverish as I gazed at the old man and then Burlein. 'He is out to change the Marcomanni, like Father was. Is. He wishes to have fewer men with Aristovistus's noble blood riding with the tribes, and none who have ruled before. Gunhild will give him the right to rule, even if she is already married, but he brooks no rivalry from Balderich. He can be harsh, I found out, when we spoke of the future. So, of course, we agreed it would be so.'

'We need him,' Ansbor said mournfully.

'Yes,' I agreed. 'Yet, Burlein will not stand second to anyone. Balderich understands this, but Gunhild? I doubt it. She has been a pawn of sinister powers for so long; she would deserve some true happiness. I will miss him, Balderich, Grandfather. Gods know we would have needed his authority over all the Marcomanni, but for now, this nation is divided, and in war. But, Burlein would have none of that. You saw what he did to the old families. He is an axe indeed. So we war until Father dies. Finally. And, I think it is a good thing Grandfather is not here, for I trust neither Father nor Burlein.'

'Did you regain your fame?' Fulcher smirked.

I spat, terrible agony ripping through my face. 'Did I?'

'You regained some honor,' he said ruefully.

'By burning the hall?'

'By saving the woman,' he corrected.

'They were part of the reason I was here. And Grandfather,' I said. 'They will make fine stories of my deeds. Men shall follow such deeds.'

He shook his head. 'I mean Tear. Sparing her. That was honorable.'

With that, we rode south.

PART III: SPRING TIDES

'The manes, spirits of the hall, are watching us, no doubt, and I say we forgive him. Let any man mocking the Oath Breaker leave with a bleeding face!'
Burlein of Hraban to the gathered Marcomanni revelers

CHAPTER X

I suffered during the trip to Grinrock. Much of the time, I was too pained to care for the news and the riders that rode around Burlein's column. I cared little for the words of rebellion against Maroboodus, and little for the bloody skirmishes Nihta apparently led to put down the breaking away of some of the northern clans. I did catch the news that Vannius had led his Quadi back home, north of the Moenus River, towards the Quadi ancestral home. They blithely concentrated on their own civil war against dogged Tallo, keeping an eye on the north lest Tudrus the Older should try to reclaim his lands during the Marcomannic turmoil.

Burlein and Maroboodus. They would be like a pair of fighting pit animals, left to settle the thing for good.

Maroboodus had suffered a terrible blow. His hall was a burned down husk. The trade it had enjoyed, and the influx of great warriors disrupted. His fame was tarnished like a blade that had been pissed on. The secrets he had kept were out in the open, though unproven. I had shed doubt on his motives, his true allegiances, even if he lived. I survived doing that to him. Few did with Maroboodus. I was not only the Oath Breaker. I was also Vago's Bane. I was the Hall Burner. Many thought of him as a liar at least, and that was thanks to Balderich's speech. These thoughts kept me warm.

Burlein was in a position of strength. He would have to be decisive, and harry Maroboodus mercilessly, whip up confrontation after confrontation against the great man, brew discontent, not unlike Bark had done before for Isfried. I was young, but even I knew this. It ran in my blood. War.

I developed a fever, went unconscious, and awoke to full consciousness. I was lying on a bed. Stubborn, merciless fingers were probing the wound in my face, and then a finger ran the length of it, from my forehead, splitting my eyebrow, over my lips to my chin. I roused myself, feeling angry at the intrusion. I grabbed the finger, expecting Cassia to be administering to the wound. She had during my feverish dreams, of that I was sure of. 'Your face looks like an ugly fungus, swollen and rotten,' said a rasping voice.

The finger was old and rough.

'Stay still, fool,' Tear said angrily, as she continued her probing.

My eyes popped wide, as large as bull's balls. I whimpered as bright sunlight stung my eyes wickedly from an open doorway. Despite her instructions, I struggled and pushed her away. She sat there, in a clean, gray dress, her hair combed. The hunger and suffering during the imprisonment had left her lean.

'It will mend. Cassia did a commendable job sewing it, but there will be a fat scar,' she told me frankly, and I pulled myself up, noted I was nude under the wolf pelt, and scowled at her. She was a völva, and such creatures were servants to Freya, goddess of seidr magic, ladies of seduction. I shrugged at the impossible thought, for she was as old as time. She pushed her chair back, rolling her eyes. 'Even the old think about such things.'

'How did you know what I was ... ' I began, but the pain in my face stabbed at me suddenly, and I winced.

She waved her hand. 'You are too young for me, likely would be a terrible disappointment should I care to cast the spells. Gods, but I have suffered enough for men, anyway. All my children carry the blood of Lok, as you know,' she sighed. 'All are perilous, as are you. Besides, you wetted your bed last night, Hraban, and I wiped you down. Hardly an inspiring thought, is it?' She cackled, and I lay back, cursing her vilely. The room was warm and cozy, dark in the corners, and a gentle fire was burning in the middle of the room. I had stayed earlier at Grinrock, and in the same house. There was no sign of Ishild. Or anyone else.

'She is around. She is fine, though she did cough greatly the first day. The girl inside her is very much alive,' she said guardedly.

'The girl Odo might or might not find useful. Tell me, Tear, is my child part of the prophecy?' I asked.

She looked at her gnarled hands, and shook her head. 'You tell me. We used spells to find most of the stanzas. They say you saw Shayla? She told you the full verses?' she asked gruffly, but her voice faltered. 'We learnt much from Goddess Sigyn, but not all.'

I nodded. 'I did. She is dead.'

She stiffened. 'Shayla? Dead? Why?'

'I wanted to live. Simple,' I told her, and she looked at me with disapproval. 'She killed herself,' I added. 'But, there is much more to the story. Don't judge me.'

She contemplated it, nodded, and took a ragged cloth to dab my face with. It came away bloody. 'All our enemies dead at your hands. Wulf, Bark, and Shayla, even. What do you think you learnt? That you are impregnable? Survived Vago, and your father? Don't grow cocky. Odo is out there. You remember he wished to take you to Gulldrum, where we come from, far in the north. He thinks you will do all the deeds necessary, no matter what, but he still wishes to hold all the strings in his hand. That you slept with Ishild, well, that hurt him. He did wish to cut you for that. He figured you would still serve the purpose. Cut or not, he thinks you will lead us to our lost Veleda, his youngest sister and my daughter. Is this what Shayla told you as well?'

'Whose side are you on now?' I asked bitterly.

She smiled like old women do, crookedly. 'I think Odo is now the power behind our clan. He escaped that night Maroboodus betrayed us, captured the unsuspecting Koun with him, and did not ask for my return for Koun's. Only the ring and Ishild.'

'He did ask for Ishild, then,' I whispered. 'I am happy Father denied him that, at least.'

She cackled. 'She was with Maroboodus on the war with the Matticati. Your father wished to see Koun's head before giving her over. Then, nothing. You escaped, and all saw you, but Odo never sent him any word. You apparently took the ring.' She flicked it in the air before my eyes, and I grabbed for it, failing as she was fast. 'And then, Maroboodus was just waiting to see what to do with Ishild. He did not know where the ring might be. He rued the day he had to give it to Odo to begin with. Now, you have both, and he has naught. Not even his wife. Lok laughs, no doubt!'

'Give it to me,' I demanded, and she shrugged and flipped it to me. 'Why am I unguarded anyway?'

She smiled, as I made sure it was mine. 'I am guarding you. Such power in such a small thing. Woden's Ringlet that Veleda's blood must be spilled on. On Woden's Plate, and we don't even know where that is. Then Lok is freed. Men will fall, gods as well. Your father needs it to control the Suebi, in order to fight Rome. You need it for you wish to deny it to both. Gods must be wagering a lot of wealth on who ends up with it.'

'Armin wishes it for the same reason as Father,' I grinned briefly, and then regretted it as my face hurt terribly. 'He wishes to control the eastern Suebi, the Langobardi, and the Semnones, but he does not wish my father to have any part in their plans.'

She cackled. 'Oh, he hates the idea of sweet Thusnelda marrying your father. And, I think young Armin will want to rise above his father, Sigimer, the corpulent Segestes, and the gloomy Inguiomerus, who agreed on such a deal. I see much thirst for glory in that young man. Like I see it in you. Only difference is he has an unblemished fame. He is not that different from your father. Suffers more from dishonorable acts, but is not loath to betray and cheat.' We sat in silence for a while, until she breathed hard. 'You believe in the prophecy now?' she asked.

I shook my head carefully. 'I do not. I do. I do not know. All I know is my child is safe, but I still have to kill Maroboodus and murderous Catualda. And your son, if he does not leave us be.'

She grunted. 'Child, not Ishild?'

I hesitated. 'I do not know if we like each other. Guthbert told me she is asking for Odo. Odo, who will make children with her, if he can. Is she even sane? Yet, at one point, she saw me as the man for her, the one thing to rip her far from her family, meaning you and Odo, the man to save her. I did not know if she was merely trying to manipulate me to help you with the damned prophecy, or if she truly had some feelings for me. I don't know.'

Tear grunted gruffly. 'She tried to betray us. For you.'

I shook my head at her. 'Then, she slept with me, hating Ermendrud for what we had, and testified against me, nearly dooming me. Had it not been for the old bastard … '

She laughed hugely. 'My old man Adalfuns, the damned Crafter! A fine husband he was, wise and keen, gentle even, saving me after Bero and Bark's bastards hurt me those decades ago. He gave you permission to marry Ishild, and so you were saved. I was there that day when your father was foiled, and the look on his face kept me going in my sufferings.'

'It was a bad day,' I told her with a small smile, 'but it was not all bad, I agree. Did you love him? Adalfuns?'

She nodded wistfully. 'Yes. But, I had a destiny elsewhere, this prophecy, the foul things our god demands,' she said, tiredly, putting away the cloth. 'It will take time to heal, Hraban. She testified against you, but she had no choice, boy.'

'I take your word for it. And don't worry about the face. Just a wound,' I said, though I dreaded to see how my face looked. 'As for your question, I found out the full prophecy. I remember you wanted me to go far away when we met for the first time. You did not know if Veleda's blood would be enough for Lok, or if she should die. You needed to know if you would have to see your daughter slaughtered.'

She nodded. 'I still do not know the truth.'

'I can tell you,' I told her carefully. 'The lines—'

'Perhaps you did not understand what she told you?' she said quickly, apparently dreading the answer.

'I understood it,' I said, and pointed tiredly at my gear. 'A scroll over there, as old as time.'

She got up on shaky legs. 'Does it say … ' she began to ask, then shook her head and got up to fetch my scroll. Her hands were faltering, as she rummaged in my discarded pile of gear. She stood up to her full height, with the crumbling scroll in her hand.

'Read it,' I told her tiredly. She opened it, read it, and after a long time, slumped. 'Read it aloud, Tear,' I told her. 'Let me hear the wonderful words of your god, Lok, as he cursed our family, the first of men.'
She did.

'The Bear will roar, beware you gods,for time is come to break the bars, sunder the rules, break the words.
The road from the shadow will begin,the Raven to bleed on the evil, rocky skin.
A sister, a brother, wrongful act share,a deed so vile, two children will she bear.
The Raven will find the sister,the gods to look on as blood spills onto the Woden's Ringlet.
A raven will show the way, a bear is slain,cocks will crow, men feel pain.
Youngest sister's blood is needed, her heart rent,onto the plate of Woden, her life is ended.
Released is the herald, the gods will bow.After doom, life begins anew.
A selfless act may yet the doom postpone.'

I nodded, remembering how Shayla had recited those words to me, and I missed her. 'Her heart is rent. I am sure Odo will not sacrifice a drop of blood from her damned fingertip, Tear. He will rip her heart out, and smile as he does. If he is capable of smiling.'
She sobbed. 'So it is true.'
I nodded. 'Yes, if Odo gets his way, Veleda will truly have to die by his hand. This has to be present. Woden's gift.' I lifted my hand, and the ring on it. 'Sigyn spoke with me, by the way. Before Bero died.'
'She did?' Tear said with amusement. 'She hates her husband,' she smiled. 'Sharing his prison is not something she imagined their life would be like. She is a frivolous goddess, not a dutiful slave, serving his needs. Lok is not a very good husband, but a false one and a scheming shit bucket. She likes to see him under guard. Of course, this end of the worlds and of the gods' business makes her uneasy. Perhaps Lok's new world has a new queen? Perhaps Lok is mad enough to fall in his own Ragnarök?' Tear mused. 'This scroll says a selfless act may change things.'

'Yes,' I told her. 'It is something I think about as well. But, as you see, there are a lot of shady, hard to understand, easy to misinterpret lines and—'

'You are not a selfless man, Hraban, remember? Your family has ever evaded—'

'The bloody prophecy by either killing themselves or going into exile, and here I am, dancing with wyrd. Yes. But, perhaps one day I will be selfless. I have hope.'

'She was very pretty, was she not?' she asked. 'She was selfless, no? She was not happy, and would have died, anyway. Shayla?'

'Yes,' I said simply, remembering the sucking maw that swallowed her, and the pain I endured when the vortex of her goddess claimed her. Tear sat back down, and I rubbed my smarting face, discreetly wiping away a tear.

She looked at me tiredly. 'A man to thwart the destiny has to be a strong man, an unselfish man. It will always call for a sacrifice. Always. That means he will not find happiness. Be aware of the hold Draupnir has in you. Your pride is a terrible thing. Your need for vengeance, your position? This fame Fulcher is worried about? All this tells me my daughter will die, and the world will end.'

'Gods. Fulcher and his foolishness. Yes, I wish to be a lord of the Marcomanni. I will not run away. I trust I shall make the right choices at some point, but I am not one to live in a cabin, hunting and fishing until old age claims me. As for Ishild, I will marry her, for she is the mother of my child. It is just I do so. Is that not a right decision? Adalfuns—'

She shrugged. 'He is a poor judge of men, or women. Look at me. I loved Adalfuns, but I loved my gifts and fate more. She will not make you happy, for a reason. One I cannot share.'

'Why not?' I asked.

'It would hurt her,' she told me. 'I will not have her hurt more.'

'You do not trust me?' I nodded carefully, wondering at her words. 'So, Adalfuns. You must have been prettier than you are now?' I dared to tease her, and was rewarded by a wicked smile.

172

'I was. I was prettier than Ishild,' she said with a sigh, and we laughed. She seemed like a likable old woman, despite everything that had passed. 'What now, Hraban?' she asked.

I got up painfully to stoke the ebbing fires, but I did not remember I was still nude and slumped back with a scowl. She grinned and huddled next to the fire, working the embers and logs so they burnt higher. It was odd to be at peace with her. 'I will fight with ... for Burlein. The question is, what will you do?' I asked. 'Burlein might not let you go.'

She sighed. 'He will. He is a powerful man now, and many men flock to his banner. Maroboodus lost face, thanks to you, even if he took a piece of yours with the blade. He is weaker, not enough, but a lot of the finely shining fame is gone. Men whisper vile things about him; even Sibratus the Quadi is an uncertain ally. He is weak for a good while, his plans slowed, perhaps even destroyed if Burlein is not a fool. I suspect he is. In any case, Burlein has no use of me. I will go, and be free for a while. After my granddaughter is born. Lif.'

I shook my head. 'I will name her—'

'Lif,' she said. 'You will see.'

I groaned at her ramblings. 'I will kill Maroboodus, or have him killed. Then I will keep them both, Ishild and her, far from Odo. I'll be a famous man in this land, and she will be safe. They will both be. I will lead men for Burlein, and enjoy life for once. Of course,' I stretched my face carefully, because it hurt from talking, 'I have other promises to keep.'

She nodded. 'Do not do that. You'll break the stitches. It is best you make plans in the spring, Hraban.'

'I will kill your son, Tear,' I told her brutally. 'If he ever runs near me. He told my weak brother, Gernot, to kill a friend of mine, Hagano. He is responsible for many deaths.'

'Just as long as you keep my girls alive,' she said tartly. 'Beware of Odo. And these lines,' she gestured for the scroll. 'We did not know many of them; Sigyn did not share them. This one that says you will bleed on evil, rocky skin? That the road begins from that event? This is the one we knew about, but much of the rest is unknown. And we did not know what a rocky skin is either. Most of these lines in the prophecy are slippery, Hraban. Lok is a god of schemes; he rarely tells us how things will work out. No matter what you try to do, you might play his game.'

'Is my child one Odo will spare?' I asked her. 'Can you tell that much, at least?'

She scanned the scroll. 'They are to share an act, Hraban, Ishild and Odo, but it only says she will bear two children. Not two children to Odo. I think Lif is the girl. The boy—'

'Fine,' I said heavily. 'I will not let her near him. Ishild, nor the baby.'

'I thank you for that,' she said sadly. 'But, spring will be perilous.' She left me sitting, and Ishild came in slowly from the side room. I got up dizzily and walked to her, holding a blanket around me. She looked drawn, tired yet strangely beautiful, and her gray and white dress looked fine over her large, rounded belly. I fought the desire to place my hand on it; she saw this and helped me by taking my hand, and guided it on the mound.

There was movement under it, and that, my lord, changed my life.

I stared at the life growing inside her, the bulging, moving creature that was part of me, and she smiled gently. I was curious, I wanted to see the creature kicking under the skin, and I felt betrayed, for things would not be easy with Ishild. Yet, at that moment, many of my priorities seemed foolish.

'You are uglier than I remember,' she told me gently.

I ignored that, and took a deep breath. 'Your mother told me you have a reason for the things you did. For supporting Odo,' I began.

'I don't support him. I have issues to deal with him. Did she tell you this ...' she began, truly alerted.

'No, she said this would hurt you,' I told her. 'But, I need to know. Why did you sleep with me? Was it because you wanted to get pregnant before your turd of a brother did this to you? For he is to whelp children on you. At least, until he gets a boy. Did you know this? When I lost you for those many years in our childhood, did he tell you about these things? The prophecy speaks of it. Did you know?'

She shook her head. 'I know not why I slept with you. Perhaps to have what that evil mouthed hussy had. Ermendrud? You threw me aside.'

'You were too desperate, too fey, too secretive, deeply entwined in their schemes, and I did not want to be tied down by seidr-using maniacs.'

She smiled. 'I am no völva. I have no magic other than my blood. I see things sometimes, but they rarely come true. Once I saw a dream that I will ride a horse, and it will bring death to people I love.'

We breathed hard as we looked at each other. I finally shrugged. 'I did not trust you then. And now, I hear you still wish to go to Odo? So I do not trust you now. Yet, you carry a child; my child.'

'Yes,' she said huskily. 'Wyrd. Yet, I do love you.'

'You do? Still?' I said carefully.

'I have a lot of love in me, Hraban,' she said with a breaking voice, and I held her. 'For you, for my child, for those I cared for when I was young. I love so much that I am very tired.'

'So, rest with me, and we will see what comes out of it, no?' I told her softly.

'There are dark valleys between us and happiness, Hraban,' she sobbed.

I said: 'Hush. Let us not speak about the valleys. You are with me, and safe for now.' We held on to each other, near desperately, and I thought about her. She had deep secrets, still, and I would keep an eye on her. I had the ring, and my damned father was shamed, and pushed to a very tight spot. I was, for once, on top of my enemies, able to control my future and not running from them panting and out of breath. I took a deep breath, unsure of my words. 'Will you marry me? They will think ill of us, if we do not. In a normal tribe, they would not allow us to—'

She stirred. 'Let us marry, if life gives us some mercy. Give it a year, or two.' She breathed heavily, and I nodded carefully, worried.

'So be it.'

She sensed I was not happy with her answer, and was gentle as she touched my face. I let her do so, driving Shayla's specter far from my thoughts, and I pretended to love the mother of my child. There would be mountains to climb soon, valleys to cross, and I was determined to do so.

Gods laughed, but we made careful love, and had peace for a while.

I spent the evening and the night holding my hand on her belly, wondering at a tiny foot moving under it.

CHAPTER XI

Winter arrived with a brutal force, unleashing the times of frozen death upon us and all the Marcomanni, no matter whom they called their lord. They all fought the same enemy: hunger and stinging frost. For our Grinrock, our relative success against Maroboodus brought unexpected issues. Many a Marcomanni from the north took shelter in Grinrock and the south, and Burlein's people were hard pressed to provide food and shelter for such families. Yet, he welcomed them all, buying what he could from across the river. He sent hardy men, hunters and travelers, to scout the northern lands and to gather news. Some men he sent to Hard Hill itself, pretending to be supporters of Maroboodus. From these brave men, we got a wealth of news. Many villages around the Hard Hill were empty, their people having fled, but my father had returned to Hard Hill, and sat there, brooding amidst dust and ash, trying to rebuild his fame. Men told us he was sick from a spear-made wound, the one Burlein had thrown, and there was hunger and disease making the once formidable lord nearly pitiful.

We burned our dead ones, and mourned. I gave neither Guthbert nor Leuthard a holy pyre, but hoped Father would send their ashes north to the faraway lands of the Batavi, at the end of River Rhenus, near the fabled sea in the north. I prayed to high Woden for Guthbert, and knew he was waiting for me in the halls of the god, bickering with Vago, likely, on who gets to slay me first, for in Valholl, men engage daily with each other in the joy of battle, and feast in the evenings, happy and carefree, swapping stories.

I felt like I was aging at double the normal rate, and the scar in my face made me feel self-conscious, no matter if the face itself was no longer puffy like a rotten fish, and I started to gain back a semblance of a normal man's looks. For once, though, I was not poor. Bero's long lost riches saw to that. We had a bag of Roman gold, and even more glittering silver; bronze aplenty. With that, we purchased precious food and even some small cows. We all had horses, and two ill-tempered pigs.

And, when I say pigs, I meant Ansbor and Fulcher.

Ansbor was not happy with his lot. He rarely was. I spoke to him often about Wandal, and what we should do to regain him. I planned on sending men to find if the Matticati held him. It was also possible the Vangiones or even Romans had captured the dolt, and we both went quiet when we thought about that. How we would find his trail in the Roman world was a mystery to us.

Of course, he could be dead.

Eventually, we promised each other we would find a slave trader in Moganticum, and start there. We would venture in a world we did not understand, and we would be in danger for our friend. We nodded at that, but Ansbor was nervous, for Maroboodus had to be dealt with first.

Also, he was in love.

He did not admit it, but it was clear as rain when the woman passed by in the room. He was utterly stricken by Cassia, and deathly afraid of losing her. She was a striking woman, and disturbed me as well. She had been strange in Bero's tower, but I chased the husky words she had uttered there away, and hoped Ansbor the best of luck with her, though that thought bothered me as well. I did not think he suited her, but felt like a bastard for thinking like that, for I did not truly know her. I suspected I was jealous.

As for Fulcher, he brooded. He had taken to visiting Hunfrid, the unhappy king of the Vangiones, and had found out from him the man who had led the attack on his hall, Bricius, was not even a Germani, but a Celt of the west, and he commanded a motley crew of vagrants who tracked men. Mercenaries, obstinate, never in one place. They had likely left the Vangione lands, the brooding Hunfrid confided to Fulcher after my friend had drawn a seax. They worked for pay, and Hunfrid could not pay them. This made Fulcher his morose self again, and it was impossible to draw even the off-smile I had so enjoyed out of him.

Bricius could be anywhere.

So, we had two brooding pigs in the house.

Pigs, for Ermendrud was utterly furious when they tracked mud and twigs in to the great hall she and Cassia kept religiously pristine and clean. The women quickly formed a trinity of unholy leadership in my Hall, one that us, the divided men, could not cope with. Euric had wisely purchased a hut for himself, snorting at the antics of the three horrible creatures, whenever we hid away at his place.

As for the coins, Cassia pushed me quickly aside, and took hold of my fortune. I did complain for having to beg for a piece of bronze to purchase a dozen arrows, for example, but in truth, I was lucky to have her in the house, even if Ansbor was grumbling and nervous when she walked past.

'Why don't you tell her how you feel, you idiot?' I asked him finally, when I grew tired of his sighs and groans. 'You had months to do so, and here you are, miserable as a near drowned dog.' His face took on a suffering look as his eyes tracked the movements of the dark-haired beauty, and his hands made inconspicuous movements as he tried to tell me it was not my business. The dolt was dead scared.

As for me, Ishild and I lived a lie.

It was a nice lie, full of odd, tender feelings, despite all that had passed. I still did not know her secrets, and Tear would hover around, but overall, the pregnancy and her company gave me strange peace I had lacked. I was happy, happy enough, I suppose, though dreading the future.

Euric surprised us before the Yule feast, for he bid us farewell. Winter was no time to travel, but the damnable fool was adamant to go to the east, being so close to the people inhabiting the high mountains. He wished to live there for a while, and learn new things about iron. He also wished to forget his constant worry over Wandal. He would spend the winter in the east, amongst the high hills of the Black Forest near the mountains, and Fulcher bought a guide to show him the way. Well, Cassia gave him the coin to do so, but Fulcher dealt with the practicalities for he knew the hills and the best guides.

Wrapped head-to-toe in dark furs, Euric stopped by before leaving. 'I will be back in the spring, Hraban, unless the filthy gods take me. Then, we will find Wandal, or at least his bleached bones,' he told me, sitting on a sturdy horse. I nodded, unhappy to lose him. It was strange how a man who was once a distant father of my friend was now a man I had taken oaths with.

As for the spring, Burlein was preparing.

He had changed. He was no longer the drunk merry third brother, a useless wastrel, nor the spineless, beaten man, but now he was a warlord, a man with the weight of the world on his shoulders, as if he was the giant Atlas himself. He had turned into a lord of men, though he was spending too much wealth, perhaps on needless endeavors. Yet, he was also generous with praise. He was dispensing justice, taking care of his people, and meddling in Maroboodus's affairs, as he made inroads towards the north, finding allies amongst the Marcomanni who formerly bowed to Maroboodus. Tear had reservations about him, her bony shoulders shrugging when Burlein passed, but for me, that Yuletide was time of hope. Burlein was doing almost everything right. His blunt axe-like brutality had honed itself to wiser ways.

And then, there was Gunhild.

Oh, he courted Gunhild patiently, and with respect, but it was hard going. Gunhild had dead Koun on her mind, her shame over the many humiliations still vivid in her thoughts. Had it not been Melheim, Burlein's bullnecked brother, who had tried to take her by force? She must have seen Melheim's mad face in Burlein as well. However, she had a history with the south. Had not the lords of this very village wanted her for marriage? Indeed, she had once been married to a noble of Grinrock, until the man had died, and so the village itself was no den of pain for her. Yet, she had truly loved Koun. Sometimes she would sit with us, listening to Cassia and Ermendrud bickering with Ansbor, then asking me softly if it was true, absolutely certain that Koun had died. I would hold her as she sobbed. She would have to move on. That was the rule of life. Not to do so is the road to slow death. That was something I would have to remember myself many times in later life.

Then, one night, Fulcher and I saw her talking with humbly kneeling Burlein, deep in the wintery scene of shadows and light near the riverside. They spoke at length, and in the end, she embraced him. He was a good enough man, and so her healing began.

It was a good winter.

CHAPTER XII

That Yuletide, we celebrated raucously. We gathered in Burlein's hall, the hall where I had deceived Isfried, luring him to attack Hard Hill. It was much the same kind of a celebration, for that distant night we had been very drunk with Burlein, and had gambled like fools. We did it all again that Yuletide, and he was in a greatest of moods, and not only for the gentle Gunhild.

Men travelling south had brought him great news.

A great many chieftains in the northern and eastern lands of the Marcomanni had declared neutrality in this war. Burlein's men were competing with Maroboodus's men on swaying some chiefs to our way. Father had sent men on the same mission. They had fought bitter skirmishes, and even if Maroboodus had hung some of Burlein's men in the villages of the Moenus River, Burlein had had great success with few others. Some said the Quadi had not abandoned Maroboodus yet, but neither were they entirely for him. Vannius was still with the Quadi as well, apparently until spring.

I nodded at the news, and his face was flushed with the excitement, his fears in the background. I pointed a finger at him. 'Vannius will not fight us, as long as Hunfrid is prisoner. In fact, if you give him his older brother, he will lick our asses.'

He grumbled. 'Peace. We have some time to think about the Vangiones. Didn't you already promise Vannius he would fall, should he let us deal with Maroboodus? We tried and failed, but Hunfrid still lives, despite him doing his part. He might not be happy with us, if there are more demands coming his way. He might not believe us. I would not.'

I shrugged. 'We have not dealt with Maroboodus, really. And Hunfrid is your prisoner.'

He roared happily. 'Gods, I didn't realize what kind of strange games Isfried had to deal with. In any case, we have your father by his hairy nut sack.'

'How do you know it is hairy?' I asked mischievously. 'Romans likely shave them.'

He hummed uncomfortably. 'I have not seen his, if you are trying to imply something filthy like that. No. And, this claim of yours, that he is a Roman more than Germani—'

I slammed my mug on the table, and pointed a finger at him. 'He is a damned Roman. I heard a man tell me this is so, and he had no reason to lie. He hopes to use the Germani in wars that benefit Augustus, and when the time is ripe, and the internal enemies of Augustus have grown weeds, my father will subjugate us all to Rome. It is—'

'Fine!" he said tiredly. 'But, few think that far in these lands. What the chiefs out there think about is Balderich, and his lie over the old man's fate. They don't care a goat's ass for Rome. It is all too far-fetched for them.'

'Fine,' I echoed him, brooding as I took more ale. 'But, it is true, nonetheless.'

He shook his long, glimmering hair back, as his mood was ruined. We watched as men roared happily, some who had celebrated with Maroboodus not a month before. 'Vannius is alive, and they say he is fighting with Tudrus's relatives, Tallo especially. He is busy for now,' he noted. 'Too busy to help us. Too busy to go home to his Vangiones, even. He will, I am sure, but perhaps he is gathering men for his attempt to take over the throne of the Vangiones.'

I grunted. 'We can decide this thing with the Marcomanni alone, but we should seek outside help. I don't care to take any chances with the bastard.'

He shook his head. 'We will see. For now, we are doing well on our own. Come spring, we will take stock of the situation, and decide what to do with Hunfrid, Vannius, the Quadi, and the Vangiones. Nay, the gods themselves.'

'Come spring, it might be too late. We are harassing Father all across his dominion, but we should make decisions about allies now,' I told him. His face screwed up with worry, and then, he brushed the sentiment aside, clinging to confidence as he toasted men around him. 'Use Vannius to gather either the Quadi, or the Vangiones, to us. We need help.'

'I will try to find some allies,' he allowed unhappily, and I toasted him.

Then, despite the heaviest snows that had arrived and very bitter cold, we spent a very happy Yule. Ishild laughed every day. Tear and Ishild had made peace, and I felt there was some part of the old Ishild in the house, the merry child I had run around in and around our village when I had been young, before she had disappeared and reappeared as a woman.

A Yule celebration was a ten-day long affair of plenty and enjoyment, and every one of those days Fulcher, Ansbor, and I feasted. Despite a tearing hangover, I would endure Cassia's nimble fingers as she checked on my wound. She seemed strangely happy, and talked about the house, and how it could be enlarged. Yuletide was ever the happiest time of the year, and this was no exception. I nodded at her plans, and finally grabbed her hand. She sighed resolutely. 'You are going to be asking about my plans? With him?'

'Ansbor is a fool for you,' I told her with a nod. 'He will likely propose. Soon.'

Her face took on a marble-like quality as she sat back, her eyebrows cutting a severe line on her brow, not giving away any hint of her feelings. 'Yes,' she said huskily.

I gazed at her carefully, treading like a lynx into a guarded henhouse. She might be easy to speak with, but she might bite my head off as well. She was a striking woman, with hips to make any man stop, bosom to match a goddess, and like one, she could likely eat a man alive, should she be displeased with him. 'You are here, in these undecided lands, risking life and limb. And, yet, you have riches across the river, vast lands, and a husband-to-be. Is this not so?'

'Yes, it is so,' she said. 'But likely my riches are gone, and should I go back, I'd have to fight for them. My husband-to-be has married another, and I think he might be happy it is so, for he never searched for me. Was there ever a request, or a messenger trying to, nay, begging to buy me free? There is as little true love in that story as there is between you and Ishild.' She looked shocked at the last words, and then she got up, visibly calming herself.

'You have no idea what Ishild and I share,' I snarled at her, aroused by her words.

'A baby,' she told me severely. 'You have a baby between you. Not even that, yet. Ermendrud told me about you two, and what Ishild did to you, the trick she played on you. You had rejected Ishild. It was wise. Despite her looks, she is not destined for this world. There are women, Hraban, that will make you smile, but she will always make you uneasy. She is not whole.'

'This is none of your business, Cassia! And what will you tell Ansbor?' I hissed. 'He is my friend, and I worry for the craven fool.'

She shrugged, as cruelly as only a beautiful woman can. 'I will consider it.'

'You will?' I asked, surprised.

She laughed dryly. 'Ah, my, you have a small opinion of your friend if you are surprised that he might win my heart.'

'I'm not sure you have one, ' I mumbled, and she fixed me with a cold stare.

She leaned forward, and tapped the scar in my face painfully. 'I feel alive here, Hraban, with you lot. If you are displeased with this, we can move with Ansbor, and find a fine hall for ourselves. Is this how you want it?'

I opened my mouth to say, 'yes,' but just shrugged. She was very useful in the hall. 'No. I will need you.' I felt uneasy as I said that and gazed in her eyes. Our looks lingered, very close, and finally she got up, and I felt disappointed. I felt I was a poor friend to Ansbor.

'Fine,' she said carelessly. 'I will handle Ansbor, and he will be happy, no matter what we decide, so do not worry. He is a grown man. As for your Ishild, she has all sorts of uncomfortable problems, some nausea still, and her weird eating habits are hard to satisfy. She desires half-raw millet, pinched apples, and even the sweetest of mead, sometimes at the same time, but this is normal. I will handle it.' She smiled, and was about to leave.

I stopped her. 'When you said there are other women who could make me happy, do you mean Ermendrud? She was very disappointed in me, you see. There was a baby—'

She looked at me, her face strained with anger, then she slapped me hard. 'Not Ermendrud, you idiot. Besides, she has principles. She is not the sort to crawl to a man who hurt her. And, yes, she lost a baby. Something you should talk to her about, perhaps,' she said with freezing anger, and left. I lay back, utterly confused.

On the last day of the feast, I was pleasantly surprised.

While sitting on a long bench, Ishild next to me, her face pale from nausea. I held my hand on her belly to steady her. She grabbed it, smiled at me, and nodded at a young man with thin hair sitting at the end of the hall on a high platform, and Burlein pelted me with a pig's bone. He pointed at the man, and bowed my way.

The man was a poet, one of those few rare talents, who can dress an average man in glory, and cover foul deeds with honor. This gentle poet was singing songs in praise to our recent victories. Burlein was prominently placed in the songs, as was Isfried and even Melheim, though Gunhild had to leave when his name was uttered. This was so, for Burlein was building his family legacy again. A wise leader makes himself look like the most brutal lord in battle, yet a fair, merciful ring giver in peace, and the poet was burying past shame that weighted down the family. He sang about the heroics, and the battle of the Hard Hill, the burning of the Red Hall, the liberation of fair Gunhild, and men were praised for valor, even my father mentioned in a line of praise, for he was no coward, even if he was the enemy of all the men in the hall. He was hailed, which left a taste of sour bile in my mouth.

Then, Guthbert's stand was mentioned.

The poet gave whole lines to our heroics, the battle of the small room, where the man of great deeds fell bravely, and he named me the hero. I shrugged, for I had not slain the man, but Burlein's deed was kind, nonetheless. I felt grateful for Burlein and flashed a smile his way, but the men in the hall looked down. I had to stop myself from gazing at Fulcher, the longhaired man of too accurate predictions, for men did not wish to hail me. Burlein noted this as well and looked troubled, his eyes lingering on me. I wondered if he was calculating if I was crippling him, rather than aiding. I cursed such thoughts away, and endured the awkward silence, and Ishild held on to my hand. Despite the disappointment, the poet made a good work of the song, and I was determined to enjoy it.

We listened to the song many times that night, and men wept shamelessly, thanked high Woden and terrible Donor, Tiw and Freyr, and made pledges and oaths, some making peace with men they hated or had a feud with, for such was the power of song.

At last, the poet nodded at me, and sang one final song. His face betrayed emotion and his weak beard shook with the power of his song. It was a wonderful little song of high praise, honoring a man who braved all for his family. It spoke of the perilous Raven and the harsh choices of men, of my bravery, and the Woden's terrible rage I carry in battle. It named me Vago's Bane, and bravest of Aristovistus's blood. It named me many fine things and grudging mugs, and horns were finally raised, Burlein's being the first.

'He did err, my friends. He erred, for he served his father, the liar,' Burlein said loudly. 'The manes, spirits of the hall, are watching us, no doubt, and I say we forgive him. Let any man mocking the Oath Breaker leave with a bleeding face!' They cheered him, and saluted me. Others just nodded, for I was a vitka slayer, and a man who had schemed against them. Delicate fame was like a small flower, lord; when stepped on, it was impossible to make it blossom, but I was set on the path of recover, and I threw the poet silver I had stolen from Cassia earlier.

That evening, Gunhild wed Burlein, and Tear was the one to do it.

Men had heard the rumor, and looked at Burlein strangely, but they struggled against the old, holy ways for Burlein's benefit, and overcame the fact she had already been married to Maroboodus and her husband was still alive. Burlein took a terrible risk. She would be doomed if Maroboodus got his hands on her. Burlein was wagering some of his honor as well by breaking holy ties, but he was also giving the Marcomanni a subtle message. Maroboodus was not her real husband, but a man who had forced her into an unholy matrimony, having captured her father, and buried them all in lies. Burlein loved her, and as she was Aristovistus's blood, this also elevated the blond man, who was much younger than fair Gunhild.

I glanced at Ishild, who gave me a cold smile. Men were staring at us during the celebration, as most knew we were not married. Few things make a Germani feel nude like disapproval and suspicion, and I had a lingering suspicion the song I had heard that night was not to be a popular performance. Yet, Ishild had her secrets, and I endured the looks for her benefit.

After Yule, we endured hunger, and waited for war.

CHAPTER XIII

Spring was coming, but it was agonizingly slow to do so. People suffered cold, severe sickness, and there were many corpses carried aside and hoisted up high to a shed set on a sturdy old tree to keep the wolves away. We would burn and rise a mound over them later, when the land thawed, and life returned to vibrant colors. Ishild's belly was still growing, and she was no longer happy at all, but increasingly sarcastic and terribly cranky. This sporadically evaporated in a sudden burst of loving and caring chatter, but only for a moment's time.

The old, toothless woman taking care of her needs snickered at me, and told me this was normal, when I asked. I grew bored with hearing that, but no doubt, they all grew bored with me asking the question. Ansbor and Fulcher had gambled for a month, barely taking outside, with Cassia mocking them for their apparent uselessness, and all their nerves were wearing dangerously thin. Cassia was spending much time with Ermendrud, whispering with her, and I tried to ignore the lot, and find out what Burlein was planning. He had been secretive, and I did not like secrets. They often got me into trouble.

It was late Martius as the Romans called it, or Lenzin-mánód as the elders knew it in our lands, the spring month. The stubborn snow seemed to disagree, and sweet spring felt like a faraway dream as the frozen ground and windswept tops of the trees swayed in the northerly wind that made all living things miserable to the bone. One day, I burrowed my way to Burlein's hall, cursing the bothersome snow, and wondering why the hell we lived in a land where the air was colder than an ice jotun's ass, when they said the warm winds blew in the south, and men laughed at the thought of a freezing, deathly cold white blanket covering the ground.

I kicked open the door, and Burlein welcomed me, though he looked haggard and feverish. When he spoke to a servant, asking her to fetch mead, he sounded overly happy, though strangely agitated. None of the other chiefs were there. 'Shrug the snow off. My dogs hate the stuff.' He waved his hand at two large greyhounds he had bought from a greasy merchant from Illyria.

They growled at me. Dogs did not like me, I thought, remembering my ugly foe from the time I ran from Burbetomagus. I glared at the two resentful mutts, and shook some of the snow off, though not all as I walked forward. The dogs still growled at me, and one got to its feet. I scowled at it, holding a hand on Nightbright. Burlein sighed, and grabbed them by their necks, dragged them cumbersomely to a small room near his seat, where we usually held food and drink, but not now, since it was all mostly gone. He latched the door, and the two unhappy animals growled unseen.

'Thank you,' I told him, 'though they would likely make excellent dinner.'

'If the snow does not melt by next week,' he muttered, 'I'll eat them myself in secrecy. How is Ishild?' he asked carefully, as he pointed at a bench.

I sighed. 'She is sore, in various pains, and complaining pretty much all the time. And this is all normal, they claim. But, other than that, she is fine.' I lied to him, for I was concerned about her, and unhappy about her condition. 'Do you have any food that is not still walking about? Ansbor stole some of the gruel Cassia had left me this morning, though I cannot prove it.'

He nodded carelessly. 'Some old bread, stale wine, surprisingly nice ale. A bit of mutton, too, though it's not very good anymore. It made a man sick yesterday. He has been taking a shit since, and complains his haunches are getting sore.'

I nodded, sat down, and ate the bread while he stalked around me. I eyed him with trepidation, feeling something evil was afoot. I did not turn to look at him, as I munched on the dry wheat. 'Should I have brought my shield and spear? You look like you are about to have me sacrificed to Donor, or at least giving it some serious thought.' I asked him merrily, as I experimentally chewed on the mutton, which really was not very good, and I wondered how long ago it had been roasted. I would suffer for it, but I was hungry, and there it was.

'Gunhild is the same,' he quipped.

'What? The same? She wishes to sacrifice me?'

He laughed and plopped down, his beard in tangles as he tore at it. 'No. Like Ishild.'

'You mean … ' I asked, perplexed. 'But, she didn't have any children with her first husband! She thought herself barren!'

He laughed raucously. 'Well, you remember we spoke about it. He was not a very good ploughman, a sloppy one. He rarely ploughed, in fact. And Maroboodus,' he said, clearly regretting bringing up my father's relationship with the woman he seemed to adore, 'apparently spent his juices on slaves. The bastard.' He visibly tried to calm himself, and barely managed it. 'But, there we have it, Hraban. My skills in this art are unsurpassed, and so you and Gernot will not be the only ones to carry Aristovistus's blood.'

I nodded, carefully. Was this the reason he was so nervous? That I would feel slighted, or threatened, even? It was possible. I smiled at him, slapping his hand carelessly. 'Lord, I am happy to share the blood. I trust you with my daughter, you trust me with your … whatever comes out. I have no plans of ruling these lands, no. It is for you, and for the brats to decide, later. For Gernot, I make no promises. I just want my fame and home down the road.' I grimaced at the thought of my brother, fawning on Odo. 'So, she is terrible to you? Gunhild?'

'Yes, she is,' he said with a shudder, and gave me some more ale and raised a horn. We drank to both the happiness and unhappiness of our lives.

'Now.' He set down the horn, letting it spill on a table. 'The war. We have to keep them alive, our wives and children, to make them rulers.'

I nodded gravely. 'The others? Your council?'

He waved his hand towards the door. 'They were here already. I wanted to share this news with you privately. About Gunhild. But ... ' He looked around, as if a sly spy might pop out of the shadows. 'There is news. Come spring, the Hermanduri will attack the Quadi again, as is their way, Suebi or not. They have no love for their neighbors, and Tallo and Sibratus will go at it, leaving a huge opportunity for these bastards. Yet, for what your father did to the Hermanduri last spring, they have a gigantic grudge. So, they will go easy on the Quadi, and send a sizable army here. They will send us men. I am to command them.' He grinned happily. 'So, I did find us some outside allies.'

I opened my mouth, but shut it. He noticed my uneasiness and brooded. There was ever some uncertainty in Burlein, lingering doubt over his greatness and Tear's words came to my mind. I grunted noncommittally. The Hermanduri were numerous and savage. They had more than fifty thousand men spread out from the mountains to the east of us to the great rivers of the north, and though they were not a united people, a relatively small tribe like a Marcomanni would need to tread carefully, if they were to survive. That was why we had defended the Quadi against them since time immemorial. Hermanduri were known to war with the mighty Cherusci, the dreaded Chatti, and the Quadi at the same time, in addition to whatever they did in the east, the lands we rarely heard of. I briefly thought of Marcus Romanus, the Roman who had taught me Latin, the man serving Maroboodus and travelling those lands for Maroboodus, serving his dark plans, and wondered what part he had played in the deaths of my family.

I sighed and rubbed my face. 'Lord—'

He looked perplexed. 'This is a solid plan, Hraban. I know you would wish to use Hunfrid to lure Vannius and some Quadi to our side, making the bastard a veritable king of the mongrels, but would it not be possible he would war on us next? It is good, I think, to hold Hunfrid a prisoner here, giving us peace from both Vannius and the Vangiones. We need another ally, and I have been promised it,' he said with a clipped tone.

'You didn't tell me this during winter,' I told him unhappily.

He nodded, fury playing on his face for a moment. 'No, Hraban. I did not. I have to rule on my own. You planned what happened in Hard Hill. Men know it. This has to be my war.'

'I messed up in Hard Hill. There is no cup in my hand, one made of Maroboodus's head bone,' I told him back. 'Hermanduri are treacherous. We don't even know who rules them.'

'This lord told me he will bring three thousand men here. Men Maroboodus will not expect,' he grinned. 'It will be dreadful for your father.'

'Was it costly?' I asked scathingly.

'Yes, well ... ' he stammered.

'Well?' I asked, dreading his answer.

'It cost us the Quadi.' He laughed uneasily, and I stared at him. 'We will not aid them in the future, what is left of them.'

'And you think they will let us be after the Quadi are evicted from the rivers?' I asked him incredulously. 'They will—'

'We will work with the Chatti to contain them,' he mumbled, but he knew it would be nearly impossible to have the Chatti help us against the Hermanduri. Then, I stared at him. He blushed.

'What?' I asked.

'You are not married to Ishild, not really. And you have complained she is capricious, fierce, and strange. The Chatti and your father wanted to marry you to Gunda, the Chatti princess. So, why not now? It would bind them to us.'

'You presume too much!' I told him. 'I might as well try to make love to a goddess than tell Oldaric and Ebbe I would like to marry her now! After all the trouble, they don't trust me. Yes, adeling Adgandestrius is my friend, my fine friend, but their fathers think he is a fool, and—'

'This is something we should do, nonetheless,' he yelled, and slammed the table with his heavy hand. 'We need you.'

'Gods,' I told him, eyeing the blackened rafters in desperation.

'You would move there, of course,' he said, looking down.

193

I nodded, as I tore some meat off the bone in my hands. 'So, you wish to be rid of me as well?'

He sighed. 'You remember Yule. The poet praised you in two songs and the men? They do not trust you. They think you bring them bad luck.'

'It is my tribe as well,' I told him frankly. 'I feel no inclination of leaving it.'

He opened his mouth and closed it heavily, rubbing his face. 'People do not trust you. That is important. And, as I wanted Balderich gone, perhaps it would be best if you were gone eventually. To a happier place. I do think it might be for the best. After the war.'

'Do you?' I asked softly and dangerously.

'I do not know,' he said frankly. 'There. You have it. I think of you as a friend, but there is a bloody history with you and Grinrock, and also, you are Balderich's grandson. And I will have a child I have to protect.'

'I said I do not wish to rule,' I said, incredulous. 'I said it, and I mean it. I am no threat to your child.'

His eyes glinted. 'Very well. But, perhaps, even if you are not, the people who are after you are? There is the prophecy, and I believe in it. Tear? Perilous. Ishild? As perilous. They could go with you to Gunda after your father is dealt with,' he told me prudently. 'There is the mad god to consider, and the servants to the creature are a danger and are in danger here. Her mother especially ... there are solutions, that ... are permanent,' he suggested. 'They did work against us, did terrible things, and men hate them.'

I growled, and put a hand on my sword. 'No.'

He shook his head tiredly. 'Fine. Think about it. We have little we can do right now. But, the deal with the Hermanduri has been sealed. I will keep Hunfrid, and let the Quadi die to the Hermanduri, this coming summer. It will be a terrible summer, Hraban, but this is my decision. And then, we will discuss your future.'

'Very well, lord,' I told him, still angry, and he looked ashamed. He was growing into a ruthless man, quickly, and I worried about him. I had not expected him to entertain such thoughts about Ishild and me, and as it was with many insecure men, he took rash actions to cover up his inexperience and uncertainty. I wondered if my daughter would be safe, and thought about smuggling Ishild and Tear to Euric.

He got up and stretched. 'Times change, Hraban. I will manage the Marcomanni and mold them into a stronger nation. The Quadi do sadden me, they do. Sibratus and Vannius have split them up like a ripe turnip. A dying people they are, and we must think of ourselves now,' he said languidly as a pretty slave walked past. I heard Gunhild throw up in the far rooms, and Burlein stammered and smiled wistfully. 'You did not warn me of that,' he said, as he listened to her terrible moans and bitter curses. 'I thought pregnancy was a pretty, serene thing, not something resembling what I pushed out of my ass this morning. Horrible.'

'Ishild was not with me in the beginning of the blessing, so I could hardly warn you,' I shrugged. 'But, I tell you it is possible that it gets much worse!'

He mumbled something as he sat down. 'A blessing for us it will be, but not yet, it seems,' he said softly and then cringed as Gunhild cursed all the men in the earth to Hel for the suffering she was going through. I poured some ale for Burlein, sympathetically clapping his hand, despite my worry for his plans. He drank it down, gray of face. 'Gods, let the snows melt, and give me an escape!' We laughed softly and moved to a room that served as a guest quarter, and he waved his hand towards her quarters. 'Gunhild has swayed some more of the old Marcomanni families and even stray men on our side as well, men who remember Balderich. She is powerful, especially now when she is pregnant. Men see it as a sign of godly favor I managed to make her vomit so. I should be able to field some four thousand fine men, if we summon all from the forests and further valleys. Your father might have some five thousand, if he gathers some from the Quadi as well, but many are unwilling to serve either. Some thousands are neutral. Thus, we need some three thousand Hermanduri. Simple. It will be about numbers.'

I nodded, and took a deep breath, giving up. 'And me?'

He roared happily. 'I need you on my side this spring. You are his true heir; his men see a heroic son against a false father. His former wife in my hands, his son in my ranks? It might cost him hundreds of men.'

'She is still his wife—' I reminded him, and he growled.

His happiness was gone in an instant. 'No, the marriage was not legitimate. Balderich was imprisoned, and would not have accepted it, it was not ... ' He stopped speaking and sat down. 'I will fight, and I will win, and men will come to me, and your rewards are going to be great.' He went on, looking around. 'We will march during Drimilchi,' he said nervously, and I felt gloomy foreboding.

I stretched. 'They are making plans as well. He is a crafty one, has good warriors, despite the ones we managed to kill. Perhaps he has some five to six of his riders left? Nihta will be a terrible man in the field of battle. Are you comfortable with leading the men in a shield wall?' I asked, and he looked down. 'You are?' I asked again, and he shrugged, his face flushed with shame and anger.

'I am a lord, Hraban, but you know me. I know you have doubts—'

I shook my head. 'I have doubts as well. It is normal, I think, and I am sure we will all know what to do when the time comes. If you are bent on using the Hermanduri, you have to be able to control the bastards. Can you?'

He shuddered as he collected himself. 'I am not a grand strategist. Isfried was a fair one. Hermanduri are sending chiefs, and you are right. They will need decisive leadership, and I can give them that, should you help. As for the battle plans? Perhaps you would come up with one?' He looked red-faced and deeply ashamed, and I nodded at him, horrified he had none.

'You have kept the spies in Hard Hill, yes? Father has men here, I am sure,' I said carefully.

'We have men there, yes,' he nodded. 'We lost some in the winter, but we have many reliable men there. One especially is very good.' I shook at the responsibility and leaned back, unhappy. He gestured with his hand towards the north. 'We will draft a plan on the assumption we shall march on Hard Hill. We will need supplies and stockpiles, like the Chatti do when they go to war. We will need cavalry and scouts all around the troops when we march, and we will need to know exactly where the enemy is from the moment we march. Nay, from this moment onwards. This will take a lot of men. And, despite that, the battle we will eventually fight, no matter our well-laid plans, will be a surprise on both sides. I hear they always go wrong. I need you to help me with this, and most of all, I need you to lead men in the battle itself. He will have Roman training. We need surprises.'

'Yes, I can help with that,' I told him sourly.

'So, let us plan,' he told me happily, 'and keep in mind it will be a terrible, messed up plan from the start.'

Later on, I lay on my bed, which was filled with wooden chips. I idly kicked them off the bed, as well as I could, but it was hopeless. Ishild was leaning on the doorsill. 'Ansbor was sitting on it today. He was carving something. Bored. Ermendrud told him to clean it up, and he did, but—'

'But, this is the best he could do. I don't care,' I grumbled, and nodded at her. 'Getting close?'

'The old woman says it is so,' she told me with a shudder. 'It's not long. What did you discuss with Burlein?'

'Plans. Plans for the melt, what we will do. Things he has done.' I wondered what to tell her about his plans for Gunda and the Chatti.

She sat down heavily, and kneaded my hand gently. 'You will conquer him, Hraban. Maroboodus. One way, or the other.'

'We are riding to him when we can, and then we will see, indeed, if it is so. We planned for some surprises for the battle, but we are children playing war,' I told her judiciously. 'Then, if we win, I think we will find fame and honor and a hall with the Chatti. We will see.'

'I ... very well.' She got up stiffly, trying to hold her spine erect. She smiled at me wistfully. 'Sorry I cannot enjoy this pregnancy. It is not a feast to carry it. This is harder than last ... ' She shut her mouth.

I laughed and waved her off, and she ambled out, looking dour. Ermendrud came to the doorway, eyed the mess around the bed and the floor incredulously, and stepped in. She had been wary of me the whole winter, avoiding being alone with me, and I understood her. Much water had passed in the swift river from the time I had contemplated on marrying her. After that, she had taken with Wandal, but now Wandal was lost, her father dead by Nihta's hand. She stooped to pick up the pieces of wood on the floor, but I swung my legs around. I took her hand, and she looked at me, astonished. 'If I can, Ermendrud—'

'If you can, indeed,' she said bitterly, tore her hand out of my grip and wiped hair from her face. 'I trusted you.' This was a discussion we had not had since the day I left her.

'I was a bastard,' I sighed. 'I was being caged by my father, by Armin the Cherusci, hunted by Tear and Odo, both mad dogs, and then there was Gunda.'

'The Chatti princess,' she mimicked my voice, and her face took on a semi-idiotic look as she groped the air as if reaching for the stars. I could not help but giggle and then laugh, and she slapped me in fury, but could not help joining me. When we were done wiping tears off our eyes, our eyes met.

I gave her my hand, and she took it with a huff, looking down. I spoke as well as I could. 'I thank you for sending Wandal with me to my exile. He saved my life. Now, I shall do all I can to find him. Ansbor and I, perhaps Fulcher, will help as well. Euric, of course. We will find him.'

She nodded, about to say something, but then shook her head with some kindness. 'It is well. After this business with Maroboodus is done, yes?'

'Yes,' I told her wisely, afraid she might fly into a frenzied anger again. 'He will chase after us, if we just leave. Burlein will not survive alone, either. It has to be done. For more reasons than my dead family.'

She nodded. 'He did kill mine, too, so do it well.'

I pulled her up from the floor. 'I think the weather will turn warm very soon. Euric needs to be found.' I gazed in her eyes, and she understood I was planning something.

She observed me suspiciously nonetheless. 'And you want me to go there? To find him.'

'You go and tell him to stay away, for now. Tell him to keep you, Ishild, and the baby safe,' I told her. 'I think it would be best if you were somewhere in the mountains.'

She shrugged, as her eyes flickered to the other room. 'I do not trust her. Ishild.'

'Is it because of Tear?' I asked.

'No, I actually trust the old skins better than her daughter. There is something about her that reeks of falseness,' she said slowly. 'But, I will do as you asked. And when you bring Wandal back, I will be thankful. Not before!'

'Ermendrud,' I told her as I held her hand. 'You were pregnant?'

She clamped her mouth shut, and blushed, looking away. 'Yes.'

'How did you lose it?' I asked, treading a strange road. If it had been mine, I should feel sorrow. I should feel sorrow anyway, but I was unsure of my feelings.

'It was yours, Hraban,' she said bitterly. 'And I lost it like babies are lost. They are weak as leaves in autumn wind, especially so early in pregnancy, and I was afraid, always afraid, and so the gods punished me. I bled, and Cassia helped me.'

'Afraid of Wandal not coming home?' I asked.

'Yes. And when you were missing,' she told me miserably. 'When they said you were dead and so was Wandal, I cried for days. I was a coward, you see, unable to brave life alone, and I did not eat, hoping to die. I had nobody. Euric forced me to, but the baby died.'

Her words were sad and bitter, and I pitied her. I pitied the baby as well, and cursed myself for the misery I kept causing people. I wiped tears from her eyes, then mine and felt wretched. She had deserved much better. 'I wish I could make it up to you.'

'I don't think you can, Hraban. I cannot forgive myself for starving myself, punishing myself. Perhaps I tried to die as well. I was a coward. I ever was. And you cannot forget you used me. It will have to be carried around all our lives, our pain.'

'Aye. I think you are right,' I despaired, holding my temples, and she clung to me. An adult carries many mistakes on their shoulders, and mine were already terrible.

She smiled at me and turned to go. 'Clean this wooden scrap from the floor. This is no pigsty. Only hay allowed. As for Burlein, Hraban, try to make sure he knows what he is doing. I will go with Ishild and the baby, and try to be braver. I swear I will keep an eye on her. I will not let her die. I shall not fail. I promise.'

'I thank you for that. Keep everyone safe, if I cannot,' I asked her wistfully, and she smiled. 'I will find Wandal.'

'I will. You keep yourself alive.'

'Yes, by gods,' I told her, and liked her fine and myself less so. I could be married to her then. She might have delivered me a son or a daughter, but wyrd, my choices had killed the baby. I felt ashamed, and spat at fame. Gunda, a princess. I left Ermendrud for a promise of fame, and a woman I did not know. She suffered for me. Damn Fulcher anyway, but he was right. I hated myself, and did not like it.

CHAPTER XIV

The snow was finally melting. What remained was ugly gray, the fog was as thick as water, and all of our clothing chafed with the moistness and dirt. While the sun was still shy, hiding behind banks of heavy, puffy clouds, the people were out, enjoying themselves, staring at rivulets of water running for the river, the occasional greenery reaching up from surprising places. Overall, it was all hopeful, and the diminishing snow banks revealed wonderful hints of summer, especially the first yellow flowers, soon followed by the white ones. There was something wonderfully joyful about spring, but this wa only so if you had endured a real winter. In Rome, the misery was different. There, the floods covered parts of the city, the heat of the high summer was terrible, or the moist misery of the spring were child's play compared to freezing months of hunger in the north.

Fulcher came to me as I was dressing. He sat down with a huff, wiping clammy sweat off his forehead. I lifted a brow. 'Well?'

He smiled. 'Burlein got word, and news. From Hard Hill. Some for you, one for me. The bastard who killed my family, Bricius, is there with some of those mercenaries of his. Your father is scrounging up men as best he can.'

I grunted. 'We will both get what we need, then. Soon.'

'Or die forgotten and humiliated,' he told me gravely.

'Yes, of course. Can you find a guide that can take ... ' I asked loudly, and then lowered my voice. 'Ishild, Ermendrud, and the baby to Euric, after the baby is born?'

He looked shocked. 'Yes. I suppose so. I know where Euric was likely wintering. There is a mining village days away, and I told him about it, but—'

'Things will get dangerous, very much so,' I told him. 'There will be Hermanduri here, by the thousands, likely. This place won't be safe.'

He shook his head so his red hair flew. 'Hermanduri? Yes, yes. But, what of Cassia?'

'I—'

'Forgot about her?' he said sternly.

'No, not really,' I told him timidly. 'And Ansbor—'

'Does not own the girl,' he spat. 'I will do as you say, but wonder at your thoughts at the same time.'

'She is a healer, and might save our lives. A hardy girl,' I told him sternly.

'And very pretty,' he said darkly. 'Don't do things we all regret.'

'I—'

'Don't risk her for her pretty face,' he told me nastily. 'She should survive this war, like the other girls. Even if you entertain thoughts of taking her from Ansbor.'

I stared at him incredulously. I pointed a finger at his nose. 'Look. You give me advice on honor, or lack of it, on fame, and the uselessness of it. I need no advice like this. She is a friend.'

'So were Ermendrud and Ishild,' he said, looking down, and I slapped my thigh.

'You might be older than I am, but you know nothing about that,' I told him, as I girted Nightbright on my hip.

'I think you might be blind.' He wiped his incredibly long hair away from his face as he stood. 'I have sight, Hraban, and I fear there will be tears, one day. Either make your move, or let her go, but do not keep them guessing. Best to break hearts quickly than to let them rot.' He walked away, mumbling in anger.

I cursed deeply and went out, retrieving a roan stallion from the stable, his mane steaming as he walked out to the mud and slosh. He was not

Minas, but still a beautiful, sure-footed animal, mighty restless after the winter. Like I was. Gods, Cassia. Ansbor liked her, not I! She was a healer. We needed healers. I cursed Fulcher, and sulked on the back of the horse, but the horse was happy, utterly happy, as he galloped hard on a patch of trampled snow, and I was giving him much needed exercise while brooding over the many unknowns in our lives.

Then, a filthy, fat man, with long brown hair in a ponytail, rode into the yard. He had a brutal, scarred face, a coarse beard, and he was wearing gray furs that were strangely practical, not constricting, cut in a way to keep him warm, and allow him great freedom of movement. He was a man who had obviously spent most of his time outside. By his garb, he could have been a trapper or a hunter. I knew his face though, and I knew he was a hunter.

Of men.

He stopped his thick, sturdy horse, removed his mittens, and scratched his tangled, dark beard. It was indeed Hands, the Chatti who had once been employed by Father, until he had disappeared while taking after Veleda, the girl I was now determined not to find. Had he found her? I turned the horse carefully, and put my hand on Nightbright. The man saw this, grinned at me, and jumped down, muttering a curse as he shuddered with a pained limp.

'You! What are you doing here?' I asked Hands, but he didn't seem to understand as he ambled forward, and I drew my sword.

'No need for that, lad,' he said as I got down from my horse and walked towards him.

'I am not a lad. I am Vago's Bane, Hands, and I didn't kill him while he was squatting down for a shit. I bit his hairy throat out. I have well-deserved scars and wealth. Address me as I am, you damned, blood handed bastard,' I said with a growl, but he raised his hands and rolled his eyes tiredly.

He smirked at me. 'Very well. Relax, O Lord Bane. I mean you no harm. None have paid for your head, and since you are such a dreaded lord, I am sure to attack you only when you are squatting on a shithole. I'm not above such tactics. I have no scruples, you see. Sword away, lord.'

I did not sheath my sword. 'You are a creature of my father's. Why are you here?'

He grimaced. 'I know you might think so. Nevertheless, I work for coin, or even cows. I am not exclusive. And your father was likely upset I failed to deliver Veleda to him. Gods know things got harder for him after that cur Odo was not happy. No. I don't work for that one either. Neither for Odo, nor your father. Not this time. I am here for someone else.' I regarded him with slitted eyes, and he grinned. 'Veleda? The girl?' he said. 'Remember?'

'What about her?' I growled.

'Donor's blue ball-hairs! I work for her!'

I sneered at him, blinking, unbelieving. 'She is ten. What does she pay you with? Good advice?'

His smile disappeared. He adjusted some of the gear on his horse while glancing at me repeatedly. 'You gave me a permanent limp last year. What are you, seventeen?' He smiled to himself.

'Eighteen, I think. You should expect such wounds when you underestimate your prey, young or old,' I sneered, and he nodded.

'You are right. I did not expect you to have that seax.' His smile was overly sarcastic as he shook his head in disbelief. 'Neither did I expect what happened after I went after Veleda.' He looked embarrassed.

'Do explain,' I said, tapping Nightbright to my thigh.

He gestured vaguely towards north. 'The girl you spared, that night. Veleda. I tracked her in the forest after you … persuaded me to leave. I didn't leave, of course. I set my hound on her.' My eyes narrowed, and he shrugged. 'I know you expected me to renege on our agreement, come now.'

I pointed my sword at him. 'She told me you would not harm her, but I thought she was just wise to the ways of the woods,' I told him with a scowl.

He snorted. 'No, she is not wise to the ways of the woods. The dog found her in a few minutes, panting in damned excitement as she was running. He barked softly, making enough noise for me to find her; that mutt had some style, and I loved it. A good hunting partner for a man like me. Yet, when the stupid bastard caught up with her, he went quiet. I found the two nuzzling, for Freya's sakes! She patted the dog. She was calling him cute! I was furious. It is her dog now, by the way.'

'And you followed the dog, and let Veleda pet you?' I said. Veleda. She had been a wise, careful little girl, one who did not speak like a child. She had told me we would meet one more time, and that it would be terrible, for Odo would find her then as well. Wyrd, if we did, but I would fight for her, should that happen. I shuddered at the thought, and decided she was wrong.

Hands was peered at me under his eyebrows, smiling and laughing softly. 'Yes, she is a queer creature, wise to the ways of men's hearts.' He laughed for a moment, like a bear would, his greasy, barrel-like chest heaving under the fur. He continued, 'Veleda. The little mysterious alf. I tracked her indeed to my damned dog, and I was going to do something that I am good at, what I was told to do, and paid for.' He put his face on his hands. 'I had a sturdy spear, a nice pair of manacles that I would have put around her damned, thin neck, and she was worth a fortune, and I could not. She left the dog rolling on the moss, happy as a damned wood fairy, and then she shook my hand, spoke to me, of high Woden, and fierce Donor, gentle Frigg, and the rest of the sodden gods, and told me that I am needed. I do not know how, but I could not open the manacles. She was too … honest? Kind? Above my threat. She touched my heart in so many strange ways. I know her mother is Tear, the völva, and perhaps she put a spell on me, but I do not think so. And so, I took her away. Not to Maroboodus, and certainly not to Odo.'

He walked towards me and pushed down my blade. 'Come, offer me something to drink. Something with spark, spirit, and fire, if you have any left after the winter.' He walked past me to the house, went in with cool familiarity, and I gaped at him incredulously, as he plopped down on my seat.

I followed him in and chuckled at his hairy face. 'You have gone soft, Chatti. There is a man's heart under all that dirt, fat, and hair.'

He slammed his fist on the table. 'She has a way to move men's hearts, and I remember you didn't take her, either!'

'What in Hel's name is this?' Ermendrud shrieked, as she came to see who was making the racket, but Hands gave me a long-suffering look. I shrugged at Ermendrud and made a begging motion with my hands. She fumed and disappeared, soon rummaging around the cellar, trying to find something edible, and the last of the mead.

Hands chortled, as I dragged a seat in front of him. 'So, Vago's Bane has to beg for a woman to do what she is supposed to do.'

I laughed at his face. 'Coming from a fat bounty hunter who obeys little girls, this is quite an observation.'

'Fine!' he told me sourly, and nodded with confusion, as it was Cassia who brought him some mead, and he smiled at her as sweetly as a greasy older man can. Cassia looked at me with some doubt, and I indicated to the other room. She went, muttering unkind things.

Hands shook his head, looking at her amble away. 'My, my. Perhaps I misjudged you. A saucy blonde, a ravishing brunette, and then, there is Ishild, of course. Quite a number of women you have under this small roof. I hear your Ishild is pregnant?' He glanced at me with humor as I indicated in the affirmative. 'And you are not married to her? You know, that will cost Burlein some men. Your father might be a traitorous piece of rot, but Marcomanni do love their old ways. I am surprised Burlein has not forced you to marry! Would make sense. But then, he is married to a married woman, and that will cost him even more men.'

'I ... ' I started, nearly spilling the news of Burlein's plans and Gunda, but decided it was none of his business. Instead, I glowered at him, hoping he would get to the point of his unwanted visit. Or had he? Was it Ishild? I sat up, but he continued, taking a swig from the mead horn.

'Gods, that is still good. I actually like them like this, my drinks. Old, and a bit rancid. Like I am,' he chortled. 'Burlein. I hear he is getting ready for war. Maroboodus, as you know, likely has men here, just like your lord has men there, and it will be a damnable mess.'

'I am not willing to discuss Burlein, thank you,' I finalized. 'Your visit had some meaning, my unwanted friend?'

He pointed a stubby finger my way. 'I still work for those who pay most, occasionally, but for her, I work for something else. I work for her survival; Veleda's. And she has a message for you.'

I shook my head. 'No, I have a message for her. Tell her I do not wish to find her. I know about the prophecy, the full verses, and she will die, if I should, one day. Tell her she should hide, far away, and also tell her,' I growled as I leaned forward, 'that I think she should ask your former dog to bite your nuts off and leave you dead. I do not trust you. No matter if you have had a temporary change of heart. Or just found a heart, anyway.'

'She does not think it can be avoided,' he told me tiredly. 'The part of you finding her, not the part about my lovely dog. It is wyrd. You have to decide what you do when that day comes. She says it might be avoided, if you did a deed. A hard, harsh deed. She says you owe her. You owe her a life. A life that is a relative of hers.' He looked hard at me. 'You have to find compassion in your heart for others than yourself. You have to think hard on what is best for your child. Your baby might need a father who knows how to give her up.'

'You teach me compassion, bounty hunter?' I said, troubled at the subject. Surely, he did not think I would give my child to her. I kept a grip on my sword. 'I thought you were here for Ishild.'

He waved his hand. 'Veleda says she has her part to play. But, she has obligations elsewhere, and we cannot help her.'

'Really? What obligations?'

'I say no more of that,' he told me as he tore into an old bit of meat, something I had hoped to consume for my mid-day meal. 'Odo is making plans for Ishild and your unborn daughter, but Veleda says she can protect your daughter from Odo while the game plays to the end. Nevertheless, you need to trust her. This is what she said. You need to believe her when she says this is the only way Lif will be free of Odo, until the end at least, when this business is decided. If you do this, then it is possible Odo will never find them. For this is a selfless act, Hraban. Utterly so. If the baby stays with you, she may suffer. If Odo gets her? She will not die, but I doubt he is a fatherly type. It might be the prophecy will come to pass no matter what you do here, but your child can be happy until it does. With Veleda. Give her up as soon as she is born.' Hands looked hard at my eyes. 'Lif will thrive with her, even if things get hard. If you do this willingly, she said, you would avert much evil. Fewer people you know will die. You'll be less hurt. The prophecy is untouched by this act, but it will be a kinder road for her. Give her up, and leave here. Veleda told me to tell you this. Travel north, soon, very soon, flee the Marcomanni, and you can find yourself with your own people, the Gothoni, or with the Cherusci, perhaps. Forget the Marcomanni, and your father. Stay, keep a hold on to her, and you will ride a perilous, strange path that will claim lives for decades.'

'That I would give away Lif ... my child? How could Veleda know something like this?' I was kneading my forehead with a fist.

'This is a compassionate, selfless act, my lord Bago's Bane,' he confirmed. 'Veleda is a powerful völva; she speaks with gods and spirits.'

'Vago!' I told him, and realized he had mocked me. There was a small, slimy smile on his face. 'And I have business here, with the Marcomanni.'

'Yes, Vago. This is the road, Hraban. Fine. Wage your little wars over Ishild and the damned Marcomanni, avenge the rotten corpses of all the men and women you loved, maybe become a great man, but spare Lif much trouble, and let go of her. If she is taken away when she is born, and you let this take place, it will all be much less painful.'

'Except for me,' I said skeptically. 'I will be a father.'

'You have not tried to raise a child yet,' he mumbled. 'They are fine when they are all grown up. I am sparing you much suffering.'

'You? I am to give her to you? A bounty hunter with a fancy tale to tell, and then, one day, I have to go to either Odo or gloating Maroboodus on my knees, to spare her?'

'I am no liar, Hraban,' he told me, with a large, rumbling voice.

I spat. 'I doubt Veleda is a safe guardian for my daughter. She is what, ten, no matter her fine skills with dogs and vermin.'

Ishild entered. She did not look at me, but walked to Hands, who hesitated, watching her empty hands and her rounded belly. She sighed, her beauty striking, and leaned over the fat man, whispering something to him at length.

'I will not let her go anywhere near Veleda! Never out of my sight,' I told them both, but Hands ignored me with disdain, and I rapped my sword on the table. Hands got up, as surprised Ansbor and Fulcher entered, with their weapons out.

He looked imperious as he walked towards them, pushing through with little care, but he turned at the door. 'When the time is nigh, trust, Hraban. It will be bitter, dangerous, but trust. I am sorry for your coming losses.'

Ishild nodded, and came to me, squeezing my hand. 'Wyrd, Hraban. Time will show what happens,' she said sadly and left. Ermendrud, unseen by us, harangued her about what Ishild had told Hands, to no avail.

The fat man mounted his horse, and rode east as I went to the door. 'Happy day of your birth, young raven! In a bit over a week's time! She told me, Veleda!'

I thought about the words and stood there for a long time and a terrible foreboding grabbed me with its choking tendrils. Shayla's last words reached for me. She had warned me. Beware my birthday.

CHAPTER XV

Next day, some weary Hermanduri envoys rode to Grinrock. They were a savage-looking lot, having travelled in the Black Forest for a week through banks of muddy streams and snowy hills, but they brought Burlein what he needed: confirmation of an alliance. An army of Hermanduri was riding our way. Burlein sent words of explanation to the Marcomanni villages that would be on the Hermanduri trail, and the news was taken in with nervousness and hope. They were to gather all their men in Grinrock in a bit over a week. Men began to hunt, traders were sent to buy what food could be found, no matter what side of the river. The war to settle all things between the ancient Marcomanni families was coming, and many would die. The worried women prayed, and even the children were restless and joyless.

That evening, I was shining Nightbright with a rag and some grease, and Ishild was asleep with her head on my lap. I was careful not to wake her up or cut her when she suddenly did sit up, her eyes wide with surprise. I nearly cursed her for I had a sword in my hand.

She looked over at me. 'It's time,' she whispered with a small grimace, and I found the floor was wet. 'Go and get Gunhild. Get the old woman Cassia hired. Get Cassia! Ermendrud, perhaps. She promised to help,' she was gasping now at me as I tried to help her up. 'Go already, fool!' That was uncannily like the less fateful Ishild I had known as a child, and I grinned at her as I sprinted for the next room, where the women slept.

'Up! Help her, dammit!' I yelled like a man possessed and ran for the door. I would be a father; no matter what dangers came our way. The muddy track was slippery, as I ran like a maniac for the hall of Burlein. I kicked the door open and fell on my back with a curse. Gunhild was there, sitting on a stool, being massaged by Burlein, who looked down at me in stupefied surprise, but Gunhild put a hand on his chest and nodded at me. Some slaves were summoned and so we went, her belly rounding with a baby as well, slowing her down.

I tailed her; my eyes round, pestering her with questions she refused to answer. 'You should not come inside,' she said sternly as I babbled, I cannot remember what, but I ignored her. I was there for a few moments, looking at the miracles of birth, and then Cassia threw me out bodily after I begged them to help Ishild, with tears in my eyes.

'Stay away, cur, and come back when it is done, and try not to get too drunk,' she said with disdainful anger for my weakness, and slammed the door closed on my toes, which hurt, but I was happy as the thick door muffled the suffering voice of Ishild. I slunk back to Burlein's hall and walked inside, weakly cursing the whole of Midgard for the misery such a simple thing as birth forced on a man.

'It was like battle,' I told Burlein, who had procured a jug of mead from somewhere. Fulcher and Ansbor ran in, their faces white, expecting bad news, but I waved them down, tortured in my mind with the images of Ishild's suffering, her breathless pain.

'We went to the house, and there was something horrid happening; it's your ... ' Ansbor stammered.

Fulcher sat down. He put his head to his hands. 'I never saw that before, even though I am a father. I was wise enough to find an excuse to work in Grinrock when this happened. It is a woman's world, and thousand times more terrible than a shield wall. But, you will be a father.' He cried for his lost son, we sat there, all grieving, yet strangely hopeful, and soon, all very drunk for the jug was a large one, and the mead very powerful. It was not alone, the jug and Burlein was generous enough to sacrifice everything he had to ease the evening's slow passing.

I am not sure what happened that evening, but I remember holding Burlein by his shoulders, shaking him gently. 'She screams, and twists and sweats terribly, and curses horribly. She hit me with a log while calling me a god abandoned mule,' I said with a slur, shaking him some more.

'My mother threw a knife at my father from my birth bed, and they said my grandmother fetched the knife, and tried to improve her aim,' Burlein said drunkenly, smiling at the memory he did not have.

I nodded sagely. 'Ishild did not have one. Only the log. No weapons for Ishild, thank Woden,' I mourned as I reached for more drink, and an old slave woman snorted in disgust as she listened to us. 'It was horrible,' I repeated several times in various tones and voices, and Burlein looked uncomfortable, knowing his turn would come.

After ten hours of this, we were reduced to throbbing hangovers, red-eyed as drowsy foxes, and ultimately a silent band of sorry fools. Suddenly, I was shaken by the exhausted Cassia, her eyes red-rimmed like ours, though not from worry and drink. When I saw her, I paled in fear. She smiled, exhausted, and shook her head. 'Lif is well. Ishild is weak, but should live.'

I stormed out. 'I thank...I do thank you, Cassia!'

Cassia ran after me. 'It was hard for Ishild, though. Wait, you.'

I stopped and took some deep breaths. She stopped in front of me, and wiped a strand of errant, sweaty hair from her eyes, looking at me wisely. She took my hand. 'The old woman says she cannot have more children. She has seen this before. She was hurt in the birth. She will be weak for some time. But, she should survive.'

I absorbed the news, and while this was sad for her, I was relieved. That meant Odo would not whelp his brood on her; the boy meant to populate Lok's world. *The prophecy was dead,* I thought, *it was gone.* However, I would never have a son, unless I married some other woman, and thoughts of Gunda returned to haunt me. I was a true bastard, but tired to the bone, exhilarated and afraid at the same time, and I forgave myself quickly. I shook my head with a small smile, embraced Cassia and gave her a kiss on the cheek. I went home, leaving her sputtering after me. I entered the hall, went to the room that was Ishild's, and quietly sneaked in.

There she was.

The tiny fingers, the small, strangely happy sounds, and the pinched face that was both ruddy and pink made me stop in my tracks. Ermendrud, after a suspicious glance at my generally disheveled condition, was forced to hand the baby over by muttering Gunhild, who stalwartly took my side. So I held her for the first time, drunk on her little hands, her pouty lips, which I swore she curled in an exclusive smile at me. I would not easily let go, until Gunhild swatted at me painfully and explained that she needed to eat. I reluctantly parted with her, and Ishild took her, guiding the sweet lips to her nipple. She was utterly exhausted, hurt, having lost a lot of blood but happy in ways one can never be unless they experience the same thing. She had a faraway look on her face, one of sorrow, but we were all a bit strange that evening, and so I did not give it much more thought. I hugged Ermendrud as she wept, and we both knew why. I wept as well.

I sat next to Ishild and rested, observing the baby, my head finally ending on her lap. I fell asleep as she caressed my hair in her thoughtful mood. There was love in her touch, despite the many dangers we were facing, and I was happy that early morning.

The next day, around midday, to be exact, I woke up and spent the entire day staring at the girl, not even noticing my ravenous hunger. Germani wish for boys; in fact, most men of any nation do, for boys make your line immortal, keep the family strong, and give you pleasure in ways a simple girl could not. Yet, that day, I disagreed.

I thought she was magical.

I snorted, for being Ishild's child, and mine, a combination of the old blood, she certainly was. The prophecy was doomed, I thought as I gazed upon sleeping Ishild. She would bear Odo no children.

However, that did not mean the bastard would not try. Odo would not give up.

I smiled, despite Odo, for I was truly happy. She was a breathtakingly beautiful baby, rubbing her face on the coarse linen she was wrapped in, her hands moving around, as if groping for her parents, and her toes were lovely and small, and I got endless enjoyment from holding them, warming her. Her eyes were piercing blue, though the old slave woman grunted that it might change, but I did not believe her. She cried softly and sucked constantly on half sleeping Ishild's breasts, one after another, slept soundly, and finally pissed and pooped all over me. This made Gunhild very happy, though not for my discomfort. She claimed she was a very healthy baby.

Ansbor laughed at me hugely. 'Finally, a woman managed to shit on him, not the other way around!' Fulcher clapped my back all that day, smiling like a fool, and they looked sheepish as they observed my happiness.

Tear came in through the door. She saw the baby and held out her hands. I felt my throat tighten, but Ishild handed her over, and the old woman walked back and forth in the hall. She thanked the gods, and she blessed the baby, and while I watched her warily, she seemed satisfied by her.

'What is her name, Hraban?' she asked, as she gave her to me.

'I ... ' I began to deny her, but could not. 'Lif.'

'Lif,' she said unhappily. 'I wish it was not so. And she is one of those that might populate Lok's world.'

'Ishild cannot have more children, unless the gods heal her,' I spat angrily.

She gazed at me with sadness. 'Beware of Lok. There are more creatures of his out there than Odo. Give her away. Today. Forget Ishild. Go out with her to the edge of the woods and wait. Hands will come. Do not, and it will be terrible,' she said as she gave me a cold smile, and left, heavy-hearted. I shifted my eyes between Ishild and Lif, and lifted her. I walked around the hall, gazing at her eyes, her beautiful face.

I could not go out. I could not.

She would stay with me. I was anxious, afraid, but I would be her future, not Veleda. Certainly not Hands. She would be lady of the Marcomanni, not a homeless wonderer, at the mercy of the woods and hostile tribes.

Tear left that evening. Hiking to the forest, Fulcher told us. She did not say goodbyes to anyone but Cassia, who escorted her a way, and I found it strange that I missed her. When I asked Cassia about her, she smiled. 'She was not alone, Hraban. An old man was waiting for her by the trees. Gnarled as an oak, the same color nearly. Strangely keen eyes, white and gray hair. I walked to him to welcome him in, but he was wise, and told me he wished no words with you. Called you a tedious young bastard. He took her away.'

'Was his name Adalfuns? Adalfuns the Crafter?' I asked her, in awe. He had been her husband, the famous crafter, who had promised to help me three times for letting Veleda go the year past.

'He did not say his name,' she told me, 'but he did tell me to disagree with you, and to foil your plans, if you were a total idiot in my opinion. I shall try. Hraban?'

'Yes?'

She shrugged and blushed. 'For many months, I have wondered about you. There are so many sides to you. Stubborn as an old pig, noble and brave, like a famous king. Crude and handsome at the same time. But the way your eyes shone when you saw her? I liked that. I like that man.'

'I ...'

She laughed and went, and I shook my head in doubt. Women were impossible to understand, yet we tried to.

Later, even years after, people claimed they saw the famed Adalfuns the Crafter with Tear, guiding her to the east, and in some strange way, I was happy for her, though I greatly desired to see Adalfuns. I felt I would need his help very soon, again, and cursed him for not providing it, as he had promised. He had once, but gods knew I needed it then. That day.

For I was weak.

I stared in awe at my daughter and feared for her, and so I asked Fulcher to find guards and guides to take her, Ishild, and Ermendrud away from me, to Euric, and likely safety. I would not give her to Hands, ever. But, I would trust Euric.

It was the beginning of Aprilis; the last vestiges of the snows were melting fast, the water was running in rivulets for the river, past year's dry leaves spinning along for the river, and none knew where they would end up. That was how it was with our lives as well.

While the village celebrated the beginning of the month of Eostere the goddess, Ishild fell sick, and could not travel.

CHAPTER XVI

Days went past, and she writhed in pain. It was a week after our child was born, and our entire household was packed and ready to go, but she was still sick. I fumed, worried, and forgot about the war and Father. While Fulcher, who was forever worried about my morals, must have thought this a great sign, I was doing nobody any favors by letting Burlein work on our plans alone.

However, I was a father, and felt a changed man.

The truth was, I was not thinking about the songs echoing in the halls, praising me. I was not thinking about Hulderic's or Mother's pyre, or even Wandal's plight. I was an Oath Breaker, and I was breaking my oaths of vengeance. I felt worry and love for the little, exposed girl, and I think I was finally an honorable man, for the first time in my life. None saw it, none knew about Hraban's changed soul, except for the people around me, and I was happy with myself. Even if deadly worried.

Yet, life did not stop and wait, as I loved Lif.

A delegation of opportunistic traders came to Grinrock, which was a testimony to the lack of surprise in the warfare we were to engage in. They knew Burlein was gathering precious food, and apparently the motley crew of traders had left Moganticum discreetly to trade with the Marcomanni. They were mostly Mediomactri Gauls, led by a big, smiling man of strange origins, his face as dark as a lightless cellar. They put in to the harbor with the assurance of a conqueror.

It was my birthday, and I peered at them from the corner of my house, nervous to the bone.

Cassia found me staring at them, and I noticed she wanted to speak with me, but I shook my head at her. She nodded, unhappily. She had been nervous all week, helping sick Ishild tend to the baby. Cassia had insisted they leave without her, with or without proper guards, but I had denied her that. Ishild would be needed; she was Lif's mother. Gunhild had attended her, and Cassia had had many arguments with Gunhild, one terrible one, and the house had been an unhappy one, except for the gentle little babe.

Many men came to wonder at the Roman style river ships, navis onaria, the sleek hulls with a single bank of oars, for all Germani love ships. While not clinker-built like ours, and susceptible to sinking in the rock-infested rivers, they were deadly fast, and could reach even the shallowest shores. The goods they carried to our winter-savaged village, mostly food but also the fine examples of swords with exorbitant prices, pieces of leather and iron mail, even fantastic fruits not seen before, made the whole wet season like a fine feast. They were terribly greedy men, yet the winter makes any man a generous customer. They were doing a brisk trade with our lot, the men who had stolen much of the wealth in Hard Hill. You could not eat gold and silver, so our men paid anything asked of them.

Men flocked through the deep forests for the traders, including many of the higher warlords with their guards and champions and even the humbler chiefs, who would take part in the war against Maroboodus, all bringing their retinue days earlier than Burlein had requested. The Hermanduri would arrive in around week. With the Marcomanni came dozens of eager women, and rowdy children, and they all yelled with surprise and joy. The ships brought with them strange short men, who's antics made everyone laugh helplessly. There was also a massive man, dark as night, very like the captain of the group, able to break boulders on his chest, a feat some of our warriors attempted, maiming one of them hopelessly.

I joined the groups of men exploring the wares set in the harbor; I browsed the rare jewelry, and found things of delicate beauty on the long tables. A well-dressed Gaul sold me a silvery brooch, with a raven and a flower, and I left the market and gave it to Ishild. She took it with thanks, as happy as a sick woman can be, and there were tears in her eyes. I left her to recover.

Then, Burlein called for me.

I went to him, and found him drinking happily and toasting with some of his men and the Hermanduri chiefs. The Hermanduri ambassadors who preceded the army were there, tentatively joining the feast, having groomed themselves. They still looked a savage lot, men of the deep hills and woods, tall and gangly, dangerous and treacherous. He gave me a twisted horn full of precious wine, which I smelled carefully. His wide face was like that of a man who has managed to empty his bowels after a week of pains. He leaned over me, smiling hugely, tears in his eyes. 'Hraban, I am sorry but you are an orphan. Try not to cry! News from the Gaul.' He pointed a finger at the sleek, dark-haired and skinned man, with a rich tunic of red. He nodded at me, his eyes glinting. Burlein roared happily. 'They visited Hard Hill. In fact, they were going to set shop there, but the hill was in mourning, for your father is dead! He died, and I killed him! The wound I gave him, last year? It festered, it rotted, and the man died an unworthy death. They saw him! These men … many other saw him! Pale-faced corpse of a man, blood dried on his lips and chest. We will ride! We will ride, and clean his men out of the lands. Hail Woden for this joy! The Hermanduri will get their due, of course.' The hard men from far east smiled at Burlein stiffly, saluting his promises, and I shook my head softly, determined not to rest until the sly bastards were gone.

My father was dead.

The thought left me subdued. I wanted to see him burn, with my own eyes, and I wanted to piss on the embers of his burial fire. It felt unreal for the man to have died so easily, without the carnage his sword and treachery usually caused. There would be no heavy shield wall, rent spears and butchered corpses, widows mourning for their lost ones.

There would only be a … change.

I drank with Burlein, and nodded at him. 'Have your own men seen this?'

He nodded, entirely drunk, but pulled me close and pointed at a man, and I knew the man. 'He hitched a ride with the traders. He was there all winter, and saw your father wither away. Gunnvör! Tell him!' Our eyes met, and it was the man in a fur cap, the one who had shot Guthbert. Gunnvör nodded at me, merrily hoisting his cup and grinned. I answered his greeting, grunting.

'And, for the proof,' he laughed, 'here!' He gave me a large thing wrapped in a blanket of wool. It was a sword. I opened it up, anticipating the sight.

It was Hulderic's sword.

It was my grandfather's blade, the one I had coveted all my life. The ancient blade of the Gothoni, old as our ring, the blade that had rent my face.

Maroboodus was surely dead.

'He stole it?' I asked.

'Yes,' Burlein said. 'Took it off his cold, dirty fingers. Hah!'

'They did not guard him?' I asked Gunnvör.

'They did guard him,' he chuckled, and patted his bow. He took two bracelets from his pouch, heavy golden ones. 'These I took for myself from the guards.'

I swallowed in anger, and nodded at him as I stroked the blade. I hated Father, but looting his body did not seem honorable, and I blithely forgot I had wanted to piss on his skull. Yet, I was his son, and felt that was my right. But, Gunnvör, he was a nobody. Nonetheless, I drank with them, enjoying as they enjoyed, the small men entering at some point, their ridiculous antics making men laugh, but I left soon, worried. It was my birthday, after all, and I felt very, very uneasy as I stroked the blade in my hand.

He must be dead. He would never willingly let go of the blade. I turned it in my hand as I went home.

It was very late evening, and Ishild was likely sleeping with the baby. She still occasionally bled after the birth, and she was uncommonly weak, barely strong enough to walk. I could not sleep, nor did I try. I stopped before I entered the hall, and gazed forlornly at the harbor. There was a feast, a happy merrymaking outside in the harbor area. Women were laughing, furiously celebrating, it seemed, for their men and sons would be spared the spears of the north. Gods seemed to be on our side. I hated myself for my doubts as I sat in the dark, fingering the damned blade. It did not make me happy, and I had loved the blade. No, it felt malevolent. It felt cold, like I was petting a half-frozen snake, about to spring up.

It did not feel like mine.

It whispered warnings to me, with the rasping voice of Grandfather, stern and kind, but reprehensible, nonetheless, for he was dead and I was hearing things. Hands and even Shayla, warning me of my birthday? Wyrd, said Ishild? Was it our Wyrd to go seek Wandal, free of my father? Or was there something else afoot? Where was Nihta? Where were his men, who would likely pay their respect to their fallen lord, and try to smite down the men who killed their master? It was a man's duty. I turned and went to the main hall. Cassia was sitting there, alone as well. She nodded at me, and she held a precious axe, one she had worn the day we killed Leuthard. 'I cannot sleep,' I told her, glancing out of the door toward Burlein's hall. 'They are all celebrating. Tomorrow, you must take them away.'

She said nothing, until I sat next to her. 'We are mostly packed,' she told me nervously, wringing her hands. 'Have been for a week. All the gear is in the stable. I asked Fulcher to pack some more rations, and prepare the household so you will manage. For the war,' she added, as she saw me look at her with a question.

'For the war, right,' I said, looking at her. 'You know there might not be one?'

'I heard. I am sorry,' she said.

'Sorry? Need not be, if it is true,' I said, 'yet ... ' She did not say anything, nor react in any way. I poked her, and she scowled at me, her pretty face screwed in anger. I smiled at her. 'You do not think he is dead.'

She shrugged. 'I am not a man. Not a warrior. I have neither sight, nor spells. Nevertheless, I do not like rumors. Trust is for the peasants, and rulers must see the corpses of their enemies with their own eyes. This is a warm wrap, made of sheepskin, and should keep her warm.' She nodded at the table, and I took up the warm clothing, fingering it. I grunted thanks for it was for the baby. She smiled wistfully. 'Spring brings ever strange tides, Hraban. It is always so. Rarely good ones, save for the sun. I hope that will keep her warm. Even if Ishild does not wish to leave.'

'What do you mean?' I asked with a tired shake of my head. It had been an unhappy hall that week. I wanted no more quarrels between them, though I was not sure what they had quarreled about. 'You have tried to speak with me, but I have not listened. So spit it out now.'

She snickered. 'Oh, now? Yes, why not? Gunhild is a fool, Ermendrud hates to travel, and Ishild, whom Gunhild thinks is too weak and weary to travel, is a liar.'

'Liar? Are you saying she is pretending to be weak?' I scoffed as I looked at her.

'Yes. I have seen plenty of births—'

'Come, now. I doubt she would fake weakness. Why would she?' I reasoned. 'She bled so much. She was very, very hurt. You told me she will never have—'

She rubbed her temples, as if trying to explain something to an idiot. 'She bled like a pig, Hraban, but so do most others. It was not as terrible as the idiot Gunhild made it sound,' she fidgeted, agitated by the discussion. 'Life begins with birth, and hers was hard, and hurtful, but she is strong, and able to travel. Has been for days. But, she says she cannot, that she is too damned weak.'

'She is weak, Cassia, and I think you are paranoid,' I told her sternly.

'Really? So why does she sneak out when the night comes?' she asked me with bitter amusement.

'She what?' I asked.

'Sneaks out. At nights,' she told me. 'She meets with someone.'

'She is too weak to walk,' I insisted.

'Ah, well, then she has crawled out this very night, for she sure as Hel is not in her bed. Oh, before you panic, she leaves the baby here. I make sure of that.'

'What!' I asked, and rushed to her room. I opened the door briskly, scanning the room with puzzled fear. *It was true,* I thought. She was not there; nothing was in the room. I checked under the bed, unwilling to believe what was before my eyes. I walked back out, and leaned over Cassia with a scowl, as she grabbed her axe hilt. I stared at her in shock. 'You would pull that on me?'

'Only if you don't believe me,' she said frankly. 'Was she there?' she asked sweetly.

'No, she is not there, and I admit you might have a point. I have kept an eye on her before the birth.'

'But, not after, for she was too weak to be a danger. Moreover, you were too happy, you utter idiot,' she told me. 'You failed.'

'Where is she?' I half shouted. 'Since you seem to know so much about her.'

'Ermendrud and I have been keeping our eyes on the baby, Hraban; she was your responsibility,' she told me brusquely. 'But, if you must know, they have seen strange men lurking in the woods these past days. Not Marcomanni. Not the men of the north, or the south. Ragged. One was found dead. He was ripped open, gnawed upon.'

'Men are found dead all the damned time, Cassia. And there are strangers and ruffians all over the woods.'

'This one was devoured. Ripped and torn.'

I laughed. 'Wolf? Bear? You are saying Ishild eats men?'

She nodded, afraid to the bone. 'This was happening in Hard Hill, remember. There is something out there that is not sane, not ... like us. But, the corpse is not the point, it is the fact he was out there and looked like those furred filthy shit-bags Odo orders around.'

'You saw the corpse?' I said softly.

She nodded. 'I think Ishild is trying to get back to Odo.'

I sat down heavily. It was true she had an obsession about Odo, the gaunt, dirty mongrel of a vitka, her brother, and the bastard who wanted to make a child with her, and who wanted me and the ring for the prophecy. 'If she is trying to get to Odo, if she is meeting with something out there, why didn't she just go? It's not like we could have stopped her.'

She leaned forward. 'That is why I am watching the baby.'

'And he wants her, not Ishild alone,' I nodded. 'If this is true, she must be desperate.'

'She won't take the baby,' she said grimly. 'Besides, didn't Odo also want you?'

I spat in anger and nodded. 'I do not know if you are right,' I told her gently, 'but I thank you for thinking about Lif. And me.'

She looked away. 'Yes, yes. And I still do not think your father dead. Nor do you,' she said casually, now looking at the sword in my hand. 'That sword. Evil. The Winter Sword, I call it, cold and deadly, full of deceit. It has lost its master before, and now you have it. I do not trust it. Nor do I trust your father. So, go and find out if we are in trouble, will you?'

'I will try to repay you, Cassia, one day,' I told her as I got up. Her eyes glimmered in the dark as she got to her feet, her womanly shapes brushing past me.

She smiled as she turned. 'I will go to Ermendrud and the baby, and see how they fare. She will make a terrible mother for Wandal's children. She is constantly fussing over her small problems. As for paying back, I would like to be considered a friend, Hraban. Friends help each other. I'll also alert Ansbor and Fulcher. I have a bad feeling.' I nodded and squeezed her hand, and she smiled as she went, letting go of me.

I pulled on a stiff leather shirt, and then Leuthard's former mail. I looked at my old Athenian helmet as it was staring back at me from the table. It was whispering unworldly things to me, of like mind with the suspicious sword, and spoke of trouble. I hoped the night would end and morning would come, my birthday gone.

I picked up the grinning helmet, and hiked for the harbor. It was very late.

The Gauls were still there, as they should be, for no sane men rowed the river in the dark. But, when I looked at the ships, I noticed there was a nervous bustle on the decks. Things were being packed and moved off the shore to the pier, then to the ships, and the items on sale were growing few. A small Gaul in a leather hat and a large featureless cloak was gathering coins from the sales, and their dark leader, tired now and smiling less, was pointing toward the hall of Burlein. Evidently, they paid a tithe of their sales to the lord. Burlein was not wise with money, I had learnt, but was making some profit from the merchants. A wise trader knew whom to please, especially if the lord was to lead the whole nation of the Marcomanni.

I waited in the shadows, uneasily, brooding over Cassia's words, and wondered as one of the small men walked by, throwing colored wooden balls up in the air. I decided I had waited and brooded enough and roughly grabbed him, the balls falling all over the road. I dragged him near empty shed by the riverbank. Amidst his many shrill protests, I pushed him against a weak plank wall and scowled at him from inches away. He scowled back and laughed.

I slapped him.

'Hey! You cannot hit me; I am smaller than you!' he shrieked.

I slapped him again, much harder, and he yelped and cursed softly.

'Bastard elk humper,' he said in bad Latin, and I corrected his pronunciation, though mine was not perfect at all. His eyes rounded in panic, knowing what to expect, and I rewarded him and struck him again, this time balling my fist and driving it to his belly. He threw up violently and I placed a foot on his back, pushing him to his vomit, holding him down like a landed trout.

'Now. Questions,' I told him.

'Why is your mother a filthy prostitute? Why do you smell of old sweat, even older piss, and fresh fish, all intricately mixed up together?' he tried, and before he could ask another one, I stepped on him hard, so hard he flattened on the ground with a crunch, and groaned in panic as his leg thrashed wildly.

'All right! Ask! Your turn!' he whimpered.

'Where did you come from?' I asked as I kicked him.

'From our mother's cunts!' he said stubbornly. I drew Nightbright, and frowned at a pair of boys peeking at us from behind a corner, and they disappeared.

The small man sobered as he turned his head to look at the sleek blade on his face. He nodded his head. 'Sorry. A bad habit! Yes. From Moganticum.'

'Not Hard Hill?'

'Yes, but Moganticum is our home!'

'Who are you?' I asked.

'We are a travelling group of actors! The best in Greek drama,' he said proudly and adopted a look that he apparently thought passed for an ancient Greek hero, or a fool. I pushed the blade closer, and he went quiet and abandoned the heroic face in favor of a meek one.

'The best in the backwoods of Moganticum?' I sneered.

'Best in Moganticum, certainly!' he explained. 'This mud is cold, and there is my dinner here as well, so can I—'

I poked him, drawing some blood from his nose, and he was happy in the cold mud and the remains of his dinner.

'Who are the Gauls who do the trading bit?' I took my foot away, and he stayed put. He learnt slowly, but he learnt.

'I do not lead the troop, nor am I friends with the big, dark man and his Gaulish friends; I just followed them onboard when they paid us to join them.'

'Why would traders in fine arms and precious food want a troop of horribly bad actors with them on a trip to a dangerous shore?' I inquired.

'Your hairy kind have never seen a good act; it is good to have men amuse your customers, for they pay more that way. It is unfortunate for the actors. We have to endure the smell of men sleeping with their cows, and the cruel pinches of their mongrel children,' he sniffled in indignation.

I laughed at him. 'I suppose so. No, do not get up. I laugh when I kill men, so we are not friends yet.'

'Fine, my lord, fine!'

'What did you see while visiting Hard Hill?'

I walked around him, grouching and looking at him from above. He shuddered and answered quickly. 'There was a ruined hill, with burned buildings and a somber number of half-starved people! A king dying. Not a few days past,' he said carelessly.

'A king?' I asked.

'A mighty lord! King or a lord. A strong body he once had, now broken! We were called in to a meeting with him, to make him happy. He barely moved; he did not see the act!' he said. 'Though he paid.'

'He is sick then? Not dead?' I asked with alarm. 'I thought the Hill was in mourning?'

'It mourned later! We held a play for him. Then, when we finished, he choked out a gout of thick blood and did not move, even when they tried to rouse him. He died, and they cried. Placed his sword in his hand and wailed. The dark Gaul grumbled, and wanted to come here to trade. Lots of silver here, he assured us!' he said, daring to look up to me.

'Very well.' I let him go, gave him a bronze coin, and the dwarf thanked me. 'More than you deserve, if your plays kill lords.'

'The lord gave me a silver coin before he died. Perhaps you can give me the same? He was not as wealthy looking as you, his locks gray and face dirty,' he said slyly.

Gray. Not red like father.

I felt my stomach churning. 'Do you know why they went to Hard Hill first? Surely they knew it was ravaged?' I pulled out a silver coin.

He shrugged. 'Now that you mention it, they did not even unload the merchandise. Did not make many coins from the lord. I suppose they charged something from the men who boarded the ships there.'

'What kind of men? A man with a furred cap? Archer?' I asked, as I threw the silver to him. 'Do not try my patience.' He was holding out his hand for more, and put it down.

'Him, yes, and his friend. A small man, short, neat beard, moved like a cat,' he said, shrugging, uncaring. 'Held a Roman sword under his tunic, armor. Warrior. Running from his dead lord. Probably has enemies.'

'Did he come with you?' My heart was racing. 'To this town? In here?'

'Both did, but I have not seen them in the crowd. Wait, the fur cap was with your lord Burlein, when we performed. He was there with the dying lord in Hard Hill as well. Not sure where the small one is,' the man said with a chuckle, and judged his own height ludicrously. 'I'm big enough down there,' he assured me.

I ran off, leaving him stupefied, groping in the mud, because I ran over him in my haste.

In the muddy shore, the merchants were pulling off, waving lanterns, having packed their last gear, and the dwarf ran for his life, screaming for them to come back. Men laughed at him, but the men on the ships ignored him, their faces grim. I turned around to look at the crowds. I did not see the man, the archer, and our former spy in Hard Hill. Gunnvör.

The man who had arrived with Nihta.

The hall of Burlein was not far. I jumped on a horse, the owner cursing me for a filthy thief as he ran after me unsteadily and deep in hic cups, hanging on to my foot for the moment it took me to kick him off. I rode like a feverish maniac, kicking the horse so hard it neighed in fear and pain. Mud flew crazily as I navigated halls, begging no child should get in the way. At the hall, I jumped down and drew Head Taker, holding it with both hands. I considered Nightbright, the lighter blade, but I missed my shield and the reach of the heavy killer blade gave me comfort. My helmet gleaming in the torchlight, as I stalked for the door. Then my heart was racing, for a guard was dead in the nearby shadows, nothing but a bloody heap, his belly cut and the guts steaming on the muddy ground.

I entered the hall to see my hopes die.

Nihta and Burlein had fought, that much was obvious.

He was not caught unawares, or alone. The savage Hermanduri envoys had been feasting there, and had tried to defend him, but they were dead. One had an arrow in his head; the other one was as pale as snow, artery slashed in his leg as he was stretched on a table. In the corner, the dark part of the old hall, a struggle was going on. A man was hissing soft encouragements to another, who was weeping, struggling, holding on to a blade of a gladius that was deep inside his belly. The dying man's eyes turned to me, and I shuddered, as it was Burlein, his eyes terrible. He was gibbering in fear. His hair was matted with blood. He was constantly being pushed to the bloody floorboards by the murderer, even if he pushed back up bravely.

'Hraban!' Burlein said with a sob, and the man holding the gladius turned to gaze at me.

It was Nihta.

It was the lithe man I had known, the man with sharp eyes and a lean face, trimmed brown beard and a small frame, deadliest of the deadly, a former slave and Maroboodus's lieutenant who had trained me, who had been a friend, sort of, but who had no heart, no more than my father. His eyes flickered to the end of the room, away from me, and I instinctively went to my knees as an arrow thunked to the doorway, spinning out to the darkness. It was Gunnvör, the traitor, and he pulled another arrow, his face betraying shock at my rage.

For it was rage that was hammering in my temples, Woden's Dance filling me with animal-like speed as I turned towards him.

'Bastard,' he hissed, 'fame stealer, coward. I killed Guthbert, and they made a song about you? Shit walker. Die.' He pulled the arrow back and then fell back. The Head Taker had sliced into his temple, splitting his skull as I had charged him with vengeance, scrambling forward with berserker speed. I grunted over him, laughed at his dimming vision, and grasped and freed the blade with two hands as I turned for Nihta.

Oh, gods, how I feared, despite the rage hammering in my heart.

Burlein was gone; his fingers sliced through as Nihta pushed his gladius maliciously to Burlein's chest and out, leaving no doubt the last lord of the south was gone. He wiped the blade crudely on Burlein's face, smearing him in thick blood. The blade glinted dangerously. He regarded me as he moved to the light of the hall. He had grown a bit thinner, a touch more merciless. There was cold disdain in his voice. 'Hello, boy. It does look like your father Maroboodus is again the one Marcomanni lord who can make this shitty tribe achieve something more than growing ugly, small cows.' He swished the sword in the air, droplets of blood hitting me. I said nothing, just staring at Burlein's face, feeling sorry for him, and for our lost friendship. 'Did you two get close?' Nihta asked, walking around me, nodding at Burlein's direction. 'Is this terrible for you?'

I nodded at his coaxing, Woden's rage thrumming in my head. I hissed at him and laughed in his face, braving the terrible warrior's wrath. He was a snake that was now slithering around me. 'He was a fine friend. Better one than you turned out to be,' I told him, as I turned with him, the Head Taker anxious in my hands. I would die. I would die in an eye blink, and the rage would drain, leaving peace, but I wanted to live, and I was very confused as I faced the nightmare of any warrior, a practiced killer with rare gifts with a blade.

'He is not vengeful, Hraban, despite the surprise you served him. Your father, that is,' he faked a lunge at me, but I ignored him.

'Is he not?' I questioned, as his eyes laughed at me. We had sparred many times, but this would not be a game. 'I'm disappointed.'

'No,' he told me matter-of-factly. 'He told me to slaughter you, and make it as quick as it pleases me. He has bled you once, you see, and there was no challenge in it. So, I shall do as he asks. I shall kill you as quickly as it pleases me. Perhaps not as quickly as one might hope, but certainly it is not going to last for hours. Minutes, perhaps. Oh, that scar must be nice, they tell me. Gives you character. Show it to me.'

'Come then, my former friend,' I laughed spitefully. 'Come and see it.'

'You don't have a wolverine around? Or help, like you did with Guthbert? No?' he asked scornfully.

'No, I am alone, like I was with Vago and his son,' I spat and cursed him profusely. 'You gave me a sword to fight Odo. I thank you for that, though I doubt it was given because of compassion. No, you have none, Nihta. You are an empty husk of a soul, a turd on the snow, a worthless creature no real men would toast with, causing misery where you go,' I told him. 'And you will not take Gunhild and her baby.'

'Ah, the child that carries the blood of these traitors. That is ill news for the baby, another one for Maroboodus to hate,' he laughed, 'after he is reunited with her.'

'He won't be,' I spat.

He laughed happily. 'You are a tenacious, surprising little pawn. Odo and his mad schemes, you and your willingness to hang on to something that was never in your reach, like a father who is Roman with Roman agendas. You think yourself so special you will not give up,' he mocked me. 'You are a fool, boy. You could be somewhere else, living a happy life, but instead, you run around these lands, trying to slay men who are as high above you as the clouds are to a rat.'

I shook my head. 'Vengeance is a dish even a rat enjoys. I find it sad that you have no such passions. The Semnones who crushed your family? Do you not think about them at all? Nay, you are but a tool, and tools have no meaning. You are an obstacle between my father and I, and soon it will be a family affair, and you will be dead.'

Nihta stiffened and licked his thin lips. 'I keep my oaths, Hraban. You do not. Now, where is Gunhild?'

'She is safe,' I lied, for I had no idea where she was.

He nodded grimly. 'No man or woman is safe tonight, my little raven. All oaths will be held tonight, the ones broken avenged. Tell me where she is, and she will be spared, at least.'

'I—' I began, but his words were just a nasty ruse, and he scuttled forward so quickly a lighting would have been left gawking. He appeared there, in front of me like a wraith, his face brutally twisted as he thrust his sharp sword forward. I was still hearing Woden's Dance, the battle rage giving me heightened reflexes, the heat of rage churning inside, but despite this, I could barely follow the blade. I threw the Head Taker into a sweep before me as I stepped back, dodging as well as I could and slashed my blade at him. He was nowhere near, and I rolled away, hearing the blade part air where my face had been. 'Gunhild deserves peace, not the mad bastard's tender affections,' I told him savagely and attacked. 'And you will meet Guthbert and his ugly brother, if a heartless man is even accepted in Valholl.'

He played with me like a sated cat swats at a mouse. Some of it was like the times when we were training. I tried to conserve my strength, to hold back the rage inside me for it would not help with Nihta. It would only force me into mistakes for him to exploit. I grew tired as the armor was heavy, and he was so good it was hard to understand. There were terrible heroes and famed champions running wild in our songs and stories, but this small man was closer to legends than any man you knew from the stories.

'Drop the blade, Hraban. It is too heavy for you. Perhaps you should use your teeth like you did with Vago?' He cackled as he danced left, then right, and then right at my face and under my blade.

His hand clipped my chin. I stumbled back and twisted desperately as he jabbed at me, splintering the wall under my armpit. I kicked away, rolling, dropping as he laughed and slid after me, always so I had to turn, turn. I despaired, for I would only very rarely get a stab of my own his way. Whenever I tried to hit him, the blade danced around me and I took hits and scratches in the chain mail and my helmet. I did the best I could to keep my feet and arms away from his deceptive moves.

I defended, ran and dodged, sweating, the rage playing futilely inside, for this man was greater than any berserker. Soon, I would have to take risks, as I was tired, and he was not, and he expected each one of my few futile stabs and slashes. This became evident when I staggered and a deceptive stab at my feet turned to an upward slice, which nicked my throat and he hissed in anticipation. 'You need the chaos of a battle to kill me, boy,' he laughed and came at me again, enjoying himself. 'I will find your Ansbor next. And any cur that follows you. The women I will give to the Gauls; oh, they will enjoy them.'

I swallowed and roared, pushing at him, dodging a slash, and tried to think of something that would save my life. I felt my throat, trying to decide if the blood oozing on my chest was from a fatal wound. Likely not.

'Come, Hraban. You do well against most men, even more experienced ones thanks to the gift Woden has given you, but you are no match for me, burdened with armor. Die on my blade now, and I'll tell your father it was a hard fight.' He looked serenely composed, and I remembered something. The last time I had seen him angry was when Odo had probed into his past. He had lost control then. In addition, had not Nihta himself told me to find the weaknesses of one's foe, if one can, much before a battle?

I might know his.

I grinned at him bravely. 'I am rather burdened by armor than shame. Do you know what the men say when I tell them the champion of Maroboodus has been a man whore for his former Roman slave master? A pleasure boy? Do you?' His eyes narrowed as his serenity disappeared, and I came forward, slashing with the Head Taker. He blocked it casually, kicked me back savagely, stumbling as he did and came at me, his eyes wild. I fell away, breathless, as his sword clanged on my helmet. 'They ask me if the woman was a beauty? I say no, she was no woman, it was a *man*, a fat, wart-ridden Roman master, part *Celt*, perhaps? Imagine their surprise and disgust as I tell them you enjoyed it, while he was humping away at your ass in front of the other slaves,' I mocked him, watching his reaction, which was no longer that of a cool-hearted killer, but one who would charge headlong at a shield wall, risking all.

And so he did. Nihta did.

He attacked, his face a mask of fury. He was very, very fast, and my helmet deflected one attack again. I thrust back, puncturing his tunic, but he did not care for his danger, pushing me back relentlessly, snarling. I was panting very hard now, but found strength to slice and dance out of his way, and a swift overhead cut of the Head Taker took a hank of his hair. 'I tell them that you liked it so much you chirped at his feet, thanking him as he was cleaning himself up, and you were hugging his knobby knees, a pitiful, sated thing. Roman ways for Roman dogs, eh? And the songs they sing about you? Have you heard them? Not one for fragile nerves and sensitive ears! Gods, the poets do make you seem like filth. For once, they do not lie!'

I dodged again as he roared, moving like a wraith, uncaring, trusting his speed. I rolled over a table, slipping on blood as he jumped on the table.

'They do not laugh; they shrug. They say you look like a woman, small and weak, pretty as a girl virgin,' I panted, and Nihta jumped down, slipping on the same blood. I stabbed the Head Taker down at the blur that was his torso, already regaining his balance.

He screamed like an angry spirit, recoiled away, rolling and panting. There was a ripping wound on his side, running to his hip. He looked at it in shock, grabbed a torch off the wall and threw it at me, readying to fight me to the death. I stepped back, prayed what I was about to do would save me, and I swung the blade at a latched door.

It opened, and the two hounds flew out, panting and snarling, and Nihta blanched. They both stared at him ferociously, and I could swear Burlein's corpse grinned. They jumped forward with a howl, latched their slavering teeth on his leg and arm, and he howled as they rolled on the hay. He roared; a dog whimpered and slumped to the floor, its neck broken. I charged him, but far too late as I saw him skewer the last hound through its throat. He aimed his gladius my way, shaking, cursing softly as he took stock of his wounds, retreating for the door. He shook his head, face pale from blood loss. 'Run, Hraban. Run. He will be after you. The man-eater. He has a job, Hraban, but he hates you and will come after you.'

'Who?' I asked, but he was gone, a trail of blood on the floor and ground outside.

'The man eater!' he yelled from the shadows, laughing wildly, and I charged outside.

Somewhere, ominous horns sounded. I ran out, thanking gods for Cassia's diligence. We would have to flee.

Maroboodus had come.

CHAPTER XVII

When the mournful horns blared, the revelry in Grinrock had reached the point of tiredness as drunken lords and their men were heading for their bedding. The night mists of the deep swamps and the woods always harbored secrets and beasts, but nothing made men feel more terrified than the sound of the horns, not so distant.

My father was not dead, nor dying.

He was there in the mists, sitting on a prancing horse, capricious and vengeful, and it would mean death and destruction. Only the fleetest and the wisest would survive to see the day. I swore, for I had not sent Ishild and the baby away in time, and now she was in danger indeed. I cursed and swore more. I was a perfect fool. I bade poor Burlein goodbye in my thoughts, mounted the horse I had stolen, and rode away wildly towards my house, praying Gunhild was safe, and Cassia had prepared our horses. Burlein was dead, and our dreams were dead, but we were not, not yet.

But, we would be, if we tarried.

I saw the harbor, where a hundred very confused, entirely drunken men were milling on the shore, some still drinking, wondering about the horns, and then suddenly aware of a distant rumble. A vast number of cavalry was approaching swiftly under the cover of the night and mists. I turned the corner only to see Fulcher galloping down from the house. Ansbor was riding after him, whipping a horse, and they were leading Ishild and the baby. Cassia was holding on to a horse's mane behind her, packed with our wealth and food. Ermendrud was mounting her horse, her face pale with fear. I gazed at Ishild, and decided it was the wrong hour to accost her for her absences.

Ishild shrugged. 'He is come, then.' Her face had no guilt or fear, and she pointed for the eastern woods. 'There will be chaos, and we must run.'

I was about to curse her when Fulcher grunted. 'Horns, Hraban. Cassia insisted they are not ours. What happened to you?' he asked as he regarded my bloody countenance. 'Where is Burlein?'

I waved him to keep his voice down, as men ran past. 'We need to run, now. Nihta killed Burlein. Do not ask me to explain,' I said, looking suspiciously at Ishild, who was not surprised by father's arrival, her face not betraying her feelings under a fur cap and tunics. 'Can she travel?' I asked, regarding Lif. I cursed myself for not having listened to Cassia. Or even Hands.

Cassia spat. 'Yes! You know she can!'

Ishild put a hand on the forehead of the child. 'If she is part of the prophecy, she will survive even this cataclysm. So, we go, Hraban. At least for a while. We must not be captured by your father.'

'Where is Gunhild? Have you seen her?' My horse started to prance as the horns sounded shrilly again, and the ground shook a bit.

'I have not seen her; perhaps the harbor? Burlein was going to buy some weapons, and she has his wealth,' Cassia told us. 'He is truly dead?' Her voice cracked.

'Yes, he is truly dead, and so are the lords of this village soon enough,' I spat, hating the traitors who put us in such a situation. That damned song, that stupid poem. Gunnvör had been robbed his fame, feeling his honor insulted. Like I had been by Father. Betrayed. But, I no longer cared for the fame, only Lif. I was happy I had managed to slay Gunnvör, at least. All around us, men were running for their homes, worried for their children, while others were convinced it was the Hermanduri arriving to join us for the war. Some had weapons, and they were staring at the mists carefully; nobody were leading them.

'Which way, Hraban? Quickly now,' Ansbor asked.

From the north, dark lines of horsemen rode up.

They were but shadows in the deep mist until the familiar standard could be seen emerging over a small hill. It was a red rampant bear on a dark cloth, and a wrathful man rode in front of it, wearing a helmet that was formerly Hulderic's, my grandfather's. The line stopped for a while, rippling into a shape, the horses prancing, the men enjoying the moment of surprise, the foe at their mercy, savoring the cruelty of the moment before the butchery begins. I guessed many were from the east, men Maroboodus had begun to train in the Roman way. They had unusual discipline and did not yell out, as would any other Germani army.

Then, they attacked, a thousand men.

All were hungry men, lean as hunting wolves and eager for revenge, for many had likely lost family in our rebellion. The men of Maroboodus poured into the village and the sloping banks of the river, their shields banging on saddles, thick spears and quick darts clutched in eager hands. Some carried fluttering torches and others bows. None were drunk. We had been lulled into a mortally false feeling of security, and now we were to pay as his men charged through the deep mists, scattering fumes and anyone who stood before them. They started to dismount and form packs of killers, and our men fled or fell before them.

It was my fault, I thought. I had been enamored by Lif, and had forgotten Father.

There were many men in Grinrock, but they were in no way prepared for a fight; most had celebrated all evening, some had no weapons in hand, and those who could, would fight in small, isolated groups. I gazed as a chief of Burlein's built a shield wall of drunken and tired men. Many others joined that wall, until a hundred and more were there, facing out from the harbor. They were backing off towards the woods, and Gunhild, to my horror, was amongst them.

My father saw her as well.

He yelled and screamed, and a group of two hundred bloodthirsty men formed around him, led by him and his fighters. He was in a rage, battle mad as a bloodied boar as he pointed his gladius at the retreating band. They dismounted and formed a cunus, a bristling column of spears. They did it uncannily quickly, horses bolting wildly, and the lot charged, my father's standard bobbling in the air above them, Father and his well-armored men aiming for the middle of the line.

The defenders yelled encouragement, shields banging on top of each other, men bracing, but the foe was brutal and strong, shields getting hammered by axes as the men met. Maroboodus's men were jumping on top of the foe, and breaking it in a jumble of sundered shields and stricken men. They started to butcher Burlein's men, who saw their chief dead, half his face missing. Screams filled the night as Hard Hill was avenged, blood spilled for bloodshed, insults answered with a point of spear. Women suffered in the shadows, fiendish laughter drifted through the town, most children were tied down for slavery, and oldsters butchered without emotion. The Gaul's Roman ships rowed back to the shore, the traders turning into slavers, ready to buy the merchandise with their newly made coin as warriors herded captives that way.

Fulcher and Ansbor were turning their horses around, looking for an escape. 'The woods, as she said? What the Hel else is there?' Fulcher asked desperately, but I did not answer. I saw Maroboodus walk towards Gunhild who was on her knees, apparently begging amidst the many dead and dying. Then. he struck her. Hard. She fell. and blood flowed from her face. I swore as the bastard dragged her off by her hair, her pregnant belly mocked by the men they passed. He would hurt her.

'Hraban! We cannot do anything! We must go!' Ansbor yelled at me while poking at my horse to get my attention. Finally, I nodded, spitting phlegm out of my throat. I longed to ride down and kill him, falling in the attempt, no doubt, but could not. I had Lif. I shook my misery away. as I stared around the strangely ethereal chaos around us. and there seemed no way out of the trap. Many wary men were riding around the perimeter, and they were not from the south. They were viciously herding back those who tried to escape, killing any who resisted. One spied us, riding closer.

'Take him,' I told my friends, and Fulcher screamed a challenge and rode to the man, who was not prepared for him. My friend speared him so hard it seemed he folded over the spear. 'We have to go, to the woods!'

Fulcher screamed, as another bearded man converged on us, but blanched and rode away, calling for more men.

It was a desperate escape.

There were fleeing people everywhere, wounded men fighting and rolling on the grass and sticky mud, sudden fires springing up, and all sorts of ungodly chaos. A group of Maroboodus's Marcomanni found us, and saw the women with us, hoping to capture them. They would be both very entertaining for the night and then, profitable in the morning. We nodded at each other, then to them.

'The women are ours. We are not going to share,' I told them, and the helmet and rich sword made them think they had made a mistake. One shook his head, trying to encourage the others to charge us, and I heard him whisper my name. So, we spurred the surprised horses at them. I slashed one out of the saddle while another fell to Ansbor's dart, but the rest charged us back, and my shield was torn apart by a vicious axe. One toothless man spurred for Ishild, seeing an opportunity. I screamed a warning at her, but my foe was skillfully guiding his horse before me, and I could not disengage while my horse was furiously trying to bite his.

More of Maroboodus's riders spied us from afar, some guiding their beasts our way.

We fought, we fought hard, and Fulcher finally killed one enemy in his saddle, Ansbor intercepted the axe man fighting me, clobbering him insensible from behind, and I turned to see what had become of Ishild, feeling terror to my bone.

Cassia was tearing an axe from a man's skull, bloody to her elbows, a fierce look on her face. She then mounted and grabbed Ishild's reins, as Ermendrud shook in fear and shame. The baby was crying. We rode like mad men and women for the deep shadows.

'You wounded?' I asked Cassia, as I spied her near me.

Cassia spat. 'Men tend to underestimate women. He ignored me, but that was fine. He did not see me coming.'

I laughed, but Ishild looked ill. I stopped and steadied her. 'Take the baby, Hraban. I cannot be sure I can hold on to her.' I did, cradling her gently.

'We must hurry,' Fulcher hissed from nearby. 'Must not stay.'

'Ride,' I told him, and pulled Ishild after me.

Ermendrud was up ahead, dodging a thicket. We plunged in to the woods, some fugitives following us, men on horses. Horns sounded angrily behind us, few raiders taking after us, but Ansbor pulled up and threw one dart to impale a horse that fell heavily on its side in to a tangle of roots. The rider howled in pain, and he hopped back towards the dying village. The rest scattered, and did not come near. The screams and crackle of fiery inferno behind us began to fade, as we rode hard. We went east as far as we could, then turned south. We soon spied the Marcomanni riding the far valleys, blocking that way, though we could not be sure if they were father's men, or men riding to help their lord. We could not risk it.

'North?' Ansbor asked dubiously

'Yes, that is the only way for us,' I told him worryingly, for that way took us deep into the lands of Maroboodus. In the west, the Hermanduri were coming, unaware of what had taken place, and no friends to us in any case. Therefore, we flew North like a flock of terrified birds, riding through flowery valleys and clear streams of the springtime, searching for a peaceful way out. We had four men with us. They were all looking back ruefully, all carrying shields and spears, survivors. My father was sure to look for us, and the Marcomanni living in the lands of the north would keep an eye out for us. We avoided all the people we could, and saw only a few, thankfully.

For now, we were flying free.

Cassia rode next to me that afternoon. 'He has not given up. I saw some men on horses not long ago.'

I had been looking around, but trusted her. 'I saw none. Where?'

'Behind us. Where are we going?' she asked, her pretty face worried.

I shrugged, trying to seem hopeful. 'I will ride to the lands of the Chatti. Then, I hope to find Tudrus the Quadi in the lands of the Sigambri.

Perhaps go northeast to the Cherusci. Any place where Ishild, you, Ermendrud, and the baby are safe,' I was scowling at the hills and woods behind us. 'I see nothing.'

'There as well,' she said and pointed at a low hill to the west, where a flock of birds flew to the air, angrily circling their disturbed home.

'Yes, I see. We will camp at night, and I shall go and see,' I told her.

We crossed some farms, the fields forlorn and ugly, and the cows were out after the long winter indoors. There were occasional riders, and most waved at us. They suspected little, but Father was sure to be on our trail.

Ansbor was grunting as he was observing the land around us. 'Wonder why they didn't take after us immediately? Surely they knew your helmet.'

'Father likely wanted to deal with the pressing problem,' I told him, thinking about Nihta's words. Someone was coming after me, for sure. 'He can lose anything but his hold on the Marcomanni. He had settling to do. Then, there are the Hermanduri, somewhere out there.'

'But,' he said, 'he should have sent men after you, harried you mercilessly.'

I nodded, not mentioning what Nihta had said. I gazed behind at our sorry troop, riding forlornly forward. The women, Ermendrud and Cassia, were calm enough, but Ishild was miserable. I handed the baby to Cassia, who took the small one happily enough. One man of the four was lagging, his face a red mess as he was bleeding from a cut. He slowed his horse, and I knew he wanted to go on his own way. I turned my face away, and let him go.

I rode next to Ishild, who was not saying much. 'Odo. You have met with him this week? During nights when the fools slept. Your friends.'

She said nothing, gazing ahead.

'Why?'

'I cannot tell you,' she told me with a small voice.

'Did you betray us?' I asked her.

'I did not, but when the time comes, trust,' she whispered.

I cursed and feared, for there were many men after us, and likely they belonged to my father and Odo both.

That first night, we stopped by a small pond. I sat next to Cassia and the baby. The small one was crying some, whimpering really, very gently, and it did not seem she was doing badly. I was fidgeting as I hesitated, giving Fulcher meaningful looks. He was nodding, and so was Ansbor, who was standing guard a little way off.

'You going to go back to see who those men are?' Cassia asked as she glanced at my horse, which had not been prepared for the night.

'I will go and see who they are,' I agreed, 'and then I will slit some throats, Cassia,' I said as I kissed Lif's hand.

'Slit one for me, and please remember to search them; we need food,' she told me in all seriousness. 'Oh, yes, be careful,' she added.

'Not sure how careful I can be, but I will try,' I said and patted Nightbright. I decided to leave the Head Taker with Fulcher. I watched the horse and then the fire. 'Where is Ermendrud?' The three men with us jerked up and squinted into the dark.

'That one blonde girl?' said one tall man. 'I do not see her. She was here.'

'She went to check on Ishild,' Ansbor said. 'Just there in the bushes. She was feeling sick.'

'Where?' I said thinly, as Fulcher's face grew alarmed. We rushed forward, the spears brushing aside some ferns, taking steps further into the darkness. Somewhere up ahead, I heard running steps, a person crashing through the underbrush. A curse, it was Ermendrud. Ishild had left us, and Ermendrud had taken after her.

'Woden's fiery shit, damn it,' I cursed. 'Make the camp ready, Fulcher. I will fetch them back.'

'Let me come—'

'Take care of them, with Ansbor,' I said with rippling anger. 'You two, come with me.' I pointed at two of the Marcomanni, who nodded.

'Has she left?' Cassia asked, with a told-you-so tone of voice.

'I'll fetch her,' I spat, and whirled my horse around savagely, and rode like a madman to the night, followed by the two men. I was cursing Ishild and cursing Odo, for I had no doubts about what, or who, was following us.

I tracked in the moonlight, finding broken twigs and a footprint, as I stopped by a copse of fir trees on a small hill, looking around carefully. There was not a trace of the women anywhere. I lost the tracks in the dark, and my companions did not see them either. The land was quiet, the wind fair and gentle, and stars twinkled across the sky. There were some fires burning all around us, signs of life. I sat on the horse for minutes, my companions growing impatient, all staring at the dark surroundings. I was feeling hopelessly anxious about the women in our lives. Then, a man appeared in a grove of wood, followed by another, not very far, both seated on ponies, or very small horses. I put a hand on my horse's mane, begging Tiw the beast would not neigh in greeting, and I sat as silent as a corpse. They were following something, and I bet these were the tracks I had lost.

I grunted and dismounted, led the horse aside, and tethered it to a tree. The two men followed suit. I pulled out Nightbright, and walked forward vigilantly, choosing a spot behind a large tree, one that we had passed. The men's voices could be heard in the night, hissing and whispering. One was very upset, and another was demanding something, in a surprised tone. There was an argument, a violent one as they shouted briefly, and then I heard Ishild answering. She was protesting, and I took a step forward.

'Show us their camp, now, and then we will go, not before,' said one man loudly and imperiously, and I froze. They would come my way. Soon, I saw them walking, pushing petite Ishild before them. She made a meaningless gesture towards the north, and the man behind her pointed his spear that way, making clear what he wished. They wanted to see us, scout our camp, and then they would heed her request.

To go to Odo.

Where the hell was Ermendrud?

'What shall we do?' asked one man, when I spotted Ermendrud, squatting on a hillside not far, watching the men. She was shaking with fear, but trying to conquer it, her face pale in the moonlight.

I grunted at the two men. 'Go and get her.' I pointed at her. 'Go, and do not alarm the two. I will deal with them, but keep Ermendrud safe.'

'Fine,' said the other one, grinning at me, and they sneaked to the dark.

The two men escorting Ishild walked briskly, and they were closer; I saw their faces and gear. They looked ragged, and were wearing animal furs and old clothing, and even their spears were untended and in bad condition. They were Odo's men from the north. Servants to their clan, from Gulldrum, or whatever it was. Cold shivers went through me as I stalked the men, trying to get ahead of them. Skull-faced Odo was coming for little Lif and me, and the idiotic, willing Ishild as well. Animal-like fear filled me, and I licked my lips, as they got closer. I would have preferred the men of my father, even Nihta to be there. Well, not Nihta, but anyone else. There was no running from men driven by a god. They would be heedless of danger, mad to the bone marrow. I managed to get ahead of the men, and waited as I saw they would pass me by. I leaned on a tree, hoping they would not smell me.

They did not.

The first man passed cautiously, stalking after Ishild, walking his horse, almost bent to the ground, swearing as he was trying to see any signs of danger. I let him pass, even when his horse sensed me and whinnied. The second man rode after the first one, tired and bored, picking at his tooth, for he only had one I could see. The horse ambled past me; I stepped up and stabbed the man in the side, pulling him down from the saddle. He was dead as a sack of barley.

I turned and faced the white, scared face of the tracker. He fumbled with his spear, but I shook my head at him. He looked at his horse, but I slapped it on the rump. It bolted madly.

I ignored Ishild, who was taking a small step backwards.

'Where is Odo?' I asked the man harshly. He shook his head dutifully.

'Odo. Where is he?' I said as I poked the sword in his face, drawing blood from a thin wound.

'Odo is near, and your brother and his man are the ones chasing you,' he told me, carefully.

'His man?' I asked, dreading the answer. Gernot and Ansigar. Both had escaped death, despite their wounds.

'A scarred man, Ansigar,' the creature answered carefully, confirming my fears. 'Bent as a storm-battered tree.'

'I was the storm. They want me, the ring, and the poor child,' I stated maliciously, glancing around in the dark that suddenly felt sinister danger looming near. 'And her.'

'Odo wants these things, yes,' he said, grinning briefly at my apparent fear.

I grunted as I quickly crouched and cut the tendons in his legs. He stared down in horror and shock, and then he tried to take a step, but the legs would not budge and he fell down on his face. He screamed himself hoarse, and Ishild watched me as I stood over the man, thinking. Finally, I turned to her. 'I will do the same to you, if you try to run again.'

'You hold me against my will,' she said, with a small whisper, holding her other arm with a clutching grip, scared. 'Why would you do so? I have my fate, and it is not with you. Never was. Not after you rejected me.'

'With Odo? Why? Don't you think now is the time to tell me? No?' I yelled at her until she shivered with fright. I kicked at the screaming man in frustration, and he went quiet. I stood over her, until I felt ashamed and turned away to check on the two men. I rummaged their pouches and the horse's bags, and took their food and a horse, which I gave to Ishild. Behind me, I saw a wolf look at the man from the shadows. It howled, and I heard it had friends. 'You will not run again.'

'Don't threaten me,' she whispered, wiping a tear. 'You do not understand.'

'No, Ishild, nor do I care to guess.' I spat, and she turned to look at the grove of wood the men had found her in. 'Where the Hel is she?'

'Who?' she asked. 'There is something up there.'

'Ermendrud.' I was gazing at the edge of the hill where the two Marcomanni had gone to fetch her. 'She was hiding there.'

'There is something else out there,' she whispered. 'I sense it.'

I took a deep breath, and guided our horses that way, Ishild clinging on to hers. There, a small clearing that was still, untouched and pristine. Then there was a tiny hissing sound in the night as wind ruffled through the hill full of wild barley. A fox was stalking its perimeter and somewhere up the incline, something hissed. It was a sibilant voice, full of malice, and I heard a crack, a meaty crack of bones. The hissing voice sighed, and spoke terrible words with a slur, almost singing. I had pulled Nightbright, as I listened to the voice.

'Whisper the pleading words in this deeper night and ask if you would:where is the morning's saving might?
Far, far from these chopped bones, my meal, that is what I shall tell you, and I will add:here there shall be no hope nor light.
Sleep, my mutton.'

I dismounted, and walked up the hill, Ishild in tow, Nightbright glinting in my hands. Up there, on the summit, a large shadow was hunched over a corpse, blocking the stars and the moon. I knew it was a corpse, for the arm was there by me, lying on the grass, drained of blood and gnawed on. The two Marcomanni were in sliced heaps near the shadow, one missing a head. The corpse jerked strangely as the thing tore at it. I was not sure if it was eating it, or just ripping it apart, sated by the very act of defilement. The thing raised its head as I approached, and it looked darkly furry, though much of that was filthy clothing. It rose up to its full height, though a bit stooped as it regarded us ferally. Its right hand was a mass of scabbed scars, looking like gray and scarlet rock. My heart was beating like it was about to burst through my chest.

It was a man, certainly, but one that was possessed.

It was horribly scarred, but the scars were not the cause of the man's debasement. This creature had been guarding the chosen of Lok, so commanded by Maroboodus, and I prayed to Woden for mercy. I thought something had crept inside him in that tower.

It was Leuthard, huge and menacing.

He chortled a bit as he regarded me, his hands still holding Ermendrud's flesh, and I nearly sobbed, as I stared at the near unrecognizable body. 'I am happy tonight, Hraban, but I am after you.

Don't you worry. We shall meet soon again.' Leuthard pointed a scarred finger my way, and loped away, nearly animal-like.

He was a possessed man. Mad.

I turned to regard the white-faced Ishild. 'What do you know of this?'

'He is your father's creature, Hraban, not Odo's. When I met with … Odo, that one was hunting the woods. He is looking to make sure you do not escape. Your father need not chase you. He set this hound on you. He has some other mission to perform as well for Maroboodus, since he spared you now. Some deed. Something for later. He is not stupid; don't underestimate him.'

'What deed?' I asked, as I wiped tears. Ermendrud was dead, and I cursed the words of Hands. Had I given Lif away and left a week ago, she might be alive. Others might die yet. 'Never mind. What is he? He is not human.'

She licked her lips. 'He never was, not fully. There are many creatures of the gods in Midgard. Many. Spirits, unhappy dead. And older things. You and I are of god's blood. He is as well.'

'Which god?'

She smiled wistfully. 'Lok's creature.'

'What?' I asked her.

'Lok sired many monsters across the Nine Worlds,' she said with a small voice. 'But, that one does not obey Odo, no. He is proud, chaotic. While Lok's creature, he does not serve him, willful, proud. He is—'

'Mad. And he now follows us for my father? As does Odo for me and Lif?'

She nodded. 'As does Odo. And I must go to him.'

'Ermendrud is dead. She was a friend,' I snarled. 'She was here for you.'

'Not my friend,' she murmured, looking down, and so it was that I struck her across the face, and she fell to the ground.

She lay there, shocked as I gazed down at her. I wanted to kill her, I truly did, but I stayed my hand. 'I regret you are the mother of our baby. But, then, you are no mother. No. You left her. You ran for the bastard. Why did you not take her, and leave us earlier?'

'Because,' she shrieked desperately, 'he demanded Lif. He demanded you! The ring as well. I only wish to give myself.'

'You kept us in the Grinrock, you did,' I hissed at her. 'And now, they will get us indeed.'

She pointed a finger my way. 'Fool. If we had left earlier, Odo would have captured us! Only with Maroboodus's men causing chaos across the lands did we have hope of escape. They had to retreat from the vicinity of the village, as thousands of your father's men attacked. Only so we could flee! And here we are!' she sobbed.

'You knew Maroboodus was coming?' I sneered.

'A fool would have known he is coming. Any fool, save you and Burlein,' she sneered back viciously, and got up, wiping her lip.

I shuddered at her words and spat, but she was right. I glared into the black, where my enemies were preparing. 'It is almost as if you wish to be humped by him. What are you, I wonder? Odo is your brother, you work to extract us from him, but you slink to him, knowing he will punish you. He will rape you. Yet, you go.' I spat at her feet. 'Go to him, then. Next time we meet, we shall not know each other. He will be disappointed you are barren. The prophecy is broken.'

She turned on wobbly knees, then struggled up and walked for the woods. She was sobbing, and glancing at Ermendrud's corpse and at me and at the edge of the woods, she turned. 'What is the one thing, Hraban, that can make a mother give up on a child, and a man she loves? For I do love you.'

'Madness?' I ground my teeth together.

'Aye, madness. Love for one's child is madness indeed.'

'You left her,' I told her bluntly. 'And I have asked for reasons for months.'

She smiled. 'You so worry he would bed me, Hraban. Odo. You have guarded me, been afraid for me, and you were happy when you heard I could never have more children.'

'I ... '

'You were happy,' she whispered. 'So happy. He would not whelp children on me, though you thought he would try. But, Hraban, my dear man, Lif is my second child. I have been a mother since I was thirteen, Hraban. I am a mother whose son is with the mad creature, my brother Odo. My son is not safe, no, never with a bastard who thinks of Lok and himself first. I fear for my son, so much I am gibbering with fear when none can see. Years ago, I was but a child really, I gave him the boy who will marry our Lif, should the prophecy come to pass, and a mother cannot let Odo raise him. So I have to go. Lif is safe with you, if you escape.'

'Why,' I asked bitterly, bewildered, 'did you not tell me?'

She sobbed, and shook her head. 'I do not trust you. You rejected me, remember? I gave my love to you, and you thought I did it to bewitch you. And after you left me? I was alone. Had you accepted me? I would have trusted you, loved you, we could have saved my son from Odo. Yet, it is wyrd you did not want me, and I was bitter. So bitter, hurt, alone. Bitter enough to sneak to your hut that night, and take you at least once. Now, that bitterness serves Odo, for Lif is in danger. I am a cursed woman, Hraban. Keep Lif safe. Trust, when time comes. Care for our daughter, as I care for my son. Goodbye, Hraban.' She ran to the woods, and left me there, with my self-loathing.

I fell on my knees, tears running down my cheeks.

I was an utter fool, a jester of the first degree, not unlike the small men we had laughed at. I was a joke, something the gods amused themselves with.

I had thought to save her from him, to spare her his filthy attentions, yet Odo had already raped her, when she had been helpless and alone, and I had been but a youth. I did not love Ishild, but had failed her as a friend. She was gone. Gone to her son, not Odo. Now, Odo wanted Lif and me, and they were very close. He wanted the ring as well. He would read the lines; drag me from one place to another until the prophesized events took place, and Lif would suffer. I would bleed on evil, rocky skin, I would then eventually find Veleda, and he would be there for his god's joy and freedom. Poor Ishild.

It looked desperate.

I still had a sword. I clutched it, and took comfort from it. No matter the sorrows and shit, it still stood between the bastards and me, and I would use it to cut off Lok's face, if I had to.

I walked up to the horrid mess on the hill, and looked down at poor Ermendrud. She had been afraid, then she had run bravely after Ishild, and now she was dead. It all felt meaningless to me as I stared at her. The corpse had no resemblance to the spirited woman I had known, the face cold and bloodless, eyes staring to the stars utterly uncaring of my sorrow. Flesh and bones. They were just building blocks, pieces of bricks and lumber scattered on the hill, and what she had been was gone.

I closed her eyes nonetheless, and shuddered in fear, as I thought of the animal Father had unleashed on us. I blessed Ermendrud softly, and ran down the hill and rode away, for we were in a desperate hurry. In the camp, I told them Ishild was gone, that Ermendrud and the Marcomanni were dead, and Odo was out there. I did not mention Leuthard. In the morning's pale hint, the softest of light, a stream of riders was approaching across the horizon.

CHAPTER XVIII

For a few days, we avoided them by riding hard. I risked much when I stopped by a long, rich hall. There, I told a young, battle-hardened chief of the raiders in his land. I pointed to their general direction, and he set about raising his men, happy for some activity, and forgetting entirely to ask who I was. Then, we rode away, and begged the lord would be enough to buy us time. It would not stop Leuthard, as he served Father, lord of the land, but Odo's ill-disciplined men would suffer, or at least be slowed down. We whipped our horses, and dared not rest for more than a few hours.

Leuthard's face haunted me, and while I realized the terrible man had turned into a possessed creature of nightmares, part of me wondered if he had always been one. I could not understand how he had survived that night we attacked the tower atop the rock. That Odo, and likely Gernot and Ansigar, were there after us, felt like a paltry thing indeed to endure, in comparison to the terror of the mad creature stalking us. Sometimes, there were signs behind us of a large number of men. Fires burned in the night, closer and closer. We would take a few hours of forced sleep, save for the one standing guard. We ate frugally in the saddle, and we were sore all over the place, and in a foul, frightened mood. Ermendrud's death and Ishild's disappearance merited explanation, but I had not been able to give it so far. Cassia had hissed at Ansbor to remain silent, as he pressed the issue.

For that, I was grateful. Their fate tortured me. She had a son. With Odo. She feared for him, and I feared for her, tired of running away. I glanced at the baby in Cassia's lap; sometimes fully awake, staring at the land around her with keen wonder, other times asleep, after sucking some milk from a gourd Cassia had secured. We would need more, soon. I worried for the small one, that she might fall, the fragile thing she was, as she was bouncing up and down, carried by Cassia. The horses were restless and powerful, and our need for speed dire.

Yet, despite all, we kept moving resolutely forward.

Finally, after two restless days and long nights, we were closing on the Moenus River, where we would cross to reach the troubled lands where the Quadi made their home. The Matticati had been thoroughly trounced not too long before, but Sibratus and Tallo would be fighting in the east, and the opportunistic Chatti and the merciless Hermanduri would take sides, or just their own. I would try to reach the Chatti, their capital Mattium being somewhere over the hills and vast woods, past many pastures and glittering lakes. It was desperately far away, and I was depressed as I regarded the river that ran East to West, my former home banks. Moganticum, the great Roman fortress, stood at Rhenus River, at the end of the Moenus River, and for a moment, I hesitated, thinking about turning our horses that way.

Then, the choice was taken away from us.

We heard a distant whinny of a spirited horse, and turned to look behind us. 'They are here,' Fulcher said softly, as we saw a group of forty riders crest a bridge, looking around. They were riding hard. They had a dozen empty horses with them, and I guessed the young warlord had made things interesting for them, at least. I hoped the man was alive. There were some twenty of the enemy, and men were riding madly from the woods, meeting them. One was gesturing wildly in our direction. They knew we were there, and the chase was on.

We rode for an hour, hoping to lose them again, but soon, we could see their first riders reaching for us, very close. A hunched figure was leading them, and I recognized Ansigar, my old friend, one of the Bear Heads, our childhood war party. He had ever been jealous of me. My grandfather had been the leader of the village, a famed warrior, and I had been the scion of the old blood, whereas he had only had the tunic on his back, and saw himself poor and unlucky. He chose to follow Gernot when they received their spear and shield, and ever since, he had guided and helped my brother in the service to Odo. Had they reached the riches and honor they imagined, I did not know, but should they capture us, Ansigar would not go unrewarded. Of that, I was sure. Of the main culprit, there was no sign, the red-headed scarecrow Odo was out of sight.

Nor was there any sight of Leuthard.

I saw Ansigar grin, his thin brown beard braided and whipping in the wind, his eyes in slits as he regarded our flight. I pulled on my helmet with one hand, nearly dropping it. Cassia was whipping her horse madly, holding on to Lif. I cursed the lot chasing us. I should have stabbed both Gernot and Ansigar when I had the chance, but I had spared them, and gods knew why. Then I saw also my brother. Gernot was there, behind Ansigar, heedlessly guiding his horse, the weak face featureless as he barked orders. The enemy spread out left and right. We heard their screams split the air, as we finally came to the muddy, rocky shores of Moenus.

It was early spring. The river was wild, devilishly unpredictable, and very dangerous, in a state that would make it hard to cross, even on a dry summer day. Sodden logs and debris were racing for the west. There were no bridges. There were no boats either. The crossing might be a suicide.

I looked at my friends helplessly and then behind us. We would never beat them.

'I would rather die with a blade in my hand,' Ansbor said, with a scared voice, glancing at the axe Cassia was holding, then pulled Leuthard's sword from his back. The blade was too heavy for him, and he had no training with it, but it was his. Fulcher was nodding carefully. I understood them, of course I did. Few Germani would rather drown, if death was inevitable, and there were spears to fall into, enemy to slay. I shook my head sadly. 'I also, but for Lif. So, I will attempt to cross. I will not force you to join me. Cassia, perhaps if you ride East or West, right now, they will not bother with you.'

She was licking her dry lips in fear, but shook her head, and guided her horse to the riverbank next to me, handing chortling Lif to me. 'Take the baby, Hraban. Keep her dry, out of the deathly water. Do so, for you are stronger than I am.' She guided the horse to the icy, turbulent river, the horse shivering and muddy up to its knees, and she cried out as the cold water enveloped her hips and legs. We were staring at the woman, and she scowled at us, her beautiful face glancing at the approaching troop of demons. 'Best come then. Will you follow me?' Then, she forced the horse fully in. She gasped as the water tried to kill her with its icy fingers, but guided the terrified beast across. 'Come, boys! We have had no bath for days!'

'She is mad, out of her wits,' Ansbor was whispering, fidgeting in his saddle. The last of the four fugitive Marcomanni snorted, as he whipped his horse after Cassia.

'No, she is braver than most men,' I grinned, prayed, and nodded at them.

I wrapped Lif with anything I could find, thanking the gods, and Cassia, for the sheepskin. Her tiny face was poking out from under the myriad of garments. 'Please, Woden,' I grimaced, and went after Cassia, holding the baby against my shoulder, guiding the horse with one hand and legs. Fulcher and Ansbor blanched at the desperation of it all, but they followed me, risking losing their place in the afterlife, the fine tables of the gods and goddesses, braving a trip to Hel's, or Rán's, kingdom. We rode to the cold Moenus, the tired horses faltering and neighing, but they started to swim instinctively, though we had to force them over rather than to follow the shore. Soon, beside me, Ansbor was gasping, and I struggled to hold the baby above the water as I was forced to lean forward.

'Are you fine? Can you make it?' I yelled at Cassia, who was swooning on the horse, her lips blue, and then I cursed as the horse turned sideways. I tried to turn the beast, but the current dragged the struggling animal downstream. I finally managed it, though it was near impossible. I saw Cassia's horse make it out of the river, dripping ice-cold water, shivering, and Cassia half-conscious on it, crying. My teeth were shattering from the cold, but Lif was chortling happily and I thanked Woden for that. Fulcher and Ansbor were next to me, their horses overtaking me. Cassia was glancing behind us, and she looked barely conscious and very concerned, as she looked at the evil men behind us.

Horses neighed, men yelled, and I heard soft curses and commands. An arrow flew by. The last of the four fugitive Marcomanni was struggling with his horse in the current, as an arrow hit the horse. The beast screamed like a human would and went under, and the man cried as he followed it. He disappeared under the surface.

I struggled, kicked the horse. Looking back, I saw Odo standing on the bank. The haggard creature was wearing a white, long tunic; oddly clean in comparison to his greasy red hair, his snake-like face staring at me maliciously. He walked forward, holding his hands out to his sides, barking prayers, and I knew whom he was praying to. He was casting some sort of a spell, or likely a curse, now using his wand, which danced in the air. He had some other men and women dismount, and joining hands, they started chanting. They tried to stop us, and I snorted at the fools. Some of his braver men guided their horses to the river's edge, but none tried to follow us.

'Hraban! Come! It is time to pay your debts now!' Ansigar was screaming, and I saw his face, savaged by the beating I had given him, his frame bent and crippled. I had whipped him so hard the bones had been bared. Apparently, I had hit him in the face as well, though I did not remember that. He was not crippled enough to be unable to use a weapon; he had a sword and a long bow, which he pulled out, nocking another arrow. Gernot was behind him, his missing hand wrapped in a red cloth, an unreadable expression on his face as he stared at me. Another victim of Father's, and of his own insecurities, I thought, as I tried to keep conscious.

An arrow splashed near me, and I heard Odo screaming at Ansigar. Dutifully, the next one smacked near Fulcher. They wanted me alive, and Lif as well. I struggled to get my horse across, but it obeyed, barely managing the current. Ansbor was nearly level with Cassia, reaching the shore, and Fulcher was behind me, trying to help me, while keeping a nervous eye on Ansigar, who was now afraid to shoot, for he might hit me. I had to look back, feeling familiar eyes on me.

I noticed Ishild's horse reach the bank, where the fur-clad men were milling. On her lap sat a boy of five years old. He was no ugly brute like Odo, but a blonde-haired boy with inquisitive eyes and a gentle face. Odo was stalking the riverbank, and pointed a finger at me, then snapped fingers at the men around him. Ishild rode to him, speaking gently, pleading, and he was silent as his men whipped their horses, dark-furred and dirty, long hairs streaming as they rode to find boats. He was coming; I would not be safe, and neither would Lif.

My horse pulled itself up from the water, stumbling, and I struggled to stay on it. Lif was only slightly damp, now crying gently, her eyes searching my face for reasons for all the insanity around her. 'We must go, for they have men searching for boats or rafts. They will be after us very soon,' Ansbor said weakly, looking at our former friend. Ansigar made a throat-slitting motion our way, dancing on the riverbank ferociously.

I turned the horse towards Odo, his eyes glittering darkly. 'You sister-raping, dirty mongrel! Bastard!' I screamed at him. 'Do not follow us, you damn filth.'

'Or what?' Odo yelled back. 'This is your wyrd, Hraban. Your wyrd is to serve us, and you shall not escape. Never you shall. Never could. We always knew that. We knew you when growing up.'

'And you will hound me to the end of eternity?' I told him. 'Threaten Lif and me?'

'Lif, you idiot, will marry my boy, and is safe and precious. I will only need you, and that ring. I know you have it. Ishild tarried and lied to keep you safe, gave you this gift of brief flight, but it is done now. Stop suffering, Hraban, and let this thing run its course.' I spat, and eyed Ishild, as I was shivering, trying to get the blood flowing in my limbs. Odo saw my look and smiled at her briefly. 'She will marry, Hraban.'

'You?' I spat.

'Gernot! She will marry Gernot for her lack of commitment to our cause. It is just, is it not?'

My brother made no move at that, his face still, but when Ansigar nudged him, he shuddered and nodded carefully. 'We shall share a woman, brother,' he called out.

'Come here, Hraban, and you will fight for her,' Odo smirked. 'Fight your brother for her virtues, and then submit to me. I shall hurt you. You have challenged me so many times, but you shall live a while, perhaps, knowing Ishild is safe.'

I considered it. Fulcher was trying to revive Cassia, but Ansbor rode next to me, wiping water from his neck, as he grabbed my horse. 'No. We will find a way.'

'We have been trying to find ways as long as we have fought them, but always we fail,' I sobbed, as I clutched Head Taker desperately, longing to go and kill the bastards.

'Then we have to wait a while longer,' he said. 'Ishild chose this; we must choose something else. Wait. We shall wait. I wish you had told us. What happened to Ermendrud?'

'He did not get her,' I told him. Leuthard had.

Fulcher was watching our discussion as he spoke, rubbing Cassia. 'This is not good. She needs help. She is blue and white in places. And the horses? Shit. They shiver, and are already exhausted. We should find shelter.'

'There is no shelter,' I told them hollowly, feeling Odo's eyes on my back. 'Let us find a place to die at.'

I began to ride for north. Cassia was behind me, half-conscious, Fulcher supporting her. Ansbor rode behind us, rubbing his frozen legs, his teeth chattering. I did not think about the inevitable. The Quadi in that land were gone. Villages were half empty, people afraid of war and terror. Few would aid us. Gods, I prayed for Adgandestrius, my Chatti friend, to appear again with a troop of his terrible warriors, but such miracles only happen once in life, and so I lost hope, even if my body fought on. Lif watched me happily, and I smiled at her, loving her. Over a wooded hill and in a small homestead, we found some poor herdsmen, and they mercifully gave us some milk, asking for nothing in return, and so we rode again. We had to stop for the night, nearly reaching the hills of the ravaged Matticati, and the land where the occasional Chatti ventured, considering these hills theirs. Quadi disagreed with them, and so it was a warlike place.

That night, nothing disturbed us.

We headed north, towards the Matticati lands, and I was feeling unrested despite some sleep. Cassia was recovering a bit, breathing fairly well again, shivering less, though she was silent as she brooded in her saddle. It was not a merry troop, and I did not remember anything amusing or pleasant from that trip, only worry, and the cold.

We stopped, and had to rest for a few minutes, and Ansbor grunted at me awkwardly, as I was giving the baby milk by a small, sputtering fire, staring at the flames. He was fidgeting by the flames, crouching to warm his hands.

I nodded at him, feeling drowsy and hopeless. 'So, in trouble again, eh?'

'Yes, that we are,' he chortled. 'We need to find some allies. Stronger ones than Burlein.'

I shook my head at him. 'It was my fault as much as his. I should have known Father would not sit idle. Nor die in bed.'

'Winter was over,' Ansbor said somberly. 'We were all happy to enjoy the wares of those damned merchants, the possibility of an easy war. They made everything pleasant for us. We made it so easy for them.'

'Burlein was happy to hear Father was dead, but we should have done many things differently,' I cursed as Lif was sputtering with the milk. 'We let them lull us into sleep. And that one bag of lies. That man.'

'What man?' he asked, mystified.

'The man who shot Guthbert, Gunnvör. Burlein's poet gave me credit for it. And so he—'

Ansbor laughed hugely. 'You, and your fame. One way, or the other, someone gets hurt. Now, even tribes topple. Hraban's Dark Hand, the poem should be called.'

'I doubt it will ever be sung again,' I told him broodingly. 'No matter what, we should have been on our guard. But, he was not. He was relieved. I was worried for her.' I nodded at Lif.

'How is she holding up?' he asked, staring at the baby and changing the subject, and I sensed he was critical to me.

'She is likely to survive us all.' I grinned, for she truly was. Odo would not let her get hurt, no matter what he would do.

'Do you think we should give her to Cassia, that she might slink away in the night, and we draw the Hel humped shit-bags after us?'

'How do you propose we draw them after us? Odo is out there.' I thought of Leuthard, and would never let the two run to the woods at night. Had we left earlier, had I listened to Hands and Veleda? Wyrd. 'They have scouts; they know where we are.'

'I say she goes,' he told me, looking down at his hands. 'And—'

'And? You shall go with her?' I asked him with a sneer.

'Perhaps?' he told me, gazing at me.

'No,' I told him, and I saw he was struggling with his patience. He shook his head, and looked disgusted.

After a while, he spoke again. 'That boy before her? It is—'

'Ishild and Odo's,' I said, with spite. 'That boy, Lífþrasir, is to marry her.' I nodded, indicating Lif. 'Over my rotting carcass, of course.'

'Over ours as well,' he said prudently, and then grunted as he gathered his courage. 'I blame you for not sending them all away. They should have gone with Euric, when he rode East for the winter.'

'They should have, yes,' I told him. 'But, we were on top of our world then.'

'Yes, I know,' he uttered forcefully. His fat face was humorless and harsh, as he eyeballed me, and I shrugged.

I growled at him. 'Cassia. Of course she is free to go. Who am I to hold her here, against her will? But, she will not go to the night alone. We might leave her with a homestead, some larger house that can defend itself, and she can get to safety from there, eventually. However, Lif comes with me,' I told him, with a hint of a warning in my voice.

He was hugging his knees, and rocking back and forth, looking at the sleeping woman. 'I love her. You know that?'

'Everyone does. Even she does. But, have you told her?' I asked him. 'I told you before to make it known. I have no part in what you have left unsaid.'

'I need you to tell her to go,' he told me, staring at my eyes, desperation and resentment playing there. 'Because she says she does not wish to go. And it is your fault.'

'Mine?' I hissed. 'Mine? How?'

'She has always avoided the topic of love. She is a friend, the best of friends indeed, but she does not wish to go, as she says she is your friend, too.'

'I think she is, but—'

'Is she more?' he asked spitefully. He grabbed a rock and threw it to the fire, staring at it, as if ashamed for the words he uttered.

I opened my mouth in an angry retort, but for Lif's sake, shut up. I shook my head at him, and searched for an answer. The truth was, I did not know what I thought about her. I had loved Shayla. I had cared for Ishild. I had once liked Ermendrud. But, Cassia was close to my heart. I respected her. She was courageous, beautiful, and intelligent. She was different in my heart, different from the other women I had known that past year. I stared at Ansbor's face, one of my last few friends, and wanted to tell him she did not think of him that way. It was not my fault. It just was so. I drew a ragged breath from my guts.

Ansbor waited somberly. 'Does that mean yes? This is the thanks for all the help I have given?'

I let the breath go, and shook my head. I resented his tone. I sneered at him in disgust. 'We are running across this hostile land, chased by Odo and others, gods wager on the hour of our demise, I am trying to save a baby, and we are lost. And you are jealous. Yes, Ansbor, she is beautiful and willful, intelligent and braver than most men. She has a biting personality and a warm heart, she is intelligent and loyal, but she and I? We share respect. What you wish to have with her is for you to build. If she does not love you? You will have to handle it.' I saw my words left him unhappy, even more jealous. Ansbor would be my enemy, perhaps. Like Ansigar, he would hate me. His eyes glared at me suspiciously, and I grew even more annoyed. 'For now, neither Hraban nor Fulcher are a threat to you. No words have been spoken. I am not a lover to her. But, someone else might be, one day, unless you stop guarding her like a fat, lazy dog, and tell her how you feel. She might say no. It is possible and likely, for you do not respect her wishes and independence. Now, scamper off, and thank you for all the help you have given me.'

He got up unsteadily and turned to go, but did not. 'You know, I do not follow you for the silly oath I gave you that day last spring, not anymore. You have lost so much honor since then, no man would be ashamed to leave you. Yet, my father died in that same battle as your heroic grandfather and brave mother, and I have vengeance to take, as well. Therefore, I shall follow you, for we have common goals. One day, we might not have them. I am not sure I wish to die a sad, useless death for the many dangers you bring us, but I shall fight for you still, for now. In addition, I thank you for slaying Vago. That somewhat alleviated my need for vengeance.'

'Thank you, Ansbor,' I told him tiredly, fully understanding my friendship has been perilous for him. 'Let us hope we don't face each other in a shield wall one day.'

He laughed. 'Wouldn't it be nice to fight in one, for a change? All we have been doing is burning halls, and fighting spirits and bastards in the thickets.'

'Yes, a shield wall would be terrible, perilous, and nice, all at the same time. I'd rather shit myself while waiting for a battle I know is coming, rather than suddenly shitting myself for all these surprises,' I told him, and glanced at Cassia. 'Speak with her already, or lose her. Someone will take her, as I said.'

He nodded, his face dark as he gathered himself. 'If you take her, it will break us,' he said. He walked for her, his steps hesitating and heavy, until he plopped down next to her. She awoke with a startle, half-pulling at the axe next to her, but then she relaxed. Ansbor spoke to her at length. He was calm enough, apparently spilling his heart finally, and she was nodding, and then holding his hand gently. She was not a cruel woman, one insensitive to someone else's needs. Then, she both nodded and shook her head, throwing her hand around the northern hills. Ansbor's face was anxious, and he argued, but she was adamant, and he looked suspicious, his eyes flickering my way. Finally, she squeezed his hand, and he relented, getting up and walking off while cursing softly. Cassia took a long breath, holding her hands on her face, and then looked startled, as she saw me watching.

I could not turn my face away.

Her eyes were moist and shining, and she blushed, and then turned to lie on her side, her eyes on mine. She was beautiful and I felt my heartstrings move. Gods help me, but she was more than a friend, but could not be, for Ansbor. 'Your father,' I told Lif's curious face, with a sad shake of my head, 'is like a vortex of shit. You are caught up in it, you are smeared. Woden did not do a very good job when he created our family, did he?' She smiled, I was sure, and shut her eyes. I laughed gently, and took a deep breath. 'I hope you make it, love.'

In the very early morning, we got on our horses. We would try to get some distance between us and the enemy, but it seemed Odo had not rested that night. Far in the morning mists, savage men were yelling questions. Then, like shadows, I spied them sitting on horses below us, in the trees we had ridden through the night before. They had crossed the river in force, and spread out to find us, Hel bent on capturing us. There were but ten of them, down there, but surely more were out there somewhere. They sat still as some of the enemy went on their knees, searching marks of our horses' passing. One looked up, his hand on a churned bit of grass and mud. He pointed our way. I spat, for while Odo was not with them, Gernot and Ansigar were. The latter rode forward, as if he had seen something. Then, he yelled, his finger pointed at Fulcher, whose red hair was like a halo as he moved for me, not having noticed the danger. He pulled back, but the damage was done.

'Haiyaah!' I yelled, and we rode.

For hours, they rode after us relentlessly, and slowly caught up to us. They had fresher horses, and I could see in the distance Ansigar mocking us. We were closing up to the small mountains and rolling, craggy hills of the Matticati, and there were light beech woods spreading around us. I could hear their horses now, and knew they gained us every minute. They were as patient as wolves, tracking a bleeding auroch, ferocious in their quest to find us, and their rewards would be great. We would fail, Lif would suffer. Ansbor and Fulcher would die, hopefully, and I was to be a prisoner they would barely keep alive.

And, Cassia would suffer, I knew she would.

She would suffer like women do, when caught by immoral men, and there was nothing else in Odo's troop but such men. I prayed to Woden as well as I could, subjecting myself before the god, then cursing his fickle nature, but all he would give me was the battle rage, and that started to hammer inside my head.

'We have to face them soon!' Fulcher yelled at me breathlessly, as I spurred my horse on the mossy ground, the horse staggering as I held on to Lif, who was gurgling happily.

'I know. We will,' I said hollowly, fearing the moment, as I was looking for a defensible position.

'It's Ansigar. He and your brother are cowards! We might make it, if we kill the two!' Ansbor yelled as he joined us, guiding his horse next to me. I shook my head. The black-garbed men would not run. They were there to kill and capture, or they had no going back.

Then, in front of us, stood a sturdy, shaggy stallion, happily eating early green grass.

Hands was sitting on it, looking at us carefully, swathed on furs.

I reined my horse to a halt, remembering how he had parted from our company, and how Ishild had been whispering to him.

'What are you doing here?' I hissed at him, as Fulcher and Ansbor pulled their spears out, surprised.

'We have not the time,' Fulcher urged, guiding Cassia to the side.

Hands ignored them. 'Time to make a choice, Hraban. You owe Veleda a life,' he said, staring across the woods, where my filth of a brother was getting steadily closer, navigating a rough, ragged cliff we had passed just a few minutes earlier. 'Had you agreed, and given her to me earlier, they would not be here. She would be safe. It will be hard for me to save her, and men will die. Perhaps the prophecy itself takes bounding leaps forward, but I can save her.'

I sat there on my horse, with my smiling baby daughter in my arms, wrapped warmly, and tears welled in my eyes. Gods know such a terrible situation would make any loving parent, most people, mad with anxiety and fear. I wanted to kill him. I wished to ride my horse at him, and over him, bleeding, and dying even, I would ride on, until the end. But, to give Lif to that beast?

'Do not,' Cassia demanded. 'He cannot be trusted,' she spat.

'I am my own thing,' Hands said tiredly, looking over his shoulder as if trying to see if there were any threats blocking his way out. 'And I am helping both my Veleda, and your poor Ishild. Your Ishild asked me to stay close, and now I am here, irate and battered, having slept in lice-infested barns and old bundles of hay for too many days. You don't know how many men I have strangled in the dark, as they were hunting you. Many!'

'Surely you know the trails around here, and can lead us all away?' I asked desperately.

He shook his head. 'No, Veleda wants her. She does not want you. This is where you choose. Give her to me, and I take her to safety.' He fished out a piece of meat from his bags, and he chewed on it happily. 'You decide,' he added, the tough meat being ground to paste in his ruthless mouth. He observed me for a moment and sighed. 'Let me tell you something, and should you speak of this to anyone else, I will hunt you down. I have a daughter, too, Hraban. A sweet wee thing, lovely as an apple. None know where she is, for she would be in terrible danger, as I have enemies, and so I know what you are going through. As for your sweet little one there, I will not hurt her, and I have slaves who will look after her while we travel,' he told me, looking mildly embarrassed while sneaking looks behind me, his chewing getting a bit more erratic. 'One minute, Hraban, then you are out of choices.'

Fulcher stirred, and was about to say something, but I rode forward, tears filling my eyes and dripping into my beard. I slowly lifted her, and her little hand had a hold on my finger, her clear eyes gazing at me, as if trying to remember my face, until Hands pulled her away from me, gently but resolutely. 'Will I see her again?' I asked, with a shuddering breath.

He snorted, amused as he grinned at the little girl, who had a very serious look on her face, though she seemed unafraid. 'Do I look like a damned seer? I know not. Everything is possible. You might. Depends on the wyrd, and those bastards down there, and so many other things in this damned world. However, she is Veleda's now, and she is a wise girl. She will be fine, unless you find Veleda for the whore-mongering bastards. Think on that,' he said, peeking at the girl and smiling at me. 'Takes after her mother, thank the gods. Take care now.'

'How will you get away from them? They are going to come after you, when they find we do not have her!' Cassia asked spitefully, guiding her horse forward.

'Oh! That. Yes, here,' he said, and grabbed something from the side of the horse and savagely launched a javelin that spun into the air before anyone could move. It pierced Cassia's horse and she fell off the saddle with a surprised scream. Hands laughed like a mad man, happy with the quality of his throw, and kicked the flanks of the horse. 'Heyaah!'

'Hands! Siegfried!' I bellowed, as I whipped my horse.

'I am true, Hraban, but I will not risk Lif,' he yelled, 'Veleda will hold her safe, but you see to your woman, and fight well! Perhaps you should leave her and run, but I suppose you found honor with Lif!'

I staggered in my saddle, and turned the horse. He was riding away, to Veleda; I hoped and spat after him. I cursed and whipped my horse to Cassia, who was being helped by Ansbor, her leg under the horse. 'That piece of lice-ridden fat!' Fulcher exclaimed, now also off the horse, then pushing and prying to get her out of the vice-like grip of dead flesh, blood, and churned mud. 'He betrayed us!'

'He is an opportunistic stink bag,' I growled and helped them. 'Quickly!' I said, and then a horn rang out. It was a mournful, sad sound of reverberating threat, and it rang through the distant valleys amidst the surrounding Matticati hills. Even Hands turned to look around, but then whipped his horse again, and I lost sight of Lif, as he plunged to the foliage and took to the trails known only to the hunter of men.

A line of men rode out of the south. It was Gernot and Ansigar, and they were there, very close. 'Get them!' yelled Ansigar. 'Now!'

'Mount up,' I said with trepidation, as a crescent of ragged enemy bore up towards us. I climbed on my horse, and turned it downhill towards the enemy. Ansbor pulled Leuthard's blade, and Fulcher, in a mail I had given him, followed with his thick spear as they vaulted on their surprised horses. I gripped out the spear of Balderich, Wolf's Tear, loosened the swords on my hips, hitting the flank of my faltering horse and nodded to Fulcher and Ansbor.

'Don't hurt the child!' Gernot yelled. 'At them, disarm them!' Our horses lurched forward.

Then, five men rode out of thickets to our left. Three held bows, two javelins, and they all aimed at Cassia, who was scowling at them.

'Drop the weapons, or she is dead,' Ansigar ordered as his horse galloped closer.

We hesitated, our horses confused, and Cassia shook her head at us. 'Do not,' she mouthed, but the archers were all aiming at her, and there was no choice but to surrender or to ride away, hoping to escape and sacrifice her.

I looked to the sky, terrified at what I would suffer. I dropped my spear. Fulcher grunted and dropped his, and as Ansbor refused, staring at the enemy sullenly, Ansigar rode to him and pushed him off the saddle. I dismounted and stared at Gernot, who was riding for me, his face unreadable, his weak brown hair tangled and dirty.

'Quite a chase, brother,' he said, as his men rode around us. His men collected our weapons, and as Cassia refused to give the axe, Ansigar hit her with his spear shaft, and she fell on her back, and said no more, whimpering in pain.

'Let her be, turd eater,' I told him, but he lifted his eyebrows at me. I was in no position to make such threats.

Gernot gestured at us. 'Tie them down. Not him.' He pointed a finger my way. A veritable avalanche of men jumped on Fulcher and Ansbor, hitting and kicking them until they were side-by-side on the mud, cursing, tied like sacrificial pigs. 'The child, where is it?' Gernot mused, looking around.

'Where is the baby?' Ansigar asked Ansbor savagely. 'Where in Hel's name is she? You men! Find the child! You two, track back where they came from. Find anyone hiding the brat!' Men turned to obey him.

Gernot rode around me, gazing down. Then he stopped his horse, gazing down at me, and a man handed him my Nightbright. 'Where is Lif, Hraban? Did you leave her for the wolves?' Gernot asked, his voice grating. He gestured at his men, and Fulcher screamed as someone hit him. I gazed at Ansigar's leering rat face as he enjoyed every moment, and he vaulted off his horse and walked around the captives. More of the ragged men rode up the hill. Odo was not there, but the men whispered to Gernot. He nodded and then approached me, calm as gentle rain.

He was no longer his impatient self, desperate and angry. He had grown with his wound and exile. He nodded, and men pinned my hands behind my back. Cassia moaned, and men leered at each other. Her turn would come. I prayed she would stay unconscious. 'Your friends, Hraban?' Gernot whispered tiredly. 'Do you wish to see them bleed for this? I have no choice, brother. Lif?' I spat at him; he did not even wipe it off. 'The men told me there was a fat rider here, just before we got up. That you gave him something. They saw this, but could not track him. Where did he go?' My brother looked at Cassia, then at Ansbor and Fulcher, who were tied down, their faces desperately trying to keep their calm. Gernot was thinking on which one would be hurt next.

Cassia grunted as Ansigar stalked around her, poking her with the spear shaft, and then she moaned in pain.

'You animal. Come and fight me, bastard,' I cursed him.

'You should not have left me alive, Hraban, and she will not appreciate it,' Ansigar told me coldly.

'Speak, and spare her the humiliation,' Gernot told me. 'We will kill them cleanly, take you and the ring,' he said, and tapped it as his eyes gazed at the great prize of our family, 'and they need not suffer. But, we will need Lif.'

'I will give no such promise,' Ansigar said softly and stepped over Cassia, ripping at her tunica. Gernot's face finally showed emotion. He hefted Nightbright, and thrust the blade under the chin of Ansigar, pushing him away from Cassia.

'I said. She will die a clean death. You will have to learn how to listen,' Gernot hissed at Ansigar. Cassia looked at them, afraid, inching away, and Ansigar nodded carefully. Their relationship had changed as well, and I wondered how much Gernot blamed Ansigar for his misfortunes.

'I do not know where Lif is. The fat one had his own agenda,' I told Gernot's back.

Gernot shrugged. 'Perhaps Lif need not be found at all. Odo asked for her, certainly. But, you know, he will be happy with you. And the shitty ring. Perhaps he would be happy with nothing at all. He is strange and mad, and it is possible the prophecy is already moving as it should, and all this is just necessary, tedious dance. But, he will still hurt me for failing him.' Fulcher struggled a bit, and a man hit him again. 'Lie down,' Gernot told me. I laid down on my belly, and he smiled sadly as he squatted before me, speaking so softly none others would hear. Ansigar did not like it, his thin face screwed up with suspicion. 'All my life, Hraban. Your shadow has blocked the sun for me, all of it. In Mother's eyes, in Grandfather's many plans. You denied me everything. All that I am, and should have been, you stood there to stop it. Then came Father. Finally. Finally, I had my share.' He ambled closer. 'You know what happened. We were both sorry for it, all the things we did to each other. Now, we have nothing more left than to finish this. You did not take my life that day, and so I have to live a vagabond, a lord of the filthy rabble. I am the small ruler of larvae, and Odo, Hraban, rules me with hate and hurt. I failed him, you see, and he is not happy. So I need Lif. Not for respect or power. I need her in order to keep breathing, even if I despise myself for it.'

'Why not leave him then?' I spat. 'Like you left Father.'

'I had to leave him; Odo had me by the balls. He has ever manipulated me, and I did kill Hagano for him. As you remember, the deed you took my hand for,' he showed the stump to me.

I smiled. 'Well, if it is any condolence, you were never any good with a spear. And perhaps god Tiw approves, as he, too, lost his hand to an animal. I was not a man the day we fought.'

'You fought well, brother,' he agreed. 'But, now, you are caught like one. An animal.'

'Father would laugh at this, his two unwanted sons killing each other,' I smiled at him.

'He would,' he agreed with a grin. 'You burned his hall? I guess he paid back, eh?' He traced my scar with his left hand's finger inside the helmet. 'Fancy. Odo will make it pale in comparison, though. You will have terrible time with this bastard.'

'In Gulldrum,' I stated blandly.

'Ah, yes, their ancestral home,' he said, licking his lips. 'He'll perhaps take you there. I am not sure. I've been to the place. It is an altar to suffering inside a hill, under the root, and over the underworld. Perhaps there he will rip your eyes out and eat them, then he will break your arms, and gods know what else. If nothing else, he keeps such promises. And then, he will let you go, and you will wander the world until you run into Veleda, and he will give her blood to the ring, and we shall all pass away, as will the gods.'

'You speak much, brother,' I said calmly. 'Why not just make a stand, if you wish to be rid of the liar?'

He smiled. 'Well. You were always right about me. I am not brave. That is why I need Lif. But one thing remains from the boy you used to know,' he said maliciously. 'It is that certain bit of meanness and nastiness, and I know I was both mean and nasty. So, let us even the score. Ansigar!'

'Lord?' our former friend answered sarcastically.

'Take his hand,' he said maliciously, as he got up and his men sat on my back. 'Put it in front of you. This is what Father planned on doing to you, before you were exiled. Now, there is none to save you. We shall be the two brothers, my friend, both as crippled and torn. You will lose one hand here for certain, to pay me back, and then the other one, if you do not tell me where this fat man is taking the baby. Put it forth, bastard Hraban, or I will indeed let Ansigar deal with the fabulous woman there.' His eyes flickered to Cassia, who was looking on bravely, angry as Freya the goddess before a battle.

I prayed to Woden for strength and nodded, and putting out my left hand, looking at his eyes.

'Your right hand, brother. Right one. Like it was for me,' Gernot said softly, and I grimaced and obeyed him, terrified.

Ansigar smirked at my helplessness, and grabbed the Head Taker and walked next to me. He spoke to me. 'You left me crippled as well. I'm not very strong nor is my aim very accurate. This might take time. You be strong for me!' Ansigar smiled at me sadistically.

'Let him be! Ansigar!' Ansbor was saying, and was rewarded by a smack from a burly tower of filth.

'I have not yet decided what to do with you, Ansbor, but do not claim you never wanted to see this bastard humiliated,' Ansigar told our friend. I prayed to Woden as he raised the blade, wondering how I would survive without my hand, horror tearing at my insides. Then, I heard the horn again, blaring a challenge, but as I looked around, none of the enemy was holding one. They were all looking around.

'There it is again,' Gernot said, mystified. 'What—'

A steady, small line of men came to sight over a small hillock just next to us. They were men on horses, very large men on very large horses, well-helmeted all, with large spears and shining armor and thick, wide shields. For a second, I saw the image of my father that fateful night he charged to Hulderic's village, and saved Tudrus and the remains of our village from

Vago, as his men had looked like these men, but these were not men of Maroboodus.

There were only five of them, and my brother had fifteen, but Gernot was taken aback. His men looked at him in confusion, but he waved them down, walking forward to see the men better.

'Who are you? Matticati?' Gernot yelled, as Ansigar was motioning his men to pull us into a heap and the rest to make a shield wall, save for one who was supposed to watch us. They made a semblance of a line, though not all had a shield or even a proper weapon, but now one held Grandfather's fabled spear, a lanky, broad-shouldered man in a brown tunic and furred pants. Another had Leuthard's former sword and looked ridiculous holding it, his filth mocking the fine blade. Gernot's left hand held Nightbright; Ansbor was clutching the Head Taker. One man was watching us, but he paid little attention, his eyes transfixed on the silent men facing us. I got up to my knees, quietly and softly, observing the guard.

The strangers rode forward, casually, looking from side-to-side, seeking trouble, but likely not fearing it. Leading them was a bronze masked man, with a barrel-like chest and golden hair spilling from under the rim of the helmet, and a fine mist was coming through the mouth hole. He rode towards us, stopping some twenty feet away, his men spreading out around him. A casual attitude of practiced killers emanated from them. The leader punched his spear to the ground and held up his hand. 'We are no Matticati, but who are you, a ragged-looking lot? What are you doing to the woman?' His voice was mockingly arrogant, and his horse seemed to echo the sentiment as it whinnied spitefully.

'This is none of your business, friend. This is an evil man, offending my lord who is a vitka of might and dread. Do not cross him, fool!' Gernot said, with as much conviction as he could gather, gesturing towards me.

'Is it your sister?' the rider asked.

'No, a prisoner,' Ansbor said wisely, gazing at the large men like a small dog would at a pack leader. With fear. 'He is our target.' He thumbed my way.

'If she is not a relative of yours, then we have a problem,' the rider stated with a grunt and shook his head at Gernot, who was about to speak. 'No. Shut your trap. I asked about the woman, not the man, but by all means, let us talk about him in a bit. As for the woman. I saw him.' He nodded at Ansigar. 'A rapist. I hate such men. I am thinking your vitka is a fable and a filthy lie,' the man gestured at Gernot's men, 'and a group of rag tag robbers and mongrels do not make a favorable impression on me.' The shield wall shuddered nervously. I peered at the guard as I got up. He had a thin knife on his belt, and I stepped forward silently, grabbed the blade, and impaled the guard so hard the blade went through his side, breaking rib bones. A man moved for me, but stopped as I pulled the blade out, and retreated back to the shield wall. Men now glanced at the riders, and at me nervously, fingering their weapons and waiting for Gernot to command them.

He said nothing, licking his lips.

'So they got no balls, do they, boy?' the leader yelled the question at me. I stared at Ansigar and my brother, and both were now whispering angrily. I stalked to my friends, and released Fulcher and Ansbor with savage jerks of the blade, and not a man in the shield wall moved my way, but they shuffled back to form a sort of a huddled group. My friends were up, despite their many injuries, and Ansbor dragged Cassia aside, who seemed revived as she got up on unsteady feet. Silence was oppressive, until one of the enemy dropped his spear, then fumbled as he tried to get it up. The leader of the riders and his men laughed at that.

The leader asked again. 'Balls? Do they have them?'

'No balls at all,' I explained, and sneered at Gernot. 'Nightbright, the Head Taker, and the spear. The large sword as well.' They made no move, and I growled, Woden whispering to me of violence.

'And if I meddle in this, they will run, right?' the rider continued, snickering with his men.

'They will run like rabbits, lord. And you have already meddled in it,' I answered. 'My weapons, cur!'

'Are you worth anything, boy?' the rider insisted. 'Something to reward my meddling?'

'I'm a man who pays his debts,' I told him. 'Happy to bow to you, my lord. As are my men.'

'Ah, you offer service?' he asked curiously.

'I offer much, should you help me,' I told him morosely. The rider's eyes were glittering, as he regarded the enemy. Ansigar was whispering furiously to Gernot now, but my brother was shaking his head, looking towards the south. He was hoping for more of Odo's men to arrive. 'We do not have time, lord.'

'We have some. Is that your spear?' the rider asked, pointing at Aristovistus's spear. The man holding it blanched, and nearly hid it behind his back.

'Yes,' I said miserably, for it was a fabulous weapon.

'A fine, old one. And that old sword as well?'

'It was,' I said, with anger, 'my grandfather's.'

He smiled. 'I want it. And then, you shall follow me, until we figure out a place for you,' he said happily. I grunted with an animal-like anger. Finally, I nodded, and he pointed his spear at Gernot. 'So be it. Drop the weapons, or use them,' the man said with spiteful anger. His men shifted their shields, and held their spears in an overhanded grip, their eyes boring at the men in the shield wall, choosing targets.

The shield wall was shuddering with indecision.

Ansigar looked like he was going to explode, as he tried to convince Gernot to fight, but Gernot, disappointed by the turn of events was walking for his horse, and he threw down Nightbright as he did. The others followed him, dropping the looted weapons, and I walked after them, picking up Leuthard's blade and handed it to Ansbor, then Balderich's spear and my Nightbright. Finally, I took the Head Taker and walked to the lord, and reluctantly handed it hilt first to the man who saw my suffering, and grinned at me under his bronzed helmet. He judged the motley lot of sullen enemies, and pointed the blade their way. 'You! Dogs. Run off, or you join your dead friends. I will have my men show you how to rape, and they are well built, I tell you. You will cry, as they have not seen a woman in long months. They won't be gentle, not even if you are virgins!' His men spread out, grinning as Odo's men ran and chased their horses, mounting them as quickly as they could.

That was the last hour for Gernot to show his mettle. Men were whispering angrily as they mounted their beasts, as they were still many, and we were but eight, and they could have won, possibly, but Gernot did not have the heart for such a combat. He spat at my direction and trembling, turned his horse, and his men hung their heads in shame, following him. Odo would be very displeased with him.

'Well, quite a bunch of cowards they were,' the rider spat, as he raised his helmet a bit while admiring the blade. 'An old one. They don't make such any more. Did you lose anyone to them?'

I nodded, my face clouded over as I looked at the tall hills.

He shrugged. 'Worry not. Your Woden will look after the dead.'

'I lost friends and companions over the river. And here, my own blood. My daughter lives, but she is gone,' I told him with a trembling voice. 'I thank you for your timely help, but I must go after my daughter.'

'Hraban,' Ansbor said tediously. 'We need rest.'

The rider's eyes enlarged, and then he clapped a hand on my shoulder as he leaned over me. His men were suddenly alert; their spears pointed our way. 'Well, rest you shall have. I say you give me your weapons, that helmet, all the rich armor, and we take you with us to safety. Besides, what kind of a man would I be, if I let you go seek your death? The curs ran without a fight, but in numbers lay their courage, and they have men all around us.'

'You know who I am, then?' I asked him, brooding at Ansbor.

He grinned warily. 'The son of Maroboodus is not a prize I can let go with good conscience!'

I observed the stern men around me, men who had just saved us, and now suddenly were perhaps an enemy, and I shook the battle rage away. I eyed the slopes and prayed to the gods, all I could name, that Lif would be safe until I saved her. And screw the prophecy, but I would.

274

'What are you?' I asked the rider.

'We are Batavi. Romans in a sense. And we shall take you to Castrum Luppia, where your father had a victory feast last year,' he said, and I cursed. Roman auxilia. Gods hated me.

But, we were safe for the moment.

CHAPTER XIX

'Yes, we swam the river and escaped them, for a moment,' Ansbor told the merry warrior, as we rode towards the familiar northern passes for the Matticati lands. The previous year, Wandal and I had chased Catualda there, all the way to the Castrum Luppia, where Father had sprung his trap on the Vangiones and Hengsti, taking the fort. I glowered at Ansbor for fraternizing with the enemy, but he blithely ignored me.

The man was shaking his head in wonder. 'Swam? The river? Only we do that, in full gear, that is. And not when it's running so high. Deathly cold, that is.' He looked at me dubiously.

'Why is it your privilege to swim rivers in full gear?' I asked him tersely, feeling miserable, fighting the urge to ride off at a full gallop.

He snorted. 'Because we are the Batavi, the best damned horsemen in the world. I am Chariovalda.' He put out his hand, and scowled at me until I gave mine, grasping his forearm. He nodded grudgingly, as he pulled hard on my arm in a warrior's salute. He let go and snorted. 'So, we hear you are quite a rascal. Maroboodus trying to build the Marcomanni in a proper fighting force is the news we keep hearing about over the river, but there are people who sing songs about you.'

'Ah, yes,' I said, knowing he meant my dishonor. 'Do they sing the song on how I burned his hall last year?'

'They do not,' he laughed. 'Truly? They only say you betrayed him, killed unwary holy men, and slept with unmarried women. Any of that true?'

'Yes, all of it,' I told him hollowly. 'Though he himself has done much worse deeds, and all I did was obey.'

'Did he order you to whelp babies on young women?' he asked with a small laugh.

I said nothing, for Ermendrud's fate was pressing heavily on me. Leuthard was out there, I was sure, tracking us, and I begged to gods he would not find Hands and Lif. I had lost Ishild as well. I had lost her long ago, before I even knew I might have her. 'I have nothing to say to that, lord.'

'Nothing? Fine,' he said calmly, his eyes on mine. I turned away first, and he rode on calmly. We were navigating the deep chasms and tall crags of the Matticati hills, and would soon witness the wonderful valleys, green pastures, swaying woods, and fields of barley we had ravaged the past year. 'Did you betray him?'

'He made me give oaths,' I told him severely, 'against my own family. We made friends later, but it was but a lie, though I gave him the many victories he needed. He was always set on sacrificing me, even after pretending to love me. He did not even think I was his son. A dog, perhaps?'

He was nodding as he rode on, giving swift commands to some of his men. 'Do you think,' he rumbled, and took off his helmet. His face was heavy and scarred under each eye, his eyes hazy like water, with blond curls around his face, interweaving with his huge moustaches and beard, 'that he might have treated you differently if your hair was red?' He reached out to my dark hair and I guided my horse further from him. He let me and chuckled. 'And I do not think you are a dog, Hraban, but a wolf. Wolves are not the type to let anyone kick them around, even if they are treacherous.' He smiled enigmatically, and I was not sure if he was giving me a compliment, or not. He grinned and continued. 'Now he is strong. He wishes to start his life anew here in Germania, to wash the shame away, shame of having served Romans.'

I laughed. 'No, my lord. He is more Roman than Germani. He is going to betray the lot of us to Rome.'

Chariovalda was staring at me in stupefaction. 'He is our worst enemy. He razed the fort we are now riding for. He is uniting the tribes.'

'He,' I spat, 'unites them so they are malleable and easy to betray later. And there are Roman men who have to fall in this war, as I hear Augustus is nervous of his legacy.'

'Men who have to fall?' he inquired.

I knew I should have been careful, but I was too tired to care. I waved my hand to the south. 'In Rome, they need these wars, for the Wolf has to feed. But, I was told the truth by a fat bastard who thought I was to die. He told me Maroboodus serves Rome. Roman lords who threaten Augustus's state, this new hegemony of his, are going to suffer in this war. Only when they are dead, and Augustus is safe, will the Germani suddenly collapse. My father, my lord, is a bastard, who will do all of this. He is Roman, serving certain unsavory Romans who wish to kill other Romans so Rome can become even more corpulent and decadent, and less honorable. And Maroboodus will be left in charge of the lands in here, a Roman lord. Faugh!'

He was nodding his head, as he stared ahead, his eyes flickering my way, likely thinking I was mad. 'A fancy plan. To think I learnt of it from a dung-smelling barbarian out of the backwoods. I suppose you speak Latin, too?' he asked with a grin.

'I do,' I told him in Latin, my pride prickled. 'And you smell of piss, my lord, so I suppose we complement each other.'

He chortled. 'And you say old Augustus is pulling the string of Maroboodus, hoping he will hand over the Germani to him, after Republican leaders are dead?' he wondered.

'No, the merchant told me there are others who would benefit from this new reign of Augustus. The old man apparently does not know about Maroboodus,' I reiterated, with a tired, bored voice. 'Someone is out there playing dangerous games. It has cost my family blood.'

'Oh, I think it is possible,' he said darkly. 'But, why would they not just stab the Republicans, and this is what they are talking about lout, men who wish for the Republic to have its old powers, the rule of many over the rule of one. Why not just slay such men?' he asked me sweetly.

'They want no martyrs, I suppose. There has been lots of blood spilled in Roman civil wars? No. A Germani must do this deed, an enemy Augustus will then conquer and be loved for,' I said.

'Ah, but you are a wise one for a shit digger,' he smiled, as he rode easily.

'I don't feel wise, Chariovalda,' I told him. 'And your horse looks wiser than you.'

His men snickered, and Ansbor grumbled something about shutting my rotten mouth, but Chariovalda was only chuckling at me. 'Indeed. You are a strange man, Hraban. A very strange one.' He pulled out the Head Taker. 'I shall keep all these weapons of yours until we decide what is to become of you. You are, after all, no friend to Rome. By your own words.'

I chuckled. 'I wonder who is my friend.'

He nodded towards the north. 'The Cherusci, the Sigambri? Tencteri and the Usipetes? They all fight hard up there, and look in suspicion at Maroboodus and us, both. Fiercely independent, they are. Perhaps you should go there.'

'Yes, there are some of the Quadi out there I would like to meet with,' I told him. Veleda had told me to go up there. To the Cherusci, to Armin? The man I had betrayed for Father? Was she right? Was it too late?

'Tudrus is a nasty bastard,' he told me with a grimace. 'He is up there these days, that Quadi and a thousand of his people. We had a cavalry battle early spring, and they nearly routed us.'

'He is much like you,' I told him, for it was true.

'Only much older,' he added with a sniff. 'Now, shut up, we deal with many issues soon. I am happy I fished you out of the trouble.'

I nodded at him impatiently.

Lif.

I would find her.

We were taken to a hill beyond the passes of the Matticati, and a brilliant sunlight tried to permeate the misty woods below. On that light, we saw glittering men on the hill. They were a war-torn contingent of Batavian cavalry, apparently scouting. The Romans had been so impressed by my father's slaughter of the Matticati and the Vangiones and the decimation of the cohort of Romans that the commanders had sent the sturdy Batavi to find out the true manner of the suebian threat.

The Batavi seemed Germani enough, all with beards and a dangerous squint in their eyes, blond and red-headed, some as dark as I was. Unlike the average Germani, the Batavi were heavily armored in ring- and chainmail, and armed to the extent they resembled travelling arms merchants. Most had a heavy spear and wicked darts, and a few hefted thick bows with deadly arrows. Some, the better warriors, sported fat, dangerous axes and sharp swords, all made of the best possible Celtic iron. All their shields bore the same symbol of a star and a bull, and I admired their discipline, as some men rode out on light scout animals, while others cared for the tough, muscular Roman horses.

'We look like servants,' Ansbor told me morosely.

'Or prisoners,' Fulcher added, 'which we are, in truth.'

'Thanks to Hraban,' Ansbor said gloomily.

'Shut up,' Cassia whispered. 'He lost his child.'

Ansbor nodded savagely at her, angered as she was defending me. 'We all lost something! A home, at least. Wandal lost Ermendrud, even if he does not know it. Loss is to be born these days, and so is blame,' he told me, and vaulted down from the horse and walked off briskly to take a piss.

Chariovalda was talking with some of the men in the camp, and then put on his helmet, motioned for his men, and got up. He pointed his finger at us, and I nodded. We would ride on down to the lands of the Matticati, and some of the scouts led us to trails that skirted streaming, clear rivers. They took us to the trails down the hills, occasionally stopping, dodging war parties of strange nature. Once, two men went back after quick consultation with Chariovalda. We sat still, getting bitten and savaged by the mosquitos, and the horses grew irritated at the flies buzzing around us. Soon, some screams could be heard, silencing the birds, but then the men returned, sheeting their bows, and the birds began to chirp away again. A ragged horse, with a bloodied flank raced past us, a man dead on the saddle.

'Your tormentor sent men after us,' Chariovalda said casually, chewing on some dried meat as he guided his horse onwards. 'We rule these lands, not they.' I shook my head, for the dead man had had the scarlet scar of the Red Finger on his forehead. They did not work for Odo, but Maroboodus. Did they accompany Leuthard?

In the woods, there were skeletons picked clean by animals, as many forgotten battles had taken place there during my father's campaign. Our eyes gazed at the fox-gnawed bones, as we rode in silence over corpses left behind in the woods, unburied and unfound.

'I knew some Batavi. Recently. One is dead now,' I told Chariovalda heavily.

He nodded. 'Brutal campaign they had here. Your father stepped on a trap, but in fact trapped the overconfident mud eaters. It cost him some, I bet, but it cost our allies more,' Chariovalda said sourly, examining the skeletal carnage, disgusted by the ineptitude shown by the usually stalwart Matticati.

'He sacrificed old men, and Burlein's men, a man he did not like,' I explained, 'as that is his way. But, now, Burlein is dead as well.'

'I see,' he crumbled, his eyes flickering my way. 'Who were the Batavi you knew?'

'Leuthard and Guthbert. Their father lives in Batavorium? I know not his name. Guthbert is dead. Leuthard is … changed. He is my father's creature.' He rode silently, nodding. 'You knew them?

The man nodded profoundly, startled, as if torn from his thoughts. 'Yes,' he said. 'Their father died last winter. They are all there now, by Hercules, save for Leuthard. He is changed, you said? We will see them in Woden's halls, or Freya's, I suppose.'

'Guthbert was a fine man,' I told him morosely, not mentioning he had a family in Rome as well.

'You killed him?' he asked with humor.

'No, but I helped,' I told him. 'Another shot him, and that man, my lord, betrayed us to Maroboodus. Gunnvör.'

'You bragged of killing him, then?' he grinned.

'I did not. Burlein paid a poet to sing my praises, and the man took offence,' I explained, as I guided my horse over a rotten timber.

'We take offence easily, Hraban. Wyrd,' he said.

'Wyrd,' I agreed, and hoped my wyrd was different.

Cassia rode next to me. 'You worship both Roman and Germani gods? Wyrd is—'

'They are all the same,' said Chariovalda and I, together. Shayla had taught me this. We glanced at each other in surprise, and laughed. I quickly shut my mouth, and glanced at Fulcher. He nodded. It was hard to feel happy when you should be grieving, but sometimes grief had to give room to joy. Lif was not dead yet. Not that I knew of.

'Hercules, Donor, I think they are the same, and I worship the smiter in any form he chooses to take. Did he not take a woman's form to slay a stupid giant once?' Chariovalda said happily. 'Bet he was a looker. Women say I am as pretty as a maid, some do.'

'This does not offend you?' Ansbor asked, surprised.

Chariovalda leaned on him. 'If Donor used ruses to kill giants, I happily use my beauty to bed women who admire pretty men.'

'You do look like a handsome woman, lord,' Cassia said happily, and Chariovalda gave her a calculating look, one Ansbor did not enjoy. 'Though, perhaps, not a maid, but a grandmother,' Cassia allowed, and he cursed her with a chuckle.

We came to the valleys of the Matticati, and Chariovalda took us directly to the old Roman fort, thundering up the forlorn hill where a thousand men had died, and entered the crow-filled woods of that embattled hill. Around the fort, there were alert Matticati, guarding the legionnaires rebuilding the destroyed fort, and another hundred Batavi, flitting in and out of the woods. They guided us inside the perimeter, forcing us to dismount, as riding in camp was against the rules of men and gods, and we walked.

The agger and the fossa were sternly rebuilt, and the part of the stockade I lost Wandal at was again in place. There was another cohort of legionnaires building the fort, immunes most of them, all from Moganticum, craftsmen of skill. We were shown to squad tents, very similar to what my father had when he first came to us. I got my own, Fulcher and Ansbor another, and Cassia slept with the Batavi women. They split us up on purpose. She was the only one of us allowed to walk outside, free but for one guard, a young beardless and blushing Batavi, who got extremely nervous when she appeared.

There we stayed for days. Our wounds were administered to and bound, our clothes cleaned, and Fulcher and I had our armor scraped of rust and weapons sharpened, because we saw this from afar, as they would not let us go around armed and armored. We were happy to be receiving food, though the legionnaires woke up dreadfully early to the sharp blast of the cornu, or some other horn they used in the camp.

As for me, despite the relief of food and care, I suffered alone, and refused to see anyone. I thought of mysterious Ishild and her terrible dilemmas at the mercy of her brother, I thought of unhappy Gernot, my brother who had no strength in him to either flee his masters, or even fight me, and I thought of Ermendrud and Leuthard, the latter ripping into her with his hands. He had eaten her. I was not sure of that, but it was possible, for she was missing an arm. I could not repel the sight from my mind, and I knew I would face the beast one day, as he would not rest until he did slay me. And he was not alone, no. The Red Fingers were out there with him.

Most of all, I thought of Lif.

I cried bitter tears, as I thought of her little fingers, her perfect nose, keen eyes, and enigmatic smiles, and I cursed the wyrd sisters for the fate they had sown together.

Lif.

Lif.

She tortured me, for no man who loves a daughter, could enjoy life after losing such as Lif.

By the end of the second day, I heard Cassia argue with the tedious Ansbor, and then she came to me and sat with me for hours. She said nothing, and I stared at her, having asked her to leave many times. She stared back at me. Then, finally, something moved inside me, and I put my hands on my face as I wept. She was patient, not asking for anything. She did not demand a cease to my weeping, or for me to take heart, or to let go of the grief. She threw a satchel of kindling at Ansbor and Fulcher, who came to insist I was to be left alone.

So, in the end, I spoke with her. I wondered what Ishild was going through. I told her of Ermendrud, as I had not told anyone what I had seen. She shook her head in disbelief, as she held my hand. Of Lif, I needed not say anything; I only wept, and she could merely hold me, as I let go of restraints and raged. She stayed with me, as I prayed to Woden to keep the baby safe, as it was a brutal world that did not love the weak and the young. She joined me in such a prayer, reaching out to her Celtic deities, and even to our Frigg, wife of Woden, renowned for her wisdom and care, and to Siff the Golden, lady to Donor the Smiter, as she was a strong, wise goddess and would make Lif strong as well. She slept next to me and kissed my forehead, holding me to her bosom, and I stayed there, curled in sorrow and gratitude.

The next morning, we woke up as the trumpets blared, and the legionnaires stomped out to hear their orders, and to eat their frugal breakfast of vegetables and water.

She looked me up and down, as I sat up, groggy with nightmares. 'Do you feel any better?' she asked.

I shrugged, ashamed for my weaknesses the night before. 'Not really, but—' I began, but then she slapped me.

She grabbed my beard painfully. 'Now, it's time to start living again.'

'How do I do that?' I asked her, after a brief and unsuccessful struggle to release myself. 'For what?'

'See your friends, and get drunk,' she said calmly. 'Then, start making plans.'

'Gods know my plans—'

'You cannot give up, you dung heap,' she told me sternly, and I was released.

'I—'

'Go!' she told me, and I got up to my feet, wobbly as hell, and she slapped my rear so hard I winced. I filed out of the tent, staring back at her disbelievingly. The guard who was in charge of me dropped his mug of ale as I rushed by him. He ran after me until I found my wits, and asked him where Ansbor and Fulcher were holed up; I found out it was in the tent next to me, and so I went in there.

She was right. I would have to start making plans again. Impishly grinning Cassia bought us very sour ale, and we drank ourselves senseless during that day, and we discussed our plight, most of which we had forgotten by the evening.

A man entered the tent the next day, stalking around me, taking stock of senseless Fulcher and Ansbor. 'Greetings, how are you doing?' I asked him brusquely, as he had not said a word, nor introduced himself. He was a very young man, with lively eyes and a smooth, horse tattooed face that hinted it might be pleasing if he smiled. He did not.

Instead, he left without a word.

I followed him outside, and realized we had slept through the bleeding trumpets, as the sun was high, the day was uncomfortably hot. My eyes stung from the bright light so badly, I forgot the many questions I had for the young man. When I could see properly, shading my eyes, I saw a line of men leading their horses. It was exhausted-looking Chariovalda. He nodded at my disheveled condition as he stopped his horse.

'Alive again?' he asked carelessly as he spat through his helmet's mouth hole, accidentally hitting my tunic. I stared at the spittle. He wiped his helmet clean and shrugged. 'A good reason to get cleaned up, eh? There will be a small feast, and you are going to be there, tonight. See you there. Don't drink more before that. Cassia demanded you were allowed to feast alone, but we don't like morose people huddling drunk in our tents. We drink together. And not too much when we are at war.'

I got cleaned up, taking a bath in terribly cold water, and so did my friends. That evening, we were escorted to a red, mud-spattered tent outside the fort, one decorated with bedraggled furs and skins.

Chariovalda saw us coming, and detangled from a discussion with a lanky man in armor, giving reports. He waved his hands happily. 'Welcome, our unwilling guests. Welcome. We have plenty of food, we eat some juicy, stolen pork, and some even less honestly acquired lamb, for our friends, the Matticati, love the Romans, but dislike all others, and we have to eat as well. Leave the fat one outside, for we cannot abide gluttony, though.' He pointed at Ansbor, who was heavyset, strangely so, despite the harsh winter and our late troubles. He likely hid stolen food somewhere when he could.

'Do not worry, just give him some gruel, and set a guard on him,' Fulcher told Chariovalda, and pushed the glowering Ansbor inside, as his eyes lit up in anticipation of the food.

'We should let him join the Sigambri! They would starve ere winter,' said one of the men in the tent.

We had a good time with the merry men of the Batavi who told us stories. They told us their tribe was originally of the mighty Chatti, like the Matticati were, but had found home near the sea, far in the north. It was a fertile land, though light in woods, but the vast pastures were rich and bountiful, raising strong horses, and the wheat gave them excellent ale. They all lamented the piss they had to drink there, but told great stories of the mighty feasts. Rome loved them. The god-like Nero Claudius Drusus had befriended them year past, and their men had served Caesar and Octavianus, the current Augustus, for decades.

Mainly, they told us about Nero Claudius Drusus.

They would follow him to Hades. They were his clients, his personal friends, and these men loved him like they would their father.

'Toast to the small bear!' Chariovalda yelled. 'Toast to the foreign man who could not be more like a Germani, like a Batavi! He will conquer for Rome, and gods see we will be his ferocious arms!'

'Aye!' they yelled, and we echoed their sentiment and smiled.

'So, he talked you out of your freedom, and now you toast him?' I asked Chariovalda scornfully.

He sputtered. 'No, we are his clients. Willing ones.'

'Do you pay taxes then?' Cassia asked shyly. 'I remember when the Mediomactri were special friends to the god Caesar, but now we are just ... upset.'

Chariovalda got up, and plopped between Cassia and me. He placed a careful arm around her and shook his head at her. 'I know not what the future brings, girl, but the stepson of Augustus—'

'He is related to the bastard?' I asked.

'Yes, yes,' he said heavily, 'they are sons of this hag; well, they say she is a pretty fine-looking hag, Livia by name, and the hag is married to Augustus. Don't have children between them, some only from previous mistakes. Now Drusus does not enjoy his mother's company, so she is a hag to the lot of us. He has a brother, Tiberius? Yes, that's the one. More a mamma's boy that one, but Drusus loves Tiberius, so we love him as well, I suppose. As long as Drusus lives, lady and lad,' he said, giving Cassia a wet kiss on the cheek, one that made Ansbor get up and walk out briskly. Chariovalda grinned as he continued, 'Then we are safe, the Batavi. For now, we serve in their armies, and fine service it is. Nevertheless, no cows, nor slaves, nor silver do we give them. Only spear service we so much enjoy. The fawning Ubii pay, now the northern tribes too, like the Canifetes, but not us. Not without a fight. And we can fight.'

'Vangiones say they do not pay either.' I raised my eyebrows, and wondered what became of the Hunfrid, as my father had found him in Grinrock. Perhaps Vannius truly was the king now.

'Well, I don't trust a Vangione's words, but we really do not pay,' Chariovalda claimed, and threw an angry look my way. He pointed a bone at my nose. 'We boast less than they, and need not lie. Romans tax the shit out of the weak. Gauls sell their daughters to the wily merchants, but Germani are different. We fight; it is that simple. We have always fought. We fight better with their training and their weapons, with their legions. With them, we are much more. In addition, they are much more with us.

Our cavalry and their infantry complement each other, something the tribes this side of the river will one day find out. We help them with the things they lack. Ferocity of the northern gods, skills born in savage lands, and horsemanship we learn as children. Gods help them, if they ever try to tax us!' He laughed hollowly. 'Our weapons are too sharp for a taxman to ignore.'

'My swords?' I asked him. He ignored me. 'My spear?' I continued.

He shook his head. 'Sword. The short blade is still yours. Safe. All safe. Mine for keeping now. Perhaps one day, yours again? We will see.'

'What exactly do you plan to do with us?' I insisted, and he sighed.

'Hercules, let a man eat in peace!' he complained loudly, but then looked at me. 'Wait.' A man entered the ring, the same man who had come to our tent, saying nothing. He was seated in the middle, a position of honor. Chariovalda grunted. 'Hengsti's son, Thurwag. A young whelp, trying to rebuild his father's tribes. He sits here, and eats food we have stolen from his people. And he thanks us. He needs us, you see, to silence lords who are no longer loyal. We serve Thurwag for now.'

'Him, or someone else, if he is not smart enough for the job. Basically, you are here to make sure someone with less than amicable feelings for the Romans should not come to power?' I asked.

He raised his thick eyebrows in surprise and laughed. 'Yes. Thurwag is still being evaluated, and there are others we might like as well. You are not as stupid as you look! You might have uses, Hraban. I will take you to Drusus. Then, we will speak of your sword and spear.' Drusus. The name made me uncomfortable. He sounded like a man to turn hearts, and gods knew I did not trust myself with the poor judgment I had shown. I wanted to leave. To go and search for Lif. He nodded, as he saw my soured face. 'Your daughter is fine, no doubt an elfin thing of beauty, and I see your dilemma. No daughter is ugly to a father, eh?'

'She is pretty, and you dare to suggest she is not?' I growled indignantly.

He sighed. 'Mine are like mules, I admit it freely. Teeth sharp and small, and sour looking lot. Will be hell to marry them, will cost me lots, by

Hercules. In any case, my lord Hraban, I think you must come to him. You can offer him things. He can offer you things as well.'

'What kinds of things?' I asked.

'He can make dreams come true,' he whispered. 'He will love you.'

'Why would he love me so much as to lick my toes?'

'You will lick his ass first, and he returns his favors,' he laughed, and clapped me so hard I hit my jaw on the table. He leaned on me. 'If you speak the truth, then Nero Claudius Drusus is one of the men your father is supposed to send to the pyre. I am sure of it.'

I was about to ask him to speak more, when Thurwag pointed a finger at me. 'You were the one on the wall of this fort in the battle? The berserk whom all saw? The helmeted one, who danced swords with dozen Romans?'

I nodded. 'Our host has my helmet hidden somewhere, just like he is hiding away your food.' Thurwag snorted, and came to sit next to me, and we shared stories that night. In the end, Fulcher carried me to bed, drunk again, and I dreamt of Veleda. Yet, I slept, and I was grateful for that.

The following days, Chariovalda took me out on a horse, and gave me permission to walk the area around my tent, though not too far, and his guards made sure I knew the limits. Before the sun had risen, he trained with me. He gave me a wooden sword, like Nihta had used, and he put me through a hard routine. He was good with his weapon, older by fifteen years, and even if I was as fast as a fox and cunning enough, not entirely new to war after the past year's many fights, he had me on my back many times. He would goad me to simple rage, showing me how our kin fought, and what Romans had taught him. Woden would not dance with me, for this was no real fight, but I cursed myself for my ineptness. I knew how to fight, after all; I was just too angry.

He would grunt happily after he humiliated me. 'I can see you have been explained this. Fight with the point, son. You have a weapon made for it. It's not meant for felling trees! But, you still try, when you get angry,' he laughed, as I tried to hit his foot with a deceptive, low slash. It was a trap; he pushed me over, and I spat mud as I got up.

He spat. 'Come, son of the Marcomanni. I am a Roman citizen. A man higher than you, like an eagle is to a sparrow. There, you see. Only a peasant would swing like that! Ha! Is that something your grandmother showed you? With a broom, perhaps? Let me see, yes, that is it. That was good. For a boy. It was good but this is … better!' he said with a grin and ended my furious attack routine abruptly.

I was on my back again.

Nihta had been a dispassionate teacher, Chariovalda was all happiness and laughs, and where Nihta had made me disciplined and strong, Chariovalda made me skillful and clever. He helped me channel my rage away from the losses of Ermendrud, Ishild, and Lif. It worked for the day, but by evening, I would be sober again. But, I did not wish to be sober.

It was evening, two weeks after we had arrived to the Matticati lands. We were sitting outside our tent, by a raging fire. Chariovalda had gone to suppress a mutiny of some local Matticati with sturdy, dogged Thurwag, and we had been lounging outside of the tent all of the scorching hot morning and afternoon, looking on as the legionnaires were making a permanent fort, one built with thick timbers, high towers, and stone reinforced gates.

Cassia was infuriatingly happy, for she liked the carefree, equally happy Batavi women. She joked with them, often shamelessly about us men, and the handsome creatures made us feel like cleaning ourselves up. So, we had a bath arranged in strange, tiled tub and sat down in mild water, scrubbing out dirt and grime.

Fulcher looked supremely happy to do so. 'My daughter usually insisted we have a bath a few times a week. We had a fine, clear spring not far from us. My son and I … ' he said, and choked into silence.

'One day, we will find that man,' I told him reassuringly, for my Lif had made his loss seem insignificant.

Ansbor grunted away the unhappy moment, and replaced it with another. 'Here we sit, in a mildly warm water, but surely soon in a hot one again. Shall we wait here still when your father comes for a visit? Surely he knows we are here.' Ansbor spat. 'Or Odo.'

'Odo has no army,' I told him tediously. 'Only abominations.'

'So are you,' Ansbor muttered, and got up to dress. 'What else is this business with Odo but struggle and fear, as the rest of us wonder what will come to pass? Fight of the abominations.'

'Is this about Cassia again?' I asked him, tired and bitter. 'Not one of us have died yet, save for Hagano.' I remembered our young friend, the first victim of the events leading to the return of my father.

'Save for Hagano. And possibly Wandal,' Ansbor sneered. 'But, Hagano does not matter, does he? And now, they are taking us to the Romans? What happens to us, should this Drusus dislike you? And it is likely he does! Most everyone does! We will be sold into slavery. All you have left is that damnable, cursed ring.' I stared at the ring, and wondered how little it meant to me. But, it meant a lot to others.

Fulcher shook his head at me, as Ansbor went, huffing. 'He is choosing his own fate, Hraban. It is not your fault if he leaves. As for me, I am still waiting for the blood that is mine.'

'I hope we find it, friend,' I told him. 'Have some ale. Pour me some.' He did, and we lounged in the tubs, and the water was now getting cold.

Fulcher grunted, and a slave hurried to heat some more. 'What do you think your father is doing now?'

I waved my ale horn around, still peering at my ring. 'He is subduing the South for good. He will bleed any chief he does not like, and he will not like many. Then, he will crush any opposition threatening him from the outside, likely the Hermanduri Burlein invited. Perhaps he will be busy this summer. And he has Hunfrid. Gods fear what he will do with that cur.'

'If he is picking a fight with Rome, he will behead the fool, like a chicken,' Fulcher suggested, and we giggled at the thought.

'In any case,' I said, 'I have to find Lif. No matter what the windbag is doing. I do not know the North.'

'You have a plan?' he asked.

I fingered Woden's Gift. Draupnir's Spawn. He stared at the ring as well, and I sighed. 'I just don't love it as I used to. Thanks to you.' I smiled to take the edge off the comment. 'I feel I am lost to the Germani. But, I must stay for Lif, don't I? I do not love the ring.' I took a deep breath. 'But, Armin does. I will have to find Armin. He will give me resources to find Lif. It is a mighty gift I take him.'

'Ah, the mighty relic,' he mused. 'But, now, we go to the Romans?'

'We will escape, my friend,' I said heavily, 'but only when we are not surrounded by the Matticati, who war on each other. They would make leather shoes off our hide.'

'Thurwag is friendly with you, though?' Fulcher noted laconically.

'Thurwag is a pup,' I told him, 'but a friendly pup.'

'He is older than you!'

'He,' I sneered, 'has not been ground through Helheim, like I have.'

'Your Helheim,' he told me sadly, 'is yours. He has his own. He lost his father, and likely half his family here last year. I hope you have grown enough to see the turmoil of others, not only yours and mine.'

'I hunt for Lif now. Not fame.'

He shook his head. 'I know you saw what your fame is like already, how hard it would make people love you. And I saw you with your daughter. You have started to find honor only you know about, and I love you for it. But, there are other tests for you. Ones you might fail.'

'Why do you say that?' I asked him with rising anger. 'Is there not enough sorrow with Ansbor—'

He nodded. 'You have to settle the issue over Cassia. She cares for you,' he blurted and blushed. 'She is mad for you. It is growing, this problem.'

'What?'

'She feels burning love for you, my lord Heart Breaker. And you know it. Send her home, or it will end badly. Or love her, and deal with it. This cauldron is just festering until it spills on someone.' He got up to leave before I could dispute him, and then Chariovalda arrived.

He walked in slowly with his men, a few less than had left that morning, and his blond eyebrows were burrowed in concentration under some crusted blood. He was reading a scroll, and by him, walked a young man pulling at a sweaty light horse. He noticed us sitting around, burrowed his eyebrows into a purposeful scowl, and gestured impatiently at me. I gestured at the tub with an exasperated look, and he rolled his eyes, as he walked over to me. I handed him a horn of ale.

'Ale again?' he said. 'You are too young to drink it so often. Addles your brains, and gods know you cannot afford to get more addled. I told Cassia it is a bad idea to make a suffering man rely on drink.' Fulcher grunted in agreement, and Chariovalda continued, 'Better let me,' he said and quaffed it all down, grabbed mine, and emptied that as well, while kicking over the vessel that held more. 'Ah. Much better.'

I scowled at him, unreasonably angry, and I suspected he was right in claiming drink was not good for me. But, I did not care. He did not care for my scowl, and threw the scroll to me, and I barely caught it before it reached the water.

'Can you read?' he asked. I nodded uncertainly.

'Latin? I did not ask you to decipher pictures,' he sneered. I scowled at him and nodded again. 'Read,' he gestured, as he stretched and smiled at Cassia, who was heaving to sight. 'Ah, she always appears when I arrive.'

Fulcher sighed. 'Are you not married, my lord?'

'I am, but I cannot help being handsome. Only women turn into coarse, milk-swabbed creatures of broken nerves when they have babies, when us men will look better and better as time passes.'

'We thank you for these words of wisdom,' Fulcher said sarcastically. 'She can use an axe, lord, and you had better remember your wife.'

'What?' Chariovalda asked. 'I? Freyr forbids I could ever forget the terrible creature. Have you read it already, lout?' I took my time and ignored him, and he rolled his eyes. He grabbed it back from me. 'Very well. I will spare you the trouble. Nero Claudius Drusus is summoning the tribes of Germania to a Thing. This very month. We are going there. Perhaps we figure out what to do with you then. And you will meet him.'

I nodded, sure I would not. But, then, I thought of something.

'Are the Cherusci invited?' I asked timidly.

'The Masters of the Two Rivers? Yes, why?' he asked prudently.

'A man owes me cows, was just wondering if I get to call his debt in,' I told him earnestly.

'He won't be bringing cows, you idiot, only spears and his words, if this man of yours comes.' He yawned, and walked for his tent. He turned around, and yelled at me, 'If you try to escape, boy, I will clip your balls. And stop dipping into my mead and ale, or I will give you to a slaver. I would not want them to see how I make adelings into bastard drunkards.' He left.

I scowled at his back, and spoke to Fulcher. 'If Armin is coming to this thing, then we are going as well.'

'If your father comes?' Fulcher asked.

'Then I shall challenge him there,' I said grimly. 'And hope to survive.'

'Gods bless you, lord,' Fulcher said. 'I shall bury you well, then.'

'Dip your head into a horse's ass, Fulcher, and get us more mead,' I told him, as I got up to dress, making a slave girl blush.

'He said no ... ' Fulcher told me, but I cursed, and so we drank, as I had come to appreciate its healing powers. Few other things made me happy, few things silenced Lif's soft cries in my dreams. I did train each morning with Chariovalda or even Fulcher, but the thought of Lif in some remote hut, or even a grave, drove me mad. Cassia, apparently feeling guilty of my newborn thirst, tried to stop me, but I ignored her angry words and even pleas.

One week passed. Even Fulcher and Ansbor ignored my company, but I growled at their backs, and told them all to go to Hel and drank myself senseless. So, on the day before we were supposed to ride to Moganticum, Chariovalda came to me while I slept, kicked me awake, and when I growled and tried to slap his offending foot, he gave me a proper feast. He sat heavily on my chest, forced my hands down to the sides, and beckoned to his grinning, fiendish men, who brought jar after jar of wine, heavy mead, and some stiff drinks I didn't know, apparently made of fermented horse milk. He forced so much drink down my throat I was left insensible.

Later in the morning, he forced me on a horse, and I threw up long into the afternoon; I cannot remember feeling as miserable. For some reason, I did not even remember Lif.

The Batavians laughed helplessly at my vomit-sodden face and beard, my desperate eyes, and the poor beast carrying me likely felt as miserable as I did. We were riding for Rhenus River, with many a rebellious, captured Matticati lords in tow, and Chariovalda was constantly sending scouts ahead and behind and smirking at my red eyes. 'I told you, son. No more mead. No more ale. You had better know whom to obey. I mean you no evil,' he said, and smirked as I retched again. 'Drink without permission again, and we shall do this again. I shall lead you around Moganticum's two Gaulish towns, nude and drunk, and tell all it is Hraban of No Sense, and you will never forget that. Mourn Lif, you bastard, your daughter. It is what a man is supposed to do, not to escape the fears and sorrow.'

'Yes, lord,' I told him, retching. 'You never saw her, and—'

'Yes, the name is all I know,' he told me morosely. 'Now, your men tell me nothing of worth. I serve Rome; Hercules knows whom you serve, but at least the woman told me of your life a bit more, so I do feel some pity for you.'

I turned to look at Cassia, who stared at me imperiously. 'She would make a terrible enemy,' I blurted. 'She knows too much about me.'

'Any woman would,' he rumbled. 'No sense destroying yourself. Sweet wine, sweeter mead, it will do that to a man. You grow weak as a kitten, your limbs do not answer your call as swiftly as they should, your muscles groan at the simplest of tasks, and you die a rotten, pitiful death at the backyard of some inn, utterly despised and forgotten. The only time they will take note of you is when they have to bury you for the common good. World is full of adelings, abandoned by their fathers, and men who have lost a child. Even Drusus does not get along with Augustus, these days!' He chewed some dried meat, and laughed at me as he eyed me.

'How badly are they—'

He shrugged. 'Drusus is … an old Roman. He is fury as Donor himself in war, but in his ways frugal and austere. Of course, when he feasts, he is like us, happy and boisterous. His wife is a goddess as well. But, his adopted father does not care for him.'

'And yet, he commands the war?' I questioned.

'Oh, yes, he is allowed legions here, in the frontier. It is a risk. For Augustus. Should Drusus will it, these troops might not hesitate to turn on Rome; after all, it has been so in Rome for decades,' Chariovalda said. 'Drusus is a good son to Livia and obeys her, but he has his own thoughts. And I wish you to share with him what you know about Maroboodus.'

'You said Drusus is one of the men the bastards in Rome wish to see die?' I said, feeling sick.

'It is irony, you see, that Drusus, Augustus's own adopted son, thinks the Republic is the finest thing that ever fell out of Juppiter's ass, and I am sure there are a lot of tensions in their world. Now, if Maroboodus is raising the tribes against Drusus, then Drusus should not underestimate the danger. I worry for him. They dare not attack him publicly, so I do believe your story. They will use a Roman to slay Romans, and will reap Germania as a nice bonus,' Chariovalda said softly. 'You have to—'

'Tell him someone in Rome wishes to see him dead? I should tell him this? He would laugh. Then, sell me to slavery,' I said, and then retched.

'For the sakes of the bastard dogs of Cerebus! Stop torturing the horse! Yes,' he said more calmly. 'Just tell him what the bastard told you. Who was the bastard?'

'One Antius,' I said. 'Trader for the legions.'

He turned in his saddle. 'The producer of munitions for the army? Negotiatore for annona militaris? What? That fat creature?'

'He has a servant, some ugly mule of an optio? Cornix. They are there, and serve some other purpose than ... taking care of annona miliaris.'

'Militaris,' he crumbled. 'There, see. This will be interesting. You shall tell him.' He turned in his saddle. 'If you are planning an escape, of which I warned you about, then at least see him before you try. He might not understand your words, if your voice is very high.'

'What?'

'If I clip your nuts, boy, I told you, and you will not speak like a man again,' he chuckled, and I trusted his expertise. 'And remember, Drusus is a powerful ally. One who takes his favors and honor seriously. Trust him, but do not betray him. Tell him everything, as he is like a god. Swift to reward and to love, but stubborn in hate.'

'Not unlike Maroboodus,' I said. 'They know each other?'

'Likely met in Rome, your father guarded Augustus, remember?' he told me as he observed the Rhenus River coming to sight, the long streak of silver amidst greens and myriads of browns, as we passed fertile valleys and tight copses of alder trees. 'His father died when he was young. Loved him, I think, anyway.'

'I am past caring for my father. He abandoned me the moment he saw me.' I spat.

We rode in silence for a while, until he grunted. 'So what? You lost your woman and child? I hear you were not even properly married! It is a brutal world. I have rarely seen a young man so prominent, and most of the Matticati whisper about your fight in that there castrum. You should be strong, and stop worrying yourself into a drunkard!' he pushed me, and I tried to slap his arm feebly.

I could not help it, but his concern got through to me. 'I had a beautiful baby, and a woman I did not understand. She betrayed us, or saved us, I don't know. In the end, I had to give up the baby to a man I do not trust,' I said. Tears filled my eyes, and I tried to wipe them away so as not to shame myself, but Chariovalda clapped a hand on my shoulder.

'So tell me everything. Everything about fathers, brothers, sisters if you have them, sons and daughters. It will be good to share aches with a man, not only to a woman.'

And I did. Cassia rode close by, protectively. It took time, but he never once interrupted, but kept nodding and grunting. I saw his face harden with anger, and even his tears flow with grief, and I told him what had come to pass the past year. I told him of the prophecy, and what I had to do to survive Wulf, Bark, and Shayla, and how I had loved Shayla. I told him of my losses of grandfathers, mother, and even father, whom I had come to respect. I told him of the vile deeds I performed for him. I told him of the loss of Wandal, and what happened to Ermendrud.

When I was done, he was silent, watching the thickets around us. Then he smiled sarcastically. 'And here I thought you were wet behind the ears. Gods know you have suffered, but you have also caused grief.'

'Yes, lord,' I told him with misery.

Ansbor shook his head nearby. 'And you did not tell us of Leuthard.'

Chariovalda spat. 'He told me, as he knows I won't start crying. Shut up. Here,' he said, and handed me Nightbright. 'Sounds like you need to be armed in sleep.' I gratefully accepted the fine blade and grasped it in my hand. 'And, before you ask, I am keeping the long blade. You will tell me its history, one day. It is a mighty relic we do not wish to see amidst a horde of Germani charging us, should you go back.'

'I gave them freely,' I said hollowly, looking over at Head Taker enviously.

'No, you gave them because you had to,' he corrected me. 'As for this poor Ermendrud? There are stories of their family.'

'Ermendrud's? His father was Fulch the Red,' I said, addled indeed.

'No, no! Leuthard's. But Fulch the Red? Oh. He was a nasty one in a shield wall. Smelly, but also deft with an axe. Split one of my friends from collarbone to belly, and then—'

'Lord!' I nearly shrieked. 'Leuthard?'

'Yes, well,' he said, guiding his horse so it would not step on horse dung, dropped by the beast in front of him. He failed. 'Gods! I am sorry, lovely one. We will clean it later, yes. As for Leuthard's family, Guthbert left for Rome, long before Leuthard was driven from Batavorium. His father, I hear, had it. What Leuthard has.'

'An illness?' I asked.

'A curse, not unlike yours, except you don't eat man flesh,' he giggled, and sobered. 'They do. They eat humans. They tear the meat, crack the bone, and it fascinates them. They cannot subdue their thirst for such things. A woman was killed when Leuthard was but fifteen. The Thing condemned him to exile, after his father paid the wergild.'

'He is what, exactly?'

Cassia was riding close, listening in. Chariovalda glared at her.

'Why are you with him? Next in line to be his wife?' Chariovalda asked her with a grin.

'I've never been married,' I interrupted, and noticed Ansbor's face darken. His brown beard shook in anger, and I knew Fulcher was right. I'd have to deal with the problem, though I had tried already. It was not my fault Cassia did not think of him as a future husband. Had I not told him to tell her he loved her a long time ago? He had done so near Moenus, finally, I reminded myself. Had Cassia left him hanging, giving him some hope? Gods, women were terrible.

She blushed and choked. 'He is my friend. And I don't wish to get married. That is exactly why I am here.'

'Ah,' he said, confused. 'You are hiding from your fiancé? With this god-cursed boy? A brilliant plan. As for Leuthard,' he continued. 'As you just told me, your family is blessed, or cursed, with the blood of the high one, Woden the Wanderer, the Wise God, but there are other creatures the gods made.'

I agreed. 'Odo, the mongrel who tries to make this world a drowned land devoid of life, claims Lok cursed our blood, and then created theirs. I have heard Sigyn speak, so—'

He made warding signs, and knocked on wood we were passing, startling a fat squirrel to run high up to the boughs. It was yipping agitatedly. 'Do not mention ... very well. Mention away. But, Lok made many creatures, inspired by Woden. We all know Lok is spreading his seed profusely across all the worlds, and he has bred quite a host of monsters into this world of ours. The Midgard Serpent, for example. And Vánagandr.'

'Ishild mentioned something before she left me,' I said softly.

Fulcher was nodding. 'Vánagandr. The Wolf?'

'The same, the wolf. Fenfir, by his other name.'

'Woden's bane, come Ragnarök,' Ansbor grunted.

Chariovalda nodded sagely, as he picked leaves off the trees. 'Fenfir bred two wolves, one that chases the sun, Skoll. Another chases the moon. When these are swallowed, Fenfir is freed, as is Lok, and so—'

Cassia was smiling. 'You have so many legends.'

'You share these … dreams,' Chariovalda spat. 'Your druids hide them, that is all, keeping the signs and many of the stories to themselves. As for Hati, this moon-chasing mutt, this wolf is a savage one. A night creature, and it is said he does not chase the moon dutifully across the sky, as a good dog would. No, he has the taste of man flesh, but also can take a man's form. It is said he lives amongst us, sullenly serving Lok in small ways, spreading his seed, and growing his brood of half-men.'

'Guthbert never had this … urge?' I asked, terrified now.

'No. But, Leuthard was ever strange. What did he look like? When you saw him.'

'Bloody,' I told him. 'Very tall, but he is tall. Dangerous. Delighted by his meal. Above—'

'Human needs and thoughts, yes,' Chariovalda said, with a chuckle. 'He was caught that day, when he was fifteen, holding the heart of the woman he had killed. He was exiled, and became a shield breaker for the Marcomanni. Your father bought him easily enough, for he loves, loved Guthbert, even if they often fought. Now, you say he is after you?'

'He is,' I spoke hollowly, eyeing Fulcher and Ansbor who were riding sullenly near us, unhappy with this news.

Chariovalda put a heavy hand on my shoulder. 'As I said, Hati is a wolf that follows few gods, and only occasionally chases the moon in the sky. Leuthard is like that. Odo's service to Lok does not matter to him. I would fear, both whatever Maroboodus has asked him to do, and what he will do to avenge Guthbert. He wants revenge, at some point.'

'I will try to survive him,' I growled. 'Last time I fed him to a wolverine.'

He laughed hugely. 'I know, incredible. But, likely, that saved your ass.' He nodded at me. 'You are all crazy, but I like you lot. Let me mull things over, Hraban, and see if I can help you in any way, after you have had a chat with Drusus. End of the world? You fighting a powerful prophecy with a Wolf, and this awkward rot-skull Odo after you? Your father's games? All this is a hard tale for a simple man like me to understand, but I will try!'

300

That evening, we were close to Rhenus River, and Chariovalda kept glancing at me. I knew not what he was thinking, for he had been mostly silent after my story, though he did not shame me for my tears. He had shed his own, as he was an empathetic man. I gazed at the small fort on the eastern bank of the river and across the water; Moganticum's mighty fort atop a bluff was shadowing the filthy harbor and the two Gaul villages. Fulcher and Ansbor came, and wondered at its many lights, the torch light rafts, and the larger ships. The Roman power was evident.

'Rancid tit,' Ansbor said softly. 'God's piss, but it is four times Hard Hill.'

Fulcher and Ansbor stared at it awestruck. Chariovalda was grinning at their reaction. 'Tomorrow, we cross. And you are Romans. At least, until you run away.'

I smiled at him. Only until I met with Armin. I fingered the ring in my hand.

PART IV: THE EAGLE AND THE FOX

'Roman laws concern us. Roman trade we do not need. Your words? We should not heed.'
Inguiomerus the Gaunt to Drusus.

CHAPTER XX

We were standing on the deck of a simple raft. We approached the harbor, wondering at the terrible business of slave trading, the miserable creatures huddled on the deck of a boat, some being ushered to sit by walls, all tethered like animals. We glimpsed long, busy warehouses full of jars of all sizes and shapes, even colors. Curious looking men were arguing, making hard bargains, and the beggars peered on, as vast sums of coin changed hands. The nauseating smells hammered our senses, and I remembered what Nihta had told me of the harbors of the southern seas. Part of that was evident, even in this backwater fort; the terrible sights of poverty and wondrous riches. They were all there, mixed together.

The town itself surrounding the harbor was growing, which was apparent by the harried craftsmen running wood to the town, the horse drawn carts a virtual line on the muddy roads. A tall wall was being erected around the town area, wooden, but in places already made of stone, and high up on the bluff overshadowing the town, the castrum had another village growing around it. Up there, I spotted a fabulous building, made of gray stone, a temple of Mercury. I had seen similar building in Burbetomagus, but this one was much larger, with real marble and stone on the walls, and a brilliant white statue hunkered over the doorway, overlooking the town, castrum, and the harbor.

Fulcher was looking at the massive fort with disbelieving eyes, and Ansbor was cursing. 'How did you take the fort in Matticati lands?' Fulcher asked, with a small voice.

'With surprise. We are not here to take this one. We are here to find a refuge inside it. I suppose we are guests,' I said neutrally.

Chariovalda snorted. 'You are guests, who are closely watched, my friends.'

Fulcher spat, and whispered to me, 'They are Romans. Not to be trusted.'

'Chariovalda is to be trusted, indeed. And they are our Roman hosts now,' I said. 'Until I find Armin,' I whispered.

'Until what?' asked Chariovalda. 'I couldn't hear you.'

'Until we know what Drusus will want to do with me,' I smiled, and lied to him.

He grimaced back, not entirely sure he should believe me. 'That, or until I decide I don't like your treasonous mutterings,' Chariovalda rumbled, as the ship moored to the planks with a jarring crash, and shrill curses from a thin harbormaster rang out, as he tore at his thinning hair.

Cassia was beaming. 'There is the warehouse my father owned!' Then, she squinted. 'It has been given to someone else now. Bastards. I should—'

I patted her back. 'Perhaps you should see what became of your estates. Get it back? We cannot help you, likely. Being non-Romans.'

'Peregrini,' she said, as she gazed at the warehouse. 'That is what you are called. The Romans do not truly see us local citizens as equals, either. There are many shades of respect and rights in these matters, and if my estate is gone, it is likely gone for good. And as I said, my former fiancé is likely married already. Hopefully.'

I snickered. 'You'll need a husband with a forceful war band to wrest it back, should you wish to.'

'Are we talking about my dreams now, finally?' Cassia asked. 'You never wondered about them.'

'I have asked why you stayed,' I growled, and bowed sarcastically. 'What are your dreams?'

She took a shuddering breath. 'I had dreams to make the estates something much more than they were with Father. We have apples and wheat, lumber and ore, and he was a hopeless idiot with the prizing and

305

timing as he traded it. Yet, now? I have different dreams. You meet someone, and then, you are hopelessly stricken. So, now, I have different plans. I'll stay with you. As for Lif, we are all with you. For, we love you.' She went silent, and put a hand on mine for a second. I stiffened, and stared in her eyes. 'And I am not some fawning fool you can mistreat, Hraban. I will hit you with an axe, if you do not appreciate me. So far, you have. But, I want more.'

'What did you tell Ansbor that night we were running away from Odo?' I asked her breathlessly.

'I don't know how to break his heart, Hraban. You must, if you feel the same,' she told me, smiled, and moved away.

Gods, help me, I thought, as despite our hardships and my sorrow, I did love her.

'What did she say?' Ansbor came over and asked me, somewhat desperately. 'You held hands. As friends? Did she—'

'I spoke to her about our business, of Lif, and other things. And they are our words, Ansbor, not yours.' I marched away, hoping he would not follow. I felt guilty, but we were heading for trouble, and I had no time for his moods. I would have to break him. Fulcher was right.

Later.

We disembarked after the Batavi, and walked by to a sad slave market. Vendors hawked their living wares, Germani youths being particularly sought after by a Roman merchant, and of course, the young women were fetching handsome prizes. One young, red-headed girl was looking at us, huge eyed, with misplaced hope.

'Bless the girls, if they go to Rome,' Chariovalda crumbled, as the horses were disembarked, and he swatted a slave who had pushed his horse disrespectfully.

Ansbor stopped me. 'Why do they hold them out like this?'

Cassia turned to him. 'They are flesh, that is all. Slave in Germania is a happier creature than one in Rome, or even Gaul. One has to obey, but here, they have no rights. I was his slave, remember?' She thumbed towards me.

'You never were! I needed a healer for the dolt. I fetched one,' I nodded at Ansbor. 'One of the better deeds Felix ever did for us.'

'There are many, many slaves here, young Ansbor. You will find it different to your home,' Chariovalda told him good-naturedly.

'I miss it already,' Ansbor grumbled.

I could only agree. I remembered my unwilling visit to Burbetomagus. Despite the fantastic shops full of fabulous and unusual wares, and strange looking traders from afar, I had not loved it. Home was where you woke up to a slight chill. It was where you walked to the hall for a quick bite of cold meat, or bowl of warmed gruel, and outside the birds sang in your own language, the fat cows complained as slaves milked them, and you were your own master.

Yet, I had no such home. Nor would I, unless with Armin. And even then, I would be shunned and reviled.

There, in the Roman lands, none knew me. I cursed and corrected myself. The Romans did not know me. The Germani, like the Vangiones, did, and were not friends to me either.

Chariovalda was finally ready. We mounted up. 'Come, Legate Saturninus waits!' he yelled.

'Saturninus?' I asked, as I followed him.

'A legate to the XIX Legion up north with the Ubii, but here to deal with many issues with the infrastructure. He is a master in logistics, and should be in Syria fixing the tax system, not in here. But, he is needed. Drusus trusts him. A fair man as well, as long as he does not dislike you,' he said. Children chased after us, and Chariovalda enjoyed a game of torture and threw them bronze coins that landed in hard to reach places. He enjoyed a particular success when a child had to climb to a jar, or over something bigger than they were to reach the coins. 'Builds up character,' he explained sheepishly, as Cassia scowled at him, after a dog had nearly bit a girl for coming too close. She got the coin though, and smiled impishly after us. 'See?' he asked Cassia. She did not answer.

Before us opened the clear space in front of the huge fort. This was the area where you were not allowed to build anything; the killing field for missiles, should an enemy lay siege to the fort. The legate sat on a small horse outside the gate. He had on his brilliant, sculpted armor, and his guards were glistening in the sun in their metal helmets with feathers sticking up, their lorica hamata shined to the sheen. We approached the legate, who was an older man, weather-beaten, white-haired, and looked like he would be able to eat a brick. 'So, how did it go?'

Chariovalda saluted the man. 'The Pup should have the Matticati under his weak thumb now. I left some commanders there, and brought back some of the more rebellious chiefs. The lot are to be jailed. That should keep their families controlled, at least until the Pup is seen as a legitimate ruler.'

'Losses? Maroboodus?' he asked.

'Infinitesimal. Lost a few men. And I did scout the lands of the Quadi,' he said, with a smile.

Saturninus was scratching under his chinstrap, then he took off the helmet, and his sweaty gray curls were plastered to his head. 'So? Tell me more. You look like a dog that stole a snail pie.'

'I could kill for one!' Chariovalda said, but did not draw a favorable expression from the legate, who was a short man, as were many Romans, but wide of shoulders, and his eyes missed little. He was like flesh beaten into iron by rigors and pain. Men like this would wreak havoc on our side of the river. My fingers brushed Nightbright, and his eyes bore into mine.

'You found a wild wolf out there?' he said carefully, nodding at me.

'Ah, yes. Him. He is an interesting creature, Legate. I saved his hide, as he was running from some scoundrels. Fights well, and I am thinking about keeping him,' Chariovalda said, with a wink.

Legate was nodding. 'And?'

'And … ' Chariovalda said, throwing his hands around. 'Nothing, legate. He is my pet. I'll show him to Drusus, perhaps.'

'I see,' the legate said. 'What does he have to say to Drusus?'

'I—'

The man was consumed by sudden rage, and he hit his four-horned, silver-etched saddle savagely. 'There is this meeting coming, Chariovalda, and it is driving me crazy. Absolutely mad. So what news does this one have for Drusus? I know you two, Drusus and yourself, are close friends, and now you wish to show this dark-haired bastard to him. Now, cough it up. You know he is my friend as well.'

'Is there one Antius in the camp?' I asked him, with broken Latin, and his rage turned into astonishment.

'My, my! A Germani who speaks civil. Like a demented child, but still! Antius? The negotiatore? Yes, he is here,' Saturninus said. Then, he raised his hand. 'Wait. The man is as slippery as a prick after a good night with a woman, and none like him. He is getting rich with his business, and he is not known to be very honest. Likely sells some of the food meant for the troops to the enemy, even. Is this about it?'

'No,' I said.

'Good, for that would be beneath Drusus to handle,' he crumbled. 'So, it must be some sort of a conspiracy. No?'

'Yes,' I said calmly.

'In that case, feel free to stay, young man,' he grinned. 'There are a few of us keen on keeping the young lord alive, and he does need to be warned until he hears and obeys.'

'He is not that young,' Chariovalda said softly.

'Be that as it may, that fat turnip Antius has a lot of power, boys. He should not be called a traitor, at least to his face, nor to anyone else's, now that I think about it.' Saturninus let his face adopt a gentler look. It made him look strange, as if kindness was painful to him. 'You will let Nero Claudius Drusus decide what to do with him. He might not listen. Big things are afoot.'

'I am honored to meet him, if he has an hour to spare,' I said, seething at the lost time. 'When is this meeting, and will the Cherusci come?' Chariovalda glanced my way suspiciously, but I ignored him.

'Oh, I am sure he has time for men who fight. He likes the grease of the saddle, loves even the lazy soldiers, so you will see him. Now, Chariovalda, talk to me on the side.' They rode off near the wall, where Chariovalda laughed as he gestured towards me. Saturninus sighed and started to argue, and they had an animated discussion. After a while, they came back. 'I assume you will make sure he goes nowhere without guards. I have things to do before Drusus arrives. They made him an urban praetor in Rome for this year, but he cannot keep his hands off the Germani, so he is here,' Saturninus said, dismissing me with his hand. 'That means I cannot leave to Ara Ubiorum for the XIX legion yet, either.'

Chariovalda was playing with one of his moustaches and winked at us. 'Yes, our sponsor is looking to kill a great chief in a single combat, so he can offer Juppiter Spolia Opima the enemy's armor in Rome. Glorious goal, though his pregnant wife will likely curse him for his dangerous hobbies!' Chariovalda looked at me and smirked. 'Perhaps he shall hunt your father in the field? And he has other reasons to be here. You will see.'

'My father is mine. He has to get in line,' I growled.

'He's got a split face, and he is still full of hot air.' Chariovalda jerked a thumb in my direction.

'Who is his father? Never mind! Drusus will put him in his place,' Saturninus said and left, cursing all the Germani to Hades. Then he cursed again, as he could not ride to camp, dismounted stiffly, and took the rightmost gate, Porta Principalis Dextra, as he huffed away. 'Find one Cornix for me!' he screamed at a guard, and I smiled. 'The optio with no face. You know him, Antius's lapdog. Find him!' A guard ran to execute his orders.

'I told him he should hold Cornix, Antius's helper, though I did not tell him what for. He did not appreciate it, but agreed. But, I doubt he is to be found,' Chariovalda said. 'It is very hard to pin that fat Antius down, and I doubt his man is easier to find.' He squinted my way. 'Puppet for so many mighty children, that is what you are, Hraban.'

I spat. 'Puppets sometimes get pulled apart by naughty children. I am no puppet, not anymore.'

'Being a puppet to Drusus might be the first time you can make the most of yourself,' he told me, and burped. 'Forget the Cherusci, and whatever you plan with them. Yes, they will be here.' He led his men to the outskirts of the fort. 'Fossa,' he said before we went through the brooding gates, pulling at our horses, pointing down at the deep pit surrounding the fort, deeper than most. 'Agger!' he said, and pointed at the elevated wooden and sturdy stonewalls and I grunted. Tall and thick. 'More than agger now. Used to be a rut in the sand.'

We entered the fort, leading the horses to a stable area near the gates, where the men of small detachment of cavalry were fixing up some broken harness. Chariovalda was smiling. 'Look, there, the Via Principalis takes you across to the parade ground in the middle, after that the praetorium, and there, boy, sits our Saturninus and the other legates.'

Inside the gate, the castrum was very similar to the fort the Roman cohort had been building in the land of the Matticati, but larger, much larger, made for more than one legion. There were lines of barracks, many with patios. A straight stone road ran for the praetorium, and at the end of the street, I could see finer houses, the ones for higher officers, or tribunes. On the right and left, just after the gate, there was a clear space, so it would be easy to run to the walls, and legionnaires were living in barracks just next to this space. There were corrals for cows, and sheds for other animals.

We walked forward, and I admired the quality of the road. So smooth and well-placed, it actually felt crafted by gods. It felt strange to walk on it, and I tried to use the mud tracks beside it, but Chariovalda jerked me back to the road. We passed the numerous barracks, where men of the legions lounged, gambled, and laughed, their officers cursing, trying to find them things to do. A Germani chief would have to cajole and exhort their men to get out and do some menial tasks, and even then, they would be poorly done, but here, they tried to excel. Yet, the men seemed happy.

I would see these men fight, one day, no longer happy but angry and bloodthirsty.

Chariovalda grinned sadly. 'Our Germani pride is based on the individual, theirs on the nation. An individual will go on through centuries, unchanged, feeling insulted by the slightest slight, and thus will Germani conquer slowly, for they will obey no one. Rome conquers swiftly, for they say, "we will," instead of "I will." We brag of individual victories, they of common slaughter. Their soldiers, if not the generals, will share the spoils gladly, as well as the pains. If a Roman soldier ever lost their pride in their nation, these men would turn in to mercenaries.' I shrugged it out of my head, but would think about it in the future.

We walked all the way to the fifth street, where we noticed locals had set up a small market, and they could go no further than this. The Gauls had set up a forum, where they sold anything from clothing to weapons, love potions, and tools. There was food, all kinds of meat and vegetables, and brazen women as well, though the final part of that business was to be conducted outside. Legionnaires and Gauls looked up at us with brief interest, and went back to bantering.

In the middle of the camp was a very austere looking building, with marble columns, small ones, but still, and other buildings meant for the standards and officers. 'Praetorium,' Chariovalda said patiently. We turned north, and walked briskly to the auxilia barracks, similar in style to every other building we passed.

'This is like a dream,' Ansbor said. 'Was Castrum Luppia like this before your father burned it? Surely not?'

'No, they were tents only,' I said. 'The way you saw it. Some hundred soldiers.'

'They are like ants,' Fulcher said, as he ogled the marching men in chain mail. 'Merciless and precise. Do they enjoy themselves?'

'I do not know,' I said somberly. 'But they fight doggedly.'

Some men were working on building a smithy and setting up workshops, and there were some who were cooking bread in clay ovens. Legionnaires stopped and smiled at us, and I decided they knew how to enjoy life as well. They were an interesting lot. I gazed at their faces, and there were young boys full of wonder, old grizzled veterans, with scars and scowls to match, rat-toothed men, with skinny faces, fat men, with swarthy complexions. All men different to each other, of course, yet all similar in dress, and especially in bearing. Proud. Indomitable. Capricious and gay at the same time. The best men there are, they obviously thought. And they were right.

I envied them, and understood how a man could find a place for themselves amongst them.

Around us, the sturdy legionnaires came and went, hundreds working on hauling gear and building materials, hundreds were out training. And running. Gods, like Nihta had trained me. Some men were waiting in lines for food, and others were fixing gear. A man was hollering, running a gauntlet of grim-faced, determined men. His mates were punishing him, brutally, and whacking his with cingulum belts, studded ones, and blood flew.

'A thief!' Chariovalda told us, as the squad beat the man, led by a sadistically grinning centurion wielding a stick. We were shown a barracks, one that held supplies, but we were happy to rest, though I despaired at the lost time.

That evening, I saw a man staring at our door from the shadows. It was Cornix. He noticed me, and disappeared. Antius's supply master. My enemy. Men my father worked with were watching us.

CHAPTER XXI

I despaired more, as two long weeks went by without Drusus, and I thought Lif was far, far away. I was begging she would be alive, but felt hopeless, and I was brooding. Then, Chariovalda's men celebrated Drimilchi at the end of the month. It was one year since Hulderic and Sigilind had died, and everything was different. I was scarred in face and body, and I was a father to a lost child. I had tried to kill my own father. I still would.

I thought about these things as they took us to the feast, as the Batavi celebrated outside the Roman camp, in the deep night by a fire. They made fine offerings to the old gods, a fat cow, and one of his men was a priest, as well as a warrior, and they sang songs about their past deeds. They were Germani, through and through, but they served Roman Gods as well, and I admired their character, as they lived a life on the edge of old and new, navigating those murky waters easily, and without a care. Woden was with them, I was sure, and I doubted any Roman god would think less of them for their long beards and merry ways, even if a Roman noble would smirk at them with amusement, and arrogance.

Chariovalda sat next to me later in the evening, put a hand on my shoulder, and smiled.

'Where is Cassia?' he said, surveying the crowd. 'We do not mind having a pretty face amongst us.'

'She is at the camp, a bit sick, she told Fulcher. A man of yours is watching her.'

'Not pregnant, no?' he asked, and I shook my head, remembering Ermendrud's lost baby. 'Perhaps I shall visit her, and make sure she is fine,' the old lecherous bastard suggested, and immensely enjoyed the startled look on my face.

'I am thinking about Lif, not Cassia,' I pouted after I recovered.

'Lif. Yes, yes. Anything to ease your thoughts, boy? Do not hesitate to ask. Anything, save for freedom, and an excessive amount of my mead,' he laughed. 'Except this very night. The mead, that is.'

I shook in tired anger. 'Lord, I do not think I am good company. My sorrows weigh me down. I can only think about riding out there, finding them, and getting back what is mine,' I started to leave. He grabbed me, and pulled me back so hard I fell over the log I had been using as a seat. He let me scramble up on my own.

He grinned. 'Now, shut up, and enjoy our company, even if yours is miserable. Don't want to force my men to abandon the feast, and look after your sorry ass. We will have even more company this night ... wait. They are here.'

I started to ask what he was talking about, but he didn't have time to answer. A line of ghostly horses was approaching from the south, the riders' faces shrouded in mists, only their silhouettes in sight, as if they were dead and stalking the living. They looked like shadows, with an occasional glitter of armor, not daring the flames and light.

Yet, it was not so.

They did brave the light, and we saw they were a dusty line of men seated on great horses, Romans in chain armor, a cavalry unit one hundred strong, with a great purple, red, and gold banner. A silver and gold eagle was perched inside a circle of leaves, and gazing imperiously from the lofty perch. Then, a less glamorous sight at a first glance rumbled along, a wagon, four-wheeled raeda was rolling forward with them, and then under the dust, we saw it was shiningly silvery and breathtakingly beautiful, led by white horses. The column stopped by us. The Batavi got up, and Chariovalda nudged me with his foot. We joined the Batavi. A man jumped out of the wagon's side, pulling aside a dirty curtain. It was an ugly man, with a strange hunched back and a scowling countenance of a suspicious beast, its hair matted with grease.

315

Chariovalda leaned on me. 'Better bow to Drusus, boy. That is his standard. He will want you to bow low, for he does not know you. A fool gawking like you do, while he stands before you, a bad idea.'

'But is—'

'Suit yourself, Hraban,' Chariovalda said, shaking his head in dread. 'You are a brave one, to be sure.'

I gave him a very evil eye, and scrambled forward. The beast-like man turned to squint at me in return, a bit of drool escaping his lip, and I shuddered. *Gods, where was Armin*, I thought, hoping to be rid of Rome, though I liked the Batavi just fine. I avoided looking at the thing, and went on one knee before the ugly man. A wave of snickers rose around me as a handsome, short man rode up on a grimy gray horse, while dusting himself off. He gaped at the sight of me on my knee, and jumped down like a true rider, agile as a cat.

I glanced his way and wondered, for he was apparently in his forties, but looked boyish and springy, as if he had just run and won a race with a youngster, utterly dusty and happy. I noted his eyes were very light brown, his hair dark and stiff, his chin strong, and there was a certain nervous energy about him, as he fidgeted, staring at me. He noticed Chariovalda, and pointed a curious finger my way, while he scratched his temple with his other hand. 'Who is the young scar bowing to my slave?' Then, he spoke to the slave, without waiting for Chariovalda to answer. 'Garmix! Is there something uncouth going on here? I don't abide my slave having affairs I don't know about!'

'No, lord,' said the ugly man, with a bow. My head was spinning, as I realized what had happened. I turned to look at Chariovalda, who was wiping his eyes as mirth helplessly shook his body, and even Ansbor and Fulcher were laughing raucously. The slave continued, 'He is not my type, lord. I like mine more docile. This one looks as mad as a bull with a thorn in its nut. Not the loving, cuddly type, no.' The glorious man laughed as his slave, the ugly man, grinned at me. I got up, my fists balled, scowling.

'Lord … ' I began. 'I am—'

'Yes, yes, a Germani. I am sorry, my friend. I know you are not his lover, and abhor the thought. In Rome, such things are more common, though a free man should never be the one who submits. If you do desire him later, make sure he is the one bending over, and have him clean himself. Come.'

I sputtered and reddened, and he laughed hugely. The man, Nero Claudius Drusus, placed a hand on my shoulder, calming me. Despite the nervous energy in him, there was a strange quality to his face and eyes. While he had been making a joke not a moment before, now his eyes scourged my soul, and I could not look away. The orbs did not move, nor did they blink; they stared at me as if they were alfish eyes, strange and inhuman. He was formulating opinions, wondering and making up decisions, and gods forbid, if he did not like me. I stood tall as we walked to Chariovalda, who was still breathless.

Drusus nodded at me, tearing his eyes off, and then grinned at the bastard Batavi. 'Chariovalda. Well met. You should not play such tricks on such a formidable youngster. He is all knotted muscle, has the temper of a badger mother and a very thin patience, and might split your head for such affronts, you utter fool,' drawled the man, as he let me go. I felt somehow sorry for it, but the two men embraced warmly, Chariovalda bending down to the great lord.

The man laughed heartily at Chariovalda, and then threw off his dusty cloak. Underneath, he wore glorious war gear, an intricately sculpted metal cuirass, with fat medals of gold and silver. He bore himself like a god, as he spoke at length with Chariovalda. They were talking about many things, and I was unsure if I should stay, but somehow I managed to stand still. They mingled, some riders went on, a plumed legionary leaving a brace of guards with Drusus to stand in the shade, some ten men. They trusted the Batavi explicitly. Finally, the feast continued, and Chariovalda nodded my way, his face stern.

Drusus walked to me, calmly, his hands spread. 'Nero Claudius Drusus. That is I. Chariovalda calls me many names, but friend is the one I like. Just call me that, nothing what the pompous, toga-wearing fools try to push down my throat. Praetor, your highness, mighty general, most wise lord, or such nonsense. And you are ... Hraban. Raven,' he said, and I nodded. 'A Raven who understands Latin.' Again, I nodded. 'Well, speak!'

I shook myself and nodded. 'Yes, I am Hraban, and I do write and speak some of your language. My father had me taught by this Roman exile,' I said awkwardly, and the Romans laughed at my discomfort.

'He sounds like a damned mule,' someone quipped from the darkness, one of the legionnaires and the rest laughed with humor. I scowled that way, but Drusus turned me away.

'They are good men, and mean no evil,' he said calmly, his eyes on me. 'Hraban the Marcomanni. Son of Maroboodus.' The last words were spoken with a tightly strained voice.

'Yes,' I told him.

'Maroboodus, the man I know very well. The guard of our family, one of the Tall Ones, the iron fists of my stepfather. You know, I think he was assigned to my guard once. And to Julia. Often to Julia's guard.'

'Julia?' I said, with a small voice.

'Augustus's only daughter. Julia Caesaris,' he said, as he shook his head, walking around me. I stood still, feeling the urge to grasp Nightbright, but I noticed I did not have the sword, and my eyes sought Chariovalda in the feast. The man's eyes flashed mirthfully, as he scratched his back with my blade. He had grabbed it when he pushed me over. So, I stood still. Drusus came to eye me again. 'Yes, I know your father. I used to trust him. Now, he has turned the Marcomanni into an enemy. He is a dangerous one, he is. And the man who killed Julia's husband as well, old Agrippa. The Wall, we called the old man. Your father butchered him, they say.'

'So they say,' I agreed. 'Or, perhaps—'

'He did not,' Drusus said cautiously. 'Agrippa was sick when he travelled to Illyria. I saw him go. He was sick, and snot was flying as they carried him. But, off he went, for my stepfather ordered him to go. Something happened, indeed. Suddenly, Augustus was raging, beyond angry. He was in tears of hate, as he tore through his house on the hill that day. The funeral was furious, rather than serene.'

'I wonder if they were tears of joy?' I breathed, and his eyes stared at me dangerously.

'Go on,' he said. 'I won't bite. Talk about my family, as if you knew them.'

I had a hunch the discussion was not going well, and felt cold shivers run up and down my spine. 'I hear Agrippa had ever been the one to win Augustus's battles. Mayhap it is time for Augustus to do his bit, and he was happy to be rid of Agrippa?'

He observed me like a carnivore. A bear of small size, but immeasurable power. Finally, he smiled wistfully. 'Perhaps. But, why is it so I am here, and not Augustus?'

'Did they not name you the urban praetor for this year? I understood you should be there, and someone else here?' I said arrogantly, afraid I would make a fool of myself. 'Possibly he cannot come here, if you are here against his orders? He would lose face. He might come later, when the war is nearly won, and grasp the honor?'

'Yes, that might be so,' he agreed with a smile. 'I am here because I like it here, and I did defy some thinly veiled orders to go home. They say I should stay in Rome, but in truth, they do not fight me, for I have wars to finish. Here, the stench of Rome is far. And so are my stepfather's schemes. In truth, he killed Agrippa, by sending him all over the world. Gods know what diseases the old man had concocted. But, I agree Augustus resents his tarnished military fame. Perhaps he will appear here for the final battles, for I am sure there will be wars with your people.' He laughed hugely and sighed. 'He has before. Agrippa gave him many victories. Most, in fact. Agrippa was his soldier, his brave sword, his bravery in battle. Augustus should hate Maroboodus for the murder of his friend, enough to see Maroboodus dead at least, for he truly believes the wounds in Agrippa were made by your father. Even if they were made after the old man died of snot.'

I smiled. 'Father brought Agrippa's head home, did you know? A great deed, and many wondered at it.'

'Indeed?' Drusus smiled. 'I have heard it was so. Though the Agrippa I saw burnt on the pyre had his head very much attached. Mystery, if any. Do you know whose head it was?'

'I know the skull my father brought with him belonged to a Syrian male prostitute,' I told him awkwardly. 'This is what I was told, before I was to die. For he did not kill Agrippa, but it was decided claiming the head as the old man's would be something to make him look mighty and heroic with our tribes.'

'Who decided it?' he smiled.

'A Roman for whom Father works. I know not who that is,' I told him gravely.

'Oh?' he inquired. 'Indeed? A Roman? Chariovalda hinted at this just now. So there is some sort of a conspiracy at work.' He waved his hand dismissively. 'Such things are always likely. Rome is made of war and politics, and both are bloody and filthy. I care not. Maroboodus is an enemy to Rome, that much he has shown.'

'He has two things to achieve,' I said slowly. 'One, he will make a coalition to fight you.'

'He has been doing well with that. I hear he has spoken with the Chatti and the Cherusci, and agreed on marriages. I am holding a Thing to see where we are. And to smear his ass on mud while I do so.'

'I was there when the marriages were agreed on.'

'You were? And then you had a falling out?' he asked with a small smile.

'He came home, Drusus,' I braved his name, and he smiled like the sun, 'betrayed, and schemed to walk over our legitimate chiefs, my relatives all, promised me love for service, and in the end, I also was betrayed, and exiled to face death. But, I did not wish to die and went home, gave him King Vago's head, and burnt his hall.'

'What?' he asked softly with curses. 'You killed Vago? Do you know what kind of a turmoil there is down there right now? Some youngster is trying to take over, and there are damned cousins and warlords vying for power. I should hang and crucify you,' he spat, his eyes dangerous. 'What have you got to say for yourself?'

'I am sorry. I did not like lord Vago,' I grunted mulishly, and he started to snicker, shaking his head. 'He is to create a powerful army, Drusus, and then he is to—'

'To fall?' he smiled incredulously. 'Fall to the Roman blades easily, betray his people? My, that would ruin my honor and fame both. An arranged war. Bah!'

'Yes, he will hand the Germani to you. Or whoever it is that commands,' I told him softly.

'I command here, Hraban, none else,' he smiled dangerously.

'Not if you die in the war. That is what he has been tasked with,' I said. 'His master in Rome has high hopes for certain men to fall, men who would reverse what your stepfather is building. Chariovalda told me these are men who love the Republic of Rome, and do not embrace the rule of one man. He thinks you are such a man who loves the Republic.'

His face had a pallid look, his eyes flashed in anger, and his wide jaws tightened. He looked to the flames dancing in the feast fire and nodded slowly. 'Most Germani love to gossip; are you a gossiper?' he asked, with a small snicker, but his eyes were unchanged. They were weighing me, my soul, my words.

'I do. I also like to say plainly what I know, as it is. I do not lie,' I snarled at him, he gave me a cold smile, and I continued. 'I so swear, by our gods.'

'Woden?'

'Yes, Woden,' I said. 'All-father.'

He smirked. 'Juppiter promises us Romans victory; so does Mars. Do your gods do this for you?'

'The vitka claim they do,' I told him, hesitating.

'But, you do not believe it?' he asked, his eyes betraying his astonishment. 'You do not?'

'I think,' I began, cursed, and continued forcefully. 'I think the gods promise we have a chance to win. No gods step to the battlefield and decide things for us. That is our job. If we are brave enough, we have a chance.'

'Our gods claim we cannot lose,' he stated slyly.

'They are monstrous liars,' I told him, and he laughed hugely, his eyes filling with mirth, as he clapped his hand on my back. I noticed Chariovalda take a long breath, one of relief.

'Indeed, boy, indeed. They are liars, the lot,' he told me happily and sobered. 'Very well. There has been much bleeding in Rome, Hraban, over this great issue. My father fought for the Republic. Many families have fallen, and the whole nation is exhausted by civil wars. Some men still fall, either ruined financially, or by poison. But, few are as liked as I am. Perhaps it is so, Hraban, they seek to destroy me by enemy hands. Those who love me in the army might have to fall as well. They would happily accept the humiliation of some legions, if only I died. Then, one day, the Germani would just fall. It is a long shot for one man to achieve something grand like this. Maroboodus is taking great risks, not likely to succeed, not even with his military training. It is, I think, an impossibly long shot that would be well rewarded. But, if he fails, there will be murderers travelling from Rome one day, and poison will be poured in my wine, no matter if Rome howls and blames Augustus. What has he been promised? Lands?'

I nodded. 'Lands. He is looking southeast, I hear. They say he has a Roman son as well.' I spat, as I remembered the words of Antius.

'Ah,' Drusus said, his eyes flashing with keen intelligence. 'I know now why he would take on this desperate mission. I think I do.'

'Lord?' I asked, confused.

'He has a kingdom to win, your father. But, he might also lose a son, should he fail,' he mused sadly.

'He lost us without an eye blink,' I spat. 'After milking us like cows.'

He placed a strong hand on my shoulder. 'He did not see you grow up. He did this one boy. Even if he was not married to the mother. I shall tell you this story, one day,' he told me, and I fidgeted, for I wished to know of Maroboodus, to understand why he had done the things he had done. Drusus watched me knowingly. 'He is here to work the will of some who hate me and what I love. He is here for power. And he is here, for he loves and fears. He is attempting a desperate mission for all of these things, and gods know which truly motivates him. He is not a total beast then, even if he is that to you.'

'I was betrayed by my father. I was cast out,' I said. 'That is all that matters.'

'For you, it might be so,' he said sadly, and wiped his face. 'But, none of it matters.'

'Why, Drusus?' I asked him, upset at his words.

He shrugged. 'I won't let him combine the tribes against me. I will keep him busy and alienated. I will conquer swiftly and without humor, Hraban, and he can sit and rage in his burnt hall. You have disgraced him enough for me to make sure there will be no grand Germani strategy to fight my legions, only scattering of bickering Germani tribes. This man was Antius the Negotiatore? The man who told you these things? Chariovalda mentioned him.'

'Yes,' I said sullenly. 'I hate him.'

'Hate silently, Hraban, patiently. It will be sweeter than nectar when the time comes to step on his throat,' he murmured. I nodded, and we stood there, silent for a while. He was looking at me and thinking.

'What will you do? Will you make war on Rome?' I asked boldly.

He shook his head at the question. 'I will not speak of such matters with a man called the Oath Breaker. But, should I do so, Hraban, I will do it for the Republic. It is a thing to fight for, our legacy, what set us apart from the Greeks, the east and the south alike. Now, we have the discipline of the armies, superior weapons, and favor of the gods, liars all as we agree. Back in the days we had more. We had less of an army, but boasted a purity of mind, unyielding honor to guide these lesser armies, and yes, Hraban, all that is going away. Honor is dead.' He gazed South, as if he could see Rome crumbling down. 'We have fame of arms and bloody victories, but our greed shames our ancestors,' he continued, and I smiled. Gods. Fulcher would marry him, if he heard him speak thus. He continued, with some humor. 'Unless some of us survive and turn back time, it will grow worse. Augustus is a schemer, Hraban, my mother's husband. But, there are true schemers who see the benefits of Augustus's legacy, but without the blood of Augustus. Both hate the Republic. And me.'

'Yes, lord,' I told him, as he spat phlegm in his sudden anger.

He turned to go, but glanced at me. 'You lost your daughter? There is suffering in your face.'

'Yes, my lord,' I told him miserably.

'A father who loves so is a man I trust, despite what people call him. We will get her back, my friend,' he said happily, and it was so easy for me to love him. He was a great lord, but even more, he was a great man. He walked away, mounted a horse, blew a kiss to the Batavi, and left, leaving me standing alone.

I met Chariovalda's eyes, and he nodded wistfully at me. I understood his dedication now. I walked to him, kicked him in the balls, making his men roar with joy, took my sword from his belt, and walked back, guarded by some unwilling Batavi; I went back to our housing and took care of Cassia. She was shivering with stubborn fever, and I slept next to her, warming her. She did not mind and snuggled closer, and I thought of Drusus and his eyes, and felt there was a man who could change destinies of men, and huge nations, alike.

Gods, I would leave the Romans with Armin, but Drusus, I would never forget.

Cassia kissed me, half asleep. It was a gentle kiss, and I answered it; I knew I loved her.

Ansbor would hate me.

CHAPTER XXII

A week crept past, and the Germani nobles, with their adelings and war bands, trickled to the suddenly busier Moganticum. There were the haughty lords of the northern tribes. Many of them were Roman allies, some unwilling ones, especially the Frisii, who were the neighbors of the Batavi, proud and poor men whom Drusus had humbled bloodily, and their gaunt lords, the only Germani who paid true tribute. Then, there were the Canifetes from the coast, and the Ubii, who arrived grimly, the large tribe that old Agrippa had welcomed over the Rhenus to join Rome, now willing friends, close allies to the Roman Eagle. The Chauci, the greatest tribe of the far north was there, some of the chiefs who had succumbed without a fight to Drusus the year before during his northern expedition. Ampsivari sent a small delegation, the neighbors of Chauci and Cherusci.

Some of the more stubborn lords of the north and middle lands came in. The small tribes, the Marsi, the heroic people, sent some men to hear Rome out, and they said one of their greatest leaders rode with them, though others said there were only some minor nobles there. The dwindling Bructeri were there, all scarred men, brutally tattooed in face, too thin for lack of food, unconquerable in spirit, ever ready for war, yet interested in what the Romans had to say. A chief named Wodenspear was rumored to ride before them, a terror of Rome himself, now under the flag of truce.

I was sitting by the river, staring at the men riding in with their families. They would gather north of the town, and come in all at the same time for the Thing, but those who arrived visited Moganticum profusely before the meeting. The wind was whipping across the river, raising ripples, and sometimes making curious rings as something plopped in to the water,. I felt lost in my choices. I needed clarity, and so I waited.

The mighty Cherusci, lords of the two rivers, were expected, and I dreaded their arrival. Segestes the Fat, Inguiomerus the Gaunt, and Sigimer would surely come, and with them, hopefully, Armin. But, if he did not come? I would have to find the way with Sigimer. He had liked Maroboodus, so I was skeptical of my chances with him. Catualda, my foe and relative, served Armin, and that would be a problem, should Armin or Sigimer agree to my service.

But, I had the ring.

The Cherusci needed it to pacify the eastern Suebi. That would weigh more than Catualda's scrawny neck, I decided. Armin was ruthless, not unlike Father, though with an honorable streak in his young character. Would he let me duel Catualda? If not, I would find a way later. To kill him. To kill Father.

I spat, and felt so tired. Killing and running, and hunting for fame. Fulcher was right.

All I needed was honor.

But, that would be sullied in whatever event would take place soon.

No deal I would make was to be enjoyable or honorable. I would not become Roman. No matter if Drusus haunted the recesses of my mind, his nobility having made a great impression on me. His plans and fears moved me, his belief in the Republic thrummed in my soul. He believed in something so greatly, it could not fail to move a man. He commanded armies, but he was also a target in a cruel game. He needed help. I could stay; I could fight for him. I knew that. But, I had Lif.

So I would go.

Armin would own me. What would he ask of me? I had betrayed him for Father once. It all tasted stale to me. Lif was the only thing that mattered truly, but the web of betrayal felt heavy on my shoulders. I had felt brilliant as the summer sun when Lif was born. Many things were clearer, made more sense. I felt good about myself. Now, I was preparing to let honor go again. I was not sure how I would find it once more. In

Germania, I would be despised; I would likely be asked to do deeds that shamed me, but I would have Lif. In Moganticum, I would not have Lif, but I would gather fame, and keep my newly found honor. And Cassia. If Ansbor would understand, which was not likely. Gods. 'They hate me,' I said with a small voice. 'Except the Romans.'

Men were riding forth on the other side of the river. I roused myself from my thoughts, and gazed that way, but shrugged, as I understood it was Thurwag. The Matticati were there, preparing to cross, and eventually the Chatti would show up, having some sort of an agreement with Rome, though Father had persuaded them to join him, should Rome invade that year. Most tribes of the east, the unknown lands beyond the rivers of the mystical lands, were not coming, the enemies of the Cherusci. The Hermanduri were not going to appear. Most of the Suebi nations were too savage, or unpredictable, to travel that far. The Marcomanni had not been invited anyway. Of the contested areas of the central and northern lands, only the stubborn Sigambri and their allies the Tencteri and the Usipetes were missing, having no interest in what Drusus were to offer, or say, having suffered greatly for years at the hands of Rome. They expected to do so this year as well, proudly. No doubt the Marsi and the Bructeri would join them, even if they were there.

No Cherusci, I thought, and I waited impatiently in the barracks, while the Romans prepared themselves, as if for a battle. There was a nervous energy in the camps, the men running between the barracks and their chores with springy steps, proud in their tunica and sandals, hobnails clipping the via praetorium mercilessly. They were fixing gear, replacing what was irreparable, and brutes of centurions were snapping their vine staffs on many a slow ass and unhappy back, as the legions prepared.

There were two full legions in the huge camp; the XIV Gemina and XVI Gallica.

The next day, I was fixing a sheath for Nightbright, one to fit it nicely, made up of thick, oiled leather and furred edges, and Ansbor was oiling Nightbright, as Chariovalda stomped in. He threw down our gear, my helmet rolling in the dust. No weapons, just the armor. 'Dress up like whores, my friends. Wear your helmet, Hraban. Your horses are at the gate, groomed by slaves.'

'They are all here, then?' I asked him.

'All are here. All of them. All who will come. Drusus will parade them so they have to pass two legions in arms. No better opening statement than staring at steel of twenty thousand bastards.'

'They will be suitably impressed, I am sure,' I sneered at him. 'After all, most are tribes that succumbed with no fight.'

He hesitated at the door, and then pointed a finger my way. 'Drusus likes you. Do not over-tax his mind with sarcasm, should he speak with you again. You know he is facing many challenges.'

'I will try to behave,' I told him, and he farted as he left. I snorted, and we dressed. We wore our old gear, patched and cleaned, leathers greased and the armor shined brilliantly, the shoes were the traditional Germani ones, with overturned leather on the outside. We walked to the gate, and stared at the main road. It was thronging with brilliant legionnaires, and they were spread all over the place.

'My gods,' Fulcher murmured as we made our way out of the castrum.

We exited, staring at rows and rows of brilliant men behind the gates. Outside, we mounted up, and I put the helmet on my head. A harried optio pointed a finger, through a bustle of officers and men carrying vases and food, towards a group of men sitting in a loose formation outside the castrum. When we reached the men, who were Batavi and Ubii officers, trumpets rang out harshly, and the ground trembled. We turned to look at each other; the horses grew fierce, and we calmed them.

The legions appeared, and marched out of the castrum with a half step.

We stared at the wonder of the power that had humbled the least humble nations in the world.

You have likely never seen such a sight, my lord Thumelicus, not even in Roman areas as we did that day, when the troops marched through the two gates. Few battles looked as splendid, the ones I would witness later, for there the men would be grimy and grim, but these men were not soiled. Brilliantly gleaming chain mail, sturdy metal helmets, adorned with arrogant red and white crests and plumes they only use in parades, tunics mostly red, though here and there white, for the newer men who had not yet washed them in the common tubs, where they would harmoniously assume a shared color. Their shields were freshly painted. For XVI, a snarling lion adorned the oval shields. For the XIV, the Capricorn, a creature of the faraway lands.

Chariovalda found us and pulled us with him, and as we rode with him, entirely bewildered, he described the beast to us, but we called him a liar. No goat could live under water. He took us to the hundred or so Batavi, and we tried to stand our horses next to theirs, in smooth lines.

Endless lines of stern, armored men, streamed from the gates, and we could only wonder at them and their way of going to a parade. We had seen thousands of them the past weeks, but all together? In a massive fist of death? Never. The ground shook as they came, in military step, like a single living creature snaking around the gates, walking resolutely, turning by barked orders. They filed out of the fort, in lines of steel, bronze, and iron, not like men, but silent statues, disciplined, jaws shaved and set, their swords and pilum spears clanking in unison, as their steps matched those of the man next to them. Like things from Hel, undead, emotionless, some wondrous constructs of the alfs or dwarves, they marched on.

We admired them, and then hated them, for soon, the dust covered us as they stomped past, and no grooming would make us stand out.

They marched to the huge clearing north of the castrum, led by their first, the finest cohorts, which were twice the size of a normal one, and they were followed by the nine others. The legion's standards proceeded them, carried by tough and smart men, who sometimes were part of the leadership council of the whole legion. The standards glittered in the morning sun, the golden eagle awash in the pale sunlight, the battle honors and symbols of the grass crown held high. Less distinctive than the golden eagle, all the cohorts carried their standards, centuries as well, making it a splendid, martial sight of gilded, bronzed, and silvery honor. I spotted a tall man carrying a pole, with a shell made of silver, and there was a face inside it; while I nearly fell off the horse gawking at the face, Chariovalda said it was Augustus. We tried to peer at the face, but could not see it properly. The face would be familiar to us, later.

'Look at those men!' Fulcher said. 'They mimic our champions!' Indeed, men with trumpets, buccina and cornicula, marched with them, their heads framed by bear pelts, leather armor covering their chests.

'It is a new habit,' Chariovalda said sheepishly. 'They wish to look a bit more barbaric and distinctive. The standard bearers wear them, too, sometimes beast skins from the south, spotted or striped. Ah, the nobles. Look at the young cocks!'

With the legions rode young men, glittering tribunes, all clad with sculpted armors, young men making their political careers by serving the state, and the people. I had seen one of them once, in the battle of Castrum Luppia. A scarred man, a military tribune, rode beside the legions, overseeing the march. Chariovalda had told us they were second-in-command of the legions, and today, they directed the marching troops, for the legates were coming out at the gates with Saturninus and Drusus, proud officers under his purple banner, which was adorned with gilded letters spelling out his many glorious names and titles.

The legions deployed in a triple axis, three lines. The first cohort was the first one the Germani approaching from the north would see, its centuries of eighty men taking their places, with the legion's most prestigious centurion, primus pilus, the first spear, standing before the first cohort, unmoving, eyes harsh as death. Best men were there in the first cohort, and following it came the next four, their centuries marching to take their place in a panoply of steel, bronze, bright plumes, and red shields. Soon, all the centuries of the four cohorts were lined abreast, their centurions and optios subtly beating the lines straight, helped by a tessarius in the back of each century.

Then came the next two lines, having three cohorts each. Like an army of insects, emotionless and efficient, they spread out, some centuries and cohorts having far fewer men than the other, since the legion was never fully stacked. Men died, left on missions, or on furloughs, for which they paid their centurions dearly. Many men ended their commissions, free to go, or enlist again. It was a powerful statement nonetheless. The two legions coming together in huge lines, standards in the air, the terrifying power of these trained men, not as tall as our people, or the Celts, yet sturdy, implacable enemies, proud and unyielding, men who would hold Rome on its feet forever, if it were up to them.

And, of course, it was.

So deployed the army of Drusus, a small part of it, for he had six such legions under his command in Germania to hold sway over the Gauls, to keep us in check, and perhaps, to conquer us. I saw them, and wondered how different they were from a Germani army. An army of the Hermanduri, facing you in the field, would be a rowdy group of individual lords, with hedonistic, self-serving champions prancing around, proclaiming their many honors to the foe. They would yell insults, curse crudely, and in battle, they would be ferocious, in a shield wall, or a cunus. You would fear some of the lords under their banners of bones and simple symbols. You knew whom to look out for when Germani marched for you. Here, the Roman army. They all looked equally deadly.

There were a few hundred glinting Roman cavalrymen riding their horses behind the right wing, to guard the flags and contingents of the Vangiones and of the Ubii, mostly cavalry, as well as strange looking archers and slingers from Syria and Crete, deployed near the fort.

How was one to conquer such men? To attack such power, discipline? Madness. My head swam.

Fulcher and Ansbor sat next to me, their mouths open. 'They all have armor? Iron and bronze, steel? And swords?' Ansbor asked, and Fulcher nodded prudently. 'All of them?'

Fulcher inclined his head toward the men, as he calmed his horse, having sensed his uneasiness. 'They conquered most of the known world with those swords. Even the nations who had similar units. It's not all about steel and iron. Some of these standards have seen a century, or two, of war.'

Ansbor shook his head. 'Not about steel, huh? It helps, though.'

I said nothing. My father would oppose these men? I could see how, and why, he had started to break the Marcomanni traditions and teaching our men to war this same way. He had a trover of armor, of course, for he had taken a fort the year before, and even our burning of his hall would only delay his plans. But, should these men march on the Hard Hill? Not too far from there?

Madness to fight them. Father's mission was a suicide mission. His Roman boy must be made of gold for him to try toppling this army. And more like it. I shook my head, as I stood next to Chariovalda, near the castrum gate, looking at the lines and lines of men in armor, with swords and helms, which our men rarely had.

However, there was something wrong.

I felt a flutter in my heart. My terror was fading, the despair changing into something else, and I scowled, only to be interrupted. 'You don't approve of them?' asked Drusus, who boasted a youthful smile on his handsome face. He walked up to the Batavi, as his horse was being saddled still. His light brown eyes were alight with fire. He looked at his men with keen pride, and so I shut up, stopping myself from answering. 'Well?' he asked, gazing up at me. My mouth twitched under my helmet, and he saw this. He motioned for me to speak.

'Lord? Why would I not approve?'

He squinted at me. 'Call me friend, or call me Drusus. I told you. I do not wish my ass licked. You don't approve? Of the troops? There is something wrong with them? I wish to know what it is.'

I swallowed. 'It appears to me, lord, our tribes should find it in themselves to forget their petty wars quickly, or die,' I said honestly, and Drusus grunted. 'In that, my father is right, no matter his true motives.'

He laughed. 'Indeed? We should be happy your lords don't see as clearly as the young scarface scowling at them here today.' He softened the words with a clap on my leg, and then shrugged as he gazed past the legions. 'Your father will not be here, but the mighty Cherusci and our dubious allies, the Chatti, are coming, down that road, passing the silent troops. I shall wonder if they don't shit themselves. I nearly do when I

332

witness these men in a parade. Usually the legions would train right now, but today, they serve a higher purpose. Do you think they will be impressed?' he inquired, and I realized he was genuinely puzzled.

'Lord? It is a mighty sight,' I ventured, as I finally understood what I felt.

He looked exasperated. 'Drusus, for Juppiter's sakes! You called me Drusus when we had our chat. Yes. A mighty sight, indeed. And yet, the Sigambri, Usipetes, and Tencteri again defy me, and have not appeared.'

I shrugged at him. 'They are Germani.'

He threw his hands up to the air. 'Germani! Germani? What in Hades's name does that mean? Eh? That they are mules that enjoy a whipping? Last year, I humiliated them. I punctured their shield lines, slaughtered their best warriors, and what do they do? They try to make an alliance to kill me. Is there anything one can do, short of exterminating them all, to make them yield?' he mused bitterly. I did not say anything, and he scowled. 'Despite what your father's plans are, whether of uniting the Chatti and Cherusci for the good of your nations, or his own ends, even those of the one we spoke about, the plans will not come to anything. The Cherusci are divided, some would fight, and others love us. Now, after they see this, they will know why it is wise not to cross me.' He looked very pleased with himself.

'You? Or Rome?' I asked him casually. Chariovalda was shaking his head slowly. Drusus mounted his horse, not answering my question, scowling mightily. I swallowed, and ignored Ansbor, who reached out and pinched me, knowing I was going to say something foolish. But, I had to, for what I felt when I had gazed at the army marching was *greed,* and so I spoke. 'They do look fine, my lord … Drusus. I do think they could make a god piss their pants. Yet, for some reason, the fear left me soon enough. Now, I look at the men. I see them. They are like the Rhenus River. Impossible to beat, but possible to harness. I hear you built a river up north? To gain safer access to the northern seas? Like the river, in their discipline, there are opportunities. Men who do things the same way are predictable. And so, all the loot they carry is a great lure to attempt many dangerous deeds, should we see them wandering around the woods.'

He snorted, and Chariovalda's eye had a tick, as he listened to my arrogant answer. Drusus shook his head at me. 'That is why we have generals, like myself. It is our job to make sure they are not predictable,' he said slowly and grinned at me.

I shook my head. 'I love the way they stand and gleam. If I was a Germani lord, with a vast, hungry army, the only thing I would think about is how I would want to loot their fabulous supplies, piles of precious armor, and their sharpest weapons, and make a strong tribe with them. We do not think like the Gauls,' I said to him, and he was silent. 'We have nothing worth defending, but we do enjoy taking.'

'The Gauls?' he inquired, his voice having a dangerous edge.

I nodded. 'They live in an oppidum; they have their cultivated, fortified lands, and things they can lose. Our people need little.'

He smiled, mulling it over as he walked his horse to Chariovalda.

He poked at the Batavi. 'Chariovalda. Do you see why we have a hard time trusting even our allies, like yourself? A boy is thinking about how to kill our men. Do you see?' he asked. 'And the Gauls did not give up easily, boy. They still fester with rebellion. My officia just found out about a plan to kick us out. That is why I am here. And so are they,' he said, and pointed at the legions. He fixed Chariovalda with a questioning eye. 'Are you going to rebel, Chariovalda?' he asked mischievously.

'Tax us, and find out, lord,' Chariovalda said, smiling.

'Frisii are paying taxes now.' Drusus gloated.

'They will run out of gold and silver soon, and cattle, then their children. Then, they will only have their weapons, lord,' Chariovalda said neutrally.

Drusus nodded. 'Gods help us all when a man less amicable than I am takes over here. You will bring the boy, today. He will sit next to you and me in the meeting. I will want the Cherusci and the Chatti seated, so they can see him. Now, wear the helmet, son. You are known for that, they tell me.

' I shook my head softly. He would parade me before the Germani. He would ruin the last shreds of my fame. For Lif, I would do it. I would suffer happily, if only I could find a solution.

And so we waited.

The legions didn't move. And you could tell they were alive by just looking at the small movements their heads made. I wondered if they thought they were to present arms to Augustus himself, not the barbarian aristocracy.

Then they arrived.

The Ubii cavalry came galloping through the woods, aiming directly for Drusus, and an officer in a gorgeous helmet rode towards them, talking to them quickly, and then nodded calmly at Drusus, who waved his hand. The Ubii took their place amongst the auxilia on the side.

Far in the north, down the hill and near the villages, a road stretched towards the horizon. A line of men appeared, many of whom had already visited Moganticum, but who would now join a train of proud men, coming to meet their host in a procession of Germani.

First, came the mighty Chatti, formally allies to Rome, yet nervous allies, a mighty nation careful of its independence. I saw Ebbe swaying on his horse, his beard braided and head swinging from side-to-side, and there was also Oldaric, the fierce, tattooed man, both in their war glory, bronze and golden panoply of war and huge spears held in powerful hands, silver glinting amidst barbaric furs. I saw Adgandestrius, and I smiled, for I liked him. The man had saved my ass when Odo and Gernot would have taken me, mutilated me, and I would be a man like Bero now, somewhere far in the north, whimpering and delirious, Odo's toy. The young fool with twinkling eyes and a cropped, blonde beard looked good with his forehead bared. The Chatti cut their hair as a sign of killing a man.

With them came champions and their men, large and tough, much like the Batavi but less armored, wilder. The Chatti looked at the vast array of men, and I chuckled as I noticed them whispering to each other, exchanging upset words, for every man there much desired such gear. Drusus glanced my way, and gave me a small cold smile, which I answered. Finally, the vast Chatti delegation passed the legions, their eyes constantly glancing at the massed men staring back at them, with steely eyes, red shields out, spears in precise angles, and swords at their sides.

We were on the right flank, just before Drusus's officia and the legates, who were waiting by the gate to the castrum, and I saw the Chatti scowl at the Batavi, all of them the same nation formerly, now bitter enemies. Then Ebbe fixed his eyes on me, staring in utter stupefaction, and whispering something to Adgandestrius. I raised a hand to them, and the adeling gawked, and started to whisper and nod at his father. 'Do not do that, stand still. In the Roman army, discipline is all; this is not a market where you dilly-dally with girls,' Chariovalda said grimly under his breath.

'I'm not in the Roman army,' I answered equally grim, but he just hissed at me to be quiet. 'And I at least moved them. Unlike the legions.'

'Infamy tends to rock men,' he whispered, and I cursed him.

Next arrived the Cherusci, the northern neighbors of the Chatti, your people, lord, and my throat tightened. They were the mighty lords of the Albis and Visurgis Rivers, east of the Sigambri. Mighty people like the Chatti, they rode with their heads held high, dressed in their best.

Armin, he had to be there. I did not see him.

And then my prayers were answered, for first came Armin indeed, his blond head bared, and his tall body covered with a glittering, rich ring mail, a long sword on his side in a red leather belt. He rode in with the standard of his father, Sigimer, a round bronze disk with a painted axe. He looked like a young god, a hero returned from the dead, his cheeks rosy and his eyes bright, as he flashed wolf-like glances over the enemy lines. A small, fat horn was on his hip, and I wondered how he would react to me, for he had schemed with me to overturn Maroboodus. I had obeyed Father and tricked him, and so had toppled Isfried and Melheim, and many Matticati as well for we had fooled him.

He had escaped.

Catualda had tried to take the precious ring to Armin, but I did not see Catualda with him. Sigimer, Armin's powerful father, followed, his armor a plain leather jacket. He held his axe loosely, the beautiful weapon with a wolf insignia, a famous weapon of much honor. By him, rode a dark man, very much like Armin, yet different; where Armin was radiant, he was gloomy, all dressed in black and grey. His fair hair brought contrast, for it

336

was almost white. It was Rochus, his brother, and the man I would know well one day.

Next followed Segestes, his fat face smiling benevolently at the Romans, his corpulent body contained inside a loose and rich tunic, gold glittering around his neck and his fat jowls bouncing prominently when he was turning his head around, clearly admiring the legions. He was carrying a large metal shield, with a carved and sculpted face, and wondrous chiseled beasts, a guard fit for a warrior but ludicrous on him. Indeed, there was a slow murmur of mirth rippling through the legions, though quickly repressed, but Segestes was oblivious to the fact. Or he was beyond it. He was no fool.

Inguiomerus came last, his black skull standard held aloft by someone who was likely his son, and he eyed the legions like a wolf would look at a wounded prey. I saw Drusus furrow his eyebrows for a second when he saw the gaunt man. Inguiomerus had fame as a flayer of his foes, and Rome feared him, much more than his brothers. They passed, and I noticed Armin suddenly turn his head and look directly at me, his face uncommonly serious and thoughtful, but he was gathering looks, too. There were many appreciative murmurs amongst the Batavi on his stature, and I could see the young man also impressed Drusus as he approached.

'He looks like Vercingetorix about to surrender his arms to Caesar,' a Roman said to another near us.

'Except he is not about to surrender,' answered the other with a hawking laugh.

His eyes followed me, and I struggled not to wave at him. I stood still until he was gone.

After this came the Marsi and Bructeri, allies to Sigambri, but more willing to talk terms. Wodenspear led them, a Bructeri war king, and a tall muscular man, with weird tattoos around his eyes, black beard strangely tarred, disdaining armor and fancy clothing. He did not even look at the legions. He knew them well. The Marsi did not have a high chief with them after all, just minor ones. An insult to Rome, perhaps.

The rest did not matter, the northerners and the insignificant, and I kept my eyes on Armin, wondering what would come to pass.

The Germani rode up to Drusus, and greeted him, bowed heads, nodding as if to an equal. He was fairly young, Drusus, but not young enough to be insignificant to these Germani leaders. Drusus nodded back with lavish smiles. Sigimer led the Cherusci, Ebbe the Chatti, and they talked softly, and I could not hear what about. Then, the play was over, for the Germani were led away to their quarters outside the castrum, but Armin lingered, passing the standard to one of the tall men in his father's party, a man with a very high forehead and red hair.

I looked at Chariovalda. 'He wants me.'

'Who is he?' he asked carefully. 'The young god.'

'Armin, son of Sigimer,' I said hollowly.

"Ah, the man who you spoke about. He does not look like a cow herder, and I doubt he owes you anything. Lord of men to be, by the looks of him, a spear king. Go ahead, talk to him, you liar, and I will wait here,' said Chariovalda, not giving me freedom, yet giving me some trust.

'Stay with Chariovalda, Fulcher and Ansbor. I have words to say to the man,' I said, and guided my horse away.

I rode to Armin, and took off my helmet.

He flinched at my scar. 'Your father?'

I nodded. 'I do not hold it against him. I tried to kill him. I only rue that he survived.'

'You gave him your oaths. Is that how you honor them?' he asked, and smiled at me. 'You certainly obeyed him well enough as you tricked me. I thought you might, but I had little to lose.'

'Trickery is hardly a gift a guest should give his host, my lord,' I reprimanded him. 'And I know Catualda was to bring you the ring, no matter what was to pass. He tried.'

'He did, yes,' Armin said neutrally, giving me a small smile. 'We actually had it for the autumn, until he took it with him to meet with Vago. And then you escaped. And you retook it, Hraban. It was upsetting. Catualda

338

was hurt badly.' He glanced around uncertainly, and stared at the legions. 'Fancy looking boys, are they not?'

'Indeed. Killers, the lot,' I said glumly.

'So are we,' he remarked coldly and shook his head. 'And now you are here. A Roman.'

I shook my head. 'I still seek vengeance, Armin. And something else.'

'And Romans are happy to help you, no? Maroboodus is their great enemy,' he told me happily.

'Maroboodus is, and is not, their enemy,' I said slowly. 'And I need something.'

'Indeed?' he asked. 'But, your father is the one clamoring for war, right? War we should lead in, since the Romans are coming our way.'

'He has his agendas, and I shall not speak of them,' I told him. 'Perhaps later, if I find a safe haven for me while I search for the other thing I need.'

'A safe haven?' he asked softly, his eyes flickering towards Chariovalda. 'Surely you are not trying to lull me into believing you? I tried that once.'

'As I said, neither of us is blameless, Armin,' I said darkly. 'I am no Roman.'

'Ah,' he nodded, and eyed my finger. 'And you know we shall need that.'

'Yes,' I said, fingering Draupnir. 'I have it now.'

'You nearly killed Catualda for it, and he is kin,' he smiled dangerously, but looked away for a moment, gathering himself.

I spat. 'He is bad news, my lord, and a worthless shitty piece of gristle, a murderer, and a schemer, and I was his victim,' I growled. 'And he is my kin as well.'

'Yes, he is. Bero's son,' he smiled. 'So, you are offering that for a position in our lands, in our troops.'

'I am.' I felt tightness in my belly, as I fought the urge to fidget.

He was nodding again and shrugged. 'The thing is, Hraban, I could do this. You could start anew with the Cherusci. My father and Inguiomerus have deals with your father, as you know, deals they still might consider valid, but they also see the benefits of what you might bring to our side, the ring included. But, I am not sure, Hraban, not yet on what I will do.'

I nodded carefully. 'So, you make no promises nor oaths to the Oath Breaker.'

'I did once, Hraban, but I admit the situation was ... complex. I shall have someone speak with you, Hraban, very soon. Don't lose heart,' he said, and turned his horse. He rode forward, but stopped for a moment. 'Should we fight each other one day, Hraban, it is a sorry thing, and sure to lead to blood we regret.'

'It is, lord,' I told him heavily. 'I do not hate you, and regret trusting my father. But, I will not lie to you. Catualda is my enemy. One I will not spare. But, I shall need a home, no matter how many people detest me.'

He smiled. 'They do. But, a home is a dream you might find, indeed. Let us talk. Later.'

He rode away, his young face turned to the gloriously armored legates, the younger tribunes, and especially the tough centurions standing in front of their cohorts, the souls and arms of the legions. The legions might bear fantastic, frightening beasts on their shields, emblems that had seen a hundred wars through centuries, but Armin smiled at the devices, his blue eyes flashing, for he was the lion of these woods.

Chariovalda passed me on his horse, and laughed briefly. 'You will have to decide soon, Hraban, on whom you serve.' He left some men to guard me, as I sat there on my horse.

Fulcher and Ansbor came to me. 'So who will we serve?' Ansbor asked dryly.

'Wyrd,' I said, and gloomily followed the Batavi to castrum.

CHAPTER XXIII

Ansbor and Cassia were talking in the room that evening, arguing about how to care for a rash, when Fulcher walked in and came to sit on my bed. He kneeled next to me. 'One Antius wishes a word with you.'

I sat there, with Nightbright in my hand. 'Antius? A fat—'

'It is him,' he said. 'The man who works with your father.'

'Is he alone?' I asked, mystified.

Fulcher snorted. 'There are thousands of men in the camp. None are alone here. But, you won't be alone, will you?'

I perked up and nodded, as I pulled on a tunic and my armor, which was shining prominently. I walked outside, where the Batavi guarded us. A man looked at me in alarm, as I strode past him with Fulcher, but two of them started to trail after us. Fulcher kept in step next to me, his red beard swaying, as he pointed towards the fifth street, where the locals were packing up the daily market. There, near a wheat merchant, stood the man I hated.

He was corpulent and ugly, his hair short, dyed with blond streaks. He had a half amused look on his face, as he regarded the simple merchants packing, most of whom knew the man. He was speaking Gaulish with them. He was intelligent, despite his foppish looks, I reminded myself. Had he not manipulated Tear, and Odo even, and worked with Catualda and my father to change our world? Oh, how he must regret speaking with me, thinking Vago would have killed me.

Something alarmed him, as he turned to look at me. His face fell for just a moment, as he regarded me, taking stock of my scar and my frown, and the blade on my belt. He made a lavish gesture, his stained toga giving away hints at the man's nature, for he was not afraid of physical toil and dirt in his lofty position. He was the mind and eyes of some far away menace, a game piece in the finer, deeper games of power. Fulcher was following me, observing the cluttered area cautiously, but Antius just pointed him to a space farther away. I raised my hand at my friend, who obeyed reluctantly, conversing with the Batavi guards.

I stopped to scrutinize him, my fingers playing on the hilt of Nightbright.

He looked like a fish left alive on a hot rock. He sweated, and fingered his toga, trying to straighten out some wrinkles.

'Well, we meet again,' I told him bitterly. 'Despite Vago and your treachery. You filth.'

He sighed. 'Hraban, Hraban. It is true I did not think to meet the wayward, insignificant boy of Maroboodus again. Now, you are here. Saturninus has questioned Cornix. He did it today, in fact, surprising us as we returned to Moganticum. Nothing came out of it, of course. And I had a chat with our friend Drusus. He has no proof.'

'No proof at all,' I agreed. 'Only my word.'

'And your father is not likely to speak.' He smiled. 'I suppose Felix is gone?'

I nodded. 'Likely he would not believe Felix either. But, he suspects, does he not?'

'He does,' Antius said softly. 'He knows he is in danger. And so, Hraban, he is looking for proof, something to justify his fear of Rome. Cornix, of course, won't speak, will he? He is as mad as a bat in sunlight, and scarred like an ant ravaged bough, much worse than your pretty face, but he has undoubting loyalty. He is still an optio in the XIX Legion, my servant, and you, Hraban, should run far, far away. This is my warning. Go away.'

'Ah, that I cannot do,' I said with a cold smile. 'I have men to kill.' *But, more so, Lif to save,* I thought.

'Yes, men to kill. People to find.' He smiled back.

342

I stiffened. Could he know about Lif? Yet, I dared not say anything about her, in case the fat mound of perfumed lard was just fishing.

His eyes flickered to Fulcher and searched him, and I hated him. Then he gazed at me and pointed a finger my way. 'That you escaped Vago was unexpected. Impossible, in fact. That you escaped and took Hunfrid prisoner? Incredible. You burnt your father's hall? You killed some of his most reliable men? Yes? Gods laugh! But, now, it is over.'

'What happened to Hunfrid? I know you speak with my dear father, so I am just wondering,' I drawled to his annoyance.

'Matters not, Hraban. All will be clear one day. You know what I am doing here, and I know you have warned our young urban praetor he is the target for Maroboodus. Unfortunately, for you, he is just one man. His fates are beyond you to change.'

'This one man,' I told him, pushing him with my finger to his astonishment, 'is a man unlike any I have seen. I think that men like him, and others, these Romans your Augustus so fears and this employer of yours wishes dead, might be the man to cut a bloody swath through lard-filled shits like you. But, as for Drusus, I am not his savior. I have business elsewhere,' I said forcefully.

His eyes went to slits. 'Where is that baby of yours? Cornix has not seen her. I know what the Wolf did to that one girl.' He stared at my eyes. 'And you were speaking to Armin?' I opened my mouth, knowing he was only trying to fish for information, and had, possibly, succeeded, for he grinned. I punched him in the face so hard he spun to the ground with a crash.

Men turned to look at us, and I waved my hands, my breath strangled with fear. He knew I did not have her. 'He is drunk,' I told men coming closer cautiously, and they nodded, smiling impishly. I kneeled next to Antius. 'You are on my list, Antius, and just like these men do not care if you live or die, Drusus might not mind you falling. He might be of the old, honorable blood of Rome, but he is also a player in this game. If all things fail, I shall be his sword in the dark. And he cannot prove you an enemy, yet he knows it is so. I will be in your nightmares, Antius.'

'You cannot prove anything,' he hissed. 'And you just made a mistake. Again.'

I grabbed his face, and noticed the Batavi take a step forward from the corner of my eye, Fulcher pleading with them. 'You fear, fat dog. You fear for you know there is one player in this game who knows you. Drusus. He knows what you are. And when Maroboodus fails to kill him out there in the war, he shall have no need to prove anything to anyone anymore. He shall be so strong he will lead his army to Rome, and let the gods decide who is just, who is false, and no lack of proof will spare you then. Nor will I.'

I got up, and his face glistened with sweat as he struggled to his feet. I walked away, and he spat after me, his spittle hitting my neck. 'You made a mistake, Hraban. A mistake.' I turned back, punched him so hard I heard a tooth crack, leaving him insensible in mud, where a dog stopped to piss on him. Gods, was the violence the mistake, or did he know I was desperate for Lif? I was a fool.

Tuba woke up the camp with the brazen cacophony. I poked my head out of the barrack, shading my eyes as men were marching. The tough centurions were already at the praetorium with the noble tribunes, receiving orders for the day. Legionnaires were breakfasting on some vegetables, getting ready for a long day. Soon, the unlucky ones would march forty Roman miles, or jog some ten in full gear. Others would train battle skills and other equally important legionnaire duties, and raw recruits would do so both in the morning and the afternoon. Many immunes would work their sometimes nearly exclusive trades, especially the scribes and the clerks, and the carpenters. Naval soldiers would train the seamanship at the river. Day as usual.

Except, that day, four cohorts would guard the meetings of Drusus.

Fulcher came in from the outside, shaking his incredibly long hair enthusiastically. 'Chilly morning, my friend. The Batavi sent us some nice rations again. The legionnaires seem to munch on some fruits and vegetables and a piece of bread every morning. Wine with water, no ale, no mead. No wonder they are killers. They probably see a man trying to stop them from the first proper meal since forever when they face the spears. The Batavi eat well though. Beef, vegetables, ale. Porridge. Cannot complain. Ansbor is getting too fat,' he told me, as Cassia appeared wearing a white tunica and silver bracelets, and she giggled as she watched me, combing her hair.

'You look like a mole that has woken up in the middle of the winter, Hraban. Your beard is in tangles, rings under your eyes. You been drinking again?' she inquired sweetly while nodding at Fulcher.

'Rough night, Cassia. Much will be decided soon,' I told her. 'Be careful as you move around. In fact, please have a guard with you, never far.' Antius and Cornix. I felt Father's hand reaching for us from afar. Her eyes met mine, and she nodded bravely.

So we ate well, dressed up, and waited. I thought of Armin, of Antius and Catualda, feeling fates tug at me. Soon, things would change for all of us, and I eyed my friends, Ansbor's sullen face as Cassia was chatting with Fulcher, who was embarrassed as she teased him for his inability to tie a knot at the hem of his armor. I felt wind blow through the room, and thought it was Woden's warning. Men would die. Wyrd, the three sisters spinning our future were hard at work, and some strings would be cut. I would fight so that none were ours.

We were taken out in the late morning, and had to dodge a hundred recruits who were jogging in formation, full kit on. Wicker baskets, the bedrolls on the end of the long poles, the pilum and shields were clanking, dolobara digging tools clanking, and helmets bouncing in their heads, their mail dusty. The youngsters were huffing along with rounded eyes, wondering when the pain would end. A pair of ruthless centurions jogged next to them, wearing a tunic alone, and holding a well-used cane that danced on unwary shoulders every now and then. The bastards were laughing. We walked calmly with our Batavi guards, and came outside in the wake of the dust cloud from the hapless recruits.

Outside the gate, a familiar sight greeted me.

The Quadi exiles had arrived.

Bohscyld stepped towards us from the side, and grinned in a way a hideous monster from abyss might grin. Fulcher looked surprised, groping for a weapon, Cassia nearly screamed as she regarded the boulder-like Quadi, but I waved them down and walked to him. He had grown, not fatter but stronger, if possible. He was like a rock, as wide as a pony. I gave him my arm, and he took it, and he grinned at Ansbor, for we had fought each other through our childhood. Then he stared at Fulcher uncertainly. He also noticed Cassia, and went entirely red in the face, looking up and down.

I laughed at his sudden timidity. 'He is with me. So is she.' I pointed at Cassia, and he mumbled something incoherent, distressed. 'Where are Agetan and Tudrus the younger? Where is your father, Tudrus the Elder?' I asked.

He grunted and hissed while gazing at the Batavi, and I understood I should not name the men. They were with the Sigambri after all, and I followed. 'Hey!' yelled one of the Batavi guarding us and rushed to follow us, suddenly followed by some ten of them. Chariovalda was taking no chances since I met with Armin, and my meeting with Antius was common knowledge. My friends ran after me. 'Hey! We are ordered to attend the meeting.'

'When does it start?' I asked a tall Batavi in leather armor.

'In two hours! So—'

'So, I will speak with my friends first,' I grimaced at him.

'But—'

'They are my friends, man, and I shall speak with them,' I told him tiredly and walked on.

'You shall not punch any of them,' he told me prudently.

'Only if they punch me first,' I snickered, for we had previously hurt each other countless of times.

'Who are they?' he demanded.

'They are Gauls, Mediomactri Gauls. I used to know them in Hard Hill.'

'They don't look like Gauls,' he said uncertainly, but I did not answer him.

346

We walked the length of wall of the castrum towards the village, and I followed Bohscyld to a busy house near the road, an inn by the looks of it, for food was being served from a stone table with steaming vats sunk on holes. I saw that Tudrus the Older was sitting at a table, eating a pig. A whole pig. His son, Agetan, was with him, near identical to Bohscyld, who stopped me with his arm, growled, and took us to the side. A man was talking with Tudrus, and Tudrus, seeing us, discreetly dismissed him on some errand. He motioned for me, his eyebrows shadowing his face as he regarded the Batavi guard clambering after me. His face was leaner than it had been, the old man's hair gray and in a ponytail. None wore the Suebi knot. We went to the table, and he looked up at me. 'Sit, Hraban.' Brusquely, to the point. I frowned at him. Had I not saved his wrinkled rear?

Tudrus the Younger walked up from around the corner and grinned briefly, his long hair framing his face, the lithe and muscular youth, my former, terrible enemy, now happy to see me. He sat down like a cat, and gave my hand a painful shake, looking at my face and the scar, and Agetan was clapping my back, smiling stupidly, and I had to grab his arm before he broke a bone. I never heard Bohscyld or Agetan speak properly, but they had a way to make themselves understood. Tudrus the Younger gazed at his father, who was now sitting there on the table, with a half-eaten leg bone of a pig crunched in his ham-like fist, his eyebrows furrowed.

'Father is being unhappy, Hraban. He is like that these days,' Tudrus the Younger said, glancing at the old man who grunted, and noticed the food in his hand and tore off a chunk with his teeth.

The old chief spoke. 'You saved us. My boys and me, Hraban. I give you that. Despite this, we lost relatives. We lost our lands to the pup Vannius and traitor Sibratus. And you were working with your father then. Would you have stayed with him, had he not betrayed you?' he asked, while pointing to the table.

347

'I ... yes.' I gazed at him. 'He was very likable then. He was ... is my father. But, I did send Ansbor to warn you, for you are my friend. I am sorry for your losses. How do you like the Sigambri?'

He snorted as he gazed at Ansbor sitting with the Batavi, and gave him a near imperceptible nod in thanks. 'Like living with the pigs. They have a fertile valley or two, but they are at war as often as the warriors of Valholl. Unhappy land, and our few thousand people face losses every spring. We might have done better fleeing to Rome. Here. Like you did.' He slurped at a horn full of steaming ale. Then he inspected my face. 'Your warning was not entirely groundless. I believed you. I hate him. And now, your father and you seem to have an irreversible fall out.' He tapped my face with a pig bone. I slapped the bone so it flew and hit one of the Batavi, who only sat down as Fulcher begged him to.

'Makes you prettier!' said the younger Tudrus, ignoring the guards arguing with my friend.

'You should try it! Can I fix one for you?' I asked him. 'And I am not here for good. I fled here after I lost Burlein, and I lost other things as well. I need...'

'Help,' Tudrus the Older said. 'This meeting here is moot. The Cherusci are here only to see what they are facing. The Chatti are still undecided, it is true, but nothing will come out of this.'

'So, where is Wandal?' asked Tudrus the Younger eagerly. 'I have not trashed his ass for a while.'

'He was lost in the battle of Castrum Luppia,' I said with sorrow. 'Something I have to deal with yet.'

'Gods, you have a lot on your lap,' Tudrus the Older said.

'And Ansigar?'

I looked away. 'He is with Gernot and Odo.'

'Odo? The bastard's still alive?' Tudrus the Younger asked. 'Father told us of this prophecy.'

'Yes, they are still after me. It is a long story. I shall never have my own hall, and even if I miraculously manage to fix everything else, I shall drag my feet through the Roman world, trying to find Wandal. I lost his bride. I lost my tribe, and I lost—'

'Your daughter,' Tudrus the Older said grimly.

'How do you know that?' I said with a small voice.

Tudrus was munching on his pig leg, and he took a swig from his horn, then a swig of mead from unsuspecting Agetan, but he did not seem drunk at all. He was searching for words. 'You made my helmet famous, boy. I am proud of you. I have been bragging shamelessly that it's my helmet,' he laughed, but his voice was nervous. 'Eat, and I do not care if it is your second breakfast,' he grunted.

'My daughter,' I growled.

'Eat,' he said tiredly, and I did, holding the turmoil inside me in check. Tudrus bought the Batavi a meal as well, and it was a noisy and loud group watching over me, full of mirth and happiness I did not feel.

I played his game, and took a long breath. 'So, what have you been up to? I have not seen you since last year,' I asked, while eating the last bit of pork.

He showed a basic gladius to me, and I admired it. 'We have been fighting alongside the Sigambri. When we moved there, last fall, we had nothing to offer but our spears and lives. Maelo took us in. Now, we serve him. I got this blade off an exploratore scouting our side of the Luppia River.' Tudrus the Older nodded many times and then licked his fingers. 'Your father changed the world for us all, Hraban. The Quadi will have to find a new place to live. Tallo, my relative, is still free of your father's schemes, but he is weaker than traitor Sibratus who follows your father. The bastards,' he slammed the table with his fist so hard the Batavi rose up as one man. I waved at them, and they sat back down, though they did not let go of their weapons. 'In the north, however, there is hope. The Cherusci. Armin especially, I think, even if he has no lands other than Sigimer's. He will fight Rome. He will fight Maroboodus. And so, we are thinking about joining him. As are you.'

'He sent you here?' I asked breathlessly.

'He did,' Tudrus the Younger said carefully.

349

'What about Armin? What is he planning?' I asked him desperately.

His eyes went into slits. 'He says yes. Will you serve him? He and his father are going to fight, if these dog-faced turds invade,' he stated. 'I like him. Ruthless bastard he is, but I do like him. Suffice it to say, with or without your father, the tribes in the north will stand. Even without the Chatti. You would do well to serve the young man. He is a worthy warrior, and has an uncanny way to convince older, prouder chiefs to heed him. But, you know this already. He is here to see the Romans, and has done that. He is here to charm the Chatti into joining them. He is here… to hurt your father. Though I think your Drusus will do that as well. Neither wishes the Marcomanni anywhere near this war. And so, Armin has many uses for you. The ring, of course. Then he needs the Chatti, yes, so he hopes you would help him with that, and many other things,' Tudrus said. 'Your Gunda still thinks you are her future husband.'

I groaned and cursed, for while I was pleased and my ego soothed by the thought of a Chatti princess thinking like that, I was not planning on marrying anyone, not for anyone. I had desperate feelings for Cassia, and she came far behind Lif. Another duty to hamper me, another thing in my way. I shook my head, making no comment.

'Or,' he continued, sensing my reluctance, 'the ring will be enough. He is your sanctuary, like he will be ours. He forgives much. But, as I said, he is ruthless.' He looked down.

'And what is needed?' I asked him, feeling doom pressing its heavy hand on my shoulder.

'An ill deed for an ill deed,' he said softly, looking down, the honorable man suffering, and I felt my newly found honor was about to be irreversibly destroyed.

'Armin will give you everything you need,' Tudrus the Younger said, scowling at me. 'He will give you Lif. He found the bounty hunter Hands, and Hands had a baby with him. He was thought a spy, captured, and he is with the Cherusci. She is a beautiful baby, Hraban. We saw her, when we prepared to travel here.'

I got up, but Agetan grunted as he pulled me down. 'He has Lif?' I asked softly. 'He has Hands?'

The old chief nodded. 'I do not like this. She is your child, Hands admitted it freely. He was taking her away to safety, he claimed, hunted by strange looking men, and took refuge with Armin's men to save her. He was lucky, Hands. He was running when he had to take refuge with the Cherusci army near the Luppia River. Armin was grateful.' Odo had gone after Hands, I thought, but failed. Thank gods.

'The Cherusci are already with the Sigambri?' I asked, my mind whirling. Lif.

'Yes, and no,' Tudrus the Younger said suspiciously. 'Listen. He will reunite you with her. You will bring him the ring, perhaps serve him, and he will forgive you. But ... '

They looked down.

I shook my head, for I knew what they wanted. 'They want Drusus dead.'

They nodded softly, ashamed, and I roared with laughter, nearly hoping Antius would be seated there, laughing with me. Gods laughed at least, I was sure of that, as I shook with mirth, and they stared bewildered, thinking I had lost my mind. What Father wished for, what Antius craved for, I, the man who admired Drusus, was to deliver. Such irony I had not imagined. Drusus, a man hostile to Augustus would fall, and now, son of Maroboodus was expected to do the deed. For Lif. Damn the spinners, I thought, and cursed myself, and wyrd.

'They expect this, Hraban,' Tudrus the Older said with some anger. 'What is so funny about it?'

'I ... my father. Rome. Things I care not to explain. So, I am to be a murderer. The Oath Breaker is a fitting man for the job, eh? None will love me, no matter what I manage to do. My fame and my honor—'

'Are Armin's. He can rebuild them.'

'Not my honor,' I said bitterly. 'Only I can build my honor. And I have seen how little lords can do to unsoil one's fame. I will be a fugitive with blood on his hands. Drusus will join Bero and Balderich in the line of the dead men who liked and trusted me.'

'You will never be high, nor loved,' Tudrus the Older told me. 'But, you will have vengeance, we will have our lands, and you will be a father, Hraban. Your honor will heal.'

I rubbed my forehead, and stared at the brothers in front of me, then at Fulcher and Ansbor, who were wondering what was going on. 'Is this the way Armin wants to win? By killing this man?'

Tudrus the Younger leaned forward. 'He is realistic. There has to be a lesser man leading the Romans. Or there will be no victory. It is that simple. The men out there are half the men without him.'

'Can you reach my daughter?' I asked Tudrus the Older. 'Can you get her out and safe, and can you spare me this burden?'

Tudrus the Older shook his head. 'Armin is adamant, Hraban. Ruthless as you are. He can give us our lands back. But, he does not trust us, nor share his full plans. He only hints and promises vague dreams, and we are grasping at those dreams. He is the enemy of your father as we are. So, no. I cannot get to the girl. If I could, I do not know I would.'

I drank, and sat there for a good while until the Batavi started to look anxious. I finally nodded. 'I so swear.' Gods, I loved Drusus, and he loved me, but he would die for Lif.

He did not look pleased, but grunted in agreement. 'So, fine. This Roman army will move north, Hraban, and stage for invasion of the Luppia River. Make yourself his friend, Hraban, and slay him at Ara Ubiorium, day prior to them marching. That night, preferably. They will likely march anyway, with a lesser man leading them. If you die, I will care for her. Or Armin will.'

Woden, but I hated Armin then. 'You. You will do so.'

So we gave oaths, and swore to be true, and I agreed to perform the murderous deed. For Lif. For vengeance.

Tudrus grunted and nodded. He scratched his grayed hair and nodded at his boys, who got up like small mountains and left. He looked at Fulcher and Ansbor sitting with the Batavi, and the Batavi stopped drinking and eating as they spied the Quadi leaving, half staying at the table, half getting up. The older man was looking at me steadily. 'I want an oath from you,' he said silently, and I choked.

'An oath? You? Why?' I asked bitterly. 'Did I not just give one? It tasted bitter as shit, Tudrus. I do not wish to wash it down with piss.'

He smiled wistfully. 'We are homeless, Hraban. You and I both. If we fail and all things go to Hel, if I die, help my boys. I want an oath from you that you will help them survive the turmoil. They will follow you, and help you stoutly when things go dark, and in return, you will help them find their place. No matter where that is, help them as they would help you.'

I was playing with my drinking horn. 'Have you been following my life, old friend, and noticed how little control I have over even my own wyrd?'

He bent over and clapped the bag on my belt and the bronze helmet. 'Yes. It looks bad now, but one day, you will be a mighty lord of these lands. That much I know. Even if you are hated, you will rule as a lord.'

'Don't tell me you have sight as well,' I groaned.

'I do not, but Woden is my friend, and surely he does not wish for the sisters to cut your strings, my boy; he must enjoy this great poem too much,' Tudrus the Older rumbled, and I noticed how tired he was. Heart broken, torn. He noticed my look and shook his head. 'My wife died this winter. So forgive me my moods.'

'Yes, lord,' I told him, and mourned with him. I gave him the oath, and he was happier for it.

'I thank you. If Woden tires of you, Hraban, then let Freya guard you with her ready blade, for I hear she loves desperate causes and homeless vagabonds. And next time you tell anyone we are Celts, I'll slit your belly. Stay close to your Drusus this night, Hraban, and you will be his man. Guard him, not at the feast, but after it. And for all the gods' sakes, kill Vannius and Sibratus for me, should my boys also die in battle. Just add them to your list, at least.' He walked off with a tired grin, and I got up.

I never saw him alive again.

CHAPTER XXIV

I walked off with my sated, if unhappy, entourage, as a man ran to the Batavi leader. He was summoned to the temple of Mercury, and he cursed me generously for the delay, despite their unexpectedly full bellies. I felt weak as I walked on, thinking about the terrible oath. We soon neared the austere temple, and the men murmured in awe. Few Germani tribes had temples, and thought only the Romans built the massive buildings and worshipped in them. Romans were wise enough to preach how their gods were our gods, and all the men serving Rome knew Mercury was Roman Woden.

I gazed at the temple, where a statue of a young man, wearing a winged helmet, his ankles adorned with smaller wings, was staring over the multitude of men milling before it. I cursed him, as I stared at his stony countenance, for I could use some help outside a battle as well. Oh, he gave me the will to fight like a mad dog, a berserker, but he also made it so I was constantly being drawn into filthy plans. And I was of his blood? Bah. I spat as I walked forward.

Bastard. He likely laughed.

I remember Bark telling me he was a complicated god. The vitka had not lied. From misery to victory, from victory to exile, from exile into a promise, one that would make me a murderer in order to be a father again. 'Wyrd take me,' I cursed, as I walked the Roman road, wondering at the well-fitted stones and sand that would make the way so durable, it would last for decades. Ignoring the god's gaze, I studied the temple. The columned wonder ahead was in some strange way a simple, sturdy, powerful, and ominously holy complex next to the castrum's north wall, easy to reach from the northern gate. It boasted some slabs of marble, tastefully arranged so the plain concrete under it was pleasing to the eye. Six columns of gray-shaded stone were guarding the portico.

Before the temple, a huge row of benches was apparent. They were arranged in a square and the spot before the temple was clearly left for the Romans. On the sides, bonfires were burning, and harried slaves were roasting meat, mounds of dead animals prepared for the feast, and ale and mead was abundant, though there was very little wine. It was much like our Thing. Many of the Germani were already there, milling in tribal groups, avoiding the others, for most had feuds. The Batavi gazed at the preparations, and the leader grunted at me and guided my steps for the temple and the area behind it. There stood a horde of merchants and artisans.

'What is this?' I asked.

'You will look presentable,' said the tall Batavi darkly. 'Your tunic is shredded in places; you stink of piss and goat. Your men look like shepherds.'

'I was fine enough for the parade, though!' I said.

He shook his head. 'Chariovalda was reprimanded by Lord Drusus. And your woman gave me this.' He handed me a small pouch of coins. 'Old Roman coins to buy you fineries.'

I groaned and dismounted. Cassia had guarded my wealth ferociously for long months, and so I would look like a perfumed man-whore. I bought a clean Roman tunic, made of wool. It was a legionary tunic, white, slightly lower behind the knees than in the front. It felt uncomfortable and tight in the chest, and they were all the same size.

'One size fits most!' cackled the merchant, eyeing Ansbor's belly dubiously, but they were to go with their old gear.

I also bought brown leather pants and dressed behind the wall, guarded by the tall Batavi, who did not let me out of his sight. I had my beard trimmed by a crippled Gaul specializing in doing this for the Romans, and another merchant, a red-cheeked young woman, sold me a pair of caligae, military issue, well-made with no shafting edges on them, all the hobnails in place. I walked about with them awkwardly, to Fulcher's and Ansbor's silent amusement, until I made them wear similar things, though I did not fuss with the quality in their case.

The hobnails were awkward; I felt like a horse. Cassia appeared with a guard, looking splendid with her hair braided and pulled high, her neck bared, and gods curse me, but I stared at her until she blushed. I stumbled in some slabs of rock, the hobnailed sandals treacherous, and she giggled with a high voice. 'Grace of a three-legged horse,' she mocked me, until I finally slapped her in the rump. It was a mistake, of course, for Ansbor's face turned from unhappy into sour, and both Cassia and I went silent. He was festering with jealousy.

Next, Chariovalda rode up, grunted appreciatively, and dragged me after him, as I was tying my belt and sword. Fulcher was at hand, with my chain mail and helmet. He was gazing at the sun, wondering how much time we had. 'Who was the ... Gaul you met?' he asked, and I shook inside. If I killed Drusus, this man I liked would be my enemy.

'A man who used to visit Grinrock, a Gaul trader. He— '

'I thought you said he visited Hard Hill,' Chariovalda said amusedly, as he focused on a low building, with steam escaping from small crags.

'There as well,' I told him sullenly, and hated Armin, and myself.

'I am keeping an eye on you, Hraban. I have a feeling you are lying to me. Those Gauls of yours disappeared, my boy, and by the description I heard, it was Tudrus the Older. I have fought him, you know.'

'I am not sure, my friend, what to think of your suspicions. Surely there are plenty of men who have fought with you,' I told him, and he glanced at me.

'I like you, Hraban. I hope you make the right choices. I do not wish to fillet you, son. Now, let's clean you.'

I stopped walking. 'I just dressed myself!'

'Now you undress,' he growled, and I was pushed forward. I was allowed to use the legionary bath situated behind the temple, and stepping inside the hall, I stopped to gaze at many tubs full of water. Chariovalda shook his head at me, as I gaped. 'Usually there are baths made of stone, but this is temporary until the one in the camp has been rebuilt. There was a fire. That one is cold water, that one is hot. That is the scalding one. The slaves will throw you in each one of them; they will scrub and massage you. We have to hurry. Thanks to your ... Gauls.'

'I think I don't—' I began, but he snapped his fingers, and the Batavi grabbed me, stripped me, and helped the slaves torture me.

The Germani bathe. We do so in warm water, as well as cold rivers.

However, for the Romans, bathing is a way of life. Off-duty legionnaires lounged in front of the building and on the benches around the tubs, gambling as they enjoyed one of the two places where all ranks were somewhat equal. Some muscular men, who were legionnaires on duty, worked huge bellows, warming up the waters. These men spotted the struggle first, as the cursing, slipping Batavi carried me across the hall.

I received gawking looks from the soldiers, and amused by the spectacle of a struggling group of Germani, they encouraged me to first dip into the scalding bath. I, of course, had no choice, and was thrown in. I came up sputtering, and the hands grabbed me and pulled me out of the tub like one would pull a snail out of its shell, and they promptly pushed me to the ice cold one, even if I managed to drag one man with me. The shock of it nearly made me squeal like a rabbit, but I did not, for I was underwater with the Batavi. I came up, pushing the bastard off me, and did manage to preserve some of my dignity by cutting off my scream in the middle.

I spied Cassia laughing by the door, holding her belly, and even Fulcher and Ansbor enjoyed themselves immensely. I shrugged the grasping Batavi off and walked myself to the hot waters, where I slipped in and glowered at the bastards staring at me.

Chariovalda spat. 'I asked you once not to over-indulge yourself and drink my mead. You did not heed me. I asked you who the men were. You lied. Next time, you lose my confidence.'

I nodded at him, for he was a great man and felt sorry for what would come between us, the bloody act still hidden in the shadows. I got up as a slave oiled me, and I blushed as Cassia's eyes lingered in my naked body, but I decided to forget her impish smile, as she was chased from the door.

The oil was scraped off with a curved strigil, and I did feel clean. Finally, a pretty girl guided me to lay on a stone slab, and the massage, lord, was one of the best things in Rome and the nations she stole the habit from. The girl left me standing by a row of tables, and an older, bent backed man approached me, showing me a table, but next to the table, there was a dark, large-bosomed beauty oiling a man, and I decided that I would wait for her, which the old man took surprisingly well. The girl gave me a flash of a smile.

She was skillful. Her nimble hands searched my body for painful sprains and unusual knots that I did not know were there. She kneaded all my aches away, and a surprising surge of energy and strength filled me. I moaned and squirmed under her administrations, and some legionnaires made lewd comments, which they thought I could not understand, but I just grinned at them.

Seeing these men, our enemies, soldiers and men at the same time, made me think about my choices. Tudrus had asked me to guide his sons, should he fall. He believed I would tangle on long into this story. My father had betrayed me; I had betrayed others. I had led my friends astray, and now, they held poor Lif, mine again should I slay a great man. I was a killer. I was a man with no honor, and they expected me to act like a bastard, but this time not for fame. I had learnt to appreciate my inner happiness, at least a bit more than the thoughts of fame and glory, but now they, the gods, were truly testing me. I had failed. I had chosen, my orlog; the choices of my life making up my wyrd had been ill-favored ones.

Could I renege on the oath?

Would I be happier with these men? Would Lif be safe with Armin, should I fail to slay Drusus?

I could never be sure. Odo was after her. Armin did not understand that creature. And Leuthard? What was he doing? Antius asking questions, in the dark?

I had to do it.

With these thoughts, I paid the young girl who smiled at my shyly, and my eyes took on her generous bosom. I felt vaguely guilty for Cassia, and thought of our kiss, when she had been ill. I smiled at the girl, knowing there was a difference between lust and love. I wanted to dress, and a Batavi handed me my weapon.

I walked to the meeting next to Chariovalda, with a Batavi shield, with Nightbright on my hip and the bronze helmet on my head, the mail of Leuthard glimmering on my torso. Fulcher and Ansbor walked with us, and their beards were trimmed, their caligae new, though they were spared the bath and pristine tunic that was chafing at my armpits. They looked strangely clean nonetheless, as I had gotten used to seeing them blooded, grimy, and sullen. The Thing of Drusus would begin soon, and on the field, a vast assembly of Germani chiefs were sitting uncomfortably on the cushioned benches, being served good ale and sweet mead, and they were gorging on sweet meats and steamy vegetables. The afternoon was warm, and many were in their tunics.

I spotted our host as we drew near the Roman end, before the temple. Drusus was clad in a white garment, with long sleeves and a voluminous fabric billowing around him, similar to what I had seen Roman nobles and Antius use, a toga they called it, but this one had purple stripes on it. He looked fresh and clean, his curly hair oiled, and he had similarly dressed men standing behind him, five of them, with curious rods ending in small axes.

Chariovalda leaned over me. 'Lictors, former soldiers, and centurions, men who should keep Drusus alive. He has many, for he is the Urban Praetor of Rome, a famous general, and a governor. He often travels without them, not wishing to insult the locals, but the lictors are the men in charge of his life. They have a terrible job.' The lictors looked ill at ease, as they stared over their master's shoulder at the bearded men, who would like nothing more than to kill their general. Yet, Drusus seemed perfectly at ease, as he addressed familiar men who came to greet him, some soon laughing with the young lord.

Around the perimeter, before the temple, was at least a pair of cohorts of Roman soldiery, a handful of Batavi cavalry, and some tough Ubii infantry, and a few Vangiones lounged in the area. Further, two cohorts were spread around the woods and hills, protecting the proceedings.

Nero Claudius Drusus took no more chances than he had to.

I saw Armin standing tall amidst the Cherusci, his eyes scourging me as I followed Chariovalda. He was whispering to a man with a high forehead and piercing eyes, though his eyes never left me. I cursed him. How could a man so noble looking ask for such things as he had?

Chariovalda walked towards Drusus, bowed to him, and he was shown a seat nearby. I stood there for a second, until Drusus beckoned for me, and I took heavy steps forward. The general's lion eyes held me as I came to him, and he nodded at me, placing a hand on my shoulder. The Germani went silent, for many knew me, and they saw I was with Drusus, a traitor to my people. I was not sure what Drusus had in mind showing camaraderie to a man they despised, a womanizer, an apparent traitor, and the man called the Oath Breaker. The mood was brooding; I heard small voices from the crowd of the mighty lords, none pleasing but subtly mocking.

Drusus nodded at me and pointed at a chair near Chariovalda, a strange thing as it looked rickety and delicate, but I found it sturdy enough. I observed the men in the crowds, and they stared at me with mixed feelings. Ebbe, the older Chatti, had lost weight, and his cheeks were hollow, but he still nodded my way. They had once held my side over Gernot, and despite what happened, Adgandestrius had likely spoken well of me.

'Lord Drusus! Let him take his helmet off at least, so he may eat!' the grinning adeling hollered at Drusus, pointing a finger at me. Drusus roared with laughter, got up to fetch me a plate, stunning all present and presented it to me, with a silver goblet of mead.

I got up to bow to him, but he waved me down, and so I took off my helmet and the scar in my face drew a buzz from the multitude. I growled at them instinctively, but then tore at the meat in front of me.

Drusus was urgently talking with a military tribune. Chariovalda was shaking with amusement as men stared at me. He whispered, 'It is told the

Sigambri have made a sortie this side of the river. Bloodily beaten back, of course. Perhaps they wanted to make a point while Drusus is trying to seduce their fellow chiefs.'

'Where did they attack?' I asked him, drinking calmly, trying to ignore the looks. 'Gods, they think I am Roman now,' I breathed.

'Yes,' he snickered. 'But, as for the Sigambri, up north. Ubii lands, against Castra Vetera.'

'Castra Vetera? What is that?' I asked him, pretending not to know, but Tudrus the Older had told me already.

He answered without care. 'North, where the war will start. Now, Sigimer is the war king of the Cherusci this year, so listen to him,' he hissed, as the old warlord was getting up, and Drusus faced him. The patience was growing thin with the Germani, and Drusus was nearly robbed of the opening statement, but recovered amiably.

Drusus called out. 'Hold, my lord Sigimer! Let us bless the meeting first.'

'As you please,' Sigimer said calmly, but the thought of invoking the Roman gods was not pleasing to many. Men made hammer symbols in the air, invoking Donor's protection.

Despite this, a group of thin Romans strode next to Drusus, swathed in white ropes with hoods. Chariovalda snorted. 'Haruspices, marsi perhaps. Not a pullarii. No, haruspices, there comes the sodden cow.'

'What are you talking about?' I saw Sigimer hesitate and sit back down.

He snorted at my stupidity. 'Priests. Omens. Reading omens. Like our vitka and völva, they too think it suitable to read omens, and they are most often favorable. There are many kinds of magicians with the legions. Marsi, they have the same name as the tribe in the Luppia River, but are healers, often legionnaires. Pullarii are fools, who read the clucks of the holy chicken and their erratic movements and feeding habits! Imagine. Chicken eating habits. They eat anything, for Juppiter's sakes. What can they tell you? Will we win the war? We will if the fat hen eats that grain. She did!' He laughed too loudly and sobered quickly. 'In our tribes, he would have no use, the birds would be eaten, and their bones picked clean before he farted!'

361

I nodded and chuckled with him.

He pointed at the thin man directing the cow's placement, which was proving hard for the cow was not cooperative. 'That is a trio of haruspices, man who reads entrails; look at signs from the livers. Etruscan way. Do not ask what that is. But, they are fairly much like our vitka. Drusus always sits with them the night before a campaign. He is more superstitious than a maiden trying to get pregnant. He ... ' Chariovalda stopped whispering, as Drusus squinted at him.

The cow was finally led to the priest, a man in a clean white robe and a cowl over his head. Drusus stepped forward, and the Germani toasted him, knowing he would do the honors. He took a Germani-style horn of mead. 'To your health, allies and friends! Let it be so, let us be friends!' he saluted the men in a passable Germani dialect. Most understood most of what he said.

Wodenspear grunted, the tattooed man gesturing for the priest. 'Let the priest read the omens, and then we know better whether we shall be friends or enemies! And we will not bow to this cult of Augustus.'

Drusus smiled coldly at the famous warrior. 'This is not the altar of Rome and Augustus, like the one in Lugdunum, just a place where men gather to discuss life and death.' There, it was clear what the agenda was. War or peace, life or death. Drusus was going to dictate, some would bow their heads, and others lose theirs, eventually. Drusus smiled to take the brunt off the words. 'I am the governor of this land, a superior legate, Augustus pro praetor for my stepfather, and I promise, no man is forced to bow.' He gestured for the priest. 'We do what you do before a Thing, ask for gods to help us.'

Wodenspear grunted uncertainly.

The priest hopped next to the wary animal, as we watched on inquisitively. He then took out a long, sharp pugio and, stroking the animal gently, slit its throat without further ceremony. It was a messy death, as any sacrifice is. The cow broke free, ran around crazily squirting blood, and finally fell before Ebbe. The men around him looked at him with pale faces. He kept his face stoic as the priest approached. The belly was expertly sliced open, and the man tore at the entrails, eyeballing the liver carefully, comparing it to a dark liver-sized rock with inscriptions in it. His white clothing turned grimy and red, and his voice rose to explain his favorable findings, but none listened to the man telling Drusus about the omens, or how Juppiter blessed the meeting. A torch was fluttering in the suddenly chilly afternoon air, and there was a reserved mood when Drusus thanked the priest. Ebbe looked troubled, but brave, for it had been a terrible omen to the Germani that the animal had fallen so before him.

Drusus tried to lift the heavy mood. He raised his hands in welcome. 'It is but a cow, and likely it fell at the feet of the hungriest of the guests.' A small ripple of laughter, none from the Chatti. Drusus continued, 'Let us forget the omens, and the gods. Let us speak as men. My fine lords, I welcome you. Summer is fast coming, and so often the summer has seen brutal wounds of battle and deep scars or war, the unhappy, newly made slaves and widowed women crying. It is not the wish of Rome to be thus.' I noticed Wodenspear grimace at the claim but Drusus pressed on. 'I would much rather be in Lugdunum in Gaul, with my beautiful wife and newborn daughter.'

Chariovalda nodded and smiled, smacking his lips, and glanced at me apologetically. 'He has a pretty wife, and it seems to many that he enjoys her company overmuch. Many babies!' I smiled, as Drusus spoke on. Little did I know some of those babies would grow into men I would loathe, one day. And women.

'Rome wishes nothing more than to trade fairly, and live alongside you, as equal powers. This is what Augustus has told me. He told me he wishes nothing but your hands, held out in friendship.' Men eyed him, listened to his broken Germani, the power in his voice, the well-practiced gestures empowering his message. Drusus was walking back and forth slowly, and it was the first time I saw a true orator in action. This was a skill a Roman noble must know, the fine art of how to persuade his audience. Drusus was a great warrior, but he was also a likable man, who could turn nearly any man's heart.

'Our hands, and perhaps, arms?' asked someone from the Cherusci, and Drusus laughed with them.

'Arms, if we must, though it is not an easy feat taking them,' he said, and the Germani could be seen swelling with pride. Chariovalda snorted. Still, Drusus did not relent. 'Last year, I did more than build large towns and fancy villas, and initiated the cult to Rome and Augustus. I built forts, created markets, supported crafts, dug ditches, and laid roads, and I upheld peace.' He held a dramatic moment of silence. He pointed north. 'I did these things, things any Roman is to do with his fief. More, I also dug a river to get my men to the north, as speedily as we could. This is what the Sigambri wanted to stop, the reason we waged a terrible murdering war amongst them,' Drusus said, his face honest. He pointed a finger at the assembled men, who had their mead horns and goblets filled. 'I also made pacts with some of your brothers. Some of the Chatti, some of the Cherusci.'

The Chatti looked unhappy, as many glanced their way, and I also noticed Segestes the Fat shift his massive ass.

'If you made such a deal with our friends,' Inguiomerus asked in a sly voice, 'then why did you conquer the north? Did they say no? Or did you even ask for their friendship? Though the north,' he said, with a nasty sneer, 'fell with no fight.'

The Chauci and their dependents rose up as one man to spit curses at the lank Cherusci, who seemed to enjoy their spite, but Drusus slammed his fist on the table, silencing everyone. Mercury looked over the multitude of men, foreboding as a god could be. Flies buzzed around the dead cow, and men sat down slowly.

Drusus commenced his pacing. 'As for the valor of the Chauci? It was never tested. They are wise, not foolish, and see the benefits of Roman friendship.' Many of the wilder Germani shook their heads in disgust at the comment, but Drusus kept talking. 'I have heard rumors that I took the north to gain easy access to your backs, via the glowing, glittering northern rivers. Albis and Visurgis, we named them. I found the rivers.' This stopped men from eating, mulling over the implications of the claim.

Drusus could come at them over the hills and forests, or he could sail the precarious sea and wild shores of the Mare Gothonium to reach their backs over the many rivers of the north. Perhaps both. Drusus progressed with his speech, having made his point. 'I did find them, and they are useful, my friends, for war. Yes, very much so. But, the reason was trade, exploration, and peace. We are curious people.'

'Perhaps too curious,' Sigimer stated bluntly, scowling.

'Perhaps not,' Drusus answered spitefully, 'for our spears give us the right to be as curious as we wish to be. Is it not the same with the strong Germani tribes? How many clans and weaker tribes have you pushed against Rhenus River, sometimes over it? Like the Ubii? We are the same. We have power, much power, maybe too much for those who seek to oppose our will. Ask the Sigambri how many legions they have seen. What you saw on the field was paltry compared to my full force. And that is trivial compared to all the legions of Rome.'

If men had not thought of Roman spears before, now they did. Romans could come at them from many places, many directions. In addition, the war with Sigambri was rumored to have left so many Sigambri dead that whole villages were empty. What would a large war be like? That was the thought riding through their minds, a fear of war coming at them from the north and west, maybe even south? Killing thousands?

Drusus laughed, dismissing the threat. 'Here, today, we have the honest Chauci, and the finest men of the Chassuari, even the implacable Frisii. Many others who wish nothing more than peace with us. They will benefit greatly, for while they will not suffer wars with Rome, we will give them peace from their neighbors.' The Cherusci looked at each other. They were the closet neighbors to the Chauci. Drusus smiled benevolently. 'So, I summoned you here, the great chiefs, no vile brigands or thoughtless villains, to discuss a peaceful end to the constant war. Is that not desirable? Loot and slaves, we all can have elsewhere. Why make us your enemies by raiding our lands, like the simple Sigambri and their subjects do?' Drusus made a fist and turned to the Germani. 'See the difference between the Chauci, and the Sigambri. The former are alive, their grandfathers sit their grandchildren on their knees, smiling in feasts, gazing around their long halls happily. They have much wealth, and a great future. Sigambri lack grandfathers and many fathers, some, if not all, of their wealth, many halls, and very soon they will lose the rest,' he said, evenly and calmly.

Wodenspear spat. 'And they lack mothers and grandmothers, and to be honest, even the children, for your legion spares none.'

'Yes, that is so,' Drusus told him coldly.

The Germani looked down to their mugs and each other. Some were nodding slowly, like Segestes, his corpulent body shaking, his gaudy tunic smeared with mead, and sinister eyes scanning the other Germani. Others gritted their teeth at the not-so-veiled threats. Wodenspear, close ally to the Sigambri, was whispering something to the Marsi, their neighbors, harshly and without care. He was aggressive, and the Marsi seemed of like mind. Drusus looked at them, gauging the mood. He looked uncaring, and I knew he wished to make sure the largest tribes stayed out of the war. Surely, he did not think that threats would make the proud warriors trusty allies, a man so like the Germani himself?

No, I shook my head. He only cared about the Cherusci and the Chatti.

Drusus ignored the unsettled lords. 'We have an alliance with the Matticati and with the Chatti,' he bowed to Ebbe and Oldaric, 'an understanding with the Cherusci, some of you at least. Hermanduri of the Suebi talk with us peacefully. Yet, we hear troubled rumors.' He fixed an eye on Sigimer. 'We hear a deal was made, a deal with the Sigambri present, between the Chatti, the Cherusci, and the Marcomanni and their Quadi friends. A cur named Maroboodus put a concern forward. That Rome is a common enemy to all of you? Is this so? Did you listen to him? I hear you did.'

They all shifted their gazes to me, remembering I had been present in the meeting, and they assumed I had spilled my guts to Drusus. I shifted in my seat. I had not spoken much of the meeting I had attended, but little did it matter. I would be the hole all shit would be thrown in.

Silence. Drusus did not move.

Finally, Inguiomerus got up, and Drusus turned his head towards him.

The gaunt man made no lies. 'We did speak. We are no subjects to Rome but men of our own laws and customs. You offer prosperity and peace. We are prosperous, after our own fashion.' Segestes rolled his eyes at his brother. Inguiomerus walked forward. 'You bring laws. We have them. Passed to us by Esla and Aska, the first men, and the gods who gave them life. Our laws respect men, and their rights. Man is to be respected, no matter his stature, nor is his death a commodity for judges to give or take. No, it is for his peers to decide. Death we deal, but only if the crime is great enough.' The Germani banged their shields. 'Roman laws concern us. Roman trade we do not need. Your words? We should not heed.' Rap of spear on shield echoed in the meeting for a long time. 'As for Maroboodus? Perhaps you should fear him. He knows you better than any.'

Sigimer came to stand next to his brother. 'We have spoken with the Chatti, and the Marcomanni. We have agreed to marriages and aid; in case we are threatened. We are friends, Roman, if there is no such threat to the nations who love freedom. But, there is, is it not so? You speak of the Sigambri and war? Are you going to take their lands? Come over the river? Should you do so, where will you stop? Will you stay in the lands of the Sigambri? Will you stay near us and the Chatti? Will you build forts? Maroboodus maybe spoke true words of wisdom.'

Drusus's eyes and voice hardened. 'Rome has a grudge against Maroboodus,' he spat. 'A grudge we will settle. However, we cannot settle it if the Sigambri attack us, every spring, every summer, like rabid dogs. They did, not week past. We wish peace with you. But, Rome will have Maroboodus's head, and the Sigambri humbled. Will you stand with him? With them?'

The Germani spoke animatedly with each other.

Ebbe of the Chatti got up heavily. 'Lord Drusus. We can make our mutual alliances, and still keep peace and treaties with you. If you invade our great nations one-by-one, as your armies have done all over the world, as they tell us, the backwater mud swallowers,' he said sarcastically, 'then I doubt you can blame the Chatti for throwing their lot in with the free people.'

367

Drusus was about to speak, but Oldaric the Chatti stood up next to Ebbe. 'Our agreement with you stands, but we will not look on idly at these wars.' He sounded sour, the father of Gunda, his tattoos crudely wrinkled as he scowled. 'Answer Sigimer. Are you, my lord, going to take the Sigambri lands? Do not, and we are friends. Do, and we might not be.'

Drusus shook his head, as he walked up and down the field. He laughed, throwing his hand towards the east. 'His words echo here, even if he is not here. Maroboodus is not to be trusted,' he said tiredly, as if he was an utterly misunderstood wise man, surrounded by tedious children. 'I do know him. Better than you. Did he not serve my stepfather? He is a snake. A murderer of the elderly and the unwary.' He continued, 'Will you let Rome avenge itself? That is all I need to know. Will you let Maroboodus win you over? Here, look at his son!' he said, and pointed at me. 'Come here!' Drusus ordered.

I was mortified, but got up, slowly.

'Hraban. The boy he called the Oath Breaker, a boy whose hands he was going to cut away, then turn over to be sacrificed and tortured,' Drusus said spitefully.

I glanced at Chariovalda, the only man who knew this. He shrugged, bewildered, shaking his head, and then my eyes snaked to Cassia, who was looking down. Drusus had spoken with her? She was blushing. I cursed her under my breath, and turned to look at the multitude of men staring at me.

'His son,' Drusus said, with spite, and pulled me next to him, 'served him, worshipped him, yearned for his return. When Hraban found out Maroboodus had set up his so-called rescue of the village they lived in, causing the death of his noble mother and famed grandfather, imagine his rage! Imagine it! He had done great and dark services for the man. He trusted his father! Like you trust him.'

My mouth was open, and I croaked something unintelligible, finding I could not say anything. I flushed with anger, and tried to take a steely gaze. Drusus was flaunting some very dirty laundry in front of everyone. For now, that of Maroboodus.

368

Drusus placed a hand on my shoulder. 'In his face is a terrible scar; it is the scar he got for trying to fight back. Where is Hraban's honor? Still here.' He tapped my chest. 'He is my prisoner, but a trusted prisoner. His story rings true, for I know Maroboodus.' I was wondering if he would speak of Maroboodus's deals with Rome, but this Drusus did not do. Instead, he shook his head. 'Such a brave boy he was, now a self-made man. Slayer of his foes.' The Vangiones scowled at me, standing at the edges of the meeting, fingering their weapons. 'Lost! Lost! He is a good man; so do not hate him for serving Maroboodus, for the many crimes he had to commit. His weakness was love for his father, and are we not supposed to obey our fathers?' Drusus's voice was dripping with sarcasm, and I knew he was thinking of his own stepfather, but now there were some voices from the Germani side agreeing with him, Adgandestrius one. Others were voicing concerns over Maroboodus and his many ill deeds, especially the Matticati, who had suffered unusually high losses in the war this past year.

'Lord,' I whispered at him, as he was silent for a moment, listening and looking keenly, making plans.

Drusus leaned on me, and whispered. 'They admire you, Hraban, a bit at least, though if they would forgive you for the womanizing and lies, we shall not know. For you are mine. I am sorry for what I have to do now.'

'What—'

'What he did, my friends,' he raised his voice and the men went silent, 'was to obey his father. And his father, a cur if there ever was one walking around on two legs, told him to murder your holy vitka. He told him to murder the völva. He told him to give false oaths. He made Hraban an accomplice to his crimes. And soon, he will do the same to you. He has done worse to Rome, betraying his oaths to our lords.'

Drusus pushed me to stand there before my kin, confirming the terrible crimes I was guilty of, and there was both hate for my father, and disgust for me, in the bearded faces. I stood as tall as I could, and gazed at Armin's face. He gave me a brief smile, for I was close to Drusus now, even if his father was looking away from me spitefully. They were discussing, divided, arguing like children, the loudest and rudest bullies, as they both cursed and praised Maroboodus, and I spied a small smile on the face of Drusus. What Father had accomplished last year with the might of his arms and wisdom of his words, what he had finished this year, final cementation of the Marcomanni, was for naught. Drusus had sown seeds of discontent to the hearts of the tribes. The Marcomanni might not ride with his enemies.

Drusus glanced at me apologetically, and put his hand on my shoulder, flinching as I flinched, feeling betrayed. 'You have a new home now, Hraban. Embrace it, and it will embrace you. I give you my word Rome will not abandon you. And do not hate your woman. She helped you. She wanted a new home for you. She is thinking about your best interests. Keep her close. We shall speak more.'

'She is not my woman,' I told him woodenly, feeling naked and alone as I turned and walked to my seat, my feet dragging. The eyes of the many of the arguing Germani followed me. I felt like a fool and a tool, and I slumped on the seat, pouring myself a goblet of wine.

Fulcher leaned over my shoulder. 'You have to change your name and face, if you wish to live on the other side of the river now. Keep the honor, lord. We know it is there.'

'Shut up,' I told him, and he went away. I felt like I needed another bath. I gazed at Ansbor, who was whispering something with Cassia, leaning over her, and she finally pushed him back. I shook my head and looked ahead sullenly.

Drusus walked to peer at the Germani nobles, who went silent, brooding, agitated and angry, only Armin in control of his emotions. 'I have been preparing for a terrible war, for when have you not tried to steal the wealth from this side of the Rhenus? Sigambri, Tencteri, Bructeri, Marsi; they have all attacked us in the past, as they did last year, as the Sigambri did this past week. Whether in pre-emptive strike or not, I know not, nor do I care. War confuses minds, and who began it? Gods know. Yet, all we want is peace, and it can finally be had when Maroboodus the Warmonger and the Sigambri and their troublemakers, Maelo, Baetrix, and Varnis, are peacefully in their mounds. After that, we shall all prosper. It is

370

war and then peace, should you so desire. The Sigambri do not. They are not here.'

Men were nodding sagely, even some of the more warlike chiefs, and Drusus smiled, for they seemed content with this, not pressing the issue of the Luppia Valley.

Yet, a single man pushed through the Germani nobles.

Armin walked up to Drusus, and everyone looked at him, going silent as he was tall and fierce, his blue eyes burning, and some of them knew he planned to resist Rome. Armin spoke, waving his hand around the seated men. 'Ever it is so that our men make war on each other. It is our way. I see the justification of Rome waging war on Maroboodus. I see your concerns for the Sigambri,' Armin said, and Drusus smiled. They looked like dark and light-skinned brothers. Warriors both, schemers and spear lords. 'Yet to ask for peace from the Cherusci, while you have subdued our northern neighbors, have an alliance with our southern ones, the Chatti, and plan to crush and occupy the Luppia River, our western friends. This is a great thing to ask for. Peace. Ever has it been so that our people talk of peace after the battle. Not before it. How could one speak of peace without a war? None know who is truly stronger. It might be so in Rome that words are weapons, but the Germani think deeds by spear mightier than words. And I say you shall not war on the Sigambri, no matter what you think is right or wrong.' Many men nodded at his words, mainly Marsi and Bructeri and the glowering Inguiomerus, though reluctantly, for he had little love for his nephew. Sigimer looked down, waiting for his son to speak.

Drusus sighed. 'Luppia. Always about Luppia. Why is this river as a dividing line such a great thing for you, my friend? We keep crossing it, but the war will not end until one of us pacifies the other. Sigambri, or us. And they cannot.'

Sigimer got up, stretching. 'I am the war king, the thiuda. My son, my advisor. What he says is this: if you come to take Luppia, if you build your forts and harbors along the Luppia River, if you lay a stone on the ground for your roads, we will rise up and fight. Then you will have a proper war on your hand, young lord. Instead, attack Maroboodus, and forget the Sigambri. Let them be. We will help them live in peace, tell them to stay their war bands. We can, perhaps, suffer the traitors to our north,' he said, with a hostile glance at the Chauci, 'but you are aiming for the heartlands of our kindred, and this is where it should stop. We agree with you that Maroboodus is not a man to trust, but the Sigambri are not your prey to hunt.'

Drusus was glaring at the two men who stood before him, making threats.

Armin shook his head and pointed north. 'It would ease our minds, Lord Drusus, if your legions did not concentrate on Castra Vetera, and you let us speak to Maelo this year. Bring your troops here, drive the Suebi off. But, do not come to Luppia. That is all there is to it.' He stood before the high Roman noble, one of the highest men in the Roman Empire, and spoke with casual strength and straightforwardness that left even Drusus in shadow. Armin's eyes, usually kind, were keen and sharp.

Finally, Drusus spoke. 'This is a harsh choice you offer. Sit and wait, hoping you to keep the wild Sigambri at check? They attacked us again, not a week past—'

'They did not, lord,' Armin said, with a sneer. 'But it would seem convenient, if someone burnt a few houses in the lands of the Ubii to make it seem they are hostile.'

'Are you saying I staged a farce? That I lie?' Drusus asked Armin mutedly.

'Yes,' he told him back, and the men around him whispered at his bravery. 'I do.'

Drusus stood there for a long time, but Armin did not flinch, nor apologize. Drusus had sown seeds of distrust between the Marcomanni and the Cherusci, and now the Roman looked to the Chatti, I noticed, wondering what they thought and nodded carefully. 'Rome shall take on the Sigambri and their allies, for a lasting peace. I will take Maroboodus's head as well, though not this year.'

'You will war with the Sigambri for their fertile lands,' Inguiomerus spat. 'That is the truth.'

'And we will make slaves of even their children. We keep the offer alive, my friends. After the conquest of Luppia is accomplished, we offer peace to all who did not appear on the battlefield. Stay off Luppia, and you shall be friends. Fight, and you shall be visited by the evil boys you passed the day you arrived. For now, our business is concluded. Now, we shall feast and boast, as is your way, and soon, we shall see whose boasts come to pass. Trust me, my lords. My boasts rarely fail to impress in their accuracy. I am honest.'

Wodenspear laughed spitefully. 'A man told me something like this last year when he sold a sick horse to my son. He boasted he would rather die than pay us back. He said the gods had promised him a long life. Now, he is dead by my hand. So, we shall hear your boasts, my lord.'

Drusus shrugged at him. 'I am not selling you a horse, Wodenspear. I need mine for war.' There was a general laugher. Men liked him, even if they distrusted Rome.

Segestes, worried over the escalating situation, got up, not gracefully, and his hands fluttered. 'Perhaps we could exchange hostages? If Rome takes the lands of the Sigambri and leaves them unfortified, and we have some hostages, then perhaps—' Men scoffed at him, and even Drusus shook his head.

He waved his hand lazily. 'I will not do so. A Roman word is better than hostages; few receive it though. You did. War we will have, if you will have it. Germani women will wail in the woods, should you decide wrong.'

Wodenspear grunted. 'You have taken quite a few of our women, Roman. This time, there will be men to welcome you.'

Drusus nodded. 'Some of you will be enemies, others friends, and so the dice is cast. Tonight, we feast, and in the morning, finish the talks with those who love us better than our swords.' The young lord mingled with the Germani fearlessly, and I dare say, few disliked him.

Armin walked to Drusus. They were discussing in quiet, rumbling tones, standing at first, then sitting, like two fighting pit dogs sizing each other up, and it went on for an hour. They were leaning close to each other, like the best of friends gossiping about the harvest or some woman who had broken their hearts. One looked happy, the other unhappy, and then the roles switched as the two spoke. Drusus did not speak with Sigimer, nor Segestes. He avoided Inguiomerus, who hovered nearby, hoping to catch a word, or two, with him. He even avoided the Chatti, nodding at Ebbe and Oldaric briefly, and complimenting Adgandestrius with a short sentence, for the fool blushed. *Like a maiden,* I thought and chuckled.

None came to speak with me; most looked troubled when my eyes met them.

I drank ale and mead, looking at the faces intermingling around the clearing. More food, steaming meats, juicy fruits we had never seen before were served. Wine was offered, and that was a novelty for the Germani, going straight to their heads. Some men got into fights, and the cohorts looked at them uneasily. They had been told to stand ready, but not give the gathered nobles any excuse for bigger trouble. There would be trouble, no doubt, for Wodenspear and the Chatti were discussing and even without my father's men, these nations could brew trouble for Rome. They had many tens of thousands of men, after all.

But, my father was needed to beat Rome. I knew this.

He would know how to fight Roman armies; he would bring the discipline and the strength of arms into any set piece battle.

Unless Armin could do so as well.

I decided that was what Drusus was trying to determine. I snorted. All bastards, the lot. I turned to look for Cassia, but she was not there, and so I drank more. The lictors of Drusus were groaning at the feasting barbarian lords, many getting drunk and teasing the toga-wearing men brusquely, trying to steal their axes and rods. Drusus's eyes twinkled at all his enemies and friends, as he drank and ate with them, and the evening turned into night, when he approached me. I sat up, stood up, feeling dizzy on my feet, for I had drunk much, and I lurched as I took a step. I gazed at his eyes carefully, and he nodded for me to walk with him. He was leaving.

'You countrymen,' he grinned, a bit drunk, 'are a happy sort. I love the Batavi, I do, but I think one day I will love the Cherusci and the Chatti and the lot of them as well.'

'You certainly loved Armin,' I told him suspiciously, slurring a bit.

'Hraban!' yelled a man, and I turned. Drusus stopped uncertainly, about to speak, but I shook my head at him, and faced the man. It was a wide man, his face ruddy and red, with a dark beard plaited in silver, wearing elk leathers and a ring mail, his hand on a two-headed, two-handed axe on his back. 'I say you are a piece of traitorous shit,' he grinned, very drunk. I gazed at the man and deduced he was a Cherusci. I glanced at Armin, who was standing further away, looking at the confrontation, and he shrugged. It was not his doing. Men were turning to look at the drunken warrior, as he made a mocking bow to me. 'A traitor and a liar. A piss-soaked pup.'

'Who are you?' I asked him with spite.

'Ragwald. That's who! A champion of Segestes. And I dislike your face,' he smiled. I ignored Drusus who tried to grab me and walked for the drunken man, carrying my helmet. Ragwald grinned as he walked forward, a man larger than I was. 'Do you have something to tell a man who is a champion of a hundred fights? A bark? A whimper? Come, show your measure! Sandal-smelling rodent, you.' He grabbed me by my armor. 'I say—'

But, he did not, for I smashed his face with the helmet so hard he flew around and onto his belly. Segestes got up ponderously. 'Step back, son,' he told me sternly.

'Drown in your lard,' I told him thickly, and kicked Ragwald so hard he yelped. I was angry and disappointed, and decided to humiliate the bastard. I untied my pants and took a long, clear piss on Ragwald's neck. He tried to get up, but I stomped on his right hand, something cracked, and his eyes showed whites as he passed out in agony. 'So you all can see my measure,' I growled at them, finishing my relief, and Ebbe laughed raucously and many joined him. I was done eventually, feeling much relieved, and left Ragwald unconscious, Segestes cursing me softly, and walked to Drusus. 'Shall we go?'

He looked troubled and nodded. As we walked off to the dark, he shook his head. 'I wish I could do that to some men I know in Rome. It would be a shock, it would. They would smell of perfumes, strut around like peacocks, speaking like they were gods. Then I would smash them in their faces and piss on their mouths. Ah! Wonderful. Perhaps I shall hire some Germani to do it for me. Never ceases to impress how you people can piss when everyone is looking. I would likely stand there with a limp dick, trying to get even a drop out, until forced to give up in shame.' I giggled like a girl with him, and the lictors and the grinning Batavi followed us, their hulking, armored bodies taking the sides, as we walked for the gates in the darkness. 'Armin. I like him. I think he might be a dangerous man. If he survives the war. But, I don't think he is a good general. He is too young. He had no training.'

'Only training in lies,' I slurred, and Drusus laughed, as he took a wrong step on horse dung, nearly falling over and grasping my shoulder in his distress. He waved the lictors off, and kept on walking.

'One has to learn how to lie, if one is to rule. As for the keen art of strategy and war? Lies are essential in these as well, but he lacks the deeper skills in management of war, I think. He is not ready. Not yet. He has a lot to learn. But, he certainly is different from the other young men in your tribes. He would learn new ways quickly. Like your father did. Like you will,' he told me, and then I saw movement in the dark, men raising their heads not too far off, training bows, and so I did what Armin wished for, and tried to save Drusus.

I jumped in front of him, for gods' sakes.

Arrows flew around us. There were many, and one Batavi bellowed in pain and anger as he was hit. An arrow struck the wall near us, and guards shrieked warnings up on the battlements. The lictors jumped forward as one man, but two arrows flicked through them, and one hit me on the belly, as I covered Drusus who fell on his rear, astonishment clear on his face. I fell over him, looking at the shaft in horror, felt blood trickling under my tunic to my pants, and I ripped at the shaft, as the lictors pushed us to the ditch surrounding the fort, a long drop as we tumbled down. There were screams of warning in the dark, as men rushed to find the attackers, but they were gone.

Drusus was over me, muddied and sodden, his finger grasping the arrow. He was grunting, and then slapped my hands so he could work in peace, and failing that, he slapped my face to calm me, and I did as he lifted the mail. His face lit up in a happy grin. 'Flesh wound, Hraban, just that. Your mail stopped it.'

I groaned and lay back, only to land on watery mud. I was not drunk anymore, not in the least bit, and I let the chuckling general pull at the arrow and then snap it, and he slapped his hand on my chest and pulled me up. He gazed in my eyes. 'Thank you, Hraban.'

'I ... ' I began, but only nodded instead. Woden's breath, but Armin had shot arrows at us. Had he succeeded in killing Drusus like this, would it have served him well? Had he not asked me to kill Drusus, just before the campaign? Perhaps he had meant to kill me, then. Or both. Armin played many games; I knew this already from his schemes earlier against Father. Had it been Catualda out there, actually hoping to slay me?

I grabbed the arrow. The point was blunt, not sharp at all. Deadly still, but not against the armor of Drusus, for he was bound to wear it under the toga. I got up, hating the dangerous game. The grateful lictors dropped to the ditch and clapped my muddy back, without any heed to their voluminous garments getting dirty, and cheered me as a hero. Eventually, I was shown to my barracks, where my friends were already asleep. I sat down on the bed, thinking about Lif and begging Woden for luck, for it would be needed. How in Hel's name could I slay the man?

For Lif, I reminded myself, and liberated a jug of wine from the guards and renewed my stupor.

In the morning, I woke up soiled in piss, and could never be sure if it was Ansbor's, or mine.

Fulcher sat next to me, as he avoided sitting too near, and explained why it was possible it was Ansbor's. 'Ansbor confronted her last night.'

'Ah, that is why they were gone,' I told him, sniffling at my clothing. 'I suppose I should he happy it is not my blood.'

'She told him something he did not wish to share with me,' Fulcher told me darkly. 'But, you likely know what this was. It would have been better, Hraban, had you done this months ago.'

'Gods help me,' I said, miserable. I changed my clothes, feeling ill, for the moons were not favorable, and I felt a change was coming.

CHAPTER XXV

That morning, we stood in Chariovalda's tent.
'So, what am I to do with you?' Chariovalda said, as he stalked around the tent, holding my grandfather's sword, the Head Taker glinting in the dim light.

I said nothing.

'It's a nice sword; perhaps I shall give it to my cousin,' he mused. He slumped down on a wooden bench.

'I am to serve Drusus?' I asked him. 'He seems to have plans for us.'

'Plans for us,' he simpered at me, rubbing his lobes. 'You are a worm, Hraban. Men, such as he, have plans indeed, but you think he is wondering about you, day and night, wishing you good night and morning in his prayers, and likely you are waiting for him to serve you sweetened porridge for breakfast. He is preparing for war, not babysitting you, singing your praises in his dreams. No, you have your part to play, but you shall have to learn things first.'

'What things? We are proficient ... ' Ansbor said with a wince, his head splitting with pain.

'You are to learn to fight like the Romans first,' the Batavi snarled, and Fulcher and Ansbor shuffled their feet in protest. Cassia just grinned at him, and he looked away from us, and struggled with a budding smile. He liked women overmuch, the dog. He took a deep breath, and poked me with the sword, again properly stern. 'You can swing a sword, but your boys cannot. But, you know nothing, nothing. You are not fit to fight for the Batavi. You know nothing of discipline, nor the way Romans wage

379

war! You likely could not march fully packed and geared, but would fall in a ditch and die of exhaustion!' he spat, and took a swig of wine.

'I was trained by a man such as you for weeks,' I told him morosely. 'He made me run like a dog, swim—'

'In full gear?' he asked skeptically, and I shut up. 'Indeed.'

'Why march when you can ride?' asked Ansbor glumly, glaring at Cassia resentfully.

'There, there! That is exactly what I mean! Arrogance! Every one of my men knows how to swim like a salmon, and can do what those steel-clad Romans can do twice over. They can fight a pitched battle, then march twenty miles in cold mud, pitch a fully guarded camp, and do it again the next day after burying the men who died of the wounds during the few hours of sleep they got. You, and yours, cannot!' he mocked us with a woman-like saunter, making Cassia scowl, and then laughed like a bastard.

I shrugged at him tiredly. 'Well, it seems the war is coming. I am sure we will learn.'

'Prisoner, you do not make plans for yourself. I make them for you. I am the master of Hraban, the Oath Breaker!' he moaned. 'Because Drusus told me to give you training and position, I am stuck with you. I hear you saved his life yesterday? A man of mine was hurt there, so I know, but he has kept it a secret from the others.'

'I am not sure if he was in any real danger; he was armored under the toga, no?' I told him, as my friends gawked at me. It was news to them as well.

'You lot keep your mouth shut about it!' Chariovalda said threateningly. 'Yes, he was, but it is always possible to catch it hot when you are at the wrong end of an arrow. They could have been poisoned, no?' he said maliciously, and lifted my tunic hem with the sword. 'Apparently, they were not.'

I slapped my former sword away. 'Apparently not.'

'You were hit?' Cassia said in alarm, as she rushed forward.

'He is fine like a virgin apple, untouched, nearly so,' Chariovalda said. 'So, the war will start, and you will learn new tricks.'

'But, will I serve Drusus, or you?' I asked, nervous they would post me far from the man I was supposed to slay, even if the thought seemed distant and impossible. I cursed Armin softly, and Chariovalda stared at me peculiarly for a while. I danced away from Cassia, who cursed as well, still hanging on to my chain mail.

'You are a strange one, my boy, always mumbling. Try not to do anything foolish,' he said sternly. 'I know not what, and whom, you will serve. Perhaps me, one day, and I serve him, so you serve both. '

'What happens next?' Fulcher asked him. 'With the tribes, and the war?'

He mused, and shook his head. 'They know a fight is coming. The most important thing was to discredit Maroboodus, and Hraban, the hapless bastard here, helped. And Cassia.'

She blushed. 'He said he wanted to help Hraban. He did, and I think we have a home here.'

'You have a home already,' Ansbor began sullenly. 'You have estates and fine lands, and the lord is sure to help you get back anything you have been cheated out of. You are charming enough for that.'

Cassia spun on him, but Chariovalda struck the wall so hard a guard vaulted in, but went out as he noticed the mood was not welcoming and there was no danger. Chariovalda continued, 'I see you have issues gods themselves would fear mingling in. My advice for you, Ansbor, is to respect her as a friend and find yourself a woman. More than anything, Drusus wishes for the Chatti to stay out of the war. Cherusci, we can handle, and I think Drusus wishes to humble them in any case, but the Chatti have to remain calm. And so they shall.'

'How do you know this?' I asked, stupefied.

'Oh, he has taken Ebbe as a hostage.'

'What?' I asked, now shocked.

'A guest? Whichever you prefer. The old warrior is here until the war is over,' Chariovalda said, uncomfortably. 'He wishes the Chatti to remain peaceful, after all.'

'You think this is the way to prove friendship?' Cassia asked, incredulous.

'It is necessary,' Chariovalda said doubtfully. 'They spoke the words of Maroboodus yesterday, and Rome does intend to build fat forts in Luppia, collect taxes and slaves, and settle in. It cannot be changed. It is ordered by Rome, and Drusus has no saying in it. But, I admit, it is a total, and utter, mess. The opposition will be mottled. The Bructeri will fight like maniacs, the Marsi as well. We will see if the Cherusci will stay out of it. They are fools, if they do! That Segestes is such a fool, but the others are not. They have wars with the Suebi in the east, but may have a sizable army available for this war. Mayhap not. We can keep them busy elsewhere, I think. The Chauci might have their tails up for the insults yesterday.'

'And you think Oldaric and Adgandestrius, and the hundreds of honorable Chatti warlords will sit still like children while their honor is broken so?' Fulcher noted with a sneer.

'Ebbe is ill,' Chariovalda said slyly. 'He is ill, and has to rest, before going home. That is all the Chatti need to know.'

'They are no fools,' I snarled. 'They will let Ebbe hang, and make songs about him, while they march to gain vengeance.'

'Well, we will see,' Chariovalda said. 'But, it will be decided soon. They should be glad it is not Stone Jaws here.'

'Stone Jaws?' Fulcher asked curiously.

'Tiberius, brother of Drusus. Or Augustus? Yes. Augustus would have killed the lot, all the trusty fools who travelled here, and so would Tiberius, but Drusus and that Saturninus, the legate you have become briefly acquainted with, would never do so. No, Drusus needs these men for the future,' Chariovalda sighed, and got up. 'As you know, Hraban, he might wage a different kind of war soon, at some point. He believes you about your father, yet he only has your word, but he is wary of his family. No, he needs men to respect him after the war is done with and won, and he will need the Germani to serve him. He needs allies and willing friends from the surviving enemies. Gods! Why explain this to you backwoods numbskulls? Just nod.'

We did.

'Now, go and speak with Drusus, Hraban. The day he agrees you are Roman, is the day I will return the sword and the spear to you. I'll keep them for now, for I do not entirely trust you,' he told me, and I bowed to him, liking the man. We filed out and followed a Batavi, and I had to slap Cassia's probing fingers, as she tried to put her hands under my tunic to feel the wound.

'Scratch!' I told her scathingly. 'Just that.'

'I am sorry I told him of your life, but I could not say no. He is very persuasive,' she told me unhappily.

'I wish I had his skills of persuasion,' I told her, as I glanced at Ansbor, who refused to look at me. 'He thinks you and I—'

'I told him yesterday,' she said heavily, giving up on trying to check the wound, 'that I am not meant for him. That I would be a friend, and even then, he would have to be happier, for all we have shared since you returned are bitter, unhappy words.'

'I'll try to speak with him,' I told her worryingly. 'Again.'

'It will do no good. I told him I am taken.'

I gazed at her. 'Taken?'

'My heart is taken, has been for a year,' she whispered, and I knew what she meant, unable to deny it as she gazed at me. I nodded. She peered up at me from under her beautiful eyebrows. 'So, will you stay with Rome then? Drusus can help you with many things, and after the war is over—'

'It will never be over, Cassia,' I told her seriously, as I stared at Ansbor. His eyes had a vacant, hurt look, and he did not smile nor frown as he held my eyes. I shook my head and walked on, enjoying the sunlight and occasional blast of reviving wind, and tried to find ways out of the dilemma. Ansbor. He was my friend. Gods help me.

We found Drusus in a simple tunic, his hair disheveled as he was guiding his horse in skillful circles over a grassy field. I walked forward and my friends waited, and Drusus waved at me happily, enjoying the moment of solitude. The horse was lathered, spirited as a young fox, and I was happy to watch him ride. Could I slay him?

For Lif, yes.

Saturninus walked over, and watched the lord with me. He was gray of face, having worked all night. He shrugged as Drusus made the horse vault a small trunk, half rotten, the horse huffing as it came down. The legate was not looking at me, but handed me a carving on wood. I gazed at the letters, and then spoke. 'It says, "Inimica." An enemy.'

'Yes,' he told me dryly. 'The Cherusci left this night, during the celebrations. The Chatti left this morning. Not sure who left this in the Thing. But, they are gone.'

'Minus the poor, ill Ebbe,' I sneered as I handed him the wooden message.

'Yes, he is still here,' Saturninus said dryly. 'Thank you for keeping our man safe. Suffice it to say, he is not safe. Not from yours, not from ours. He does not have enough proof on who is conspiring against him. He knows, of course, but cannot prove it. And if he did? He would face war in any case, no matter the evidence of treason. He needs more fame, more allies, more tribes to commit for peace. For alliance. For now, he goes to war, and hopes to conquer, for he needs the fame should he tackle … higher targets.'

'He is a dangerous man,' I told him. 'Ruthless, like my father. But, I like him better.'

'Better than you like Armin?' he inquired sweetly.

'I do not like Armin,' I blurted, and realized it was true. No matter if he could remake me into a Germani, I distrusted him. 'What do you know of Maroboodus and his son in Rome?'

He thought for a while, and then spoke. 'Drusus will tell you. I do not know more than rumors. As for you, I know from Chariovalda you are contemplating on leaving us as soon as you can. Perhaps to join Sigimer and the enemies of Rome. Can they help you with your vengeance and your lost family? They might. I know not.' He clapped me in the back. 'But, Drusus has honor as well as ruthlessness. I love him. He is younger than I am, and I love him like a son. Trust him.'

'I will serve him,' I told him hollowly. 'Even if I have to train like a dolt.'

'You did not just call the legionnaires dolts?' he breathed. 'No, that is impossible.'

'Dolts and lazy mules,' I growled. 'I could outmarch them two times over.'

'What?' he asked, mortified as Drusus rode over and vaulted from his horse with a laugh. He spied Saturninus ashen, shocked face, and cocked his head at the legate. The man twitched as he whispered at length to Drusus, who just laughed hugely and guided me away, keeping his hand on my shoulder.

He spoke to me merrily. 'I will ask you to join my army.'

'Yes, lord,' I said softly.

'Drusus. Friend,' he reprimanded me.

'I am but a boy from backwoods of Germania, Drusus. Why do I call you a friend?' I asked him bluntly.

He chuckled. 'I need you. I like you. And we have things in common, no matter if you have hay between your toes.'

'Lord?'

'Friend or Drusus, can you not remember?' He blushed, and hung his head. 'I am a leader of hard men, Roman, first and foremost. But, my friendship to you is no lie. The day you bowed to my idiot slave, and mocked our gods as liars, I liked you. Your story is not unlike ours, mine and my brother's.'

'Really?' I asked. 'Your mother and grandfather were killed by your father, too?'

He shook his head. 'No, but it is rumored Augustus killed my father, and he certainly ruined him. I was still a baby in my mother's womb when Augustus married her. My father had to attend the marriage. Imagine that!'

'Really?'

He nodded. 'It is true. We have both been misused, hurt, and thrust into a vortex of betrayals and pain. Yet, I have a goal. It is to serve Rome. The real Rome. My Rome, for which my father gave his life for.' He looked troubled, and waved us on. He looked grave as he walked. 'I seem like a brutal, grand lord to you, and indeed I am. But, I am not immune to betrayal. Observe what happened to my brother. When Agrippa died, and Augustus's daughter Julia was widowed, he had to divorce the only woman he could ever love, and marry the flippant Julia. He, Augustus, wishes to cover all his bases. What is in store for me?'

I nodded. 'Your brother—'

'Stone Jaws. Tiberius,' he smiled. 'Call him either.'

'Is unhappy?' I asked carefully

He nodded. 'He is indeed. I would be, too. He marries a whore, and sees the woman he loves soon married to another, a man who sits in the senate and meets him nearly daily, arrogant in his ways!'

'I would kill the man,' I said, truthfully.

He laughed. 'I serve Augustus; we loved each other in some ways. He taught me to be a man who keeps his words, he often played with us when we grew up, gave us a life like most could only dream of, education, position, and wealth to make kings weep with envy. But, the price? Imagine if he told me to divorce Antonia! We have two children, more to come, as soon as it is possible,' he smiled at me, and I smiled back. 'But, imagine, if Tiberius was to die, who would Julia be forced on next? Would I lose my wife?'

'I doubt you would allow that, lord,' I told him, but he shrugged.

'A lord now, tomorrow but a puppet. In Lugdunum, where I govern the Tres Galliae, my wife sits, trusting me. I hope I am worth that trust. I have the new Urban Cohort there to guard the mint and her, but Gaul is a festering cesspit of discontent. If that was to explode, and I lost it?' He laughed. 'Augustus would enjoy seeing me humbled, somewhere in the back of his mind.'

'Surely, the Gauls see the war in Germania as a good thing? Rome fighting the bothersome Germani will unify them under you, certainly?' I asked.

'Gauls hate both the Germani and Rome, Hraban. I am facing a festering rebellion, war with your people, war with the Roman traitors. I can fall easily enough, should Augustus become overly suspicious of me. Then Antonia would be used to marry someone he needs. I tread carefully, Hraban. So I cannot blame him, or anyone, for their plots to kill or discredit me, not on your words alone. I will grow strong here in the north, Hraban, and when the time is right? I will, perhaps, make the Republic shiny and bright again. But, it will be hard and bloody.'

'And you need men like me for this?'

He placed a hand on my shoulder, making his lictors jump. 'I have status, wealth, and an army, Hraban, but my family is truly my treasure. Livilla, my beautiful girl, our little imp, how she loves to hug me, and to play with my fingers. In addition, my boy,' he said, with tears in his eyes, 'also Nero Claudius Drusus, he is a clever one, planning war already. We will have more.' He pulled me with him. 'Antonia, my wife. Never was there a woman so virtuous, so much unlike her father, Marc Anthony. She is the virtue itself, and likely the one common thing Augustus and I love. However, she is more; she has my heart. For them, Hraban, I will never cease fighting. I understand your choices.' We walked in silence for a minute. 'I held a census in Gaul. I know how much money we can have from there, perhaps I should use it to create a new Rome, and there is the mint in Lugdunum,' he mused and smiled, looking back at his lictors. 'Do not speak freely in front of them. I know some spy for my stepfather,' he nodded towards the men, looking at us pointedly. 'But, I will need men like you for the future. Many men like you.'

'Would the legions follow you?' I asked him dubiously.

'Perhaps, if I give them victory. They would after this war, and the loot I will give them,' he said scornfully. 'One earns such devotion. Besides, many have served with me, or Tiberius, in the past.'

'Indeed, few seem to dislike you, Drusus,' I told him, and he clapped my back.

'So, I ask you. Stay with us, and I will reward you,' he said, and glanced at me. 'I will give you power, and help you with your daughter.'

'Because you like me, or because I am useful?' I asked boldly.

He put his forehead on mine, his eyes burning. 'Because I like you, but also because you will be useful in the wars of the north. Because you are Maroboodus's son, and because Armin wants you. I spoke with him last night, and his eyes lingered on you so many times. He has plans, and I will be careful. And because I will need a friend and a skillful man when I go home.'

'What am I to do for you? Be another soldier?' I asked.

'Soldier for now. You will sign papers, Hraban. They are just papers. They tell me nothing. One day soon, I will want you to come and tell me where and whom you will serve. I will have work for you, for I sense I could trust you, if you finally made up your mind.'

'You do not trust me now, Drusus?'

'No, Hraban,' he said. 'It is not Chariovalda who whispers evil little thoughts in my ear. I do not trust you as long as your daughter is missing. When that terrible situation is cleared, for good or for bad, I will trust you with my life.'

'If you do not trust me, how can I serve you?' I asked sullenly.

'You will serve Chariovalda for the time being. I will keep you from this war. I will face an enemy out there, and I do not know yet who. I cannot think about blades behind my back.'

'I am sorry you do not think more highly of me,' I told him miserably, hating the whole situation.

'I think you are like me, I told you. You love your family most of all. And your Lif is lost. Out there. When you have decided, Hraban, you will be my sword.'

'What does a sword do?'

'Slays my enemies. The ones who play dirty games in the shadows. I need a man who goes to those shadows with a sword, and comes back to me, still my friend.'

'You need a liar, and a murderer,' I told him sullenly.

'Yes, but one who is on my side.'

I nodded, blushed. He asked what my father had asked, yet for some reason, I trusted he would not throw me into the abyss. I nodded at him. 'I will sign papers. Then, gods willing, one day soon, I will tell you these words you wish to hear. When Lif is safe.'

'Good. For now, sign up with the army, and do your best. We will try to find your daughter after the war. For now, I am sorry, I have to be the lord who fears everything. And so there will be swords on you, and also on the woman who loves you. Whom you love, for I know you love her, Hraban. I do. This Cassia.'

I did not move, for there were tears in his eyes. 'Swords,' I said with a soft warning in my voice.

He nodded. 'You will be treated as a Roman soldier, Hraban, but until the war is over, you will stay where you are safe. She will be in danger until I trust you. One day, we will let our children play together, and I hope you will forgive me.'

He would hold Cassia a prisoner.

I shuddered in indecision, but calmed myself and bowed to him. 'I accept this, Lord Drusus. And let us be friends, even if you have swords on the woman I ... love.' For he was right in that.

'You will be Roman,' he said, relieved, and walked me off to Saturninus. 'And my friend.' Saturninus took off his military helmet as Drusus spoke with him and Chariovalda rode up, summoned as well. The legate did not address me but Chariovalda. 'Very well. You have a day to leave with the boy. Take him, train him, and keep him alive, in Xanten, at Castra Vetera. Hold him for me. He is a valuable Germani, and perhaps soon one of us.'

'We do not,' Ansbor growled, 'need training from the Romans. We are warriors, not parade soldiers.'

Saturninus heard him and scoffed. 'Oh, are you now? It matters not, son, what you think about Roman army and your imaginary feats and playful deeds. You had better be careful, even on our side. The kingless Vangiones hate you already, Matticati do not trust you, and the Ubii wants nothing to do with you. But, war is coming, and you might have fewer enemies soon!' Saturninus left, laughing like a demented jackdaw, as he put his helmet on his head and rode off. Chariovalda took me back to the fort.

I turned to him. 'So, Drusus loves his brother a great deal.'

He nodded. 'A great deal. They have gone through a lot together.'

'He speaks of remaking Rome.' Chariovalda put a hand on my shoulder, squeezing it, and shook his head.

389

'He will make you an important man, Hraban. He knows you are a sort of a boy to get things done. Keep alive, and his friend. And I am sorry for Cassia. Do not think those swords are dull, or in any way not real,' he told me sadly. 'I will keep men watching you, as well.'

Lif.

Armin had Lif. Not one word they spoke mattered, as long as Armin held Lif. I would find a way. At Xanten. At Castra Vetera. Drusus promised me wonderful things, fine friendship, happy life, wealth, and position. But, he did not have Lif. And so, he would fall. But, Cassia would suffer.

PART V: THE GATHERING STORM

'I am Hraban! Son of Maroboodus! The Oath Breaker! The Bone Breaker.
Come, and be corpses, curs!'
Hraban to the Usipetes survivors

CHAPTER XXVI

It was late in Maius when we reached Xanten. We had ridden down the banks of the unusually turbulent Rhenus River, with hundreds of mounted, heavily armored Batavi and the lighter cavalry of the Ubii, and the latter parted ways with us to go summon more men to Xanten from their various villages. We passed Castra Ubiorium, the city the former Germani tribe had chosen as their own after they escaped out lands. It had been a tribe that had been starving due to the Chatti and Cherusci, hunted by the Sigambri. XIX and XVII Legions were marching before us for Castra Vetera, having left the fort of Moganticum with some tall auxilia from the Alps, along with a regular cohort, or two, from the Roman army.

The summer was scalding hot. We drank warm water and soured ale from gourds. Flies were a constant nuisance, and men cursed the trip that seemed to drag its feet. It was not that far on the horses, along the Roman roads in the making, but we spent a week on it due to heavy army traffic and orders Chariovalda had to deliver to various commanders in small forts and watch towers along the way. On the way, I noticed many discreet men guarding us, keeping an eye on Cassia especially, blades casually on their sides, others holding well-used bows and javelins. Fulcher had noted them as well, and raised his eyebrows at me, and I faced away. I prayed Woden to give me a way out of the predicament, and then begged Mercury, the Roman god of thievery, for the same, should he listen.

It seemed hopeless.

The riverbanks were quiet on both sides of the river, save for sweet birdsong, and we entered the part of Rhenus with steep, rock-strewn sides. The river was flowing resolutely through these rocky formations, a fantastic sight of calm pools and rushing torrents combined. Noble hawks and eagles soared far above, and many Romans thought it a good omen. On the other side of the river, the lands of embattled Sigambri spread out, smoke rising from the settlements, and I imagined them getting ready for war. With them were Tudrus and the Quadi exiles. It looked no different from any other land, wooded and fertile, but this land would turn heads around the world very soon.

Finally, we arrived at Castra Vetera, the fort guarding the way to the Luppia River. Roman shipping was busy, as it rowed up and down the river, but ominously, the Luppia itself seemed devoid of boats. Great hanging trees covered the banks where dark water flowed to Rhenus from the east, the deadly yet beautiful access to the heart of the Sigambri, Bructeri, Marsi, and the poor Usipetes and Tencteri, forever stuck on the banks of Rhenus. Luppia reached a long hundred Roman miles inside the most warlike frontier lands of Germania, and there, Drusus was mobilizing his army, an army that was to change things forever in the land.

The fort itself was an ugly, stone, and wood-entrenched thing of high, brooding towers and busy gates on a fat, low hill, and muddy huts of the locals were hunched on the sides of the stone-laden military roads. Castra Vetera was a fort for two legions, Legion V Alaudae, the ones who had lost the eagle to the Sigambri years past, the shame forever theirs. The other one was the XVIII Legion.

The Batavi calmly headed for the gates, and Cassia and I rode up after them, following Fulcher and Ansbor. A fresh wind was billowing on the hillside, gently ruffling the cloaks of the Batavi, giving relief to the oppressive heat, and we enjoyed it, as we navigated past some cohorts.

'It is the wind of the north, Hraban, from the sea,' Chariovalda told me, as he rode with us.

'We are from Gothonia, my family, and so there is something familiar about it,' I told him, and indeed it was so, for our family, the first of the men, Woden's own blood were spawned in the northern sea shore, on the rocky sands of Gothonia's many islands. The wind had a strangely effect on me, a light tug on my soul that made me smile briefly. I had never seen the ocean, but its smell was there in the wind, vaguely titillating. I felt a strange yearning.

Chariovalda smiled happily. He had been suffering on the tedious journey, his horse letting gas mercilessly to the amusement of the Batavi. 'Will get him some proper barley,' he told us sheepishly as the beast farted loudly again, to all our discomfort. He stroked the horse's neck. 'Bastard's been fed moldy hay. In two weeks, Drusus will arrive here. And we go to war.' I grunted and stroked my horse. I said nothing, staring at the castrum and enjoyed the momentary caress of the cool air. 'Only two weeks, Hraban, then things will surely look up. If you behave,' he continued. 'And you will enjoy this muddy place, I am sure. Oh, you will. In the meantime, we have business elsewhere. Behave while we are away.'

I looked at the Castrum, and the tuba called out unsteadily, the camp waking up.

'Are we to stay here?' I asked him unhappily as men rode around us.

He nodded. 'I hope you care enough for the girl, and don't do anything utterly stupid. And yes, despite the love we all have for her, she will die, should you do so. But, it will be quick, if it comes to it. That much I can promise.' I held his eye, not giving away the turmoil inside of me and nodded. He nodded back. 'And yes, you will stay here. Come.'

We rode to the gates, and a nervous tessarius of the XVIII Legion met us there, asking for a password while looking at the mass of XIX Legion marching past, dust-covered and parched. Chariovalda took out a scroll and handed it to him imperiously, and the tessarius took it and ran inside. We stood there for half an hour, until after the morning inspection in the castrum was over, and the legionnaires were sent to their various duties. Then, a string of young legionnaires marched out with an optio, fully packed with thick spears, cumbersome shields in leather covers, carrying a long pole, a furca with fat pots, sturdy dolobara, their personal gear, a leather rolled-up sack and two pila one longer, the other shorter. They had full gear, not exactly uniform, as some wore bronze helmets; some made of steel or iron, and their tunics were of the same color only by a stretch of a wild imagination.

Ansbor and Fulcher smirked at them, and pointed at how some of them were already limping, their caligae substandard. An optio sauntered after them, barking high-pitched orders. He was a tough man with darkened skin, knotted arms, and a well-used stick, followed by an arrogant centurion, whose squat build looked nearly comic, until you looked at his pig-like brutal eyes, which burned with a promise of Hel's fires.

'Manlius, stop the men, have them stand there,' the centurion said, as he swaggered to a stop.

Chariovalda leaned on me. 'Just remember, Hraban, that despite the next two weeks, one day, you will be a high, respected man. I do not know how much you have suffered and crawled in shit previously, but, in Rome, the high have crawled as well, often. A man must learn to serve, before he commands.'

'What?' I asked, as the centurion pointed at a brutally sunny spot of parched grass where the miserable recruits went to stand like hapless mules. Then he spat, and greeted Chariovalda with his vine stick.

'These are the bags of vomit?' he asked, his jaws chomping like he was about to chew through a helmet. 'The girl cannot join them.' He frowned at Cassia, who was about to argue.

I turned in my saddle to gaze at Chariovalda. 'I thought you were to train us?'

Chariovalda smiled and ignored me. 'Yes, the lice-ridden louts here are your boys. And Cassia will stay with me for the time being.' Cassia was a prisoner, for now. The Batavi straightened in his saddle. 'Boys, you are to remain here, and train a bit, like the Romans do. Manlius there, the optio, and do not mistake him for a legionnaire, will make sure you do well. Sabinus, the centurion there, will make sure it is painful. We will go home to fetch fresh men, change clothes, make love to our wives, and we will be back! Have fun, for you will make love to pain and her sister, humiliation.'

'I wish to stay with Hraban,' Cassia hissed at him, but he shook his head.

'Do not worry, Cassia. They will be fine, but I'm not sure we will be. You will cook for us! Follow my men,' Chariovalda laughed with a warning look at me.

I shrugged helplessly at Cassia. She was fuming as she turned her horse to follow the first of the Batavi, her eyes lingering on mine, while Chariovalda lingered on for a bit. The men who had been guarding her rode after them, and I felt helpless rage, but there was nothing I could do.

'Dismount. You will not need your weapons. You will train, Roman style. With their weapons,' Chariovalda said, and we did as he told. Reluctantly, I handed him Nightbright. He took it, and the horses. 'And the armor as well. All of you.' We basically stripped down to our tunics and caligae, and they took our gear. 'Regards from legate Saturninus, who was a bit miffed about your comments over the quality of the Roman armies!' the bastard Batavi remarked, and Sabinus's eye twitched at that, and he looked like he was ready to pummel someone, or rather, us. Ansbor went gray in the his face.

The Batavi rode out and left us there with Sabinus and Manlius. One young Batavi, the last man, stopped with a grin on his face, and threw a sack of coins to us. 'You will need to buy your gear! Enjoy!'

Then, they were gone.

The optio took the recruits away, marching briskly towards the north and hilly grounds, where he would grind them to weeping sacks of meat, but the centurion, his eyes glinting evilly, pointed his vine stick towards a hamlet near the castrum.

He started the training immediately.

'Now, lads, usually the master-of-arms is the one to arm peasants like you, but since you are not legionnaires, we will buy this gear from the market in the town. Same gear, likely stolen from the fort by these merchant bastards, no? But, I don't care, and neither will you. Now, march and sing!' he told us, gruffly.

'We don't know your songs,' I told him gruffly.

'Cannot sing? At least you can grunt some Latin. You filthy man-whores, I'll make you sing with my cane. Mouths open! Croak!' he barked, but we stayed mulishly quiet. 'Fine, sing after me, my lovelies!' And so he sang, with a deep bass voice that reverberated and grated on our frazzled nerves. 'For a loss of one man, we cut thousand, thousand, thousand heads... ' he hollered.

As we marched, he ordered us to repeat the words, and I did, managing Latin fairly well, but Ansbor and Fulcher sounded like imbecilic lambs, and men we passed howled with mirth. He struck our calves, stopped us all the time, showing how to start with the right foot, end with the left, and our protests were answered by the accursed cane. He called us turds, ass sores, cow humpers, girly boys, and other such things, and finally, Ansbor had enough of his antics and turned on him, his fists balled and teeth gritted, as he was trying to grab the vine stick. The squat centurion promptly punched him in the face, and kicked him with his hobnailed caligae while singing a bawdy song about a whore and a senator. He kicked Ansbor a few more times, and I shook my head at Fulcher with a warning.

The centurion pulled Ansbor up by his lice-ridden tunic. 'You ass, a big fat Germani ass, I kick a thousand, thousand, thousand times, like that, and that, and end it with a smack!' He cracked his vine stick on Fulcher's head as he was trying to stop him, despite my warnings. Fulcher fell back, holding his bleeding nose. 'You are now in a legion. The legion! I care not if you are just pretending, but if Saturninus asks us to train you, and show you how proper soldiers train, I will humor the good legate!' he said, as he kicked Fulcher in his turn. I was grinning at my unhappy comrades, for it was a rare case I stood by to see them bleed, and not the other way around. The centurion was scowling at them. 'No, why would a lord so high bother with scum like you? Seems like a terrible waste of my precious hours, but I am a generous man, and so it shall be. Show the assholes how the Roman Army trains, he asked. And so you, Hraban, *will* learn.' He kicked Ansbor.

'I am Hraban!' I said indignantly, and then froze, for clearly the centurion had made a mistake, and he was not a man to leave mistakes stand.

'I am sorry. I thought you were the fat one. Here.' And the stick started to dance on my back, as I struggled not to defend myself, knowing it would only make things more difficult. When he was done, he pulled a new stick out of the back of his belt, a pristine one still in one piece, unlike the one discarded in dust, and kicked us into a bleeding, bruised line. 'So. Singing and marching. Let us go, you pig-faced charlatans!' We reached the market with a semblance of marching steps, singing raucously, and the sight must have been hilarious, since everyone we came across were left with a happy grin. The giggling women in the market, the squabbling merchants, and the customers all stopped what they were doing, and made a rude joke, or two, at our expense.

'Give it to them, Sabinus!' yelled a merchant, with huge red moustaches, an ex-legionnaire who straightened up as he realized we were coming to see him.

'I will. Happily. I have a toothache, and I need to whip something anyway. Here, outfit these into semi-proper gear. Here is the payment.' He stripped the pouch from Fulcher and threw it to him.

'Can I keep the rest?' he asked hopefully, weighing the pouch.

'No, you cannot,' I said in passable Latin, and he was taken back.

'A barbarian speaking civil. How interesting. How about I keep it all and help you to the best gear, not the crap I usually pass to newcomers who have lost their gear?' the merchant suggested slyly.

'If you leave us coins for mead, we are happy,' I told him unhappily, for I had no idea how much it would cost, since Chariovalda was no longer there to provide us with our meals and fine drinks.

The centurion stared at me in shock. 'No, you give the rest to me! They cannot seriously think I will let them drink while in training! Give them the shit,' laughed Sabinus, and so we were outfitted with very substandard gear.

We squabbled a lot, fought over the fringes of the caligae, for we were to abandon the fine footwear we had bought. We argued about the quality of the shields, some of which had seen battle. We fought over the badly cast tips of a pilum, the age of a sword blade, and of the length of the cingulum belt's straps. The merchant looked as haggard as we did after the ordeal, but we stepped out of the shop looking fairly identical to the soldiers we had seen marching that morning, complete with entrenchment tools, cups, and bedrolls hanging from a furca. We were armored, looking like soldiers, save for our long hair that streamed out under the helmets, but our self-esteem puffed strangely.

Ansbor laughed at his gear, hefting it. 'I could carry this for five miles, and not get a serious sweat!'

Sabinus asked me politely to translate, looking like a man-eating bear sneaking up to an infant, and I did, cautiously.

He grunted and popped his head back inside the merchant's house. 'Marcus! We will need a full tent as well! A cooking kettle? Yes.' So we got a tent, a heavy thing that was impossible to carry with any form of grace, and a large kettle that we had to drag with us, and it bruised our sides and legs, and Fulcher and I cursed Ansbor, who was sullenly quiet.

'You will march twenty miles today. Not five. Let's go,' Sabinus said happily, pointing downriver, towards the hills where the other recruits had disappeared earlier. He started singing, and Ansbor was the first to carry the tent.

In the evening, we were shown an empty barracks, and we fell into deep, painful slumber, our feet featureless lumps of molten pain, full of angry blisters. We did not think about food or complaints, nor did feel shame for the raucous laughter that had greeted us at the gates when Fulcher and I carried Ansbor inside, tent and kettle tied to his belt, my friend unconscious and exhausted beyond care.

The feet were no better the next day when we did it again, and we even tried soaking them in urine, which seemed to have no positive effect on them.

The day after we arose to the blaring trumpet, we ate something so inconsequential it left us hungry, were hustled to the morning orders, and then Manlius, the optio, told us to fetch the tent and the kettle we had deliberately forgotten and hidden, and off we marched, our feet bleeding already.

For a few days, we hiked in a rain, and if the heat had been bad, rain was no better; turning the cloaks into smelly and heavy burdens, the ground slippery and stealing what strength we had, and any food we carried was reduced into horrid, wet clumps of unappetizing taste and looks. For the first few days, we were marching some twenty Roman miles, and then on the fourth day, we did it in quickstep, and our minds numbed, as we cast aside all hope of survival.

The optio was an easygoing man, not reluctant to using his cane, but he did not force us to sing. We did sound rather disturbing. The centurion was deaf, apparently, for he forced us to croak all the time. By the end of the first week, when we started to do forty miles in quickstep, we hollered again like idiots, and Ansbor did not make it back that time, and we had to carry him to a wagon. We had not hope of carrying him like we had the first day. The next day, we did it with the grinning elite first Cohort of the XVIII Legion, and none of us made it, vomiting in dust and waiting for a wagon, while disgusted Sabinus was calling us hopeless dogs. The following day, we barely hung on with the less elite eight cohort, in quickstep. I noticed how my mind was growing less rebellious each day, my feet hurt less, and I was proud like an enthusiastic puppy when one of the officers said something complimentary, even if it was something like: 'Well done, shit walker. You threw up in the gutter, not at your feet!'

It was hard to understand two weeks had passed, but it was so, for Chariovalda sent us word he would be away for one more week, and that Cassia sent her love. I actually cried, for the torture would go on, and did not have the heart to share the news with my friends, who had been counting days. They would understand the issue soon enough, of course, but I could not break their childlike hopes.

So we marched, cursed, and grew stronger and angrier as the days went past.

The accursed trumpet, or tuba, played the early notes, indicating the beginning of misery in the morning, and we made ready to march, but week three was different. Painful, but different. We were taken to a large indoors barracks, told to wear our armor and shields. They put a wooden sword on our feet, and we were told to do as the others did. Fulcher and Ansbor had never trained with a sword, and so this was very new to them. As I picked up the wooden sword, I found out it was actually heavier than any normal blade, just like the one Nihta had trained me with. After a few hours of stabs, always stabs, our arms grew slow, numbingly weak, and our knees were trembling. This was when we had some bread, a bit of olive oil, water to wash it down with, and were put up against live opponents, while our wrists screamed with pain.

Here, however, was finally our time to shine.

By our nature, a Germani fought duels rather than battles. We fought in shield walls, we rushed the enemy in a heavy cunus, but the battle easily turned into a chaotic melee, with no semblance of order, as soon as the blades started to fall. For the Romans, strength lay in discipline, for us, in courage and rage, in superior strength and speed, and god's favor. Some young fighters in their armor and shields squared off with us, eyeing the officers curiously.

Manlius shrugged at them. 'Here are some barbarians for you to clobber. Make them bleed, and you will not have to march tomorrow.'

They all grinned, and nodded to each other. We stared at each other in confusion. Sabinus was lounging on a discarded jug, picking his toes with the cane. He glanced at us. 'You lot will march no matter what, but perhaps I shall get you some wine if you beat them? I make no promises, boys.' He might have promised us Valholl's many women, for we, ale-drinking, mead-loving barbarians would kill for some watered wine at that stage. We stepped forward, trembling happily with anticipation, and I think Fulcher even drooled, likely tasting the wine already. Sabinus shook his head in disgust, as he continued with his toe picking.

An optio pointed our adversaries to us. I was to face a lanky recruit, a man with very small eyes and a peculiarly wide chin. I waited patiently as men around us were cheering our upcoming fight. Manlius spat. 'Go at it,' he said, and before I could say a word, my friends charged their opponents.

I noticed Ansbor slam his shield with a huge force to a swarthy legionnaire's shield, making a terrible booming sound as he vented his rage on the poor man. Fulcher went in more cautiously, dancing away as his foe, a thin boy, tried to foolishly rush him with his wooden sword hacking down. Then, I was embroiled in my own battle, and I walked for him, casually holding my shield at my side and observed his nervous face, which told me he would try to finish the battle quickly. True enough, the man grinned and suddenly rushed forward, as he tried to gut me, his wooden sword deceitfully rushing from behind his shield, but I sidestepped it and with an overhand slash on his shoulder, a kick on his leg, I had him on his side, cursing in pain.

Looking around, I could see Ansbor slamming his sword in his opponent's arm, and the fight ended abruptly. Fulcher was sitting down as I looked at him, but he shrugged and pointed at a man who was holding his foot.

Manlius and Sabinus looked at each other and grabbed a shield apiece, gesturing at a tall legionnaire to join them. He addressed the men staring at us glumly. 'Boys, as you see, the barbarians,' he pointed a sword at us, 'excel in one-on-one battle. Let us show you why you never leave the shield wall.' They stood, took a place in a line, three feet from each other, and gestured us to break them. 'Come, barbarians. Attack as you would usually, with no sense and full of fury.'

Everyone stopped and looked at us. Buoyed by our easy victories in one-on-one battle, we formed up as our men would, locking the shields and then nodding to each other, we walked forward, then we ran, swinging our swords, and slamming our shields forward. The Romans strode a step forward as well, blocked our wild swings and shields, and gutted all three with the sword thrusts coming deceptively from under a rim. Ansbor was throwing up, Fulcher cursing, and I just glowered at the centurion, who made an elaborate bow to the men around him, all staring at us agog.

Sabinus, the centurion, dropped his weapon. 'That is what discipline is for. You are savage, canny fighters in man-to-man battle, but in war, where nations disappear, you have a lot to learn. Now, again!'

And so, we started to learn what discipline was, keeping our shields together, timing our charge meticulously, guarding our friend faithfully and keeping our mouths shut, suffering if we failed. In a week's time, we knew more. We learned to throw spears in unison, at the right moment, not before, not after, but when it was required. They were wooden spears with leather knobs, and we also learned how to receive them, often painfully, as the sadistically grinning veterans used us for target practice. We learned drill, and the terse commands of the tuba, cornicula and buccina, how to turn together, how to charge, march, and retreat with semblance of order, feeling like a flock of hens. Deadly hens, but hens still.

We were allowed to go to the town with the other men, and there, we sat and drank wine, which the jolly legionnaires offered us. I did not drink, for I was looking around the village and found an establishment that might be useful one day. I remembered what Drusus had said about shadows and swords. In any case, as the training went on, we forgot time and our complaints, and then Chariovalda came back, and Drusus arrived with more troops.

CHAPTER XXVII

W
e were on the banks of Rhenus, and Manlius and Sabinus were laughing so hard their eyes were running with tears. I did, too, and for once, despite his unhappiness, so did Ansbor. 'So, Hraban. You look less arrogant.' A dry voice behind us noted, and I found Saturninus was standing there in brilliantly sculpted armor, and I had to squint as I tried to look up at him.

'I have an inkling that I might have been wrong,' I said, as I climbed to my feet, and Ansbor hooted as Fulcher sunk under again. We were learning to swim, as all legionnaires do. I knew how, Ansbor as well. Fulcher did not, but he was busily learning.

'He is going to drown,' Ansbor laughed. Some men watching exchanged coins, as Fulcher had not surfaced yet.

'Drusus is arriving, boy,' said the legate, and we turned to look at a stream of river galleys coming along, with flags flapping brilliantly in the wind. There were a dozen ships, majestically gliding over the river, birds racing around the hulls, chasing insects. Such ships had once ferried Vago to slay my family, and I felt apprehensive as they came forward, usually the sign of raids and slaughter. But, these ships were truly fabulous, and the man I had come to respect was perched on the prow of the leading one, a gilded ship of lighter hull, his purple cloak billowing behind as he gazed on to the Sigambri side of the river.

'Rivers are the key, son. And we know how to use them. Soon, they are ours,' Saturninus exclaimed gleefully, as the ships approached. 'Some auxilia are coming with him from the south.'

405

They docked, one-by-one, many waiting for their turns. Men jumped off from the ships, sailors and slaves receiving them, yelling instructions to gather their gear and troops. Many men, dozens, were forming up in the piers and marching off, the auxilia from the south. Drusus got off from a gilded boat that was rowed ashore near us. He was cursing a questor. 'Next time, I will board a normal ship. I looked like a whoremaster in that thing. What was it called?'

The questor kept a stony face. '*The Harlot*, sir.'

Drusus laughed. 'Find out who built it, and throw him to the river. No, I was just ... never mind.' He was laughing again at the distraught questor, and then he noticed me. He hooted, happy and nervous, full of barely contained energy. His worries seemed a thing of the past, and I guessed the coming war gave him the purpose and distraction he truly enjoyed. 'Well. Did they make a legionary out of you yet?' he asked, as he clapped my back. He was not truly expecting an answer, as he was staring around at the pier at the confused auxilia unit amassing on the shore, slowly moving to inland.

'They try to, lord. However, it is not a task for a few weeks,' I told him, while two legionnaires pulled Fulcher out from the water. He was gagging and praying.

Drusus smirked at Fulcher's prone body. 'No, it is not. It is a lifetime of learning. When the cute boys have turned into grizzled veterans and leave after twenty-five years, many enlist again. It is all they know. Killing and building. Man's world, that.'

Sabinus, the centurion, spat, thrumming his leg with the wine stick, as if about to whack his commander with it. 'When will they let the men marry, sir?'

Drusus winked at the officer. 'I hear you are married. To an Ubii girl? A fair-headed, plump girl she is, I am told. Gossips terribly. I hear she echoes your opinions of the legates quite willingly in the market.' Sabinus flinched but said nothing. Drusus chuckled as he strode next to me. 'At ease, centurion. I know nothing about such matters, and if I did, I'd let you complain. Gods know we all make mistakes.' Drusus, of course, knew much of what was going on with the troops. A rare mark of a true leader, he remembered everything he heard.

The optio, Manlius, nodded. 'She is not fair-headed.' The centurion cursed him, and the optio just stood there, eyes glinting mischievously.

Drusus placed a hand on my shoulder in shock, as he saw a man in armor fall to the river with a shriek. The man did not come up. 'Cannot afford to lose any. Optio! Go and tell them to take their time! We have no hurry before we cross the river!' Drusus turned to me, and I saw he had not slept much, for his eyes were ringed with dark rings, despite his apparent energy. 'Well, Hraban. Have you forgiven me?'

'The threat that still hangs over Cassia?' I asked him angrily. 'Or the speech you gave the gathered nobles of my world? Confirming my ... crimes? Or that you wish me to become a murderer for you when you go home?'

He shook his head, gazing at me cautiously. He took me aside, adjusting the chain mail around me. 'Yes, Hraban the Marcomanni. All that.'

I took a shuddering breath as the great man walked next to me. Had my father not manipulated me? So many others as well? Yet, I could not remain angry with him. I gazed across the river, thinking of my homelands, my tribes, all strangely distant. 'Was it truly Saturninus who asked the bastards to train us? Or did you? For my home feels rude, the people strange now, that we have suffered and learnt to love the army.'

He chuckled. 'I did, and he begged me to. I wanted you to love this army, if not Rome. The army is home to so many of us, its honor crossing nations and tribes, binding one to a single cause. That of its general.'

I hardened my soul, for Lif, but I loved the army indeed, and I loved Drusus, and could not explain it. He was one of those men you would risk your life for. 'I forgive you,' I told him generously, thinking how I would slay him and rue it forever. Armin's promise felt hollow, but Lif was not something I could forget.

He nodded happily. 'I like you Hraban. I truly do. You will be stationed here when the war begins.' I nodded. He would be dead, if I managed it. 'No complaints about missing a war? Fine. We will have one, and it will change things. I dream of killing a great chief in one-on-one combat. Haruspices read the signs to me last week. I will manage it. It will be a red-haired man. He told me to take the chance if it comes. We will see if it was your father he was talking about,' he mused. 'I respected him once, but now he is an enemy to me, and my men.'

'He won't duel you fairly. And the chiefs come with bodyguards, lord. Champions,' I told him, wisely.

He smiled at me. 'That is why I have men like you to keep them busy next year. Though not in this war, not before we can trust you.'

'I would rather kill my father myself, lord,' I told him morosely.

'I know. But, I am a higher lord than you, and get to try it first! You had your chance, I recall.' He grinned at Fulcher, who had been dragged out of the river, and found the strength to stand up straight, while being berated by a legionnaire, who was trying to teach him the strokes. We both laughed hugely as the sodden man flapped his arms in an amusing mockery of the legionnaire, who groaned in desperation. Drusus clapped me on the shoulder, and left to oversee the various workings of the camp, and I stared after him, hardening my soul.

Chariovalda arrived at the afternoon with the Batavian auxilia, along with Frisian troops and some Canifetes. He had two Batavi auxilia alae with him, around one thousand men, 1st Batavorium, and the 2nd, merry strongmen in chain mail, with dazzling bronze cavalry helmets, long spatha swords, and sturdy hastae, and all were riding large horses from Gaul. Trained and deadly, disciplined, the two alae were a terrible enemy. They were like an army of men, like my father had when he came home last year. The brooding woods across the river waited, unimpressed by their splendor.

The Frisians were just a regular cohort, some clad in the Roman army way, but wearing trousers, sorry looking men, barely trained, and the Canifetes were light cavalry, men like our Germani, with decurions trying to keep them in line, an utterly hopeless task. Chariovalda set up camp, and received me in the evening. He was sitting in a Roman chair, dressed in woolen finery, and there was a woman on his lap when I entered, and he looked at me sternly, as I had a startled look on my face.

'It is mine, not yours,' he said drolly, guessing the reason for my confusion. 'Cassia is alive, and chaste.'

I grinned. 'You know, my father used to have slaves sit on his lap. He was deeply despised for it, seeing how he was married.'

Chariovalda slapped the girl on the rump and grinned. 'Cassia would not sit on my lap. I tried, she screamed at me. She is one loyal girl! As for your father, I like his style, but let us leave my wife out of this, hmm?' I grunted and looked around. The tent was sprawled with armor and weapons. 'I like your legionnaire look, Hraban, makes you look martial, instead of a rogue,' he laughed, and I spied my helmet, sword, and spear amidst the gear. Also Leuthard's sword was lying in the corner.

'Yes, they are safe, do not worry,' he grinned, and poured some wine for me. I took it, sniffling at it experimentally, as the girl left to fetch more. He shrugged. 'So. We will go to war this week. Sigambri will be ready. Tencteri and Usipetes, and perhaps Bructeri and Marsi, and gods know how many others will dance with us. I—'

I interrupted him. 'Marcomanni and the Chatti?' I asked. 'Have you heard anything from Oldaric, and my father?'

'Your father will be busy with the Hermanduri. We paid them good coin to harass the Marcomanni this year,' he smirked.

'Bastards,' I told him with a smile.

'Yes, your father will beat them, but he will be busy. Drink,' he said, and I drank. 'Ebbe's imprisonment will keep the Chatti pacified.'

'So our lord hopes,' I said, grimacing. 'Perhaps this year, but—'

'All he needs is this year,' Chariovalda grinned. 'Drusus is not an idiot, even if he trusts you enough to give you some small freedom. You will get your weapons back.' He poured me another cup. 'I am to give you a commission. Gods know what use you are, but there it is. Loot, and revenge!' he told me, and drank.

'To loot, and revenge!' I saluted him, happy Drusus thought so highly of me. 'But, he will keep an eye on Cassia still?' I drank as he bade me to.

'Cassia is a guest,' he told me softly. 'No more, but a guarded one. To blades and honor, and a large amount of wealth!' he saluted again. 'I am starving of coin.'

'Really?' I said, trying to stop him from refilling my cup, but he slapped my fingers painfully.

'Really. Gods, by Hercules, I do need this war. I need coin. A lot of coin, a large number in slaves! I have a wife and mistresses to pay for, men to reward, and bribes to pay, after all!' he laughed, and very soon, we were a bit drunk.

'Does Drusus's priests promise us wealth?' I wondered.

He waved his hands and spat. 'Not sure yet. He will seclude himself to the temple the night before we march. What he does there, gods know. But, I know he is not alone.'

'Oh?'

'He has a priest who reads the omens for him. They ask his ancestors for guidance. Those bastards better tell us how to get rich.' He looked slightly disgusted, and we drank more, happy to swap stories, and I remember having a mock fight with him, using nasty cudgels before I fell asleep on the corner of his tent, curled in a ball at my new lord's feet.

The next morning, Cassia threw water on us.

'Pigs! What in Hercules's name are you two doing? There is an army out there getting ready to war, and you two sleep and drink, and sleep again!' She kicked me painfully.

'Cassia, how nice to see you,' I told her and grinned, and she could not help but grin back, though she turned away in mock disgust.

I looked at Chariovalda, who was groaning. 'You hit me with a stool, Hraban.'

'Cudgel, lord, and you hit yourself, I remember it. How many men will I lead?' I asked.

Chariovalda was getting up, massaging his head. 'You are a trooper. You only become a decurion in an alae with knowledge, experience, savagery, if you are lucky enough to survive a few wars! In your case, and judging by the number of enemies you have made, I would not hold my breath!' he laughed more, and nearly choked on phlegm.

He gave me back my weapons and armor, and I gave him an oath to follow him, and to serve him and Rome. Him foremost, Rome second, I felt after the oath, but it did not matter. I signed papers, and so, too, did Ansbor and Fulcher, the next day, with awkward marks that made no sense. I abandoned my Roman gear, and Ansbor and Fulcher wore what the Batavi wore, trousers and the mail, with shoes and Roman helmets. We looked the part. We were mercenaries, being paid two hundred and fifty denarii, and I had a plan on how to kill Drusus.

Outside, I walked and talked with Cassia, happily hearing her stories of Batavorium, and I told her of our weeks of pain.

Men were following us, a constant reminder of what would soon take place.

CHAPTER XXVIII

Castra Vetera was situated in a lush, beautiful valley by the sparkling, swift waters of Rhenus River, defined by rolling pastures of emerald green grass swaying in the northern winds. We could see large deer, lazy moose, and swift foxes peering at us from the hazy birch woods surrounding it. At least this was how it used to look.

Now, it was all different.

The pastures were patchy and trampled, the deep emerald green turned to brown mud, as huge armies concentrated on Castra Vetera. A veritable town had sprung up around the fort and the native village, kept out of the walls by the camp prefect. It grew daily, bringing with it temporary inns, cheap wineries, opportunistic weapon vendors, busy smiths, many doctors, strangely attired fortunetellers, and, of course, whores. There was little peace to be had. Hundreds of men milled around, and temporary legionary camps sprung up, as if summoned by a vitka. I Germanica had arrived one night, and XIX had built their camp on a hill, the XVII in the woods.

I Germanica raised our curiosity. 'They don't look like our people,' Ansbor said, as he spied some of the men of the legion, hoisting bull emblem shields. We were waiting for Chariovalda to give us our orders.

A legionnaire of the V Alaudae grinned at us, apparently of a Germani origin. 'They are a Roman legion, from northern Italy. They were I Augusta, but lost the title after the Cantabrian War. They nearly left the old man in hot water during a battle, retreating like scared rabbits. His guard saved him, but the old man stripped them of the title.' The man enjoyed their disgrace, and smacked his lips. All in all, in the area was massed some sixteen thousand men, some legions and cohorts were, of course, understrength. Some had a lot of new recruits, but it was a massive number of men, nearly one in seven of all the troops in the empire milling in the formerly beautiful plateau.

Then, there were the auxilia. Like in Moganticum, some legionary cohorts and few units of the Alps auxilia would be holding the Castra Vetera, tall men who rarely smiled. The Ubii were not to join, nor the Vangiones, but there was a vast array of other auxilia cohorts, many from Aquitane, Gauls all, strange archers from Syria and Crete, skillful slingers, and even a cohort of Thracian horsemen, forever jealous of the Batavi for the preferential treatment.

The Batavians who were to act as horsemen guards of the legions, exploratores, riding the vulnerable flanks, scouting ahead, seeking out the enemy, preventing them from finding us. These men trained hard. They ran daily, rode after, and fought with arms so wide in range, I didn't even recognize some of them. We trained with them now, Fulcher, Ansbor, and I, serving under a decurion of the second turma in the 1st Batavorium. Junius was halfway gone, the campaign season already far. Then, Sabinus came to see us, waving his wine stick at me while I rode through a set of obstacles, sharp stakes on the ground. He distracted me, and I fell off the horse in full armor, and landed near him. He smiled and walked over. 'You can't ride for shit,' he informed me.

I got up, bristling, and dusted my armor off. 'You are really a pain in the ass, you know that, Sabinus?'

'I am not Sabinus; I am a centurion to you. No, you cannot ride for shit. But, if you become a Roman citizen one day, you are welcome to join my troop. I will give you a letter of recommendation. You and your friends are good lads, even if the one fool will never learn how to swim,' he spat, embarrassed, and shook my arm. 'Now, get on your horsy, and ride to Chariovalda. He has been summoned. The war starts.' He grinned and left, leaving me standing there.

I looked at him going, smiling wistfully at his words. He had beaten me many times with his damnable stick, but now, I would fight for him ferociously. I cleared my head, for Armin would not let me enjoy the trust of Rome. I excused myself from the training, rode by some huge granaries where thousands and thousands of tons of grain were secured, and from where other thousands were consumed each day. The army had to march soon.

As I rode near the castrum, I saw some Batavians riding by in light gear. One had a huge gash in his arm, and he sat in his saddle, ashen-faced. Others were dirty, bloody, and grim. They were scouts. They had already started the war.

A bridge had been built over the river nearly overnight, the skilled legionnaires planting sturdy stakes in the river at angles, men swarming like ants to make the thing hold together. A river was nothing more than a minor obstacle for them. For Germani, going over one was a major undertaking.

On the other side, I saw teams of archers and a cohort of infantry on guard duty. There, under the shade of sparse trees, nothing moved. The woods looked uninviting, dangerous, and deadly. The free Germani were there. They were still silent. Waiting.

Men who wait have plans.

I could imagine Varnis and Maelo, Wodenspear, the lords of Tencteri and Usipetes, all of them preparing. Tudrus, and his sons as well. They would be waiting for us.

Perhaps others. Like the Cherusci.

They knew how many men there were coming over. They knew very well. The Luppia River was the arrow aimed at their heart, ending in hills and mountains that separated the Rhenus tribes from the Cherusci. They must have feared, their Things filled with angry voices, with chiefs arguing how to counter us, and ending up with no other plan than to amass their troops and give a few good battles, asking poor Woden for help.

Or someone had mastered them, and they were waiting with devious plans, as a seemingly unbeatable army would march against them, one that nonetheless was predictable. Armin would be doing just that, planning and inspiring the Germani. And Drusus thought he was a pup. *Perhaps he was*, I allowed. We would see, soon.

My chest tightened. I asked Woden, Donor, and Tiw for help, but I could not be sure they were on my side. I had my sword, Nightbright. In the end, by obeying Armin, I would be free of Father. Armin would not stand Maroboodus. I would be a father again, holding Lif. These things would have to do, even if I had no honor or friends left under the skies of Midgard. I left my horse outside the castrum, the guards checked my orders, and I walked through the wide streets, passing barracks, and turned for the principia, where the standards were held, where the leaders gathered.

There was a nervous energy in the legionnaires streaming back and forth from the various barracks. Some were writing, and many gossiping indecently. They had mostly taken on some extra pounds, as experienced soldiers did. Better to carry your extra nourishment on your waist, for there were days ahead when they would eat air and drink tears. There was a throng of men running around the general area of the principalia. Many were centurions, given orders. I spotted my lord, Chariovalda, who was on his tunic, stroking his beard when he saw me, and grinned. 'Chaos, total chaos, as always. One day, it's peaceful, the next, all hell breaks loose. They practically dragged me out of a toilet for this.' He laughed, and I looked embarrassed.

'I hate the toilets,' I told him morosely.

He stared at me. 'They have not told you how to use a toilet building? The guards tell me they have seen your ass in the woods when you have to go.'

'Yes, we do it in the woods still,' I said with discomfort. The idea of shitting with a bunch of strangers, and using a common sponge to wipe one's ass did not appeal to me. He scowled at me, and I waved my hand towards a toilet building. 'Ansbor tried it, but he couldn't use the sponge; it was disgusting,' I said, and shivered. Chariovalda burst into a huge laugh, and evidently disrupted the anxiety prevalent in the other commanders. We collected stares.

'Come. Drusus wanted to see me quickly.' We pushed through to the principia, where legates and camp prefects were doling out orders for chiefs, centurions, commanders of all kinds, and even supply officers were getting theirs. Medical personnel were packing, and being told their places.

Saturninus was talking to Drusus, pulling at his sleeve. 'The XVII will leave three cohorts here, one on the other side. The rest will march with us, as ordered. Will they take their Aquila, or march under vexillation?' he asked tiredly.

Drusus grunted. 'All the legions take their eagle; they need to be seen to become famous.'

'It is not customary to take them, if only a part of the legions marches ...' Saturninus started to argue, but Drusus waved him down.

'My army. The damned eagles follow me. See you in a bit.' He waved his hand briskly, and Saturninus left, glancing at me, and sighing as he went.

'Lord Drusus,' bowed Chariovalda to the commander.

'You were there yesterday; you know the plan. Here, your orders,' he said, giving a scroll that fell, and I picked it up. Drusus glanced at me, and gave me a quick smile. 'Serve him well, and you serve me,' he told me, then centurions, and a military tribune pushed near, and he concentrated on them.

'As ordered, the XIX shall deploy first ...' he was saying, when Chariovalda took me out.

'So you have your plan already?' I asked.

He nodded. 'Drusus held a meeting last night. He will give the army a speech in half an hour. I have sixteen decurions in the first Batavorium, fifteen in the 2nd. If you perform your duties well, who knows how many will be vacant after this war,' he said evasively.

'Any my posting, lord?' I asked him.

He pointed across to the east. 'You are inexperienced. You and your boys will stay with two turmae in the small fort on the other side of the river, and help guard it.'

I smirked. 'Drusus said he would keep me out of danger, but out of war entirely? And there is no fort on the other side.'

He looked stern, but failed. 'The fort will be there in a few hours' time.'

'And they will march tomorrow morning?' I asked, dreading the night.

'Some will go today, many Batavi are already out there,' he said, looking at his dirty fingernails. 'I know you would like to join us, but if I put you on a trained horse, set you and your boys amongst a trained alae, you will risk their lives. I would like to have you there, but I lead an army, not a collection of shepherds with spears. So, help the alae guard our way home. And our food stocks. Then, we think of your father and your wife. And child.'

'I am to guard grain and cattle?' I asked, my honor insulted, and Chariovalda nodded. I followed him out of the gate.

He placed his hands on my shoulders. 'You have your orders now, Hraban. I am not sure we will meet again, but I just wanted to tell you I am happy I took you prisoner. You are a shifty man, but I think there is an honest streak in you. At least you seem to suffer, when you contemplate on breaking the oaths forced on you. I almost think of you as a son.'

'You don't speak too kindly of your daughters,' I noted.

He grinned and shrugged. 'Farewell, and let us hope there will be happy news when this war is over.' He left, and I walked off, and found Cassia, who was binding a foot of a Batavi. She noticed me and finished her work, running after me with her guards.

We stopped near the river, our guards hovering nearby. Cassia leaned on me. 'What is wrong?'

I grunted, as the troops were moving around near the bridge. Horsemen rode over, on the other side some cohorts were glinting in the sun, as dolobara were hacking into the muddy ground, digging the moat, and heaping the mud to build the agger, where the walls were being built of felled trees.

'What the hell happened? Can I come with you?' she insisted.

I shrugged as I saw that on the Germani side, nothing moved, still no enemy was seen. It was as silent as a grave mound. Birds were likely singing, and there was a doe staring the camp builders. I took a deep breath. I had to trust my friends, and try to keep them alive at the same time. Impossible, but I had to give them a chance.

'I have to speak with you. This evening. And Ansbor and Fulcher,' I told her evenly.

'Is it serious?' she asked, trying to read some subtle sign of what I was planning.

I massaged at my temples. 'Are you happy here, Cassia?'

'Yes, I am. Despite the trouble you are in. *We* are in,' she added with a smile. 'There is order here. Things are clear-cut. At least someone is on our side. No matter the threats in the shadows.'

'Ah, but the Romans on our side are as treacherous as the ones against us,' I said with a shudder. 'Drusus had Chariovalda find men to keep an eye on you. To keep me in line. We are still being watched. And they are no idle threats, Cassia. Your life is in danger.'

'We are watched, yes,' she agreed. 'I'm no fool. I know. But, it is a small price to pay for such a splendid army on our side.' She wiped her hand across the horizon, where the Roman army was mustered, and silvery lines of men were amassing on a wide patch of land. 'What will you speak to us about? How to lose all this?' she asked sweetly, yet nervously.

'Yes,' I agreed, and we settled into silence as Ansbor and Fulcher joined us, the former brooding and staying a bit off, watching Cassia listlessly.

In half an hour, most of the army was drawn up on a field opposite of the bridge, men stretching from one end to another, armored men on splendid horses, infantry on foot, panoply of shields making them look like field of silver red flowers, and an army of glittering spear points. Near twenty thousand men. An incredible number of men. I smiled grimly, trying to detach myself from them, the men I had grown to respect and love. I could not help but think on how the shepherds and farmers in Germania were leaving their mud-caked halls, sad huts, and squat houses, grabbing a bunch of sturdy spears and a trusty shield, ready to follow their lords against this killing machine. I felt a tug of regret in my heart, for I was planning on joining them. For Lif.

Drusus arrived in his war splendor, the man I was to slay. He wore a brilliant golden, incredibly sculpted torso, a thorax sadios, a crested Attic helmet, with a purple horsehair, a cingulum belt, with bronze and golden medals, the splendor hanging around his knees, and a commander's purple cloak, a paludemanetum was billowing round him as he rode slowly so all the men could see him. He rode from one end of the field to the other, taking his time, and not a man twitched, save for the unruly auxilia, which was growing nervous. His handsome face was smiling, his keen eyes penetrated men's souls, and many stood taller, others avoided his gaze, as if he was a young god who could burn them where they stood. When he stopped in the middle of the field, his officers joined him. There stood Saturninus with the XIX, Sextus Vistilius with the XVII, and other legates in their expensive armor. I smirked. A week from now, all of them would be mud-spattered, bearded, and smell of piss. If Armin got his way, they would never come home. Drusus had the familiar questor, a nervous young man in silvery armor, next to him, and a military tribune, with a red stripe under his chest, a stern looking man with a scar, serving his tenure before moving on to greater things. All were sitting on great horses under Drusus's standard, a purple flag with his name on it, gilded on top.

There, too, strode the Legion standards, all five eagles with wreaths, decorated with legion birth signs, glittering with many phalarae for merits, and men always noted the V Alaudae eagle that had been a Sigambrian possession a few years past, when the fool Marcus Lollius had been surprised. I suddenly wondered if Adalwulf was facing these men today, or in the coming weeks. I had not thought of my grandfather's former champion since he left Maroboodus, but hoped he was well. Drusus guided his horse in small circles near the first Cohort of the XIX, and then rode next to the eagles, his purple cloak billowing in a gust of wind, the reins on his horse jingling with bells. The field was silent, as men let their eyes follow him.

He got off his horse, sitting down on a gilded chair set up for him.

A priest appeared with a toga covering his head, and the standards waved in the air. It was an old man, hunchbacked and swathed in white. I noted there was a fire burning by Drusus, and the priests walked next to it, holding a bowl, praying for a long, long time, long enough for Drusus to start fidgeting in his chair, to the amusement of some of the XIX veterans.

Finally, the priest poured the liquid from the bowl to the flames. The army, and evidently the war, had been purified. I scrutinized the men in white carefully.

Then, something familiar followed.

A set of notes were blown by aenators, the men in charge of the legion's cornu, buccina and tuba. Out came sacrificial animals, a fat bull and a thick-necked ram, which tried to break free, running erratically around, held by sweating auxilia Gauls, and there was also a pig that came along peacefully, comically staring at the ram with abject pity, as if understanding the futility of the resistance. Two haruspices went forward, and the animals were stopped near Drusus. There was no speech, only the butchery, and the animals died messily, the Gauls dripping with blood, desperately trying to avoid sprinkling any over the Roman nobilitas looking on dispassionately.

The augurs went to work. It took time, as the liver was cut out, its various knots and knobs searched by expert fingers, and when one of the priests got up, nodded and smiled, a veritable sea of cheers went up from the Roman troops. Drusus grinned at the cheering men, nodded at the priests, and got up to address the army, which slowly went silent. Not many could hear him, of course, for the army was vast, not all spoke Latin even, but they all stood in rapt attention anyway. We were close enough to hear, and he stood up high, his silvery armor and greaves sparkling in the sun, the Greek style sword, favored by the officers, in a silver sheath catching sunlight, as if designed to do so.

'Men of Rome! Our allies! My brutal boys!' he yelled. 'Last year, the XVIII Legion made a fortune! They sat here, guarding this tiresome fort, relaxing as only a legionnaire can relax, doing light training and some forced marches.' Men laughed, and yelled agreement, even the ones who could not hear him. Drusus grinned. 'The Sigambri attacked them. There were five thousand of them, a horde of angry warriors, and we didn't even count their allies.' More laughter and catcalls. 'Essentially, the lucky bastards made a fortune on Sigambri slaves, and not a few of the lucky boys are now lazy with their wealth! This is not right!' Men jeered him and the legionnaires of the XVIII. Drusus adopted a serious expression, and was rewarded by expectant faces. 'This year, we asked them why they attack us again and again, year after year. They declined to show up in the peace meeting, but attacked the Ubii instead.' Drusus looked sad. 'So, we will go, and ask them ourselves. They will explain their actions, after we are done with them. This year, we are going to be fair. All of you get your share. Romans will make a ton of money. Why should XVIII alone get the gold and women? I want my share! So we go to war, and make peace over burnt villages.'

'The bastard is good,' Fulcher told me, as he came to stand near.

'He is very good,' I agreed.

Drusus waited for them to go silent. It took time. 'It is true. Some will stay home, some will guard the new forts, but there will be bonuses to all, none shall be forgotten. Yet, make no mistake, the battle, men, will not be easy. They fight like badgers when cornered, but they lack cunning, training, and weapons. We will prevail, and I shall be proud of you. On to victory! Follow your commanders, fight well, and if you die, I shall never forget you. I will not forget your family!' Men roared again on top of their lungs, but the questor and the military tribune looked at each other uncertainly.

Chariovalda walked over and leaned on me 'He made no mention of Augustus, or Rome, which is why the two bastards are nervous. The tribune is Marcus Lollius Paulinus, a creature of Augustus; it was his father who lost the eagle.' Chariovalda nodded towards the gilded eagle moving to its legion.

'So what is the plan? Do we know who are out there?' I asked, awestruck at the massive show of loyalty, which shook a man to the core. Such energy, so many men marching for this one young general, unquestioningly ready to plunge into the woods and hills filled with enemies. And Armin planned to topple them? I would go and join him? Madness.

He spat towards the east, missing Ansbor's foot by an inch. 'We have scouts around in the east; ships have been roving up the Luppia River.

They tell us Inguiomerus of the Cherusci is busy with Semnones, and Sigimer is so with the Chauci, our allies. Segestes is, as you know, more Roman than most here,' he smiled wolfishly. 'It looks pretty straightforward. Rome versus the Luppia River Valley, and no Cherusci taking part in this party. However, we must be careful; he said they lack cunning. You know this is not true.' He was thinking about Armin.

'What will we do? Do we have targets? Plans? What of the Chatti?' I asked.

He shrugged. 'Thurwag the Matticati has been keeping an eye on the Chatti. Nothing. No report of their movements. Hermanduri have been attacking the Quadi for a month, there are reports of your father warring there. Sorry, lad.'

I nodded, cursing. I hoped no Hermanduri speared Maroboodus before I did.

Chariovalda nodded at the emerald green and topaz blue waters flowing to Rhenus from the east. 'Luppia is the key. We have the river in the middle. We will rush to the gates of the Cherusci on the left bank of the river, and build forts along the way, and then we turn north, and raze all the Marsi and Bructeri settlements until they give up. There are also Tubanti and Salii, small tribes beyond Bructeri to the north, and if they don't yield, we burn them to Hades, too.' Chariovalda examined his horse.

'Burn?' I asked absentmindedly, as I thought of Hard Hill and the night we burned it, and of Grinrock.

'Burn and kill, take slaves, until they give up. Then, and only then, we turn to the Sigambri across the Luppia, late in the campaign season, if we must, and Varnis and Maelo, Baetrix on the other side of the river, will face our wrath. They will expect us to attack them first. We attack them last. The forts will defend our back, and cavalry,' he told me, and scanned the Sigambri side of the river. 'The Ubii will sortie against them tomorrow, to keep them busy. Why have allies if you cannot expend them for a good cause, eh?' he asked.

'Like Rome used the Batavi?' I asked maliciously, and he spat.

'We are different.'

I laughed. 'Usipetes and Tencteri?' I asked.

He shrugged. 'They always fight alongside Sigambri. We will get them, too. But, we will go for the Bructeri first, flipping the river to our cause, and keeping them sliced up like eels.'

I scanned the army, deep in my thoughts. 'There will be many mules with the troops. Good for eating, perhaps?'

Chariovalda grinned. 'Yes, I suppose, though troops who have been forced to munch on their unhappy baggage animals claim it is the final revenge of the four-legged bastards on them. Terribly chewy and tasteless. See, each squad of eight has two, and some slaves to gather food and lead the mules with their personal gear. It is a city on a march!'

'Lots of wealth with a legion then,' I mused, and thought how rich a man could become by crushing even one.

'Capture a standard bearer, as he holds all the coins for their unit!' Chariovalda laughed, but glanced at me suspiciously, regretting that bit of advice. 'Luppia is around a hundred Roman miles, legion marches as fast as its pack animals, but we should make it in four days, we will range there in two on horses, depending on what is out there. We control the river, they are split, and the forts and navy will make it hard for them to cross, even if they ignore the Ubii,' he said, mounting his horse.

I was thinking. 'And the cattle and grain, it follows? There will be a massive number of grain needed?'

He shrugged. 'One legion consumes forty thousand pounds of water a day. Happily, that flows next to them. The grain need is nearly twenty thousand pounds, and our horses need forty. I do not envy the supply officers. We will all go hungry for days. However, hungry or not, we will win. And we will eat their food as well.' He nodded towards the enemy.

'And the ships here will eventually supply the forts, which will supply the troops?' I mused.

'Yes, this is why your people cannot stay on field for a long time. Germani have their women pack food for them for a week, or two, and then you go home. We will stay here until it's done.'

423

'And them?' I asked. A group of wagons was drawing close, and the jingle of chains was evident.

'Slavers. Now, I see you when I see you. Obey the Decurion, and you should be fine. Guard the fort tomorrow. Drusus will pray this night, alone, and gods will listen. Come morning, this war begins.'

I nodded, and turned to walk back to the castrum.

Many things would take place that evening. Most of them fatal. And Drusus would not be praying, but dying.

CHAPTER XXIX

I sat on a bunk, and stared at my friends as they piled in. Ansbor had had his beard trimmed, and looked soldierly in his chain mail and helmet; Fulcher's red hair was hanging over his shoulder, as he was leaning forward on the bed. Cassia waited nervously, and we sat, and said nothing. I looked at my hands; they were trembling.

'Out with it,' Ansbor grunted, grabbing a mug of wine. He had grown very accustomed to the Roman way of life. He pointed a finger at me. 'Cassia said you are making plans. Such plans usually mean pain and death for us.' He had received Leuthard's huge sword back, and he struggled with it as he removed it from his hip. 'So just spit it out, and we can discuss it.'

'You both gave me an oath,' I told them heavily.

'Yes, we did, but …' Ansbor began, but Fulcher put a hand on his chest to silence him. He looked at Fulcher incredulously and shrugged the hand off, and they glowered at each other until Cassia sighed and came forward.

'Lif?' she said. 'It is about her.'

I nodded. 'Armin has captured Hands. Hands had my daughter. Armin has them both, and he …'

'Offers you Lif, if you join him?' Cassia said profoundly. 'You would betray your promises to Drusus.'

'Ah, if that was the only thing he wishes,' I snickered and rubbed my face. 'He wants Drusus dead. This night. Just before the war begins.'

They stared at me in stupefaction. Ansbor opened his mouth several times, pointing a quivering finger my way, then drunk down the wine with loud gulps. Fulcher was scowling to himself, very unhappy, and Cassia was speechless for once.

Only for a moment, though.

'And what did you tell him?' she asked, and kicked a stool, which flew to the corner with a crack and clatter.

I stared at the wreck, and then at her. 'He *has* Lif.'

She stuttered and sat down worryingly, burying her face in her hands. 'Surely Armin would not hurt her.'

'He has Lif, and he can be a very ruthless man, the pretty Armin,' I said hollowly. 'Catualda is with Armin. God knows how many men who dislike Armin see her there. Men my father can buy. If she is flaunted there as my daughter, do you not think Odo will know? Eh?' I asked, and beat the bed with my fist. 'So I have no choice!'

'Can you do it?' Fulcher asked with a tired face. 'Can you kill that man?'

'I do not know,' I said. 'We have guards. One is watching Cassia, of course, all the time, but they are watching us as well.'

Fulcher nodded. 'Yes, I have seen them. One man for each of us. And you want me to take care of them?'

'You and I. Then you will slay the man guarding Cassia, and take her far away, to safety,' I told him. 'We shall meet later, perhaps.'

'That is a lot of slaying in the midst of twenty thousand hostile men. And where will this take place?' Cassia asked. 'This *foul* deed?'

'I ... he is going to pray at the temple this night. He usually does before the war,' I told her, looking down. 'You will stay in your barrack, Cassia. Let Fulcher silence the man who is guarding you. Then travel south, west, far from here. Change your name.'

She went to her knees and pulled up my face. 'There comes a point, Hraban, when you can no longer justify evil by the loss of your honor, friends, or daughter.'

I nodded, my eyes burning with shame. 'This is not such a point. He is, after all, the enemy of our people.'

She got up, her face drawn. 'I thought you were a good man. A man worth loving.' I opened my mouth, as she let her hands brush my cheek.

She put a finger over my mouth, as my friends looked on with stony faces. 'I'll obey, Hraban. But, nothing good will come out of this. I will swim in this mad river, for you saved me once, and I fell in love with you when you tried to help me up the hill that night they sent you away. So I will suffer what comes. For love. And for Lif.'

I stared at her as she left. Ansbor's face looked feverish, devoid of life, ashen with streaks of sweat pouring down his face. Fulcher glanced at him, and then at me, and he spoke. 'The men keeping watch at you are lax. They follow you from afar, not bothering with stealth. I know the men who take turns to watch me. I need not slay them. I can lose them easy enough.'

I nodded. 'This evening, when the night falls, Drusus will go to the temple. If he does not, I have to find him in the field, or praetorium. I will leave this barracks, and walk towards the town at first. Fulcher, there is a narrow alleyway, just past that brown hut with the reddish thatch. We drank wine there with the legionnaires. Hide there, and when I have passed, we will make these men into corpses. Then, Fulcher, you shall take Cassia far away. Perhaps to Lugdunum. Wait for me to call for you. It would be best if you stayed there, with her.'

He nodded carefully. 'I am to murder two innocent men? Three, if the man guarding me is not lazy this night?'

Ansbor spat. 'No men are innocent.'

'I need you, Ansbor, to fetch me a haruspex,' I told him. 'Ask one to meet me at the temple, tell him we need a divination done. Then stay far. Your guard need not suffer. You are just a soldier asking for divine help, and that is normal.'

'But, this priest will suffer?' he asked.

'I will need his robe,' I said hollowly, for I had slain holy men before.

'You shall come to the temple, and take his robe. You will kill the man, and then the lord. And then we ride to Armin?' he asked.

'I will get you. We flee, yes, to Armin,' I told him. He grunted, and got stiffly up, nodded at me and walked out. Fulcher gazed at me mysteriously.

He pointed a finger at me. 'You gave him oaths?'

427

'Drusus?' I asked timidly. 'Yes.'

'Burlein and Lif restored you to the right road,' he told me sadly. 'Even after all the things that took place, you were an honorable man for one winter. This is for Lif? Not for something else? Were you promised power by Armin?'

I shook my head. 'They promised me a marriage to Gunda, but I would spit on a marriage with a goddess, if only my daughter is safe with me.'

He laughed as he shook his head, getting up. 'Let it be so then. We, Ansbor and I, will soil ourselves for you, my friend. He will do so out of duty, I will as well, but more so for you saved my daughter once. And think hard on what Cassia said just now. Dedication like hers you will never find again. Hopefully, her life is not a prize you have to pay for this. Ermendrud was already too high a one. I doubt we can hide her anywhere, if you succeed.'

I nodded and watched him go. No, she would die as well. The woman who loves me. They would slay Ansbor and Fulcher as well, for none would be spared. It was very nearly impossible for them to escape, and I loathed myself. They had a chance, a small chance, and that was my gift to them. I cried, and felt thoroughly miserable.

For Lif. Wyrd.

Wearing Leuthard's chain mail and carrying my old helmet, I slinked out of the barracks. I had not moved much since our arrival, having sequestered myself to the barracks and the training grounds, taking the meals dutifully, but now I adjusted a tight caligae and then walked off towards the main gate. A mighty effort was ongoing; while most men of the legions were asleep, veteran campaigners all, the support troops were busy with preparations. And, of course, there were many men who took the time to meet with women. Rules were laxer that night. I stomped along the busy lane, and smiled at some Batavi I knew. I gazed behind me, as the tuba blared in the fort, announcing the evening meal.

It was dark, I was swift, and I noticed two young men, both apparently trusted slaves, or even soldiers, of Chariovalda, trying to keep up with me. I neared the gate, and a harried legionnaire in ring mail stopped me.

'Juppiter's left ball,' I growled at him, giving him the day's passphrase, something he had likely heard a thousand times already. I strode forward, aiming for the village, where men were enjoying last chances at peaceful existence with the local women. Near the woods by the town stood the temple, of Hercules this time, a long, if simple, wooden building, with high stone columns running around it, both Roman and Gaulish in its outlook. Drusus would come there, that night. I would be there.

I stalked down the muddy path, passing some sheds and a pigsty, then the hut with the reddish thatch. I turned abruptly, dodging some soldiers rushing for their units. A shadowy, narrow path led towards the market, and there were several dozen halls around it. Most were sad, local houses where families lived, often the illicit families of rogue Roman soldiers, blithely ignored by the officers of the camp. One was the building I had noticed early in our training, a whorehouse, where destitute girls sold their wares. I felt sorry for the girls, but their backyard would suffice for something I had to do.

I walked on; the mud was thick. I heard steps behind me and prayed to the gods things would go well. I turned.

The two men stopped to look at me, surprised. Both were armed with short swords, both bearded men with young faces and they grinned at me uncertainly. 'You with Chariovalda?' I asked them.

'We ... yes,' said one of the men.

The other one sneered. 'You know what we do,' he said arrogantly. 'Are you going to visit that establishment?' he asked with a sniffle, nodding at the whorehouse that was not far.

'No,' I told them, and prayed again, for Fulcher stepped out of the dark shadows and thrust his spear in the meek man's back, thrusting deep, twisting it out deadly quick and stepping forward. The other one stared at him in horror and ran, ripping out his sword, but I stepped forward with Nightbright out, and steeled my heart. I stepped even closer, as he slowed down and then he hissed, thrust the blade forward, and I dodged it, nearly slipping in the mud, but balanced enough to punch my blade to his chest, where it scraped on a bone, pierced muscle and meat, and split his heart. I grunted as I pulled him to the shadows, toppling him to the mud. 'Come, do as I did,' I told Fulcher.

'Chariovalda will never believe this was a coincidence, should we have to stay after all,' he told me, while dragging the corpse. 'This will spell doom for us.'

'We are Germani,' I reminded him, and myself, 'from the eastern woods.'

'We are,' he said coldly. 'And now I am to get Cassia?'

'Take her to safety,' I told him. 'Be careful with the guard. If she does not obey, truss her up, and carry her away at spear point.'

'Be careful, my lord,' he told me. 'But, I doubt I will manage to take her anywhere, if she disagrees.'

I pulled my sword through the young man's clothing, cleaning the blade. I felt dirty and hopeless, but I was determined. She would die indeed, and as long as Drusus died, and I got away, Lif would be safe. 'Fulcher?'

'Yes, lord?' he said, as he watched some legionnaires passing the alleyway.

'I am sorry I could not help you find the man who took your son's life,' I said.

He smiled wistfully. 'We are not dead yet. And there is still time. Fate will be revealed in the end.'

I smiled as he ran away. I walked away swiftly in the dark evening, wind picking up as I made my way to the temple. Many soldiers were milling by it, Hercules overseeing the activity from his lofty perch on the top of the temple, though he was not being very attentive, for I was still alive. I greeted the men I knew, some of them Batavi, and hoped there were no more men following us around. There were none, I decided, for I could not control everything.

I walked up the steps, and a throng of centurions exited the temple, the bravest men of the army, who had a terrible mortality rate in battles. I nodded at them respectfully and squinted into the dark temple. It would be closed when Drusus arrived, and I walked forward briskly on the tiled stone floor, my hobnailed caligae making clipping sounds. A brazier was sputtering in the middle of the room, and another image of Hercules, a vicious, bearded man with a club, was staring malevolently at me from the far wall. I walked by the brazier, coughing a bit as pungent smoke billowed around me. I brushed my hands over an altar where a stick of incense was burning and smoking weakly. Ansbor stepped out from behind the statue, nodding at me while watching some legionnaires, who walked briskly forward towards the altar. I made way for them, nodding gratefully, and went to Ansbor.

He was armed and armored in his Roman gear, holding a shield. He nodded back. 'They dead?' he asked softly, nervously glancing around the room.

'None know we are here,' I said deeply. 'Well?'

'I got the priest, but could not let you do this alone. I lost the guard,' he whispered.

'You lost him? Is the haruspex there?' I asked, and nodded towards the back rooms.

'He is, and eager to meet you. I had to pay him a terribly high prize, though. Says we have to hurry, he has other business this night,' Ansbor told me, and when I moved that way, he put a hand on my shoulder, smiling. 'Wait. Let them leave.' He nodded at the legionnaires, who were praying. I scowled at him, staring up at Hercules, one of the Greek heroes Marcus Romanus had once told me about, as he taught me the rudiments of Latin. He had shown me the ways and forms of the old ways and gods, most coming from faraway east, some from the Greek, and was not my helmet, gift of Tudrus the Older, from those lands? Heracles, Hercules, aid me, I prayed.

But, gods, Drusus.

He was a god.

He was a man to turn the fates of men, a vortex of glory I was to suffocate. He was a victim of his stepfather, a lord of swords and a … friend. Ansbor was staring at my face, as I struggled, and he hesitated, starting to speak, but he turned his face away, saying nothing. I placed a hand on his shoulder. 'I am sorry for the tensions between us. It has been harsh for all.'

'Mainly so, due to your family,' he grunted with some distress. 'I wonder what life would be like, had we served your father, and let you rot in your disfavor?'

'You would be happy, no doubt,' I told him sourly. 'But, you still would not have Cassia.'

'Cassia?' he asked, surprised. 'Oh, yes. She does not want me, no. Because she loves you,' he snickered, and then rubbed his face tiredly. 'I am sorry as well. Will you marry her?'

'Cassia?' I said. 'I do not know, Ansbor. I hope she will be far from here soon. It is such a distant dream, Ansbor.' He was nodding his head, anger playing on his face, cold, clammy sweat pouring on to his face. He pointed at the legionnaires leaving the temple, and I glanced at their receding backs. A woman was in the doorway, her head swathed and holding a baby, and one of the legionnaires bent to kiss her. The baby stared at the temple, and then at me. It, she or he, held my eyes.

I stopped.

Drusus was a father as well.

He also kissed their mother like that. His wife, Antonia, would be a plaything to Augustus's whims when he died. Their children would lose their father, their fate tied to the mother. Or the mother would lose the children? They might be separated. I had lost Lif. Now, due to Lif, his children would lose Drusus. The child chortled and smiled, as the father, about to go to war, took her to his arms, a husband who should not be married by laws of the army, and then they walked off.

I would, could regain Lif. I would orphan Drusus's children, let his wife and family fly with fates. I would likely lose Cassia, a woman who was brave and lovely. A woman I cared for. Loved. So much it hurt. I would lose Fulcher and Ansbor. I shuddered as the baby disappeared.

I shook my head.

Lif. I am sorry. I could not do it.

'Let us go in, then,' Ansbor said, and stepped aside, wondering at me, seeing the tears inside the helmet.

'No,' I told him heavily. 'I cannot.'

He looked exasperated. 'It is too late, Hraban. You have killed this night.'

'I will pay,' I told him. 'Ansbor, I … '

'Come, at least he must be paid,' he encouraged.

'You said you paid him?'

'I could not afford to pay fully,' he insisted. I took a step forward then another, and stopped at the door; it was ajar, and a man was sitting in a chair, swathed with white robes and a cowl. I pushed at the door, and the figure moved. It was huge, the robes stretched over the torso. Something occurred to me, and I turned to Ansbor, who was standing right behind me. 'Where is your sword?'

He opened his mouth, instinctively groping for the huge sword of Leuthard. But, it was not there. Only the legionnaire one.

'I have it, Hraban,' said the man sitting in the room, and I flashed a look his way as he pushed back his cowl. The hand was scabbed and covered with rock-like scars. The face was the brutal, scarred face of Leuthard. Bricius's lean face appeared out of the dark corner, holding a bow, and he had some men of the Red Finger with him. And Cornix.

Gods, but Antius had made his move.

I pulled at Nightbright, hoping to sprint to safety, and then Ansbor pushed me into the room, and I fell on my belly on the feet of Leuthard, who now held his old sword. Ansbor walked in, joining the men who had been our enemies, and who were now his allies. He locked the door with a bar.

I tried to get up, but Bricius stepped on my hand with a hiss of pleasure, and they grabbed my face and arms in a vice-like grip, as Leuthard chuckled and laid his blade on my neck. Ansbor did not smile but looked away. Bricius grinned over me. 'You killed my men, Hraban. My cousin. Then, you took my benefactor, Hunfrid. When Maroboodus sent us north to slay the young Cherusci—'

'Armin?' I hissed, as I gazed around the room. Cornix was lounging in the back of the room, his burned face oddly complacent.

Leuthard grunted with bear-like anger, and Bricius went quiet. The bald man glared at me, his animal-like eyes glittering in the dark, his bald head sweaty. He took a deep breath. 'Guthbert. You killed my brother, Hraban. You nearly killed me. It was cleverly done.'

'I did, wolfman,' I told him bitterly. 'And he died well, slayer of men rather than of women.'

He chuckled. 'Ah, the Batavi have been telling you stories, Hraban. Oh, yes, they are all true. I am Lok's spawn, like Odo is. Hati's brood, I am that. Yet I serve chaos, and your father sows it, and so I serve him before my father god, Hraban. I was called a beast, with the Batavi. And I am that. I feed on the weak, Hraban, not women. Most all are weak next to me, no matter their sex and age. I fed on your friend when I found her there. I took her in many ways, Hraban, and then one final way. She fought, and the two fools tried to help her, but it was useless. She was weak, like you are. I will feed on you. I will eat you, Hraban, here, after they have broken your bones, and taken your tongue.' He smiled at me as he gazed at Ansbor. 'Perhaps your friend here will join the feast? I promised to spare the woman he cares for in return for this pleasure, but there is no need for him to go hungry. He looks like he is able to swallow a war band's rations of meat in one seating.'

Ansbor said nothing, but shook his head, his face white and suffering, terrified and alone amongst the beasts surrounding him, and I cursed him softly. 'For a woman who cares nothing for you, Ansbor? This is how you think you will get her?'

Bricius chuckled as he pulled a knife, grabbing my face painfully. He leaned on me, his sinewy face close, as he ripped the helmet off and dropped it to the ground. 'Put it out, the flabby tongue, boy, and do not make me cut it out through your lips, though that would please me just fine.'

I spat at him, and gazed at Leuthard. 'So, you serve my father still?'

'Yes,' he said happily. 'I do.'

'By killing Armin? What and why are you—'

He waved Bricius back as he stared at me. 'You upset his plans. He is nearly half feebler as he was before the war. He has some thousand truly loyal, trained men, Roman-like in their ways, but the chiefs are hoping to break off him, and he has to fight the ones who would do so. Before you burned his hall, Hraban, chasing him out of Hard Hill like a fugitive, he had the ears and spears of the tribes. Over ten thousand men. Now, only half.'

'At least I achieved that.'

'Yes, you did,' Leuthard smiled brutally. 'Sigimer and Armin are the ones the rest listen to now. So, I shall go, and kill the young bastard.'

'You will get nowhere near him,' I spat.

'I will go with the Romans,' he said huskily, glancing at Cornix, 'and they will set me on his tail. I will find him. I have a hunch Armin will find the Romans, you see. But, he won't win. He will run. And I will lope after him in the dark.'

'And Antius set you on my trail as well,' I snickered. 'A coward's way of fighting me, Leuthard. Guthbert would not enjoy this.'

'Guthbert and I did respect each other, even if we disagreed on many things,' he smiled. 'But, he is not here to discuss this issue. It is pure luck I am here with you, boy. I was to come here and meet with Antius, so I could slay Armin after the Thing. Armin, the bastard, fled that night. So. I will go with the army. It will be hard. But your father asked me to do another deed, one I thought I would achieve somewhere out there. But, you are here.'

'Bastard,' I hissed.

'He wants to make sure you have gone to Hades. No matter quickly, or slowly, but dead as a stone, that is how he likes to think about you. He preferred you would suffer, though. I reckon I can serve my lord well in that by telling you I shall savage the baby after Armin is dead, for we just found out where your girl is. I shall hold her in my hands, rip her screaming head off, and eat her steaming flesh. This, I promise, and Odo and you both be damned. The god, Lok, laughs, no matter if his plans are

435

dashed for now. I shall laugh! I'll take the skull, Hraban, and give it to your father. His deserves to see his granddaughter, does he not?'

I struggled, of course. Ansbor had told him about Lif. I gazed at my friend, who shook his head in weak denial.

Bricius pushed my head to the floor while the men sat on me, and I cried and cursed as they ripped out Leuthard's mail off my torso, beating me half senseless as they did. I was bleeding from my nose, my face was puffy and raw, as they dragged me on the floor, and then Leuthard placed his heavy knee on my neck, grinning at me. 'Let Drusus be victorious, so Maroboodus will beat him next year, and let us celebrate both their victories today with a feast.' He grinned at Ansbor, who took a reluctant step towards the door, his face glistening with fear as he stared at me. Leuthard stepped on my left hand and a finger broke. I howled as he crouched to take a hold of it, a wicked grimace on his face. It was likely the shadows and the oil lamp flickering sadly, but I thought his face was changing into darker shade, an unhuman one with subtle bestiality, his eyes small and cruel, and his bloodlust was obvious by a nervous twist of his face, his teeth shimmering in the shadowy room.

Bricius stabbed the dagger between my teeth, wounding my lip, twisting my mouth open, and another man was fishing for my tongue. My legs were thrumming the floor in pain, and I prayed to Woden, but there was no dance of savagery, no help coming from divine lords, only a waiting Valkyrie after I died.

Woden had let me down.

But, someone had once promised me help, three times in the hour of my need, and so it was I received that help for the second time.

Outside of the door, Drusus was bellowing orders, and the slap of hobnails striking the wooden floor could be heard as the Romans approached. Bricius's head shot up in astonishment, Leuthard stood up as well, his face shocked. Ansbor looked utterly lost, stammering, and the men let go of me. Cornix was swearing nastily, and he started to probe the wall, and I noticed there was a door in the shadow. Leuthard grunted, as he pulled out his sword, stepped over me, and thrust the sword through

Ansbor. My friend fell back, shocked and sorry, his face blank, as Leuthard ripped the blade out. He stepped over me, hesitating for a moment as the men rushed to the back wall, where a door was opened. He turned towards me, his face brutal as the main door shuddered under repeated kicks.

'Hraban!' Drusus was screaming. 'Hraban!'

Leuthard gazed at me. 'I'll not have this end with a simple sword thrust. I shall enjoy it. So come and save him, Hraban. Armin. Save her, your daughter. I shall meet you out there. At least you get to see her before I shall break her.' He rushed and kicked me in the face so hard, I lost a molar, and I rolled on the floor, spitting blood and mucus, holding my broken finger. He disappeared out of the door to the dark, swiftly as a hunting wolf. The world was whirling around as I crawled to Ansbor, his corpse shuddering in death throes, his chain mail ripped and bent, parts of it thrust into his flesh by the terrible sword of Leuthard. He grasped my hand, my broken finger twisted crazily to the side, and smiled, as I grimaced in pain. He spat a gout of blood as the door cracked, light shining through the splintered wood. 'I am no different from Ansigar, Hraban. No different. I was jealous of you. I have paid.'

I shook my head, feeling sorry and hating him both. 'No, Ansbor. If he kills Lif, then this death of yours will never balance the scales. Never. But, you are my friend, and we shall bury you.'

'Be good to Cassia. You always had her, I know, but I loved her,' he whimpered in terrible pain and fell to his side, his guts spilling from the wound. I cried for him, and I hated him, and so it was that Drusus, his light brown lion's eyes burning fiercely, pulled me off him.

He put his hand on my face. 'Your father's men?'

'Yes,' I said, swooning. 'That, and more. That Antius's man, Cornix, was helping them.'

He nodded carefully. 'Cassia came to me, and told me everything.'

'She did?' I asked him, and gazed over his shoulder where Fulcher and Cassia were rushing for me. The Romans gazed at the carnage. A centurion ran to the open door, yelling for men to follow him, as they took after

Leuthard. They would never reach them. Cornix would see to that, knowing the camp and passwords.

'She said she had a divine warning. She insisted to meet with me. She worried about you, and thought something terrible was going to happen. I knew she was right when she told me you came to meet me here. Invited by me. I did not invite you, so I knew your father was reaching out for you, friend,' he said. 'Thank her gods, Hraban. You will rest a while, friend, and we shall catch the bastards. Oh, we will, and we will hang them. I will nail them to the tree, like you do in your lands, and we will toast their cries together. Cornix killed the men watching you, it seems. Near a whorehouse. Did you visit a girl, Hraban, when you have Cassia there? Naughty.' He smiled, and then sobered as he looked at my hurt hand, his eyes twinkling. I shook my head in denial and opened my mouth to speak. I wanted to tell him the truth, but he shook his head, smiling wistfully. I closed it, and thanked him with a smile. 'It is best Chariovalda thinks it was so, and let us not confuse matters more, Hraban. I know you are a good man, and would have chosen right in the end. You still have time.'

'I did choose right,' I told him with misery, 'but they were here, and I was too late to save Ansbor.'

'Tell me, is Armin involved with this ...?' he asked gently.

'He is,' I said. 'As is Lif.'

Anger flashed in his eyes. 'So I was right. He has no balls for war, and tries to murder me like this. I'll teach him a thing or two.'

'Remember, Drusus, that he always has many plans,' I said.

'When I find Lif,' he told me, putting his forehead against mine, 'you will be free.' He got up and left.

Cassia leaned over me, touching a wound on my lip. I grasped her and pulled her to me. 'You are a damned fool, Marcomanni,' she told me heartily. 'A damned fool.'

'I am so happy you are not,' I said, and kissed her neck and her cheek, despite the pain.

'That old man of Tear's told me to disagree with you when you were an idiot. So I figured this was the perfect time,' she said with a smile, and I laughed painfully, for Adalfuns the Crafter had helped me once more. She kissed my nose and hugged me fiercely, until they grabbed me and carried me out of the temple. My eyes were lingering on Ansbor's cold corpse. 'We will avenge him,' Cassia said sorrowfully, and I nodded, determined not to spit with bitterness. I would keep his secret, and let him die a hero.

'Thank you for not obeying me,' I told them, and cursed my wyrd, for I would have to kill a wolf to gain Lif.

I was on Drusus's side. I had a home. And a woman.

But, I would go and fight for Lif.

CHAPTER XXX

B efore the morning's pale light, the great army started to march, their shields not covered by the greased leather sheaths, their simple gear laden in the furca swinging over their shoulders. They would need the gear, especially the dolobara, their sturdy digging tool and patera, the all-purpose cooking and eating pot.

First, the cavalry passed over the river, clattering across under a thicket of swinging spears. They were fierce Batavians, skillful Aquitani, brutally armed Thracians from a harsh, war-like land. They were men raised to slay their enemies, and these were followed by swift Cretan and even strangely attired Syrian archers, jogging steadily in their chain mail. After them, the XIX legion's first two cohorts started the campaign.

We stared at the troops, standing near the bridge. We were posted on the fort on the other side of the river, and it would take a long while before we could pass. We were silent, and I felt lonely. Ansbor had been with me all the years of my life, the last of the Bear Heads, our childhood war band. Ansigar was lost to us, having joined Odo and Gernot, Ansbor was slain by his jealousy, and Wandal lost after the battle of Castrum Luppia. I stood there with a broken finger, well set in place, my lips swollen and bloody, my tongue slashed, my ribs bruised.

Fulcher had cursed, for Bricius had escaped his clutches, and we both gave each other meaningful looks. We gazed at a forlorn bonfire still smoldering at the beach, slaves waiting around it, and we saw Ansbor's bones in the midst of charred remains of wood. A mound would be raised over it. I nodded at the bones. If Lif died, I would dig the bones out and scatter them to the dogs. I would, I swore to Woden, for I was unhappy. I gazed at Cassia, who returned the look, her eye spilling a tear as she grasped my hand. I let her and pulled her closer to me, and was strangely relieved as Ansbor was not there with his sullen eyes.

Chariovalda would be in the fort. I should beg him on my knees to be allowed to travel with them. He would say no, so I would not bother.

I had a hunch the fort would not be a slow, tired place to guard. Armin had many plans, and I remember Chariovalda explaining how much food was needed for the war. All that food was there; in the town we were to guard.

No, Armin would give me a chance to ride to help Lif.

For the moment, we waited, as nearly sixteen-thousand fighting men, with the baggage, crossed the thin bridge.

After the elite cohorts, there followed a small number of wide, strong men, immunes, pioneers, men who would make sure the forts were planned and marked when the army arrived. They would take the first arriving legionnaires, and start digging the ditches and heaping the mud for the walls. After them came more immunes, a large group of grim men with a hoard of tools and sturdy horses and mules, a force that was responsible for cutting through any obstacles in the way.

And then came the baggage train, an incredible sight.

The supplies for the XIX crossed, with hundreds of mules, as well as siege equipment broken down for easy transport and any spare tools and tents that were needed. Old Saturninus followed them with his staff and the hundred men of the Roman Cavalry of the legion, and with them came the pride of the armies, the symbol of Roman gods, the fabulous eagle. After this, the rest of the legion marched up, all carrying their furca, pilum and fort stakes, seven cohorts' worth, singing lustily in the dust, the stomp of their disciplined feet beating the bridge so hard, one would think the men wished a sudden bath. Metal glittered as the men went to war, all clad in ring or chain mail, their helmets devoid of the feathers meant for parades. Gods, they looked fierce, enough to scare anyone into a headlong flight, and again I could only wonder what Armin and the Sigambri planned to use to throw these men into turmoil and death. After this, in a similar manner, followed the six cohorts of the XVII. Then a huge force of auxilia infantry, some in near-Roman gear, some in tribal ones.

The stream of men continued.

XVIII and V Alaudae crossed, bent on revenge. Then, I Germania. Finally, after hours of staring at the marching men, we were hungry and tired, sitting down, and slaves were heaping mud and dirt on Ansbor's mound, steam still rising through the earth. Happily, for us, the last elements of the army crossed, some more Aquitani infantry, even more light Thracian and Pannonian cavalry, and the undisciplined Frisian infantry. A harried-looking group of engineers had been making sure the bridge structure was not going to break, and they congratulated each other heartily.

When the men of the army were over and gone, the world seemed empty, and we got up to cross the bridge.

I rubbed my aching neck muscles, and turned to regard the harbor as we crossed the bridge. Two heavily armored Batavi followed us, and Fulcher grunted. Chariovalda had taken precautions, and we were closely watched. In the harbor, ships were preparing, some already being rowed up stream for the Luppia River. They were shallow barges, armed with ballistae, and they had archers and light infantry on them, ready to keep the Sigambri at bay on the right bank, while the Roman fist crushed the scattered smaller tribes on the left flank. I shook my head. If the Cherusci were truly being kept busy by the far away Semnones and the Chauci, they had no hope. If Armin was out there, leading with Sigimer and some few Cherusci, it would make no difference. I had failed him. He would know this. Woden and gentle Siff, I prayed and hoped to save Lif.

On the other side, the rough fort, with its unpolished walls and wooden towers, rose, smelling of fresh timber and mud. I saw Chariovalda lingering outside the gates. He hefted the Head Taker in his hands, weighing it, and as he noticed me, he stiffened. I dismounted and walked to him, and went to my knee.

He threw the sword to my feet. He eyed me irascibly as he sat there, and I picked up the splendid blade. The ring and the blade, together again.

Cassia called it the Winter Sword. As I held it, I felt it yearn for blood. I'd feed it. I looked up at Chariovalda, and he held my eyes. He spoke softly. 'The two men were found by the whorehouse yesterday. Yet they were no lax men, who would get into trouble over whores. Nor would Cornix surprise them. They were my slaves, my trusted men. One was possibly my son, for I was sloppy with his mother once.'

I nodded and groaned.

'Drusus still trusts you, but should I?' he asked swiftly, grapping Wolf's Tear, the mighty spear from a rider.

I shook my head at his words. His bastard son. I pointed towards east. 'I made up my mind yesterday. I shall serve Drusus. I shall do so in the future. My girl is out there. Any deal I had with Armin is void now. I can only fight for her, and there are no schemes left. I will fight Armin for Lif and for Drusus. I shall not deny the deaths of your men, however. Lif was all I thought about, then.'

He nodded, looking disgusted, 'So that is what Armin did. He has your daughter. Well, I did not love the boy. He was stupid, and hated me for denying him. I was ever wary of him, for he was devious and treacherous. I forgive you his death, but I won't forget it. I shall ever be careful with you. For that, I cannot take you with me, though. Nothing has changed. You shall not ride out there. Drusus and I will find Armin, boy, and get your daughter from him.' He spurred his horse. 'You will serve here, under guard, Hraban, and you will trust us to do our best for her. There is nothing we can promise, of course. And keep the sword safe. I think it is cursed. Any man who held it, since your father returned, has lost something. It has a bad history. Take your spear as well, now that you know your side.' He threw the mighty spear my way, and I grabbed at it from the air, my Roman chain mail clinking as my sore hand failed at catching it. I picked it up.

'What did my father lose?' I asked him sourly.

'His sons,' he snorted, and rode away, laughing. 'I lost a bastard, but you took the right bastard.'

I stood and stared after him, as first smoke pillars sprang up to the sky over the embattled horizon. Villages were burning; Rome was purging the Usipetes out of the way and marched for the Bructeri. Gods were watching. The war was on, and somewhere out there, the tribesmen were preparing to die for their freedom and families. The wolf Leuthard and the bastard Odo were hunting for Lif.

There were three cohorts of XVII legions left in Castra Vetera, guarding the river and the harbor with the warehouses, and one, the glorious, elite First Cohort manned our shabby fort on the Germani side. The legion's primus pilus, the first centurion, was in overall command of the new fort, camp praefectus commanded at Castra Vetera. No other battle-hardened officers were to be seen, only a junior tribune who was stomping about, a young, scared man. He tried to guide the centurion once, who just ignored him. The tribune turned into a sullen, if harmless beast, avoiding any further loss of face.

Fulcher and I tried to sort out where we should go, until a centurion pulled at us. He grinned at us. 'Don't look so crushed, boys. Yes, the lot marching out there gets the loot, the prisoners, and some get a spear in the gut. We get to make love to their wives while they are gone. Come on, and find your decurion, the bastard who is going to order you lot about. Batavi? Yes. Good. There are some Thracians, and they do not get along well with the Batavi, so steer clear of the buggers.'

We found the riders standing in serried ranks around two hulking riders, all in glittering chain mail. They turned to look at us as we came closer. I hoisted an oval shield and wore a legionnaire chain mail, my attic helmet with god's symbols, Balderich's ancient spear, and two swords. Our decurion, a man with a plaited beard and a toothless smile, gawked at us. 'Can you carry all that, lad?' They laughed merrily at us, but I was in no mood for such humor, and glowered at him.

I gazed at the men I was supposed to serve with. The two turmae had some fifty men, Batavi of all ages, and the men looked at us with mirth. Near us were some twenty men of the Thracian cavalry. Heavy men with scarred faces, all with dark armor, tall arrows and recurved bows, short, stubby spears, and nasty axes, standing under a white snake flag.

The officer swallowed his happy mood, and sneered at us. 'In this army, you do not come and go as you please. You come on time. If I ask you to take a shit standing on saddle, you do that. I don't care if you are the best friends with the lords. Here, you are as useless as a pointless spear, if you are not present,' he growled, and men laughed at us. 'And what is the woman doing here? You bring your whores to war? Or is she your sister, taking care of you?'

'She is a healer,' I told him coldly, staring at his eyes. He nodded sourly, swallowing his next comment. Healers were not to be spat on. 'And we were late thanks to Chariovalda, who had words with us.'

'And his words are to keep an eye on you, and so we shall. Get your young bones in line with the others, and you will be handing over the food to all the men this evening. Not to mention cooking it, as we shall give our women a well-deserved rest! From cooking that is!' he barked, and we looked indignant.

'I hope he knows we cannot cook for so many. They might go hungry,' Fulcher whispered. 'I can only roast meat.'

'I'll shit on the stew,' I said, and he grinned, despite the fact I was half serious. I was in a foul mood, stuck in a muddy fort, and outside, things were taking place that would, and could, break me.

The decurion gestured around the new fort, which smelled of freshly cut wood and overturned, rich mud. 'This fort is held by one cohort of legionnaires. We are to scout the Usipetes lands around us for any sign of the poor, snaggle-toothed thieves, and there will be many Ubii going through here with supplies for the army. We,' he pointed to the other decurion, the Thracian one, 'shall have one alae out there every day. Stay alert, and do not let the enemy surprise you. If you see anyone skulking in those woods, get them here alive, and we shall question them properly.'

I glanced around the wooded hill to the north. They were a mix of wild, light woods of low hanging alder trees and thicker copses of deep green firs. Some small pastures of barley peaked through the greenery, but beyond the borderlands, there would be leagues and long leagues of fabulously rich land, with plenty of places to hide in.

The blond decurion waited until my head turned back to him, and then he was glowering at us. He continued, irritable. 'The Usipetes own these lands, but the damned Sigambri are a danger. Them, and the riders of the Tencteri, live mostly south of the river. They might try to cross. Ubii are making advances to keep them occupied, but we do not know where they are currently. Before the war started, we got reports that there were the usual number of warriors in the Sigambri villages, so they likely thought we would go for them, not the Usipetes and the Bructeri,' the decurion told us. 'Keep-an-eye-out! This is no idle posting.' He dismissed the turmae, and started to figure out specific orders, guard duties, and patrols. He stopped us and pointed at the kitchen area, where pots and pans were hanging. 'Cook. Make it good.'

So we cooked for that one evening, Cassia made the gruel taste like a scorched fir tree, I overbaked the bread in a small oven, many times, leaving the loaves charred lumps not fit for the pigs, but that was not true, for some pigs ended up eating them. We were relieved of the task quickly enough, the decurion humbled. After the evening meal, Fulcher was to be on guard duty, the change of watch announced by a tuba in the fort. Cavalry rode around the surrounding countryside at regular times, throughout the night and day, and so he fetched his horse, unhappy, wordless.

I was left with Cassia.

We sat in the tent, and I gazed at her. Her dark hair was long and thick, her face full of emotion, and her eyes alive with quick wit, as she was thinking deep thoughts and stitching her tunic. I knew she was a woman worth noticing. She had followed us through storms and good times. She had helped deliver my baby. She had healed my friends, when she could have gone home. I had cared for Ishild, when we were children. I had lusted for Ermendrud, for she had been my first. I had hopelessly loved my enemy, Shayla, and lost her before I truly knew her.

But, I did know Cassia. She was more than any woman in my life, and she was also my friend.

She challenged me, advised me, saved me, and laughed at, and with, me, and I desired her, I decided, often so badly my head hurt, and only the pain over Lif and Ansbor's sullen eyes had stopped me from doing something.

Ansbor?

Wyrd.

The customs of our people screamed at me, still, even after losing my fame and respect of our tribes. One must be chaste. One must honor the family. But, I was a Roman then, at least for then. I got up, put my hand around her, and pulled her to me, enduring her shocked face. 'I am going for Lif. I have to brave Odo and the prophecy, and I have my father to slay. I might lose Drusus, and his respect, like I might have lost Chariovalda's. I cannot promise you safety. But, you know this.'

'I ...' she began and swallowed. 'I ask for commitment. To share these things. I will die one day, Hraban, but I care nothing for that, if my life has meaning. It has been so, this past year.'

'You were rich,' I smirked at her, her enticing eyes warm to look at. 'You had a husband to be.'

'He was fat as grease,' she said, and blushed as she ran her finger over my chest. 'I did not desire him. Only my father did, for he was wealthy and powerful, and my father understood only those qualities.'

'Ansbor stood between us, and my sorrow did as well,' I told her, as I leaned to kiss her neck, making her shiver as she grasped my shoulders. 'Now, he is gone, and I shall ... mourn him. But, he asked to keep you safe. I will not, for I will love you, and that is perilous.'

'I know, Lord Hraban,' she said. Her face was near me in the shadowy tent, her eyes round and tear filled, and I kissed the tears away, her cheeks, her thin, fine eyebrows, her delicate ears, and then her neck again, for it was smooth, smelled good, and she reacted with a soft moan, which I enjoyed. I kissed her lips, the painful cuts on mine opening, but we did not care as we devoured each other, entwining our bodies together.

'It is hard to see how it will end,' I mumbled, and she hugged me, her leg around mine.

'I will be there when it does,' she said, with heated blush rising on her cheeks. She opened a fibula holding her tunic up, and I helped her. She did not stop me as I undressed her, revealing her high breasts and perfect, pink nipples, which I promptly kissed, massaging her bared sides as she shed her garments. Soon, we were touching each other desperately, kissing urgently, and what her hands were doing with my manhood made me a very happy man.

Ansbor's face came fleetingly to my mind, the threat to Lif haunted me, but she was my escape that night, and I shared love with her hungrily. The urgency melted away after a while, and what followed were peaceful thrills and gentle pleasure in a Roman fort ready for war. It was love, and I was a happy bastard that night. Despite the god who usually ignored my prayers out of battle, I begged to Woden she would survive the times that would be full of sorrow and danger. I had to escape the fort, and leave her behind. While she slept, I thought of ways to leave.

I hoped Drusus would forgive me. Again.

CHAPTER XXXI

Over the next few days, ships rowed downriver and others came back, carrying news and sad slaves, mostly women, some men, quite a few children. I was not allowed on the cavalry scout missions, being relegated to wall guarding duty. From the rough wall, I gazed at the slave wagons rumbling in, the uncouth riders and the rough mercenaries guarding the cages, looking exhausted as they guided their horses our way. I glanced at some of the Batavi, who were watching the river and, of course, watching me at the same time and cursed them. Cassia and I took fierce comfort in each other every night, giving me relief from the pain and fear over Lif, but Leuthard's face haunted me all the long days.

Around us, the men of the XVII gossiped, having received news from the drivers of the slave wagons. I eavesdropped on their discussion, and we all yearned for news.

There was little to tell. The Germani were slow to war against Rome.

Had I been wrong? Was Armin out there, cursing his reluctant allies, and there was no threat to the forts we held?

There had been very few skirmishes, and then mainly with some probing cavalry, but the Bructeri had sortied some ten ships to fight on the river. There had been losses and blood on the water, as the Roman Navy had torn into them. Mostly the riders of the army had found few enemies along the river, but many empty Bructeri and Marsi villages.

After chasing the Bructeri ships away, the marines had raided the other side of Luppia. The nearest villages were alight almost the entire length of the Luppia, from Castra Vetera to the wild hills near the vast, rich Cherusci lands. The legions had already built a fort forty Roman miles away from us, and another was begun sixty miles away, with the rest of the XVII split amongst them. They were built on dead Bructeri and Marsi settlements, just to make a point.

The Batavi had found Bructeri and Marsi retreating north, thin streams of non-combatants, mostly old people, with the cattle and spare horses, and the legions had started to march after them, leaving smoke and fire behind them, and the clanking of slaver chains. Apparently, Drusus wanted to capture the elders and the families, thinking the warriors would defend them. It would be a ruthless war. Fulcher was deep in his thoughts, and I started to wonder if I should ask him to leave the army, and try to reach Armin. He was allowed outside, after all. I cursed my lot, praying as I sweated on the walls.

On the fourth day, some grim slavers brought in new slaves.

I walked outside one such cage, bored, gazing at the rare enclosure, for it was holding warriors. Fulcher was with me. 'How is it out there?' I asked him, as we looked at the men in the cages. 'Does the decurion keep an eye on you?'

He shrugged. 'The Decurion? He eats, shits, and walks his horse around us. He keeps an eye on me as well, at least when he can. I might be able to slip away, but I don't have a good horse. On purpose, of course. It is eerie out there,' he said. 'There are no tracks that we can see. It is like time stands still. Perhaps they have all gone east, and will die like heroes in some nasty battle. All the Usipetes villages are empty, devoid of life.'

'I will have to do something soon, Fulcher,' I said. 'Will you see to it she is safe, if you survive? Cassia.'

'I'll escort her to safety,' he said, with a small smile. 'Yes, of course. Perhaps she will like my wife, and we can help each other until we find a home. I likely do not have one where your father now rules.'

I placed a hand on his shoulder. 'Get her wealth back, serve her, get your wife and daughter, and sort it out, like I will sort out things with Leuthard and Armin. Odo as well.'

450

He nodded, his eyes moist. 'I will, lord. I will get them, and serve her. Ansbor? I know you are hiding something. I told you not turn your back on him. I told you to deal with it. Many times.'

I shook my head. 'He would be alive, if I had. And I did turn my back on him. Let us not speak about it.'

'Let it be some way down the road, Hraban,' he said, 'when we can mourn all the terrible choices thrust on us.'

'This shitty war will be terrible and quick, it seems,' I rumbled. 'Armin is not acting like I thought he would. He is not fighting, but running. I overestimated him.'

But, I had not.

We walked around the rest of the cages. There were sad children and a few hungry women, then another cage full of younger men. Some were lightly wounded. After I had passed it, looking at the women and crying children, a man said something to another, and so I stopped, and returned. I stood in front of the cage, looking at the man who avoided my stare. I remembered him from somewhere. He was a strong man, well-muscled, with a high forehead, and then it struck me. He had been one of the men standing with Sigimer and Armin the day of the great Thing. He had a red hair, and had taken the standard off Armin when the young lord spoke with me.

He was a Cherusci.

I stared at him for a time, shocked at my discovery. His face hardened, and he spat in my face. 'Oath Breaker. Roman shit rooting pig.' I nodded at him furiously and walked briskly to the praetorium of the camp. After being informed by a slave the primus pilus of the XVII was in the stable, I marched there. He was not there. A stable hand thought he saw him enter the latrines.

And so, I went in as well.

The stable had smelled better. The stink of all the varieties of farts and multiple forms of excrement, sauced with the whiff of rancid piss, wafted thickly in the air, as I walked in. Amidst some legionnaires, sat a grizzled man of fifty years, with a piercing, sharp nose and leathery skin, bald as an egg. I stared at him, unsure how to break his peace. He tried to ignore me, until he could not and sighed, looking at me with pleading eyes. 'What? You have to deprive this joy from me? Or is it that you think this a whorehouse, and wish to roger me? Can I wipe my ass first, or do you prefer your road a bit rocky? Huh?' he asked, and the men around us laughed raucously.

'No, sir, I—'

He waved me down. 'Sit down then. I am getting neck aches for staring up at you. Too tall, I always said of the Germani before a tussle. Easy to cut down as trees.'

'I have no need to sit down,' I told him somberly. 'Look—'

He pointed the hole next to him, resolutely. 'Sit the shit down. What is it about you people that make this so hard? Sit down and do it, for Juppiter's sakes, and tell your bowels to relax,' he growled at me, and the legionnaires laughed again.

'Sir, I—' I begged.

'I will not speak with you, unless you do it. Drop them. I realize that taking pants down is harder than an undergarment for us Romans, but seriously, do it,' he grunted at me.

I sighed, and did as I was told. I sat there with my pants on my knees, as the centurion, primus pilus of the whole legion explained to me why shitting is so very important for a soldier. 'Take one too early in the day, it breaks the routines. Too late, it leaves you hungry,' he claimed. It was all about intelligent resource management. I sat there until I understood he would never quit, and so I pretended to squeeze out a sizable turd, and he applauded me happily. He gave me some further instruction on how to sit more comfortably, and when I did not heed it, brooding at him, he snorted. 'He looks like a woman when he crosses his legs, that is all I am saying,' sneered the old man, and the bastards around us agreed heartily. I moved my legs apart with a thump.

I cursed, and tried once more as he eyed me, finally happy. 'Sir, I noted something about the prisoners.'

'The slave auctions are at the end of the campaign, lad. If she was pretty, you just have to take your chances,' he declared in the midst of exertions and relief. 'Though I hear you are having some with the healer woman.'

'No, there is a man ...' I said, and the legionnaires laughed raucously.

'Same thing, though I do not want to know more, boy. Men or goats, it's all the same to me. Live, and let live!' he winked at me lecherously.

'The man is a Cherusci. A member of Sigimer's household,' I said, with no patience, and a simple threat of violence thrumming in my voice. 'We know Armin is out there, and now a man of his is here.'

The primus pilus stared at me for a while.

'Perhaps he changed tribes?' he asked while getting up, grabbing one wooden handled sponge and wiping his ass with it.

'It is possible. Though if he is with the Cherusci, you should question him. He might know about their plans, if it is Armin who leads them.'

'Here, take it. Use it.' He handed over the sponge, and I cursed the smirking legionnaires, as I stood up, unhappy.

'They seen balls before, use it. Then we go,' he urged, and I did, flinching. He smiled wistfully. 'That cured you, young fool. Some advice though, usually we dip them in water before reusing them. That was quite disgusting,' he grimaced, as we exited. It was true I was no longer averse to entering Roman toilets. I was determined to burn them down, if I found one unguarded.

'Go to the cages with the guard,' he told me, and nodded at two men to follow me, 'and bring him to me.'

The young man was fetched, and his eyes pierced my soul with defiance as the legionnaires clamped irons on his legs and wrists and dragged him to the tent indicated by the primus pilus. What he endured there, I will never know, though I can still hear his screams today in my nightmares. But, what I wanted was to speak with him privately, and so I prayed he would survive the ordeal. I waited outside, fidgeting, feeling nauseous, thinking about Cassia, Ishild, and Ansbor. A large legionnaire came out, sweat running down his bared chest and bloody smear on his knuckles. Next, a weasel faced auxiliary with thongs and knives exited, looking pale, and he was followed by the primus pilus, who seemed unconcerned about the whole affair, eating an apple.

He noticed me and nodded. 'He is serving Sigimer. It seems that while the Cherusci have few men to spare for this war, they sent a general, as suspected. He tried to hit his head on a spike to kill himself after I asked who this commander is. Can you imagine it? He didn't succeed, but anyway, I worry. Such a fanatic.' He looked uncertain, as he gestured at the tent. 'Few men do that unless they fear they will reveal something important. I will talk with him tomorrow.'

'How did they capture him?' I asked.

'I do not know,' he mused. 'Slavers take them where they can.' He turned to me. 'They say you cannot be trusted. Chariovalda told us to look out for you.'

'I have a reputation,' I told him sourly. 'And something happened the night before the army marched.'

'That whorehouse business? I heard of it. Trouble with a woman? Eh?' he asked, bemused, finishing the apple. 'You were involved? A woman?'

'A small one,' I told him unhappily, not willing to tell him of Lif.

'Happens to the best of us sometimes. I once killed a man for a small woman; I do like them petite.' He nodded, and I cursed him under my breath. 'Well, you did well here today. Tomorrow, I'll find out what he is hiding, and if it is good, then I'll send men out with this information to our young god, Drusus. It might be nothing, but he bothers me, so we will ask him arduously. Well done, lad,' he said, and went off towards the principia.

That afternoon, I stood on the wall again, impatient and waiting for the evening. All was peaceful, the banks of the river were as silent as grave mounds, and the grass was hissing in a breeze. The wooded hills revealed nothing of the plans of Armin, the man the Cherusci prisoner had tried to cover for. But, this man knew them, and he would tell me where to find Armin, and what his plans were. He would, or he would suffer pains he had never known before.

After I was relieved of duty, I went to our tent, and brought Cassia some food. She was tired and cramped, for she had been healing men most of the day, and the hurts were increasing. The fort was situated in a wet patch of land, the air unhealthy, and mosquitoes carried fever and diseases. The sick tents were already half full. We did not speak, but we ate and made love, and I thanked gods for her as I kissed her firm, beautiful belly, then her thighs, and made life very good for her after that. That night, I awoke next to Cassia, who murmured something in her sleep, grasping at me painfully. She clutched my arm, her nails making white scratches on the skin, and I removed her claws with a brief grin, my hurt finger throbbing painfully. She looked petulant as she was left there, her breasts bared, and I resisted a very basic urge to climb back on and get close to her warmth, but I had a mission.

I dressed in my Roman chain armor, missing the armor Leuthard had taken back, girted the Head Taker on, hanging Nightbright on my other hip, and grabbed my spear. I strapped on my caligae, and pulled at my belt, with its cingulum clinking softly. I pulled out the heavy cape, smelling of lanolin oil, and considered my helmet and shield, and grabbed them, too, and my spear. I crouched on the far wall of the tent, lifting the side gently with my spear, popping my head under the rim to stare around the night. Nothing. The men who were watching us were looking at the door. I might even escape the fort, I grinned, but I needed a horse. I decided to take care of that problem later. First, I had to speak to the prisoner. I gazed as Cassia fondly, bidding her farewell, and dodged outside.

I walked the night, and thought about the uncanny, silent hills, and of the embattled Cherusci, the silent Sigambri, Varnis, Baetrix and Maelo, chiefs who had been fighting Rome for decades, now supposedly surprised and stuck on the wrong side of the river. I thought of the Germani, who would never lay down their spears easily, and felt uneasy at the memory of Armin's eyes. His eyes had not flinched before Drusus. He had travelled these lands all that spring, likely. Tudrus the Old had seen him with the Sigambri. Had he not found Hands and Lif with the Sigambri? He had planned, schemed, and now there were Cherusci at the fort, guarding the grain. I felt a tingle of warning, and thought I had not overestimated Armin after all.

Fulcher appeared out of the dark and grunted, startling me. He was fully dressed and armored and ready. I took a deep breath and calmed myself. 'I asked if you would take care of Cassia.'

'I said I will, if I survive,' he said dourly. 'I am coming along. You know why. She is a healer. They will fight for her here, and she is safe.'

'Fine,' I told him.

'Where are we going?' he asked.

'To see a prisoner,' I said grimly.

'I heard about that, yes,' he said, as he stomped along. 'Cherusci?'

'Yes, and he will tell me where Armin is,' I confirmed. 'And what the bastard is planning.'

A guard near the praetorium challenged us, and I raised my hand. 'The mother of flies!' I answered, not stopping as I walked towards the prison tent, chuckling at the passphrase of the day the tessarius of the first cohort had delivered to our decurion that morning. Evidently, the primus pilus did not appreciate the various winged insects of our homeland. The guard on the door of the tent stiffened with surprise, his eyes red rimmed, but he, too, challenged us, and nodded suspiciously when I declared that I would go in on the command of the primus pilus. 'Fine, but keep it down. Men are sleeping around us.'

'He up?' I asked before dodging in.

'He is praying or cursing, not sure which,' the guard told me, scratching at lice.

I went in.

The man was lying in a heap, his arms manacled behind his back, his foot in a strange angle. He was conscious, only by a thread, his head bleeding from his unsuccessful suicide attempt. His fingers had been mangled, and two had been skinned. I clucked my tongue at Fulcher who fetched water, and I poured it on the prisoner's face, startling him in to a seated position. I let him drink the rest of the water. When he opened his eyes, he shuddered and fell away from me.

He croaked. 'Away, traitor!'

I walked around him, the words clutching painfully in my breast. 'I? You know nothing of my past and choices, but I shall not bother to explain.' He spat, defiant. I glared at him. 'Just like the Romans made you squeal today, I can as well.'

He laughed and then grimaced at me. 'I'll suffer. I surely will suffer. But, I shall not betray my—'

'Armin,' I said, as I crouched next to him. I placed a finger on a wound in his shoulder, and he flinched. 'I tried to help Armin, you know. What he asked was too much, even for an Oath Breaker.'

'Do what you must,' he hissed.

'Where is Armin?' I asked him, and pressed the finger into the gaping wound. He flinched, and his mouth opened in a shriek of pain as he fell away from me.

'He is where Drusus is,' he told me painfully.

'Is there a baby with him, a bounty hunter named Hands? Siegfried?' I asked.

His eyes burned at me. 'He has your daughter. He is keeping her safe, and near him. And you shall not have her. You will not leave here alive. It is too late,' he said, and I frowned.

'Too late?' I asked with a low voice.

'Die, Hraban the Traitor,' he snickered. I slapped him down, and he shrieked. I got up.

The guard came in. 'There will be none of that, do you hear? I told you, I told the slaver—'

I lifted my hand. 'A slaver was here?'

'He belongs to the slaver, so he has a right to see his merchandise, no? They spoke at length,' the guard told me defensively.

I turned to the prisoner. 'You are a noble, no?'

'Just a warrior,' he sneered. 'Simple cow herder.'

I shook my head. 'No, you are a noble. A leader of men. Cherusci men. The other prisoners are Cherusci as well. Big and strong, some dozen? And the sad women are not. What about the slavers?'

'What?' he asked me, with a quiver in his voice.

'You are no prisoners, nor slaves, are you?' I asked him with rising anger. 'You are bloody infiltrators, guards and all. You were to lead them, but gave the slaver instructions on what to do, did you not?'

'No!' he said empathetically, but I turned, my mind whirling.

'Where is the slaver?' I asked the guard.

'I don't know. Sleeping near the wagons?' he answered.

The young man just pursed his lips tighter, but could not help grinning at me. 'It is too late. I shall see you soon.' His eyes glowed with a gleeful light.

I kicked him in his face, the guard yelped at me, but I growled him out of my way and ran out.

'Fulcher, go and wake the decurions and the turmae, arouse the camp!' I said, as I ran through the few barracks and rows of tents for the wall.

'If they are in the camp, the Cherusci, should we not go to the cages?' he shouted after me.

'They cannot take the camp alone! But, they can open the gates!' I yelled. 'Hurry!'

In the deep night, I saw the eastern gate, and for a second, I saw a man holding a torch high in the air, and then waving it for a few times, before the torch went out. I rushed forward, cursing. I was out of breath when I climbed up the rampart, and a young man of the first cohort was shivering there, with an over large helmet. It was the elite cohort, but they had their recruits as well. I checked the door to the gatehouse for signs of the torchbearer, but there was nothing.

'Halt! Passphrase!' he said, far too late, as I was standing next to him.

'Whore mother of all the flies, out of my way!' I said, and pushed through him, and he was sputtering when a centurion making rounds ran up.

'And screw the wasps as well,' he said, finishing the passphrase. 'What are you doing?' the youngster blurted as the centurion scowled at me.

I remembered the silence of the hills the day before. No animals out there, no birds singing in the verdant trees. That would be so when there is danger close, and nothing is more dangerous than a man. And how many hidden men would it take to silence a whole wood? I looked over the darkness from the ramparts, and cursed the torches that had half blinded me. I silenced the two men behind me, the centurion now with a gladius in his hand. He pulled at my cloak, and I tore it out of his grip. 'Shut the hell up!' I hissed at them, and they obeyed in stupefied silence. 'Was there a man here just now?'

'Yes,' said the soldier. 'A Germani. Went to the gatehouse. Took a torch. Knew the passphrase.'

'The prisoner has heard it all day, as the guard keeps asking it. Gods,' I said breathlessly, as I rushed for the gatehouse door of the wall. I pushed the door; it did not budge. I rushed back to the wall. A horse whinnied in the darkness, and there was a dull thump. I was not sure, but there was a cut off scream. The horsemen riding night guard around the camp should be out there.

'A torch! Give me one!' I commanded.

'Just who do you think—' the centurion started, but the young man rushed over to light a torch and handed it over to me. I took it, held my breath, and slung the burning branch with all my might from the wall, over the agger and the fossa, and landed with a crackle of sparks.

Frozen, bearded figures were revealed in the sudden pale light. They were a veritable horde of men staring up at me like a pack of feral, black wolves. They were lightly armed, with framae spears and cudgels; few had cumbersome shields, making slow progress in order not to alert the sleeping fort. Startled, some dodged out of the light, most stayed in it, looking up, realization striking them that they had to do something.

The Usipetes had arrived.

The centurion stared at them in disbelief, and I screamed from the top of my voice, 'Sound the alarm! Germani! Alarm!' I braced my shield, as I saw hundreds of shadows rush forward in the darkness, skittering and shoving each other, and dropping down to the fossa, the ditch, to clamber up the agger. A slingshot whipped past my head with a sickening, thrumming noise. I cursed and hesitated. This was an opportunity to leave the fort, but Cassia was in the camp.

The Usipetes were to take Castra Vetera, or at least our small fort, break the bridge, and destroy the precious supplies and any ships they could find, as I had thought Armin might plan to do. There were some two-thousand of them, a great number of their armed men, though not all came with their lords. Not all agreed with the plan, and some even stayed home, obstinate in their selfish ways. But, the iron-tipped flower of the war hardened, if poor, Usipetes were there, pushing up the agger doggedly, some screaming in pain as the guards started to throw torches and some pilum down. Ours was a small fort, like a speck of fly shit on the wall when compared to a full legionary camp bristling with swords, and so we felt terribly overwhelmed those first few moments of the assault, when their men rushed forward with deadly intent. However, it was a Roman fort, full of the best men of the XVII legion. They were not rattled by a nation of Germani, and would fight the enemy with skill and brutality.

On the other side of the river, sounds of battle echoed as the rest of the tribes' warriors had crossed the river at night. They were attacking Castra Vetera and the supplies, and the harbor. They had possibly used the same ruse there as they had in our fort In any case, the town and the harbor were on fire.

I rushed around the rampart, gazing at the enemy now reaching the wooden walls, finding easy hand holds on the roughly cut timbers. A face appeared on top of the wall, just near me. I rushed forward and speared the skull, the body falling forward, and the spear hopelessly entangled. I pulled the Head Taker, and aimed at the man climbing up next to the corpse. I whacked it down heartily on the startled man's visage, and the heavy blade cut his forehead in half. He fell to the darkness, and I waited for the next one to appear, which he did, and then I had to rush and hack at a tattooed hand, soon severed, only to rush to another place. Their only hope was to take the walls before the legionnaires mustered.

I cursed and spat as one man managed to vault over the wall, a huge grin on his face, but the grin was his last, as I impaled him. I stepped on him, ripped the blade out of his quivering body, and rushed to pummel a young man in the face. In the dark, I saw movement, and heard a muffled order, then a deep, rumbling cheer. In the dim light, I saw a heaving mass of men marching for the fort.

A shadowy Usipetes column armed with large red shields and framae were marching in close order up the road, led by a bearded, bald brute of a Germani. All the shields had a white moon painted on them, giving out their positions as the mass of men marched steadily forward.

Towards the gate.

I glanced down to the camp as I heard warnings. A legionnaire was pointing at the gateway, and then from the barred gatehouse a javelin flew, impaling the man's leg near the gate. He was howling and crawling away when some former prisoners and pretender slavers, tall Cherusci Germani, ran out to stab him into a quivering heap of dying flesh, and then retreated back out of sight. They had the gatehouse. They had the gate. I slammed the door on the battlement, the wooden construct as hefty as a boulder. It was too sturdy.

The young legionnaire shouted a warning. Turning, I saw several hands appear, pulling the men brazenly for the wall. I rushed to his side as the lean-faced, bearded wolves came up. The centurion, puffing and spitting blood with each breath, for he had a slash on his cheek that left his teeth in sight, joined us, and we pushed at the nearest enemy, now growling at us in anticipation of a kill, or their own death. So we shrieked and struck, one fell to a pilum, the centurion pushed one down while stabbing another in the face. The one I aimed at blanched and fell back voluntarily, but others had made it over the top, and were wildly trying to tear the shields off our arms. I impaled one, the centurion lopped off an arm from another with a savage sweep of his gladius, and they went down. Suddenly, the rampart was clear.

Elsewhere, it was not so. I saw savage struggle all along the wall, some dead guards lying in heaps, and shadows jumping down to the fort.

The centurion roared and slashed at another man, opening up a gash in a surprised face. 'Point is best, but sometimes the edge is more pleasing,

461

turds,' he yelled and grinned. My eyes huge as the chaos churned around us. The centurion grunted, holding his face. 'Shit, they made me ugly.'

'It's an improvement,' the legionnaire said, with a grimace, as a flurry of spears flew up from below as the enemy made ready to climb again. The white moons were marching closer, and the centurion kicked at the door to the gatehouse. We grunted, and tried to break it down, but it was held closed, and we had no hope of dislodging it.

He turned me around. 'Go down, find men. I will hold here,' he told me.

I saw some of the men of the first cohort were running up in partial gear, wakened to a night of horror. The trumpets, buccina, and cornicula were sounding brazenly now in our fort, and in Castra Vetera, where a brutal fight was ongoing. A tall Usipetes fell to the gladius amidst the tents. Gods, I prayed for Cassia's safety. I cursed the fifty marching Usipetes, and saw a tall man in front of the column, raising his spear high to the air, a helmetless man in ring mail, a champion and a chief, and his men cheered, readying to take the gate. Gods knew how many men waited behind them in the dark.

I swore as the centurion grabbed a small ballista stone from a crate, took a long breath and threw it to the dark. It spun away true, descended swiftly, then smote the chief in the mouth, dropping him to his knees, as he was howling in pain, spitting teeth and blood in agony, and stopping the column for a second.

'Nice throw, huh! Now, go!' laughed the centurion, gesturing down to the yard. 'Don't let it open the gate. If it is open, get it closed.'

Woden's wild dance was pounding in my ears, as I turned to regard the gate area. I let go of my fears, hefted my sword, and rushed down the stairs, shouting the passphrase at some gathered legionnaires, for I was not a Roman, and the first cohort men were grim and in no mood to differentiate between the Germani. I growled at them, the berserker ready to bleed and die, and kill. I rushed around to the tents, and got a better look at the gate area. The guards were slain, and the heavy doors were open, tall Cherusci ramming pieces of sturdy wood under the gate doors, trying to block them. They kept glancing back at us, cursing as they worked. I laughed at them wildly and maliciously, as a vaettir of the deep woods and nodded at the legionnaires. 'Shield wall,' I hissed at the men around me. 'Let us go, and rip open the bastards.'

They grinned under their iron and bronze helmets, the finest men of the XVII, and made a line around me. A spear thrown from the gatehouse thudded into the shield of a man near me, and he spat as he cracked the shaft with his leg, stomping on it. We walked forward, some nine of us.

'Come, let's kick the starving bastards out!' a man yelled, and we thrummed our spears and swords on the shields, making the Cherusci stop their toil on the gate and to stare at us with concern, edging for the stairway to the gatehouse. Hobnails were slapping behind, as a dozen more veteran soldiers formed with us. With them was the standard bearer of the 1st Cohort, a wide man with hazel eyes and meaty palms, his ring mail shining, wielding a small shield.

I grinned, for to fight under such a device was a great boost. 'I am not one of you, boys,' I told them, 'but I won't dishonor that.' I pointed at the standards, as I switched the Head Taker to Nightbright.

The standard-bearer grinned and clapped my shoulder. 'You are with us today, barbarian.'

'Where is the primus pilus?' I asked him.

He shrugged, uncaring. 'Gods know. Taking a shit? The gate beckons. Let's go.'

We advanced, holding the shields up to block the spears coming down, thrown by the infiltrators. The men at the gate disappeared to the gatehouse, spitting at our direction, casting glances at the gateway, where the fifty elite warriors had not yet arrived.

'Shall we follow them up, sir?' asked a legionnaire.

The standard-bearer shook his head. 'We have to hold and close the gate, and clean the upstairs after. Come!'

We marched forward, a man next to me catching a framae in his groin, dropping like a sack. A man filled his place; there were some twenty of us now. We had time, I thought; I prayed, as Woden's rage hammered at me, and I knew I was wrong.

We came under the roof of the gatehouse at the time when the fifty grim Usipetes pushed through, and were surprised to see us there with bared weapons, standing under a standard. We both stopped for a second. Then, I growled, Woden demanding blood. 'Kill them. Kill them all. Step on their cocks, and rip them open.' The legionnaires screamed, and we rushed forward for the gate. We fought like dead men, casting aside our worldly worries in an orgy of blades and blood.

Before we reached the enemy, men pumped their arms; pilum flew with terrible strength, impaling arms, legs, and unarmored torsos, though mostly hitting shields. In one case, a spear flew and went through the face of a man, nailing him to a gatepost. Nightbright quivered in my sweaty palm, the short sword perfect for nasty stabs delivered under and over the shields. Swords flashed around me, and we hit them, toppling the first line of the enemy to the dust, the second squirming in surprise, as their shields were useless by the pilum that had broken on the leather, hanging heavily at crazy angles.

We hacked, stabbed, shields high, as the milling mass of the Usipetes growled, and the lines ground together with a series of thumps and painful gasps. The Usipetes were lean, mean fighters, with a history of terrible conflicts and little peace, and they asked for no mercy, gave none, and the gods laughed. We gritted our teeth and pushed forward, taking a step, then another, groaning as we pushed at the enemy, trying to remove them from the gate.

I could hear Fulcher yell nearby, horses whinnying, and I guessed some of the Batavi were on their horses, despite the rules against riding in a fort, rushing to our aid, though they had to dismount to join the shuddering deadlock. The Germani before us were taller, proud of their red shields with the half-moon, but the legionnaires trained every day, grimly grinding their muscles into a savage strength. We held them and moved them, step-by-step, taking wounds, giving many, men falling over corpses.

We pushed for our lives; the prize was survival. More Usipetes were seen running behind these warriors.

Men behind us were stabbing spears over our shoulders at the growling faces of the Usipetes, wounding some, killing a few. They were doing the same to us with long spears, the tips punching through our shields, and some of us fell, others lost their shields. I could smell shit, piss, and gore as the man before me slipped, lifting his red, rent shield. I pushed my sword into his throat slowly, agonizingly slowly. He was nearly out of reach, but the tip was enough, and I saw life fade from his eyes. He bled to death, but the chief who had been hit by the ballista stone filled his spot, stepping up from the ranks, huge and threatening, bleeding from his mouth, eyes wild, embracing the swords and spears of his ancestral enemies.

He came on, swinging a wild axe above his head, smashing it not on my shield, but the shoulder of the legionnaire to the right of me, who went down silently, tripping the next man, and the Usipetes, eyes mocking us, beards dripping sweat, jumped on the corpses, pushed through the line, and our line buckled. A shield slammed the chief, and he fell on his back, struggling to get up. The men on my left got his shield up to block a spear snaking for me, and I grimly punched my blade through the stream of men trying to push through our line, killing them one-by-one, for their shields were in their left hands. Soon, corpses blocked the hole, but I turned to see the enemy chief again on his feet, aiming his axe, this time at me.

He missed my helmet, but the shaft hit my shoulder painfully, and I howled while the chief laughed like a hound-bitten maniac. I could smell his bloody breath, as I punched my shield forward with all the strength I had, bashing his nose flat. I cursed as I stepped forward and put Nightbright into his belly, ripping it back and forth until it went through his ring mail. He yelped like a dog, thrashing around, and finally fell back, ripping the sword from my hands. Some hands took hold of my shield and ripped it off me, and I glanced to the left. Fulcher was there, punching his gladius at the enemy, killing the shield thief and then another. I nearly fell on a corpse, and a red-shielded, lanky man tumbled at my feet, the ground awash with blood.

465

Then I saw her.

Cassia was there, pulling wounded Romans to the relative safety of the fort, grunting with exertion. I saw a Usipetes aim a rock her way. I growled and screamed, as I grabbed the axe shaft still dangling around my feet. I went to attack, unheeding all threats. The man who had been aiming the rock at Cassia turned his face towards me, frozen as I howled and pointed the axe at him.

Between us was a red-shielded wall of men. A thick one, still sure of victory, howling and baying to avenge their lord. I went to this wall, the axe flickering in the air. I remember laughing at their weak shields, splitting faces, breaking eyes and bones with the heavy shaft, smashing the crude axe into skulls, slicing off ears and flesh, leaving brains exposed. When two men wrestled the axe away from me, I slashed at them with the Head Taker, punching my fingers through the eyes of one of them, who had gotten too close. I did not know how long it took, but there was a new wall in the gate, one made of fallen and broken shields, shuddering wounded, silent corpses. I stood on top of that wall with the tentative Fulcher, who had been guarding me with his shield.

There were ten legionnaires with the standard still flying, locking shields behind us, and the enemy was pushed out and could not pass. They withdrew from me, muttering my name. I howled at them, blood flying from the helmet's terrible mouth hole as I mocked them, dancing over the corpses of their kinsmen and friends. 'I am Hraban! Son of Maroboodus! The Oath Breaker! The Bone Breaker. Come, and be corpses, curs!' I screamed at them, but all they did was stare at us sullenly. I flicked the Head Taker at their faces, droplets of blood flying in the air, as the legionnaires started to kick and remove the wooden blocks from under the gates, dragging bodies to the side. Then, finally, the gate closed on the enemy faces, and the men cheered hoarsely.

I felt tired to the bone, as I walked to the corpse garden of the gateway and found Nightbright. Blood dripped from my helmet, as I regarded Cassia, who grinned at me uncertainly. I shrugged my shoulders, as I started touching myself, seeing if I was badly hurt. I had scrapes, aches, and superficial wounds, and should have been dead. I threw up, on all fours, as Fulcher crouched next to me, handing me some water.

A ballista shot screamed from the tower above us. A brutal stone hit a heavily armored Batavi rider on the yard, breaking and killing him, and burying itself in the horse. The Cherusci had figured out how to use the Roman weapon, and a sound of cranking could be heard. I struggled to get up, but Fulcher shook his head. 'I will go. Speak to Cassia.' The standard-bearer smiled at me as he took Fulcher, some grim Batavi with axes, and led some men up to the doors of the gatehouse. I walked to Cassia and held my arms open, and she stepped into them, pushing her bloodied hair aside. On the battlements, Romans were butchering the Usipetes, gladius and pilum flashing, and we were safe for the moment. She looked at me softly, her hand stroking the helmet, and I let her remove it and drop it in the dust.

There were axes hacking into a door above us, as the Romans cursed the enemy fortified in the room above, and I gazed down at her, despite the horror of war. I bent down to kiss her lips, and felt fire burn inside me, an unexplainable moment of pure bliss and admiration, like I was touching the gods. 'I do love you, woman,' I said.

'So you do,' she answered softly. 'You chose me this night.'

'Yes,' I said.' And I would again. Life was strange.'

She smiled happily. 'We will marry, boy.'

'Boy,' I smirked. 'I just danced over a dozen armed men.'

'You are a champion,' she agreed, 'but you are my boy as well.'

I lifted her up, enjoying her face, knowing she might cause me pain and death in the future. She would never go to hiding, no. She would share my road, and to love, Lord Thumelicus, means you risk terribly much. I had already been hurt with Lif. I shrugged my pains away as above us, a crack of a broken door could be heard, then screams. A spent javelin rolled down the stairs, then a man fell down after it, a screaming legionnaire, holding a broken foot. She detangled herself from me and sighed, ready to help the man. The Cherusci above were dying, or fleeing, as I stopped her. 'I will take Fulcher, and get her back.'

467

'And I will help you care for her, when you do. Just make sure you get back, my love,' she told me worryingly. 'What we have has great worth, despite what might happen. I am happy you know it now.'

I nodded at her, and went to help the men guarding the fort. It was heavy work, but in the end, by the time the sun rose from the horizon, we were secure. I was leaning on a doorpost, when the standard-bearer whistled, and I turned. His small shield was riven, his face ashen from fatigue, but the standard was there, bloody and glittering, as he came up to the wall to show it to the foe. We said nothing, looking at the carnage. Nearby, the centurion who had sent me down was dead, and so was the young man. I grabbed my spear and wrestled it off the skull of the enemy I had slain. Grim men held the wall, a mix of Batavi, Thracian, and legionnaires. The corpses were being heaped in lines near the gate, and the enemy dead were thrown over the walls. The sullen enemy surrounded the fort, witnessing the hundreds of dead men rolling to the fossa.

On the other side of the river, gleeful Usipetes were herding hundreds of cattle north; the harbor was on fire, as was the village of the Gauls. Some ships were burning, some were rowing up and after the thieves, firing ballistae at the jeering enemy on both banks. The enemy dared them to do so, dancing before death. Castra Vetera had repelled the thousands of attackers, though part of the Castra was on fire as well. During the morning, most of the attackers on that side had flowed on to the bridge, intending to come to our side, and our exhausted men threw anything and everything at them, stones, spears, ballista rocks, and arrows, for they crossed very near to us. Their chief was dragged along the river bank, having been hurt in Castra Vetera, and they were done with the fighting for now, growling at our tiny force that had dared to attack them.

But, they had done well. Drusus's army was in the enemy lands, with its supply base besieged. And that meant there was something out there waiting for Drusus, and the prisoner had told me Armin would be found where Drusus was. And there might also be Lif.

I would take Fulcher, go there, and find Leuthard, and any bastard who stood against us. This time, Cassia would approve, and it gave me hope. Love is like that.

PART VI: EAGLES AND WOLVES

'I asked you once if this army might be a home to you. The Aquila was bright that day, shiny and fabulous. Now, the banners are broken, the eagles covered in gore, the forest wolf broken under them. I think you have a home now that you fought to make them so. No?'
Nero Claudius Drusus to Hraban

CHAPTER XXXII

Morning revealed utter chaos, and brought much sorrow. We had lost some fifty men out of the two hundred and fifty, and enemy dead were still littering the whole area, numbering in hundreds. We also had many wounded, men permanently maimed, and some who were lost entirely, evidently captured, thought the primus pilus darkly. He was right. In the early afternoon, these few men were hoisted on poles before the fort, without hands and feet, tied down by their throats and waist. They were barely coherent, mercifully too hurt to care for their pains, but the legionnaires cursed, and the few archers spent precious arrows trying to put their comrades out of misery, but with little success.

Cassia worked hard to save as many men she could, and I watched her efforts. A man reached us from the fort across the river. In the Castra Vetera, the cohorts had lost more than a hundred, and the enemy nearly a thousand men. As the fires had ceased burning, our men across the river pursued the cattle thieves, and they managed to recover some of it. Much of the grain was gone, many ships burned, and the Usipetes were still huddled around our fort, with nearly three-thousand men. They could stand there for a long time, for they had much captured wealth, their women were there to take care of their wounds. They showed no compulsion for leaving, though some wounded lords could be seen pulling out with their retinue.

The blond decurion of the turmae summoned us to the principia. He stopped me with his upraised hand, and nodded with respect. His eyes twinkled as he gazed at the gate, and I smiled at him. In the end, no matter what kind of a bastard you were, glorious deeds in battle washed off much distrust and dishonor in the eyes of the pragmatic Romans, if not our own people. I walked over to the primus pilus, the old centurion, as if I owned the sand and blood-caked mud of the fort. I entered the tent, where the old man sat on a stool. I saw Cassia there, her eyes seeking mine, and I smiled at her.

'Well, this was an interesting night,' he cursed.

'Yes,' I answered, my eyes red and shrugged.

'You fought well at the doors. Did you get wounds and lacerations?' he asked pensively.

'No, just bruises,' I shrugged. 'Some scratches,' I allowed. 'Nothing to cry about.'

He smiled. 'Soldiers cry about everything, Hraban. If they fight well, they earn the right.'

I said nothing to that, and primus pilus nodded. I spoke, 'I lost a friend the other day. He had a lot to complain about, so much it changed him.'

He nodded, rubbing his face. 'You have spirit, Hraban. Do not give it up, even when friends die. I have lost countless, and can still joke about them and this nasty life,' he told me, and walked over, putting a hand on my shoulder. 'Better to die laughing than grim. Your Valkyries like their men funny, I hear.' I swallowed my anger, and nodded at him with a weak grin. He continued, 'We will rout the mob tomorrow, as we cannot do that today. Too many men mauled, and need to reform some units. Also have to scout around their army to make sure no more of the rogues are out there skulking. I was to send men to Drusus, as you know, but I can send but one or two now. I will need to send some this very night, to tell of this ...fiasco.' He shuddered, thinking about the punishment. 'Gods, they will lack food. They will put me on half rations for allowing that to happen. They have never fought like this before.'

'They do now,' I said. 'Armin the Cherusci is a clever enemy.'

'So, shall you go?' he asked sternly, as if unwilling to admit such a thing was possible.

'I can go, but will you trust me?' I asked him, though I was determined to go anyway.

473

'Well, you led the men at the gate, but you are right, you will have two men with you, all I can spare,' he grinned and sobered. 'I know something of your issues. You have a daughter out there, Chariovalda said.'

'He talks too much,' I crumbled.

'You have a home with the legions, boy, so get your girl home, and play the part. Legions are full of boys like you. Men with many sad stories, and we love them all.'

'So, I shall go and tell Drusus he is likely going to get raped, and should be careful?'

He snickered. 'Yes, go. He does not like to be raped, I am sure. And he should be careful. There is something going on out there, no doubt.'

I looked around, seeing Fulcher enter. 'And what shall I do? Ride around, looking for Roman forces? What will I tell them?'

He threw his hands towards the east. 'The troops have two weeks' worth of food with them. We have been supplying the bases on Luppia, but now? He needs to know. Drusus, the legates, his council. As to where they are? Follow the fires,' the old man said, and scowled. 'They killed some of my exploratores last night, so I have no better answer. You have to find your way. Also, as the bastards have a ring around this palace, we cannot go out at daylight; we have to sneak out by night. If you manage it, I suggest you ride through the forts built by the river asking for directions, while I will kill these rancid whoresons. Take your man, but move lightly. I will send a ship and other riders as well, when the boys down there have been sorted, but some must get through now. I trust you. This is my gift to you, boy, for what you did last night.'

The tribune who had been holed in the fort entered the tent.

'Sir!' said the primus pilus, with a malicious voice. 'Did you notice something strange this night?' The immaculately dressed tribune nodded, embarrassed. His helmet hid a deepening blush. Rumors told he had slept through it, drunk. They were likely rumors only, and he had cowered under his bed, but it was better to be a drunk than a coward. 'We will need a proper horse, sir. I assume you have no objections?' the primus pilus continued. 'You have two, after all. No, wait, we take both.'

He was trying to catch his breath, as he stammered and fidgeted. 'They are very expensive, an Iberian breed, and belong to my father, so I should probably ...' he began, but his voice faltered as he regarded the cold eyes of the veteran soldier. 'I am an officer, my father is ...' he started again, but the primus pilus stared at him with his eyebrows arched, like an animal about to feed. The fool said nothing more, melting in to the shadows.

The centurion snorted and thumbed the tribune's way. 'The lads always think they have an opinion, snot-nosed aristocrats. They serve as fancy parade ornaments, at best! So, you go?' the old man asked, grabbing a scroll from a pile in his cluttered desk.

I nodded, grateful for once I had someone on my side.

He fidgeted and gestured towards Cassia. 'The healer will stay behind. She will treat the wounded, and be treated well. Any man trying to molest her will lose something. What that will be, depends on my mood.'

'A hostage, sir?' I asked him, sneering. 'I would not have taken her anyway, but she has already been a hostage.'

He laughed and nodded. 'She will stay with me, in her own tent, for her own good. She is safe. In addition to my gratitude, the Batavi seem attached to her. The army does not molest healers, Hraban. Imagine if you did, and were wounded, and the last thing you saw before passing out is the woman you hurt bending over you. No thank you. But, you come back, boy.'

She came to me, and we gazed at each other, entirely in love. Fulcher was smiling happily, clearing his throat, and I swear he shed a tear. I gave her a huge hug, and she smiled at me demurely. 'Obey him, and come back, Hraban,' she told me, and left.

I gathered myself and took the scroll the old man was offering. 'A report for our prefect.'

It took all afternoon to have our weapons sharpened, and the horses checked and fed in preparation for our mission. We bantered with men who had travelled the Luppia River, finding out as much as we could about the hills, valleys of flowers, and golden wheat ahead. Then, finally, Fulcher and I went to the Primus Pilus, who was preparing the fort for the siege, and eventual sortie. We carried our gear, water and food, cloaks and our weapons. I held Wolf's Tear, and the Head Taker and Nightbright were both tied on to my wide belt.

A man in white robes was milling around the principia tent, and primus pilum stood next to him. 'I will read the omens today, and you will bless the standards with waters and garlands and be happy with what I say. Agreed?' the centurion asked the priest drily, and did not wait for an answer. He came to me. 'Juppiter is fickle, and this priest is known to be a doomsayer, and so I will interpret the signs. The cohort will love that, eh? Now, ride well, and ride hard, and if you are caught, I wish you a swift death. Soldier's lot to be in these shit situations, no?' he clapped me on the shoulder, and I nodded.

The decurion of the turmae walked up, wishing us luck with a sincere smile, which turned apologetic. 'I will have those two ...' he said, and pointed at two hulking twins with green eyes and wide, shaved chins, 'to look after you. They are called Pipin. One is really called Radulf, but it is easier to call them both Pipin, as we never know which is which.' His eyes twinkled. 'Don't make them mad, Hraban.'

I scowled at them, and they scowled back, but I decided they could be useful.

I turned to the primus pilus. 'Sir, the red shields. The lord who attacked the gate? Was he famous? Fulcher made a lot of silver from his corpse, at least.' Fulcher smiled briefly at the scowling primus pilus and the decurion.

The centurion waved his hand in a dismissing gesture. 'Usually, you do not speak of such things to outsiders, definitely not to your officers, for it is expected to share the loot with the troop boy. But, I did not hear you. The lord you killed was Ingvar, a bear warrior and second-in-command to Usipetes, one of their high war nobles. You did well. His cousin is likely to lead the red shields now. You mean to take their gear? You should leave your Roman gear here; at least your man should drop the helmet, and both should shed the cingulum and the Roman capes, shields. Get some Germani footgear as well. And leave the chain mail, for Juppiter's sakes! In fact, strip.' I kept my weapons and helmet, and then we went and picked up red shields from a pile of loot, and left our Roman gear behind, reluctantly. The standard bearer of the turma said he would watch after the pricey gear, and I believed him. We wore wool and bloodied tunics of the enemy. We tore at our beards, smeared dirt on ourselves, and tried to look like men fresh out of battle. The Batavi, Pipin, and Radulf reluctantly followed our lead, looking like nobles forced to eat with peasants.

We took our horses to the gate, looking around the legionnaires, and they saluted us. The gate creaked open, we led our horses out to the dark, and we waved. I saw Cassia in the crowd, hugging herself with a small, cold smile, one forced on her lips, and I blew her a kiss before the gate closed. A legionnaire was outside, a part of the picket, and he grinned at us. 'Don't go and turn Germani now, all right?'

Fulcher snorted at him. 'We are all Germani, Roman.'

He shook his head. 'You know what I meant.'

I stroked the horse, eyeing the darkness. 'Juicy meat, sweet mead, and good ale every day, that's what we eat out there, not the cruel and hard bread, and there won't be watery wine out there, no,' I told him, and he laughed and cursed us for bastards. We bade him farewell, as we sneaked to the river, making our way slowly and quietly along the bank, praying the horses would not neigh. We stopped there, and one of the Batavi went forward on foot, as silent as a cat. We waited and waited, and Fulcher finally saw him returning.

'One man,' the Batavi mouthed, and I nodded, dismounting. 'Sitting under a tree. Muttering to himself, he is.'

'I shall take care of it,' I told them.

'No, you are on our ...' started Pipin, but I ignored them and disappeared into the dark.

There was a guard post, an Usipetes lounging on the riverbank under a tree, looking for ships and scouts, but it was late, the gray hours when men are least attentive. I snuck close, moving ever so slowly, brushing the grass aside with my feet, avoiding small rocks, listening, stalking, hunting, my prey in sight after twenty steps. The Germani burped and yawned. I was coming behind him, timing my moves to his breathing, and I closed the last feet between us. I thrust Wolf's Tear forward, and it sunk in his neck, and killed him sawing back and forth, and holding him down with my foot and the spear. It takes a long time for a man to die, surprisingly long, but die he did, a young man like me. I left him, and scouted ahead again, but there was no one there, and the silent, empty trails led north to the heavy woods of the Usipetes, and the Legion's trampled route for the Luppia valley ran to the east, towards the freshly built Roman fort somewhere in the morning's mist, some thirty to forty Roman miles distant.

I fetched Fulcher and the Batavi, and we rode out, silently.

We took to the woods of the valley, avoiding all roads, cursing the mosquitoes and sharp branches as we made our way east, passing burned settlements of the Bructeri and the Usipetes, and saw unsettling sights as few half-devoured corpses of men and animals littering the green fields and pastures by woods of beech and alder. There was no evidence of Roman hardships this far to the west, and the first day we rode was eerily silent, save for some lingering fires and surprised foxes and brazen wolfs eating the remains of domestic beasts. We spent an uneasy night, knowing the first fortress would not be far. We lit no fires, and in the night, we heard a large force of men moving east. We hid ourselves, seeing but nightly shadows, silhouettes of speeding men and horses headed for the west. I climbed on the saddle, nodding at Fulcher to do so as well, and as he did, one of the Batavi followed us in bewilderment.

'Where are you going? Stop!' he hissed at me.

'We shall fetch one, and then come back,' I told him, and we rode after the group.

'Fetch one?' he asked with confusion, and then he understood. 'A man?' he asked, his jaws open.

'Yes, we shall have a guest, Pipin,' I said, and we rode off with Fulcher.

There are always slow men in any cavalcade. So it was with these men.

Soon, a straggler came up from the mist and the night's dust. He was cursing at something, riding far slower than the main force, and we rode to each side of him. He looked up, expecting to see familiar faces, but instead he saw my fist. Fulcher dragged him across his saddle, hitting him again for a good measure. I grabbed the horse, and we rode away for our camp, which was surpassingly hard to find. Pipin was scowling at me, tapping his foot.

I grabbed the hair of the man and raised his unconscious face so I could see it.

He was an older man wearing an otter skin tunic, and had a fine hand axe on his belt, which I took and gave to one of the siblings before the other Batavi dragged him down from the horse. The man huffed as he fell, and was soon sitting in the dust, staring at us with huge eyes, his beard dusty and tangled.

'Who are you? Sigambri?' he spat in fear.

'I ask the questions. Who are you?' I prodded him with my spear, and drove him back towards a tree.

He looked at us in distrust, massaging his bruised jaw. 'You are not Usipetes,' I growled, and he shook his head, looking relieved.

'Usipetes! You are? Why are you so far from the confluence of the rivers? Scouting? No, I am a Tencteri, Brumarg's men. Part of the force besieging the Romans in the yonder fort,' he gestured towards the east.

We glanced to the dark. Besieged?

'How did the battle at the rivers go?' he asked uncertainly, sensing not all was well with the scene, after all.

'We are not Usipetes,' I said casually, and he slumped. 'The Tencteri have crossed the river?' I asked.

He gritted his teeth and shook his head bravely.

'Hang him,' I said casually, and the Batavi grunted and dragged him to his feet. Very soon the man had a thin rope on his neck, and the two hulking Batavi started to hoist him up. I watched, waiting.

The man suddenly found motivation to speak. 'Yes! Hold! Yes!' he started to babble, and soon we learned from his eager lips not only had Tencteri done so; they had done it two weeks past, and had nearly succeeded in taking the fort on the bank of Luppia. It was not a finished fort, but only had an agger and the fossa, with the stakes on top all the legionnaires carried. Yet, they were horsemen, and fighting up the walls was much harder than they had thought it would be, and so now they just tortured the Romans with nightly attacks and sleeplessness. The Batavi had to draw him up again for the next question, for he suddenly tried to be brave again, but he came around.

'How did you know to expect a fort?' a Batavi asked again.

He licked his lips, rubbing his throat. 'Rome always builds them. And … spies.'

'The Sigambri? Are they on this side as well?' I asked, fearing the answer.

'Yes, the Sigambri, too. They went north. Weeks ago!' he told me croaked.

'But, our scouts told of vast numbers of men in the Sigambri villages. How is that possible?' I demanded.

He shrugged. 'We left the women home, and moved all the old men from east to west!' he laughed at us nervously. 'The warriors left.'

'Whose idea was that? Varnis, Maelo?' I asked while eyeing the rope, and he answered willingly.

He grinned sheepishly. 'No, some Cherusci visited us early spring, just after the snows had melted. They were riding around, making deals, and they told us to do this. They argued, of course. The Sigambri did not wish to leave their lands nearly undefended. Finally, they agreed. Maelo agreed. Baetrix reluctantly after that. That Cherusci was insistent and famous, despite his age.' He blabbered for the rope was getting tight on his neck. 'Armin,' he added happily. 'A young pup.'

'And they are out there, waiting for Drusus?' Fulcher asked.

'Yes,' he answered, insulted by such a stupid question. 'They are not here herding cows, are they?'

'Where?' I asked.

'That I do not know. We were to attack the forts,' he said, with a small voice, afraid to disappoint us, but there it was. We had to decide his fate, happy with his answers, or not.

'Do it, Hraban?' Fulcher asked.

'He cannot tell anyone he saw us,' the other Batavi mused.

'I can make it quick,' growled Fulcher, eyeing his spear.

'Lord, no! Please! I would go home to my wife, and children, if the Ubii have spared them!' the man wept. 'With the old men defending the village, the Ubii have savaged many families and clans of the Tencteri and the Sigambri. Please spare me, and let me go.'

I sighed. 'Fulcher, break his left foot, then we go.'

The man screamed, and screamed even more when we left. We took his horse with us, and I soon forgot him. In war, be cruel. That was what my father had taught me.

I was thinking hard, as the sun made its way to the sky. Drusus thought he had surprised the tribes, but they knew all about his plans, and there would be perilous danger for the young god. The Germani were fighting a different kind of war now, and they were ready. Sigambri had been living out there for weeks, with little food, no doubt, but they were patient. Uncommonly so. If things went well for them, the battle would be fought on their terms.

What was waiting for the daring Drusus out there?

Wyrd, but I would find out soon.

CHAPTER XXXIII

We rode towards the west slowly, and finally spied an estranged fort from the top of a wooded hill. It was in a valley, near the bank of the river, and the ground outside was littered with corpses. Legionnaires stood guard on its walls and around it; some Germani horsemen rode around, while most sat in a haphazard camp. The siege looked peaceful enough from afar, but for the trees, where captured Romans were pinned to terrify the defenders, and for the amusement of the Germani and their gods. The enemy seemed to be a bit over a thousand strong. The fort was filled with mules and bullocks, and there was a huge number of amphorae piled on one corner of it, evidently part of the supply the army must miss terribly. A makeshift harbor had been destroyed; a plank swinging on the currents by twisted nails and ropes.

Fulcher pulled at my reins. He pointed gingerly towards north.

As we looked, a column of careful cavalry approached from the far woods, some fifty strong, flitting amidst a cover of trees, spread out, with scouts ahead. It was a fairly stealthy group of men, save a bright red cape decorating the shoulders and back of the man leading them. Clearly they suspected danger, but the leader of the men was as stealthy as a drunken thief. The Tencteri were no fools either, being some of the best cavalry in Germani lands, and had also noticed the men. From our hill, right below us, a man rode carefully towards the Tencteri camp, hoping to give a silent alarm of an enemy approaching. The approaching riders, men who had unwisely but fortunately flushed out the Tencteri guards on our hill, were Romans.

'Those men know where Drusus is,' I said, pointing at the fifty men.

'They are in deep shit. Why does that idiot wear a red cloak in the woods?' either Pipin or Radulf growled.

I smirked. 'Idiots do strange things, or they would be called something else, but how one gets to lead cavalry is beyond me. Perhaps he is just fashionable? Like the tribunes. The Tencteri will be happy to explain how brown is the preferred shade this side of the river.'

A Batavi growled in his saddle. 'We should stay clear. The Tencteri are light cavalry, some of those riders wear armor, see? They will never escape,' he said.

'No,' I told him. 'They know where Drusus is, and so we shall save them.'

One Batavi grabbed me by my tunic, and pulled me face-to-face with him. 'I am supremely tired of you doing what you please. We can find Drusus on our own.'

'I didn't know the Batavi shit their pants at the prospect of a battle, Pipin,' I told him with a grin. He spat, shook his head, and let go of me.

'Radulf,' he grumbled. 'Go, then.'

'It will be fine,' I told him, he looked sour but pulled his weapon. I felt strangely confident, nearly jubilant to be out looking for Lif, and I wanted to find Drusus as fast as possible. And I had a plan.

'I'll kill you, Oath Breaker, if I die,' he grunted, and waved his hand as he considered the comment. 'You know what I mean.'

'See you in Valholl, friends!' I laughed and spurred my horse downhill, and Fulcher cursed and followed, his horse neighing, the Batavi following after.

The scout who had started guiding his horse downhill was glancing up, for he had heard the horses neigh. He kept riding, high on his saddle, staring at the main camp of the Tencteri, looking keenly to his left at the Roman auxilia and towards us, flitting after him. I bet there were other scouts going for the camp down in the riverbank, but I did not care.

I rode wildly, pulled my sword, and crashed after the Tencteri who finally saw us, blanched visibly, and hit his calves on the side of his dappled horse, his hair flying behind. The trees on the hill thinned out, as we dodged and weaved our way towards the camp. The young warrior before me whimpered in fear, as he guided his horse for safety, low-lying branches drawing blood, his horse stumbling in rocks. My horse was a superb beast of a tribune, well-bred in Rome, and I was lucky in my choice of route, as I dodged trees and mossy stones, keeping an eye on him through the trees.

He saw a Batavi near him to the right, the brutal face of my companion grinning with anticipation, spear aimed the rider's way. He steered away from the man, cutting a swath that led closer to me. I got right next to him, holding his eyes, raising my blade to the air, but I waited while he pissed himself, mumbling prayers. I was still waiting, and then we were out of the trees. Before us, there was a churned up meadow, and an army of Germani not two-hundred yards away.

Their heads rose as one as they regarded us in surprise.

I grinned, and then struck. A tuft of hair and skull flew in the air, and the young man screamed hideously. My horse reared, as I looked at the camp of the Tencteri. There were guards on horses, and men lounging in the sun, and they all gaped at the dead man, then at my friends and me. Fulcher and the Batavi had come out of the woods as well, and Fulcher had the spare horse which he now let go. Hundreds of eyes stared at us, and I could see other Tencteri scouts coming in to tell about the Romans probing their camp, so I raised my sword in the air. I screamed. 'Your mothers are rancid bitches not fit to lick my ass!'

The Tencteri yelled, and so we were in trouble.

Hundred men ran for their horses, their guards whipped their horses and bearded, hate-filled men raced for us, their women exhorting them. I turned my horse and whipped it, following Fulcher who had gone as soon as I pushed my sword in the air.

We rode back up the hill, not looking back, through light woods, dodging large stones and mounds filled with ferns. Behind us, we could hear the screams and yells of an army of angry Germani. I turned my horse northwards, passing Fulcher, who had stopped to wait for us. The Batavi followed me.

'What was that?' one of them screamed. 'You could have slain him before he got down there!'

'We saved the Roman riders, and hopefully, they shall save us,' I told them, and galloped north along the hill.

There were horses not too far behind now. Glancing down to the valley, the Tencteri chiefs were screaming at men to return, for the Roman camp had to be guarded. Apparently, however, a large force had taken after us. A man came out a copse of alder trees, an older warrior who raised his hand in question. We hailed him as we rode by, his puzzled face making me laugh, infecting the Batavi while Fulcher just grunted. He was still looking confused when some hundred men broke out and through the forest, surging after us, bearded faces full of glee, and shields were flashing with colors. Gods, there were many of them. The Tencteri scout ran to get his horse, and joined the sport.

I glanced to the right to see if the Romans were still advancing in the valley below, and I could see some men looking up, pointing fingers and riding to the leader, who seemed an uncaring lout, even from up there. Then, he finally gestured lazily, and they started to gallop back up to the north, his cloak trailing behind him.

'Quick, over there. Follow me,' I panted, and rode after them. We went back down the hill, and surged for the valley the Romans had been occupying, and in the distance saw some of them disappear into woods. We whipped our tired horses after them.

'I thought you were supposed to avoid the enemy, and keep the scroll safe!' growled Fulcher.

'I forgot!' I screamed, and the light horses of the Tencteri surged after us, some men spilling from saddles by low hanging branches. 'They will help us.'

'What if they have been told to avoid the enemy, and they actually obey?' one of the Batavi cursed.

'They won't,' I said, hoping I was right.

A framae flew by us, and Fulcher cursed; another had scratched his ear. We whipped our horses into a greater speed, the beast trembling with fatigue and excitement.

'Why are we always in this situation? Tell me, Hraban,' Fulcher cursed as he gripped his spear, anticipating a last stand soon.

'Just ride, and save me a place in Valholl,' I screamed. The Batavi laughed, grinning like mad spirits.

'Why didn't we let them die? Tell me! Some scum of auxilia Germani cavalry putting their noses into a wrong place!' he kept on while panting.

'You sound like Ansbor!' I shouted at him. 'How many are after us?' I asked.

'Why? Should I stop and count? Batavi friends! Count the enemy. Our lord wishes a precise number, and the color of their pretty eyes!' he bawled at our fellows. The enemy was gaining on us, forming a crescent to envelop us. Then, when we passed the woods the Roman auxilia had disappeared to, a twanging of bows could be heard, and a cloud of arrows, sagitta flew in like a hungry flight of sparrows from the woods. What ensued was chaos for the Tencteri, and for Fulcher.

The auxilia were mounted archers from Syria and Parthia. They were men who used composite bows, made of wood, horn, and sinew. They could ride and fire a bow, fake flight, and shoot behind them with the famous Parthian shot while galloping madly away. Excellent scouts, armored yet agile, these men had taken the opportunity to sting the Tencteri passing in front of them. Arrows hit the column of the enemy from the right, and a dozen horses crashed to the ground, dropping men, and many had a shaft jutting in their flesh. One of the men spilled was Fulcher, for there was an arrow in the head of his fabulous, well-bred horse, making the prized stallion a meal for the wolves at best as the beast collapsed, spilling my friend hard, and he did not move.

I pulled on my reins, the Batavi pulled theirs. We regarded the Tencteri who were looking at the trees with their mouths open, some but boys with nothing but a cloak on their bodies and a framae in their hands, surprised in a way they had never been surprised. Another volley tore into them, and this time more than twenty men screamed and fewer horses fell, for the archers loved still targets. I rode to Fulcher, guarding him protectively.

An arrow hit my shield.

'Roman auxilia, you blind vermin!' I screamed, and the third volley hit the milling enemy squarely as they had been regrouping.

The auxilia rode out of the woods, led by a man in the red cape, calmly looking at the enemy, still strong in numbers as the arrows started to fall in droves, and men tumbled out of their saddles and horses squealed. The swarthy men guided their horses with their legs while shooting, letting fly from angles where enemy shields didn't protect the foe. The Tencteri were confused enough so that some attacked, some fled. It was a massacre, and only perhaps forty got out, riding for their camp. Two archers were dead, one by a thrown spear, and his horse was still guiding the man around the field, his master staring at the sky, held so by a spear.

A chorus of groans filled the field as I got to Fulcher, who still breathed, and the Batavi helped me hoist him up and tie him to a horse, sneaking looks at the archers who were now circling us, observing us dangerously.

The red-caped man rode up. 'Hello. Do you speak Latin?' he asked in a passable Germani dialect.

I nodded. 'I do. My friends? I do not know. We come from Castra Vetera.'

He brightened. 'Ah well! Perhaps you can tell us why there are Germani skulking around our forts, and the army is starving? Oh, these are the men of 1st Augusta Parthorium, a vexillation I took to war after escorting Augustus home from the east. Nice pickle the old man put us in. I am praefectus. You can address me thus.'

'You have no name?' I asked, while examining Fulcher's head.

He looked at me uncertainly. 'Are you a senator in the garb of a Germani?

I shook my head, as I lifted Fulcher.

'In that case, please address me as praefectus. It is what I am,' he sniffed.

I would later find out that he was Gnaeus Calpurnius Piso, in command of a fresh auxilia unit forever lost in the west, originally from the east. He was a senatorial looking young aristocrat, earning his way up the ranks. Unlike many young nobles, he had a cool head and a sense of crude humor. He was young, arrogant, and smarter than he appeared. It was an honor for one so young to be a prefect. He was a likable buffoon.

Unlike his father, as I would one day learn.

The Batavi, who indeed spoke Latin, explained what had happened with the Usipetes, the Tencteri, and the Sigambri, and he looked bored.

'I was sent to see where our supplies are before the troops mutiny, for there is a horde of Bructeri and Marsi waiting on a hill not a day away!' He looked around, as if expecting the whole enemy army to come bursting through the woods. 'So, Alisio is besieged?

'Yes, it is, if you talk about the so-called fort by the river,' I said, and he was humming.

He got down from the horse, and looted one rich looking corpse before his men could. He grunted as he pulled at an ornate ring, which came off with a sickening pop of finger bone. 'Nice! Silver, I think, must have belonged to a Roman lady, Mercury bless her. So, that is your man?' he nodded at Fulcher.

I grunted.

'Sorry, I told Murtaxin not to shoot at you, but he has a thick head,' he said, as he cut open the clothes of a near-dead Tencteri.

'Murtaxin?' I asked.

'Well, it's not his name, but that's the closest I can manage. A Syrian? Parthian? One of the cutthroats I led here from Syria. I guess we shall never go home. I miss Syria, I do. Pretty women, rich loot, no wet wool, and fewer trees.' He gestured at the archers who had done their share of the looting. They led off horses, carried off usable armor and weapons, and jiggled silver and rare gold, bronze, and pearls in their calloused hands, bickering over some of the more precious findings. Thin men, with robber-like faces, I liked them.

'What is your name?' he asked me, while turning another enemy around. I looked at him and saw how anxious his men were becoming. Some Tencteri were seen looking at us from afar.

'Well, praefectus. I am a horseman, and in a hurry that might perplex you. '

He clucked his tongue. 'I do get perplexed easily, but let us not be cheeky, or I shall roast you.'

I rolled my eyes at his threats. 'Hraban ... look—' I started.

He laughed. 'Hraban? What is wrong with proper names, like Lucius, Marcus, or Gnaeus, like mine? You people are impossible.'

I spat. 'You nearly rode into three-thousand Tencteri, who are, by the way, over there, behind that hill. They have few fineries, oh lord, so your bright cape would have made them happy.'

'Indeed. Would be wasted on the scoundrels. Now that we have looted our rightfully won riches, paltry that they are, and have saved your sorry asses, we shall leave.' He got up, mounted, pocketed his loot, and I could see he had a bright cuirass under the cloak. I sighed.

'We saved you,' Pipin spat in heavy Latin. 'Not the other way around.'

'You saved nothing, and sons of senators don't ride to battle in peasant garb. Besides, I wanted to attract the enemy. Only way to count the cunts is to have them ride after us. We had an ambush site picked back up that way,' he sniffed and pointed toward the north, but smiled and gave the order to retreat. 'Does not matter. We got some of them.' And so we went, Fulcher on a horse, tied to the saddle, and the archers occasionally losing arrows at some foolhardy enemy scouts.

'Sons of senators might go home in a pot when taking such risks.' I grinned at him.

'By Mercury! That would probably be the one thing to make my father smile. It would be a horrible sight, his smile, but he would grin and cry with happiness! I think he might make a piss pot out of that urn!' He laughed like a mad thing, drawing exasperated looks from the Syrians and the Parthians around him.

'Is the army hurt?' I asked, as we led Fulcher on a horse.

'No, not really. A bit scattered is all. We marched up Luppia, built two forts, and left legion I Germanicum to fortify the hills near the Cherusci lands. Then we formed a large line, and drove for the Bructeri villages and

489

burned over a hundred. Their army was on sight; retreating after thousands of their non-combatants, and we went after them. Prisoners tell us they hoped to find a proper battle site, and were asking their gods to aid them,' he said and grinned. 'Tired of running, no doubt. They won't leave their elders to die.'

'I wish the gods fought it out for once, and we could eat and drink while they went at it,' a Batavi grunted, after having convinced a stubborn Parthian the fine horse he was leading was off limits, and his. 'How is the food situation?'

He shrugged. 'We are short. We carried some two weeks' worth with us, but we left a lot on the forts so we could move faster. We have few days' worth, and the high and mighty ones have been tightening the belt.'

'The food is besieged,' I told them.

The Roman nodded. 'Guess we confirmed that. Not sure it was wise of the Germani; now the men are angry, and won't be happy when they finally fight. They will strangle the bearded bastards, for they have food. They have been flaunting it at our army.' He laughed, and shook his head. 'A hungry legionnaire is a thing made of hate. Fight a sated one, and you do fine. You'll might survive to be a slave, but these men of ours will drink their blood now.'

I did not tell him of an army of Sigambri somewhere out there.

We rode on, seeing more and more signs of a battle and war. The twenty Roman miles from Alisio were a land for unburied corpses. Hamlets were still burning, and horses and men had trampled the rich wheat and cornfields. There were more Roman patrols riding around, which Gnaeus greeted happily.

'He is a fool!' whispered one of the Batavi.

'He is a dandy. He had sense to arrange the ambush on a fly. How is Fulcher?' I asked, glancing at the unconscious man.

'He whimpered a bit, either he is dying, or getting back to us. No bones seem to be broken,' the man said carefully. 'But, I am no expert.'

'At least he cannot whine now,' the other Batavi said with a grin, and I agreed.

We had ridden half a day, and smoke was rising from several points on the horizon. Gnaeus swiped his hand across it. 'We advanced this way few days past, marching back from the east to the west after the Bructeri. They are a pretty fleet with their dirty feet. The Marsi are with them, too, though I cannot tell them apart. Some say they have noses like a bent pilum,' Gnaeus laughed. Some twenty grimy legionnaires marched up from the valley in front of us, and one could glimpse, far away, the shining armor of an army on a march. Gnaeus rode up to the centurion, and there was gesturing and cursing as Gnaeus was trying to make the veteran soldier salute him, with little success. 'Where is the commander, centurion? What was your name?' he asked testily.

'Centurion Shits-in-Your-Skull, sir. He is over there, with the XVIII,' the centurion spat. 'They are about to attack.'

Gnaeus rode up to us after some more words with the rude officer. He wiped his face. 'So. Let us go and look for XVIII. Passphrase is "Hunger and Bones." Hraab. Hraab, was it? Dismal names. I'll call you Marcus. I'll send my men ahead,' he said, and he clapped my arm and led his men towards the woods, gesturing at an officer of the troop, and the archers galloped away. He turned his horse back for us, ready to guide us.

'Where is our supply?' growled the centurion as we passed them, and looking at the men, they were lean, a bit dirty, like a group of wolves. 'What are the cohorts doing in Alisio?'

'They are eating well in Alisio and Castra Vetera. The Germani besieging them won't stop them from eating,' I told the centurion in Latin.

He spat, nodding. 'So it's like that. Better tell the lord.' He shoved my horse. 'And the passphrase is "Hunger and Victory." That idiot couldn't wipe his ass without a slave,' he said it deliberately loud so Gnaeus heard it. The young noble smiled benignly, but there was a dangerous glint in his eyes, and I decided the buffoon was not a buffoon at all, but dangerous and wily.

I liked him, and laughed as he mimicked the centurion as we trotted off. Surrounding the army were Thracian and Aquitani cavalry, but I did not see any sign of the Batavi. We rode out of the woods into a huge churned up valley, where legions were marching, silvery snakes treading mud and grass into mucus, their shields off the hide sheaths, men carrying pilum. They would settle before a wide, tall craggy ridge, with light woods and huge stones scattered on its steep slopes. It was a long ridge, its left end curving north, right one towards a river, one of the greater rivers streaming to the Mare Germanicum, through the lands of the Chauci.

On the top of that ridge, smoke rose from campfires, creating a light orange haze, unlike the heavy dark pillars that accompany the marching Roman army after they visit a hamlet or a house. The Germani were there, waiting, apparently too tired to run. The Bructeri and the Marsi had finally stopped to give battle.

The Roman army was forming a triple axis formation. Two legions, XIX and XVIII, faced the enemy squarely, their standards shining in the air, the men excited, hoping to go up the ridge and kill the foe. V Alaudae was below to their left, held in reserve, and guarding the left flank where the river and some auxilia held the right. A large number of auxilia was marching past V Alaudae, in their thousands. They would make things interesting for the Bructeri by trying to flank the battle line waiting on top. The Auxilia were footmen of the Aquitani, Frisii, Thracia, and Gauls of every nation, eager to put an end to the war. The XVII was guarding the forts, and I Germania was far away, guarding the end of Luppia and the gate to the Cherusci lands.

But, three legions should cut through gods, should they dare stand on the side of the foe.

In the middle of the field was a small fort in the making, men toiling with dolobara tools, heaping mud on the walls and placing stakes constructed recently, and it was full of unpacked tents, mules, slaves, and guards. Doctors and surgeons were preparing to receive casualties there. I gazed around, and tried to see Drusus.

Then I noticed the purple flag. There, behind the XVIII legion, was the great standard of Drusus, the man himself wearing his great plumed helmet, and I could see single men in military garb trotting to him and from him. *Officers relaying orders*, I decided, feeling excited, despite Armin and his plans. There were also Batavi and other Germani riding back and forth, many galloping for the eastern and western woods, avoiding the ridge, not unlike predators looking for a weakness in a wounded beast. They were exploratores, finding all they can about the enemy. Far beyond the ridge, a huge dust cloud was billowing up.

Gnaeus spat. 'Their elders, women, children. Thousands of the bastards. We'll trounce the men, and go after them.'

'Let's go,' I said, keen on getting the news to Drusus.

'Let us,' Gnaeus agreed. Some Thracian cavalry spotted us, and came forward. There were four of them, fur clad and in trousers, carrying broad short swords and short wide-bladed spears as they guided their shaggy mounts for us, and we stopped.

'Hunger and Victory! Let us pass!' I yelled, and they moved out of our way.

Getting closer to where Drusus was seated on his dark horse, I saw the legions begin their cumbersome march up to where the Bructeri were waiting. Buccina blared, the standards dipped, and the centurions barked orders with harsh voices. The ground trembled, as if the gods were walking up that ridge. They had archers and Roman cavalry on their flanks, and I saw the huge auxiliary force now begin to jog to the northwest, shadowing the Bructeri Ridge and apparently trying to give the Germani there other things to think about, other than the silvery soldiers bent on killing them.

The legions seemed to move like streams of living metal, and the many centuries looked like living creatures, with hundreds of feet propelling an armored torso forward and up the hill. Buccina and cornicula blared again, the Aquila standards waved, and the cohort and century ones answered, men following the orders. I saw centurions growl at the men, optios trying to keep the centuries in line, and I saw the archers and slingers sprint forward. There was no artillery present. Slaves and camp followers were mutely looking at the thousands of legionnaires from the camp.

I neared Drusus. He was giving terse orders. I saw him grin at a tribune as we rode up, and then some burly Batavi guards were challenging us.

Drusus glanced behind him, stared at me in utter stupefaction, and winked for the guards to let me come over to him. 'What's wrong with your friend?' he asked while clapping me on the shoulder, and then turned to stare up to the wooded ridge. 'I thought you were to stay in Castra Vetera? For your safety. For mine, Chariovalda still thinks.'

I put a hand on Fulcher's shoulder. 'I was. As for Fulcher, he was shot out of his saddle by some mounted archers while we were being chased by the Tencteri besieging Alisio,' I told him brusquely.

Gnaeus piped in. 'Yes, sir. There seemed a fair bunch of the devils there; we feathered some, but I think the young lad is right. Marcus here.'

Drusus took a bland look at Gnaeus and looked at me. 'Marcus? No, wait. Never mind. Tell me everything about Alisio.'

I pointed to the west. 'There is more. The Usipetes assaulted Castra Vetera ,and burned the docks and much of the supplies and stayed for a day, though hopefully the primus pilum expelled them the next day. The Tencteri are around Alisio and its supplies, and they are raiding and killing all living things between here and there.'

A scream of feral hate sprung from the top of the ridge, the enemy leaders exhorting their warriors to a blood frenzy. It thrummed through the land, silencing men and beast. It was a barritus yell, battle-mad Germani holding a shield before their mouths while shouting, resulting in a bloodcurdling sound that echoed around us and across the valleys. It stopped me for a while, and the old Hraban felt the call of his kin, the dreams of Germani victory once his.

Drusus smiled wistfully. 'A fine challenge. We will remember them. Go on.' I nodded slowly, and stared at lines of thousands of Germani on top of the ridge, brandishing their weapons, their fantastically colored shields flashing amidst the green foliage as the archers ran up the hill, and legions marched up silently, going for the enemy.

'Here,' I said, delivering the scroll. 'It should explain Vetera's issues.'

Drusus took it, and opened it lazily, while speaking. 'Tricky business, evicting them from the hill, but they have been running before us nearly a week. They took some heavy casualties by our cavalry, but they would not fight. Now, they seem eager enough. Their tails are certainly up! So, they cut off the supplies?' Drusus said quietly, and scanned the scroll. 'That must be Wodenspear up there, no?'

'Yes, he is there,' I said, gazing at a great standard, hung with blood-soaked hide surrounded by a wall of tall shields. 'And the Tencteri seem to think the Sigambri are around here as well,' I said. 'A man told us willingly when we asked. That part is not on the scroll.'

He laughed. 'Poor willing man. Do you not think our exploratores would have seen Sigambri already, if that was so?' His tone was annoyed, as he wiped his brow, and I looked at him in brief astonishment. He was short tempered and tired, and perhaps he did not wish to believe there was something strange about the war? 'The plan has worked so far.'

I looked at the Batavi, who looked away, not willing to take part in the discussion. 'Whose plan? We don't know what the Cherusci plan. And you know they are here.'

'Ah, yes. Armin. Sigimer,' he said. 'Look up there, Hraban. If he is there, he is finished. There is a river behind him, and very little room to the north and west for fleeing. If he does, our cavalry will harass them to red ruin. It will be the end of the Bructeri and the Marsi. There are no Cherusci and Sigambri, and whatever the Tencteri and Usipetes are doing are of their own devices. And they failed, did they not? We get munitions from the land, and our boys get meaner from shrinking belly fat.'

'Yes,' I said harshly. 'But, Armin is no fool either. He has made plans, complicated and brutal. He can plan for many contingencies, and has before. It might look like they are trapped, but perhaps they are trying to trap you.'

'He is a boy,' Drusus said, and sent a tribune galloping for the XIX Legion. 'He is brave and smart, but has not commanded warriors before in this kind of a war. We have, my brother and I. We took the Alps, and ransacked Noricum. If they tried to starve us by harassing our supply lines, it did not work. We are here, about to do battle.'

'No,' I said, 'they plan to win this battle, and then make your journey home a thing of hunger and horror, with no place of safety, and the prospect of battle hanging over the retreating army every minute. They hope to bathe in blood, and they are all here. It is a long day's way home if there is nothing but enemies and hunger to look forward to.'

He snorted. 'He will not win this battle. It is not possible. If he even is here. My scouts have been riding around for days. They have seen nothing but this rabble, and the thousands of women and elders. Their army is thousands strong, but as good as dead. We have three legions here. Hraban—'

'They know the land. They have been here for weeks and weeks. What if you were meant to fight them here? They would be well-hidden, and some of your exploratores dead. They might know you have no more patience—'

He turned his face towards me, anger of the noblest Roman playing furiously on it. He slapped a hand on his sword hilt, then pointed a finger my way and took deep breaths. I kept my eye on him, careful not to make any further movement. When Fulcher groaned, one of the Batavi slapped a hand over his mouth, a sheepish look on his face. The other one looked on in fascination, apparently waiting for the punishment that was sure to come, stroking his chin.

Finally, Drusus calmed. He took a shuddering breath, and ran his hand across his face.

He sighed. 'Marius! How many scouts have returned from the north? Exploratores? So few? Did they see anything? Over there, on the left flank? The same, thousands of refugees?' Drusus questioned a stoic tribune. He pondered for a while, looking appraisingly at how the legions spread out. 'I doubt they are here, Hraban; they do not fight like that, do they? They have never planned anything elaborate. Nothing like it.'

'No,' I agreed, giving him some peace of mind.

'And you wish to hunt for Armin, then?' he asked me.

'Let me fight, Drusus,' I begged him.

'Armin, if he is here, would be a fool to let his guard down today.' He squinted, looking up. 'Tribune, send more men to the woods of the west and northwest. Send men to the south as well. Even more than we already did.' He eyed me. 'Join Chariovalda. In order to get your sword to Armin's jugular, Hraban, we have to beat the enemy. When we do, you go and find him. Keep him and her both safe, if you can.'

'Yes, Drusus,' I said and nodded gratefully, feeling terribly anxious as the battle line enveloped the ridge. Drusus smacked his lips happily as the archers started to fire arrows at the Bructeri and Marsi, and some shields disappeared from the distant Germani war line. The auxilia started to cut right and climb the ridge from the left side.

Drusus dismounted to stretch and nodded with a smile. He shook his head, as if it was a huge weight to carry. 'The exploratores have seen thousands of people fleeing in those woods to the north. Soon, we shall see if there are more than shaking elders and children out there. Our scouts don't get near the refugees easily, but I grant you, there might be a surprise, or two, waiting for us. We can handle it.' The tribune, who I recognized as the man who had been uneasy when Drusus had spoken to the troops at the beginning of the campaign, was nodding and making warning gestures at me. Drusus snapped his finger at me, pointing at a copse of trees to the south. 'Go, and join the cavalry there, brother.'

I nodded and rode off.

They would go in, and try to swallow anything Armin had baked.

CHAPTER XXXIV

Gnaeus rode with me, and we wondered at the gigantic battle taking place. He was smiling at the men who were climbing the hill. 'Gods, but they must be swearing like bitches up there. Terrible to keep a line in that terrain. Don't envy the men in the ranks following the first one.' Then he snickered, as he spotted the Germani shield wall, colorful and brazen. 'Don't envy the men in the first line when they hit the bastards on top.'

'Why did he choose to send the auxilia there, instead of a legion?' I asked, and Gnaeus snapped his head towards me. I pointed to the left side of the ridge where the horde auxilia infantry were climbing in a mass of some thousands, making good time for unseen top, where more Germani waited for them.

He smiled thinly. 'Usual tactics, my boy. Saw it while serving with Tiberius in Bellorum Alps. Use the expendable auxilia to flush out traps, and make them think about other things than legions. Often the auxilia wins the battle. Drusus is trying to make them shaky, and to stare behind their backs. Make them react to us. Keep up the initiative. Even if you pulled at Drusus's hair, he is no fool. He knows what is expendable, and what should be preserved. Fewer mouths to feed, if we lose some auxilia, and they will get Bructeri attention. No offence, of course,' he added with a sheepish look. 'Your Latin is horrid, but good enough to make me think of you as a Roman.'

'Your men must love you,' I said thinly.

'The Parthians hate me; the Syrians love me. This week. Next week, it will be different, as I give the others some small advantage in the camp.

Best keep them hating each other rather than me. That, too, Marcus, is wise tactics,' he laughed.

'Hraban, I am Hraban,' I said, as Fulcher groaned in his saddle.

'He'll be fine!' Gnaeus told us cheerfully. 'Look, he is moving V Alaudae closer to the advancing legions. They'll guard the left flank all right, should there be something out there.'

We looked on as the Cretans and Syrians peppered the wooded ridge top with arrows. The Germani could be heard mocking their efforts, though many missiles found marks in the bearded ranks. Especially the slingshots which were terribly accurate and ultimately deadly, pulverizing bones wherever they hit. I thought I saw Wodenspear, with his tattoos and dark hair in the middle of the line, under his banner, taunting the Cretans with a bared ass.

'Never could understand that,' Gnaeus said dubiously, having witnessed the same sight. 'Getting an arrow in the anus, or balls, is hardly a heroic, inspiring feat. Imagine what it will look like as you try to stand in a line with a shaft in there. Ridiculous.'

I chuckled despite the terrible battle. 'You have such a thin ass, my lord. I doubt a fly could lick it.'

He looked shocked. 'The ladies tell me it is a fine ass. Muscular and strong.'

'Your ass looks like a gnawed pinecone, thin and meatless,' I told him, liking him.

'You have to stop thinking about my ass, Hraban,' he said with pity. 'Really, you have to. You are ravaged with envy.'

We laughed and sobered, for Bructeri war roar reached us, the men in a frenzy, mocking the Cretans and Syrians, who were running out of missiles. It was not long before archers streamed back down from the hill, having kept the Bructeri busy while the legions marched up.

Gnaeus adopted a stern, self-important look. 'Send them in; make sure V Alaudae keeps up. Auxilia is to charge, now!' he rumbled, mocking Drusus.

Indeed, near Drusus a man ran towards standard-bearer and the buccinators, and soon, the clear notes rang out, electrifying the XIX and XVIII. The legions marched forward briskly, walking up bravely towards the enemy. V Alaudae was deploying near the end of the ridge and a bit to their left flank, intending to support them, if the need should arise. The auxilia were already very near the unseen ridge top, far to the left.

'Let us kill the fools,' Gnaeus said sternly, with Drusus's voice.

'Where are the Batavi?' I asked, thinking where we could leave Fulcher safely, eyeing the wood, south of the left flank of V Alaudae. 'Hidden?'

He nodded. 'Yes, they are there, our rear guard, safely hidden amongst the trees with my boys. We left most of the Thracian cavalry with I Germanicum. The light cavalry is scouting west and east.' The standards waved on the hill, and bright buccina and cornu blared. The Germani answered with a spirited cheer, their voices echoing in the valley.

'They seem eager, don't they?' one of the Batavi said dourly. Pipin, this time, I thought.

'Very eager. The dogs want us to go at them,' the other one answered.

We stopped the horses, and looked at the men trudge up the hill, the leading centuries stoically keeping pace, their shields up, nearing the panoply of enemy on top. They reached the halfway, where the archers had been. Then, they went forward, streaming through trees and rocks.

After a while, a scream of dismay went up.

From the Romans.

Centuries rushed forward only to fall into cleverly hidden ditches, with nasty spear points planted on the bottom. Hundreds of men tipped forward, nearly all of the first rows of the XVIII legion, leaving the second and third line bumping into each other in confusion. XIX on the right fared better, a bit behind the other legion, but they also found the hill prepared for the battle, and men fell forward to nasty, hidden holes.

'They have had a lot of time to prepare for this,' Gnaeus cursed, as he scanned the confusion.

The chaos was horrible, men were crying in pain, and others were braving the Germani missiles while trying to pull their friends up from the ditch, while yet others pushed to the ditch, not willing to stay on the brink of the pits. They were the wise ones. The Bructeri began to throw spears in their hundreds, many landing on tree trunks, but mostly on the confused mass of southern men, and there were sounds of dismay and pain. Germani javelins, with thin iron points, were deadly against chain and ring mail, puncturing them easily.

'Shit!' Gnaeus said. 'Well, I certainly think this will be a battle, after all.'

We all saw Drusus ride forward, his standard flying in the air, drawing his sword.

'Is he going up there?' I asked.

'He might,' Gnaeus said dubiously. 'He is mad for Germani chiefs. Wants to meet one in a duel. Crazed as a blind hare.'

The Bructeri had no shortage of javelins. The powerful arms pumped the weapons downhill, halting the movement of the two legions in an orgy of slaughter and carnage. Up there, one could see there were thousands of men preparing for battle, angry lines of pointed, sharpened iron and resolute arms holding proud shields, the Germani finally fighting the hated enemy.

'Must be much of the Bructeri and Marsi up there,' I mumbled. 'Legion's worth of men? At least?'

When the spears ran out, men started to lob rocks, and the hapless legionnaires suffered lacerations and broken bones, still bravely struggling to get their friends up from the pits, or cowering in them. The standard of XVIII waved in the sparse hill forest, as a legate was seen urging his men to climb the ditch, which was cleverly built, and many men fell trying to do so, the best cohorts getting savaged by the Bructeri. Drusus was sitting in a saddle, judging the battle as he moved up. He pointed at a man, orders were relayed.

'What will he do?' Pipin wondered.

'If he runs, it will look bad,' said his brother.

'He will run,' Gnaeus said. 'He will go back, I think, hoping they will give chase. The bastards always give chase.'

It was utter chaos.

We saw V Alaudae looking up hill where their brothers of XIX and XVIII legions were unable to advance. The archers were being resupplied, and some were rushing back already up the ridge, a few lobbing arrows at the jubilant Germani lines, but for now, it was an uneven struggle. Feats of bravery were seen. Drusus was watching; the embattled legates of the legions knew this, and they rode just behind their men, begging the men to mount the obstacles. Some centuries had actually managed to climb the ditch, ripping out the nasty javelins from the mud for the obstacle was not perfect, rains had made it crumble in places, and roots could be used to climb up it. After some time, the men who were used to working together had less difficulty managing it. A centurion was seen getting up on the other side, starting to pull men up, but he was swarmed by javelins, a veritable wooden shower of steel and sharp ends, and he was left on the bank, cursing and bleeding.

Then, amidst the Bructeri, a man appeared. We all saw him.

He was a blond, young, with a face that was familiar, and yet not familiar as I looked at him. There was a halo of sunlight about him, as his horse whinnied wildly. He was looking down, and his usually benign, friendly face was lit in an unholy, savage glee at the trap his enemies were wallowing in. He laughed at the desperation of the army before him. Well, I did not hear him, but they swore it was so, and I did see him, even from afar.

It was Armin, the God Face, as Felix had called him.

Javelins seemed to be exhausted, and many stones flew in the air, as did lesser darts with but fire-blackened heads. Yet, they had done a great deal of damage already. There were not so many dead, but many bore wounds, many shields had been punctured and bashed useless. Moreover, it had confused the once unbeatable legions, hurting their resolve and honor. The first rank was pulling back with savaged centuries, and many a legionnaire was imploring their comrades not to leave them.

Drusus was looking at the young man on a horse.

So was I.

Had I killed Drusus that night in Castra Vetera, had I decided to do it, there would be a lesser general there now commanding the troops, and Armin would eat him. It was a battle of wills between the two men, and Romans had taken the brunt of Armin's first surprise. There would be others, I knew, for this had only stopped the legions for now.

He aimed to kill them.

Armin took up a horn, and things got worse.

He blew into a horn made of a mountain goat, a tiny thing, yet the noise it made was clear and strong. It was the same blare that had rung out in the battle for Hard Hill, the day Matticati had attacked the village, and Isfried had fallen.

'You think that is bad?' Gnaeus asked, with an ashen-faced grin.

'Sigambri, lord,' I said sullenly, and so it was.

Horns answered from afar, as six-thousand Sigambri, all hungry and tired, men who had lived and hidden in the woods for a long while, men who had been mixed in with the vast number of refugees, surged from the northern woodlands to the plain. They were running after their savage leaders, men following their oath lords, bearded men with thousands of shields decorated with stars, suns, and animals. They blew Celtic carnyx wildly, the dragon heads bobbling tall amongst the thickets of spears amidst tall, golden grass and ferns. There would be Baetrix the Terrible, Varnis, and old Maelo, men who hated Rome more than anyone, and they had managed to fool the Romans, and their exploratores.

They charged in a wide front, spread from the valley to the ridge, thousands surging for the auxilia still struggling up towards the Marsi on the ridge. The Sigambri would come for the V Alaudae.

Drusus looked at them, his face betraying shock at the huge number of men screaming for his men's blood. The Sigambri had left their lands undefended, the Ubii reaping easy loot, leaving the destitute even poorer, but should they win that day, they would be gods. They would be rich in loot and prisoners, and gods knew they thought they deserved the victory Armin was offering. I watched as Drusus shook his head, and adopted a determined look on his face, cringing at the terrible blare of the carnyx that were echoing across the woods. They say he screamed at the V Alaudae. *There, Baetrix, and Maelo! Their standards. Today, they will cease to be a danger. Men, form lines, and butcher the skin-wearing girls, the lice-ridden turd sacks!* they said he screamed, and the legionnaires up on the hill listened to buccina signaling the fall back. They reluctantly left their comrades to the trap, taking steps back, and the V Alaudae rippled, obeying the orders.

They would have to deploy to face the threat.

'They don't see them?' I asked, and pointed up to the auxilia, eager men who were getting near the top of the ridge. 'Woden help them.' Some heads had started to turn. Men were pointing fingers to the north, and some of their chiefs had seen the danger, as the wild, tattooed Sigambri pack surged in a wave of shields for them through the ridge and the valley below. I tried to see Varnis, the man I had taken Cassia from, or Tudrus, but there were so many standards in the air, it was impossible. Horns sounded amongst the enemy, a wild cacophony of a mad, bloodthirsty Hel.

I saw Armin was yelling, some barbaric standards dipped as men ran to reinforce the Marsi, preparing to receive the thousands of hapless auxilia who might reach them before the Sigambri did. He was happy, oh, so happy, Armin. I was sure of it. He, a young man, not a famous warrior, was winning a battle against the might of Rome, but evidently, the success made the impatient, undisciplined Bructeri careless.

The shields around Armin shook, men surging downhill, unable to resist the wealth in the form of the fallen Romans. These men dragged some high chiefs forward, and Armin's intricate plans unraveled a bit, as the Bructeri decided to ignore the high ground. They ran downhill wildly, hundreds of them, to pursue the retreating Romans, full of the pride in their manhood and strong in their evident victory, and Armin was cursing them. Their women followed them, screaming encouragements, and the bloodied Roman army ground to a stop as Drusus commanded it, while the V Alaudae shuffled to a long, thin double-line deployment to make sure the Sigambri could not outflank the army, and the archers and slingers ran to the left flank to help repel the coming horde.

504

'How they kept that rabble together for so long, I do not know. Exploratores should have spotted warriors amongst the refugees,' Gnaeus spat. 'I should have had my Syrians go and look. They are wily.'

I snorted. 'Armin seems a clever one at hiding armies,' I said with a low voice, and he glared at me and nodded. 'He shifted the Sigambri away from their homes, and now behind thousands of refugees. If some exploratores did see them, they likely fell dead.'

He shrugged. 'We have to go to offensive. This will not do. To be on the receiving end. Even the Alps tribes did not fight this hard.'

Drusus was still, as he looked at the Bructeri surge down to the trench where Romans were lying in heaps, and he saw many Germani charge down to loot the fallen, some of whom they slashed dead with their axes and knives. There were now at least thousand Bructeri there, buoyed by their good fortune, chiefs leading more down, ignoring Armin and his officers trying to force them to come back.

The auxilia on the left flank finally saw the Sigambri surging for them in the wide swath from the ridge to the valley. Some panicked, some were still running up towards the thousand waiting Marsi, others were turning tail and running for V Alaudae on the slope.

A dull clang of impact could be heard across the valley.

The Sigambri were giving little heed to shield walls, and the ridge was soon awash with blood and gore, as hundreds of men fought desperately in the most chaotic melee you ever saw. The Marsi cheered and charged down to dash any semblance of order as the auxilia's attempted to create a battle line. Like broken ants, heaps of bodies were made, and only the dead were at peace. The Thracian infantry seemed to create an iron hard ring amidst a sea of foes, while the rest fled. Surviving Frisii and Aquitani ran like rabbits, beaten and torn, and then we saw how a great chief of the Sigambri, likely Baetrix, led a bristling cunus of thick black shields against the Thracians, already battered from all directions. With a roar, the cunus scattered the thinned lines. The Thracian infantry broke like a mound of sand hit by a brisk wave.

Some thousand auxilia were running for the V Alaudae, throwing away their weapons, and the Sigambri were hot on their heels.

Drusus shook his head and likely cursed, but then he ignored the auxilia's distress, for as Gnaeus said, they were expendable. I actually heard Drusus scream at the grim legionnaires of the V Alaudae preparing to take the brunt of nearly twice their number of enemy. 'Look, this is what makes a difference between them and us. Discipline. We will never run like that, never! V Alaudae, stop them here. Right here! XIX and XVIII, go forward! Kill the Bructeri! Fill the ditch with their dead, and run over it! And bring me that blond boy! I will geld him!' He pointed at Armin.

So the legions charged back up the hill, century after century, save for elements of the XVII which turned to receive the Sigambri with the V Alaudae. The two legions ignored the Sigambri. They had a job to do. The savaged first rankers were the most eager to kill the offenders, and the many Bructeri milling at the ditch turned to gape at the enemy, though some retreated. The thousand or so Bructeri were milling around confused, and in the ditch, suddenly terrified, and many wavered as the iron-fisted, silent legions ran at them. The Romans were overrunning first the bravest of their enemies, men slow to retreat from looting the fallen. The enemy was confused, and did not hear Armin's horn trying to pull them back.

The pila started to fall as the legionnaires pumped them to the air; hundreds hitting the milling enemy in their shields, torsos, piercing legs, and even heads. Some famous Bructeri chiefs fell down in gory heaps to the terror and distress of their followers. The Romans climbed down the trench, as if it was a minor ditch, splashing in the bloodied water on the bottom of it. They moved over the dead, helped by those behind, century after century, each men forming up with their contrebentium, putting shield-to-shield, rushing up, and the Bructeri fell in the press. On the ridge top, Armin was trying to organize a defense, and a line of men was forming, slowly.

I prayed for Lif, and even Hands, for the legions would take no prisoners.

Drusus spoke to the legate of the V Alaudae, clasping his shoulder, and then he went forward, following the eagles of XIX and XVIII. We all saw him guide his horse up there. In the ditch, there was a Germani chief fighting off some legionnaires. Drusus was making his way towards the man, drawing his sword, but the chief threw down his axe, cursing the Romans, and Drusus was denied his kill.

Over the wall of corpses, men! he was rumored to have screamed as he dismounted, his council following him, standard billowing over his head, and the Batavi guarding him formed a box of armor and swords around him. He rushed forward to the mud. *Over the Bructeri, over their women, and let us turn to the Sigambri when these weak, fur-wearing cowards are dead. No man is poor after today, not before they gamble it all away!* They said he screamed, and men renewed their muddy battle uphill, over the ditch, and the thousands of bewildered Bructeri, still hit by pilum by the second and third rankers. A Batavi fell to an arrow, another deflected a spear that could have hit Drusus, but the lord just grinned and climbed up. His men helped him, with the Batavi and his officers and guards following him.

'God Juppiter, but he will die young,' Gnaeus said, and I felt a terrible pang of foreboding.

The legions pushed up, and cut savagely into the massed tribal groups, felling men and beast alike, sometimes even lost Bructeri women. A heavy infantryman is jovial, casual, if crude in peace, but there, he was a thing made for killing, and blood flowed. A head rolled by Drusus; he stepped on a twitching arm, a man was screaming in Latin, another in Germani, both dying next to each other. What made this vengeful Roman beast move were the fine centurions. Horse hair and feathers in their traversed helmets, the leathery faced centurions surged forward, ignoring their many wounds, cursing their foes, slashing with swords and even biting when down, mad for war, eager for blood. Thousands of swords stabbed by the example of these men, thousands of shields punched forward. Only isolated Germani groups were now left behind the advancing centuries, only to be mowed down by the next lines. Few were taken prisoner.

The Bructeri fell back, some fought and managed to kill many men who got separated from the legion, but the swords and shields of the legions were too much. The hill turned red with the blood and entrails of the enemy, and soon, there were hundreds of bodies wiggling on the trampled ground. The trench turned from muddy into a bloody stream.

'Victory, victory!' screamed the aquilifer of XVIII, a burly man, and the men who had been following their standards cheered. They closed on Armin's defense line on top of the hill.

I saw him. Armin.

He kept working tirelessly, cheering men, and sharing danger. Many times he was nearly hit by a pila, but he laughed with a careless, fey voice when someone tried to pull him back. I saw him ride to the edge of the visible enemy shield wall, staring down where the Sigambri and many Marsi were running for the V Alaude and XVII legion's thin line, chasing winded auxilia into a loss of hundreds. Armin hoped to hold the tiring legionnaires, and take a mighty prize when his allies smashed through V Alaudae.

'Shit, what a terrible business,' the other of Batavi siblings breathed.

'We will likely see our cavalry rout the Sigambri soon,' the other one answered.

'There are many thousands of them, much of their nation is there,' I noted, eyeing the terrific sight of a milling shield wall, full of tall Germani, pushing through the valley for Roman shields and swords, drums thumping, and the odd, tall carnyx still blasting sonorous blares. 'They must be exhausted after that run and weeks of hiding. But, they are many.'

'So?' asked the second Batavi laconically, and I shrugged. I had never imagined something like that battle.

The Bructeri had lost hundreds of men on the rout, but now they stood steady where they had left from, bearing wounds and losses. They threw down some remaining missiles and hefty stones, while bracing into a huge shield walls of men, three deep. Thousands of desperate Bructeri chanted, making the barritus yell with their mouths covered by their shields, the noise reverberating like a living thing.

XIX and XVIII had mostly passed the trenches. The three lines melded into two lines, as Drusus was seen shouting his orders. Standards dipped, and trumpets and cornu blared, as the men took a deep breath, and got ready to take their blades to the jeering, bearded enemy above.

'They are in the range now,' Gnaeus said, pointing a cane at the Sigambri, a brutal line of thousands of bearded, tattooed men. The V Alaudae started to launch its pilum, and Drusus looked behind. The Syrians, Cretans, and Balearic island slingers started to make life miserable for the exhausted Sigambri trying to overlap the V Alaudae, not too far from us. There were terribly many of them facing the V Alaudae, and the Sigambri had now driven off the last of the formerly thousands of auxilia. We saw flashes of the retreating men, running past the cohorts of the XVIII and V Alaudae, the Sigambri on their tail.

Drusus pushed forward, up the hill nearing the last lines of the centuries, their cohorts the least experienced men of the legion, yet eager to follow their commander. Some of these men leaned down, occasionally ending the struggle of some hapless, wounded Germani.

I could have been with the Bructeri that day. I, the Oath Breaker, yet a Germani, but instead, I found home with Rome. I admired them, though. That day, the Luppia tribes gave Rome a real battle. The Bructeri took the losses with raging shouts, their youngsters and leaders standing there on the ridge. I saw Wodenspear lived, for I spotted him standing, holding his weapon in the first rank. They knew what was about to happen. They knew they would have to bleed and hold.

The Romans were closing ranks tightly, and then the legions stopped ten yards off, and threw the last pilum, impaling hundreds of shields and arms, killing many, and the Bructeri line dropped their useless, impaled shields. The buccina sounded, and the men charged.

A sound of terror and clash of weapons permeated the air, as the stocky legionnaires rammed their shields to the bodies of their enemies, buckling the first men, the champions dying with their guts flowing on to the ground. It became a pushing match with sharp edges, but the swords of legions were made for massed melee, while the spears of the Germani were not.

The Sigambri reached the V Alaudae. They had driven back the archers, with horrible losses to pilum and sagitta, and sling stones, but now, the thousands of men had engaged their enemy. I could see how men would throw themselves recklessly at the Roman soldiers, sacrificing wounds and death to wrestle a man down, so his friends could kill the enemy. The Sigambri were rushing for the hinge of the legions. Along the highest ride, all the way down, all the army was engaged.

Save for the cavalry.

Gnaeus yawned. 'Well, it was exciting for a moment there. Go join Chariovalda in those woods, as this war will soon be over. The Sigambri might have more men than V Alaudae, but they will never break that legion in melee. The cavalry will break them. They will finish the job. and then ride them down and butcher them, and perhaps Drusus shall get to do what Crassus never did, present the enemy gear to the gods in Rome! Hah!'

I nodded and rode on with the Batavi, our senses overwhelmed with the sounds, smells, and sights of a major battle, one that Armin had started well enough, but Germani discipline was not enough to secure victory. The battle was much more terrible than Castrum Luppia had been, humbling and almost alive, a moment designed to sunder nations.

When we passed the V Alaudae left flank, to the land neither of Rome nor of Sigambri, a large, fat Sigambri appeared, and ran to challenge us, but died with a slingshot in his face. Back up in the ridge, the Romans pushed the Bructeri back, a cheer, another. A chief had died. Armin?

I plunged to the woods.

A line of horses stood ready in the shadows, their riders stoic and still, as if unloving things of night ready to drink blood. In the middle, a large man stood up on his horse. Chariovalda's eyes widened, and he stammered. I rode up to him. He squinted in confusion, and swore when he recognized me. 'It *is* you! What in the name of Freyr's fat pig are you doing here? Where are Fulcher and Cassia? Surely, you didn't bring Cassia here?' he rode towards me. 'Does Drusus know you are here?'

510

I nodded carefully. 'The forts on the banks were attacked by Usipetes and Tencteri, and they cut the supplies,' I said, and he just shrugged.

'Was to be expected, but no one enjoys an empty belly. My mead ran out yesterday,' he said sourly, and observed the massive battle. The Romans were pushing the enemy back all over, and it seemed there was a red mist in the air where the battle was fiercest.

'They fight hard, harder than ever, but they will be extinct after this, if they don't run, and why don't they?' Chariovalda mused. 'Nice surprise with the Sigambri, though. Hiding thousands of men behind Bructeri refugees. So their own lands are near undefended.'

I handed Fulcher's horse to a slave. 'Care for him,' I said, and Chariovalda nodded at the man.

'Trouble on the way, I see. Will Fulcher survive? I like him,' he rumbled.

'I hope so,' I said. 'I warned our lord of the Sigambri.'

'And he did not listen?' he snickered.

'No.'

He spat. 'Does not matter. Like you stole Cassia's heart from your foolish friend, we will steal their victory and heads with our spears.' He took perverse joy at the prospect.

'A heart cannot be stolen,' I told him sullenly, Chariovalda's words wounding me.

He grinned. 'Remember that when you are cuckolded. Now. Get your horse to the edge there; we are about to destroy the flower of Sigambri manhood. It is Maelo's standard in the middle, his brother to the north, don't see Varnis.' Chariovalda was looking on to the field where the Balearic slingers were retreating from a thousand determined Germani, at last enveloping the V Alaudae left flank before us, their spears and shields bobbling in anticipation. I trotted to the edge of the column, shadowed by the two Batavi. Men grinned at my Germani garb, and I could only hope to avoid being mistaken for an enemy.

'You know the passphrase?' asked a fierce decurion.

I nodded.

'Keep saying it out there,' he laughed, as he inspected the men in his troop, some fifteen rogues in iron helms and armor. On the hill, one could distantly see the eagles of the XVIII and XIX wave at the crest of the ridge. The Bructeri were slowly thinning out, shields broken, spears spent, disappearing in a dust of battle, as the tired legionnaires stabbed their way to their decimated ranks.

The flag of Drusus dipped, and Chariovalda perked. A buccina sounded.

Chariovalda raised his hand, banners waved and horns sounded in the woods, and it was then, when we realized there was another, ululating sound of a horn, coming from the hill. It fell and rose, as in distress, and then Armin's final plot became evident. We halted our horses as an army of horsemen swept up from the woods the Sigambri had vacated, more than two-thousand, running for the slope between V Alaudae and the XVIII legion.

They were dressed like the Germani, in hides and cloaks, leather helms and bared heads, hair flying behind. Their brutal standards were flailing wildly in the air, and the pale, nearly white-haired Rochus led the attack, Armin's brother. They were Cherusci, all the men they could muster from their other wars. He led Armin's last gamble on a whirlwind attack for the hinge between the two legions, their banner of an elk skull above them. It was now the Germani cheered one more time, and gave the battle one more mighty push, following their remaining chiefs, knowing if they failed now, they would be done for. I saw the Bructeri and Marsi attack again, desperately sacrificing their bodies, dragging down legionnaires, men leaping to the holes in the ranks, flailing around wildly. I was sure I could see Armin forcing them forward, and the legions were pushed back, the XVIII eagle going down for a second, as a result of a barrage of javelins and stones.

The Cherusci rode up like a whirlwind, and having no time to regroup and form lines, they dismounted, abandoned their horses, and pushed forward, thousands of dark-hearted men in a frenzy of battle, and their young adeling was in the midst of this group. The legionnaires confronting the sudden influx of fresh warriors and the heavy Sigambrian line fell into confusion under a multitude of blows from the left and right, some Romans retreating, shrill commands to stand fast echoing in the air.

It did not help.

Romans retreated in pairs, in small groups, and some who did not, fell under swift framae, huge spears, and sharp swords and axes carried by battle-hardened champions leading the Cherusci force. Soon, the dark mass had pushed through the two first ranks of centuries into the second, and here, the battle stiffened, as the Roman men braced themselves, throwing the remaining pilum at point blank range. It was told that the adeling Rochus himself, hefting a huge spear, killed the V Alaudae's tenth cohort's standard bearer, then pushed forward with his shield. Gods, but he was a hero that day.

In to this gap, the exhausted, starving Sigambri and the fresh, fierce Cherusci pushed. Suddenly, there was no man holding a sword before them but a few running legionnaires, and elated, they turned on the flanks of the V Alaudae and the rear of the XVIII legion, its men turning to face both down and uphill.

I heard later Drusus forced his men to keep at the Bructeri and Marsi, knowing they could not retreat from the ridge, and took the last rank of men downhill to attack the Cherusci, enveloping the embattled left flank of the XVIII, but men were tired, and faces betrayed shock. I prayed Armin would run out of allies, and I shivered to think what might have happened, if more of the Cherusci, the Chatti, and the Marcomanni had been there that day, as Father had once planned. His master in Rome would have been very happy, for Drusus would have died in the Germani hands. In the hands of Maroboodus. Now, Armin was to steal the glory, unless Leuthard killed him. The chaos of the battle was horrid.

Chariovalda had stared at the battle, and the incredible feat by the Cherusci and the Sigambri in silence, until woods and dust covered the breach. He spat, gave laconic orders, and the 2nd Batavi cohort rode out for the Sigambri on the left flank of the V Alaudae. The 1st Batavi went to Hel's maw, as we rode to close the deadly gap, and slay the Chatti and the

Sigambri milling there, briefly unsure what to do with their sudden victory.

'Gold for the man who brings me that standard!' Chariovalda screamed, pointing at the elk skull, and the men rapped their shields with their weapons, while the 2nd Batavi raced for the Sigambri horde. Horses were stomping down a slight hill towards the Sigambri now, beating on the shields and flesh of the iron-hard legion V Alaudae, whose men were anxiously looking at the fate of their most rightmost cohorts.

We screamed defiance. The 1st Batavi rode hard for the rupture, their faces full of bloodlust. The shaken auxilia stared at us in wonder from our right, as our horses stamped the ground to save the day. Looking up at the chaos we were riding for, one could see bright mail mixing with Germani grays and browns. There were light woods, with heavier patches in that part of the hill, and it was unclear what was going on. We briefly noticed how the 2nd Batavi hit the Sigambri on the left flank, scattering them, like a wind blows over ripe barley fields, and pressing them against the legionnaires, felling dozens on that first assault alone. We passed the intact part of the legion and turned abruptly, trotting uphill in the light, blood-spattered woods. What we saw was not encouraging.

The V Alaudae and the XVIII legions were pushed apart, second ranks of the legions stretching and rushing up and down to extend their lines. In many places, the Germani were between embattled cohorts and diminished centuries, with many more gleeful Germani pushing to the gap. Our horses were breathing hard with excitement, as we aimed for a dark mass of the Cherusci, all tough men, grim and scarred, bearing marks of practiced killers.

'Kill them, kill, and keep your oaths to Drusus, and Rome. Show the dogs what a whipping by a Batavi feels like!' Chariovalda roared, and I pulled my spear in an overhanded position.

I glanced behind me, and saw the brothers Pipin who had followed me from Castra Vetera.

'You still here?' I yelled.

One grinned. 'No other orders, boy. We were to make sure you do no mischief. Now, we will try to keep you alive.' I smirked at them.

The Cherusci saw us ride up, their chiefs pulling men away from the legionnaires, pushing them to face us, pallid-faced with fear, for three hundred heavy horsemen can rout a regiment of gods.

We charged.

Usually, our men disembark for battle for a cavalry was intractable in a battle, but the Batavi were practiced in shock warfare. Chariovalda held his huge spear overhand, as our three-hundred horses crashed into a thousand Cherusci. The sight of their eyes I shall forever remember as they grimaced, ready to die, men full of madness, many pissing themselves, as the hulking Batavi roared and bowled them over, stomping down corpses and shattered shields.

I aimed my spear for a young, tall man, struck with the spear of Balderich, Wolf's Tear, swift despite its size. His shield was not fast enough, as my horse tore through the enemy line, and my spear ripped off his throat. He disappeared, tore the spear with him, and the horse was pushed against a mass of Cherusci, their men pulling at the riders who had penetrated too far, toppling them off the saddles in the tight press. The momentum was gone, many enemies dead, but now, they sliced the horses in their legs and bellies, slashed our men in the tight quarters. Many Batavi fell, often killing the man who had attacked them as a last act of defiance.

The Cherusci were fearless, and I saw Rochus grinning at us from some files back, gesturing with his sword. His eyes flicked towards me, and he stiffened. I grinned at him ruefully. He shook his head at me and returned to the business of war, and I knew the gods were watching. We pushed and fought, killed a hundred enemy or more, lost a precious dozen, many horses being hamstrung. I saw Chariovalda hacking in despair with a hand axe, killing men trying to do that to his battle horse.

We pulled back, to the sound of a horn. The battle hung in balance.

Elements of the XVIII was taking steps back, gods knew what was going on in the ridge. V Alaudae was trying to reform in a weird crescent form, constrained on all sides, save where the 2nd Batavorium had slaughtered half of Maelos's own men, but even so some Germani were even running behind the encircled legion. The Germani fought like madmen, dying and laughing as they did. Rome was finally in a real battle in Germania, and the fiends loved it. Tenth cohort of the V Alaudae finally fell back, all the way back from the breach, the centurions mostly dead.

Our horses retreated, and the Cherusci launched javelins after us, falling several men and beasts. Chariovalda pulled us further back, and the ranks reformed, with considerable holes in them, many horses limping, men bleeding, grimly looking at the enemy. A thousand Cherusci had again formed a line across our path, and beyond that line, hundreds were trying to tear XVIII and V Alaudae into an army of the dead. It was up to us.

Chariovalda pursed his lips, looked after him, signaled one of his decurions to him. The man nodded, leaving the column, and I saw him heading down to the valley where the unruly horde of Thracians and Aquitani were staring up at us, with some surviving Frisii and Chauci. Chariovalda attacked again, but before I could force my beast to join them, I saw the decurion fall. There was a spear in the flank of his fallen horse, and the man did not move.

'Follow me!' I told my Batavi guards, as I tore at his reins, and one, battle mad with red, rheumy eyes, stared at me incredulously.

'Flee? No!' he said, struggling with me.

'We need the auxilia; we have to get it back to the battle!' I screamed, and they nodded, understanding, likely Pipin licking his lips nervously. So we rode down, reaching the unruly mob led by the Thracian infantry and some cavalry, some two hundred strong and another thousand men of mixed nations looking at the battle. I rode to them, screaming for their attention.

I saw Cornix emerge from the mass wearing a tunic and a hooded cloak, his face betraying shock as our eyes met, and then he ran.

I looked after him, the scalded brute running for the fort, pulling at his cowl. My horse reared, and fought my movements, but I could not help but stare after the man. He had helped Leuthard, and where was that one?

Disguised as mule drivers? I eyed the fort, where hundreds of men waited for the battle's end. There, on the wall, stood a man taller than most.

'Leuthard,' I whispered.

They waited for the battle to end. Then, they would go and hunt for Armin. And Lif.

Pipin shook me. 'The auxilia!'

I despaired but spat, knowing I had to help Drusus. I stood taller on the horse.

'Men, it is time to honor your oaths! We will go and rape the dog loving, ugly brutes, and avenge ourselves. Follow me there, and let us kill the famous Cherusci!' I yelled, and resentful eyes looked at me, though some of the braver men cheered and started walking to me.

Behind me, Chariovalda was regrouping again, with fewer men. Parts of XVIII were still backpedaling and under attack from below. Even the Marsi from the top and the V Alaudae were fighting a nasty gutter fight, with corpses heaping up around it, the legate of the legion evidently wounded, for his fancy horse was galloping freely through the dust, the saddle slashed with an axe. The 2nd Batavi were still pushing hard at the Sigambri, and allowing V Alaudae to send leftmost cohorts to firm up the floundering ones up the hill, but it looked bad.

A Thracian spat and shouted, 'No!'

'You are needed up there! Drusus needs you, men, so follow me!' I said with savagery, ignoring the man. Many men looked up doubtfully, for all men loved the jovial Drusus.

'I give the orders, an optio of the Roman auxilia, and I say we stay here,' the Thracian barked.

'A coward optio giving orders to brave men? It's like a weasel asking for a pack of wolves to sleep,' I asked him, and some men laughed nervously.

He spat at my horse. 'They left us to a trap.' He pointed to the battle. 'Let them fight now.'

'Get up, or stay in the mud,' I told him. He snickered and pulled his gladius. Pipin grimaced and urged his horse forward, kicking the man in his face, and sprawling him on his back, unconscious. I glanced back where

Chariovalda's men were dismounted and in a shield wall, advancing again. I pointed my sword at him. 'There is a fat headed Batavi up there who cannot break the filthy lot, and you should consider not only the rewards Drusus will bestow on you, but that nasty Chariovalda promised gold to the man who will bring him that standard. The ugly bone face of an elk. I shall try to shit in it before I give it to him. Shall we see who manages it?'

A Frisii shook his head. 'But, what if the Germani are winning! Should we not help them? Take vengeance?' The Frisii had a violent history with Rome, unlike their neighbors the Batavi. I casually rode to the man and slashed his throat. He fell down, and men looked at me with unreadable expressions.

'We gave oaths. Now, let us keep them,' I growled. 'Men are brave, not cowards who wait for their master to get sick before stabbing them. Join the enemy, or rejoin Drusus and hate them later, if you will.'

'They call you the Oath Breaker!' a Thracian laughed. 'But, I think they lied.'

'They did. Shall we?' I asked, and they could have ripped me apart then. They could have stabbed me to death, and left the war behind, or joined Armin. Only some of the men had heard me, but when the tough Thracians screamed assent, and ran up the hill to help Chariovalda, my friend, who was staging another assault on the leering Cherusci, most of the others followed us. We charged up, cavalry and infantry mixed, passed by the remaining two hundred men of Chariovalda's command, who stared at us in disbelief.

'Charge! The standard!' They roared, and shook their weapons, those without picking up what was lying on the ground, even stones. The Cherusci braced behind their few intact shields, and we smashed into them, wildly, madly, ready to earn our rewards. We had no tactics, no cunus nor a shield wall. We went to battle as a pack of animals would. The enemy gritted their teeth and died, slaying many with weapons, hands, and teeth as men rolled over each other, bleeding, pissing themselves.

Chariovalda led his men to the left of us. The forlorn Aquitani, poor Frisii, the reputedly cowardly Chauci, and the tough Thracians; all wanted to fight for Drusus, and their humiliation was forgotten, as they tore at the enemy like a wild beast. I screamed as Woden danced with me, Nightbright flicking in and out, puncturing skin and shield, ripping out guts and flesh. My vision was blocked for a while as blood drifted across my helmet's eyeholes. I realized there was a dead man lying across my back, a Sigambri someone had thrown across the swirling battle line. I pushed the corpse off me and roared forward, pushing a blade through a man, howling as someone clubbed my ribs.

I yapped and growled at my foes. Woden was loving the turmoil, as he danced his bloody dance in the recesses of my mind.

I was in a berserker's heaven.

A man in such a battle was no man at all but a primal being of tools that slay. In the fort during Matticati war, I had been a monster who ripped limbs apart, rent hearts, and so it was again. I lost Nightbright, and pulled the Head Taker, flaying around me, my eyes open wide, adding my roars to the cacophony of Hel, stalking the men who would die. A man in his death throes was groping for my leg, trying to kill my horse. He managed to puncture its belly, and I jumped down, ignoring him as the horse fell. I pushed forward, barely knowing the Cherusci and the Sigambri, and the few Marsi from our men.

Blades and stones went up. Our men yelled, the enemy answered in kind.

Then, the enemy's line collapsed in many places.

We climbed over them, all cohesion gone, scared and mad. We carried forward, and hacked at backs, not chests and faces. Horns were blaring up in the ridge, and the remains of the 2nd Batavi smashed to the back of the Sigambri and the Cherusci. Some Sigambri were seen fleeing in a dark mass, Maelo's standards with them. I was not sure, but I thought I saw Tudrus's sun disk standard amongst the enemy, far in the valley. I briefly prayed he would not come against me. I was merciless and angry, seeing the enemy before me but an obstacle to reach Leuthard, who was somewhere behind me, there in the chaos, soon looking for Armin and my daughter.

It was a Thracian who got to the elk skull standard first, ripping it from the Cherusci champion he had split in half, waving it in utter madness over the enemy corpses, dodging swings of cudgels and spears, and he stood on the corpse of a horse. The Cherusci saw this, and moaned in dismay. Many turned from their flight, and were surging to save their pride. The men of the auxilia and Batavi turned to stop them, the elk skull rattling on top of the pole madly. I do not know how many men died taking it, and Rochus made a name for himself that day, even more than he had previously. He killed two Aquitani champions at the standard, but in the end, the standard was dragged off by a half mad Thracian, and I faced off with the young prince, who was breathing hard.

'Lay down your weapon, you Hel-spawned turd,' I said, as I punched the Head Taker weakly towards his chest, but he dodged.

'My brother, Armin, told me it was unlikely you would slay the Roman,' he spat as he swung his sword at my blade. We locked weapons and struggled, and he hissed as he tried to dislodge me. 'I am happy to see he was right. Hate men who slay their hosts. A filthy plan it was, and you dodged it. Though your daughter is still out there.' He laughed at me bitterly, wiping tears while seeing his men getting slaughtered around him.

A Cherusci was speared in his belly next to him, screaming so hard I could not hear Rochus's words well. His eyes glittered, as the pale man nodded towards the north, pushing me back. 'They are at Freya's Tears. Armin holds them. Wodenspear knows … should I lose,' he said, and shook his head tiredly, shaken, and then charged me, desperation and fear burning in his eyes.

I cursed the proud fool, as the young adeling, son of Sigimer, came, and the Head Taker moved faster than his sword. I jumped aside, and my weapon drove down at him, carving his side from armpit to the hips, and he fell back, screaming. A cry of despair reached the skies from the Cherusci as he fell, his young face frozen in agony. I yelled a scream of triumph, holding my sword in the air, but it was also one of grief, for he seemed like a decent sort. The Cherusci hands pulled at him, as they tore him back. They grimaced and wept, as they fled the field, grabbing horses, many falling to the Batavi charging them from behind, and I lost sight of Rochus. A Thracian was dragging the elk standard with him, trying to find Chariovalda. I could not move; my head was spinning.

The battle was over.

On top of the ridge, Armin blew his mournful horn, and the enemy retreated all over the field. The legions cheered, their yells echoing across the land and the woods.

Wodenspear. I had to find him. I spat and picked myself up, found my weapons, took a strong horse, and headed up the hill.

I passed one of the Pipin brothers, who were both wounded.

Gods damn, but I could have used their help.

CHAPTER XXXV

L ater on, it was called a victory. A grand victory, a battle where we butchered the enemy, and the day when mighty Bructeri, stubborn Sigambri, and brave Marsi lost so many men, they would never fully recover. They had tried to work together, however, and they would always remember how well they had done, when the odds were not on Rome's side.

That memory was impossible to destroy, no matter the many dead Roman swords produced that day.

Germania had had a chance.

Rome had to make sure they remembered also the misery. Our cavalry took after them, hounding their men through the woods, capturing their wives, and slavers were the ones truly happy. There were hundreds of legionnaires wounded and dead. The auxilia lost nearly two thousand men, dead and wounded, most gravely for their wounded had been left behind on the ridge where the Sigambri and the Marsi had not been gentle with them, but the enemy dead and the severely wounded numbered around four-thousand, a terrible number for the Luppia River tribes. A moaning line of men, with twitching arms and legs, reached from the valley up to the ridge, and a primus pilus in charge of counting them by tribes quickly surmised it was a major loss for the foe, and nothing more was asked of him.

I rode up the ridge where a torn purple standard could be seen. Drusus.

He sat on a horse, not his own horse but another's, for he had lost several, and he was eyeing the field sitting amidst bloody trees. Birds were singing softly, the dead were still, as if listening to them. A slow moaning voice seemed to thrum in the air, as hundreds of incapacitated men and women struggled to stave off death. Drusus looked grave, and guided his horse to the ridge amidst the Bructeri and Marsi dead. He was staring at the deep woods where Armin had retreated. Smoke rose to the north, as Batavi chased the enemy through the villages and pastures, burning and grinding down any who resisted. They were finishing the job, but most would escape. He did not turn, but knew I was there.

'The day Romans lose their belly for such sport is the day Rome begins to die. How many years can they fight like this, the Germani?' he mused.

'Just as you said of the Romans. As long as they don't go soft, lord, forever,' I told him harshly, covered in blood from head-to-toe.

'I hear you rallied the auxilia, and killed the Cherusci adeling,' he said, tiredly.

'I know not if Rochus died, but I did,' I said, feeling no joy for my victory.

He nodded and looked as some Bructeri women were led down, weeping. 'We saw you fight. You are the darling of the army now. V Alaudae will buy you wine. XVIII as well. They were in a hot pan, frying swiftly.' He sounded bitter, blaming himself. 'The Germani will truly revile you now.'

'They surprised us, Drusus. We shall not underestimate them again. Though it will take time for them to regroup,' I told him.

He nodded. 'I did underestimate them. Yet, they lost war kings and nobles, many men. But, they will recover. They have the bloody woods to go to, and time to get back on their feet. Perhaps they see the futility of resistance now, but I doubt it. And the Cherusci are now our enemy.'

'Yes, they are,' I told him, wondering at the heaps of corpses and shattered shields.

He fidgeted, wondering if the Germani understood how well they had fought. Armin certainly did. 'We did not even face the Cherusci army, just some warlords. We lost ... many men.' His eyes flickered downhill to the fort where the wounded were being taken care of by the harried and overwhelmed medicus, capsari and chirurgii. He turned to me as some

523

Thracians rode by, dragging a warlord, a wounded man, by his feet down the hill. 'You are a decurion of the 1st Batavi now, and will receive an award. A Gold Crown you deserve, but you are no citizen. You will get a hasta pura, a small silver javelin, and gold torc. Paltry prize, but something we can give you. Cassia once told me what you suffered for Armin and your father's schemes. Now, tell me of Armin with your own words,' he asked. 'I'll believe you now.'

We sat there, amidst the enemy dead, surrounded by Roman guards, as I told of Armin, his temperament, his worries, his fears, and especially his clever and many plans. I hesitated, and told him of Thusnelda, and how her betrothal to my father had made Armin an enemy to Maroboodus. Yet, I did not tell him of the ring. Drusus listened at my horrible Latin patiently, coaxing the right words out of me.

'I am happy the Cherusci are so divided over your father. Yet, Armin will be hugely popular after this. Insufferable. We would have won in any case, but the cost would have been much more horrible, had the Batavi, you, and the auxilia not done your duty so bloodily. My dear stepfather will not like this. He gets nervous about battles,' he smiled in mild disgust. 'I must take some shine off Armin's shield before this campaign is over.'

'We go east then, Drusus,' I said, and he smirked.

'Well, we will chase these bastards, eat well, rout the Tencteri and the Usipetes, and march through the Sigambri lands back home. But, first, we will go and show the Cherusci we understand their message. I have men who know where Sigimer rules. Beyond Segestes. Between the rivers.' His eyes took a dreamy look; he wanted to see the lands.

'Is the army able to do all that, sir?' I asked dubiously.

'You call me Drusus. They are Romans. They go to Hades and back for me. And we will make Alisio and the others permanent fortresses here, and rule over Luppia Valley.'

'I met the men who will try to kill Armin,' I said carefully. 'I would like to stop them.'

He sat there silently, weighing my words. 'Previously, I thought it a humorless act. It would be best if that bastard had a Germani hound hunting him. Perhaps you should not ...' He shook his head, and took a deep breath. 'Go then. Find your daughter.'

'I thank you,' I told him, worried about his strange mood. 'Drusus. Stay alive, so you can conquer the bastard in Rome who wishes you dead. Whoever that is. You are the best lord I know.'

He grunted, and his face was clouded by sorrow. 'I have no need to wonder who they are, Hraban. I know who is to blame for Maroboodus. But, I will show her.'

'Her? Who?'

He smiled. 'There is a woman who will benefit greatly from Augustus's vision, a woman who is scheming to see all the high Roman nobles killed in wars, and by poison, men who would welcome the Republic with open arms after Augustus dies. This woman is a selfish woman, wishing to see her son in power.'

'Daughter of Augustus?' I asked warily.

'We shall speak of it later, Hraban,' he said drowsily, and rubbed his face. He glanced at me and spoke, 'Speaking of the bastards who scheme against me, Antius is meeting us at the border of the lands of the Cherusci where I Germania is building a fort, Castrum Flamma. We will take the legions there, and go raise hell.'

I said nothing. Crows were hopping on corpses, and we looked at each other, wondering how to navigate the dangerous waters threatening him. 'Yes, lord.'

'I'll deal with Cornix as soon as we find him. I think Antius will need one less claw in his hand, and so the creature will disappear, no?' he said, and placed a hand on my shoulder. 'Hraban. I asked you once if this army might be a home to you. The Aquila was bright that day, shiny and fabulous. Now the banners are broken, the eagles covered in gore, the Germani forest wolves broken under them. I think you have a home now that you fought to make them so glorious. I trust you. Will you swear yourself to me?'

I gazed at the woods of Germania. The sweet smells of the forests mixed with the stench of blood and piss, and I prayed to myself. I nodded. 'When

I made a man of myself, I swore I would do so many things. I swore I would have vengeance on my father, on Catualda. I swore to save my daughter, and Ishild. I swore I would get my position and fame back, things I lost. I swore to find Wandal. I think I shall never be famed in Germania, and so I content myself with the vengeance, finding my friend, and saving my daughter. The rest is gone. I am a Roman now. I renounce my home, and my people, and serve you in things small and large, in sorrow and glory. I am Roman, and will not betray you,' I told him, and he took a long breath and smiled.

'Go then, Hraban, and find her. Come back. Be careful.'

We embraced, the sticky, drying blood making a strange ripping sound as we separated, and we laughed grimly. I was going to leave, but stopped with a question. 'Lord, who was the leader of the Bructeri on the field? Wodenspear?'

He looked around. 'The Bructeri who fell are on this ridge. I saw him at one point, and he was fighting some ways to the right of here, but I know not what became of him. You are welcome to search for him. Look out for vermin looting the bodies, and for the bodies, too. Not all are dead, or dying.'

I hesitated. 'I need coin, lord. It might be useful with something I am planning.'

'Lord, when you need coin. You can ask by my name for such paltry things,' he laughed, and tore a large leather pouch from his belt, clinking with heavy coins. He tossed it at me, and he turned to ride to his officia and started issuing orders.

I saluted the young lord, whose dark hair was dirty with gore, as he looked over the moaning woods while couriers approached him. I moved away. I spent twenty minutes walking the ridge, searching amongst hundreds and thousands of wounded and dead, stepping carefully amidst broken spears and feverish, dying men, some of who still thought they were in battle. I bared my teeth at ragged men looting the dying, saved a few wounded men from these two-legged animals, but quickly found out I could not help them, and left them to their fates in the afternoon, hoping

Woden would look after them, the flower of Bructeri warriors. Then, I came to the middle of the line, where a dozen large blond men were dead in a wedge, and in midst of them there was a fierce looking man, lying on his belly, naked and robbed. His hair was reddish and black, coarse, and he had cuts on his back, a pilum sticking out of his spine. He was shuddering, and I knew it was Wodenspear. I turned him around, and his lips were bluish, and his eyes tried to focus on me, but he could not move.

'My men?' he asked weakly.

'Dead. Around you. Waiting for you in the halls of the brave. You fought well, lord.' I said, holding his hand. 'I was looking for you. I am the man they call the Oath Breaker.'

His eyes focused on me, but he could not see. 'You are Hraban?'

'I am, lord. I have a question for you. Do you know where is the place called Freya's Tears? Where a girl is held, a baby only.'

He looked confused. 'Yes, it is a league that way.' He was apparently pointing, but could not know his arms did not function.

'Where, lord?' I asked patiently.

'North of here, a grotto by a rock-strewn hill, just by the river and a ford. Just ride to the north, until you hit the river, and follow it north and west. It is on the other bank,' he explained, tired. 'I saw the baby, when Armin showed her to us. He kept her warm, and I laughed with her.'

Tears filled my eyes. 'Was she fine? The child?'

'She? Yes, it was a she. She was beautiful,' he smiled with blood on his lips.

'She was?' I said, my grip tightening on his hand.

'She was, and is, I hope,' he said, worried. 'The bounty hunter was her guard, for some reason, and was very protective of her. They are guarded, safe. Warm. Unless now, something happens. So many dead.' Wodenspear smiled. 'My wife was here, and I sent her away, before the end. She will keep my daughters safe, I have no sons.' He sobbed as he tried to move, his body wracked with pain. I nodded at him, but he did not see it. He calmed, and his eyes fluttered, tears conquering his cheeks. He was breathing sharply and closed his eyes. His voice was his again. 'I did well, Hraban,' he said, himself again. 'We were close. We were heroes.'

'You did, and you are, lord,' I told him, and waited with him until he died. The sun was going low, the forlorn rays flickering through woods. I looked downhill, and saw Drusus still conferring with his officia and couriers. I mounted my horse and guided it towards the north, my helmet turning around, leering maliciously at some looters. I saw one's face, and recognized it.

It was a man of Bricius, with a red scar on his forehead, and he was only pretending to loot a corpse. He was staring at me. I hefted my spear as I rode to the dark, and I knew Lok's beast was near me, following behind, for he knew I was seeking the same prey as he was.

Let him come.

CHAPTER XXXVI

The river was beautiful that evening, silvery moonlight playing on its rippling surface. I guided my horse on its bank, hailing a mix of fleeing enemy carelessly, many Sigambri and Bructeri running for the ford that was near. Many were harboring deep wounds. There were lots of men in those woods, especially the terribly wounded ones, men who stopped to wash their wounds at the river, resting a bit before going on to die, families and women helping the lucky ones who escaped the battle. I rode past them, a man like them, and they did not heed me, though many would have wanted my horse. That was why I held Nightbright out prominently, letting all see the deadly piece of metal, one they should not risk by trying to steal anything from me.

The wind had picked up, and was making strange spirals on the water. I gazed at the woods and the ridge where the battle had taken place, now hours away. Somewhere in those woods was the man who wanted to hurt me, in so many ways. Father's pet, Lok's spirit. I was weary of battle and travel, had not eaten much the past days, my finger throbbed, but I was ready for one final fight. It might be final one for me.

Before me, in the moonlight, I saw churning water, a strangely calm pool in the middle of the river, a bank full of thin reeds, and on the other bank squatted a tall mound of rubble, overgrown with moss and trees. Before the stony rubble, there was a small lagoon, and by that lagoon, there was a man. I stopped my horse to gaze at him. He was hooded and swathed in a cloak, and he was not alone. He had two men with him, and they were talking. A lock of blond hair was rippling in the wind, I saw this much, and I felt exhilaration. I gazed, focused my eyes, and saw a stubby horn on his waist. It was Armin, I was sure of it. The bastard was risking much, staying so close to the enemy army, but he was wily and clever, and also too lucky.

I noticed there was a stream of men running to the river, not far, and decided that must be the ford, or else they were very thirsty, bent on draining the clear waters. I guided my horse forward, and smiled joylessly as the men waded across, weaponless, one missing an arm, and the horse dipped his head to drink. I refused his wish, deciding it would have to wait, and guided it after the men carelessly. It floundered once, then twice, but found solid ground soon enough, neighing unhappily as it climbed out of the river. I guided the horse to where I had seen the men conferring. I was holding Wolf's Tear loosely on my palm, the blade of the spear glinting in the moonlight. I caught a sight of many men creeping to the beach opposite of me, trying to find the ford. More fugitives? I smiled. *No.*

I saw the figures ahead, in the midst of a turbulent discussion, and as I got closer, I heard them speak clearly. One was Armin. 'Of course it is a terrible loss. What else could it be? We lost thousands of men and women, and will lose more before they go home. There is a legion at confluence of our rivers, near our border. They will want vengeance for this. Now, we must get our men back, and find Rochus. He must be found.'

'The army is scattered,' one man said unhappily. 'Not easy to find your brother out there.'

'Find him. Army is scattered, and it will be so until winter,' Armin told him bravely. 'We have the rest of the army back home. But, now, it is up to us to find all we can, take them home, and we must survive. Smile, because the Chatti are now allies. They will never forget what happened to Ebbe. We will muster our men, get help, and we will fight the bastards. My father routed the Chauci, and next year, we will all stand united. Take heart! We nearly succeeded today. Rarely has the bastard wolf lost so many men.'

I snorted, and they turned to look at me. One man rode forward, his head askew, as he gazed at me. 'And who are you then? This is not any of your business.'

'It is Hraban,' Armin said heavily. 'The man I will never again trust.' His eyes were hard as he looked at me, his cowl falling on his shoulders to reveal a sweat-streaked face of a warlord.

'Trust, lord?' I asked him with rising anger. 'Ever have you tried to scheme your enemies dead with my help. The first time you wished to slay my father, now Drusus. Perhaps you should have asked me to join you openly, and not ask me do unsavory deeds for you, and you would love me better today.'

He smiled, and I saw he was exhausted. His cheeks were hollow; his lustrous hair matted to his scalp, but there was a dangerous gleam in his eyes. 'Maybe so. Yet, times are desperate. Your father—'

'Is a Roman, Armin,' I told him heavily. 'He has a deed to do in these lands. Then, he will go back to being Roman. It is he, who wishes to slay Drusus, perhaps other men like the Roman lord. Then, he will gather all the bastards to a war against Rome, and lose the lot. Many more so than you did today.'

He gazed at me without emotion, his eyes drifting to the side, where there was an opening of a hole, with water running out. It was a grotto, and Wodenspear said that was where Lif was. I guided my horse closer, but his men pulled their axes and grabbed shields, shifting protectively before Armin. Armin nodded. 'I have a hunch you are right. He will sell us all out, and then he will be rewarded handsomely. However, I shall foil him. For us all. For Thusnelda.'

'Thusnelda is likely a woman worth fighting a war for, lord,' I told him brusquely. 'I failed at killing Drusus. He is a better man than you.'

He laughed. 'Hard to say. Had you not failed, we would be harrying the Roman legions now,' he said coldly. 'Not the other way around. And my brother would be alive.' He lifted his head as a buccina rang somewhere far away. 'And had you helped me kill your father, we would have both been happier.'

'When the time comes, if I am lucky to be there, I shall slay him still. Where is she?' I asked.

'She is safe, Hraban,' he told me evenly.

'She would be safe with me, and I do not have her,' I told him, with a threat thrumming in my voice.

He said nothing, as if considering my words. 'She has this Odo after her, no? And your father likely as well?'

'Yes to both,' I grinned. 'So I want her now. It is a father's lot to defend his blood.'

'A father's lot is a terrible one,' he mumbled. 'There was a greasy bounty hunter with her. A strange man to guard your child.'

'I trust him better than you, Armin,' I snickered. 'So let him go as well.'

'I did,' he said evenly. 'They are gone.'

'They are gone?' I asked dangerously. 'Wodenspear said you are holed up here. Hiding. And you let them go?'

He slumped in his saddle. 'I have many men here, Hraban, so do not raise your voice. I owe you nothing. She is gone. In fact, I think it might be best you did not leave this place alive. She will be better off, if you are no longer hounding her.'

'How dare you tell me my daughter is better off without me? So, you will not help me get her. No? Yet, you are a ruthless bastard, are you not? Will you change your mind, if I give you this?' I said calmly, holding up Draupnir's Spawn. 'The ring you so desire? The ring to give the Cherusci freedom from the Suebi, the trinket that pacifies the Semnones and the Langobardi? It would be hard to find it in the river, Armin.'

He stared at the ring, my ring, the ring my grandfather had stolen from Bero in fear of the prophecy. It was an ancient jewelry, something many desired for the power it held over the Suebian nations. It was a mark of the gods' own favor, the first ring of the first men, and there it was. Armin had it once. He needed it. It would give him men, influence amongst the Cherusci and the Suebi, alike. 'And you only wish to have Lif?' he asked dubiously. 'No sanctuary? No demands?'

'I will one day find Catualda, but, no, I have a home now,' I told him, as I threw the ring to the air, making him grasp at air instinctively.

'Catualda is not here.'

'I said, I will find him,' I said bitterly. 'Guard him, or not. I will, one day.'

He smiled. 'You are eighteen, Hraban. A bit younger than I am. Yet, you are Woden's Chosen. A Curse Carrier, the Blade of Woden. Lord of the Bones, I name you. You have slain so many men this past year, and few champions do as much carnage during their lifetime. And here you are still. He stands no chance. I will guard him, no matter his flawed temperament and his ill deeds. He will need help.'

I nodded. 'Go, and get Lif. Give me my daughter.'

He hesitated at that as well, likely thinking about the girl and his honor. He opened his mouth to say something, but then a woman stepped out of the grotto. She was tall and willowy, beautiful, with red blonde hair, high cheekbones and wide hips, her strides purposeful and long. On her brow, there was a golden band, and her dress was an elk leather vest, with dark wool beneath. She came to stand next to Armin, who gazed at her with care. I nodded at her.

'Thusnelda, I take it? Your father Segestes approves your presence with him?' I pointed Nightbright at Armin.

She bristled. 'I am not here, Hraban. I am with relatives. And, as he is my cousin, I did not exactly lie,' she told me haughtily. Then, she turned to Armin. 'Either we find the ring from the river, or won't, but you will not treat with him. You will make no deals with this one, and stain yourself.'

I laughed. 'Has he told you what stains he already carries? What he has tried to do? He tried to scheme my father into a grave mound by using me, and asked me to kill my host, my lord. While holding Lif hostage. A mere baby.'

She looked down. 'He tells me everything. And I tell him the girl is not yours, no matter if you sired her. There is the prophecy, Hraban, and you are a hunted man. But, she will be safe.'

'Your man here, your cousin, would keep her safe? You are going to war with Rome for years on end, should you survive that long. Your father, Segestes the Fat, is a Roman sycophant. Who exactly keeps her safe?' I asked her spitefully.

'She has a sister. You know who that is. Veleda. The bounty hunger told me. She and Hands are gone. So, it will end here, Hraban,' she told me fiercely, and I admired her spirit.

'When did you let Hands go?' I asked, and then I heard a baby cry in the woods. I looked up, saw a small clearing up on a hillside, and there strode the fat bounty hunter, his dog trailing him, and he was carrying something. It was not far at all, and my heart raced.

'No, Hraban,' Armin said calmly. 'Let me have the ring, and then, I shall hold you prisoner. One day, perhaps, you will go free.' I looked behind me. There was a group of shadows moving up from the dark, and before them, walked a larger shadow than the rest. Armin's eyes shot up, his handsome face twisted in anger, as he prepared to flee. 'Romans? Your traitor auxilia?'

I shook my head. 'It is Leuthard. He is my father's beast, Armin. They have been following me, for my father wishes you dead. He needs no competition in slaying the Romans, and wishes to finish his contract with his masters. Or mistress. It has to be him who slays Drusus, you see, and he dislikes you for what you tried last year. And so, he wants your head.'

Armin whistled wildly and men rushed from the grotto. They were household guards of Sigimer, his bodyguards, men like the ones he had sent to Castra Vetera and the fort I had defended. Tall and young, strong and springy, they were armored in leather and bits of steel, ruddy and blond men, and they rushed over the water trickling to the grotto to stand before Armin, looking startled as strange men approached.

'Leuthard!' I yelled.

The line approached. It was the band of Bricius, the lank haired mercenary advancing from the dark. He grinned at me, for there were twenty men in the band, a motley crew of throat cutters, armed with axes, spears, arrows, and bows. Leuthard strode before them, his huge sword out, and the five men around Armin tightened their wall, looking hard at the enemy. I pointed a finger at the bald beast. 'Meet Armin, Leuthard. My father's prey.'

He stared at me, as I guided my horse away to the side. 'Stay here, Hraban, and we shall finish what we started,' he growled. 'If you run, I will just find you. And your brat.' He waved his hand towards the woods.

'You are not going to find her,' I told him calmly. 'For you will not survive this night.'

They laughed, and a man of the Red Finger raised his bow, gave a toothless leer, and shot an arrow at my horse. The beast screamed and fell, and I jumped off it, my helmet flying off my head. I got up, holding my spear, the spear of Balderich. Leuthard shed his cloak, revealing his huge physiology to all of us, holding his shield and sword up. 'Lok knows, Hraban, I hate you. You are not going anywhere this night.'

Armin chuckled. 'Looks like we are on the same side, then, Hraban. Fight with me, for Thusnelda, at least.'

'No, we are not,' I told him. 'And your Thusnelda,' I said with a wicked grin at her, 'wanted me dead just now.' I grabbed a bag from the horse. 'You men! The Red Finger? Come, and look at this.' I threw the sack to the grass in front of them. It spilled open, a small mound of gold and silver Drusus had given me pouring out, glittering in the sparse moonlight. 'Look at that, my friends, for it is but a paltry sack of trinkets, should you bring Armin alive to Drusus this night. Your cousin is dead by my hand, Bricius, but there will be more gold with Drusus, enough to buy a dozen cousins for a greedy bastard like you. Gold will trickle through your fingers. You will shit silver, if you capture them. And only if I live, for Drusus is my brother.'

Bricius licked his lips, as Leuthard turned to look at him with suspicion. 'You have made oaths to Maroboodus,' the beast said, turning around in swift circles, pushing a man further from him. Their arrows were pointed down now, and Bricius was trembling, looking at me in a curious way, his hatred and dead cousin forgotten. 'I said you have made oaths to Maroboodus!' Leuthard yelled.

I chuckled. 'You made oaths to Hunfrid before that! And after he could not pay you, being my prisoner, your oaths were forgotten. Who do you think can pay you better, men? Rome, or a paltry Germani chief? You have no tribe, you have no loyalty, and now, you can give Drusus Armin. Do you think he would appreciate having Armin in his hands? Let me say it again. All you need to do,' I hissed, 'is take him to Drusus.' The twenty men raised their heads at me. 'Alive.' Bricius grinned at Leuthard.

'And I take it you want his head?' Bricius asked, nodding at Leuthard.

'Yes, of course,' I told them casually. 'Spare the woman. She is valuable. Unmolested.'

Bricius smiled hugely. 'Feather the bald shit, and do what he says!' The arrows turned to Leuthard, who cursed like an animal he was. Arrows flew, splintering his shield and side, and I retreated to the woods and gripped my helmet, pulling it on. I gazed up the hill where I had seen Hands and sprinted hard. Behind me, battle was joined, as Red Finger turned to Armin's men, charging them with savage glee, and I saw Leuthard fall on his back as a few men tried to stab him with spears. I heard Bricius howl commands, and Armin as well.

This I did to your father, Thumelicus.

He had manipulated me few times too many, in his greed to stop Maroboodus from marrying Thusnelda. In his desperation at gaining victory, he had forced me to soil myself. He was a great warrior, a greater commander and a chief; perhaps he would have been a mighty king. But, for me, he was a scheming bastard, and he would have been my gift to Rome.

I sprinted up to the woods. I heard the baby cry, not too far, and ran like a lynx that way, loping like a cat indeed, cursing the loss of my horse. I had not anticipated Armin would let them go, but Thusnelda had convinced him, and I cursed her as well, the beautiful, high-minded bitch, even if I was happy to know there was a woman such as her in Armin's life, a girl with compassion to keep him sane, if he should survive Rome. She had likely cared for Lif as well. I sprung through the woods, starting to feel lingering desperation as the grass rustled mournfully in the weak wind, and I was no tracker. The sound of battle was fading as I ran, picking directions at random, and finally, I fell on my knees in the middle of a small clearing, leaning on a rock, cursing the gods.

An owl hooted. A raven croaked.

Lif cried.

I turned to look at a copse of wood, right next to me. It was thick and full of shadows, and one shadow moved. It was a large dog, barking in anger, running for me like the slavering beast it was, fangs bared, and it jumped on me so quickly, I barely got my spear up. The blade sunk to its belly; however, it flew over me, the claws drawing blood off my arms, the teeth clamping to my shoulder, and I strangled it as we rolled on the ground. I climbed over it; regarding its bloodshot eyes, and rammed my helmet on its head, so many times it lay still. I saw Hands walk from the woods. He was huge, and held a battle-axe with two hands. He regarded me, and eyed the thicket where Lif was crying, and I could not see her. He grunted in anger, as he stepped closer, and I tried to get up as he kicked me over. He was ugly and greasy, but also more resigned than angry. 'Why cannot you just let go? Had you let go of her when she was born, she would be safe. We would not be here, hunted.'

I breathed hard, and felt tears well in my eyes. 'I made a man of myself when my father would not. I killed Vago, the man who held the dagger that slit my mother's throat. I promised I would get my fame back. I promised vengeance for my family. I promised many things.'

'It is man's lot to give such promises, boy,' he told me. 'World is full of graves for men who could not keep theirs.'

'I have given up,' I hissed, 'on my fame. I have kept to my honor. But, I cannot let go of her. I could even forgo the vengeance. But, not her. I am a father!'

'Veleda wants her. I will take her to her. That Armin caught me was bad enough. Veleda told me not to hurt you, but I have no choice. Without a leg, perhaps you won't be so eager to run after us when we go east.' He looked brutal, as he eyeballed my legs. 'Without both, you won't ride either.'

'I will crawl, if I must,' I hissed, but it was then when Hands yelped, for a huge shadow jumped on him and grabbed his face, pulled him up to the air and threw him unceremoniously. The indomitable bounty hunter flew far in the air, landed hard, the Chatti ending up in a pained heap, his ear missing. Leuthard stood over me, as I scrambled backwards, and opened his hand. The ear fell to the ground. His scarred, rock-like hand was slick with blood.

'So, Hraban,' he said murderously. He had his sword on his belt, covered in gore. He had an arrow in his side, another in his chest, and he was wheezing, for there was a wound in his abdomen, oozing thick blood. He kicked a head he had dropped, and it rolled over the ear. It was what remained of Bricius, a terrible leer on his thin lips, which bespoke of a painful death.

I smiled at him. 'Thank you. I would have had to remove it myself later on. Fulcher greatly desired it.'

'Think nothing of it,' he answered with a growl. 'Lok's balls, but you have been a harsh one to kill.' He snickered, as he leered in the direction of crying Lif. 'Just what I need. Some substance before I go find Armin.'

'Ah, he got away then?' I said, disappointed, swallowing my fear at his words. 'I find it hard to understand they could not kill you.'

'Takes more than a band of mercenaries to slay me, Hraban,' he snickered. 'Armin ran with one or two of his men. They killed and died well. That girl ran as well, she actually fought with them! A woman, imagine.'

'I know a woman like that as well,' I told him, as I stood up. 'You will not have Lif.'

'A clever thing with the Roman gold,' he grunted as he spat blood. 'That was a fortune. Drusus must like you more than your father does. Gods, he resents the seed that made your mother pregnant. I will eat her while you watch, bleeding and crippled.' He looked huge and menacing, his face as dark as a wolf's, a feral look in his eyes. 'I will, and Lok will laugh, even if he will not be freed by Odo. Let it be my pleasure. He is a chaotic god, he is. He has time. There will be other Ravens and Bears to start the game anew, and Ragnarök may wait.'

'I agree, but I will stave it off my own way. I'll piss on your face, Leuthard.' I uttered brave words, I did, but did not feel brave. I was hurt and tired, and had only Nightbright with no shield, and no sign of my long sword.

He saw my face, and grabbed something from the brush and gave it to me, hilt first. 'The Head Taker. Your father sent it to Burlein to convince the fool he was dead. He never loved the blade, you see. He was afraid of it, hated it for reminding him of his crime, how he left Hulderic die. He wounded you with it, but it betrayed him then. He blamed the sword for not being able to split your skull.'

'Maybe he had a terrible bout of disgustingly soft fatherly feelings and could not finish it?' I grinned, as I pulled the blade off his grip. 'Perhaps he also is a father deep inside. A father I will slay. I will not hesitate.'

He laughed. 'I once wanted to kill mine. After he exiled me for my … appetites. I could not. We won't see if you are like me.'

With that, he roared and jumped forward, pulling his blade back with a smooth motion, the weapon swinging in the air eerily. It cut down hard, so hard I could barely move away. I did not, jumping forward, and ramming the hilt of the Head Taker to his face, making him grin maniacally as he raked his hand across my helmet savagely, throwing me several feet into the air. I scrambled back as he loped for me, more animal than man, ramming the blade between my legs, missing but barely. I slashed the blade at his mass, nearly screaming from fear, as his eyes glowed yellow, the blacks tiny, remorseless dots in the middle.

I did believe in spirits and gods, my lord, though I did not trust the vitka or the völva, thinking them charlatans. I had heard a goddess speak with the mouth of the dying, I had, but that night I knew this man was not a man, but a creature man rarely saw and survived, Hati's spawn. He danced around me, crouching, terribly strong. I scrambled up, running away from him, turning and swinging in terror as the beast dodged away, then pouncing on me.

I fell over the dog's carcass, and he was on me in an eye blink. He ripped my helmet off, and threw it to the grass. He bared his teeth over me, a sight to make man piss his pants, and I lost my sword, as I grasped his throat. He grabbed me by my face and slammed me down, and even Woden's dance could not beat his Lok-given rage as I saw dark. I groped around with my left hand, hoping to find Nightbright, but instead my hand fell on the shattered spear stump, oily with the blood of the dog, embedded in its flesh.

Balderich's words rang through my head, his lament the Wolf Slayer had never tasted a wolf's blood. I yanked and pulled at the stub, as Leuthard ripped into my chest with his rock-like hand, his scarred fingers under the chain mail, penetrating skin and muscle and Ermendrud's fate flashed in my mind as the spear point came free. I shrieked in pain and anger as I stabbed up and to his head, and felt his terrible grip go lax. He shuddered and fell over me, as if he had never lived. I pulled and pushed, trying to scramble out from under him, wondering at his dead corpse, the spear point deep in his skull. I reached for the Head Taker, and stepped unsteadily next to him, raised the blade. I swung it as hard as I could, decapitating him with a dull thud.

I was swooning in pain as I stood there, when I realized Lif was no longer crying. I turned to look at Hands, but he was not there, only a trail of blood. I took some staggering steps forward, but could not move.

From the thickets, a group of horses rode up like silent ghosts.

I stiffened and felt bottomless fear as Odo's thin face regarded me from under his red, greasy hair, his face a thing of pain and madness, pinched and ugly. With him rode Gernot and Ansigar, the latter glowering at me. I took a deep breath, grabbed my helmet, and pulled it on, grunting with pain. I swooned as Odo's men surrounded me, over a hundred of them. He regarded me calmly, as he nodded at Leuthard. 'I tried to reason with that one, you know, Hraban. I knew what he was, what his blood carried. He betrayed our one true master for your father. Only because he loved chaos. Now, he is gone, but he left others behind him. Yet, he played his part in this play.'

'I'm happy to slay them, too,' I said with little conviction, as I grasped Nightbright, dropping Head Taker. It was lighter, and I was exhausted. 'But, I suppose I won't get a chance.'

Odo smiled at me. 'The prophecy is a game for the gods, Hraban. We know the lines, but the lines can mean many things. And you had the scroll.'

'Had?' I asked. I had forgotten the scroll.

'Ishild brought it with her. She tried to save you, you see. She thought I would reward her for the full verses. So, I spared you.'

'You wanted my hands and my cock, if I recall right,' I spat.

'Oh, I was mad at you,' he smirked. 'When you made Ishild pregnant. She is not here, no, I sent her to Gulldrum. To the lands of the Two Rivers, where the Cherusci dwell. Our home. I was raging when you had her and made her pregnant, and I did wish to flay you. I wanted to blind you and torment you with promises of relief and then betrayal, Hraban, in your darkness. But, in the chaos our gods so love, there is twisted order, and I knew my hate was part of the game as well. It all led us here, did it not, Hraban? And the scroll clearly said it is enough she will spawn two children. I shall take yours. Now we are here.'

'You have not found Lif, nor Veleda. I did not take you to her,' I told him with spit.

He chuckled. 'As I said, the lines are murky. The final road will begin when you are to bleed on an evil, rocky skin, Hraban. That is when the final events will roll forward, the last road, make no mistake of it. You bled on the Lok's creature, Hraban, the man with rock-like scars in his hands.' He eyed Leuthard, and I saw my blood in his terrible hand, drying in rocky, evil skin. 'It is that simple. It is no coincidence. It cannot be.'

'But, Veleda is not found,' I insisted.

He smiled. 'I know, Hraban. But, the lines do not say it is the youngest sister you will have to find, just a sister. You bled on the skin, and now you found the trail to my boy's sister, Lif. And Lif is being taken to Veleda. Oh, there are other lines in there, a bear must be slain, a raven to find the way, so no doubt you will have a part to play yet. But, for now, all things are going as they should. We will take after her. We are on the road. Do you remember when my mother asked you to go far, far away? You should have. Everything you have done, everything I have done, it all led to this point.'

'You are a mad dog, Odo. You look like a frazzled badger, and seek the death of children. You will find yours instead,' I said angrily, my mind whirling. *I was to find Lif? Not Veleda?* It is possible. The prophetic lines, I cursed them.

'Yes, I will die when the world ends, Hraban. Only our children will survive,' he agreed. He shook the red hanks of his filthy hair and smiled. 'That bounty hunter is taking us where we must go, and I shall follow him. And as there are still mysterious lines in the scroll, I shall leave you alive, boy. I shall go, and you will follow, no doubt, and it all goes according to Lok's wishes.'

I growled in hate, and tried to run forward. Ansigar whipped his horse and kicked me down. He hovered above me, waiting for a command, as the hundred men gathered around us. 'Let me …'

'Silence,' Odo said softly, and Ansigar leered down. He spat on me, quivering in anger, but stayed quiet. Gernot was oddly silent as well, as I looked at him. Odo gazed at my brother. 'Oh, he rues he ever listened to me, your brother does, Hraban. But, I keep him, for only gods know what part he might have to play in this drama. As for you, I thank you.'

'Thank me?' I asked. 'Why you Hel spawned piece of skin?'

'You should not speak of my mother like that. I understood you became friends, after all,' he chided me. 'The one thing I will need is that ring. When we have walked this story to the end, I will open Veleda's chest, and sprinkle her heart's blood on the Woden's ringlet.'

I said nothing.

He nodded, and Ansigar jumped down with many men, who struggled and put me on the ground. He grabbed my hand, tore Draupnir's Spawn from my finger, and threw it up to Odo. He grabbed it from the air, and pondered my fate. Finally, he shrugged. 'We have a way to go yet, Hraban, so go and run. We will see you again. I think next year we shall finish this.'

'Let me take his leg, like Hands wanted to,' Ansigar begged. Woden help me, but they could have taken Lif any time they wanted. They would follow Hands to Veleda. I begged Hands was clever enough to avoid them.

'No,' Odo said calmly, and pointed a finger my way. 'But, your brother can take his hand, it is only fair, no? Gernot, do you want it? One of my few rewards to you.'

Gernot gazed at me, his weak beard twitching with indecision. He rubbed his stump with a glazed look on his face, and Ansigar was gesturing for him. Gernot's face turned into a deep brood, and I knew I would suffer as Ansigar grinned. 'No,' Gernot said. I turned my face to him in surprise, and he looked away. 'No. Let him keep the hand. He will need it before long against Father. And you.'

Odo cackled at his tone and simmering rebellion, and shrugged and pointed at Ansigar, who stepped away, trembling with anger. My former friend mounted his horse reluctantly, and looked away, cursing me softly. Odo rode past me, his men riding with him. 'Thank you for your golden ring, and for Veleda, Hraban. Lok's will be done, this year, or next. We shall meet again.'

I lay there, laughing.

Odo gazed at me curiously, as he rode to the east in trail of Lif, but I laughed. He would take Veleda, he would end our world, and he would marry Lif to his son so they would survive Ragnarök. But, in order for this to come to pass, he would have to slay Veleda, and pour her poor heart's blood on the ringlet of Woden. I laughed, for he had called the prophecy a game of the gods, the lines of the prophecy confusing and hazy. It was surely so, for I remembered Bero's words, or rather the words of the being who had spoken. Sigyn.

'Woden's ringlet is not golden,' I whispered.

Draupnir's Spawn was useless, unless the god or goddess, whoever it was, had lied. It was not golden, and Draupnir's Spawn was. What Woden's ringlet was, was a mystery to me. Mystery to Odo. But, we would find out. He had spared me. I would indeed ride after them, and Drusus would take me to the land of the Cherusci, where Hands was headed. To the east.

I got back to the Roman army in the morning. I fell from the saddle in front of Drusus, with Fulcher fuzzing over me. I handed him the head of Bricius.

CAMULODUNUM, ALBION (A.D. 42)

I had made myself a man by slaying Vago the Vangione, given oaths to regain what was mine.

I was a fool, Thumelicus, my lord. Fulcher was right.

In the end, I was left a stranger amidst foreigners, Roman rather than a Germani, reviled, rather than cherished; an enemy to my former friends. I had fought my father, and foiled his plans, and I was patient. I would meet him again soon enough. I had built my fort, and that fort was built around Drusus. By guarding Drusus, my lord, I knew I would have a vengeance on my father. Their wyrd was to meet, and my spear would be in that dance. I had not found Wandal. I had not looked for him. But, by being Roman, my chances were better than by being a Marcomanni. As Roman, I would ride to foil the mad Odo, once and forever.

I should have heeded Hand's words, and taken Lif away, immediately when she was born. Given her away, even. I should have abandoned the Marcomanni. I did not. I was a father, and I was a lord and that was wyrd. Fate. Unchangeable.

I also should have heeded Fulcher's words over Ansbor. His love for Cassia drove him mad, and in his madness, he betrayed me. He was lost to me, in so many ways, and I should have spoken to him. Even sent him away. I did not. Wyrd.

Also, Lif was in danger, but I had time. Odo did not know everything.

I was a man of honor. And I loved a good woman.

So, lord, while the druid struggles to heal you, I shall tell you more. I will tell you how Hraban the Roman fought to guard his lord and friend Drusus, the highest of the Romans. I will tell you how I met Maroboodus

545

again, and I will tell you what happened with the prophecy of Lok and my daughter. It will be the year of Veleda, my lord, and also the year I found Wandal, the last of the Bear Heads. And I will tell you more of Armin, your father, for our story was far from finished.

I will do all this, Thumelicus, or Hadewig, so you will find my daughter, Lif, an old woman by now, and tell her of me, her father. It is perilous here in Camulodunum, my lord, and I will strive to keep you safe while I write.

Wyrd, if I manage it, wyrd, if I do not. You will find out soon enough.

- The story continues in The Winter Sword -

Thank you for reading the book.

Do **sign up for my mailing list** by visiting my homepages. By doing this, you will receive a rare and discreet email where you will find:

News of the upcoming stories
Competitions
Book promotions
Free reading

Also, if you enjoyed this book, you might want to check out these ones:

Grab them from my AMAZON HOMEPAGE

AUTHOR'S NOTES

As a fiction writer, I took the liberty to change the facts a wee bit. How much I changed them is a mystery, for there is really little information on what really happened between various Germanic tribes and the Romans at this time. Much is lost, which is something of a relief for a historical fiction writer.

In the upcoming books of the series, we will see quite many of the hard issues old Augustus is facing, as he is trying to change Rome. What Julius Caesar tried to do with a battle-axe to his demise, his stepson Octavianus did subtly. He was the first man of Rome, Augustus, he shared power with the Senate, though he made sure he controlled the provinces with armies. His powers evolved slowly and patiently over the years, until the old man was powerful as an emperor of later ages, and began to worry about the world he had created. He wanted a relative of his to take over. While Rome was not so fussy about bloodlines, adaptation being a perfectly acceptable way of continuing one's family, Augustus did want his own blood to continue his story. He had only one daughter, Julia, and so Julia changed husbands regularly. Julia did have children with Agrippa, Augustus's best general and childhood friend, but the Republic was still out there in the minds of certain people, and also those who wanted what Augustus built, but not his blood.

So, Hraban is going to start taking sides in the upcoming events, and does so with Nero Claudius Drusus. Oh, there will be many men and women falling in Rome, few of natural causes, but this is where we start from. The first Germanicus, a great general, apparently a good man, grandson of Augustus and avid believer in the Republic, is his lord, his friend, and his hope.

In this book, Drusus is a man reluctantly readying for civil war, but only after he truly rules the northern lands. Armin the Cherusci, who at this time was still a boy, but whom I made a young man, was hoping to combine the tribes to fight Drusus. Maroboodus, who hopes to do the same, but only to benefit Rome in the long run, does not like competition. So, we have a harshly cold puddle for Hraban to slip around in.

Nero Claudius Drusus fought with the various Germani tribes. In 12 B.C., he had built a river in the north to shorten his route to the North Sea, and ultimately to the rivers of Elba and Weser, backdoors to the Germani lands. He pacified the Frisii, Ampsivarii, Chauci, and others during the campaign.

In 11 B.C., he did take on the Lippe River tribes, as we see in this book. That meant war with the stubborn Sigambri, Marsi, Bructeri, Tencteri, and Usipetes. There is no likelihood for such a terrible battle as I describe in this book, where the Germani all stood together against several legions, but Armin had to start somewhere, and this was it. I quite simply did not wish for the Lippe tribes to fall one-by-one, alone and without a fight. It felt unworthy of them, so a great plan and a nasty gutter fight of a battle was what I created. After Lippe River, Drusus likely scrapped with Cherusci directly as well. From this time, there are several forts built along the river, Haltern, Oberaden, and Andreppen. In this book, he has not yet fully attacked the famed Cherusci, and has not fought the legendary Arbalo battle, and that is still to come.

Later, in 10 B.C. and 9 B.C., he would take on the Marcomanni and the Chatti, and also the Cherusci again, and this will take place in the following book.

Armin was likely one of the most intriguing characters of the time. His and Maroboodus's hatred for each other was legendary. Armin's aim was to thwart Rome. It is possible he also planned for something more than to be a mere war king and a hero of the people, and he aimed for the dangerous kingship, rather like Augustus in Rome. That he achieved so much in his lifetime meant he was truly an extraordinary man. Such a man is not necessarily an honorable one, as we have seen in this book, and I am sorry if he truly was. Yet, I do not believe one destroys Roman Legions or fights for long years against a world-renowned war machine that should not lose to ill equipped Germani tribes, if one was entirely honorable and unimaginative. So, I will not make Armin seem anything less than driven, devious, and brutal, but we will get to know his softer side in the next book, for he has honor and love in him, and he will find some dark deeds too much for even him to handle.

In this book, we see Hraban struggle with honor and fame. Not all things in life are possible to gain, no matter your valor and drive. One has to make choices. Hraban fails in many of these choices, yet finds new things to fight for. The book is rife with violence, betrayal, and murder as Hraban navigates his way through Armin's schemes, Maroboodus's vengeance, and Drusus's plans. By the end, he knows where he belongs, letting go of impossible dreams. He will be in love, with two women, one but a baby still.

In the next book, The Winter Sword, we will settle the prophecy once and for all. And Hraban settles his scores with Maroboodus as well.

After Godsmount, Hraban will visit Rome. It is a city of beauty and brutality. Wish him luck as I begin to write these stories.

I also humbly ask you rate and review the story on Amazon and/or on Goodreads. This will be incredibly valuable for me going forward.

Please visit www.alariclongward.com and sign up for my mailing list. Also, there is a review competition that is surely worth your time.

Made in the USA
San Bernardino, CA
14 January 2017